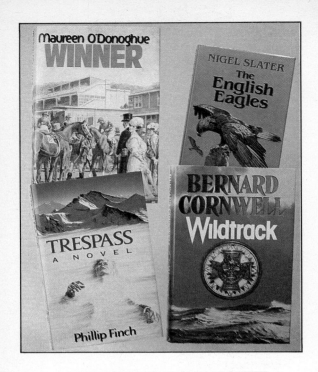

THE READER'S DIGEST ASSOCIATION LIMITED
25 Berkeley Square, London W1X 6AB

THE READER'S DIGEST ASSOCIATION
SOUTH AFRICA (PTY) LTD
Reader's Digest House, 130 Strand Street, Cape Town

Printed by Petty & Sons Ltd, Leeds
Bound by Hazell, Watson & Viney Ltd, Aylesbury

Original cover design by Jeffery Matthews FSIAD

For information as to ownership
of copyright in the material in this book see last page

Reader's Digest

CONDENSED BOOKS

WILDTRACK
Bernard Cornwell (page 9)

Though he has emerged from the Falklands War with a VC, Nick Sandman doesn't feel much like a hero. His wife has left him, he has no job to go to, and no money. What's more, his injuries have left him barely able to walk. But Nick has a dream: to sail his yacht *Sycorax* round the world. And it's a dream that he's determined to fulfil, even when he finds that someone has wrecked the boat he loves so much. As he sets about repairing her, he unwittingly enters a deadly feud between two rich and powerful men, the one accused of murder, the other obsessed with revenge.

A fine thriller, full of suspense, which combines the salty tang of the sea with a bittersweet touch of romance.

WINNER
Maureen O'Donoghue (page 163)

Irish gypsy girl Macha Sheridan has a magic way with horses: a talent for buying, breeding and racing them which she learned at her father's knee. Cast out by her own people at the age of fourteen, with only an old wagon and a few unpromising nags, she sets off on a colourful journey that takes her from Irish horse fairs to the grandeur of Epsom, Goodwood and Ascot; from disgrace and isolation to the elegant houses and high society occasions of the Edwardian era. But just as success seems finally to be within Macha's grasp, her gypsy origins threaten to betray her . . .

Winner is a saga of struggle and passion, rich in contrast, which lingers long in the memory.

THE ENGLISH EAGLES
Nigel Slater (page 307)

Robin Woodford has a past that he wants to forget, and in an effort to find a new life he has taken a new identity and a quiet teaching job in the Lake District. It's a peaceful but unexciting existence—until he spots a pair of golden eagles nesting nearby. Robin is fascinated by the birds, and passionately concerned that they should breed in safety, especially when a local farmer announces they are a threat to his sheep, and is set on their destruction. Together with pretty Jenny Stott, the assistant matron at the school, Robin starts a determined crusade to protect the eagles.

This moving novel about one man's search for peace of mind is also a tribute to the most majestic of birds.

TRESPASS
Phillip Finch (page 403)

The three desk-bound executives who join the expedition to Montana's Beartooth Mountains expect to be challenged. They all anticipate the blistered feet, aching muscles and moments of paralysing fear. What they don't expect is the changes in themselves, and in the other members of the group. For high in the mountains a man is always close to the brink, close to disaster—and to the truth about himself. As the breathtaking scenery of the Beartooths grows ever more treacherous, character flaws begin to prove fatal—and the survival of the little group hangs precariously in the balance.

A great adventure story and a haunting tale of self-discovery.

Wildtrack

A CONDENSATION OF THE BOOK BY

BERNARD CORNWELL

ILLUSTRATED BY JACK McCARTHY

During the long months he has spent
recovering in a military hospital,
Falklands hero Nick Sandman has lived
for the day that he can set sail once
again in his beautiful yacht, *Sycorax*.
His impatience grows until finally,
against his doctor's advice, he
discharges himself and heads straight
for the Devon estuary where he expects
to find the boat safely at her moorings.

Instead, he finds a battered wreck,
and a new and daunting enemy in
wealthy TV star Tony Bannister.
Before he can even hope to sail again,
Nick is forced to make a bargain. It's a
bargain that takes him back to sea—
but not quite in the way that he expects.
For Bannister draws him into a murky
world of deceit where his loyalty,
honour and courage are tested
as never before.

Prologue

They said I'd never walk again.

They said I'd be in a wheelchair till they lifted me into my box and screwed down the lid. I should learn a trade, they said. Something cripple-friendly, like computers.

They'd put a metal rod into my right thigh, and grafted skin where my thighs and backside had been burned. They'd done a mixture of rough carpentry and microsurgery on my spine and, when it half worked—which meant I could twitch the toes on my left foot—they opened me up again and did a bit more. It had all taken nearly a year and still I could not walk. You must get used to it, they said, because you're never going to walk again. You're never going to sail again. I told them to get lost.

"That's not the spirit, Nick!" Dr. Maitland said in his no-nonsense voice. He flipped the pages of a yachting magazine that lay beside my bed. "You can go sailing again this very spring!"

It was the first sign of hope he'd given me, and I responded eagerly. "Can I?"

"My dear Nick, of course you can. There's a motor sailor on the Solent that's specially adapted for your sort of case. Ramps for the chairs and a trained volunteer staff on board. And perhaps you'd let the press go along?" Maitland added hopefully. "They all want to interview you."

"Tell them to go to hell. No press."

"No press, then." Maitland could not hide his disappointment. He loved publicity.

"The last time I went sailing, Doc, I was in a friend's forty-footer

9

coming back from Iceland. She was knocked down near the Faeroes and lost all her mast above the spreaders. We hacked off the broken stuff, rigged jury hounds, and brought her into North Uist five days later." I didn't add that the friend had broken his arm when the boat broached, or that it happened in the depths of an awful night. What mattered was that we had taken on that northern sea and brought our boat home.

Maitland listened very patiently. "That was before, Nick, wasn't it?"

"Look, there's no way, Doc, that I'm going to sit on your cripple barge and watch the pretty boats go by." I knew I was being churlish and ungrateful, but I didn't care. I was going to walk again.

THAT AFTERNOON THEY SENT a new psychiatrist to see me. "Hello, Mr. Sandman," she said brightly. "I'm Dr. Janet Plant."

She had a nice voice, but I couldn't see her because I had my back to the door. "You're the new shrink?"

"I'm the new orientation therapist," she agreed. "What are you doing?"

I was holding on to the bedrail with my right hand and edging my right foot down to the floor. "I'm teaching myself to walk."

God, I was weak. My right leg was shaking. The nerves of the leg were supposed to be severed, but I'd discovered that if I locked the knee with my hands it would stay locked. So now I thrust the knee down and very gingerly pushed myself away from the bed, still holding on to the rail. My left leg took some of the weight, and the pain slid down the tendons like fire. I had no balance and no strength, but I forced myself away from the bed until I was standing, half bent. I could not breathe. Literally. The pain was so bad that my body could not find the breathing instructions.

I fell backwards onto the bed. The pain began to ebb out of me as my breath came back, but I kept my eyes closed so the tears would not show. "The first thing I have to do"—I tried to sound nonchalant—"is learn to straighten up. Then, how to put one foot in front of the other. The rest will come easily."

I heard Dr. Plant draw up the chair and sit down. She'd made no attempt to help me, which was all part of the hospital's treatment. We had to fail in order to discover our new limits.

"Tell me about your boat," she said in a matter-of-fact voice.

"It's a boat," I said sullenly. My breathing was easier now, but my eyes were still closed.

"We sail a Contessa thirty-two," Dr. Plant said.

I opened my eyes and saw a sensible, short-haired and motherly woman. "Where's your Contessa moored?" I asked.

"Itchenor."

I smiled. "I once went aground on the East Pole sands."

10

"Careless."

"It was at night," I defended myself, "and there was a blizzard blowing so I couldn't see the marks. I was only fifteen. I shouldn't have tried to make the channel, but I thought my old man would tan the hide off me if I stayed out all night."

"Your mother had left you by the time you were fifteen, isn't that so?"

"I'm a right monkey puzzle tree for you, aren't I?"

"Is that what you think?" she asked.

"What I think," I said, "is that I hate it when shrinks ask me what I think. My father's a crook, my mother did a bolt, my brother's useless, my sister's worse, and my wife has left me and married a bloody MP. But I'm not here for any of that, Doctor. I'm here because I got a bullet in my back and the National Health Service has undertaken to put me together again. Doing that does not involve poking about in my doubtless addled brain." I stared up at the ceiling. "I delivered a Contessa thirty-two to Holland once," I said. "Nice boats."

"They are," she said enthusiastically. "Tell me about yours."

I suppose it was because she was a sailor herself that I told her. The trick of surviving is to have one dream that gives you hope, and mine was *Sycorax*.

"She's called *Sycorax*," I said. "Thirty-eight foot, mahogany on oak, with teak decks. Built in nineteen twenty-two for a rich man, so no expense was spared. Her usual rig is jib, staysail, main, topsail and mizzen—all heavy cotton. She's got brass scuttles, and gimballed oil lamps in the cabin." My eyes closed again. "And the prettiest lines this side of paradise. She's dark blue, with white sails. She's got a long keel, she's built like a tank, and she's as cantankerous as the witch she's named after." I smiled, remembering *Sycorax*'s stiffness in a freshening wind.

"The witch Sycorax. From Shakespeare?"

"From *The Tempest*. Sycorax was Caliban's mother and she imprisoned her enemies in timber. It's a joke, you see, because a timber boat imprisons you in debt."

Dr. Plant offered a dutiful smile. "I hope you've had her ashore since you've been in here?"

I shook my head. "I wasn't given time to take her out of the water, but she's sheathed in copper and berthed on a private wharf. She's been battered about a bit, but I can repair her."

"You're a carpenter?" There was a touch of surprise in her voice.

"I used to be. And I was a good mechanic."

"So you see yourself as a practical man, do you?" she asked with the professional inflection.

"You're meddling again," I warned her. "You've come here to sing Dr. Maitland's song. Get a skill, Nick. Talk to the newspapers, Nick. They'll pay you for the interview and you can buy a nice little electrically driven wheelchair. In short, surrender, Nick. But if I'd wanted to do that, Doctor, I'd have stayed in the army. They offered me a desk job."

She went to the window. A cold wind drove spits of winter rain against the glass. "You're a very stubborn man, Mr. Sandman. But how will you cope when you discover you'll never sail your *Sycorax* again?"

I ignored her blunt question. "Next year I'm going to take her south to New Zealand. There's no particular reason for New Zealand, so don't ask. I'll sail to the Azores first," I went on dreamily, "then across to Barbados, south to Panama, across to the Marquesas . . ."

"Not round the Horn?" Dr. Plant interrupted sharply.

I gave her a warning look. "You think I don't want to go to the South Atlantic again?"

"That thought did cross my mind, yes."

"I don't have nightmares, Doctor, only dreams." That wasn't true. I still woke up shivering and thinking of an island in the South Atlantic.

Dr. Plant smiled. "Dreams can come true, Nick."

"Don't patronise me, Doctor."

She laughed, and suddenly sounded much more like a sailor than a psychiatrist. "You really are stubborn, aren't you?"

I WAS, AND TWO WEEKS later I managed to hop and shuffle as far as the window. It took three minutes, much pain, and my breath was rasping like glasspaper in my throat when I finally clutched the sill and rested my forehead against the cold glass.

It was a cloudless winter night and there was a full moon over the hospital grounds where the bare trees were frosted black and silver. I searched for Aldebaran among the stars. There had been a time when I would bring that far sun sweetly down to the dawn's horizon, mastering it with the miracle of a sextant's mirror. Now I was a cripple, but somewhere my boat waited, like me, to be released to the long, long winds under Aldebaran's cold light.

Because one day, whatever the doctors said, *Sycorax* would take me to New Zealand. Just the two of us in great waters, sailing south, and free.

Chapter 1

I walked out of hospital fourteen months later.

I knew that Dr. Maitland would have told the press that I was leaving, so I discharged myself two days early. I just wanted to get back to Devon without fuss and walk into the pub and pretend I'd been away for a week or two.

12

So I limped down the hospital drive and told myself that the pain in my back was bearable, and that the hobbling walk was not too grotesque. I caught a bus at the hospital gate, then a train, and another bus that twisted its way into the steep river-cut hills of South Devon. It was winter's end and there were snowdrops in the hedgerows.

I asked the bus driver to drop me at the top of Ferry Lane. He watched me limp down the vehicle's steps. "Are you all right, mate?"

"I'm fine," I lied. "I just want to walk."

The door hissed shut and the bus grumbled away towards the village, while I went haltingly down the lane which led to the old ferry slip. From there I would be able to stare across the river at *Sycorax*.

To stare at my home. For however battered she might be by the winter's ice and gales, *Sycorax* was my only home, and it had been thoughts of her that had steered me through the long months to this moment when I limped towards her. It hurt to walk, but I knew I'd simply have to live with the pain, and I'd decided that the best way to do that was to forget it and think of something else.

As I turned the steep corner halfway to the river, a watery sunlight reflected with surprising brilliance from the windows of my father's old house, which stood high on the far bank. I stopped. The new owner of the house had extended the river façade, making a great sweep of plate glass that looked down sloping lawns to the water. No flag hung from the towering mast my father had put on the terrace, which suggested that the house was empty.

I picked up my small bag and hobbled on. In summer this lane was busy with dinghy sailors, but now, in the wake of winter's cold, there was just one car parked at the head of the old slip. It was a big shooting brake filled with all the gear needed to ready a boat for the season.

A middle-aged man was stowing cans and brushes into a bag. "Morning! It's a bright one, isn't it?"

"It is," I agreed. There were a handful of boats moored out—just enough to hide *Sycorax* from me. She was on the wharf by the deep cut that led to my father's old boathouse on the far bank.

I hoped the middle-aged man would ignore me now, for this was the moment that had kept me alive through all the months of hospital and pain. I was prepared for the worst. Jimmy Nicholls had written in the autumn and said she needed work, but I had persuaded myself that it would be a pleasure to mend her.

Now, like a child wanting to prolong a treat, I did not look up as I limped to the slip's end. Only when my shoes were almost touching the swirl of water did I at last raise my eyes. And *Sycorax* was gone.

In her place, tied to the wall that was my private berth, was an ugly, boxlike houseboat.

"Excuse me?" It was the middle-aged man, who had approached me on soft-soled sea boots. He was embarrassed by needing to ask the question. "Are you all right?"

"Yes." I said it abruptly, not wanting to betray the dismay I felt. I looked into the big upstream pool where another handful of boats was moored, but *Sycorax* was not there either.

"Were you moored out through the winter?" I asked the man.

" 'Fraid so." He said it sheepishly, as though I was accusing him of ill-treating his boat.

"You don't know what's happened to *Sycorax*, do you?"

"*Sycorax*?" He straightened up, puzzled, then remembered the name. "Tommy Sandman's old boat?"

"Yes." It was hardly the moment to say that my father had long ago sold me the yacht.

"Shame, really," he said. "She's up there."

He pointed across the river, and at last I saw her. She had been dragged on her flank up the wooded hill to the south of the boathouse. I could just see her stern in the undergrowth. A deep-keeled hull like *Sycorax*'s should be propped on a cradle or held by sheerlegs if she's out of the water, but whoever had beached my boat had simply hauled her like dead meat and abandoned her.

"A shame," the man repeated. "She was a pretty thing."

"Can you take me across?" I asked.

He hesitated. "Isn't it private?"

"Not the woods, I think." I was sure, but I did not want to betray my connections with this stretch of river. I wanted to be anonymous. I wanted no one to share my feelings this day, because even if the dream was broken, it was still my private dream.

The man watched my awkward manoeuvres. I had to sit on the stones at the slip's edge and transfer myself into the dinghy as though I was going from bed to wheelchair.

"What happened?" he asked.

"Car accident."

"Bad luck." He handed down his paint and brushes, then climbed in himself and pulled the outboard into noisy life. As he pointed his boat across the river, he told me he was a dentist. He said he thought he was getting too old for the sea. In a season or two, he said, he would put the boat on the market and spend the rest of his life regretting it.

"Don't do it," I said.

"My wife wants to see Disneyworld."

We fell into companionable gloom. I looked up at *Sycorax*. "Who beached her?" I asked.

"Lord knows. It isn't the sort of thing Bannister would do."

14

"Bannister?" I asked.

"Tony Bannister. He owns the property now. He keeps his boat down in the town marina."

Anthony Bannister was a television presenter who had become the darling of the British public. His face appeared on magazine covers and his endorsement was sought for products as diverse as cars and suntan lotions. He was also a yachtsman, one of the gilded amateurs whose big boats grace the world's most expensive regattas. But Bannister, I recalled, had also known the sea's horror: his wife had died the previous year in an accident at sea while Bannister had been on course to win the St. Pierre trophy. The tragedy had prompted nationwide sympathy.

"Perhaps it's an unlucky house, eh?" The dentist stared up at the expanse of windows.

"Because of his wife, you mean?"

"Tommy Sandman lived there, too." The dentist chuckled. "I wonder how he likes his new home?"

My father, who had once been so brilliantly successful, was now in jail.

"I imagine he'll survive," I said drily.

"Better than his son. Crippled for life, I hear."

I kept silent, pretending an interest in the ugly houseboat moored at my wharf. At the stern there were railings to which washing was pegged. "Who lives in that?" I asked the question with some distaste.

"Bannister's racing crew. Apes, they are."

The presence of the houseboat on my wharf suggested that it had been Bannister himself who had removed *Sycorax*, but Anthony Bannister's public image was that of a strong and considerate man, the kind of person any of us might turn to for advice or help, and I was reluctant to abandon that image. Besides, he was a yachtsman who had lost his wife, which made me feel sympathetic towards him.

We were in line with the cut now and I could see a second craft in the boathouse: a low, crouching, twin-engined speedboat with a polished hull and a flashy radar arch. I could see her name, *Wildtrack II*, and I remembered that the yacht which had so nearly won the St. Pierre, the greatest prize for racing cruisers, had been called *Wildtrack*. There was a sign hanging in the roof arch above the powerboat: Private. Keep Out.

"Are you sure we should be here?" The dentist throttled back, worried by other strident signs which had been posted along the riverbank.

"The broker said it was OK." I jerked my head towards *Sycorax*. "He said anyone could view her."

"You're buying her?"

"I was thinking of it," I answered guardedly, staring at *Sycorax*, seeing how she had been dragged a full twenty feet above the high-water mark. There were stones in that slope which would have gouged and torn at her planking as she was scraped uphill. "Why didn't they just let her rot on the water?" I said angrily.

"Harbour Authority wouldn't allow that, would they?" The dentist held the dinghy against the end of the wharf as I clambered awkwardly ashore. "Wave if you want a lift back," he said.

I watched him take his dinghy to the upstream moorings. When he had cut his motor there was only the gentle noise of the river, but I was in no mood to enjoy the peace. My back hurt, my boat was wrecked, and I wondered why Jimmy Nicholls had allowed *Sycorax* to be moved. I had paid Jimmy a fee to keep an eye on her.

The climb was hard, and by the time I reached *Sycorax* the pain was like white-hot steel burrowing into my spine. I held on to her rudder, closed my eyes, and it must have been all of two minutes before I could straighten up and examine my boat.

She lay on her side, dappled with the wintry sun. At least a third of the copper sheathing had been torn away. Floating ice had gouged, but not opened, her planking. Both her masts and her bowsprit were gone. The teak grating in the cockpit and the brass scuttles were missing. The compasses had disappeared. I leaned on the broken roof and peered into the cabin. At first all I could see was the black gleam of still water lying deep in her canted hull, then I saw that the radios were gone, the stoves had been stolen and all the lamps were missing. The main cabin's panelling had been stripped. The engine was a mass of rust.

I was feeling oddly calm. At least *Sycorax* was here. She could be rebuilt, and all it would take would be my time and the money of the bastard who had done this to her. The damage was heart-rending, but rather than anger, I felt guilt. I felt that I had let *Sycorax* down.

I stumbled back down the hill, planning to cross the river, then walk to the pub and give Jimmy Nicholls a few hard moments. Why the devil hadn't he done something? The freehold of the wharf was mine. I'd bought it from my father because it would provide a haven for *Sycorax* and a place I could call home. It was my only address: The Lime Wharf, Tidesham, South Devon. And now Anthony Bannister had his ugly houseboat moored to it. I still found it hard to believe that Bannister had stolen the wharf by moving *Sycorax*, but someone had and I swore I would find them and sue them for every penny my broken ship needed.

I stepped over one of the springs which held the houseboat safe against my wharf. I was going to hail the dentist for a lift across the river, but first I glanced into the boathouse. And I saw my dinghy there. She lay snugly moored against *Wildtrack II*'s starboard quarter. My ownership was proclaimed in flaking paint on her transom: Tender to *Sycorax*.

I think perhaps it was the ugliness of Bannister's flash speedboat which suddenly convinced me of his guilt. So he thought his money gave him privileges beyond the law, damn him. He'd wrecked my boat, stolen my wharf, but he wasn't going to steal my dinghy. I decided I would take the tender back into my ownership, and row myself to the village pub.

The boathouse could be entered either from the river or by a door which led from the garden. I had to use the garden door, which was padlocked. I paused for a moment, balancing the legalities in my mind, then decided to break in.

My back ripped with pain as I lifted a heavy stone and hammered at the brass lock. It took six sharp blows before the hasp came away from the wood and the door splintered open. I stepped inside to find *Wildtrack II* rocking gently to the falling tide. Her bows, sharp as a jet fighter's nose cone, were slicked with chrome. She was a vulgar monster, and my father would have loved every inch of her. I walked round the boathouse's internal dock and found two oars. I tossed them into my dinghy, then climbed gingerly over *Wildtrack II*'s stainless steel guardrail. I saw that the two springs which held my dinghy close to the speedboat's flank were cleated somewhere beneath her green tarpaulin cover, so I began by unlacing the stiff material and peeling it away from the windscreen.

Once the cover was folded back, I stepped down onto the helmsman's black leather chair. And found my brass scuttles. And my VHF and short-wave radios. They were among heaps of similar items that were piled in two tea chests. Most of the items had come from other yachts. I stared down into the chests, guessing that the value of their contents must be three or four thousand pounds at black-market prices. Why would a man as rich as Bannister meddle with bent chandlery?

"Don't move."

The voice came from the door which I'd broken open. I turned.

"I said don't move!" The man was silhouetted in the doorway. The sun was bright behind him while the boathouse was in deep shadow, so I couldn't see his face, only that he was a huge man, well over six foot tall, with muscle-humped shoulders and a cropped skull. He carried a double-barrelled shotgun. "What do you think you're doing?" He had a grating voice and an Afrikaans accent.

"I'm taking my property," I said.

"Breaking and entering," the South African said. "Come here." He jerked the gun to reinforce his command.

"Why don't you get lost?" I shouldn't have been belligerent, but I was feeling mad as hell because of what had happened to *Sycorax*. I stooped to my tender's bowspring and jerked it off the stainless-steel cleat.

Wildtrack II rocked violently as the man jumped onto her bows. The movement made me stagger, and I had to clutch the radar arch for support. As he reached over the windscreen with his left hand, I clutched it, and tried to unbalance him by hauling him towards me.

I'd forgotten how little strength there was in my legs. I pulled him so far, then my right knee gave way and I staggered back into the tea chests. The South African laughed and I saw the butt of the gun coming towards me. It thumped like a pile-driver into my ribs, throwing me back. Then he contemptuously reached for my jacket to haul me out of the speedboat's cockpit. I heard myself scream as he scraped my spine over the windscreen's top edge. I hit out at him, and he must have found that amusing, for he chuckled before he threw me onto the dock. The pain forked down my legs like blazing phosphorus. The gun slammed down again into my ribs.

He stood over me and, confident that I had been battered into submission, discarded the gun. "Get up," he said curtly.

"Listen, you bastard . . ." I tried to push myself upright, but the pain in my spine struck like a bullet and I gasped and fell again.

The South African must have been worried by my twitching and gasping. "Get up!" He paused. "You're faking it." There was worry in his voice. "You're not hurt, man. I hardly touched you."

He must have leaned down to me, because I remember his hands under my shoulders, and I remember him yanking me upright. He let go of me and I tried to put my weight onto my right leg, but it buckled. I fell again, into blessed unconsciousness.

WHEN I WOKE UP I could see a cream-coloured ceiling and hear the pip of a cardiograph. To my left there was a chrome stand with a saline drip suspended from its hook. Two earnest faces bent over the bed. One was framed in a nurse's cap, the other belonged to a doctor who had a stethoscope at my chest. He unhooked it and began to feel my ribs.

"God!" I suddenly felt the pain.

"Don't talk. Can you move the fingers of your right hand?" I tried, and must have succeeded for the doctor nodded with satisfaction. "Now the left? That's good. If you speak," he warned, "do it very gently. Can you tell us your name?"

"My name?" I was confused.

"You were found without any identification. You're now in the South Devon General Hospital. Can you remember your name?"

"Nick Sandman," I said.

"That's good, Nick. Where do you live?"

"Here," I said, knowing it was not a helpful answer, but suddenly the pain was washing through me, making me arch my back. I saw the doctor's hand dart to the hanging drip and once again I was falling down the soft, dark and familiar tunnel of chemical sleep.

Where I dreamed of *Sycorax*. At night, when the phosphorescence sparkles in her wake, I like to peg her tiller and go right forward

18

into her bows. In my dream I had two good legs and I was standing on the bowsprit and staring back at the slim beauty of her hull driving through dark seas to leave an arrow's path of light beneath the stars.

SYCORAX HAD BEEN BUILT in the twenties as a rich man's toy, but built by men who only knew how to make a fisherman's workboat. She was an honest boat, sturdy and functional, with the lines of a fishing smack, but made pretty by her elegantly overhanging counter and by the workmanship of her fittings. Her first owner, uninterested in speed, had commissioned a safe cruising boat that would doggedly plunge through the worst of seas. She had been resold by a succession of owners who must have found her either too slow or too expensive to maintain. So summer by summer *Sycorax* had faded. Her brightwork had become tarnished, her sails had blown out and her paint had peeled.

My father had found her, abandoned, in the sixties. He was making his money then, pots of it. His deals on London's property market had brought him a Rolls, two Jaguars, three Maseratis, and two Nicholson racing cruisers that were moored in the river beside our Devon house. There was also a London house and a flat in St. Tropez. My father loved flash things like fast cars and painted women and a son at public school. My elder brother went to Eton but, to my relief, they wouldn't even look at me. I was too slow, too dumb, and had to be sent to a dullards' boarding school where I rotted happily in ignorance.

I only cared about boats, and I helped rebuild *Sycorax* in the yard where she'd been born. My father, like the first owner, ordered that no expense was to be spared. She was to be restored to her old and splendid beauty. Her hull was repaired with a loving and almost forgotten skill. Teak decks were joggled home, and a new cabin was made where all the brass fittings my father had collected could be lovingly installed. New masts were cut, carefully chosen from the north side of a spruce forest so that the trunk's heartwood would be central, and not drawn to one side by the sun on the forest's southern flank. We soaked the new spars in linseed oil and paraffin, then put on coat after coat of varnish. I can still close my eyes and see that finished mainmast lying on its trestles, gleaming in the sunlight.

Sails were made, sheets were rove, oil lamps polished, and a dead boat came to life on the slips of a Devon yard. A diesel engine was put in her aft belly, and the day came when she was lifted into the yard's dock. My father saw my devotion to her and was amused by it. Once she was launched, though, he lost interest in *Sycorax*. She was not the slow, docile craft he had dreamed of. He wanted a boat for long sunsets with gin and melting girls, but *Sycorax* was a stiff sailor in sea winds, and too long-keeled for easy river cruising. My father could never bear to part

20

with pretty things, so he moored her below the house like a garden ornament. Once in a long while he would motor her upriver, but I was the only person who bothered to hoist her sails. Jimmy Nicholls and I would take her out to sea and set her bows to the vast waves that came in from the Atlantic.

Six years after *Sycorax* was relaunched I joined the army, but when I was on leave I would still go down to Devon and take her to sea. I married. Melissa and I would motor down to the Devon house for long weekends but, as time passed, my father was rarely there.

Later, I discovered he was borrowing money he could not repay on the strength of promises he could not keep. He was even ready to sell me both *Sycorax* and the wharf, to raise some money. His battle became ever more desperate and flamboyant, and he lost it. He was sent down for seven years: a savage sentence, but the judge wanted to make it plain that just because a crime was committed by a businessman it was no less a crime for that.

But by then I was sailing to the South Atlantic and everything was changing.

Everything except for *Sycorax*. Because she was all that I had now, and all that I wanted.

"YOU DON'T REMEMBER me, do you?" A tall, cadaverous man in a shabby grey suit appeared at my bedside. He was in his fifties and had bloodshot eyes and a lugubrious face.

"Of course I remember you," I said. "Detective Sergeant Harry Abbott."

"Inspector Abbott now." He was pleased I'd remembered him. "How are you, Nick?"

"I'm well." The pain in my chest made breathing and speaking difficult. "I might go for a bike ride if the rain holds off."

"It isn't raining," Abbott said gloomily. "It's actually quite spring-like, for a change. Mind if I smoke?" He lit up anyway. Abbott used to play golf with my father, who loved to be friendly with the local law. My father gave wonderful parties—you could hear them a mile upriver—but there were never any complaints, not while the local police were so fond of him.

"Seen Wednesday's papers?" Abbott asked. He held a tabloid over the bed. "Falklands VC Hero Assaulted at TV Tony's Hideaway," it read. There was a photograph of me in uniform, a big picture of Anthony Bannister, and a photograph of the house.

"Bloody hell," I said.

"Mr. Bannister was in London." Abbott folded the paper away. "So it wasn't him that beat you up."

"It was a South African."

"Figured it was." Abbott picked a grape from the bunch beside my bed and spat the pips onto the floor. "A big man?"

"Built like a barge."

"Fanny Mulder. He's Mr. Bannister's professional skipper." There was derision in the last two words. "He's gone away, of course. Probably in France by now. Or Spain. Whatever. He's waiting for things to quieten down before he comes back." Abbott stared at my face. "He certainly took care of you, didn't he?"

"He nicked my wallet. And my bag. And everything off my boat."

"He tried to murder you, didn't he? He dumped you on the foreshore and probably hoped the tide would wash you away. Some dentist found you. Mr. Bannister says you broke into his boathouse."

"He had my dinghy in there!"

"Mr. Bannister wants it all hushed up. He would, of course. He doesn't want the papers saying that a war hero was scuffed over by one of his pet gorillas. Image is very important to Mr. Bannister. He's one of those blokes who straps himself into a fighting chair just to catch a bloody mackerel." Abbott laughed scornfully.

"Isn't he meant to be a brilliant sailor?" I asked.

"His wife was. She was here a lot, always sailing. I didn't like her much. American." He added the last word as though it explained his distaste, then blew a plume of smoke towards me. "I miss your old man, Nick. Have you been to see him?"

"I haven't had time," I said. Then, to change the subject, "When did Bannister buy the house?"

"Couple of years back."

"Did he take my boat out of the water?"

"Lord knows." Abbott did not seem to care. "Could have been anyone. There was some mischief on the river this winter."

"That was Mulder," I said. "There were crates of nicked stuff in the boathouse."

"Won't be there any longer, will it? He'll have shipped it all off to George Cullen. Remember George? He's still as bent as a pig's tail. We reckon Mulder's been doing business with Georgie, but it's hard to prove."

"I thought we taxpayers paid you to prove hard things."

"Not my job, Nick. I'm off crime now."

"What are you? Traffic? Giving out parking tickets?"

Abbott ignored the gibe. "I'll tell CID about the stolen stuff, Nick, but I doubt they'll do anything."

"My boat wasn't insured. My ex-wife didn't forward the renewal notice. It was hard for Melissa to remember everything when she was having fun. Besides, Jimmy Nicholls was supposed to be looking after *Sycorax*."

"Jimmy's been in hospital since November," Abbott said. "Emphysema. He smokes too much." He looked down at his cigarette, and shrugged. "Seen your kids, have you?"

"They visited me in the other hospital." I wondered why Abbott was so deliberately steering away from more pressing matters. "Are you going to charge Mulder?" I demanded.

"I doubt it, Nick. Wouldn't do much good, would it?"

"But he stole all my stuff!"

"Difficult to prove. You can prefer a charge of assault against him, if you like, but if I was you, I wouldn't bother," Abbott said airily. "Bannister looks after Fanny, he does. He'll hire him a top lawyer, and you'll end up with the court's sympathy, but they'll still pin the costs on you. Forget it, Nick."

"I don't want to. I've got to sue someone if I'm going to find the money to repair *Sycorax*."

Abbott sighed at my stubbornness. "If you insist, Nick, I'll arrange for a lawyer to come and see you." He went to the door. "You know your old man is really proud of you, Nick?" He waited, and when I made no reponse, he explained, "The VC."

"The other two earned it," I said. "I just disobeyed orders."

"It's still a Victoria Cross, Nick. It can change your life, earning a thing like that."

"I don't want it to change my life. I just want to get it back."

Abbott frowned. "Get what back?"

"The medal, Harry. Mulder stole it, along with everything else."

Abbott flinched as if, at last, he recognised that I'd suffered a misfortune. "If it's any consolation to you, he'll have the devil's own job to sell it. Any collector will know it's stolen."

"Put the word out, will you, Harry?"

"I'll do that, Nick." Abbott nodded a farewell.

THE NEXT DAY I swore out a complaint against Francis Mulder, accusing him of assault and theft. The lawyer was sympathetic but pessimistic. Mulder, he said, had disappeared and was unlikely to return to England so long as the writ threatened. He thought my chances of recovering the medal were slight, and my chances of successfully recouping the costs of repairing *Sycorax* even slighter.

After the lawyer had gone I lay back and stared at the ceiling. I felt at rock bottom and wondered how long I would have to stay there. The doctor had said I might limp again, but he had not prophesied how long it would take.

I closed my eyes and thought of *Sycorax* lying dismasted on a hill, with her hull rotting. There was no certainty that even if Fanny Mulder were found, he would have funds to rebuild *Sycorax*. The repairs would be up to me. I thought of my small bank account. *Sycorax* would take a fortune to make ready for the water. I'd have to sell her for scrap and I'd be lucky if I saw five hundred pounds. Or else I could sell my story to the newspapers. I wouldn't do that.

The door creaked and I opened my eyes. A tall man stood watching me. His long jaw was slightly jowlier than it appeared in photographs, his blond hair less glossy. It took a second or two before I realised this really was Anthony Bannister. He looked older than I had expected; but then he smiled, and instantly the imperfections were overwhelmed by beguiling charm. "Captain Sandman?" His familiar voice suggested dependability and kindliness. "My name's Bannister. Tony Bannister."

There were nurses standing behind him with silly looks on their faces; it was like a royal visit. Bannister smiled on them in gentle apology, then closed the door, leaving the two of us alone. "I think we have a mutual problem," he said nervously.

"My only problem is a boat . . . which your South African wrecked."

He nodded in immediate acceptance of the responsibility. "My fault, but I was assured the boat was abandoned. I was wrong and I apologise. Now, I imagine you want it restored to perfection?"

I found myself feeling sympathetic towards Bannister. He had shown honesty, which was the quality I admired above all things, but I also felt flattered that such a famous man was here in my room. My belligerence faded. "I can do the work on her myself," I said, "but I can't buy the materials. I'm skint, you see."

"I, fortunately, am not skint." He smiled and held out his right hand. He wore a gold bracelet, a gold wristwatch and two heavy gold rings. I thought of one of my father's favourite sayings: principles are very fine things, but they are soluble in cash. But for *Sycorax*'s sake I shook the golden hand.

"YOU HAVE TO UNDERSTAND," Matthew Cooper said, "that it's a rough cut. Just scraps of film we've assembled. We've hammered it together instead of dovetailing it."

Matthew, a nervous man in his mid-thirties, was one of a film crew sent to visit me by Anthony Bannister.

"And the film isn't dubbed," Angela Westmacott said flatly.

"Dubbed?" I asked.

"The sound isn't polished," Matthew answered for her, "and there's only ten minutes. The final film will probably run at sixty."

"Or ninety," said Angela Westmacott, "but it's a risk."

24

She did not look at me as she spoke, which gave me the chance to look at her. She was a tall, ethereal blonde, so slender and seemingly fragile that my protective instincts were immediately roused. Her hair was gathered into combs from which it escaped in cirrus wisps of lightest gold. Her jacket was a white and pink padded confection, while her trousers were baggy, white and stuffed into pink ankle length boots. She was disturbingly beautiful and she wore, I noted, neither wedding nor engagement ring. Her clothes were clearly expensive. I wondered whether Anthony Bannister's television company had sent her as bait. She made good bait.

"It's a risk," she said, "because without your agreement the footage we've already shot is wasted."

"Already shot?" I was puzzled.

"The rough cut," Matthew explained. "Tony thought you would feel happier if you could see what we had in mind."

We were in the new front room of Bannister's house. It must have been seventy-five feet long and every foot of it offered a splendid panoramic view of the river which curled at the end of the garden. Three carpeted steps climbed to the top half of the room where, rippling gently, there was sixty foot of indoor swimming pool. Between the steps and the window was a raised fireplace, built as an island. White leather sofas were scattered on either side of the fire while at the northern end of the room there was a space-age array of sound and vision equipment, including a massive television: the largest TV in a house filled with TVs. Onto the screens of which Anthony Bannister now planned to put me. He wanted to make a film of my life, my injury and my recovery, and he had sent Matthew and Angela to seek my cooperation.

Matthew Cooper took the video cassette from his briefcase. "Shall we watch it now?" he asked.

I had gone to stand at the window, and was gazing at an aluminium-hulled yacht which was running under main and jib to the moorings in the upper pool. The only person on deck was a man in a black woollen hat. I admired the exquisite skill with which he picked up his mooring buoy in the gusting wind.

"Are you ready?" Matthew insisted.

"That's a French boat." I spoke as if I had not heard his question. "He's probably run over from Cherbourg. He's good, very good."

Matthew pushed the videotape into the slot. "It's a very rough cut indeed," he said apologetically.

"Fine." I spoke as if I was content, but in truth I was struggling not to show my annoyance. I'd spent months avoiding the press, and now Bannister was trying to make me the subject of a television film. At the hospital, he had offered me everything I wanted. A refuge, security, and

25

the means to repair *Sycorax*. I should have known what the price would be when, the next day, the papers trumpeted Bannister's generosity: "TV Tony Rescues VC Hero".

None of the papers had blamed the attack on Bannister; he had come out of the stories pure as driven snow. Something nasty had happened in his boathouse while he was in London, and he was now putting it right. I'd left the hospital to come to Bannister's house where, in these last three weeks, I had mended fast. *Sycorax* had been lifted out of the trees and stood in cradles on Bannister's lawn. The materials for her repair were on order, and they were nothing but the best. TV Tony had worked his magic, but now the price for all that kindness was being exacted.

"Here it is," Angela said sharply, chiding me for being insufficiently attentive to the television screen, on which numbers counted down, then changed to show a wild and bleak landscape darkened by dusk and edged by a pink-washed sky. Plangent music played as the title appeared: "*A Soldier's Story*, a film by Angela Westmacott".

The titles went and the picture changed to a night skyline. Tracer bullets flicked from left to right, there was an explosion in the far distance and the sudden flare of white phosphorus. I looked away.

"The Falklands"—Anthony Bannister's distinctive voice was warm with a grave sincerity—"fourteenth of June, nineteen eighty-two. British troops were closing on Stanley, the battle of Goose Green and the mountains were behind them, and there was a sense of imminent victory in the cold South Atlantic air. Captain Nick Sandman was one of the men who—"

I stood up. "Do you mind if I don't watch this?" I limped to the window and stared down at the cradled form of *Sycorax*.

She'd been drained of water, and the patches of rot had been cut out of her hull. The old copper sheathing had been stripped off and the nail holes plugged with pine. The stumps of her masts had been lifted out like rotten teeth and now she lay swathed in a tarpaulin, waiting for the new timber that would be patched into her old hull.

I looked upstream to the French yacht, just in time to see the skipper take off his hat. He was a she, shaking out her black hair. Behind me Bannister's sonorous voice was telling my story.

I turned despite myself, to see my own photograph on the screen. It was a photograph taken five years before and had once stood on my wife's dressing table. I wondered how the television people had come by a copy. It did not look like me, at least I did not think so. My mouse-coloured hair was unnaturally tidy above my long-jawed face.

"We'll replace the photograph with film, of course," Angela explained.

Sergeant Terry Farebrother appeared. He looked nasty, brutish and short in his combat smock. He had been filmed at one of the

Surrey exercise grounds where thunderflashes smoked in the far distance to lend a suitably warlike background. Terry had cleaned up his language for the camera and the result was a predictable tribute to a wounded officer. He described the moment I was wounded: I did not recognise the description. I had not felt heroic, only foolish, and far from receiving a medal I had thought I would be reprimanded for breaking orders.

Dr. Maitland's pink and plump face filled the screen. "Frankly, we were surprised he hadn't died. The body can only stand so much shock, and Nick had been very badly mauled. But that's our specialisation here, you see. We make the lame to walk."

The picture changed to one of the physiotherapy rooms. "We'll cover these pictures with wildtrack," Angela said, "describing your treatment."

"Wildtrack," Matthew helpfully explained, "is an unseen voice."

A West Indian nurse described what it had been like to watch me trying to walk. "He'd be bent over. I know he was hurting himself, but he wouldn't give up."

"Nick Sandman wouldn't give up," Tony Bannister's voice broke in, "because he had a dream." The picture cut to *Sycorax* lying abandoned. "He had a boat, *Sycorax*, and he dreamed of taking her back to the Falklands. He would sail in peace where once he had marched in anger."

"Oh, come on!" I protested. "Who makes up this garbage?"

"We can change anything," Angela said. "We're just trying to give you an idea of what the final film could look like."

The film described how the *Sycorax* had chafed her warps and been driven onto a mudbank in the river. "That's a lie!" I was angry. "Bannister wanted my berth!"

Angela pressed the pause button. "What happened was a regrettable accident, for which Tony is making amends."

She released the button and the film showed the caterpillar-tracked crane which had lifted *Sycorax* out of the trees and onto the front lawn. "Boat and man," Bannister's wildtrack intoned, "would be restored together, and this film follows their progress." The screen went blank.

"There." Angela switched the set off. "That wasn't too bad, was it?"

I waved at the set. "It's rubbish. Bannister took my boat and my wharf. Now, because he doesn't want the bad publicity, he'll foist that gibberish on the public!"

"Tony rented Lime Wharf from your wife in good faith," Angela said.

"My ex-wife," I corrected her, "whose power of attorney expired when she walked out on me."

"Tony didn't know that. And you have to admit he's trying to put matters right."

"At least your film didn't mention my father," I said.

"We wanted to talk to you about that," Matthew muttered nervously.

"Bloody hell." I limped to the far end of the room where Bannister had hung a group of pictures of his dead wife, Nadeznha. She had been a very beautiful girl, with dark eyes and a happy smile. I turned back to Matthew and Angela. "Just out of interest," I said, "who exactly is paying to repair *Sycorax*?"

Angela paused. "We are, naturally."

My ribs hurt beneath the bandages. "We?"

"It's a television production, Mr. Sandman. If the programme wants to film the boat's restoration, then the programme budget will have to find the funds."

So Bannister wasn't even paying for *Sycorax*. He'd towed her ashore, allowed his South African thug to strip her of valuables, and the TV company would now pay to put it back together. It was astonishing.

"No," I said. "No way. Bannister wrecked my boat. Bannister can put it back together. Why should I make a spectacle of myself for something he did? I've spent the last two years running away from publicity. I don't want to spend the rest of my life being a man who won a medal. So take the film back to London and tell Bannister to send me a big cheque."

There was silence for a few seconds, then Angela walked to the window. "Look at it this way. You accepted Tony's hospitality. Your boat's on his lawn. The first ten minutes of the film are already shot. Do you think any law court in the land will think you didn't agree to all of that? Of course you can fight the case, Mr. Sandman. You can claim that you always planned to sue Tony, but that you first decided to accept his hospitality. Do you think you'll win?"

"He wrecked my boat!"

"He was assured by your wife that it was abandoned! She assured him very personally."

I wondered how Melissa and Bannister had met, then supposed it must have been when Bannister wanted to rent the wharf.

"Well?" Angela asked. "What's your answer?" I didn't reply. "We want to make a film, Nick. It will tell the story of a man who achieved something quite remarkable. It will give new hope to other people who are suffering." Angela's voice was sweet reason itself. "At the same time it will give you a peaceful convalescence and a beautifully rebuilt boat. But you should understand that none of the necessary materials for the repair will be delivered until you sign the contract."

I turned and looked at *Sycorax*. "Let me get this straight," I said. "Bannister took my boat out of the water because he thought it was abandoned?"

"He was told it was abandoned, yes," Angela said.

"And Melissa rented the wharf to him, even though it wasn't actually hers to rent?"

"So you say." Angela was guarded.

"And it was Bannister's thug who beat me up?"

Bannister had promised me he would try to find Mulder and persuade the South African to return the medal, but there had been no news. Bannister had also tried to persuade me to drop my charges against Fanny, but I wanted him nailed. That was a separate business from restoring *Sycorax*, and it seemed, whether I liked it or not, that the only way to achieve that was to cooperate with Angela's film.

"What control do I have?" I asked her. "I can't have you saying that I want to go back to the Falklands. I want to sail to New Zealand."

"You mean editorial control?" Angela said. "Let me explain. You'll have to understand that our skill lies in the shaping and transmission of information. We're very good at it, and we don't surrender the control of those skills to anyone. If we did, then we'd be forced to bend to the whim of any politician or public-relations man who wanted to conceal the truth. And that's what we tell, the truth. So you get no editorial control. But you tell us your truth, and we'll tell it to the world."

There did not seem to be much to say to that. "I see."

"So perhaps you'll sign the contracts?" Angela took from her bag a thick wad of documents. She separated and dropped three copies of each document onto the table as she spoke. "Head contract. The sub-contract with Bannister Productions Ltd, who will actually make the film. An insurance idemnity form. Your undertaking not to talk with any other television company or newspaper while the film's being made. And a medical form." She dropped the last pieces of paper, then held a pen towards me. "Sign wherever I've pencilled a cross, then please initial every page of the two contracts."

I took the pen and sat down. I tried to follow the good advice to read whatever I was signing, but the contracts were dense with sub-paragraphs. And the truth is that I've always found it embarrassing and untrusting to keep people waiting while I read the small print. I signed in triplicate, then initialled all the separate pages. "Now do I get the timber for *Sycorax*'s hull?"

"It will come next week." Angela pushed the documents over to Matthew, who witnessed them. "Your first call," she said to me, "is next Tuesday. The location will be the town marina. Do you know it?"

"I grew up in it."

"And you do understand you've signed to make yourself available and cooperative for the successful completion of the film? That means I'd appreciate it if you would always let me know where you are."

"I'll be in London tomorrow," I said, "to see my children. Is that permitted, ma'am?"

She ignored my clumsy sarcasm. "I'll see you on Tuesday," she said instead, "when we'll be going to sea. And might I recommend that you watch Tony's show tonight?"

They left, and I began to understand how General Menendez must have felt in Port Stanley: slashed to ribbons and nowhere to turn. But it was all my own fault.

THAT NIGHT THE PAIN in my back decided to tighten. Alone in the lavish house, I felt the temptation to despair; to accept that I would never walk properly. I swallowed four aspirins washed down with two large glasses of Irish whiskey, none of which helped, then I diverted my self-pity by switching on "The Tony Bannister Show".

It was the final programme in the present series and kept to Bannister's usual formula: a handful of celebrity guests, a rock group and an excited audience. It was a standard kind of television chat show, yet there was one very special ingredient—Tony Bannister himself. He had a natural charm, a quicksilver wit, and a very reassuring presence that made him an ideal intermediary between the audience and the gilt-edged celebrities who were his guests. I warmed to him as I watched him.

At the show's end he talked about the films he would be making during the coming summer months. Nearly all his films contributed to his tough-but-tender image. They showed Bannister climbing mountains, or diving to wrecks, or training with the Foreign Legion. This year's films would be dominated by an account of his assault on the St. Pierre. He spoke of his dead wife, recalling her loss, but promising that this year he would sail *Wildtrack* to victory in her memory. The screen showed *Wildtrack* as he spoke. She was a Farley 64, a British-made racing cruiser that appealed to wealthy customers around the world.

The picture cut back to Bannister in the studio. "And I'll be making another, very special, film this summer," he was saying, "a film about bravery, and recovery. A film about a man who has modestly refused to make any profit from his hard-won fame."

I knew now why Angela had told me to watch this show, and I cringed back in the sofa.

"Indeed," Bannister continued, "a man who has so far shunned the limelight, but who finally agreed to tell his story as an encouragement to anyone else who finds themselves in adversity." The screen showed a photograph of me. I was in uniform, sitting in a wheelchair, and it must have been taken on the day I received the medal. "In the autumn we'll be bringing you the true story of Britain's most reluctant Falklands hero, Captain Nicholas Sandman, VC." The audience applauded.

Pain scoured my back as I wrenched myself off the sofa to turn the television off. Goddamn it, why had I agreed to their film? Only for *Sycorax*, of course, but I felt a fool.

The telephone rang suddenly, and when I picked it up Inspector Harry Abbott chuckled. "So that's why you did it."

"Why I did what, Harry?"

"I told you Bannister looked after his friends. Going to be a telly star, are you? But remember what they say about supping with the devil, Nick."

"What have I done, Harry?"

He paused, evidently to gauge the innocence of my question. "You've withdrawn your charges against Fanny Mulder, Nick."

"I have not!"

"Then how come the television company's lawyer has been on to our office saying so? He claims he's got your signature, but are you telling me you don't know anything about it?"

"Bloody hell," I said softly, remembering all the pages I'd signed and initialled, but hadn't read. "I know about it."

"Long spoon, lad, long spoon." Harry sighed. "If it's any interest to you, Nick, the South African's staying at Bannister's London house. We think he's been there ever since he raked you over."

"If you knew that, why hasn't someone gone to arrest him?"

Abbott paused again. "I told you, I'm not crime any more. Good night, Nick."

I put the phone down, then found my copies of the contract documents and, sure enough, there was a clause which said that I unreservedly relinquished any legal claims, actions or proceedings that might be pending against any member of the production company. I found that Francis Mulder was named as boatmaster for the production, responsible for the supply and safe handling of all vessels needed for the filming. And all the time Bannister had sworn he did not know where Mulder was.

I limped to the window, lurching my weight onto my right leg in an attempt to convince myself that it would not buckle and that I was strong enough to sail alone into emptiness. I stared into the night and reflected on the art of committing a reluctant enemy to battle. You offer an easy victory, then you clobber him with all the nasties that you've kept well hidden. And I'd just been clobbered.

Chapter 2

It was easy to find Bannister's London address in his study. I thought of warning him, but decided against. Next morning I caught the first train to London, but I still did not reach Richmond Green until nearly eleven o'clock. I was supposed to collect my children from Melissa's Kensington house at midday, so I was in a hurry.

It was a lovely spring morning, fragrant with blossom. A cherry tree was shedding petals in the front garden of Bannister's expensive house. I rang the bell, keeping my finger on the button.

There was a rattle of bolts and chains, and a thin, balding man in black trousers and waistcoat opened the door. He was evidently offended by my behaviour, but I gave him no time to protest. "Is Mr. Bannister at home?"

He looked me up and down before answering. I did not look very impressive: I was dressed in old jeans, torn deck shoes and a frayed shooting jacket. "Mr. Bannister is not yet up, sir." He spoke with the haughty reserve of a trained servant and I saw his hand go towards the alarm system's hidden panic button that would alert the police station.

"My name is Captain Nicholas Sandman, VC." I used the full rigmarole and my crispest accent to reassure him, and he took his finger away from the button. "I really came to see Fanny Mulder."

"Mr. Mulder has a private entrance by the garage, sir."

"I've arrived by this one now," I said. "Please send him up to me. Is there somewhere I can wait?"

"Indeed, sir." He showed me into a lovely, high-ceilinged room where he drew back the curtains to let the morning sun stream onto an expensive pale carpet. "I believe Mr. Mulder also is still sleeping, sir. Would you like some coffee while you wait?"

"A large pot of it, please. Some milk, no sugar."

"I shall inform Mr. Mulder that you're here, sir." He gave a hint of a bow, and left.

I waited. The room was beautifully furnished, with a fine impressionist painting over the mantelpiece. A lovely photograph of Nadeznha Bannister stood on a side table. In front of the fireplace was an expensive glass-topped coffee table, at least twelve feet square.

"Coffee, sir." The manservant put a large silver Thermos jug on the table. "I've informed Mr. Mulder of your arrival, sir, and he will join you as soon as he can. Would you like today's paper, sir?"

"No. Is there a back gate to the house?"

He shook his head. Which meant that if Mulder wanted to escape me then he would have to leave by the front gate and I would see him run for it. If he did, I planned to phone the police.

But Mulder did not run for it. He kept me waiting ten minutes, but finally appeared in jeans and a sweatshirt that carried the name *Wildtrack* in big letters. He stood, sullen and huge.

"What is it?" he asked curtly.

"You heard that I withdrew my charges against you, Fanny?"

"I heard." He was suspicious.

"But you still owe me an apology."

A look of hurt pride flicked over the big face, then he shrugged. "I didn't know you were a cripple, man."

I suppose that passed for an apology, meaning that if he'd known I was crippled he'd have only broken one rib instead of two. I smiled. "And you've got something that I want, Fanny. Or did you find a buyer for the medal?"

He tried to brazen it out. "What medal?"

I picked up the silver Thermos jug, and smashed it down hard onto the glass table, which splintered into crazed fragments. Magazines, dried flowers and ashtrays collapsed among the broken glass. I smiled pleasantly at Fanny again. "You've got two minutes to find my medal, or I'll break up this house."

Fanny was staring aghast at the wreckage. "You're mad!" For a second I thought he was going to attack me, but he stayed rigid by the door.

"One minute forty seconds, Fanny."

"I'll get it, man! Don't do any more! I'll get it!"

The medal arrived within one minute. Just seconds after Fanny had thrust the slim case towards me, Bannister himself appeared in the doorway. He was wearing a bathrobe of flamboyant silk. He stared, appalled, at the horrid mess where his table had stood, then looked at me in astonishment. "Captain Sandman?"

"Good morning," I said politely. "I came here to retrieve my medal. Mr. Mulder was reluctant to admit that he still possessed it." I opened the lid of the case and looked down at the dull cross of bronze with its claret ribbon. "I'm sorry I had to use unfair methods to persuade him, but clearly you were making no effort at all."

"Ah." Bannister appeared incapable of collecting his wits.

"You told me you didn't know where Fanny was," I accused him.

"I . . ." He stopped, trapped by his lie.

"But, as you can see, I found him." I put the medal into my pocket.

"I can explain everything, Nick." Bannister had found his charm now, and deployed it hurriedly. "Fanny only arrived last night. I was going to talk to you about him, of course—"

"I'm in a hurry," I cut him off. "But I also want to tell you that I've no intention of making your film. None. I'll ask my lawyer to send you a bill for *Sycorax*'s restoration. Unless you'd prefer to write me a cheque now?"

"Nick!" Bannister's hurt tone suggested he had been grievously wronged. "It's going to be a very good film, very good!"

"I'd rather have a cheque," I said.

"You've signed a contract." Angela Westmacott stepped into the room. Her sudden appearance silenced me. "You've signed a contract," she said again, "and I expect you to fulfil it."

Like Bannister she was in a silk robe and she seemed to be naked under it. Her hair was cascading in a golden flood down her back. She had no make-up, yet she looked very beautiful. I understood now why she always behaved with such imperiousness: she had Anthony Bannister as a lover. She looked with disgust at the mess I'd made.

"Are you telling us that you plan to withdraw from your contract, Mr. Sandman?"

"I shall talk to my lawyer about it on Monday."

"Do that. And once you've wasted his time and your money, I shall still expect you at midday on Tuesday. If you're not at the marina, I shall consider you in breach of contract. Good day, Mr. Sandman."

I went down the front steps into the sunlight, and I was suddenly jealous of Anthony Bannister. Angela might be a cheat, and she was probably a liar, but I was jealous.

I DELIVERED THE CHILDREN safely back to their Swedish nanny at teatime. Melissa, hearing our voices in the kitchen, graciously accorded me an audience. She grimaced at my clothes. "I do hope the children don't resent being seen with you. Don't passers-by think they've been kidnapped?"

"I don't want to spend money on clothes," I said. "Not that I've got any money for clothes."

"I do hope you're not going to be frightfully boring and tell me you have money problems?"

"My money problems are no longer your concern."

"They are very much my concern, darling," she said. "School fees. You can't expect Mands and Pip to slum it in a state school." I flinched from Melissa's nicknames for our children, Amanda who was six now, and Piers who was four.

"I'm already paying their school fees," I said. "There's a standing order at the bank."

"But in a few years, Nick, Mands will want to be at a decent boarding school and Piers will go to Eton, of course, and you can't expect Hon-John to pay. They're not his children."

"But the Honourable John's filthy rich," I said, as though it was a most reasonable objection.

Melissa sighed. "And Mumsy and Dadsy won't pay."

I imagined how very relieved Mumsy and Dadsy must be that Melissa had rid herself of the jailbird's son and married the Honourable John instead. Melissa was a most beautiful rat, who had abandoned the sinking ship with immaculate timing.

I walked to the window. "You've got my army pension that I've hocked for their school fees. You've got the tin handshake which paid for their bedrooms in this place. What more would you like? A pint of my blood?"

"I see that being out of hospital hasn't helped your temper." Melissa smiled at me, evidently satisfied with her victory in the opening skirmish and now prepared to offer a truce. "I saw you on the moving-wallpaper device last night. Do you think they'll want to interview me?"

"Why don't you ask Tony Bannister?"

Melissa glared at me. She is a most beautiful woman, and I, foolishly, had married her only for those looks. She married me for my father's wealth, and once that had gone she went straight to the divorce court. By that time I was on a hospital ship. "Do I hear jealousy?" she asked me sweetly.

"Yes."

She smiled, liking that answer. "I know Tony quite well." Her voice lingered judiciously on the word "quite", investing it with special meaning.

"Of course, he's another sailor, isn't he?"

"Do you think I have a weakness for sailors?"

"All I know," I said bitterly, "is that your friend Tony has a weakness for a South African brute."

"That's hardly surprising, is it? If you had that ghastly man threatening you, you'd have a bodyguard too."

I stared in astonishment at her. My words had achieved the effect of tossing a grenade into an apparently empty foxhole and being rewarded with a body. The foxhole, in this case, was Melissa's prodigious memory for gossip.

"Who's threatening him?" I asked. The big blue eyes looked suspiciously at me. Now, upon discovering my ignorance, Melissa was wondering what advantage there might be in revealing more.

"Who?" I insisted.

She evidently decided there was no advantage in disclosing her knowledge. "Did you have a lovely time with the children?"

"We went to Holland Park."

"How very thrilling for you all, but I hope you didn't fill them up with greaseburgers, Nick?"

"I gave them fish and chips. It's all I can afford. And talking of money," I said, "when are you going to pay me the rent you've been taking for my wharf?"

The faintest note of alarm entered Melissa's voice. "Don't be ridiculous, Nick."

I turned on her. "You rented my wharf when you had no right to."

"I might have known that if I invited you up for a chat you'd become tiresome." Melissa opened her hands like a cat stretching its claws. "Actually, Nick, I had to rent the wharf."

"Why? Did Hon-John misplace one of his millions?" The Honourable John had oiled himself onto the board of a merchant bank and was already tipped as a future government minister.

"They're not Hon-John's children, Nick," Melissa said. "Mands and Pip need ponies, and I really can't use Hon-John's private account for your children's necessities."

"Why didn't you just ask me for some cash?"

"You had some?" The interest was immediate.

"I could have pawned the medal. All I'm asking, Melissa dear, is why you rented Lime Wharf to Bannister?"

"That doctor said you'd never walk again, so it seemed hardly likely that you'd ever need the boat, let alone the wharf. And your boat was nothing but scrap, Nick! No one was looking after it. Frankly, I thought you could do with the extra money—for the children, of course."

The nerve of it was awe-inspiring. I reflected that if the boat's registration papers had not been safe in my lawyer's office Melissa would have sold *Sycorax* to get herself a new hat for Royal Ascot.

The door opened, and the Honourable John came into the room. He looks every inch as expensive as his wife. He is tall, thin, very pinstriped, with sleek black hair that lies close to a narrow and handsome head. He hesitated when he saw me. "Ah. Didn't know you were here, Nick. I hear you're going to be a telly personality?"

"They want me to encourage the nation to do its duty."

"Splendid, splendid." He hovered. "And are you recovering well?"

"Fine most of the time," I said cheerfully.

"Jolly good, jolly good. I just came in," he explained to Melissa, "for the Common Market report on broccoli."

"In the escritoire, darling, with your other thrillers. Nick was being tiresome about his wharf."

"And quite right, too. I said you didn't have any right to rent it out." The Honourable John shot up in my estimation.

He dug about in the papers on the desk and found whatever he wanted. "I'm off to see someone. Will I see you for dinner, darling?"

"No," I said. They ignored me, kissed, and the Honourable John left.

"Does he know about you and Anthony Bannister?" I asked. Melissa twisted round like a disturbed cat.

"Do not be more tiresome than you absolutely need to be, Nicholas."

I stared into her face. A wedge-shaped face, narrowing from the broad clear brow to the delicate chin. With her pale, pale hair, it was a face that made men turn on the pavement as she went by.

"Who," I said, returning to the earlier question that Melissa had avoided answering, "is threatening Anthony Bannister?"

"It's only a story." Melissa opened an onyx box and took out a

36

cigarette. "There always are stories, Nick, about glamorous men like Tony." She paused to blow out a stream of smoke. "It's all to do with Nadeznha, his late lamented. You know she died last year?"

"I know."

"People were full of sympathy for Tony, of course, but there is just the teensiest hint of suspicion that he might have wanted her out of the way." Melissa watched me very carefully. "It's the perfect murder, isn't it? I mean, who's to know?"

"Overboard?" I said.

"Exactly. One splash and you don't even have to buy a coffin, do you? Anyway, Nadeznha died at night and there was only one other person on deck."

"Fanny Mulder?"

"Bull's-eye."

"But why would Bannister want her dead?"

Melissa rolled her eyes to the ceiling. "Because she was going to walk out on him, of course! And think of the alimony!" Melissa's voice took on an unaccustomed enthusiasm. "And I'm sure Tony's not exactly playing the taxman with a straight bat. Nadeznha would have revealed all, wouldn't she? Anyway, Tony's pride couldn't have endured losing a catch like Nadeznha."

"Was she a catch?"

"Only Kassouli's daughter." Melissa's tone showed how disgusted she was by my ignorance. "Oh, come on, Nick! Even you must have heard of Yassir Kassouli!"

I'd heard of him, of course. He was rumoured to be richer than Croesus. Yassir Kassouli owned ships, oil companies, finance houses and manufacturing industries around the globe. He had been born in the Levant, but had married an American and become an American citizen.

"His money," Melissa said, "will go to his son, but Nadeznha can't have died poor, can she? She was the genuine American Princess."

"She was certainly pretty." I thought of the photographs in Bannister's Devon house.

"Yassir Kassouli has never forgiven Tony for her death. I mean, at worst it was murder, and at best carelessness. And you can imagine how sinister someone like Kassouli can be if he decides he doesn't like you."

"Do you think Mulder pushed Nadeznha overboard?" I asked.

Melissa adopted a look of hurt innocence. "I am merely telling you the faintest trace of gossip, and I will utterly deny ever mentioning Tony's name to you. But the answer to your question, Nick, as to who might have threatened Tony, is Yassir Kassouli. The current whisper is that Yassir's sworn that Tony's not going to win the St. Pierre."

"Which is why Bannister keeps Mulder around?"

"Exactly. So what are you going to do now, Nick?"

"I'll see the kids in two weeks."

"I don't mean that. I mean with what passes for the rest of your life?"

"Ah! I'm going to repair *Sycorax*, and sail her to New Zealand. I'll fly back to see the kids when I can."

"I shall need security from you, Nick. You can't just abandon your children in destitution while you gallivant in the South Seas, can you?"

"I smiled. "Dear Melissa. Money, money, money."

"Who'll look after the children if I don't?"

"Their nanny?" I kissed her upturned cheek. "I'll see you in two weeks."

"Goodbye, Nicholas. The maid will see you out." She pulled the bellrope.

I left empty-handed, though in truth I had not expected to get any of Bannister's rent money. But nor had I expected to hear of a rumoured crime. I remembered Nadeznha Bannister's face from her photographs; she had been so pretty and happy. Now she lay thousands of feet deep, drifting in the sluggish darkness, and there was a whisper that she had been murdered. I told myself it was none of my damned business, but I couldn't shake it out of my head.

When I got back to Devon I searched amongst the yachting magazines in Bannister's study for an account of the accident that had killed Nadeznha. I found something even better: on his desk there was a transcript of the inquest.

It told a simple story. *Wildtrack* had been on the return leg of the St. Pierre, some five hundred miles off the Canadian coast, and sailing hard during a night watch. The seas were heavy, and the following wind was force six to seven, gusting to eight. At two in the morning Nadeznha Bannister had been the watch captain. The only other person on deck was Fanny Mulder, described as the boat's navigator. That seemed odd. I'd been told Fanny was the professional skipper, and anyway, why would a navigator be standing a night watch as crew?

Mulder's evidence stated that the wind had risen after midnight, but that Nadeznha Bannister had decided against reducing sail. In the old days a yacht always shortened sail to ride out gales, but in today's races they go hell-for-leather to win. At about two in the morning Nadeznha noticed that the boom was riding high and asked Fanny to go forward and check that the kicking-strap hadn't loosened. He went forward, wearing a safety harness. He testified that Nadeznha, at the wheel in the aft cockpit, was similarly harnessed. Just as he was rerigging the kicking-strap, *Wildtrack* was pooped. A great sea, larger than any other in that dark night, broke onto the yacht's stern. She shuddered, half swamped, and Fanny told how he had been thrust forward by the rush of the cold water. His harness held, but by the time *Wildtrack* had juddered free of the heavy seas, he found that Nadezhna had gone. The yacht's guardrails and life belts had been swept from the stern by the violence of the breaking wave.

Bannister was the first on deck. The rest of the crew quickly followed. They dropped sail, started the engine and used white flares to search the sea. At daybreak they were still searching, though by then there was no hope, for Nadeznha had not been wearing a life jacket, trusting instead to her safety harness. Her body had never been found.

The coroner remarked that *Wildtrack* had not shortened sail, and noted that this decision had been taken by the deceased, whose skill at sailing and whose bravery at sea were not in question. It was a tragic accident, and the sympathy of the court was extended to Mr. Anthony Bannister and to Nadeznha's father, Mr. Yassir Kassouli, who had flown from America to attend the inquest.

The verdict was accidental death, and the matter was closed.

"FORCE SIX OR SEVEN?" Jimmy Nicholls said. "I wouldn't shorten sail either."

"You think it was an accident?" I asked.

"I weren't there, boy. But it just shows you, don't it? Always unlucky if you take a maid to sea."

It was Tuesday. My lawyer had advised me that if I wanted *Sycorax* restored I should make the film, and so Jimmy was taking me to the marina in his thirty-foot fishing boat. It was a warm day, but Jimmy was dressed in his usual woollen vest, flannel shirt, serge waistcoat and shapeless tweed jacket that hung over thick, tar-stained trousers tucked into fleece-lined sea boots. Jimmy did not intend to discard any clothing until he was stripped for his coffin.

He had almost found the coffin this last winter.

"Bastards put me in hospital, Nick."

He coughed vilely and spat towards the houseboat that was still moored on my wharf. Mulder was supposed to live there, but I had not seen him since the morning in London.

"You should give up smoking, Jimmy," I said.

"They'd like that, wouldn't they? There was a time when an Englishman were free, Nick, but we ain't free now. They'll be stopping our ale next."

Jimmy was seventy-three. In his twenties he had been one of twenty hired hands on a rich man's racer. Jimmy's job had been mastheadman, spending his days a hundred feet high on the crosstrees to ensure that the big sails did not tangle with the standing rigging. During the war he served in destroyers and had been torpedoed twice. Now, notionally retired, he owned this clinker-built boat that hunted bass, crab and lobsters off the jagged headlands.

As we chugged downstream, I again probed Jimmy's opinion of Nadeznha Bannister's death.

"I don't reckon she'd have taken a risk," he said. "She could sail a boat right enough, I'll say that for the maid."

"Right enough to fall overboard?" I asked.

"Ah!" It was half cough and half spit. "You're all the same, you youngsters. I've seen men who knew the sea like a hound knows its master, and they still went oversides."

I kept trawling for gossip. "I've heard rumours, Jimmy, that her death wasn't an accident?"

"There are always rumours. They say she was pushed, don't they? And they say as how it wasn't that Mulder fellow on deck with her, but Mr. Bannister."

"That's news to me."

"Just pub talk, Nick."

I tried another tack. "Why does Bannister keep Mulder with him?"

"Don't know. He don't talk to me, Mr. Bannister don't. But I don't like that other bloke. Keeps bad company, he do. Drinks with Georgie Cullen."

Jimmy lit one of his stubby pipes. We were turning into the wide sea reach that was edged by the town.

A French aluminium-hulled boat was motoring in from the sea, the yacht that had been moored in the pool beneath Bannister's house the previous week. The same black-haired girl was at the tiller and I nodded towards her. "She's a good sailor."

"Boat comes from Cherbourg. Called *Mystique*."

There was very little Jimmy did not know about the river. Tourists, seeing his filthy clothes and smelling his ancient pipe, might avoid him, but his old rheumy eyes saw everything.

"The maid ain't a Froggy, though," he added. "American. She says she be writing a pilot book. I thought there were plenty enough pilot books for the Channel, but she do say there ain't one for Americans."

Jimmy spun the wheel to turn his boat towards the entrance of the town boatyard. It no longer made boats, but instead was a marina for the wealthy who wanted protected berthing for their yachts. I could see *Wildtrack* waiting for me at one of the floating pontoons. She was long, and very sleek, with a wide blue flash decorating her gleaming white hull.

"Have you heard anything about someone wanting to stop Bannister from winning the St. Pierre?" I asked Jimmy.

"The Froggies, of course. They'd do anything to keep him from winning it, wouldn't they?" Jimmy had a true Devon man's distrust of the

40

French, though he admired them as seamen. He brought the heavy fishing boat alongside the pontoon with a delicacy that was as astonishing as it was unthinking. He looked over at *Wildtrack* and the small crowd that waited for me. Mulder was in *Wildtrack*'s cockpit, Matthew Cooper was on the pontoon with his film crew, and Anthony Bannister waited to one side with Angela beside him.

Angela was wearing shorts and Jimmy growled in appreciation of her long legs. "That be nice, Nick."

He held out a hand to steady me as I went to step onto the pontoon. "Nick Sandman, you listen to me. You takes their damned money and you mends your boat. You lets them make their daft film, and then you goes off to sea. You hear me? And you don't mess about with the dead, boy."

"I hear you, Jimmy."

"But you never were one to listen, were you? Go on with you. I'll see you in the pub tonight."

I CAN'T SAY that we went to sea as a happy ship. Mulder did not speak to me and his crew were surly, while Matthew and his camera team stayed out of everybody's way. Angela retired to the after cockpit. Tony Bannister grasped the nettle, though. "I'm glad you've come, Nick."

"Somewhat under protest," I said stiffly.

"I'm sure." We were motoring across the bar, between the rocky headlands where the breakers smashed white. "I think," Bannister said awkwardly, "that we'd better let bygones be bygones. I would have told you about Fanny, and you would have got your medal back."

For the sake of peace, and because we seemed stuck with each other's company, I agreed.

We had bucked our way across the bar and Mulder now ordered the sails hoisted. He killed the engine, and instantly *Wildtrack* became a creature in her element. The sails were vast and white, swooping her gracefully southwards in the face of a brisk southwesterly wind.

Bannister and I sat in the central cockpit. Mulder must have known I was watching him and he must have guessed how I wanted to despise his seamanship. But he was good. He displayed a confident and rare skill. His crew of seven men, identically dressed in blue and white kit, were drilled to a quiet efficiency, but the star of the boat was Mulder.

And I was suddenly, unexpectedly, happy. Not because I'd made a precarious peace with Bannister, but because I was at sea. Already the small Devon beaches were indistinct, hidden by the heave of grey waves. A lobsterman coming from Start Point thudded past us in a stained boat heaped with pots and buoys, and I thought I detected a derisive expression on the skipper's face as he glanced at Bannister's fancy boat. I

41

would not have chosen a boat like *Wildtrack* to take me back to the ocean, but suddenly that did not matter. I could smell the sea and I could feel its lash in the spray and I could have cried for happiness when I saw the first fulmar make its careless flight along a wave's shifting face.

"What do you think of the boat?" Bannister had taken the wheel from Mulder. He looked marvellous as he stood at the big wheel. His legs were braced, his face tanned and his hair wind-blown.

"Impressive." The truth was that I preferred my yachts to be old-fashioned. Yet, in her way, I suppose *Wildtrack* was impressive. She was certainly expensive. The main cockpit was in the centre of the boat, but there was a rear cockpit, aft of the owner's cabin, which would serve as a sun deck when the boat was in warmer seas. She was a boat built for the world's rich, complete with digital logs, motor-driven winches, satellite receivers and running hot water.

The old seamen who had sailed from Devon—Raleigh and Drake and Nelson—would have understood *Sycorax*, but they would have been flummoxed by the silicon-chip efficiency of this sleek creature.

They would have been flummoxed, too, by the extraordinary equipment which the film crew had deployed on the coachroof. Bannister tried to reassure me. "The idea is to film a background interview today. How you learned to sail, where, who taught you, why. We'll cut it in with some old home movies of you as a kid."

The cameraman was filming general views of the boat, but was inexorably working his way aft to where Bannister and I waited in the central cockpit. I noticed how Bannister fidgeted with the boat. He constantly twitched the helm to keep the small liquid-crystal boatshape steady on the tactical screen. Mulder had not needed the electronic aid to sail *Wildtrack* at her highest speed, but Bannister was not a natural helmsman. He suddenly seemed uncomfortably aware of my gaze.

"Would you like to take her, Nick?"

"Sure."

"We're steering one-nine-five," Bannister said as he stepped aside.

"One-nine-five." I glanced down at the compass. So long as the wind did not change, I only had to keep one finger on the big power-assisted wheel to compensate for *Wildtrack*'s touch of weatherhelm. The sea was not big enough to jolt the big yacht off her course. I sensed a gust, luffed into it for speed, and then paid off with the extra half knot staying on the fancy speedometer. I did it without thinking and knew in that moment that nothing had changed. Sailing a boat well takes practice that turns into instinct, and I found, at that moment, that my instinct had not been abraded by my years of hospitals and pain.

The cameraman had appeared close in front of me. The clapperboard snapped, and I tried to forget the intrusive presence of the lens.

"Tell me when you first sailed, Nick," Bannister said.

"Long time ago." Suddenly I found it easy to talk. I spoke of Jimmy teaching me, and I described a bad night, much later on, when *Sycorax* had clawed me off the Roches Douvres, and I still swear that it was *Sycorax* who saved my life in that maelstrom of rock and rain. I must have talked enthusiastically, for Bannister seemed pleased.

"When you were wounded," he asked, "did you ever think you'd be back in a boat?"

"I thought of nothing else."

"What actually happened," he asked, "when you were wounded?"

"I got shot." Now that he was talking about the Falklands I heard my answers becoming sullen and short.

He smiled, as though to put me at my ease. "What actually happened, Nick, when you won the VC?"

"Do you want to cross the Skerries?" I nodded ahead to where the shallow bank off Start Point was making the tide turbulent.

Bannister realised that he was not going to draw me on the medal. "How does it feel," he asked instead, "to be in a boat again?"

I hesitated, searching for the right words. I wanted to say I'd let him know just as soon as I was in a proper boat, and not in some hyper-electronic speed-machine, but that was unfair to the pleasure I was having, and the thought of that pleasure made me smile.

"Cut!" Matthew Cooper called to his cameraman.

"I didn't answer!" I protested.

"The smile said everything, Nick." Matthew looked back towards Angela in the aft cockpit and nodded. It seemed I had done well.

Bannister crouched to light a cigarette with a gold-plated storm lighter. "You're going to have to answer those unwelcome questions, Nick. The reason we're making the film is because you're a hero."

"I thought we were making it because your thug damaged my boat?"

He smiled. "*Touché*. But you will have to tell us one day."

It seemed that the day's filming was over, because the camera crew began to pack up their equipment as Mulder took the wheel from me. I explored *Wildtrack*. I'd been worried before I came aboard that my injuries might have made my balance treacherous, but I found no difficulty in keeping my footing as I went to the foredeck. My right leg still shook uncontrollably and threatened to spill me like a drunk, but at least my mobility on *Wildtrack*'s deck gave me optimism.

I dropped down a hatch and saw how the forepeak had been stripped empty to make the bows light. The main cabin showed the same dedication to speed. Luxury had been sacrificed here for lightness.

The rear cabin was Bannister's quarters. Above the bunk was a photograph of Nadeznha. There was a line of print below and I knelt on the bunk to read it. "Nadeznha Bannister, 1956—1983, 49° 18' N, 41° 36' W". I stared into the dead girl's eyes. She had been no attenuated blonde like Melissa or Angela, but a robust girl with dark skin and strong bones.

The cabin's rear hatch slid forward and Bannister swung himself down. He seemed surprised to find me in his quarters, but made no protest. He nodded towards the photograph. "My wife."

"She was very beautiful," I said.

He stared at the photograph. "Greek, Arab, French, Persian and American blood. A wonderful mix. Mind you, it also gave her a fearful temper." He somehow made the temper sound like one of his wife's more endearing characteristics. "She could be very determined," he went on. "She was so damned sure she could win the St. Pierre—which is why she was pushing the boat so hard."

"Is that what killed her?"

"We don't know, not really." He paused. "I think Nadeznha must have unclipped her safety harness for a few seconds."

"She was alone?"

"She was alone at the aft wheel." He nodded towards the small rear cockpit. "The other person on watch had gone forward to tighten the kicking-strap. The rest of us were sleeping. But she was a marvellous sailor. Grew up in Massachusetts, you see, near the sea. We searched, of course. Quartered the sea for the best part of a day." Bannister's voice was toneless now, as though the events had been numbed by repetition. "But in those waters? She'd have been dead in minutes." He clutched at a handrail as the boat lurched from the starboard to the port tack. *Wildtrack*'s motion was becoming rough. Bannister plucked a blanket from the foot of the bunk and picked up a phial of seasickness capsules. "Will you forgive me? Angela's not exactly a born sailor."

I followed him up the companionway to the aft cockpit where Angela lay sprawled in abject misery. She grimaced at me, then twisted and thrust her head through the guardrails. I looked at her tall body draped over the scuppers and I saw in her long bare legs part of the reason why Bannister kept company with her.

Angela came back inboard and curled herself into the crook of Bannister's arm. He wrapped her in the blanket, then fed her two of the pills which, I knew, would do no good now.

"There's only one cure for seasickness," I said.

"Which is?" Bannister asked.

"Stand under a tree."

"Very funny." He held her tight. "What do you think of Fanny as a helmsman?"

"He's good." I tried to sound ungrudging. Mulder was gybing the boat now, swinging her stern across the wind so that the boom slammed across the hull. It could be a dangerous manoeuvre, but his control was so certain that there was never a single jarring thud.

"Nadeznha found him. He was running a charter service in the Seychelles. Very few people know just how good he is. I think of him as my secret weapon to win the St. Pierre. That's why I need him, Nick."

The hour and a half I'd spent on *Wildtrack* was not enough to tell me whether this boat and crew could lift the St. Pierre off the French, but it was possible. The boat was fast, Fanny was clearly brilliant, and Bannister had the ambition.

And he would need it, for the St. Pierre is the greatest prize for racing cruisers. It isn't really a race at all, because an entrant can choose his or her own starting time. The only rules are that a boat must be a production monohull, that it must begin at Cherbourg, sail round the islands of St. Pierre and Miquelon off the coast of Newfoundland and then, without touching land, run home to Cherbourg again. The course is around four and a half thousand nautical miles: a windward flog all the way out against currents and gales; a lottery with fog and ice at the turn; and a fast run back in heavy seas. At the end of the season, whoever has made the fastest voyage holds the prize.

French boats are good, and each autumn when the fog and ice sweep southwards to close the St. Pierre season finally, the French are still the holders and a thousand more orders go to keep French boatyards busy. If a foreigner could take the prize, even for a year, it would be seen in France as a disaster.

"I'm planning a late run," Bannister said, "and the far-north route. With any luck I'll come home just when the autumn programme schedule begins. That'll start next season's shows with a triumph."

"Is that why you're doing it?"

"I'm doing it to prove that a British boat can do it. And for Nadeznha's memory. And because the television company are paying me to do it, and because my audience wants me to win." He rattled the reasons off as if by rote, then paused before adding the final justification. "And to prove that a TV star isn't just a powder puff in an overlit studio." He laughed suddenly, perhaps embarrassed because he had betrayed something personal.

I put a hand on the small wheel that was linked to the larger helm in the central cockpit and felt the rudder's tremors vibrating the stainless-steel spokes. I was thinking of the night of Nadeznha's death. If *Wildtrack* had been running before a heavy sea then why would an experienced sailor con the ship from the aft cockpit? Perhaps Nadeznha had chosen the smaller cockpit as a vantage point to watch for the great waves looming from the darkness behind. I shivered as I imagined the tons of freezing water collapsing onto *Wildtrack*'s stern.

"Do you think *Wildtrack* can win it?" Bannister asked abruptly.

"With luck, yes."

"Would you like to be a part of it, Nick?"

"Me?" I was astonished by the offer. "You don't need me, Bannister!"

"The race rules say we must carry a navigator and Fanny, who was my navigator last year, will take Nadeznha's place as a watch captain."

Bannister turned as his crew spilt the spinnaker from its chute. The gaudily coloured sail blossomed and he turned back to me. "Why don't we end your film by showing you leaving Cherbourg in *Wildtrack*? The film will be transmitted while we're at sea, and it'll help whip up some public enthusiasm for the programme about the race itself."

"I thought the end of my film was *Sycorax* sailing into the sunset?"

"Maybe we'll use that over the opening titles. But think of it, Nick! Winning the St. Pierre!"

I shook my head. "I've never been a speed merchant."

"But do think about it," he urged me. "In a couple of months I'll be giving a big party to announce my bid for the trophy formally. I'd like to say you'll be part of the effort, Nick."

"You need a specialist navigator," I said. "Some guy who's a race tactician as well. I'm really not going to be of any use to you."

"Not in the race, maybe"—Angela forced the words out—"but you'll help the viewing figures. The VC makes you interesting enough, Mr. Sandman, to guarantee us more than twenty million viewers. That will mean we can increase the price of the advertising slots."

So my Victoria Cross was to become an advertiser's weapon? A means of selling more dog food and baked beans? I was framing an outright refusal when a violent lurch of *Wildtrack*'s hull ended the conversation. I saw the mainsail's shadow whip over us. There was a noise like a bass-string thumping, and the boat was suddenly broaching and falling on her beam. I grabbed the small wheel for support. The tall mast was bending, breaking, then falling to leeward. Water boiled up the scuppers and a shroud whipped skywards. The unleashed spinnaker billowed ahead as the mast fell. The slick hull rolled, recovered and slowed. The seas were low, no more than two or three feet, but even so *Wildtrack* staggered as if she'd sailed into a sandbank. The mainsail was shredding with a noise like the fire of an automatic weapon.

Bannister shouted incoherently. A crew member was overboard, tangled in the fallen shrouds. Angela was sobbing. Mulder's voice bellowed above the din and chaos, inflicting order on the panic.

A port shroud had parted. The stainless-steel wire, made to carry all the weight of great winds on a towering mast, must have snapped. The mast and sails had tipped overboard. It had taken no more than two or three seconds, and now *Wildtrack* lay wallowing in the gentle seas. No

46

one was hurt. The boat had pulled up short and it was a simple matter to pull the crewman who had gone overboard back to safety. The broken rigging was secured and the engine was started. All in all it had been a mild accident, harmless except to Bannister's purse.

And to his anger. He took me forward and showed me the turnbuckle that had taken up the tension of the broken shroud. It had not been that the wire had snapped, but rather that the turnbuckle had simply let the shroud go. It was threaded inside, and someone had taken a file to the threads and worn them almost smooth. The sabotage was clumsily obvious. As soon as Mulder put the spinnaker's extra weight on the mast, the threads had given way.

"Fanny!" Bannister was livid. "From now on you live in the boatyard and keep watch. All of you!"

"Does that mean I get my wharf back?" I asked. For a second I thought Bannister was going to hit me, but then he nodded. "You get your damned wharf back." He pushed past me, going back to the stern where his girlfriend was still slumped, suffering from the stomach-churning misery of the sea. For the moment Bannister appeared to have forgotten his offer that I should sail in the St. Pierre as part of his boat's crew.

I hadn't forgotten. And I wouldn't do it. There are lucky boats and unlucky boats, and I smelt the stench of disaster about *Wildtrack*. She had already killed Bannister's wife, and now someone had dismasted her. I did not care what fame or fortune might come to the crew of this boat if she won the St. Pierre, I would not share it. When I sailed my next ocean it would be in *Sycorax* and in no other boat.

Chapter 3

Inspector Abbott came to the village pub three weeks after *Wildtrack* was dismasted. He was wearing trousers made of a wide blue and pink check that looked like dismantled curtains.

"You're looking better," he said to me.

"I'm fine, Harry." I said it confidently, but it was not really true. I was swimming two miles every morning in Bannister's indoor pool and the exercise was laying new muscle beneath the scar tissue, but my leg could still betray me with a sudden and numbing weakness. Only the day before, while walking from the village post office, I'd sprawled helplessly on the pavement. But I would not admit to the weakness, lest I persuade myself that I was not fit enough to sail across the world. "I assume from the fancy dress that you're not on duty?"

Abbot plucked at the trousers. "Don't you like them, Nick?"

"They're horrible."

"They're American golfer's trousers," he said with hurt dignity. "You want a pint, Nick?"

It was early evening and the pub was still empty. Abbott sipped the top off his beer and sighed with pleasure. "Got your medal back, did you?"

"I did, and thank you."

"What do you think of the South African now?"

"He's a good sailor," I said neutrally.

"So was Blackbeard." Abbott lit a cigarette. "I haven't seen Mr. Bannister lately."

"He's on Capri with his girlfriend."

"I wonder why he's stopped going to America for his holidays?" Abbott said with an air of puzzled innocence. "Who's the girlfriend?"

"Girl called Angela Westmacott. She's a producer on Bannister's programme."

Abbott frowned, then clicked his fingers. "Skinny, with blonde hair?"

"Right."

"Looks a bit like your ex-wife: starved. How is Melissa?"

48

"She struggles on."

"I've never understood why men go for those skinny ones." Abbott paused to drain his pint. "I nicked a bloke once who'd murdered a complete stranger. The victim's wife asked him to do it, you see, so he bashed the bloke's head in with a poker. He said that it was probably the only chance he would ever get to go to bed with a pretty woman. Pretty? She was about as pretty as a toothpick. It was almost the perfect murder, wasn't it? Having your best-beloved turned off by a stranger."

The slight stress on "perfect murder" was the second hint that Abbott was not here entirely because he was thirsty. His first hint had been the gentle query as to why Bannister no longer visited America.

"Perfect murder?" I prompted him.

"The thing about a perfect murder, Nick, is that we'll never even know it's happened. Officially there's no such thing. So if you hear about one, Nick, don't believe in it."

The comments were too pointed to ignore. "Does that mean," I asked, "that Nadeznha Bannister's death was an accident?"

"I wasn't there, Nick, I wasn't there."

I had been given a message, though I wasn't at all sure why, or what it was. Abbott fixed me with his hangdog look. "Have you heard these rumours that someone's trying to scupper Bannister's chances of winning the St. Pierre?"

"I've heard them."

"And you know what happened two nights ago in the marina?"

"I heard."

Wildtrack's warps had been cut in the dead of the night, in another attempt at sabotage. If it had not been for a visiting French yachtsman, Bannister's boat might have been carried out to sea. Mulder and his crew had been sleeping alongside in the houseboat and the Frenchman's shout of warning had woken them just in time.

"Clumsy," Abbott said. "If you wanted to stop someone from winning the St. Pierre, would you knock his mast off now? Or cut him adrift now? Why not wait till he's in the race?"

Certainly, if Melissa was right and Yassir Kassouli did want to end Bannister's chances of winning the trophy, then the two incidents were very ineffective.

"Are you making enquiries?" I asked Abbott.

"No, I don't want to get involved. Besides, as I told you, I'm not crime any more."

"What are you, Harry?"

"General dogsbody, Nick."

Abbott was sailing very close to the rumours I'd heard, but always sheering off before anything definite was said. If a message was being given to me, then it was being delivered so elliptically that I was utterly at a loss.

"When's the big party, Nick?" He was referring to the party that was to be held at Bannister's riverside house in the early summer, the occasion on which Bannister would formally announce his entry in the St. Pierre. "I hear," he went on, "that Bannister's introducing his crew at the party. I do hope you won't be one of them?"

"I won't be," I said.

"Because I did hear that Bannister had asked you."

I wondered how Abbott had heard, but decided it was simply riverside gossip. I'd told Jimmy, which was the equivalent of printing the news on the front page of the local newspaper. "He did ask," I said. "I said no, and I haven't heard anything since."

"If he asks again, go on saying no."

I finished my pint and leaned back. "Why, Harry?"

"Why? Because I'm reasonably fond of you. For your father's sake, you understand, and because you were stupid enough to win that bloody

50

gong. I wouldn't want to see you turned into sharkbait. And that boat of Bannister's does seem to be"—he paused—"unlucky."

I tried to force Abbott into a straight answer. "Are you telling me that someone is trying to stop him?"

"Don't know, Nick. Perhaps Bannister's paranoid." He drained his pint. "The wife has cooked some tripe and pig's trotters as a special treat, so I'll be on my way. Remember what I said."

"I'll remember."

As THE DAYS LENGTHENED and warmed I forgot my worries, because *Sycorax* was being mended. Jimmy Nicholls and I were mending her.

They were weeks of hard work, and therefore of pleasure. We scarfed new timbers into *Sycorax*'s hull and caulked them home. We shaped new deck planks and joggled them into place. Jimmy selected trunks of Norway spruce from the timberyard and fetched them upriver on his boat. We put the spruce on the wharf and adzed the trunks down; first we turned them into square sections, then we peeled each corner until they were rounded and we had our masts, gaff and booms.

They were good days. Sometimes a spring rain thundered on the tarpaulin that we'd rigged overhead, but mostly the sun shone in promise of summer. We made a new coachroof, but strengthened it with oak beams so that the cabin could resist a knockdown in heavy seas. As spring turned into summer Jimmy and I began to lay bright new copper sheets over the finished hull, bedding them on layers of tarpaper and fixing them with flat-headed nails of bronze. The copper was expensive, but superior to any antifouling paint, and I wanted its protection before I sailed my wooden boat to where the tropical worms could turn iron-hard mahogany into a porous sponge. Jimmy and I did a good, old-fashioned job. On our rare days off we went to boat auctions on the river and bought good secondhand gear, and all the receipts were sent to the television company, who repaid the money without demur. They were even paying Jimmy a cash wage that the taxman would never hear about.

Matthew Cooper and his camera crew came down every other week to film *Sycorax*'s rebuilding. A piece of work that Jimmy and I might have finished in an hour could take a whole day with Matthew fussing about camera angles and eyelines.

"Nick? Your right arm's in the camera's way. Can you drop your elbow?"

"I can't tighten a bolt if I'm screwed up like Quasimodo."

"It won't show on film." He waited patiently till I'd finished my impression of the hunchback of Notre-Dame. "Thank you, Nick. Dropping the elbow will be enough."

Then the sound-recordist would stop everything because a light aircraft was ruining his tape. I perceived that film-making was very like soldiering, in that it consisted of hours of idle waiting punctuated by moments of half-understood panic.

I was frustrated by the delays, but in turn inflicted frustration on Matthew every time he asked the one question that lay behind the film's purpose. "Can you tell us how you won the medal, Nick?"

"Not right now. Anyone seen the tenon saw?"

"Nick?" Chidingly.

"I can't remember what happened, Matthew, sorry."

"Don't call me Matthew. Remember I'm supposed to be Tony. So what happened, Nick?" Long pause. "Nick, please?"

"Nothing to say, Matthew, sorry, Tony."

Jimmy would chuckle, the film crew would grin, and Matthew would glare at me. I liked him, though. He cared desperately about the quality of his work. He did what Angela ordered him to do, but he invested those orders with a concern for the very best pictures. He was also the conduit for Angela Westmacott's worries, the chief of which was that *Sycorax* should be off Anthony Bannister's lawn by the day of his party.

Angela need not have worried, for Jimmy and I finished the hull ten days ahead of our schedule. I phoned Matthew and told him we could launch in a week's time, just as soon as the engine was back in the boat's belly, and he promised to bring the crew down for the event. Thus we would be in the water the day before the party.

The children came down to Devon for three days and I borrowed a Drascombe Dabber to potter about off the river's mouth where we caught mackerel on hand lines. The nanny came to fetch them back to London in Melissa's new Mercedes.

"Mrs. Makyns says the children are in need of their summer clothes, Mr. Sandman." The nanny was a lolloping great Swede with a metronome voice. "She says you are to give me the money."

"Tell her I will send her a cheque."

"I will tell her. She will see you at Mr. Bannister's party, I think." It sounded like a threat.

That same afternoon a crane arrived to lift *Sycorax* into the water. The launch was scheduled for the next morning and I had a bottle of champagne ready to break over her bows. Preparations for Bannister's party were also well advanced: caterers were setting up tables on the terrace and gardeners were tidying up the lawns. Matthew arrived that evening and found me still working. The newly laid copper reflected the dying sun so that *Sycorax* looked as if she had been cast in red gold.

"She looks good, Nick," Matthew said.

"She is." I was dressed in swimming trunks and happily filthy with tar, paint and varnish stains. "One month for rigging, then she's finished."

Matthew lit a cigarette and helped himself to a beer from the crate I kept by the sheerlegs. "I've got bad news for you."

I peglegged down the ladder and took a beer. "Tell me."

"Angela wants you out of the house by tomorrow night. She says it's only till next Tuesday. Because they've got weekend guests staying, you see. I'm sorry, Nick." Matthew sounded embarrassed at having to make the request.

"I really don't mind, Matthew." I would happily move into a relaunched *Sycorax*. She had no berths yet, no galley and no lavatory, but I had a sleeping-bag, a primus stove and the river.

"Of course," Matthew went on, "you're invited to the party."

"That's nice."

"Because Bannister wants to announce that you'll navigate *Wildtrack* for him."

For a second I did not respond. I was watching the shining-hulled *Mystique*, which had suddenly appeared at Sansom's Point. The boat had been absent for the last two months and I presumed the American girl had been exploring the harbours she would describe in her pilot book.

"Did you hear me?" Matthew asked.

"I heard. I'm not doing it, Matthew."

The American girl was motoring *Mystique* against the tide with just a jib to stiffen her. She had chosen the eastern channel which was both narrower and shallower than the main channel, and which would bring her close to where Matthew and I stood.

"Angela's set her mind on it," Matthew said.

"I'll say no again."

"Then she'll probably refuse to pay for *Sycorax*'s rigging."

"Damn her!" I said. "I'll buy the rigging wire out of the fee you're paying me."

"What fee? Angela says you've been living in Bannister's house, so he ought to get some rent out of you."

"You're joking!"

The misery on Matthew's face told me that he was not. He tried to soften the blow by saying that perhaps it was just a rumour, but he was not convincing.

"Hi!" The voice startled both of us and we turned to see that it was the black-haired American girl, who had hailed us from *Mystique*'s cockpit. "Can I stay in this channel for the pool?"

"What do you draw?" I asked.

"Four foot three." Her voice was businesslike. As she glanced forward I had an impression of bright eyes and a tanned, lively face.

"When you get alongside the perch"—I pointed—"you should steer three-one-oh."

53

"Thanks!"

I crouched down to get a bottle, noting how the pain in my back was almost bearable. "You want a welcome-home beer?"

"No thanks. 'Preciate the help, though. Thanks again." She stooped to push the throttle forward and *Mystique*'s exhaust blurred blue at the transom.

Matthew chuckled. "Not your day, Nick."

NEXT DAY WE PUT *SYCORAX* in the water at the tide's height and broke the champagne across her bows, then we raided Bannister's cellar for more champagne. The cameraman was ceremonially thrown into the river, then Matthew, then me. The American girl watched from her cockpit, but when Matthew shouted at her to join us she just shook her head. An hour later she hoisted sail and went downstream on the tide.

Sycorax looked much smaller now she was in the water. She floated high so that a wide belt of her new copper shone above the river.

Jimmy had tears in his eyes. "She's a beauty, Nick."

"We'll go somewhere in her together, Jimmy."

"Maybe." I think he knew he was dying, and that he would never sail out of sight of land again.

Angela did not come for the launching. After the ceremonial throwings-in we all went swimming, then finished the champagne as we dried in the late afternoon sun. That night I sat on the riverbank and stared at my boat in the water. *Sycorax* still had no masts, rigging or sails, but she was afloat and I was happy. I could afford to forget Angela's insistence that I sail in *Wildtrack*'s crew.

I slept aboard *Sycorax* that night. I made a space on the cabin sole where I spread the sleeping-bag, cooked soup on the primus and ate it in my own cockpit. It did not matter that *Sycorax* was a mess, that her decks were a snake's honeymoon of tangled ropes, or that her scuppers were cluttered with tools and chain. I had my own boat again.

I woke the next morning to the good sound of water slapping my hull and went topsides to see *Wildtrack* moored in the channel. She must have come upriver on the predawn tide. Mulder and his crew were stringing flags up the forestay, doubtless ready for the party that night.

Later that morning Bannister and Angela arrived with the first of their house guests. Bannister strolled down to look at *Sycorax* with two of them. He treated me with jocular familiarity, though I noted that he took pains to mention my VC to his friends, and the medal went some way towards redeeming my reputation, which had been spoilt by my ragged and stained appearance.

"We'll see you at the party tonight, of course?" Bannister asked. "And

54

do bring a friend, won't you? Drinks at six, end-time unknown, and tomorrow will be celebrated as Hangover Sunday."

I promised to be there and, once they'd gone, I spent a happy day fixing the bowsprit. It was hard work, and satisfying. At around four o'clock, when I was tightening the last bolt, *Mystique* returned to her mooring. I finished the job, washed off the worst of the dirt, then rowed myself out to the anchorage. The American girl had gone down into her cabin so, as I approached, I hailed her. "*Mystique! Mystique!*"

"Wait a minute." The voice was sharp. "Who is it?"

"A neigbour."

"OK. Wait."

I was quite ridiculously apprehensive. When she appeared she had a big towel wrapped round her. She seemed very suspicious of me. "Hi."

"Hello. My name's Nick Sandman."

"Jill-Beth Kirov. Kirov like the ballet." Close up I saw that Jill-Beth Kirov had a tanned face, dark eyes and a strong jawline. "Do you mind if I don't shake hands?" she asked.

If she had offered a hand then the towel round her body could have fallen. I solemnly excused her the politeness, and said there was a party at the house tonight and I wondered if she'd like to come as my guest.

"Tonight?" She seemed somewhat taken aback by the invitation. She looked up at Bannister's lavish home. "He's a celebrity, right?"

"Right."

"Are you his boatman?"

"No."

"OK." She was clearly unimpressed with me. "What time's this party?"

"Drinks at six. I gather it goes on most of the night."

"Remind me what the guy's name is?"

"Anthony Bannister."

She clicked her tongue in sudden recognition. "The television guy, right? He was married to Kassouli's daughter?"

"That's the fellow."

"That was kind of messy." She stared up at the house again as if expecting to see blood trickling down the lawn. "It might be fun," she said. "Can I leave the invitation open? I'm kind of busy."

"Of course."

"Thanks again." She stayed on deck to make sure that I pushed my dinghy away from her boat. "Hey! Nick?"

"Yes." I had to turn round on the dinghy's thwart to see her face again. She was grimacing. "What did you do to your back?"

"Car accident. Front tyre blew out. No seat belt."

"Tough." She nodded to show that as far as she was concerned the encounter was over.

I rowed back to my wharf, disappointed. I asked myself what I had expected. An invitation to board *Mystique*? An adolescent sigh and a melting of two hearts into one?

I rowed past *Wildtrack*, watched all the way by Fanny Mulder's knowing and cunning gaze. But I was thinking of other things, of a girl with a strong face and a name like a ballet company. My boat was in the water, and I was ready for love.

Chapter 4

Over two hundred people arrived for the party. Cars blocked the driveway and two helicopters drooped their rotors on the upper lawn. It stayed fine, so drinks were served on the wide terrace that looked down on the river. The party was an evident success from its very beginning. A lot of the faces were famous: actresses, actors, television people, politicians—all enjoying being recognised. Behind the rock band was a giant chart of the North Atlantic on which a notional route for *Wildtrack*'s assault on the St. Pierre was marked. *Wildtrack* herself was dressed with flags and coloured lights.

Melissa, in a swirling silk dress, glimpsed me across the terrace. She greeted me with a kiss. "Tony wants me to look at his boat, but I told him I suffered quite enough of boats when I was married to you."

"It's nice to see you. Are you with the Honourable John?"

"Of course I am. Is that your boat?" She peered down at *Sycorax*, then stepped back and looked me up and down. "Haven't you got anything better to wear?"

I was dressed in flannel trousers and a washed but unironed white shirt, and was using an Old Etonian tie as a belt. I was wearing my only pair of proper shoes, handmade brogues. "I think I look fine."

"A trifle louche, darling."

"I don't have any money for clothes. I'm paying it all in child support."

"You'd better go on paying it, Nicholas. I told my lawyer you were planning to sail round the world and he said we might have to nail a writ to your mast. And that reminds me, your cheque hasn't arrived for the children's summer outfits."

"I can't think why. It was sent by native runner."

"It had better arrive soon. Would you be a treasure and get me some more champagne?"

I was dutifully a treasure. There was no sign of Jill-Beth Kirov coming, and every time I glanced down at the anchorage I saw her dinghy still moored to *Mystique*'s transom. I saw the Honourable John talking to a bearded MP and Anthony Bannister having an animated conversation with a young and pretty actress. It was just like one of my father's old parties; I felt as out of place as ever.

Dusk came. Jill-Beth Kirov had still not arrived. I saw Melissa teasing Bannister. Angela Westmacott, seeing the familiarity with which Melissa treated her man, waylaid me. "Do you mind your ex-wife being here?"

"Of course I don't mind."

Angela edged towards the balustrade and, out of courtesy, I followed. "I'm sorry we had to ask you to move out of the house," she said.

"It was time I moved out." I wondered why Angela had suddenly become so solicitous of my comfort. Her long hair was twisted into a pretty coil at the back of her head and she was wearing a simple white dress that made her appear very young and vulnerable.

She looked at her diamond-studded watch. "Tony's going to make his announcement in forty-five minutes. I should have spoken to you before, Nick, but things have been very busy. Tony will make the announcement, then introduce Fanny. I'd like you to be next. You won't have to say anything."

"Me?" I glanced towards the dark shape of *Mystique* and saw that Jill-Beth's dinghy was no longer there. She must have left her yacht.

"Tony will introduce you after Fanny," Angela explained. "I want to have the moment when you're named as *Wildtrack*'s navigator on film." She saw I was about to protest, and hurried on. "I know we should have talked earlier. But please, tonight, just do as I ask."

"But I'm not going to navigate."

She kept her patience. Perhaps, as she claimed, she had overlooked the small matter of my agreement, but I suspected she had preferred to try to bounce me into Bannister's crew. She clearly feared my refusal, for she fed me a passionate argument about the advantages of ending the film in the way she wanted: how it would knit the two programmes together, and how it would offer me a double appearance fee as well as the fame of being on a winning team. She then painted a heroic picture of Nick Sandman, victorious navigator, encouraging the handicapped by his achievement.

I shook my head. "But I'd be about as much use to Bannister as a pregnant pole-vaulter."

That checked her. She frowned. "I don't understand?"

"I'm not a tactician navigator, and that's what Bannister needs. Someone who'll hunt down every breath of wind and trace of current. I hate that sort of sailing. My idea of sailing is to bung the boat in front of a convenient wind and open a beer."

"But you're a brilliant navigator," she protested. "Everyone says so."

"I can generally find the right continent," I agreed, "but I'm not a racing tactician. I really hate making yachts go fast for no other reason than to win races. And I fear I don't really care about your audience ratings, either." The last comment touched her on the quick.

"You're so self-righteous!" There was anger in her voice, loud enough to attract embarrassed looks from the nearest guests.

"I just like to be truthful," I said gently, thereby hoping to deflect the threatening storm.

But Angela's patience snapped. "Do you really want my film to be truthful? Because the honest truth, Nick Sandman, is that you're nothing but a privileged public schoolboy who chose the mindless trade of soldiering because you didn't care to exert yourself in the real world. You were wounded in an utterly pointless war, and you probably went down there like an excited puppy with a wagging tail because you thought it would be fun. But we won't say that in our film. We won't say that you were an upper-class layabout with a gun, and that if it hadn't been for a stupid medal you'd be nothing. And we won't say that you're too stubborn or too idiotic to make a proper living now. We'll say you are a war hero! Doing your bit for Britain!" Her passion was extraordinary, and shocked the crowd on the terrace into awed silence. Even the musicians ceased playing. "And the real truth, Nick Sandman, is that you can't even be an eccentric rebel without our help, because you haven't got a boat. And if you ever get it, you'll be finished inside six months because you'll run out of money and you'll be too lazy to earn any more! Is that the truth you want my film to tell?"

A very embarrassed Bannister appeared at her side.

"Angela?" She shook him off. There were tears in her eyes; tears of pure rage. "I'm trying to help you!" She hissed the words at me.

"Good night," I said to Bannister, and backed off from the two of them.

I saw that Jill-Beth had arrived, but she turned abruptly away from me. Everyone was looking away. The evening was suddenly soured, and I was the focus of the embarrassment.

Then Melissa knifed through the crowd. "Nick, darling! I thought you were going to dance with me?"

"I'm leaving," I said quietly.

"Don't be such a bloody fool," she said just as quietly, then turned imperiously towards the rock group. "You're paid to make a noise, so strum something!"

A semblance of normality returned to the terrace. Melissa and I danced. Angela had disappeared, leaving Bannister with his actress. A whispered rumour that Angela was suffering from overwork circled the terrace. I forced myself to dance, but was saved by the sudden collapse of my right leg, which spilt me sideways.

"Are you drunk?" Melissa asked with amusement.

"It's my leg."

"Well, sit." She took my arm and steered me to the edge of the terrace, where she lit a cigarette. "I must say that loathsome girl was quite right. You were frightfully bloodthirsty when you went off to the Falklands."

"I got paid for being bloodthirsty, remember?" I was massaging my right knee, trying to force sensation back into it.

Melissa watched me. "Poor Nick. I thought your leg was cured?"

"It is, most of the time." But not now. I felt the old panic that I would never be fully fit again. I wanted a leg that would hold me on a pitching foredeck while I changed a staysail. For days it seemed possible until, quite suddenly, like now, the damned knee would buckle beneath me and the pain would bring tears to my eyes.

Melissa blew out a stream of smoke. "Do you know what your problem is, Nick?"

"An Argentinian bullet."

"No, Nick, your problem is that you fall in love with the wrong women."

I was so astonished that I forgot my knee. "I don't!" I protested.

"Of course you do. You were quite soppy about me once, and you're the same about that little television tart who's just clawed you."

"That's ridiculous."

Melissa laughed at my shocked expression. "You always fall helplessly in love with pale blondes, which is extremely silly of you because they're never as vulnerable as you think they are. You should settle for some sturdy girl with whacking great thighs."

"Like that one?" I said, rather ungallantly, for Jill-Beth hardly fitted Melissa's prescription. The American girl was dancing with Fanny Mulder and, to my chagrin, seemed happy to be in his arms.

Melissa watched till Jill-Beth and Mulder were swallowed up by the other dancers. "She'd do," she finally said. "Do you mind if I slither off?"

Melissa had generously salved my pride after Angela's mauling, and I was grateful for it, yet I still felt awkward. Jill-Beth was ignoring me, while the other guests treated me as though I had the plague. It was clearly not to be my evening. I saw Matthew's cameraman setting up his gear ready for the announcement and, wishing no more part of it, I gingerly limped down the garden steps.

Mulder and Jill-Beth came arm-in-arm to the terrace balustrade. They leaned there, heads close together, and my pride was offended that Jill-Beth preferred Mulder to me. I peglegged down the long lawn to where the reflected lights shimmered on the black water, and flinched with pain as I stepped down onto *Sycorax*'s deck.

I sat for a long time in the cockpit as the pain ebbed away from my spine. Damn Jill-Beth, and damn Mulder, and damn the fact that I could not slip my moorings on this high tide and take *Sycorax* back to sea.

Applause sounded from Bannister's house and I knew he must be announcing his entry for this year's St. Pierre. I opened a beer and drank it slowly. Bannister could sail without me. From this day I wanted sailing to be a whim, dictated only by wind and sea. I decided I would rig the boat with my last savings and sail south, penniless, just to escape Bannister and Angela. I would strap my right knee, lay in a stock of painkillers, and disappear.

Jill-Beth's voice stirred me from my thoughts. I raised my head over the cockpit's coaming and saw her walking down the lawn on Fanny Mulder's arm. "I won't see anything!" I heard her say.

"You'll see fine, girl."

She stopped at the river wall and stared at *Wildtrack*. "She's so beautiful!"

Mulder pulled a dinghy to the garden steps. Jill-Beth stepped down into the small boat and I heard her soft laughter as Mulder rowed the dinghy the few strokes to *Wildtrack*. He helped Jill-Beth onto its long rakish deck, then gave her the full guided tour of the topsides. He turned on the deck lights and they showed me Jill-Beth's bright, excited eyes. I stayed still, a shadow within a shadow, watching.

They stood in the aft cockpit and I could hear every word they said because water carries sound as clearly as glass carries light. And suddenly I forgot my misery, because Jill-Beth was encouraging Mulder to tell the story of Nadeznha Bannister's death.

"I'd gone forward, see?" Mulder pointed to the mast. "The kicking-strap had worked loose."

"And Mrs. Bannister stayed here?" Jill-Beth asked.

"She liked being aft in a big sea. Then a wave broke and pooped us. She just disappeared."

Jill-Beth turned and looked at the array of life buoys that decorated *Wildtrack*'s stern. "She wasn't wearing a harness?"

"She could have taken it off for a moment, you know how you do? Or maybe the snaphook bent. I've seen them bent straight in a gale. And it was a crazy night," Mulder said. "I didn't see she'd gone at first, you know, what with being busy with the kicking-strap and the water everywhere. Must have taken me five minutes to get back to the wheel."

Jill-Beth stared up at the masthead where the string of lights was bright above the floodlights. "Poor girl."

"*Ja.*" Mulder pulled open the aft cabin hatch. "A drink?"

Jill-Beth said no. "I've got an early start in the morning, Fanny, but thanks."

"I thought you were interested." He sounded hurt. "I mean, I've still got that night's log down here if you want to see it."

She hesitated, but then her curiosity about Nadeznha Bannister's death swayed the issue. "Sure."

It was like that moment when, during a calm, the water shadows itself beneath the first stirrings of a killing wind. For these last weeks, as I had lost myself in the restoration of *Sycorax*, I had forgotten the stories of Nadeznha Bannister's death. But other people had not forgotten. Here was an American girl stirring up the dangerous rumours. I shivered.

Wildtrack's deck lights were doused and the cabin lights glowed through the narrow scuttles until curtains were pulled across the glass. I thought about what I'd heard. It matched the evidence given at the inquest, and made sense. A safety harness would have saved Nadeznha Bannister's life, but they are not infallible. A harness is a webbing strap that encases the torso and from which a strong line hangs. At the end of the line is a steel snaphook that can be attached to a jackstay or a D-ring. I'd known a snaphook open simply because it was wrenched at an odd angle. Snaphooks are made of thick, forged steel, but water is stronger than steel, especially when the water comes in the form of a breaking ocean wave.

I imagined a heavy following swell lifting *Wildtrack*, surging her forward, then dropping her like a runaway lift into the deep trough. There'd have been a moment of unnatural quiet, then Nadeznha Bannister would have heard the awesome roar as the great tongue of breaking death curved over the stern. *Wildtrack* would have staggered, her bow rising as her stern was pile-driven downwards. A good boat would survive a pooping and *Wildtrack* would have juddered upwards, shedding the flooding water. But Nadeznha would already have been a hundred yards astern, helpless in the mad blackness. Her cries would have been lost in the welter of foam and wind and banging sails.

Or else she was pushed. But the cries in the darkness would have been just as forlorn.

Then, from *Wildtrack*'s aft cabin, Jill-Beth screamed. It was more of a yelp, and swiftly cut off, as though a hand had been slapped over her mouth. I detected panic in the quick sound, but the music on the terrace was far too loud for anyone but me to have heard it.

I picked up a full beer bottle and hurled it. It crashed with a satisfying noise on *Wildtrack*'s main coachroof. The second shattered a cabin window, the third missed, but the fourth bottle broke against the metal mainmast and showered fragments of glass and foaming beer onto the boat. The aft cabin door opened, and Jill-Beth came out like a dog sprung from a trap. She scrambled over the guardrail and dived into the river. Mulder, bellowing in frustrated anger, followed from the cabin as I hurled the fifth full bottle. By pure chance it hit him clean on the forehead, throwing him back and out of sight. I'd thrown the bottle hard enough to fracture his skull, but he seemed quite unhurt when, seconds later, he reappeared with his shotgun in his hands. He aimed it at *Sycorax*'s cockpit.

I ducked. He fired. Both barrels.

The noise slammed across the water and I saw the glare of flame sheet the sky above me. The pellets went high, spattering into the bushes above the wharf.

I scrabbled through the tangled mess of stores that clogged the cockpit, cursed, then found the net bag I wanted. When in doubt, an old commanding officer of mine liked to say, hit them with smoke. I had bought some old emergency smoke floats and I prayed that they still worked as I pulled the first ring. I counted, as though it were a grenade, then lobbed it out of my shelter.

There was a pause as the water entered the floating can, then I smelt the acrid scent and raised my head to see a smear of orange smoke boiling up from the river. The lurid smudge spread to hide *Wildtrack*'s hull. I leaned over *Sycorax*'s side to search for Jill-Beth. I could hear people calling from the terrace. I tossed yet another float to keep Mulder blinded, and the can landed just feet away from a sleek black head that suddenly surfaced in the river. "Miss Kirov?" I called politely.

"Nick?"

I held out my hand for her, and as I did so Mulder unleashed his next weapon. Perhaps he had realised that one volley of gunfire was enough, and that more might land him in trouble with the law, so now he fired a distress flare in *Sycorax*'s direction. The flare was rocket-propelled, designed to sear high into the air, where it would deploy a brilliant red light which dangled from a parachute. I heard the missile fizz close overhead. A second rocket followed. Either could have killed me if it had hit my head, but both went high.

I pulled Jill-Beth dripping from the water. She was panting. Her expensive silk shirt and white trousers were soaked and dirty. "Climb the wall," I said, "and run like hell for the house."

There were people streaming down the lawn, shouting, and I hoped their presence would deter Mulder's madness. I found a flare and pointed it towards the bigger boat.

"No!" Jill-Beth said in a panic. "I can't stay here! For God's sake get me out! Have you got a dinghy?"

"Yes."

"Come on, Nick! Let's go! That bastard wanted to kill me!"

I abandoned the flare and we scrambled over the stern into my tender. I had the presence of mind to toss a duffle bag of spare clothes in first, then I slashed the painter. Jill-Beth pushed us away and we drifted on the tide towards the overhanging trees beyond the boathouse cut. We reached the shelter of the thick branches just as the first guests reached the riverbank, to stare in awe at the rolling orange smoke.

"The smoke was smart of you," Jill-Beth said. Then she touched a warning finger to her lips as if to say that we could be overheard by the people who now crowded the riverbank.

"Fanny!" It was Bannister's angry voice. "What the hell do you think you're doing?"

"Fireworks, sir!" Fanny was sharp enough to find an explanation that fitted the night's mood. "Just using the old flares, sir!"

"Does your outboard work?" That was Jill-Beth, in a whisper. She pushed the dinghy along the bank, keeping under cover of the trees.

"I was cheated of ten quid if it doesn't." British Seagulls might not be flash, but by God they work. I pulled, the old engine coughed and caught, and the noise brought the stab of a torch beam sweeping round towards us from Bannister's garden, but we were now well under cover of the overhanging trees. The branches whipped at us as I opened the throttle. "There are dry clothes in the bag," I said.

"You're a genius, Nick."

I waited till we had rounded Sansom's Point before I broke out from under the trees. We were hidden from Bannister's house by now, and I curved the dinghy towards the main channel and opened the throttle as high as it would go. Seagulls aren't fast and we were going at no more than a hearse's crawl as we left the black shadows under the trees and emerged into the moonlight, where I found myself sharing the dinghy with one very wet, very tanned and entirely naked girl who was rubbing herself dry and warm with one of my spare sweaters. She seemed quite unabashed, and I had time to notice that she was tanned all over and how nice the all over was before I politely looked away.

"Enjoying the view?" she asked.

"Very much."

She pulled on the sweater and a pair of my dirty jeans that she rolled up round her calves. "Where are we going?"

"Jimmy Nicholls's cottage. You know Jimmy?"

"I've met him." Jill-Beth was searching through the duffle bag. "Got any sneakers here?"

"No shoes, sorry."

She looked up at me and smiled. "Thank you for the rescue."

"That's what we white knights are for," I said. At which point the dragon growled, or rather I heard a percussive bang and then the throaty roar of big engines, and I knew it was too late to reach Jimmy's house. I pulled the outboard's lever towards me and prayed that the little two-stroke could outrun *Wildtrack II*'s monster engines. I'd forgotten the big powerboat in Bannister's boathouse.

Jill-Beth knew immediately what the sound meant and was suddenly scared. "Fanny Mulder knew why I'm here," she said. I suspected that I knew why she was here too, but it was no time for explanations because a brilliant stab of white light suddenly slashed across the river. Mulder had turned on the boat's searchlight.

Jill-Beth cowered as the sharp prow of *Wildtrack II* burst into view. Mulder must have been doing twenty knots and was still accelerating. That was his mistake, for the acceleration was throwing up his bows so that he could not see straight in front.

"Head down!" I called out. Jill-Beth ducked and the dinghy scraped under branches. I killed the engine and the searchlight whipped past us as the powerboat slewed round into the main channel. I scrambled past Jill-Beth and tied the dinghy's painter to a low bough. "Give me your wet trousers," I said.

She frowned with puzzlement, but obeyed. I hung the white trousers over the dinghy's side, looping one leg over the gunwale and hanging the other straight down into the water.

"Breaking our shape," I explained. "He's looking for a wooden dinghy, not a brown and white pattern."

The powerboat was slowing and I heard its engines fade to a mutter as its bow dropped. Mulder had accelerated to where he thought we might be; now he would search. "Head down!" I crouched with Jill-Beth in the bottom of the boat. The light skidded past us, paused, came back, then went on again. I breathed a sigh of relief. Mulder had missed us. But he would be back.

Jill-Beth pointed to the trousers I'd hung over the gunwale. "A soldier's trick. You weren't injured in a car crash, were you?"

Her face was so close to mine that I could feel her breath on my cheek. "You're Captain Nicholas Thomas Sandman, VC. Your last annual report before the Falklands was kind of noncommittal. Captain Sandman's a fine officer, it said, and did well in Northern Ireland, but he's not very ambitious. You lacked the motivation to excel, they said. Then someone gave you a real live enemy and you proved them all wrong."

I said nothing for a moment. I had pulled away from Jill-Beth, the better to see her face in the shadows. "Who are you?"

"Jill-Beth Kirov, like the ballet." She grinned, and her teeth showed white against her dark skin. "I work for Yassir Kassouli. Heard of him?"

"Bannister's father-in-law."

"Ex-father-in-law," she corrected me, then stiffened suddenly as the searchlight whipped round and seemed to shine straight at the two of us.

"It's all right." I put an arm over her shoulder to keep her head low. The light swept on, probing another shadow, but I kept my arm where it was. "What do you do for Kassouli?" I whispered the question almost as if I feared Mulder might hear us over the growl of his idling engines.

"Insurance investigator. I work for the marine division of an insurance company that's a subsidiary of Kassouli Enterprises."

I tried to imagine her dealing with crooks, and couldn't.

"You don't look like an investigator."

"You expect the Pink Panther? Of course I don't look like a cop! Hell, if they see some chick in a bikini they don't start calling for a lawyer, do they?"

"And just what are you investigating here?" I asked.

"Nadeznha Bannister's life was insured with her father's company for a million bucks. Guess who the beneficiary is?"

"Anthony Bannister?"

"You got it in one, soldier." She grinned. "But if Nadeznha was murdered, then we don't have to pay."

There was something chilling about the calm confidence with which she had spoken of murder; so chilling that I took my arm from her shoulder. "Was she murdered?"

"That's what I'm trying to prove." She spoke grimly, intimating that she was not having any great success.

"What else are you doing?" I asked.

She must have heard the suspicion in my voice, for her reply was very guarded. "Nothing else."

"Dismasting *Wildtrack*?" I guessed. "Cutting its warps?"

"You think I'm into that kind of stupidity?" She sounded disgusted.

Then if not her, who? Yet I believed her strenuous denial, because I wanted this girl to be straight. "I'm sorry I suggested it," I said.

"Hell, Nick, I'd love to know who's bugging Bannister, but it surely isn't me. Ssh!" *Wildtrack II* had swung round, and now the searchlight slid towards us again. There was still a chance that Mulder would find us.

Jill-Beth wriggled herself into a semblance of comfort. "How long will that bastard keep looking? I need to get back to *Mystique*. I left all my papers in the cabin."

"We'll just have to wait." I paused. "Is that why you were with Mulder tonight? Hoping he'd say something incriminating?"

"Sort of. But he set me up. He knew just why I was here."

"How did he know?"

"Beats me." She raised her head to watch the light, then lowered it again. "I'm sorry to involve you, Nick."

"Don't be sorry. I wanted to be involved."

Her big eyes reflected the darkness of the night. She said nothing, so I leaned forward and kissed her on the mouth. She returned the kiss, then placed her head on my shoulder. We stayed still. I did not know just what tangle she was drawing me into.

66

We talked then. She told me she came from Rhode Island and her father was in the US navy. I told her that my father was in jail, and that Bannister's house had been my childhood home. We talked on, almost oblivious of Mulder's fumbling search. Then his light suddenly went out and the sound of his twin engines died away to an ominous silence.

"He's given up," Jill-Beth breathed.

"No," I said. "He wants us to think he's gone." I wound the starting lanyard onto the Seagull, then yanked it. The motor belched into life and its distinctive sound echoed across the river. I let it run for five seconds, then cut the fuel just as the searchlight split the darkness. Mulder had been hiding in the shadows, but his guess of where the outboard's sound had come from was hopelessly wrong.

"I need to get those damned papers! Hell!" Jill-Beth was suddenly vehement in her frustration. She stared across at *Wildtrack II*. "Suppose I swim back?" she asked suddenly.

In the end she helped me to hide the dinghy by filling it with stones and sinking it at the river's edge. We concealed the outboard under a pile of grass and leaves, then worked our way northwards. I made Jill-Beth wear my brogues to save her bare feet from nettles and thorns.

Our urgency was to rescue Jill-Beth's papers which, she said, must not fall into Bannister's hands. We planned to go as far as the ferry slip, from which we would swim to *Mystique*.

But our planning was all in vain for, as we reached the shadows at the head of the ferry slip, we saw that Bannister had anticipated us. A dinghy was moored beside *Mystique* and two men were searching her. Their torchlight flickered on the small boat's deck. Jill-Beth swore again.

"How important were the papers?" I asked.

"There's nothing in them he doesn't already know," she said, "but they'll tell him what *I* know." Then she shrugged in resignation. "You can't put the toothpaste back in the tube, so there's no point in trying."

She shivered, and I put an arm round her. She resisted for a second, then relaxed against me. "Hell," she said, "but you're a very inconvenient man, Nick Sandman. It's very inconvenient to get emotionally entangled during a case."

"Are you emotionally entangled?" She did not answer. We crouched together in the deep shadows at the slip's head and stared at the bright lights on Bannister's terrace, whence came tumbling the sounds of music and laughter.

"I'm finished here," Jill-Beth finally said, pulling herself gently away from my embrace. "But what's important now is to get you safely back. You're still kosher. Tell them that you just rescued me from Mulder, OK? We haven't talked about Kassouli, and you think I'm just a girl writing a pilot book."

"It doesn't matter about me," I said, "except that I don't want to leave you."

She smiled at my protestation, then kissed me. "If you disappear now, Nick, Bannister will think you've been working with me. How long do you think your boat will be safe then?"

The thought of *Sycorax* at risk made me silent.

"Stay with Bannister," Jill-Beth urged me, "and I'll get in touch with you through Jimmy Nicholls." She stood up. "Can I keep the shoes for tonight?"

"Where are you going?"

"I've got to reach a telephone. I'll call one of Kassouli's British executives and tell him to send a car for me. I need to go to London, I guess, in case Kassouli wants me to fly home."

"Don't leave England without meeting me."

"I've got to return your shoes, right? Take care, Nick."

"You take care, too."

She leaned towards me and kissed me warmly. "Thank you for everything." She pulled away from me and bundled up the wet clothes she'd fetched from the dinghy.

"What about *Mystique*?" I asked.

"The charterers will fetch her back. I'll call them from London." I watched her shadow disappear up the lane.

Now I was alone. The men who'd searched *Mystique* rowed towards the far bank. Mulder was still downriver and I felt suddenly forlorn. I should have been thinking about murder and proof and justice, but I had been entranced by a girl's smile.

I waited a good hour, but Mulder did not return. In the end I stripped, bundled my clothes at the small of my back and went into the river. I breast-stroked through the quicksilver shimmer of moonlight to my wharf, where I pulled myself up into *Sycorax*'s stern.

WHEN I WOKE AT DAWN the litter of the night's party was strewn down Bannister's garden, where mist curled from the river. *Wildtrack II* was back in its dock.

I took one of Bannister's inflatables and went downstream to where I'd left my dinghy. I emptied it of water, then towed it and the outboard home. If Mulder saw me, he did nothing.

I took some money from its hiding place in *Sycorax*'s bilge and walked up to the house. No one was stirring yet. I made myself coffee in Bannister's kitchen, then took the keys to one of his spare cars, an old Peugeot.

I drove north and east for three hours, arriving at the housing estate at breakfast time. Sally Farebrother was still in her dressing gown when she opened the door to me. She had a small child clutching her right leg and a baby in her arms. She looked surprised rather than pleased to see me; indeed, she must have wondered if I was in trouble, for I looked like a derelict in my filthy jersey, torn jeans and old sea boots. Sally did not look much better herself: she had became a drab and shapeless girl, burdened with small children and large resentments.

"Hello, Sally. Is Terry in?"

She shook her head. "They're on exercise."

"I didn't know. I'm sorry." I was embarrassed to find her so obviously joyless. "It's just that I left some kit here," I explained lamely. "Terry said he'd keep it for me."

"It's in Tracey's room." Sally opened the front door wide, inviting me in. "Upstairs, on the left. I'll be glad to have the space in the cupboard back."

"I'm sorry if it's been a bother."

"No bother." She followed me upstairs.

"How's Terry?" I asked.

"They want him to be a weapons' instructor." It was said unhappily, for Sally was always nagging Terry to resign the service.

I found my bergen under a broken tricycle in the child's cupboard. I dragged the heavy rucksack out and hauled it downstairs. "Give Terry my best, won't you? And thanks for keeping this."

"Sure."

I drove back to Devon, reaching Bannister's house at lunchtime. I'd filled the Peugeot's tank with petrol as amends for borrowing it, but no one seemed to have missed the old car.

I could hear voices in the house, so I took the path through the woods down to the wharf where *Sycorax* lay.

I emptied the bergen on the cabin floor. There were sweaters still smeared with dark peaty Falklands soil. There was a shaving kit, a canteen and a camera. There was a situation map and a deck plan of the *Canberra*. There was a letter from my father and photographs of my children. There was my beret, which gave me a pang of old and still bright pride.

Underneath it all was the reason why I had driven so far, a souvenir wrapped in a dirty towel. I'd taken it from a dead Argentinian officer on Darwin Hill. I unwrapped the towel to find a belt from which hung a pouch and a holster. In the holster was a .45 calibre automatic pistol, a Colt. It was ugly, black and heavy. I cocked it and pulled the trigger. The sound seemed immense inside *Sycorax*'s hull.

I did not want to use it, indeed I had hoped never to fire a gun like this again, but Jill-Beth's warning and the memory of how easily Fanny Mulder had resorted to his shotgun had persuaded me to retrieve this trophy of a faraway war. Holding the heavy gun I was suddenly disgusted that my affairs with Bannister had come to this.

I oiled and greased the pistol, loaded it, sealed it in two waterproof bags and hid it deep in *Sycorax*, beneath the water line, in a dark place where such a thing is best kept. A hand rapped on the outside of the hull and I jumped like a guilty thing.

"Mr. Sandman?" It was one of Mulder's crew. "Mr. Bannister wants to see you. Now."

It was an order. I wanted to see Bannister too, so I obeyed.

Bannister was waiting for me in his study. Mulder stood on one side of a table littered with charts and maps, while Angela was slumped in a deep chair in the corner of the room. They all three looked tired.

"Ah, Nick!" Bannister seemed almost surprised that I'd come. "Thank you for coming. Angela tells me you borrowed a car this morning?"

"I filled it up afterwards," I said. "I should have asked you before I borrowed it. I'm sorry."

"That's all right." Bannister, it was clear, did not have the guts to go for a fight.

"Is that all you wanted?" I asked. "Because I've also got something to say to you."

"Where did you go in the car?" Mulder asked in his flat voice.

I ignored him. "I've come to tell you that you can count me out," I said. "Not just out of the St. Pierre, but out of everything. I don't want any more of your film, any more of your company. I'm through."

"Where did you go?" Mulder insisted.

"Answer him," Angela said.

I turned on her furiously. "I've got nothing to say to you! Nothing! I'm sorry," I said to Bannister. "I just want out. After last night I don't see how I can decently stay. And as I understand things, you promised to restore my boat, so give me a cheque for a thousand pounds and I'll finish *Sycorax* myself and leave you alone."

Bannister hated the confrontation. "I think we should talk things over, don't you?"

"Just give me a cheque."

Mulder moved close and looked down at me. "Where did you go in the car, man?"

"Get out of my way or I'll break your bloody neck!" I astonished myself by my own savagery. Mulder stepped back. I made my voice calm again. "A cheque, please."

Bannister found some courage for a moment. "Did you go to see Miss Kirov, Nick?"

"No. A cheque, please."

"But you did invite her to the party?" Bannister insisted.

"Yes, but I didn't know Fanny was going to attack her."

"I didn't—" Fanny began.

"I want a cheque," I said to Bannister.

I thought I'd won, for Bannister walked to his desk and pulled open a drawer. I expected him to bring out his chequebook, but instead he produced a stack of cardboard folders.

"Please look at these, Nick." He opened the top one and handed it to me. My own photograph was in the file and curiosity made me take it from him. "Read it," he said quietly.

There were only two sheets of paper in the folder, both topped with a printed letterhead: "Kassouli Insurance Fund, Inc., (Marine)". My photograph was pasted onto one of the sheets, with my career, such as it had been, carefully typed out beneath. The citation for the Victoria Cross was reproduced in full. The other sheet was handwritten in what, I supposed, was Jill-Beth's writing.

"Captain Sandman's presence in AB's house is unexpected, but could be fortunate for us. Captain Sandman, like many soldiers, is a romantic. In many ways he lives in La-la land, by which I mean he's a preppy drop-out who wants to do a Joshua Slocum, but undoubtedly his sense of honour and duty would predispose him to our side."

"That," Bannister said quietly, "is your Miss Kirov's pilot book. We found these files on her boat."

He handed me another which had a photograph of Fanny Mulder doing his morning exercises on *Wildtrack*'s bow. The sparse career details said that Francis Mulder had been born in Witsand, Cape Province, on 3 August 1949. He'd served in the South African Defence Forces. He had a police file in South Africa, being suspected of armed robbery, but nothing had ever been proved. The next entry recorded his purchase of a cutter in the Seychelles where he had run his charter business until Nadezhna Bannister had spotted his undoubted talent. Again there was a handwritten comment.

"Despite being a protégé of your daughter's, there can be no doubt of Mulder's loyalty to AB. AB has promoted him, pays him well, and constantly demonstrates his trust in Mulder."

The rest of the page had been raggedly torn off, making me wonder if Bannister had destroyed comments that discussed Mulder's presumed involvement in Nadezhna Bannister's murder.

Bannister took the two files from me. "Do you understand now why we're somewhat concerned that you might be a close friend of Miss Kirov's? Do you know who owns the Kassouli Insurance Fund?"

"I assume your late wife's father?"

"Yes." He sat in a big leather chair behind the desk and rubbed his face with both hands. "Tell him, Angela."

Angela spoke tonelessly. "Yassir Kassouli is convinced that Tony could have prevented Nadeznha's death. He's never forgiven Tony for that. He also believes, irrationally and wrongly, that by making another attempt on the race this year Tony is demonstrating a callous attitude towards Nadeznha's death. Kassouli will do anything to stop Tony winning. Last night Miss Kirov tried to persuade Fanny to sabotage our St. Pierre attempt. Fanny refused. In turn he accused Miss Kirov of dismasting *Wildtrack*. They had an argument. That's when she pretended to be attacked, and when you played the gallant rescuer."

I said nothing. There was a ring of truth to her words, and I felt the confusion of a man assailed by conflicting certainties: Jill-Beth had spoken of murder, and of a million-dollar insurance claim, while Angela now spoke convincingly of a rich man's obsession with preserving his daughter's memory.

Bannister swivelled his chair so he could stare at his wife's portrait. If he'd murdered her, I thought, then he was putting on an award-winning performance. "Yassir Kassouli's never forgiven me for Nadeznha's death," he said. "God knows what I was supposed to do. Keep her ashore? All I do know is that so long as Kassouli lives he'll hate me. He isn't rational on the subject, he's obsessed, and I have to protect myself." He tapped the folders. "You can see that Miss Kirov believes that you'll help sabotage my St. Pierre run this year."

"I'm not in a position to help," I said to Bannister, "because I've resigned from your life. No film, no St. Pierre. I just want your cheque."

"And how will you account for the money already spent?" Angela interrupted. "Do you know how much money we've invested in this film? Have you forgotten that you signed contracts?"

I kept my eyes on Bannister. "A thousand pounds," I said.

He prevaricated. "I think we're all too overwrought to make a decision now."

"I'm not," I insisted.

"But I am!" He betrayed a flash of anger. "We'll talk next week. I need to look at the budget, and at the film we've already shot. I'll phone you from London, Nick."

"I won't be here," I said.

"You'd better be here," Angela said, "if you want to keep your boat."

I turned and walked out of the room.

I stumped down the lawn, and saw that Jimmy Nicholls had come upriver and tied his boat alongside *Sycorax*. He was lifting two sacks into *Sycorax*'s scuppers. "Chain plates and bolts," he told me. "Ready for the morning."

"Can you tow *Sycorax* away today?"

He straightened up from the sacks. "Where to?"

"Anywhere. Away from television people." I climbed onto *Sycorax*'s deck.

Jimmy chuckled. "Fallen out with your fancy friends, boy?"

I looked up at the house and saw Angela watching me from the study window. "Where can I hide *Sycorax*?"

He frowned. "Nowhere on this river, Nick. How about Georgie Cullen's yard?"

I picked up a coiled warp and bent it onto a cleat ready for the tow. "Have you got enough diesel to get me there today, Jimmy?"

"You don't want to go anywhere right now," Jimmy said sternly. "I've got a letter for you. Boy on a motorbike brought it from London. Said I was to get it to you, but no one was to notice, like, so that's why I hid it with the bolts, see?" He pointed to one of the sacks. "The boy said as how an American maid gave it he. You want to read it before you go."

A moment ago I had been full of certainty as to what I should do, but the sudden memory of Jill-Beth made me carry the heavy sack down into *Sycorax*'s cabin and tear open the envelope marked "Urgent".

Two things fell out. One was a first-class ticket for British Airways, London to Boston. The ticket was in my name, and the outbound flight left Heathrow the next morning. The return had been left open. The other was a letter.

"If you haven't got a visa then get one from the embassy and come Tuesday. I'll meet you at Logan Airport." The signature was a child's drawing of a smiling face, a sketched heart, and the initials J-B.

I did not consider the choices. It never occurred to me that I was being asked to take sides, nor did I think it odd that a girl should send me an expensive air ticket. At that moment, after years of nothing but fighting, pain and hospital, I was being offered a gift that seemed to imply all the things that a soldier dreams of when he's neck-deep in wet mud.

There would be no time to hide *Sycorax*, so a stratagem would have to protect her while I was away. I also asked Jimmy to keep an eye on her.

There had been precious little spontaneous excitement in my life since the bullet caught me. So I locked the cabin hatch, rode Jimmy's boat downriver to the town, and caught a bus. For Boston.

Chapter 5

The stratagem to protect *Sycorax* involved telephoning my mother in Dallas and asking her to say she was ill and that I was visiting her, should anyone call from England.

After that call I put in more coins and dialled Devon. A relentlessly cheerful answering machine responded.

"This is Sandman," I said, "and I'm phoning to say that my mother's been taken ill in Dallas and her doctors think I should be with her. I'll discuss our other problems when I get back."

I feared that Angela might interpret my disappearance as a desertion of her wretched film, and that she would then carry out her legal threats. I reckoned the fiction of a sick mother would confuse the lawyers for long enough. Then, just as soon as I returned to England, I planned to take the boat away. But first, America.

They looked at me very oddly at the check-in desk. I was wearing a pair of my oldest deck shoes, duck trousers which were stained with varnish and linseed oil, and a tatty blue jumper.

"Any luggage?" the girl asked me.

"None." But my ticket was valid, and my visa unexpired, so they had to let me on.

IT WAS RAINING at Boston's Logan Airport. There was no Jill-Beth. Instead, a chauffeur in a limousine the size of a Scorpion tank waited for me. He apologised that Miss Kirov was unable to be present personally.

We drove to Cape Cod where I was wafted to a hotel of unimaginable luxury. Despite my appearance, I was treated as a most honoured guest. I was shown to a suite of rooms which overlooked the harbour. I had a jacuzzi, a bath, a bedroom, a living room and a private balcony. It all suddenly seemed very, very unreal.

I went to the window and stared at the busy harbour where boats that cost more than an army officer could earn in a lifetime jostled on their moorings. The rain was clearing, promising a bright and warm evening. A motor yacht with a flying bridge, raked aerials, fighting chair and a harpoon walkway accelerated towards the sea, while behind me the air conditioning hissed.

In one of the walk-in cupboards I found my old brogues, which had been reheeled and polished to a deep shine. There were also four pairs of new shoes sitting alongside the brogues.

Above the shoes, and hanging in protective paper covers, were clothes. There were two dinner jackets: one white, one black. There were slacks, shirts, even a raincoat. Some ties hung on a door-rack and I noticed, with astonishment, that my old regiment's striped tie was among them. A label was pinned onto the regimental tie:

"With the Compliments of Miss Kirov". At the bottom of the paper slip was the legend, "Kassouli Hotels, Inc., a division of Kassouli Leisure Interests, Inc".

I suppose I'd really known, right from the moment when I'd opened that envelope in *Sycorax*'s cabin, who had paid for the ticket, and who wanted me in the States.

I'd deceived myself into thinking that it was love, but of course it was not. It was Kassouli.

The telephone startled me.

"Captain Sandman? This is the front desk, sir. Miss Kirov has requested us to inform you that she'll come by at seven o'clock with transportation. She suggests formal dress, sir."

"Right. Thank you."

It was madness, but I had volunteered to come here because of a girl. I ran a bath, lowered myself into it and told myself that there was no need for apprehension, that it was an adventure, and that I was glad to be here.

MY SENSE OF UNREALITY only increased when Jill-Beth arrived. She came in a white BMW convertible, and was wearing an evening dress of black and white speckled silk. Her hair seemed glossier and her skin more glowing than I remembered.

"Hi, Nick." She leaned over and gave me a kiss. "How's the jet lag?"

"As bad as yours, I imagine."

"I feel great. You'd better, too, because we're partying." She accelerated away from under the hotel awning.

"I didn't bring much money," I said warningly.

"A thousand bucks should see you through the night." She saw the expression on my face, and laughed. "Hell, Nick! You're Kassouli's guest, OK?"

"OK," I said, as though I'd known all along that it was Kassouli who'd lured me across the ocean.

Jill-Beth swung the car into a marina entrance where an armed guard recognised her and opened the gate. We drove past a row of moored motor cruisers, each the size of a minesweeper and each with an aerial array that would have done service to a frigate.

"La-la land," I said, echoing the comment Jill-Beth had written about me in the file that Bannister had shown me.

Jill-Beth understood the allusion, and laughed. "Did you see the files?"

"Only those that Bannister wanted me to see."

"I guess I'm not exactly flavour of the month with Tony Bannister?"

"Not exactly. Nor am I."

"Tough." She swung the BMW into a parking slot opposite a berth where a white cutter was moored. She kept the motor running as she nodded at the yacht. "Like it?"

I liked it very much. She was called *Ballet Dancer*, a 42-foot cutter with the solid, graceful lines of a sturdy sea boat. She was made of fibreglass, but had expensive teak decks and rubbing-strakes.

"Yours?" I guessed.

"Mine."

"She's lovely," I said warmly. *Ballet Dancer* had the good look of a well-used boat. You can always tell when a boat is sailed hard; it loses its showroom gloss and accretes the small extra features that experience has demanded. The teak decks and trim had faded to a bone white.

"All mine," Jill-Beth said happily. "Paid off the last instalment last month." She switched off the BMW's engine and opened the door. "Coming?"

I followed her onto the floating pontoon and watched as she disconnected the shoreside electricity and unlooped the springs.

"We're going out?" I said with surprise.

"Sure. Why not?"

It seemed very odd to be crewing a boat while dressed in evening clothes, but that was evidently Jill-Beth's plan. She started the engine. "You want to take her out, Nick?"

The boat's long keel made it hard to turn in the marina's restricted water, but I backed and filled until the bow was facing the channel. Once there, Jill-Beth unrolled the genoa from the forestay, then hoisted the main. I'd never seen a girl in evening dress rig a yacht before. She came and sat next to me in the cockpit where she opened a locker. "Champagne?"

"I thought you'd never ask."

The evening had been sparked with a spontaneity that matched the irresponsibility of flying the Atlantic. I felt happy, even light-headed. It was cooler out on the water where the light wind spilt down on us from the mainsail's curve.

"How does she compare to *Sycorax*?" Jill-Beth asked.

"*Sycorax* carries more windage aloft so she has to have a lot of metal under water. That makes her stubborn."

"Like you?"

"Like me. And like me she's not too hot to windward, but I don't plan to fight my way round the world."

A motor cruiser surged past us. There was a party in evening dress on its covered quarterdeck and they raised their glasses in friendly greeting. I could see the first stars pricking the sky's pale wash where an airliner etched a white trail.

"Thank you for the air ticket," I said.

"*Nada.*" Jill-Beth grinned. "Isn't that why white knights rescue damsels in distress? For a reward?"

"Is this my reward?" I asked.

"What else?" She touched my glass with hers.

We passed a moored boat which had a smoking barbecue slung from its dinghy davits. The skipper waved a fork at us and we raised our champagne flutes in reply. Then two motor cruisers passed us. Both carried people in evening dress.

"Where's the party?" I asked.

"There." Jill-Beth pointed directly ahead towards a massive white house that occupied its own sand-edged promontory. Wide terraced lawns dropped to private beaches and docks that were strung with lanterns and crowded with boats. A string of headlamps showed where other guests drove along the spit of sand that led to the promontory.

"Kassouli wants to thank you," Jill-Beth said.

"Thank me for what?"

"For rescuing me."

I suddenly felt nervous. There's something about the very rich that always makes me nervous. Principles, I remembered, are soluble in cash, and I had already surrendered my privacy to Bannister's cash. I feared that something more might be asked of me this night, but obediently steered for the dock, where servants waited to berth our yacht. I could hear the thump of music coming from the wide, lantern-hung gardens. I chose a windward berth, spilt air from the sails, and two men jumped aboard to take our warps.

We entered the garden of Kassouli's delights. A pit had been dug on one of the beaches and a proper clambake of driftwood and seaweed sifted smoke into the evening and tantalised us with the smells of lobster, clams and sweetcorn. Steaks dripped on barbecues. There was champagne, music, and seemingly hundreds of guests. It was clearly an important social occasion, for there were photographers hunting through the shoals of beautiful people. One flashed a picture of Jill-Beth and myself, but when he asked my name I told him I was no one important.

We sat at a table where we were joined by a noisy group. One of the men, after the introductions, told me how I could refinance my boat on a twelve-year amortisation schedule. I made polite noises. I gathered that a good few of the guests worked for Kassouli. The man who wanted to lend me money said that the boss probably wouldn't show himself. "Yassir's not a great partygoer. He likes to give 'em, though." He peered round the garden. "That's his son, Charlie."

I recognised the son from the pictures I'd seen in Bannister's house, but there was one thing I was not prepared for. Charles Kassouli was in a wheelchair. He was only in his early twenties, but had withered legs slewed sideways on the chair.

"What happened?" I asked my new acquaintance.

"Motorbike." The reply was laconic.

Jill-Beth introduced me to the son a few moments later. Charles Kassouli's face was startlingly handsome, but his character was distant and churlish. I felt a chill pity, for here was a boy born to the pleasures of the richest society on earth, who had thrown them away with one twist of a motorcycle's grip.

"Are you dancing, J-B?" Charles threw away his cigarette and swivelled his chair away from me.

"Sure, Charlie." Jill-Beth walked beside his electric wheelchair onto the dance floor and I watched how unselfconsciously she gyrated in front of him. She grinned at me, but I turned away because a voice had spoken in my ear. "Captain Sandman?"

The speaker was a tall fair-haired man in a white uniform coat. "Captain Sandman?" he asked again. He had a Scandinavian accent.

"Yes."

"If you're ready, sir?" He gestured towards the big house.

I looked for Jill-Beth, but she had disappeared with Kassouli's son, so I followed the uniformed manservant into the great house. A door led to a long hallway lined with superb ship models of the eighteenth century. The walls were hung with pictures of ancient naval battles.

At the end of the hall the Scandinavian opened both leaves of a gilded door and showed me into a library, where he left me alone. It was a lovely room, lined with leather-bound editions in English, French, Greek and Arabic. On rosewood tables were more models, but these were of Kassouli's modern fleet. There were supertankers and bulk carriers, all painted with the Kassouli Line's emblem of a striking kestrel. Each ship's name began and ended with a K: *Kalik, Kerak, Kanik, Komek*.

It was one of the world's great merchant fleets, run, I thought, by a modern merchant prince; a Levantine who had called me across the globe. I stared up at the paintings which hung above the bookshelves. They were not pictures calculated to reassure a nervous Briton: they showed the battles of Bunker Hill, Saratoga and Yorktown.

On a table in the centre of the room there was a handsomely mounted family photograph. Yassir Kassouli, his plump face proud, sat next to his wife. She was a fair-haired, good-looking woman with laughing eyes. Behind them stood Nadeznha and Charles, the finest products of the world's richest melting pot. I saw how their father's Mediterranean blood had dominated in their faces.

"A photograph taken before the tragedies." The voice startled me.

I turned to see a tall, thickset, balding man standing in the doorway. It was Yassir Kassouli. His skin was very pale, as though he had seen little sunlight in the last few months, and he had the look of old age. Only his eyes, dark and suspicious, showed the immense force of this immigrant who had made one of America's great fortunes. "I have to thank you, Captain Sandman, for coming all this way to see me."

I muttered some inanity about its being my pleasure.

He crossed to the table and lifted the photograph. "You met my son?"

78

"Indeed, sir."

"I raised my children according to Western tenets, Captain Sandman. To my daughter I gave freedom, and to my son pleasure. I do not think, on the whole, that I did well." He said the last words drily, then crossed to a liquor cabinet. "You drink Irish whiskey, I believe?"

"Yes, sir."

He poured my whiskey, then helped himself to Scotch. As he finished pouring, the door opened and his son wheeled himself into the room, escorted by Jill-Beth.

Kassouli brought me my whiskey in a heavy crystal glass. "Allow me to congratulate you on your Victoria Cross, Captain."

"Thank you." I felt clumsy in the face of his suave courtesy.

"Shall we sit?" He gestured at the sofas in front of the fireplace.

Jill-Beth and Charles positioned themselves at the back of the room, as if they knew they were present only to observe. The son's earlier surliness had been muted to a respectful silence and I suspected that Charles Kassouli lived in some fear of his formidable father.

Yassir Kassouli thanked me for rescuing Jill-Beth. He asked after my father and expressed his regrets at what had happened. "You will pass on my best wishes to him?" I promised I would. Kassouli then enquired what my future was, and smiled when I said that it depended on ocean currents and winds.

"I've often wished I could be such an ocean gypsy myself," Kassouli said, "but alas."

"Alas." I echoed him.

The word served to make him look at his family portrait. I watched his profile, seeing the lineaments of the thin, savage face that had become fleshy with middle age.

"In my possession," he said suddenly, "I have the weather charts and satellite photographs of the North Atlantic for the week in which my daughter was killed. Perhaps you would like to see them?" He clicked his fingers and Jill-Beth dutifully opened a bureau drawer and brought me a thick file of papers.

I spilt the photographs and grey weatherfax charts onto my lap. Each one was marked with a red-ink cross to show where Nadeznha Bannister had died. I leafed through them as Kassouli watched me.

"You've sailed a great deal, Captain Sandman?" he asked me.

"Yes, sir."

"Would you, from your wide experience, say that the conditions revealed in those photographs were such that a large boat like *Wildtrack* might have been pooped?"

I insisted on looking through all the papers before I answered. The sequence of charts and photographs showed that *Wildtrack* had been pursued, then overtaken, by a small depression that had raced up from New England. The cell of low pressure would have brought rain, a half gale, fast sailing, but the isobars were not so closely packed as to suggest real storm conditions. I said as much, but added that heavy seas were not always revealed by air pressure, and that rogue waves had been known to happen.

Kassouli sighed. "The best estimate of wave height, at that time and in that place, is fifteen feet. You wish to see the report I commissioned?" He clicked his fingers again, and Jill-Beth brought me a file that was stamped with the badge of one of America's most respected oceanographic institutes. I turned the typed pages and found what I wanted at the end: an appendix which insisted that rogue waves, perhaps two or three times the height of the surrounding seas, were not unknown.

"I do not believe," Kassouli spoke as though he summarised our discussion, "that *Wildtrack* was pooped."

There was a pause. I was expected to comment, but I could only offer the bleak truth. "But you can't prove that she wasn't." I tried to remember the evidence given at the inquest. *Wildtrack* had lost her stern guardrails, and with them the danbuoys and life belt. "Are you saying the damage was faked?"

He did not answer. Instead he leaned back in his sofa and pressed together the tips of his fingers. "Allow me to offer you some further thoughts, Captain. My daughter was a most excellent and highly experienced sailor. Do you think it likely that she would have been in even a medium sea without safety harness?"

"Not unless she was re-anchoring the harness," I said.

"You are asking me to believe," Kassouli said scornfully, "that a rogue wave just happened to hit *Wildtrack* in the two or three seconds that it took Nadeznha to unclip and move her harness?" It sounded lame, but sea accidents always sound unlikely when they are calmly recounted in a comfortable room. I shrugged.

Kassouli still watched closely for my every reaction. "Have you seen the transcript of the inquest?" he asked.

"Yes, sir."

"It says that the South African—what was his name?" He clicked his fingers irritably, and Jill-Beth supplied the answer. "Mulder," Kassouli repeated the name. "The report says Mulder was on deck when my daughter died. Do you believe that?"

"I don't know." I hesitated, and Kassouli let the silence stretch uncomfortably. "There's a rumour," I said weakly, "that Mulder lied to the inquest, but it's only pub gossip."

"Which also says that Bannister was the man on deck." Kassouli, who had clearly known about the rumour all along, pounced hard on me as

80

though he was nailing the truth at last. "Why, in the name of God, would they lie about that?"

I was beginning to regret that I had come to America. The trip had turned into an inquisition. "We don't know if it was a lie," I said.

"There is something else." Kassouli closed his eyes for a few seconds, as if his next statement was painful. "My daughter, I believe, was in love with another man."

"Ah." It was an inadequate response, but my army training was not up to any other reaction.

Kassouli, oblivious to my embarrassment, turned to his son. "Tell him, Charles."

"She told me there was another fellow." He was laconic.

"But she did not say who he was?" his father asked.

"No."

"Isn't it odd," I said, "that she sailed with her husband if she was in love with someone else?"

"Nadeznha was not a girl to lightly dismiss a marriage," Kassouli said. "And, also, she shared her husband's ambition to win the St. Pierre. It was a mistake, Captain. She sailed to her murder."

He waited once more for me to chime in with an agreement that her death had been murder, but I did not oblige.

Kassouli gave the smallest shrug. "May I tell you about Nadeznha, Captain?"

"Please."

Sometimes, as Kassouli spoke, he would glance at the family photograph. "She was a most beautiful girl, Captain. You would expect a father to say that of his daughter, yet she was, in all honesty, a most outstanding young lady. She was clever, modest, kind and accomplished. I believe that I spoilt her as a child, yet she possessed a natural balance, Captain; a feel for what was right and true. She made but one mistake."

"Bannister." I helped the conversation along.

"Exactly. Anthony Bannister." The name came off Kassouli's tongue with an almost vicious intensity. "She was dazzled by him. I warned her against a precipitate marriage, but the young can be very headstrong." I noted this first flaw in the perfect image Kassouli had presented of his daughter. He looked hard at me. "What do you think of Bannister?"

"I really don't know him well."

"He is a weak man, a despicable man. He was unfaithful to my daughter, and yet she persisted in offering him the love and loyalty which one would have expected from a girl of her sweet disposition."

Now Kassouli turned on me with a direct challenge. "Do you believe my daughter was murdered, Captain Sandman?"

The truth was all I would offer. "I don't know how Nadeznha died."

The truth was not enough. I saw Yassir Kassouli's right hand clenching, Charles made a hissing noise and Jill-Beth stiffened. I was among believers, and I had dared to express disbelief.

Yet if Kassouli was angry, his voice did not betray it. "I only have two children, Captain Sandman. My son you see, my daughter you will never see." His enormous grief was suddenly palpable. I felt for this man, but I could not offer him what he wanted. There was no proof his beloved daughter had been murdered.

"It was murder," Kassouli said to me now. "The perfect murder. But that does not mean that it should go unavenged."

I stood up and limped to the far end of the room, where I pretended to stare at a model of a supertanker. She was called the *Kerak*. It struck me, as I stared at the striking kestrel on her single smokestack, that despite Kassouli's Mediterranean birth he had one very American trait: he believed in perfection.

The *Mayflower* had brought that belief in her baggage, and the dream had never been lost. But a large part of Yassir Kassouli's dream had died in the North Atlantic, in nearly two thousand fathoms of cold water. I turned. "You need proof," I said firmly.

He shook his head. "I need your help, Captain. I will pay you two hundred and fifty thousand dollars if, on the return leg of the St. Pierre, you navigate *Wildtrack* on a course that I will provide."

Two hundred and fifty thousand dollars. The sum hung in the air like a monstrous temptation. It spelt freedom from everything; it would give *Sycorax* and me the chance to sail till the seas ran dry.

Kassouli mistook my hesitation. "I do assure you, Captain, that your life, and the lives of *Wildtrack*'s crew, will be entirely safe."

I did not doubt it, but I noted how one name was excepted from that promise of mercy: Bannister's. I saw that Kassouli would not be content until his enemy was utterly destroyed. Something primeval was at work here: an eye for an eye, a tooth for a tooth, and now a life for a life.

Kassouli picked up the framed photograph and turned it so that I could stare into the dead girl's face. "Can you imagine the terror of her last moments, Captain? Now Nadeznha is among the *caballi*, the souls of the young dead, the untimely dead." Kassouli's voice was very matter of fact, almost casual. "They roam the world, Captain, seeking the consolation of justice. Who but their families can provide such solace?"

But neither ghosts, nor weather charts, nor even two hundred and fifty thousand dollars could make me accept. God knows *Sycorax* and I needed the money, but there was an old-fashioned dream, as old as the dream that was carried in the *Mayflower*, and it was called honour. There was no proof that Bannister had done murder, and till that proof was found there could be no punishment. I shook my head. "I'm not your man, sir. Besides, I've already told Bannister I'm not sailing with him."

"But that decision could be reversed?"

I shrugged. "It won't be."

He half smiled, then carefully replaced the silver-framed family portrait. "You are a patriot, Captain?"

The question surprised me. "Yes, sir."

"Then I think you should know that I have given myself one year to avenge my daughter's death. So far, Captain, I have tried to achieve that satisfaction through conventional means. I pleaded with your government to reopen the inquest, but they have refused. Very well. If no Englishman will help me, Captain, then I will wash my hands of your country. I don't flatter myself that I can bring Great Britain to its knees, but I will withdraw all my investments out of your country and I will use my influence, which is not negligible, to deter others from investing in your economy. Do you understand me?"

I understood him. It was blackmail on an enormous scale.

Kassouli raised his voice. "Every cent of every investment I have in Britain will be withdrawn. I will become an enemy of your country, Captain Sandman. Whenever it is in my power to do it harm, that harm will be done."

Then Kassouli smiled. "But this is a nonsense, Captain Sandman! Fate has sent you to me. Fate has put you into Anthony Bannister's confidence, and I do not believe that fate is so very capricious. I am asking you to take on trust that my daughter was murdered. You must reflect that not every course of action in this world is underpinned by cause and proof. Sometimes, Captain, we have to trust our God-given instincts, and act!"

I closed my eyes. "You cannot prove it was not an accident." I opened my eyes to see that, surprisingly, Kassouli was still smiling.

"You have not disappointed me, Captain. I like strong people. They are the only ones on whom I can rely. And Miss Kirov assures me you are a brave and resourceful young man. So, I wish you to do one thing for me."

He held out a hand to indicate that I should accompany him to the door. As we walked he made one last effort to sway me. "I want you to consider everything I have said. I want you to search your conscience. I want you to consider the damage I can cause to your country. And when you have done that, then I want you to inform me whether or not you will help me. Will you do that, Captain?"

"Yes, sir," I said lamely.

He pressed a button beside the doorframe and the tall Scandinavian servant appeared instantly. Kassouli gripped my hand. "Good night, Captain. I will send for your answer in due time."

IN THE MORNING I walked about the harbour and tried to persuade myself that Kassouli's threats had been nonsensical. I could not convince myself. I walked back to the hotel where I was informed that a car would be taking me to the airport that afternoon, and that Miss Kirov was waiting for me in the Lobsterman's Saloon.

The saloon was decorated with old-fashioned lobster pots, nets and plastic crustaceans. I found Jill-Beth sitting alone at the polished bar. She smiled happily. "Hi, Nick! Irish whiskey? How did you sleep?"

"Alone."

"Me too." She shrugged, and I knew I had been brought to this town only to meet Kassouli. Jill-Beth had been nothing but the bait, and I'd bitten. "So what did you make of Yassir?" she asked me.

"Mad."

She shook her head. "He's a grieving father, Nick. It isn't madness. You want to eat lobster?"

I took the menu out of her hands and laid it down. "He isn't talking about sabotaging Bannister's attempt at the St. Pierre, Jill-Beth, he's talking about killing him!"

She shook her head disapprovingly. "You're talking out of turn, Nick. Maybe Yassir just wants a signed confession so the courts can take over? Hell, he probably wants to save his insurance company paying out a million bucks!"

"He's mad! He can't declare economic war on a whole country!"

"Sure he can! Hotels, chemical works, computers, investments, oil, shipping. I guess his companies employ thirty thousand people in Britain. And he's a very, very angry man."

I sipped a whiskey that was drowning in crushed ice. "Who was Nadezhna Bannister in love with?"

"Goodness knows."

"But that's part of Kassouli's evidence," I protested. "A love affair that no one even knows existed, a weather map that doesn't describe the sea conditions, and the probability that she'd have been wearing a safety harness. That's it, Jill-Beth! On that thin basis he's predicating murder!"

"You got it, Nick."

"You can't believe it," I challenged her.

She stirred her drink with a lobster-shaped swizzle stick. "Who knows? Bannister doesn't want a divorce, he's kicking around with that new blonde of his. He knows Nadezhna will give him grief with the taxman, so he pushes her over the edge five hundred miles out on the return leg? I'd call that the perfect murder."

"It isn't me who lives in La-la land," I said bitterly. "Kassouli goes on about unquiet souls!"

Jill-Beth smiled. "La-la land, my dear Nick, is where everything is

84

simple, where the virtuous always triumph, and where honour rules. This isn't La-la land. You're dealing with a guy who's very angry, very frustrated, and who wants justice. He only has two children: one's crippled, one's dead. And his wife's got cancer. Dying, very slowly."

"Oh, God." I flinched.

"People envy Kassouli. He's rich. But he's been dealt a bad hand with his family and he wants to hit back."

"Suppose I went to the police?" I said. "Suppose I told them that you're trying to make me an accessory to piracy on the high seas? Or murder?"

"Try it," she said cheerfully.

"I'm not helping you. When I get back to England I'm moving *Sycorax* to a hiding place. Somewhere a long way from Bannister and a long way from you."

She ignored me. "I'll be over in England soon. I'll get in touch, OK?"

"You won't find me."

She touched my forearm. "Don't be a pain, Nick. Chivalry died with Nadeznha. Stay with Bannister, say you'll navigate his boat, and buy yourself a calculator that goes up to four hundred big ones. I'm empowered to increase Kassouli's offer to four hundred thousand dollars." She picked up the menu again. "You want to eat?" I shook my head.

"OK." She slid off the stool. "I'll see you soon, Nick, and I'll have one hundred thousand dollars cash with me. If you're not there, then kiss a lot of British jobs goodbye. Safe home."

I turned as she reached the door. "Why me, Jill-Beth?"

She paused. "Because you're there, Nick. Because you're there." She smiled, blew me a kiss, and went.

I felt like a frog that had sought out the princess, been kissed, but stayed a frog all the same. In short, I felt damned foolish. And up to my neck in trouble.

Chapter 6

The Honourable John Makyns, MP, pretended that he was not embarrassed by lunching with his wife's cast-off husband, but I noticed how he had chosen one of the West End's less prestigious clubs for our meeting. He seemed rather sombre, but perhaps that was understandable. It isn't every day that you're telephoned from Heathrow to be told that a major foreign industrialist is declaring economic war against your country.

He fussed over the choice of wine and recommended the lamb to me. I ordered it, then listened as he told me a long and disjointed story about the problems of finding craftsmen who could repair Tudor brickwork. He

85

was avoiding the subject, which was Yassir Kassouli. He'd tried to ignore it on the telephone, but as soon as I threatened to call the newspapers he hastened to suggest this luncheon. He was still evasive, though, asking about Devon, the weather in America and my health.

"Tell me about Kassouli." I decided to cut through to the reason for our meeting.

"Ah." The Honourable John speared a piece of meat with his fork. "Kassouli did approach HMG. Not officially, of course. As a private citizen of a foreign state. I think he wanted us to put Bannister on trial, but there really was no justification."

"A dead girl?" I suggested.

He shook his head. "An incident happened on the high seas, beyond the limits of anyone's sovereignty. Agreed that the boat is British-registered, which is why there was a British inquest, but the coroner's findings were quite clear. It was an accident."

"Couldn't you have given Kassouli another inquest? Just to satisfy him?"

"There was no legal reason for doing so. There would have had to be fresh evidence, and there was none."

"Kassouli told me he'd pull all his investments out of Britain, and then persuade all his rich pals to do the same thing. That won't do any good to the unemployment figures."

The Honourable John concentrated on chewing, but finally decided he would have to reveal something from his side of the table. "You aren't the first person to bring us this message, Nick."

"Could Kassouli hurt us?"

"Not as much as he thinks. But he could embarrass us, yes. And he could damage confidence at a time when we're working hard to attract foreign investment. If all Kassouli's jobs went to Germany or Ireland or Spain, we'd never see them again."

"So what do I do?"

The Honourable John swirled the wine round in his glass, trying to look judicious. "What do you feel is best, Nick?"

"I'd hardly be coming to ask for your help if I knew what to do, would I? I've got some madman threatening economic warfare against Britain unless I help turn Anthony Bannister into fish food. Wouldn't you say that was a matter for the government rather than me?"

He looked immensely pained. "Did Kassouli say as much?"

"Not exactly, but I can't think what else he wanted. I'm supposed to steer the good ship *Lollipop* straight to point X on the chart. What do you think is going to be waiting for us? Mermaids?"

"So far as I know, all Kassouli wishes to do is deny Bannister the chance of winning the St. Pierre."

"Don't be pompous, John. The bastard's up to no good. You want me to go and squeal this tale down Fleet Street? Someone is bound to listen to me."

"They'll listen only too avidly, I fear." He stared at me helplessly.

"Then reassure me! Tell me the government's on top of this problem. Don't you have friends in Washington who can tell Kassouli to rewire his brain?"

"Not with the amounts of money he contributes to members of Congress, no." He shrugged. "And you forget that Kassouli has never made these threats openly. Nevertheless, HMG is forced to take them seriously."

"Then give him his enquiry! Why ever not?"

"Because HMG does not actually control the judiciary. A new inquest can only be instituted if there are fresh revelations of fact."

"Hold it!" I said. "Here's a revelation of fact. I'm not going to help Kassouli, because I don't fancy joining my father in jail. What I'm going to do is go back to Devon and, if Bannister's mistress hasn't stolen my boat, I'm going to tow it off to a nice safe place where I shall rig it. Meanwhile you'll be losing lots of jobs, but don't blame me, I've done my bit for my country. And you can tell Melissa not to try to find me before I sail. The kids' school fees are in the bank, and there isn't any more money."

"Nick, Nick, Nick!" The Honourable John held up a hand. "Of course we're not asking you to adopt responsibility for this situation. We just need to know a great deal more about the nature of Mr. Kassouli's threats. HMG would be most grateful if you were to keep us informed of his intentions. Nothing more, Nick. Just information."

"How grateful would HMG be?"

"I don't think we're talking about fiscal remuneration, Nick. Shall we just agree that we would privately approve your patriotism?"

"The only way I can keep an eye on Kassouli is by going along with his plans, isn't it? Why don't I just go to the police?"

The Honourable John gave me a very small, very tight smile. "Because you would discover that the matter was beyond their competence."

"God, but you're a slimy lot." I stared at him. "Do you think Bannister murdered his wife?"

"I think it would be unscrupulous to make any conjecture."

"But HMG would be jolly grateful if I helped knock off Bannister, and you're telling me, in the most roundabout manner possible, that the police will turn a blind eye."

"You may put whatever construction you choose upon my words, Nick, and once again I entirely deny any imputation of a conspiracy to murder. All I am prepared to say is that we would like you to be helpful to a most important industrialist who could bring a great deal more investment and many more jobs to Britain."

"Kassouli's as mad as a hatter, John. He talks about unquiet souls. He's probably chatting to his daughter right now, through some spiritualist!"

The Honourable John looked at his watch. "Good Lord. Is that the time? Now Nick, not a word to the press, there's a good chap."

He paid and left me. I had gone to the government for help, and I'd been abandoned. So I did the one thing they did not want me to do. I phoned Fleet Street.

THE PUB WAS DINGY and smelly but it was close to the newspaper offices, which was why Micky Harding had suggested it. Harding was one of the reporters who had marched every step of the Falklands with my battalion which had, inevitably, nicknamed him "Mouse".

Mouse now brought four pints of ale to the table. Two for each of us.

"You look bloody horrible, Nick."

"Thank you."

He downed the best part of his first pint. "Saw your face in the papers. Who beat you up?"

"Friend of Anthony Bannister's. South African."

"Well, well, well." He looked at me with interest, sensing a story.

"But you can't say that," I said hastily. "If you do, I lose my boat."

He closed his eyes, clicked his fingers irritably, then gave me a look of triumph. "*Sycorax*, right? God, but you were boring about that boat," he went on. "Still afloat, is it?"

"Only just. I need Bannister's money to repair it."

"So tell me all."

I told him everything, and that I now had a problem: I wanted to head Kassouli off, not because I was on Bannister's side, but because it was impossible to do nothing, when so many jobs were threatened.

"Why don't you just play *shtum*?" Micky asked. "Clearly the government's happy for Bannister to get knocked off, the jobs get saved, and you keep your boat. What do you need me for?"

"Because there's no proof that Bannister did kill his wife."

"Oh. You want to be honourable as well, do you?" He said it in friendly mockery. He was a big man with a battered face, a coarse tongue and a mind like a suspicious weasel. Now he looked dubious. "It's the word of a convict's son versus the British government and one of the world's richest men?"

"That's about it."

"The VC will help, of course"— he thought about it some more—"but Kassouli will deny talking to you?"

"Utterly."

"And the government will say they never heard of you?"

"I'm sure."

"Dodgy." He went silent again for a few puffs of his cigarette. "Do you think there's a chance Bannister did it?"

"I haven't the first idea, Mouse. That's the whole point about a perfect murder. It's so perfect you don't even know if it was murder."

"But if we hint at it, Bannister will slap a libel writ on us, won't he? It just can't be proved that he murdered his wife, can it?"

"No."

"The perfect murder," he said admiringly. "A damn sight cheaper than divorce." He lit another cigarette. "I want it. It's a lovely little tale. Just right for a low-life rag like mine. Cheers, Nick."

"So can you help?" I felt the relief of a weight being lifted. If the British government would not take a stand against Kassouli's obsession, then the press certainly would. Kassouli's threats would disappear, for he would surely not dare acknowledge that he was trying to blackmail a government or plan revenge on the high seas. I would let the newspapers stir up the sludge and make a huge stench. The stench might even give Kassouli what he wanted: another enquiry into Nadezhna's death.

"I'll help," Micky said grimly, "but I need proof." He wrinkled his face as he thought. "This Jill-Beth Kirov. She's coming back to talk to you?"

"She said so. But I'm not going to be around to be talked to. I'm planning to move my boat tomorrow. Bannister's threatening to repossess the boat, and I've had enough."

"No." Micky shook his head. "You'll have to stay there." He saw my unwilling expression, and sighed. "Look, mate. If you're not there, then the American girl won't talk to you. If she doesn't talk to you, then we haven't got any proof. And if I haven't got proof then we don't have a story."

"But how does her talking to me provide proof?"

"Because I'll wire you, you dumb hero. A radiomike under your shirt, and your Uncle Micky listening in with a tape recorder. I have to get the boss's permission, but we do it all the time. You have to go along with it all, understand? Tell Bannister you'd love to navigate his bloody boat. Tell Kassouli you're itching to help him trap Bannister. String them along!"

"But I've already told Bannister I'm through with his damned film," I said unhappily.

"Then untell him. Say you were wrong." He was insistent and persuasive. "You're doing it for Queen and Country, Nick. You're saving jobs. It won't be for ever, anyway. How long before this Jill-Beth turns up with the hundred thousand? Within a month, I'll wager."

Micky persuaded me to stay on to be filmed. But only till the story broke, and after that I would rid myself of all the rich men into whose squabble I had been unwillingly drawn.

I TOOK THE TRAIN to Devon next morning, and *Sycorax* was still at my wharf. I had half expected to find her missing, but she was safe. I climbed into her cockpit. The gun was still in its hiding place.

If Mulder had been willing to search *Mystique*, I wondered, why not *Sycorax*? I went topsides, but there was no sign of Jimmy. It was raining.

There was nothing to eat on board, so I trudged up to the house, only to find that the housekeeper was out. I knew where she kept a spare key, so I let myself in and helped myself to bread and cheese from the kitchen. I ate the meal in the big lounge, staring out at the rain falling on the river.

The sound of the front door slamming echoed through the house. I turned, expecting to hear the housekeeper go towards the kitchen, but instead it was Angela Westmacott, who came into the lounge. She stopped, surprised to see me.

"Good afternoon," I said politely.

"I thought you'd resigned," she said.

"I thought we might talk about it."

"Meaning you need the money?" She dropped armfuls of shopping onto a sofa before stripping off her wet raincoat. "So are you making the film or not?"

"I thought we might as well finish it," I said meekly, true to the promise I'd made to Micky Harding.

"And how is your mother?"

"She's a tough old bird," I said vaguely, feeling somewhat ashamed at the lie I'd recorded on the answering machine.

"She sounded quite well when I spoke to her. She did eventually say you were in Dallas, though not actually in the house just at that moment. I said I'd phone back, but she said I shouldn't bother."

"Mother's like that."

"You are a bastard, Nick Sandman."

I turned to watch rainwater trickling down the window and prayed that Jill-Beth would come to England soon so that I could get the charade of entrapment over with, and free myself of all these obsessed and selfish people.

A sob startled me. I turned and, to my astonishment, saw tears pouring down Angela's face. Her thin shoulders were shuddering. "All I want to do," she said, between sobs, "is make a good film."

"You use funny methods to do it," I said bitterly.

"But it's like swimming in treacle!" She ignored my words. "Everything

I do, you hate. Everything I try, you oppose." She sniffed, then wiped her eyes on the sleeve of her jacket. "Can't you see what a good film it could be, Nick?"

"Good enough to blackmail me for? No supplies till I do what you want?"

"For God's sake! If I didn't force you, you'd do nothing! You're like a mule! The film crew spend more time reading the union regulations than they do filming; Matthew's frightened of them; and you're so bloody casual! I've taken the company's money, their time, their crew, and I don't even know whether I'm going to be able to finish the film! I don't know where you *are* half the time! And if I do find you, and want to talk to you, you look at me as if I'm dirt!" It was as if a great chain had snapped inside her. She found a packet of cigarettes, and lit one.

"I swore I'd give up cigarettes," she said, "but how can I, with people like you around? And Tony."

"What's wrong with Bannister?"

"He's frightened of you! He won't tell you what's expected of you, so I have to do it. Always me! He's lazy, you're obstructive, and I'm just tired!" She shook with great racking sobs.

I limped towards her. "Is it such a good film?"

"Yes. It's an honest film, though you won't see it!"

I put my hands on her shoulders, turned her, and held her against me. She did not resist. I took the burning cigarette from her and flicked it into the swimming pool. "I'm sorry," I said.

"I'm sorry, too." She sobbed the words into my dirty sweater. "I didn't want this to happen." But she did not pull away from me.

"I did," I said. From the very first I'd wanted it to happen, and now, on a rainy afternoon, and to confuse everything, it did.

IT RAINED ALL AFTERNOON, all evening. For all I knew or noticed, all night too. We talked. Angela told me about her childhood in the Midlands, about her Baptist minister father, and about the redbrick university where she had marched to abolish nuclear weapons and save the whales.

She had met a glib older man who claimed to run a summer radio station for English tourists in the Mediterranean. She'd abandoned university and flown south, only to find that the radio station had gone bankrupt. "He didn't want me for that, anyway."

"What did he want you for?"

"He always said it was my legs."

"They're excellent legs."

She lifted one off the bed and examined it critically. "They're not bad."

"They'll do," I said.

She had landed herself a job with a real radio station in Australia. "It was cheeky, really," she said. "I didn't know the first thing about radio."

"Legs again?"

She nodded. "God knows what would have happened if I'd been ugly." She thought about that for a time, then frowned. "I've always resented my looks, in a way. I mean, you're never sure whether they want you for your looks or your abilities. Do you know what I mean?"

"It's a problem I have all the time," I said, and she laughed, but I was thinking that her passionate drive to make a good film must have been part of her answer to that question. She desperately wanted to prove that her abilities could match those of a clever and ugly person.

Not that Angela had ever been coy about using her good looks. In Australia she had met Anthony Bannister. He had promised her a job on his programme if she should ever return to England.

"So I came back. I wanted to work in English television."

"And Bannister was the price?"

She looked at me. "I like him, Nick. Truly. He's so vulnerable. He's very good at his job, but he doesn't have any confidence outside it."

"He's weak," I said.

"It's easy for you to say that. You're strong. Tony doesn't think anyone likes him. That's why he tries to be nice to everyone. That's what makes him good on the telly, I think."

We lay quietly for a while, listening to the rain. I pulled a strand of her long hair across my chest. "Will you marry him?" I asked.

"If he wants me to, yes."

"Will he?"

"I think so. I'm efficient, you see, which is good for his career."

"Do you love him?"

She appeared to think about it, then shook her head.

"Then why marry him?"

"Because he can be good company." She spoke very slowly, like a child rehearsing a difficult lesson. "Because he's very successful. Because I can give him confidence when he meets people who he thinks despise him. He thinks you despise him. And I'll marry him because it will make me feel safe."

"I don't understand."

"I'm tired of being chased by men. Now, because people know that I belong to Tony, they don't try. And I'd never have any more money worries, would I?"

"Would he be angry about this?"

She nodded. "Angry and hurt. He's unfaithful to me all the time, but he never thinks that it might hurt me." She shrugged. "He has a terrible pride. That's why I think he might ask me to marry him."

"Because he thinks you'll stay faithful to him?"

"And because I'm decorative." She twisted her head to see if I thought her immodest.

I kissed her forehead. "You're very decorative. The very first moment that I saw you, I thought how decorative you were."

She smiled. "You were very gaunt and frightening. I didn't think I was going to like you, and I was sure you were going to hate me."

"I was just fancying you," I said, "but I was nervous. I thought television people would be much too clever and glamorous."

"We are," she said with a smile, then went back to thinking about Bannister. "It's very important to Tony to have a beautiful wife. It's like his car or house, you see: something to impress other people with."

We lay in silence for a long while. I heard an outboard on the river as someone made a dash through the rain towards the pub. Angela fell lightly asleep. I thought she looked very young and innocent; all the tense anger had drained out of her face. I kissed her warm skin, and the kiss woke her.

She blinked, and recognition came to her eyes. "Now tell me about you," she said.

THE GOOD TIMES BEGAN THEN. Anthony Bannister was commuting between his London house and the Mediterranean, where *Wildtrack* had been entered for a series of offshore races. Fanny Mulder was with the boat, so I had Devon to myself.

I also had the nonsailing Angela. Matthew and the film crew must have realised what had happened between Angela and me, but they said nothing.

Sycorax's rigging wire arrived and we borrowed a buoy barge so that its onboard derrick could lower the varnished masts into their places. Before stepping the mainmast I carefully placed an antique penny in the keel chock where the mast's heel hid and crushed the silver coin. It was a tradition, supposed to bring good luck to the ship, but love brought better fortune as Angela freed all the materials for *Sycorax*.

Day by day the rigging took shape. Wire, rope, timber and buckets of Stockholm tar were hoisted aloft and turned into the seemingly fragile concoction that could withstand the vast powers of ocean winds. The film crew gave up trying to understand what was going on; they said I was becoming nautical, which only meant that my vocabulary had become technical, as Jimmy and I worried about deadeyes and gantlines, robands and leader cringles.

Angela made *Sycorax* a gift of some antique brass scuttles. She called them portholes. They were beautifully made, with thick greenish glass and heavy brass frames. They had hinged shutters that could be bolted down in bad weather. The sails were repaired in a Dartmouth loft and came back to the boat on a day when the film crew was absent. Jimmy and I could not resist bending mizzen and main onto their new spars. The sails had to be fully hoisted if they were to be properly stowed on the booms, and I felt *Sycorax* shiver beneath me as the wind stirred the eight-ounce cotton.

"We could take her out?" Jimmy suggestly slyly. "Put on staysails, boy. Let's see how her runs, eh?"

I was tempted. It was a lovely day with a southwesterly wind, and *Sycorax* would have revelled in the sea, but I'd promised Angela I'd wait so that the film crew could record my first outing in the rebuilt boat.

I told Jimmy it would only be a day or two, no more, before we could film the sequence I had dreamed of for so long: the moment when *Sycorax* sailed again. Two months before, I would have taken Jimmy's hint, but now I was as committed to the film as Angela herself. I had even begun to see it through her eyes, though I still refused to contemplate sailing in the St. Pierre, and Angela had agreed that we'd devise a different ending for the film, one with *Sycorax* beating out to sea.

I telephoned Angela at her London office that afternoon. "She's all ready," I said. "Sails bent on, ma'am, ready to go."

"Completely ready?"

"No radio, no navigation lights, no stove, no bilge pumps, no anchors, no . . ." I was listing all the things Fanny Mulder had stolen.

"They're ordered, Nick," Angela said patiently.

"But she can sail," I added warmly. "*Sycorax* awaits your bottle of champagne and your film crew."

"That's wonderful." Angela did not sound altogether pleased, perhaps because I was finishing a boat that would take me away from her. There was a pause. "Nick?"

"There's a train that leaves Totnes at twenty-six minutes past five this afternoon," I said, "and it reaches London at—"

"Twenty-five minutes to nine," she chimed in, and did sound pleased.

"I suppose I could just make it."

"You'd better make it," she said, "or there'll be no radio, no navigation lights and no stove."

"Bilge pumps?"

"Definitely no bilge pumps. Ever."

ANGELA'S FLAT WAS A GLOOMY BASEMENT in Kensington. She only used it when Bannister was away, but the very fact that she had retained it spoke for her independence. At least I thought so. The flat had a somewhat abandoned feel, the flat of a busy young woman who spent most of her time elsewhere.

"Next Tuesday," she told me, "we'll film *Sycorax* going to sea."

"Not till then?" She must have heard my disappointment.

"Not till then."

"High tide's at ten forty-eight in the morning," I said from memory, "and it's a big one."

"Does that matter?"

"That's good. We'll go out on a fast ebb."

"There's another reason it has to be Tuesday." She did not look at me as she spoke. "Tony wants to see *Sycorax* go to sea. I mean, the film is partly about how he helped you, isn't it?"

"Does he want to be on board?"

"Probably."

I said nothing, but felt jealousy tug at me like a foul current, threatening the day's perfection.

Angela turned in her chair. "I'm sorry, Nick. It's just that . . ." She shrugged, unable to finish.

"He has prior claim?"

"I suppose so."

"And you have no choice?" I asked, and wished I had not asked, because I was betraying my jealousy.

"I've got a choice." Her voice was defiant.

"Then why don't we sail *Sycorax* out on Sunday?" On Sunday Bannister would still be in France. "You come with me," I said. "We'll be in the Azores in a few days. After that we can make up our minds. You fancy exploring the Caribbean?"

"I get seasick."

"You'll get over it in three days."

"I never get over it." She was staring into the mirror as she pinned up her long hair. "I'm not a sailor, Nick. Do you think I haven't been tempted to get away from it all? But I can't do that. If I was twenty years old I might. Isn't that the age when people think the world will lap them in love, and all they need to do is show a little faith in it?"

"Twenty-six is not old."

"It's too old to drift around the world like a gypsy. Who's going to pay you? What will you do when your leg collapses? What about your old age? You don't seem to care, Nick, but I'm not like you."

"It's just that I'm in love with you, and I don't want to lose you."

She stared at me. "Get a job, live in Devon. Can't you talk yourself into a job, with that medal?"

"Maybe."

"You'll stay tomorrow?"

Tomorrow was Friday. "How about the whole weekend?"

"You know I can't."

Bannister wanted her to go to France for the weekend. After *Wildtrack*'s successful series of races he had moved to the Riviera where he had been a judge at a television festival. He wanted Angela to fly down for the festival's closing celebrations. The plan was that she would fly to Nice on Friday evening, then return with Bannister on Monday morning and drive down to Devon that same afternoon. We thus both sensed that this might be our last night of stolen freedom.

Angela left early next morning, going to the studios where she was rough-cutting the film that had been shot so far. I made myself coffee in her tiny kitchen, bathed in her tiny bathroom, then sat and made a list of the charts I wanted to buy.

The phone rang. I did not move. The telephone was connected to an answering machine and when I was in the flat I left the machine's speaker turned up. If it was Angela calling me then I would hear her voice and know to pick up the telephone and switch off the machine. This time I heard the usual tape of Angela's voice apologising that she could not answer the phone in person, there was a pause after the tone, and then another familiar voice sounded.

"Hi. You don't know me. My name's Jill-Beth Kirov. We met at Anthony Bannister's house, remember? I'm looking for Nick Sandman and I gathered you were filming him, and I wonder if you'd pass on a message? My number is—"

She broke off because I had switched off the answering machine and lifted the telephone.

"Jill-Beth?"

"Nick! Hi!"

I was angry. "How the hell did you know I was here?"

She sounded pained. "I was just trying to reach you. I didn't know where you were. I was just going to leave messages everywhere. I need to talk with you. OK?"

For a second I forgot my careful recording arrangements with Micky Harding. "I don't think we've got anything to say to each other."

She sighed. "I once had to investigate a guy who had a boat pretty much like yours, Nick. He was real proud of that boat. It burned. It was a real tragedy."

"Are you threatening me?"

"Nick!" She sounded very hurt. "I just want to talk with you, OK? What's the harm in that?"

Micky Harding had promised that the newspaper could ease me off Kassouli's hook. "All right." I spoke guardedly.

She suggested that very lunchtime, but I didn't know if I could find Micky that quickly. "I can't meet you till Monday," I said, "and I'll be back in Devon by then."

She paused. "OK, Nick." She named a pub that I knew, and a time.

I put the phone down. It seemed that Yassir Kassouli had not given up his pursuit of Bannister. The hounds of revenge were slipped and running, and now I had to head them into the light where they would be dazzled and confused by publicity.

I telephoned Micky and told him where and when I was supposed to meet Jill-Beth. "Can you make it?" I asked.

"I'll make it."

Angela came home and played the message tape on the phone. I'd rewound the spool after Jill-Beth's call and her voice had been overlaid with a message about flights to Nice.

"What kind of a day did you have?" Angela asked.

"I bought two charts, and discovered a million things I can't afford."

"Poor Nick." She reached out a long thin hand and touched my cheek. "A friend has said I could borrow a cottage in Norfolk this weekend. There's no phone there, and he's got a Heron dinghy in the creek. Does that make sense?"

"A Heron makes much sense." My joy at having Angela to myself all the weekend must have shown, but I still wanted to make certain of it. "And Nice?"

"I'll tell Tony I'm too busy."

I did not tell Angela about Jill-Beth's call. I wanted to, but I didn't know how to explain why I was meeting the American. Angela would have bridled at the thought of the bad publicity that would be flung at Bannister, and anyway, I told myself, I was only meeting Jill-Beth to end Kassouli's interference.

Chapter 7

Micky Harding and I drove down to Devon on the Monday afternoon. I was nervous. "We're taking on one of the richest men in the world, Micky."

He glanced at me as I twisted awkwardly to look through the back window. "You think we're being followed?"

"No." I had been looking for Angela's Porsche. She had gone to meet Bannister at Heathrow and if they left directly for Devon, they could well overtake us on the road. I did not want to see them together. I'd just spent a weekend of gentle happiness with a small sailing boat and Angela to myself. She had not even been seasick.

Micky lit a cigarette. "You're chicken, mate, that's what you are. I could do a story on that. 'VC revealed as a wimp'."

"I'm not used to this sort of thing."

"Which is why you called in the reinforcements?"

"Exactly."

The "reinforcements" were waiting for us at a service area where the cafeteria offered an all-day breakfast and where Sergeant Terry Fare-brother was mopping up the remains of a fried egg and brown sauce with a piece of white bread. His moustachioed face was impassive as the two of us approached his table.

"Bloody hell," he greeted Micky Harding, "it's the Mouse."

The Mouse, who had known the Yorkshire sergeant in the Falklands, shook Terry's hand. Terry was a bullock of a man: short, stubborn and utterly dependable. It was good to see him again.

"No trouble," he said when I asked if he'd had difficulty getting away from battalion. "They owed me leave."

As we walked to the car he asked, "So what are we doing?"

I told him that I was meeting this American girl, and it was just possible that she might threaten my boat if I didn't agree to do whatever she wanted, and so I would appreciate it if Terry sat on *Sycorax* until Micky and I got back to the river.

"Nothing's going to happen," Micky added as he accelerated back onto the motorway. "You just get to sit on a boat while it gets dark outside."

Terry, eating the first of his cold bacon sandwiches, ignored Micky. "So what will these bastards do? If they do anything?"

"Fire," I said. Jill-Beth had hinted at arson, and it frightened me. A hank of rags, soaked in petrol and tossed into the cockpit, would reduce *Sycorax* to floating ash in minutes. If I turned Jill-Beth's proposal down, which I planned to do, *Sycorax* would be vulnerable.

We reached the river two hours later and I took Terry down through the woods to *Sycorax*. I saw two of Mulder's crewmen preparing *Wildtrack II* in the boathouse, ready for tomorrow's outing when she would be the camera platform for *Sycorax*'s maiden trip. I assumed, from their presence, that Mulder must have returned from his victories in the Mediterranean offshore races.

The tide was low. Terry and I climbed down to *Sycorax*'s deck and I unlocked the cabin. I did not tell him about the hidden Colt.

"Any food, boss?" He asked hopefully. I've never known a man eat as much as Terry. He wasn't so much a human being as a cholesterol processor.

"There's some digestive biscuits in the drawer by the sink, apples in the upper locker and beer under the port bunk."

"Bloody hell." He looked disgusted.

"And you might need these." I dropped two fire extinguishers on the chart table. *Sycorax* might lack a lot, but I'd taken good care to buy fire extinguishers. She was a wooden boat and her greatest enemy was fire. "And if anyone asks you what you're doing here, Terry, tell them you're a mate of mine. I should be back by nine, and we'll go over the river for a pint. They do a very good steak and kidney pudding, too."

If there was one certainty about this evening, it was that *Sycorax* was safe. Kassouli would need an Exocet to take out Terry Farebrother, and even then I wasn't sure the Exocet would win.

I limped back up through the woods and got into Micky's car. We drove north, threading through the maze of deep lanes that led onto Dartmoor. Low dark cloud was threatening from the west and I knew there would be lashing rain before the evening was done.

We left the hedgerows behind, emerging onto the bleak upland where the wind sighed round the granite tors. We were over an hour early reaching the village pub where Jill-Beth had said she would meet me.

Micky took me into the pub's toilet where he fitted me with the radiomicrophone. A plastic-coated wire aerial hung down one trouser leg, a small box the size of a pocket calculator was taped to the small of my back, and the tiny microphone was pinned under my shirt.

"I'm going back to the bar," Micky said, "and you're going to speak to me." He had the receiver, together with a tape recorder, in a big bag. To hear what was being recorded he wore a hearing aid.

The device worked. After the test we sat at a table and Micky gave me instructions. If I went more than fifty yards away from him he'd lose the signal. He said the microphone was nondirectional and would pick up every sound nearby, so I should try to lean as close to Jill-Beth as I could. "You won't mind that, will you?" Micky said. "You fancy her, right?"

"I used to."

"Fancy her again. And keep an eye on me. If I can't hear what she's saying I'll scratch my nose."

"Is this how we trap one of the world's richest men?" I asked. "With nose-scratching and toy radios?"

"Remember Watergate. Now, what are you going to say to her?"

"I'm going to tell her to get lost."

"Nick! Nick!" he groaned. "If you tell her that she'll do a bunk and what will we have? You have to chat her up! You've got to say all the things she wants you to say, so that she says all the things we want her to say. Above all, you have to ask her just what Kassouli plans to do out there. Is he trying to knock Bannister off? Or is he just trying to scare the bastard? Got it?"

"Got it," I said. "What about the money?"

Micky closed his eyes in mock despair. "You take the ruddy money! It's proof!" He drained his whisky. "Are you ready for battle, my son?"

"I'm ready."

100

"To war, then. And stop worrying. Nothing can go wrong."

I waited nervously. If I was successful this evening I would stop an obsessed millionaire from pulling thousands of jobs out of Britain. I would start a scandal in the newspapers. I would also drive Angela away, because I knew she would never forgive me for bringing Bannister's name into the story. I had so often, and often unjustly, accused her of dishonesty, now she would say that I had been dishonest. But tonight I would render Kassouli's threats impotent, then I would leave Bannister to make his attempt on the St. Pierre. Afterwards I would be free, and *Sycorax* and I would go where the wind willed us. I waited.

"Hɪ!" AFTER ANGELA'S slender paleness, Jill-Beth looked tanned and healthy. She was wearing tight jeans and cowboy boots, and carried a raincoat and a handbag over her arm. She stooped to offer me a kiss, then sensed from my reaction that such a gesture was inappropriate. Instead she sat next to me.

"How are you?" she asked. Her back was towards Micky, who offered me a surreptitious thumbs up to indicate that he could hear her through the concealed microphone.

"Would you like a beer?" I asked.

She shook her head. "How about going for a walk?"

"In this?" I gestured at the rain that was now blurring the window-panes.

"I thought you were a soldier! Are you frightened of rain?"

I was frightened of getting out of range of Micky's radio, but Jill-Beth would not take a refusal, so I followed her outside where she pulled on her raincoat and tied a scarf over her head. "Yassir says 'Hi'."

"Great."

She seemed not to notice my lack of enthusiasm; instead she opened the handbag and showed its contents to me. "One hundred thousand dollars, Nick. Tax-free."

I stared at the tightly wadded notes. I'd never seen so much money in my life. Did Jill-Beth really believe I could be bought?

"It's all yours." She closed her bag. The rain was getting harder, but we crossed the bridge and headed towards Bellever Forest. I dared not look behind in case Jill-Beth also turned and saw Micky Harding's ungainly figure following us. My jacket was getting soaked and I hoped the microphone was not affected by damp.

"Do we really have to walk in this muck?" I asked.

"We really do." She said it very casually, then frowned with a sudden and genuine concern. "Are you hurting? Is that it?"

"A wee bit."

She took my arm, as though to help me walk. "I just couldn't abide all that cigarette smoke in the pub." She glanced up at the sky which was threatening an even heavier downpour. "Perhaps we'd better get under cover?"

She led me into the pines of Bellever. The rain was too new to have dripped through the thick cover of needles and we walked in comparative dryness. I once heard a footfall behind us and knew that Micky had kept up. He'd be silently cursing me for dragging him out of the pub.

Jill-Beth let go of my arm and leaned against a tree trunk. For a moment neither of us spoke. I was awkward, and her self-assurance seemed strained. "It's nice to see you again, Nick."

"Is it?"

"You're being hostile."

I supposed that if I really was being hostile then I was risking all the hard work that Micky had put into this meeting. I was here to convince this girl that I would help her, however reluctantly, and so I forced a smile. "Are you here to get me wet or rich?"

She smiled back. "Does that mean you're going to help us, Nick?"

"I don't know, Jill-Beth. I just don't share your conviction that Bannister's guilty. I don't like him, but I'm not sure that's sufficient grounds for ruining his chances in the St. Pierre." I was pacing up and down to cover my nervousness, then I realised that I was constantly turning the microphone away from Jill-Beth. I stopped and faced her.

She sighed. "All you have to do, Nick, is sail on Bannister's boat. You agree to do that and you get one hundred thousand dollars now, and another three hundred thousand when it's over."

"I've already told him I won't sail," I said.

"Would he believe you if you changed your mind?"

"He'd believe me," I said reluctantly.

"So tell him."

"And if I don't do it—" I was trying not to make my voice stilted, even though I was stating the obvious "—Kassouli will pull all his jobs out of Britain?"

She smiled. "You've got it. But not just his jobs, Nick. He'll pull out his investments, and he'll move his operations to the Continent. And a slew of British firms can kiss their hopes of new contracts on American projects goodbye. Kassouli's a determined guy."

With any luck, all that damning evidence must be spooling silently onto the take-up reel of Micky's recorder. All I had to do now was cross the Ts and dot the Is.

"And Kassouli won't do that if I sail on *Wildtrack*?"

"Right. You're our one chance, Nick."

It seemed odd to me that Yassir Kassouli, with all his millions, had only me to rely on, but perhaps Jill-Beth was right. My arrival at

102

Bannister's house must have seemed fortuitous. I was a very convenient weapon if I chose to be so. "And exactly what do I have to do?" I wanted her to spell it out for the microphone.

She showed no impatience at the pedantic question. "You just navigate a course that I'll provide for you."

"What course?"

"How do I know? That'll depend on the weather, right? All you have to do is keep a radio watch at the times we tell you, and that's it. The easiest four hundred thousand you ever earned, right?"

I smiled, "Right." That word had been hard to say, but I seemed to be convincing Jill-Beth with my act. Yet it occurred to me that she herself was just as mannered and awkward as I was. I should have taken note of that, but instead I asked her what would happen when I had navigated *Wildtrack* to wherever I was supposed to take her.

"Nothing happens to you. Nothing happens to the crew."

"But what happens to Bannister?"

"Whatever Yassir wants." She said it slowly, watching my reaction.

I was silent for a few seconds. Jill-Beth's words could be taken as an elliptical hint of murder, but I doubted whether she would be more explicit. "And all this," I asked in a tone of reluctant agreement, "on the assumption that Bannister murdered his wife?"

"You got it, Nick. You want the hundred thousand now?"

I should have said yes, but I baulked at the gesture. It might be a necessary deception, but it was distasteful.

"For God's sake, Nick! Are you going to help us or not?" Jill-Beth thrust the handbag towards me. "Or are you just wasting my time?"

I was about to accept, knowing the money was the final proof that Micky needed, when a strangled shout startled me. It was a man's cry, full of pain. I turned, but treacherously, as had happened before, my right leg went numb and collapsed. I fell, and Jill-Beth ran past me. I cursed my leg, knelt up, and forced myself to stand. I used my hands to straighten the leg and then, half limping and half hopping, staggered from tree to tree.

I found Jill-Beth twenty yards further on, crouched beside Micky. There was vivid blood on his scalp. He was alive, but unconscious. The bag lay spilt beside him and I saw the radio receiver, but no sign of the small tape recorder. Whoever had hit Micky had stolen the evidence.

"Did you bring him?" Jill-Beth looked at me accusingly.

"Get an ambulance." I snapped it like a military order. "Run! Dial nine-nine-nine! Hurry!" She would be twice as fast as I could be. "And bring blankets from the pub!"

She ran. I knelt beside Micky and draped my jacket over him. I tore a strip of cotton from my shirt-tail and padded it to staunch the blood that flowed from his scalp. Head wounds always bleed badly, but he'd been hit with much power, and I suspected a fractured skull. I stroked his hand for, though he was unconscious, he would need the feel of human comfort. I felt sick. I'd guarded *Sycorax* against Kassouli, but I had not thought to guard Micky. So who had done this? Had Jill-Beth brought reinforcements? Had she suspected that I might try to blow Kassouli's scheme wide open? Those questions made me wonder whether she *would* phone an ambulance, and I struggled to the edge of the trees and stared towards the village. My right leg was shaking and there was a vicious pulsing pain in my spine. I wasn't sure I could limp all the way to the village, but if Jill-Beth let me down then I would have to try. I cursed my leg, massaged it, then as I straightened up I saw headlights silhouetting running figures at the bridge.

Efficient men and women, trained to rescue lost hikers from the moors, came to Micky's aid. There was no need to wait for an ambulance for there was a Land-Rover which could take him to hospital. He was carefully lifted onto a stretcher, wrapped in a blanket and given a saline drip. I limped beside him to the Land-Rover and watched it pull away towards the road. Someone had phoned the police and now asked me if I'd wait for their arrival. I said I wanted to go to the hospital and Jill-Beth said she would drive me there in her car.

"Who is he?" she asked

"A newspaper reporter."

"You're a fool," she said scornfully.

"Not me!" I snapped. "You're the fool! Just because Kassouli's rich doesn't mean that he's right! You brought your thugs along, didn't you?"

"No!" she protested.

"Then who?"

She thought about it for a few seconds. "Did you drive straight here from London?"

"No. I went . . ." I paused. I'd gone to Bannister's house and seen evidence that Fanny Mulder was there. I hadn't thought to check if anyone had followed Micky and me to the moor. "Oh God," I said hopelessly. "Mulder."

We drove in silence until we reached the hospital where the Land-Rover was standing at the entrance to the casualty department. An empty police car, its blue light still flashing, was parked in front of it.

Jill-Beth killed her engine. "I guess this means you're not going to help us, Nick?"

"I won't be the hangman for a kangaroo trial."

Jill-Beth shrugged. "It wasn't meant to be this way, Nick, Americans against the Brits. Kassouli truly believes his daughter was murdered. If you shared that belief you'd be helping us."

104

I opened the car door. "It isn't America against us, it's just a conflict of old-fashioned honesty, that's all. You don't have proof. You don't have anything but suspicion. You're playing games to make a rich man happy."

She watched me get out of the car. "Goodbye, Nick."

I didn't reply. She started the motor and drove away.

THE HOSPITAL SMELT OF DISINFECTANT. It brought back memories I didn't want.

News was, at last, brought to me by a very young detective constable. Mr. Harding had a fractured skull and three broken ribs. He was still unconscious. Did I know who had assaulted Mr. Harding? No. Privately I was certain it was Mulder, but I could not prove it. Would I go to the police station and give a statement? No, I would not. I refused because it would be so utterly hopeless to explain. I felt suddenly tired. And scared. Mulder, if he had the tape, would already be on his way back to Bannister. I needed to reach the river and stop Terry Farebrother murdering Mulder, because Mulder, as likely as not, would look for me on *Sycorax*.

The policeman, professionally suspicious, closed his notebook. "I think you're coming to the station whether you want to or not."

"No," I said, "I'm going home. And what you're going to do is telephone Inspector Harry Abbott. Tell him I need a lift home, bloody fast. Tell him the Boer War has broken out."

I knew Abbott would give me hell when he got the chance, but he came through like a trooper on the night. I got my lift home. I told the copper to stop the car at the top of the hill and that I'd walk the rest of the way.

I stopped halfway down the wooded slope. The rain was lessening now, but I was soaked to the skin. There were lights in Bannister's house, but none down by the boathouse or near my wharf.

I went like a wraith down that slope. It was hard, for I was out of practice and my limp made me awkward, but I went as though I was on night patrol. I stared for a long time at the shadows behind the boathouse but nothing moved there when I flicked a piece of earth into the rhododendrons to stir a hidden watcher's attention.

I crept down the last stretch of the hill and hid myself in the boathouse shadows. "Terry?"

"Been listening to you for the last ten minutes, boss. Noisy, aren't you?"

Relief flooded me. "Any trouble?"

"Not a bloody flicker. How did you get on?"

"Mouse got stitched up. We should have had you there, not here." I

105

climbed down onto *Sycorax*'s deck. "He's in hospital. Lost the tape, too. Anything happened here?"

"One car arrived about ten minutes after you'd gone. Another came an hour ago."

The first car would have been Bannister and Angela, the second Mulder. I suspected Mulder was in the house now, with Micky's tape. The tape would suggest that I had been plotting against Bannister all along, but it was also possible that it would serve to warn Bannister of the real danger of attempting the St. Pierre.

At this moment, though, I cared more about what Angela might be thinking of me. "I'm going up to the house," I said to Terry.

"Want me?"

"Yes, but keep out of sight."

I could not let Angela think that I had betrayed her. I wanted her to know why I had met Jill-Beth. I would explain everything, not only to her, but to Bannister as well. Now was the time to let truth untangle the mess. That's the advantage of truth: it cuts through all the deception and muddle.

Terry and I climbed the steep lawn and went onto the wide terrace. Terry whistled softly when he saw the luxury through the big windows.

Angela, who looked expensive and beautiful in black trousers and a lilac shirt, was sitting, head bowed, apparently listening to a tape recorder. Bannister stood behind Angela's chair while Mulder and two of his crewmen stood respectfully to one side.

"Stay hidden, Terry," I said. The sliding doors were not locked and everyone in the room jumped as I pulled one of the great glass panes aside. I heard my own voice coming from the tape recorder, then Angela switched off.

They all seemed frozen by my appearance, as if caught in a flash photograph, then the tableau broke as Mulder moved towards me.

"Leave him!" Bannister's sudden command stopped Mulder. Tony shuddered as though he found it hard even to speak to me. "What the hell are you doing here?"

"I came to explain." Rainwater dripped from my clothes onto the expensive carpet.

"You hardly need to explain." Bannister clicked his fingers at Angela. "Rewind it, then play it to Captain Sandman." He paused, then added with withering scorn, "VC."

"I know what's on the tape . . ." I began.

"Shut up!" Bannister shouted.

But if Bannister was showing a new, commanding side to his character, Angela's demeanour was how it used to be. Her face was a cold mask of dislike. She leaned forward and listened to the babble of a tape going backwards; there was a click, then Jill-Beth's friendly American voice filled the room. "You're our one chance, Nick."

"And exactly what do I have to do?" My voice was much louder than Jill-Beth's, but the microphone had worked only too well and her words were quite distinct.

"You just navigate a course that I'll provide for you."

"What course?"

"How do I know? That'll depend on the weather, right? All you have to do is keep a radio watch at the times we tell you, and that's it. The easiest four hundred thousand you ever earned, right?"

"Right." There was a pause before my voice sounded again. "And what happens when we reach wherever it is that we're going?"

"Nothing happens to you. Nothing happens to the crew."

"But what happens to Bannister?"

"Whatever Yassir wants."

"And all this on the assumption that Bannister murdered his wife?"

"You got it, Nick. You want the hundred thousand now?"

Jill-Beth's voice sounded eager, then there was nothing but the magnetic hiss of empty tape.

Angela leaned forward, turned off the tape recorder and stood up. "You bastard!" She turned away from me and stalked out of the room.

"It isn't . . . ." I had been going to say that the truth was not what they had heard on the tape, but Bannister, goaded to fury by hearing the damning evidence once more, shouted that I was to be quiet. Mulder took one threatening step forward and rubbed his hands in gleeful anticipation.

Bannister repeated Angela's insult. "You bastard."

"I turned the offer down," I said. "I only wanted to hear what they planned to do. Ask the police about a man called Micky Harding who's unconscious in hospital right now! He's a newspaper reporter."

"He's lying," Mulder said laconically.

"So how the hell did you get that tape?" I demanded. "And why would I be wired for sound? Why would I risk doing that if I was on their side?"

"To make sure they wouldn't double-cross you, of course." Mulder's staccato voice was bleak.

"Micky Harding's a newspaper reporter," I said to Bannister, "and your thug beat him half dead." It was clear from Bannister's face that I was wasting my words. My betrayal was proven by the tape.

"I'm through with you, Sandman."

"You know Harry Abbott," I said. "Ask him!"

Mulder moved so that he stood between Bannister and myself. "Why did you go to America?" he challenged. I was surprised by the question and I hesitated. Mulder mocked my hesitation with a smile. "You said your mother was dying. So what about this, liar?" He reached into his jacket pocket and took out a folded glossy newspaper. On the front page, ringed in red ink, was the photograph of Jill-Beth and me which had been taken in Kassouli's Cape Cod garden. The caption said that Miss Jill-Beth Kirov had been squired to a reception at Mr. Yassir Kassouli's summer residence by Captain Nicholas Sandman, VC.

"Well?" Mulder's voice reeked of victory.

"Who the hell sent this to you?"

"What does that matter?" He stepped towards me. "You've done nothing but lie. What else have you done, Sandman? Filed down a turnbuckle? Cut some warps? I think you just lost yourself a boat, Sandman. How else is Mr. Bannister to recoup his losses?"

"What are you planning to do? Kill us all at sea?" Bannister asked.

"I was trying to save your miserable life!" I shouted past Mulder's hulking figure.

"And where's the hundred thousand?" Mulder demanded.

"There isn't any money! I turned them down."

"You pathetic cripple." Mulder was triumphant in his victory. "The money's on your boat, isn't it?"

"There isn't any, you fool!" I tried to think of an argument that might convince Bannister of my honesty, but the evidence against me was too overwhelming. I backed towards the window.

"Stop him, Fanny!" Bannister said. "Then search his damned boat."

Fanny lunged towards me and I twisted aside. "Now!" I snapped the word and Terry Farebrother appeared as if from nowhere. He must have been waiting just beside the window and he had been keyed up for this moment. He crouched in front of Mulder who, dismissive of the much smaller man, went to push him aside.

Mulder stopped dead, then screamed. It was a horrid noise. Terry straightened up and I could not see what grip he was using but I could see that Mulder was sinking to his knees.

The two crew members started forward and I snatched up a stone statuette and swung it like a short club. I noted that Bannister made no move; he just gasped at the sudden violence, which suddenly became more sickening as Terry felled the big South African with a blow to his sternum. Mulder collapsed in breathless pain and Terry turned on the two crewmen. They, seeing Mulder's agony, hung back. Bannister was white-faced and motionless.

"Come!" That was me, shouting to Terry. He had utterly cowed the room with his swift violence; now it was time to get him out. "Come on!" I discarded my unused club.

"Phone the police!" Bannister shouted.

Terry and I were already in the rainswept darkness. I was limping as fast as I could and Terry was staying with me, covering my retreat. "Did I do the right thing, boss?"

"God, yes." Why hadn't Bannister believed me? And Angela! The look she had given me before she stalked from the room had been one of hatred, because she believed I had betrayed both her and Bannister.

I slipped on the grass and thought for a second that my damned leg was about to fold up on me. The sudden movement caused pain in my back, but the leg was still strong. I looked to see if anyone was following us, but Terry had plainly terrified them. Terry himself, high on the adrenalin of a successful fight, chuckled. "Orders, boss?"

"We get out of here. On *Sycorax*. You do the springs, then cast off the bow warp. Leave the stern till last."

Terry had sailed with me before and knew what he was doing. But did *Sycorax* know? She had been out of commission for months, she was untested, and I had to take her to sea in a fretting wind against a flood tide. I dragged the mainsail cover back, lifted the boom, and fumbled with the topping lift.

I saw Angela appear on the balcony of Bannister's bedroom. She was staring down at me. "Micky Harding!" I shouted at her. "Phone Inspector Abbott!"

She turned away.

"Springs and warp off!" Terry shouted at me. "Standing by!"

The tide was swinging *Sycorax*'s bows off the wall. She was moving in the water at last.

"Let go!" The stern warp splashed off the wharf and *Sycorax* was unleashed. "Peak halliard, Terry!"

I did not trust the engine to start quickly, if at all. We were drifting on the tide and I needed a sail to give me some power. "Haul her up!" I heard the rattle of the halliard and the flap of the big sail. It rose stiffly, stretching in the night wind, and there was a sudden creak as the starboard shrouds took the mast's weight. I felt a surge of joy. It was not in the least how I had dreamed of it, but *Sycorax* and I were going to sea.

Terry swore as he tried to swing the engine into life. "Why can't you get a decent motor?"

"Can't afford it." I pegged the tiller. "Throw the yellow sailbag over here, Terry."

He found the sailbag and heaved it into the cockpit. I struggled forward with the heavy load. I hoisted the jib, tied the sheets on the sail and threw them back towards the cockpit. I heard Terry swear at the motor again and told him to abandon it and hoist the mizzen. I drove the foresail's sheets through their fair-leads and took over the tiller. We had no running lights, no compass, nothing but the boat, the sails and a pig of an engine that wouldn't start.

The wind was made tricky by the western hills. At moments it seemed to die completely, then it would back suddenly to gust in a wet squall. *Sycorax* was in confusion. She had not been ready for sea, but to sea she was going. I heard the blessed sound of water running by her hull. We were clearing Sansom's Point, which at last hid the lights of Bannister's house from us, though I was uncomfortably aware that *Wildtrack II*'s sharp bows might appear at any moment.

Terry, who had hoisted the topsail, came back to the cockpit. "What happened back there, boss?"

"Two rich men are having a row. Both tried to involve me. Bannister thought I'd joined the other side. Now he wants *Sycorax*."

Terry went back to his struggle with the engine, swung the handle again, and by some miracle it banged into protesting life. "Give it some throttle, boss!" I gave it some throttle, the cylinders settled into a comforting rhythm and *Sycorax* thrust forward against the tide. "Where are we going?" Terry asked.

"I don't have a clue." The only refuge I could think of was George Cullen's boatyard on the Hamoaze. "Plymouth," I suggested. "When do you have to be in barracks?"

"Fourteen hundred. Tomorrow."

"It'll be tight. You want me to drop you off at the town quay?"

He glanced behind. "Will those bastards chase you?"

"They might."

"I'll stay."

They followed us. The first I saw of our pursuers was a gleam of reflected lamplight from *Wildtrack II*'s polished bows. We were already abaft the town quay and the powerboat was a mile behind. It could close the gap in seconds, but clearly Bannister, or whoever was at *Wildtrack II*'s helm, did not want to make an interception in full view of the quay.

Our engine began to run rough, but Terry coaxed it and we limped on. The headlands that marked the mouth of the river closed on us. I could feel the wind's uncertainty as it was confused by the masses of land. There was white water at the bar and it would be a rough passage. The engine thumped horribly in its bearings. "Kill it!" I shouted. I didn't want the shaft to shake the gland loose and let in sea water.

The engine died just as the bows juddered over the first breaker. *Sycorax* was free at last, running to the ocean she was made for. She took the steep, breaking seas like a thoroughbred and I whooped for the joy of the moment.

Terry grinned. "Happy, boss?"

"I should have done this weeks ago!"

"And what about those bastards?" Terry nodded towards the river mouth, where *Wildtrack II* had appeared.

111

"Forget them." I gave him the tiller and set about trimming the sails. We were heading westwards along the coast and we were hard on the wind. We went perilously close to the Calfstone Shoal, from which a breaking wave shredded foam across our bows. The rain was slackening, and there were gaps in the southern clouds, edged by silver moonlight. I was happy, except that *Wildtrack II* still threatened us.

I'd deliberately put *Sycorax* head to wind and close to the Calfstone, in the hope that *Wildtrack II*, emerging at speed from the river mouth, might run aground on the shoal. It was a slender hope, and one that failed.

The night was not my helper. The sky was clearing. Soon we would be thrashing west under moonlight and would be in full sight of *Wildtrack II*, without a hope of losing the powerboat. We were wet through and shivering. I told Terry to go below and find some warm clothes.

I fell off the wind slightly to put the flood tide on the starboard bow. I trimmed *Sycorax*, belayed the sheets and pegged the tiller. She could sail herself now until we had cleared the transit of Start Point and could turn due west again. I trained my monocular on *Wildtrack II*. I could see three men on board.

"Could that fellow you clobbered be walking by now?" I asked Terry.

"Hell, yes." Terry tossed me up a sweater and oilskin. "I only tapped him."

I wondered if Mulder had brought his shotgun, but surely they would not plan murder? Then the thought occurred that if Kassouli was right, these men had already committed one murder at sea. "Terry?"

"Boss?"

"If you feel under the engine you'll find a wooden box screwed to a frame on the starboard side. There's a package in it. Can you get it?"

He lifted off the companion steps and I heard him grunt as he groped in the bilge's darkness. He had obviously felt the shape of the package. "Is that the bloody Colt I kept for you?"

"I don't want to use it, not unless I have to, but unwrap it."

Wildtrack II was still holding her distance. There were two fishing boats in sight, and I wondered if their presence was inhibiting Mulder. The beam of the Start Point light slid across the sky. I was sailing south now, aiming to go outside the tidal race at the point. *Wildtrack II* was shadowing us. The powerboat was showing a white light at the top of its radar arch, another at its stern, and the proper red and green sidelights. My pursuers were letting me know where they were, and letting me know that I could not escape them.

They kept abreast of us for the three hours it took to claw past Start Point. *Sycorax* felt hard and good, well rigged and confident. But in the morning, I thought, just as soon as I put into shelter, Bannister's lawyers

112

would descend on her with a writ. I had a talent, I reflected bitterly, for making wealthy enemies. First Kassouli, now Bannister. And all I had tried to be was truthful.

An hour later *Wildtrack II* was still within easy visual range. I was certain now that Bannister only wanted to discover my destination, but I was determined to lose him. "I think," I said slowly, "that it's time to scare them off. I'm going to tack." *Sycorax*, never graceful in a tight turn, lurched round and settled onto the starboard tack. I let her off the wind, slackening the mainsheet so that we were running directly at our pursuers. "Be ready for some smart manoeuvres, Terry. And get the gun. You'll need a couple of extra mags."

He gave me a surprised glance, but said nothing. He fetched the Colt and worked a round into the breech.

"What we're going to do," I said, "is scare them witless. Aim for the water line or the engines. If you think there's the least danger of hitting any of the crew, don't fire. You understand?"

"Yes, sir." The "sir" was unconscious. He put the safety on, then thrust the pistol into a pocket of his oilskin jacket.

I used the monocular again, and this time I clearly saw both Bannister and Mulder standing in the powerboat's cockpit. They were staring at *Sycorax*, and must have decided that we meant no good. I saw Bannister bend down to the throttles and the boat dipped her stern as she accelerated away.

"Tacking!" I shouted. We tacked. The breeze seemed stronger, slicing over the coachroof and bringing a sting of spray from the bows. The waves were building and the wind was noisy in the rigging. I was still aiming *Sycorax*'s bowsprit like a spear at *Wildtrack II*'s flank. "Where is he?"

"He's putting his foot down."

The powerboat was going inshore for us now, perhaps planning to circle round to take position on our stern. I matched her move, running north before the wind and banging into the cross-seas. She was a hundred yards away, running across our bows, and I could see three faces staring from the cockpit.

"Turning to port," I warned Terry. "Get ready to fire!"

He brought out the gun and cradled it in two big, capable hands. I turned back into the wind and hardened the sails. Now it looked as if we'd stopped playing games and resumed our westward progress. As I'd hoped, *Wildtrack II* also slowed and her bows began to turn towards us. She was circling to follow us and her turn would bring her to within thirty paces of us.

"You're going to have ten seconds!" I shouted at Terry. "Go for his hull! Aim as close to the water line as you can."

"Got it, boss." I heard the snick of the safety being released, then the sound of the gun being cocked. Terry crouched on the starboard cockpit thwart, steadied by the coaming and the cabin bulkhead.

The movement of the boats would make accuracy almost impossible and I prayed that he would not hit any of the three men. When we were just thirty yards from *Wildtrack II*, a wave heaved her up and I saw an expanse of her antifouling revealed in the moonlight. "*Fire!*" Terry held the gun two-handed, braced himself, and opened fire at the speedboat's belly. The noise was just like a sail flogging in a gale. The muzzle flash leaped two feet clear of the boat and I saw a streak of foam reflect red, then I looked at the powerboat and I saw the three faces disappear beneath the coaming. There was no way of knowing where Terry's bullets had gone, but water suddenly churned white at *Wildtrack II*'s stern and she shot away from us like a startled deer. Her bows thumped the waves as she spewed a high wake sixty yards long. Then she circled towards us and accelerated. I guessed they planned to swamp us with their wash as well as loose a broadside at our sails. They would have to be dissuaded, and I decided against waiting to make our own broadside shot at them.

"Into the bows, Terry. Get ready. *Fire!*"

The powerboat's bows were high and its belly, pale against the night, reared vulnerably above the water. Terry stood, legs spread, and emptied a magazine at the approaching boat. I swear I saw a scrap of darkness appear in the hull where a heavy bullet ripped the fibreglass ragged. Terry changed magazines then braced himself, fired again, and this time the powerboat's windscreen shattered in the night. The glass shards were snatched away like spindrift, and I saw the three heads twist away in panic.

"Cease fire! Cease fire!" I was scared witless that the final shot might have hit one of the three men. The powerboat veered off. I thought I saw three figures still moving in the cockpit. That was a relief to me, but not for them, for the powerboat would be taking water, and now their own safety lay in reaching harbour as soon as possible.

I sat down. "Make the gun safe, Terry."

"Already done it, boss."

We tacked again, and clawed into the southwest wind. The tide had long turned and the surging channel current was at last coming to our aid. I thanked Terry for his help, and pegged the tiller. There was nothing to do now until we turned for Plymouth breakwater.

We were a darkened ship sailing a black ocean. The cliffs to the north were touched with moonlight and the water broke on them in wisps of shredding white. Everything had gone awry, but at least *Sycorax* was back where she belonged.

Chapter 8

George Cullen fidgeted with his pipe. "Times are hard, Nick."

"I'm sure."

"No one wants a proper boat any longer, do they? They just want plastic bowls with Jap engines." He lit the pipe and went to the dusty window of his office. It was years since the yard last built a boat; back, indeed, in the time of George's father. Now the yard survived on a dwindling supply of repair work. It also survived on crime. George was a fence for every boatstripper between the Fal and the Exe. "Seen your old man?" he asked me.

"No."

"I ran up there before Christmas. Said he was missing you."

"I was in hospital, George."

"Course you were, Nick, course you were." He was a vast-bellied man with a jowly red face, grey hair and small eyes. I understood George's attraction for my father. There was no knavery on the coast that George did not know about, and he could spend hours regaling my father with the tales of rogues and fools that my father so relished. "Your old man's dead proud of you, Nick," George said. "The Vicky Cross, eh?"

"I was just lucky," I said.

"Rubbish, boy. They don't give that gong away with the cornflakes, do they? So what do you need?"

"VHF, short-wave, chronometer, barometer, anchors, lights, batteries, sea loo, compass, bilge pumps . . ."

"Spare me, for God's sake." He sat down again, flinching from some inboard pain. George was forever at death's threshold and forever ingesting new kinds of patent medicines.

Sycorax was tucked safe into a narrow dock beside George's office. He'd moored a wreck of a fishing craft outside, to hide her. Terry Farebrother had been put on a train in nearby Plymouth, and for the moment I'd found shelter. George's price had been to hear the story, or as much as I cared to tell him. "I know Fanny Mulder," he said. "Brings me in a bit of business from time to time. You know how it is, Nick."

"He nicks the business, George. He nicked a lot of stuff off my boat. You've probably still got it."

"Wouldn't surprise me," George said equably. "I'll let you have a look later on, Nick, and if anything is yours I'll let you have it at cost."

"Thank you, George."

"Fair's fair, Nick," he said, as though he was doing me a great favour. "And you are Tommy Sandman's boy. Anything for Tommy. And for a hero, of course. What sort of anchors do you want?"

"Two CQRs. One fisherman's."

There was a sudden commotion in the outer office where George's secretary, a shapely girl whose typing speed was reputed to be one stroke a minute, spent her days polishing her fingernails. "You can't go in there," I heard Rita squeal. "Mr. Cullen is in conference."

"Mr. Cullen can get out of conference, can't he?" The door banged open and Inspector Abbott came inside. "Morning, George." He ignored me.

"Morning, Harry. How's things?"

"Things are bloody." Abbott still ignored me. "Would you have seen young Nick Sandman anywhere, George?"

George realised that Abbott must be playing some sort of game.

"Haven't set eyes on him since he went to the Falklands, Harry."

"If you see him, George, tell him from me to keep his head down. He is to stay very quiet and hope the world passes him by while his Uncle Harry sorts out the mess he has made." Some of this was vehemently spat in my general direction, but mostly it was directed at George.

"I'll tell him, Harry," George said hastily.

"You can also tell him, if you should see him, that if he's got a shooter on his boat he is to lose it before I search his boat with a metal detector."

"I'll tell him, Harry."

"You can also tell Master Sandman that it isn't the Boer War I'm worried about, it's the one between us and America."

"I'll tell him, Harry."

Abbott walked to the window, from where he stared down at *Sycorax*. "I'll tell the powers that be that after an exhaustive search of this den of thieves there was no sign of Master Sandman, nor of his horrible boat."

"Right, Harry." The relief in George's voice that there was to be no trouble was palpable.

Abbott, who had still not looked directly at me, whirled on George and thrust a finger at him. "And if you do see him, George, hang on to him. Tell him that I'll let him know when he can leave."

"I'll tell him, Harry."

"And tell him he's bloody lucky that no one got killed. One of his bullets went within three inches of Mr. Bannister's pretty head. Mr. Bannister is not pleased."

"I'll tell him, Harry."

"They always were rotten shots in that regiment," Abbott said happily. "Unlike the Rifles, of which I was a member. You needn't tell him that bit, George. But tell him his newspaper friend is out of danger."

"I'll tell him, Harry."

Abbott left. George closed his eyes and blew out a long breath. "Did you hear all that, Nick?"

116

"I'm not deaf, Harry."

"Bloody hell." George leaned back in his chair and his small, shrewd eyes appraised me. "A shooter, eh? How much do you want for it, Nick?"

"I don't know what you're talking about, George."

He looked disappointed. "I always thought you were straight, Nick."

So did I.

A HOT SPELL HIT BRITAIN. It was not the weather for an attempt on the St. Pierre. In the yachting magazines there were stories about boats waiting in Cherbourg for the bad weather that would promise a fast run at the race, but *Wildtrack* was not among them.

Rita brought me a selection of the daily papers. There had been reports of a shooting incident off the Devon coast, and the *Daily Telegraph* said that a man was being sought. The police knew his identity but he was not being named. England was being hammered at cricket. The City pages reported that Kassouli UK's half-yearly report showed record profits, despite which there was a story that he was planning to pull all his operations out of Britain. I smelt Micky Harding behind the tale, but after a day or two Kassouli issued a strong denial and the story, like the tale of gunfire off the Devon coast, faded to nothing.

I worked for George Cullen, mending engines and sanding decks. I was paid in beer, sandwiches and credit. The credit bought three compasses and two big anchors. I nagged George to find me a good chronometer and barometer. And every day I tried to phone Angela. I left messages on her home answering machine, and at the office. The messages asked her to phone me on Cullen's number.

Angela never returned the calls, so I finally asked to be put through to Matthew Cooper.

"You've caused some trouble, Nick!" He sounded aggrieved.

"I've done nothing."

"Just aborted one good film."

"Wasn't my fault, Matthew. How's Angela?"

"She's not exactly top of the pops here. She keeps saying that the film is salvageable, but Bannister won't have anything to do with you. He's issued a possession order for *Sycorax*."

"Will you give Angela a message for me?" I asked.

"She's stopped working, Nick. She's with Bannister all the time now."

"For God's sake, Matthew! Use your imagination! Write her a letter on your headed notepaper. She won't ignore that."

"OK." He sounded reluctant.

"Tell her to find a guy called Micky Harding." I gave him Micky's home and work numbers. "She's to tell Micky that he can trust her. She

117

can prove it by calling him Mouse and by saying she knows that Terry was with me on the night. He'll understand that." Matthew wrote it all down.

"And tell her," I said, "that Bannister's not to try the St. Pierre."

"You're joking," Matthew said. "We're being sent to film him turning the corner at Newfoundland!"

"When are you going?"

He paused again. "I'm not allowed to say, Nick."

"OK. Just give her my message, Matthew."

I SPENT THE SUNDAY after that salvaging a galley stove from a wrecked Westerly that George had bought for scrap. I manhandled the stove across the deserted yard. As I reached the quay above the boat I saw I had company. Inspector Harry Abbott was sitting in *Sycorax*'s cockpit. He was wearing his checked golfer's trousers, had a bottle of beer and a packet of sandwiches in his lap, and my Colt .45 in his right hand.

"Afternoon, Nick." He aimed the Colt at my head and, before I could move, pulled the trigger. It wasn't loaded.

He chuckled. "Naughty, Nick, very! You know what the penalty is for possession of an unlicensed firearm?"

"A golfing weekend with you, Harry?"

He tutted. "Ungrateful, aren't you, Nick? I save you and all you do is insult me. I thought you'd like to know," he added, "that there is no longer a warrant out for your arrest. We searched for you high and low! Do you know what you have cost Her Majesty's government in police overtime?"

"Is that what you're on now, Harry? Overtime?" I saw it was my beer he was drinking, and climbed down to the deck. He courteously offered me a bottle, which I took, then sat opposite him.

"The funny boys are in on this one, Nick. They're not kind and gentle like me. They're full of self-importance and they talk impressively about the safety of the realm. They have nevertheless decided that your life should be spared." Harry lit a cigarette and flipped the dead match over the side. "I mean, it's unthinkable that one of Her Majesty's VCs would be carrying an illegal shooter."

"Quite unthinkable," I agreed.

"But there is a condition. You're going to sail this heap of garbage round the world and you are not going to try to stop Mr. Bannister sailing on the St. Pierre."

I finished the beer and opened another. The day was blisteringly hot. "Is that the condition, Harry? That I leave Bannister alone?"

"Took a lot of time to fix it." He spoke warningly. "Mr. Bannister lodged a complaint about you. He says you dismasted his boat, cut his

118

warps, all in practice for the day when you are going to sink it at sea. Do you know he's even got a tape recording?"

"That tape's a—"

"I know, Nick!" Abbott held up a weary hand. "We've spoken to Mr. Harding. He hasn't got any proof now, so there can't be a scandalous little story which would upset our American cousins."

"I understand."

"I don't suppose you do, Nick. Who was the little bloke with you on the night you put nasty holes in nice Mr. Bannister's speedboat?"

"I can't remember, Harry."

"Make sure he forgets all about it, too."

I offered Abbott another beer. He took it. "Mind you," he went on, "Mr. Bannister had a mind to aggravate things. He was unleashing the lawyers on you, but we pointed out that if they found you, and if he pressed charges, then we'd naturally insist that he and his Boer would have to stay in England and give evidence."

"Which he didn't want to do because it might jeopardise his timing for the St. Pierre?"

"Exactly."

I wondered if I was understanding too much. "You want Bannister to die, don't you?"

Harry tutted. "You mustn't talk about death, Nick."

"You want to keep Kassouli's jobs?"

"I imagine the Prime Minister wants to, yes."

"So Yassir Kassouli gets what he wants?" I said.

"The rich usually do, Nick." He paused. "And between you and me, and no one else, Mr. Kassouli wanted you arrested. But we've persuaded him that we can look after our own. That's what I'm doing now, Nick."

"This comes from the bloody government, doesn't it?"

He heard my anger. "Now, Nick!"

"Suppose Bannister's innocent?"

Abbott frowned. "Hell, Nick, since when were you the white knight?" I said nothing, and he sighed. "Why did you go to the press?"

"I wanted out."

"You should have talked to me." Abbott shook his head sadly. "Nick, it comes from the top, and you're powerless to do anything. So forget it." He drank some more beer. "I saw your dad last week. He misses you. When are you going to see him?"

"I wasn't planning on it."

"I think you should, Nick. In fact I think I'll make that another condition of not arresting you."

"I thought you said there was no warrant for me any more?"

Abbott hefted the gun. "Three years?"

"How did you find it?"

He smiled. "Did George tell you I threatened to use a metal detector?"

I smiled back, remembering the charade. "Yes."

"Which meant that you'd hide the gun near a piece of metal, so as to confuse your Uncle Harry. So I just had a look at your engine, and hey presto."

"It's a souvenir, Harry."

He looked at the barrel. "*Ejercito Argentina*. Didn't do them a lot of good, did it? So, are you going to try and warn Mr. Bannister?"

I hesitated.

"Do you think he'll listen to you, Nick?"

"No."

"So I'll take it you won't try. Are you going to see your father?"

"Probably."

"I'll take that as yes." He fished in his jacket pocket and brought out two Monte Cristo cigars in their tin cases. "Give him these from me, Nick."

"I will."

"And, having seen him, are you then going to float off in this junkyard?"

"Yes."

"Welcome back to the human race, Nick Sandman." He dangled the gun by its trigger guard. "I assume this is a piece of yacht safety equipment."

I smiled. "Yes, Harry, it is."

"Then hide it where a middle-aged copper doesn't trip over it." He tossed it into my lap and climbed to the quayside.

"You're an awkward bastard, Nick, but I don't dislike you. And I do like your old man. Tell him I sent my regards."

"I will."

"*Bon voyage*, Nick."

I fitted the stove after Harry had gone, then celebrated the achievement by making myself a cup of tea. I sat on *Sycorax*'s stern and read the newspapers Harry had left behind.

Angela's photograph stared at me from one of the gossip columns. Bannister sat beside her in the picture. There was a story alongside. "Almost a year since the tragic death of his first wife, the American heiress Nadeznha Kassouli, Mr. Tony Bannister, 46, has announced his engagement to Miss Angela Westmacott. Miss Westmacott is a producer on Mr. Bannister's programme." There was more. The wedding would take place very soon, probably in Paris and certainly before Bannister set off on his St. Pierre attempt. The bride was planning to give up her job in television.

She looked so very beautiful in the photograph. She wore the hesitant smile that I'd come to know so well, though her eyes were cool. Her right hand rested lightly on Bannister's shoulder, while her left, hanging over the sofa's arm, bore a big shining diamond. She looked leggy and elegant, a girl fit for a handsome celebrity. A girl it was ludicrous for a broken sailor in a broken boat to want. I suddenly felt forlorn and bereft. She had surrendered to safety, and I was alone.

MY FATHER, WHEN I WENT at last to visit him, seemed to be in a private heaven. He showed me the workshop where he made ship models, and his room, and then he walked round the cricket field with me. The county police force were playing the inmates of the open prison. The police had been bowled out for 134, while the prisoners' team had so far scored 42 for the loss of just one wicket. It was like a boarding school, only the pupils were middle-aged men rather than boys. The warders called my father "Mr. Sandman", and he had clearly charmed them all.

"They're good fellows," he said happily. His black hair was touched with grey at the temples, he was suntanned and he was fit. "The gardening helps, of course. I swim a fair bit, but they keep the pool damned chilly. I do recommend an open prison if you're ever in need of a rest. Admittedly the admission procedure is tiresome, but after that it's a very decent life. Oh, well done!"

This was for a fine late cut that left a policeman running vainly towards the boundary.

"The batsman"—my father pointed with his cigar—"is doing three years for computer fraud. Not very clever to be caught, was it?"

"Wasn't clever of you," I said.

"Stupid." He smiled at me. He'd been arrested for fraud and God alone knows what else.

We found two deck chairs in the shade of a fine oak tree and sat down. "So what have you been doing, Nick?"

"Recovering, mainly." I told him about *Sycorax* and he thought it was a wonderful jest that I'd found a refuge with George Cullen.

"Is he making you pay for all this gear?"

"Through the nose."

"Nick, Nick!" I had disappointed my father, who possessed the haggling skills of the bazaar. He frowned in thought. "Ask him about Montague Dawson."

"The artist?" I was puzzled.

"George sold a few Dawsons," my father said. "They were fakes, of course, but George used to find American yachtsmen and spin this yarn about Dawson having been a friend of the family." My father chuckled. "The paintings were done by a fellow at Okehampton. Anyway, point of it all, one of George's fake Dawsons ended up in the wrong hands, the police were tumbled out of bed, and officially the case has never been closed. George won't like to be reminded of it, and he certainly wouldn't like it if you suggested you might drop a line to Scotland Yard."

The cricket ball flicked across the grass towards our chairs. I fielded it with my foot, then flinched as I bent to pick it up. I threw it to the nearest fielder and my father watched me sadly. "Is it bad, Nick?"

"It's all right. I can sail a boat." He was quiet for a moment or two. His cigar smoke drifted up into the oak leaves. He'd been pleased with Harry Abbott's gift. He gave me one of his shrewd, amused glances. "Harry came to see me a week or so back. He gave me some news of you."

I was watching the cricket and said nothing.

"Been in the wars again, have you, Nick?"

"Harry should keep his mouth shut."

"You know Kassouli was setting you up, don't you?"

For a second I didn't react, then I turned to look into his eyes. "What the hell do you know about it, Dad?"

He sighed. "Nick! Do me a small favour. I may not be able to sail a small boat through a hurricane, but I do know what makes the wicked world go round. I did some business with Kassouli once." He drew on his cigar. "Tell me about it, Nick."

"I thought you knew the answers already." I was defensive.

"Just tell me, Nick." He spoke gently. "Please."

So I told him. I hadn't planned to tell him about Angela, but I did in the end, because I wanted to tell somebody. I missed her horribly. I kept telling myself that she was not for me, that she was too urbanised and ambitious, too elegant and difficult, but I could not persuade myself that I would be better off without her. I missed her, and so I found myself telling my father about the visits to London, and then the recent news of her engagement and forthcoming wedding. I told him about Mulder and Jill-Beth and Bannister and Kassouli.

He rubbed his face. "This Kirov girl. You say she phoned you at Angela's flat?"

"Yes."

"Why would she do that?"

"She wanted to reach me, of course."

He shook his head. "Ostensibly she wanted you to be Kassouli's man in Tony Bannister's crew, yes? The whole essence of that, Nick, is that Bannister wouldn't know that you were Kassouli's man. So why risk alerting him by leaving a message on his girlfriend's answering machine? There's only one answer to that, Nick. They wanted Bannister to know you were dodgy. They gave you a high profile, didn't they? The girl makes sure you rescue her from Mulder, she flies you to the States, and she smudges a damn great fingerprint on Angela's answering machine. Why?"

"Someone sent Mulder a picture of me, too." I spoke slowly. Seeing the sense of my father's words, I felt foolish. "It was a photograph taken at Kassouli's Cape Cod house. He didn't say who the sender was."

My father gave me a pitying look. "It was the Kirov girl. Or Kassouli. And who do you think told this Mulder fellow where to find you and Jill-Beth Kirov on Dartmoor?"

"She did?" I said it hesitantly, not wanting to believe it.

"Of course! They want Bannister to believe that he's found the fly in his ointment: you. So they set you up to be the threat. You just happened to be convenient, Nick, so they pointed a damned great finger at you. And all the time the real man was lying low."

"Mulder." It was obvious.

"Bingo. How did Bannister meet Mulder?"

"His wife found him."

"Who took the tape recording?"

"Mulder."

"That was just a happy accident, of course," my father said. "He probably had a camera with him, and planned to take a snap of you and the Kirov girl together. So who, my dear Nick, do you think Mulder works for?"

"Kassouli." I sat there, feeling very foolish. "And Mulder beat me up because he had to prove his loyalty to Bannister?"

"I would imagine so, wouldn't you?"

"But the rumour says Mulder helped with the murder!"

"Who's spreading the rumours?" my father asked patiently.

"Kassouli?"

"And who has convinced Kassouli that his daughter was murdered?" my father asked, then answered the question himself. "Mulder. And why? Because a rich man's gratitude can be very bankable. Mind you, I'd have smelt a rat the moment Kassouli offered four hundred thousand! The going rate for a killing can't be much over twenty grand."

"But Jill-Beth brought it with her!" I protested. "I saw it. A hundred thousand dollars."

"Which Mulder would have taken from you as proof that you were betraying Bannister." My father spoke gently. "My dear Nick, they were stitching you up. Kassouli hoped you might help him by being a back-up to Mulder, which is why he laid it all out for you in America, but once he saw you were going to be boring and honourable he danced you like a puppet to distract Bannister." He saw my face. "Don't blame yourself, Nick. Kassouli's played for higher stakes than this. You mustn't feel bad at being beaten by one of the best."

But I did feel bad. I'd never been clever, not as my father and brother and sister were. I lack subtlety. Only a fool would have charged straight up that hill in the Falklands when there was another company working their way round the flank. Still, I had saved that company some casualties.

"Damn it," I said. My father did not reply, and I tried one last protest. "But Kassouli doesn't even know if his daughter was murdered!"

"Perhaps he does. Perhaps Mulder has the proof. Perhaps Mulder has been blackmailing Bannister *and* taking money off Kassouli. Whatever"—my father shrugged—"You can kiss Bannister goodbye. Yassir Kassouli will get his perfect revenge."

"At sea," I said bitterly.

"Far from any jurisdiction," my father agreed. "There'll be no messy body, no murder weapon, no witnesses who aren't Kassouli's men, nothing."

"But I'll know about it," I said stubbornly.

"And who would believe you? And if you made a fuss, Nick, just how long do you think Yassir Kassouli would tolerate you?" He touched my arm. "No, Nick. It's over now as far as you're concerned."

I stared at the cricket, but saw nothing. So the night that Jill-Beth had screamed, and I had thought Mulder was attacking her, had all been part of a careful construction to trap me. And I, believing myself to be full of honour, had fallen for it. I knew my father was right. Now, according to the yachting magazines, Fanny Mulder was to be the navigator on Bannister's boat. From Kassouli's point of view it was perfect.

"What time's your bus?" my father asked.

"Five."

We strolled slowly towards the prison entrance. "The world's a tough place," my father said softly. "It isn't moved by honesty and justice and love, Nick. The world is run by very ruthless men who know that the cake is very small and the number of hungry mouths is growing all the time. And Kassouli means jobs and investment."

"And Bannister?"

"He married the wrong woman, and he carelessly lost her. At the very least he'll be sacrificed for carelessness. You think that's unfair?"

"Of course it is."

"Good old Nick." He rested a hand on my shoulder for an instant. "So what, my favourite son, will you do about Angela?"

"There's nothing to do. They get married on Monday in Paris."

"There's everything to do!" my father said energetically. "I'd start by buying every orchid in Paris and drenching them with the most expensive perfume, then laying them at her feet. Like all beautiful women, Nick, she is there for the taking, so take her."

124

"I've got *Sycorax*. I'm sailing south."

He shrugged. "Will Angela sail on the St. Pierre?"

I shook my head. "She gets seasick."

"If I were you, then, I'd wait till she's a rich widow, which can't take very long, then marry her." He was being quite serious.

I laughed. That was vintage Tommy Sandman.

"Why ever not?" he asked, offended.

"I'm sailing south," I said stubbornly. "I want to get to New Zealand."

"What about Piers and Amanda?"

We stopped at the prison entrance. "I'll fly back and see them," I said.

"That takes money, Nick."

I held up my hands that were calloused again from the weeks of good work. "I can earn a living."

"With full remission, Nick, I'll be out in a year. You'll let me know where you are?"

"Of course."

"Perhaps I'll come and see you. We can sail warm seas together?"

"I'd like that." I could see the bus coming up the long drive. I fished in my pocket and brought out the flat box. "I thought you might like to keep this for me," I said awkwardly.

I might not have bought my father cigars, but I took him the one thing I knew would give him the most pleasure. He opened it and I saw the tears come to his eyes. He was holding my medal. He smoothed the claret ribbon on his palm. "Are you sure?"

"I'll probably lose it. Things get lost on small boats."

"They do, yes."

"Look after it for me, will you?" I asked, trying to make it a casual request.

"I will." He turned it over and saw my name engraved in the dull bronze. "I'll have it put in the governor's safe." The bus turned in a wide circle in front of the gate, and stopped.

"I'll see you, Dad," I said.

"Sure, Nick."

There was a hesitation, then we embraced. I walked to the bus, paid my fare, and sat at the back. My father stood beneath the window. A few more returning visitors climbed in, then the door hissed shut and the bus lurched forward. My father walked alongside for a few paces. "Nick!" I could just hear him over the engine's noise. "Nick! Paris! Orchids! Scent! Seduction! Who dares, wins!"

I INSISTED ON TWO BILGE PUMPS, both manual. One was worked from the cockpit, the other from inside the cabin. George grumbled, but nonetheless he provided them.

"Tommy shouldn't have told you about the Dawsons," he said.

There was a letter from London waiting for me on Rita's desk. I eagerly tore it open, half expecting it to be from Angela, but of course she was in Paris. The letter was from Micky Harding. He was recovering. He was sorry that the story had died. There was no evidence to support it and such a story couldn't run without proof. If I was ever in London, he said, I should call on him. I owed him a pint or two.

On Tuesday *The Times* had a photograph of Bannister's Paris wedding. The bride wore oyster silk and had flowers in her hair. Her Baptist minister father had pronounced a blessing over the happy couple. Angela was smiling. I cut the photograph out, kept it for an hour, then screwed it up and tossed it into the dock.

I spent the next few days finishing *Sycorax*. I installed extra water tanks, two bunk mattresses and electric cabin lights. George found me a short-wave radio. I began stowing spare gear and equipment in the lockers, and took pride in buying a brand new Red Ensign that would fray on my jackstaff in faraway oceans.

The hot weather had gone. Cyclones were bringing squalls and cold air that made the Channel choppy and promised a tumultuous wind in the far North Atlantic. The first hopefuls set off from Cherbourg to take advantage of the gales. An Italian crew went first and made an astonishing time to the Grand Banks, but their boat was rolled over somewhere east of Cape Race and lost its mast. Two French boats followed. I read that Bannister was honeymooning in Cherbourg while he waited for even stronger winds.

I went to London and took the children to Holland Park where we played hide-and-seek among the wet bushes. Afterwards I insisted on seeing Melissa. "They're going to kill Bannister," I told her. "He won't listen to me, so would you phone him? He'll listen to you. Tell him he mustn't trust Mulder. Just convince him of that. I've written to him, but . . ." I shrugged.

I had broken my promise to Abbott in writing to Bannister. I'd written because there was no proof that he was guilty of the crime for which, I was certain, he was about to be punished. Doubtless my letter had been pigeonholed with all the other nutcase letters that a man like Bannister attracted.

Melissa ran a finger round the rim of her wineglass. "Tony won't listen to me now, Nick. He's married that ghastly television creature."

"I'm serious, Melissa."

"I'm sure you are, Nicholas, but if you think I'm going to make a fool of myself by telling Tony to give up his little boat race, you're wrong. Anyway, he wouldn't believe me! Fanny Mulder may not be everyone's cup of tea, but he's completely loyal to Tony."

I told Melissa everything, including my new certainty that Mulder was Kassouli's man and would navigate *Wildtrack* to disaster. I closed my eyes for a second. "I'm not mad, Melissa, and I'm not shell-shocked. Would you believe it, my love, if I was to tell you that it could suit me hideously well if Bannister were to die? But I just cannot stomach the thought of murder!" I shook my head. "I'm not being noble, I'm not being honourable, I just want to be able to sleep at nights."

"I do hate it when you get into a Galahad mood."

"So phone him," I urged her. "Say that you think it's all nonsense. Blame me, if you like. Say I'm mad. But say you promised to pass on the message. The message is that Mulder is Kassouli's man and always has been."

She looked me up and down, noting my dirty trousers and creased shirt. "You're being very dramatic, Nick."

"I know. But please, my love, please?"

She wavered, but plumped for safety. "I'm not going to make a fool of myself . . ."

"You want me to tell Hon-John about you and Bannister?"

She considered me for a few seconds. "If you withdraw that very ungentlemanly threat," she said acridly, "then I will consider telephoning Tony for you. I won't promise it." She frowned. "On the other hand, it would be decent to congratulate him on his wedding, would it not? Even if it was to that vulgar little gold-digger."

I knew I would get no more from her. "I withdraw the threat," I said, "and I apologise for making it."

"Thank you, Nick. And I will promise to consider talking to Tony." She looked pleased with her tactical victory. "So what are you going to do now?"

"I've got a job," I said, "in the boat trade." I fabricated my casual work for George Cullen into a fantasy of yacht-broking, which pleased her.

I made her promise once more that she would try to phone Bannister, or at least think about it, then I took a bus back to Plymouth, and another one to George's boatyard.

I saw George had moored the fishing boat so that it was hiding *Sycorax* again. "You're not going this weekend, are you?" he asked me.

"Monday or Tuesday."

"I'll be glad to have the dock back," he said. "So you've got everything you need, Nick?"

"I still need fenders, A danbuoy, jackstays, fuel filters, medicines . . ."

"All right!" He checked the flow. "I'm going home. Look after the yard."

It began to rain. I went into *Sycorax*'s cabin and made myself a cup of tea. I screwed a framed photograph of Piers and Amanda over the navigation table and tried not to think of how many months it would be before I saw them again. Instead I wondered whether Melissa would telephone Bannister, and decided she probably wouldn't.

I had done all I could to preserve his life bar going to France and confronting him. Yet Bannister undoubtedly would not believe me. He would not believe Melissa either, but I had tried. Kassouli would win.

I told myself I had behaved decently in trying to save Bannister. Melissa had asked me why, and I'd given her the answer truth and justice, which she believed, for she knew how important those things were to me; but the truth was that I had also struggled to warn Bannister because that was my only way of staying in touch with Angela. Each attempt to reach Tony was a way of reminding Angela that I lived and loved. Each high-minded attempt to save his life was a pathetic protestation of my love. For Angela had lodged in my desire, and life without her seemed flat.

I needed to go to sea. I needed winds and waves to blow that flatness away. I sipped my tea and jotted down what equipment I still needed.

Through the rain outside, coming from George's locked offices above me, I heard a phone start ringing. I could not concentrate on the list of supplies, so instead I teased my anticipation by unfolding my chart of the Azores. I smiled in anticipation, then noticed that the phone in the offices still rang. And rang. And rang.

I banged my right knee as I scrambled up the side of the wharf. The curved coping stones were wet, throwing me back down the wall, but I seized one of *Sycorax*'s warps and scraped my way over the top. My knee was numb and my back laced with pain as I limped across the yard.

George never trusted me with the office keys in case I made phone calls that he could not monitor. I pulled at the door, but it was locked. I swore. The phone still rang. I told myself it was probably only a customer asking about one of George's jobs, but it was a stubborn customer who'd phone at this time of the evening.

I found an abandoned stanchion and swung it to shatter the door's pebbled glass. I reached through for the latch. Knowing the phone would stop before I reached it I limped upstairs, stumbled into Rita's office, and fell headlong. My right hand grabbed the telephone's lead and the ancient bakelite instrument slid off the desk and shattered on the floor. I prayed I had not cut the connection.

"Hello!" There was silence. I twisted myself round so that my back was against Rita's desk. "Hello?"

"Nick?" The voice was very small and timid.

"Oh, God." I felt tears in my eyes. Then, stupidly, I was crying with relief. "Angela?"

"Nick."

"I'm crying," I said.

"So am I," she said, "for Tony."

I closed my eyes. "Where are you?" I asked.

"Cherbourg. Melissa telephoned."

I said a small prayer of thanks for Melissa's compassionate soul. "I told her to."

"I know. I don't know what to do, Nick."

"Stop Tony sailing."

"He's already gone. They caught the afternoon tide."

"Oh, God."

"Melissa called just afterwards, and then I spoke to that journalist you told me to find and he said you'd been telling the truth. I've tried Tony on the radiotelephone already. It wasn't any good. He says I'm being hysterical. He says you're just trying to stop him winning the St. Pierre because you work for Kassouli."

I scrambled to my feet. "What time is it now?"

"Nearly seven o'clock." I subtracted one hour to get British Summer Time. "Nick?" Angela asked.

"I'm still here."

"Can you stop him, Nick?"

I thought for a few seconds. "What time did he leave?"

"He crossed the start line at twenty past three exactly."

"Local time?" I asked. She confirmed that and I told her to wait.

I went into George's office and ripped pin-ups off his wall to reveal an ancient chart of the Channel. I dragged open his desk drawer and among the corkscrews and patent medicines found an old pair of dividers. I went to the window. The wind was southerly, gusting hard enough to slap the rain against the dirty panes. I picked up the phone on George's desk. "Are you still there?"

"Yes."

"Wait." I walked the rusty dividers across George's chart. I knew that *Wildtrack* would be going like a bat out of hell to clear the Lizard before she swung up towards the Mizzen on Ireland's southwest coast. The only place I could stop her was in my own back alley: the Channel. I added a divider's stride for the fair current and reckoned that, by three in the morning, and assuming *Wildtrack* had taken a slightly northerly course to clear the traffic-separation zone, Bannister would be in an area about twenty nautical miles south-southwest of Bolt Head. I drew a circle on the chart to limit the search area. It's easy to posit such a search on a chart, but out in the Channel, amidst a squally darkness, it would be like trying to find a dying firefly in the Milky Way. I shortened the dividers to compensate for *Sycorax's* pedestrian pace, then pricked them north from my circle to Plymouth. Eight hours of windward discomfort.

"I might intercept him if I leave now," I said dubiously.

"Please, Nick?" There was a pleading eagerness in her voice. "Will you stop him?"

"Listen, Angela, I can't even promise to find him."

"But you'll try? Please?"

"I'll try. I promise. What will you do now?"

"I don't know." She sounded helpless and frightened.

"Listen," I said, "fly to Exeter. Hire a private plane if you have to. Meet me at Bannister's house tomorrow. I'll be there about midday."

"Why?"

Because I want to see you, I thought, but did not say. Because I'm about to flog myself ragged on a bloody night for your rotten husband, and the least you can do is meet me afterwards and say thank you; but I didn't say that either. "Just be there, Angela. Please?"

She paused, and I thought she was going to refuse. "I'll try," she said.

"I'll try too." I put the phone down. The wind rattled George's window-panes. It was a south wind, and still rising, which meant that tonight's sail would be a windward slog to nowhere. The chances of finding Bannister were negligible, but that was no reason to break the promise I'd just made to Angela.

Chapter 9

I moved George's half-wrecked fishing boat, primed my wretched engine, and hurt my back turning the flywheel. I needed a self-starter. I needed self-steering. I needed my head examined. I supposed that this was the manner in which knight errants had arranged their disappointments: one bleat from the maiden and the fools galloped off into dragon land. The motor caught eventually and I let it get used to the idea of working while I dragged the foresails through the forehatch and hanked them on their halliards. I hammered the gear lever into forward and *Sycorax* set her bows against wind and water.

I prayed that the engine would keep running. Once out of the river I hoisted all the sails, but left the engine running so I would not have to tack my way past the breakwater. The sky on this English summer's evening was low and grey.

Sycorax jarred at the first wave beyond the breakwater, then she seemed to realise what was expected of her and she tucked her head round and heeled to the wind that was flicking the tops of the waves into tails of white spume.

Sorting out the tangle of sheets in the cockpit, I was soaked through. Once clear of the Draystone I'd go below and find rough-weather clothes, but for now I knew I must stay with the tiller. I hunched low in the cockpit, reflecting that I was only making this gesture to impress Angela. I was meddling in her life because it gave me a chance to be close to her, but there had been no sign on the telephone that she reciprocated that wish. She had sounded desperate for her husband.

There was a small part of me that was offended by what had happened. I'd been warned off by people who did not give a toss for the justice of their cause. No one knew how Nadeznha Bannister had died, but that ignorance had not prevented them planning a callous revenge.

So tonight, despite the warnings, I would sail, out of bloody-minded-ness. I remembered another night when I had been told—ordered—not to do something. There'd been a sniper and two bunkers with bloody great .50 machine guns. The sniper was the real bastard, because he had a brand new nightsight and had already hit a half-dozen of our men. The boss had radioed that we were to get out of there, but to do that would have been to jeopardise . . . I was jerked back to the present as *Sycorax* crashed her bows into a steeper wave and the spray rattled along her decks. I shivered, pegged the tiller, and went below for sweater, boots and oilies. I switched on my navigation lights, called the coastguard on the VHF and asked for a forecast: strong winds tonight, but falling off towards dawn, then another depression following quickly.

I went topsides briefly and checked that no merchant ship was about to turn me into matchwood. None was, so I went below again and emptied two tins of baked beans into a saucepan. It was all the food I had, and it tasted good. I filled a Thermos with tea and carried it to the cockpit. Now it was simply a question of letting the wet hours pass.

Sycorax sailed herself. Her tiller was pegged and her sheets cleated tight. Sometimes, as the swell dropped her hard into a trough, the mainsail would shiver, but she picked herself up and drove on. I still had no radar-reflector and hoped that the big ships which were bashing down from Amsterdam and Hamburg were keeping a proper watch.

Midnight passed and the wind dropped and veered. Just before one o'clock, when I should still have been well north of *Wildtrack*'s course, I saw the lights of a vessel under sail. She was travelling west and to intercept her I unpegged the tiller and hardened *Sycorax* into the wind again. I took bearings on the yacht, which told me she was sailing fast.

I opened the locker where my flares were stored. Bannister would not stop if I radioed him on the VHF, and if I tried to sail across his bow I invited a collision that, though it would stop him, could also sink *Sycorax*. Instead, I planned to cross his stern and loose red emergency flares into the sky, because even a racing boat would have to help a boat in distress. That was the law. Bannister might curse, but he would have to gybe onto the new course and come to my rescue.

The approaching yacht was on the port tack, so it was his job to stay clear of me. He'd seen my lights, for he steered a point southerly to give me room. I hardened again, and he thought I had not seen him and shone a bright torch beam up onto his mainsail to make a splash of white light in the darkness. At the same time another of his crew called me on the VHF emergency channel. "Sailing boat approaching large yacht, do you read me, over?" I thought I detected a French accent in the crackling speaker. I was close enough to see the sail number in the torchlight and, because it was not *Wildtrack*, I fell off the wind to go astern of him. The torch was switched off. A voice shouted a protest that was made indistinct by the spray and wind. The yacht's stern light showed me the name *Mariette* on the white raked transom. I waved as I passed, then the wind tore us apart as I headed south again.

By three o'clock I knew I must be well inside the rough circle I'd sketched on George's chart. The night was black as pitch and the wind was still dropping. I turned westwards and searched for an hour. I saw two more Frenchmen, a Dutchman, but no *Wildtrack*.

I turned north. There was already a lightening to the east as the false wolf-light of dawn edged the clouds. I was bone tired, cold and hungry. I had failed, but I had always known how slim was my chance of success. *Wildtrack* could have run past me at any time in the darkness. Bannister was gone, to the Lizard and to death.

Dawn showed the sea heaving in a greasy, slow swell. Patches of fog drifted above a sludgelike sea. If the fog lifted, it rained. I was just praying to get home. Sailing isn't all fun in the sun. It can be rain and fog and cold and hunger. It can be a sulky sea and a listless sky. It can be failure, and then the only consolation is to remember that one volunteered for the misery.

So, in misery, I crawled north. The wind was negligible and sullen. I told myself time and time again that I should not be disappointed if Angela had not returned to Devon. I told myself that the two of us had no future and that I really did not care whether she was waiting for me at Bannister's house or not.

At midmorning, reluctantly at first, a wind scoured the sea and creaked the port shrouds. I seized the tiller, listening to the growing sound of water running past the hull. It was midday before I passed the Calfstone Shoal. The wind carried me up the river and round the point. There on the terrace above the river, and in front of an empty house, Angela was waiting.

SHE HAD BEEN CRYING. She was in jeans and sweater, her hair bound in a single plait that hung to her narrow waist. "It's a hell of a way to start a marriage." Or to end one, I thought, but did not say as much. She was distraught, but I was too cold and famished to be a gentle listener. I made myself eggs, bacon, coffee and toast, which I ate at the kitchen table.

Angela shook her head despairingly. "I tried to talk to him . . ."

" . . . but he wouldn't listen." I finished the sentence for her.

"He thinks you put me up to it. He thinks you want him to fail." She was restless and confused, and I did not blame her. She had only my word, and that of Micky Harding, that her new husband was sailing to his death.

For a time she tried to convince herself that it was untrue. I let her talk while I ate. She talked of Bannister's belief that he could take the coveted St. Pierre, and of his happiness because she had walked up the aisle with him. She spoke of the future they had discussed and, because that future was threatened, it only seemed the brighter to her now. "Tell me it isn't true." She meant Kassouli's threat.

"As far as I know," I said carefully, "it is true."

She shook in sudden anger. "Kassouli always hated Tony. He hated him for taking his daughter away. How dare people say Tony murdered Nadeznha?"

"Perhaps because they believe he did?"

"He didn't! Do you think I'd have married him if he'd killed her? Tony isn't a murderer. I don't think he ever could kill someone, not in cold blood."

"Why did you marry him?"

She lit a cigarette. "Because I love him," she said defiantly.

"Good." I hid my disappointment.

"And," she said, even more defiantly, "because I couldn't marry you."

I smiled. "I'm not a very good prospect."

She smiled back, the first smile she'd given me. "I watched you in the film rushes. I used to go to the cutting rooms and run loops of your ugly face. You messed up my lovely film, Nick Sandman."

"I'm sorry."

"No, you're not. I've given up the business, though, haven't I? That was one of the promises I made to Tony. No more telly." She looked at her watch. "Where will he be by now? Off southern Ireland?"

"Yes."

She had begun to cry very softly. "He can't give up, can he? He's got cameras watching him, so he has to be a big, brave boy. Men are so bloody stupid." She blew her nose. "Including you, Nick Sandman. What are you going to do now?"

"I'm going to provision *Sycorax*. After that, on tomorrow's tide, I shall sail away."

"Just like that?"

"You think I should lay on brass bands and cheerleaders?"

She gave me a flicker of a smile. "I'd want seasick pills."

"Goldfish get seasick."

She laughed. "They don't!"

"No, it's true. If you take them to sea as pets, they get seasick." I poured myself more coffee. "I wouldn't mind a cat."

"Truly?" She sounded surprised.

"I've always liked cats," I said. "You're a bit catlike."

She stared down at the table. I'd thought the last few minutes had been too relaxed and, sure enough, her mind was still with *Wildtrack*.

"I've thought of phoning the coastguard. But it won't do any good."

"No. They'd just laugh at you."

"I've tried the radiotelephone again, but he just gets angry. He thinks I'm trying to stop his moment of glory. And the last two times I tried, it was Fanny who answered."

"I'm sorry," I said. "Pray that he lives."

She stared bleakly at me. "Perhaps I should go to Canada? I could go, with the film crew."

"Do you think you can persuade him to give up there when you couldn't do it here?" I suddenly realised that my pessimism was doing her no good. "Maybe you should try. Anything's better than doing nothing."

She sighed. "Tony may not even reach the turning point. God knows."

"He'll reach St. Pierre," I said, thinking of something Kassouli had said to me. He had wanted me to steer a certain course on the return leg. "Oh, God," I said softly, "I've been so bloody stupid."

"What do you mean?"

"They're going to take him to the exact place where Nadeznha died! On the outward leg he'll have to go much too far north, but they'll let him turn, because the perfect revenge has to be at the same damn place!"

"What place?" Her voice was urgent.

I couldn't remember. The only places I remembered seeing the co-ordinates were on the frame of Nadeznha Bannister's portrait in *Wildtrack*'s after cabin, and on the papers that Kassouli had shown me. "Forty something north," I said helplessly. My memory had failed me. Then I remembered the inquest transcript.

Angela ran to Bannister's study and found the transcript. She turned the pages quickly, but seemed to freeze when she came to the evidence she wanted. "Forty-nine, eighteen north," she read aloud, "and forty-one, thirty-six west." She turned to me. "Where is that?"

I used an atlas to show her how *Wildtrack* would have to sail an arching parabola westwards, then a shallower curve back home. I put a cross on the point where Nadeznha Bannister had died. Angela used a ruler to work out the distances. I watched her thin fingers and I knew, in the room's silence, what would come next.

"Nick . . ."

I had gone to the window. "It's about three thousand nautical miles for *Wildtrack*," I said. That was the distance from Cherbourg to the turning point at St. Pierre and back to the pencil cross.

"And from here? By the fastest route?" I could hear hope in her voice.

"Seventeen hundred, say."

"How long would it take . . . ?" She did not finish the sentence. She wanted to ask me how long it would take *Sycorax* to reach that cross on the map.

"Sixteen days," I guessed. "It would be faster if I had someone to crew for me."

She seemed to think of something that drained the hope out of her face. "It's your leg, isn't it? You're frightened that it'll collapse."

"It hasn't happened for weeks," I said truthfully, "and even if it had, it wouldn't stop me."

"So . . ." She could not bring herself to ask the favour directly.

"Yes," I said. Yes, I could reach the killing place, and yes, I would try.

I'VE NEVER VICTUALLED A BOAT so quickly, nor so well. Angela used her car and credit card to go to the town, while I raided Bannister's larder and boathouse.

"I can't let him die!" she said to me as she pushed the wheelbarrow of food down to the wharf. She said it as if to justify the insanity of what I was doing. I didn't care to discuss the motives; it was enough that I'd agreed to go for her. "What's in the barrow?"

"Coffee, dried milk, eggs. Tins of everything."

"The eggs need to be dipped in boiling water for five seconds. It preserves them." She took the eggs back to the house while I stored the tins in freezer bags to keep the bilge water from rusting the metal and obliterating the labels. I'd finished my rough list of perishable stores and hoped I'd forgotten nothing essential. I wasn't victualling only for a North Atlantic run, but also thinking of what would follow. My own suspicion was that I would never find *Wildtrack*, but once I had failed I would turn *Sycorax*'s bows southwards, and so I provisioned for a dog-leg voyage that would take me from England to the Canadian coast, then southwards to where the palm trees grew.

Angela brought the parboiled eggs and I gave her more errands. "I want some coal or coke, sweaters, socks, warm weather-gear. I want the best oilskins in the house. I need a sextant and the best sleeping-bag you've got. I want an RDF and a self-steering vane."

I ransacked the house for things I might need. I found charts of the North Atlantic and the Canadian coast. I took a fancy hand-held radio-direction finder and a pack of spare batteries. I took the fenders off

Wildtrack II. Crammed provisions into *Sycorax*'s every locker. There was some broken self-steering gear in the boathouse and I put it all aboard. It could be mended and rigged at sea.

I still needed medical stores. I told Angela to go to the doctor and get prescriptions for painkillers, local anaesthetic, tranquillisers and antibiotics. I scribbled a note to the doctor explaining my needs, and Angela brought everything back.

By six o'clock it was almost done. The wind was blowing hard now, coming from the southwest. If the weather pattern held then I'd have a stiff beat out of the river, and a rough sea to the Mizzen Head, but after that I'd be reaching fast into the high latitudes. From there I'd drop down to the rendezvous. My tender was still in the boathouse. I hoisted it onto *Sycorax*'s coachroof where I lashed it upside down. It was my only life raft; there were not even life jackets aboard. As I tied the last lashing to the starboard handrail it began to rain and suddenly there was no more to be done except to say goodbye.

I kissed Angela. We stood in the rain beside the river and I kissed her once more. I held her tight because a part of me could not bear to leave. "I can't promise anything," I said.

"I know."

"You just have to wait now," I said. "I'll write. Some day."

"Please do." She spoke stiffly.

"I love you," I said.

"Don't say it, Nick."

It was a miserable parting; a miserable departure. The engine wouldn't start, but the jib tugged *Sycorax*'s bow away from the wharf. Angela let go my springs and warps as I hoisted the mainsail and mizzen.

"There's a present for you in the cabin!" Angela shouted.

Sycorax was moving fast now, snatched by the ebb and the river's turbulent current. I waved to show that I'd heard, but I couldn't go below to find the gift until I had *Sycorax* settled into the main channel. Once there I pegged the tiller, went down the companionway, and found the last two boxes that Angela had loaded. One was filled with cat food, the other contained a small black female kitten which, as soon as I opened the box, greeted me with needle-sharp claws.

I went topsides. I looked back, but the rain had already driven Angela away from the wharf. The kitten, astonished by its new home, glared at me from the cabin steps. "I'll call you Angel," I said. Angel hissed at me. The hair on her back bristled. I hoped she was a sea cat. I hoped she'd bring me luck.

Ahead of me now was the river's mouth, where the half gale was smashing waves white across the bar. Car lights flashed from the stone jetty by the town boatyard. As *Sycorax* drew closer I saw the blue

Porsche parked there and knew that Angela had come to see us off. She ran down to the fuel pontoon and waved both arms at me.

"I like the cat!" I shouted as loud as I could.

"Nick! Nick!" Then I saw that she was beckoning. I pushed the tiller over, sheeted in on the new tack, and let the boat glide up towards the pontoon. Two big motor cruisers were moored there and I watched as Angela climbed into the larger boat. She stood by the quadrails, holding on to a stanchion. She was carrying a bag.

I put *Sycorax*'s head to the wind and let the tide carry me alongside the cruiser. Angela threw the bag onto *Sycorax*'s foredeck, waited a second, then caught my hand and jumped into the cockpit.

"Are you sure?" I asked her.

"Of course I'm not sure, but . . ." Her eyes were red-rimmed from crying. "It's your leg. You're going to kill yourself out there, Nick."

"I'll be fine, I promise."

"And you said it would be quicker with two people on board."

"That's true." I let the sails flap. "But not if one of them is seasick." I wanted her to come more than I could possibly say, yet I was using arguments to make her stay behind.

She bent back her left ear to show me an adhesive patch. "The chemist says they're infallible."

"It's going to be rough out there," I warned her. I was letting *Sycorax* drift on the current in case she wanted me to take her back to the pontoon.

"If you give me a choice now," she said, "I might not stay."

I did not give her the choice. Instead I gave her the tiller and hauled in the sheets. "Hold this course. See the white pole on the headland? Aim for it."

I fetched her bag from the foredeck and hoisted the staysail. I was so happy I could have walked on water. Then *Sycorax*'s bows hit the waves at the river's bar, the first cold spray shot back like shrapnel, and the three of us were going to sea.

Chapter 10

Angela was seasick. For hour after miserable hour she lay shivering and helpless. I tried to make her spend time in the cockpit where the fresh air might have helped, but she stayed in the cabin's lee bunk, wrapped in blankets and retching into a zinc bucket.

The kitten was fine. She seemed to think a world permanently battered by a half gale was a perfect place. At night she slept in Angela's lap, giving Angela the one small pleasure she could appreciate, while in daylight she roamed the boat, performing daredevil acrobatics which made me think she was bound to be washed overboard, but the little beast had an instinct for avoiding the rush of the sea. Once I saw her leap up onto the mainsail's tack. She clung to the cotton, legs splayed, as a wave thundered over the coachroof, breaking onto the tethered dinghy. She seemed to like the mainsail after that. Her other favourite place was the chart table, and every time I opened a chart she would leap onto it and curl up by the dividers. I navigated from cat hair to cat hair.

There was little else to steer *Sycorax* by. The sky stayed clouded, the nights dark, and once we had left the Irish lights behind we were blind. I could not make Bannister's fancy radio-direction finder work. I told myself, as I had told myself a million times before, that if the *Mayflower* had reached America without a silicon chip, I could too.

Like the *Mayflower*, we thrashed northwest under a press of sail. I made Thermos flasks of soup that Angela pushed irritably away. I had never been seasick, but I knew well enough what it was like. For the first day she feared she was dying, and thereafter she feared she was not. So much for the chemist's adhesive patch.

Sycorax thrived, though the short-wave radio gave up the ghost after just two days, and no amount of coaxing, banging or cursing would bring it back to life. The lack of the radio was more serious than the loss of the radio-direction finder, for without the short wave I could not check the accuracy of my key-wound chronometer.

My greatest problem was my own tiredness. Angela could not help, so I was having to sail both day and night. I still had not rigged the broken self-steering gear which was stowed under the tender, but *Sycorax* had always sailed well enough with shortened sail and a pegged tiller while I slept. Such a procedure presupposed a constant wind direction, and entailed frequent waking to check the compass headings.

The worst moment came eight nights after we'd put to sea. I woke to feel the boat pitching and corkscrewing and went topsides to find that the weather was brewing trouble. We were far north now, so the night was light and short and I could see that the wind and heavy rain were creaming the wavetops smooth and covering the valleys with a fine sheet of white foam. *Sycorax* buried her bowsprit twice, staggered up, and the water came streaming back towards the cockpit to mix with the pelting rain. I pumped the bilges every few minutes.

For the rest of that night, all the next day, and into the following night, that wind and sea pounded us. I slept for an hour in the morning, woke to the madness, pumped for a half-hour, and slept again. By the midnight of the gale's second night the wind was slackening and the sea was lessening, so I pegged the tiller, left the sails short, and crawled into my bunk.

I slept five hours, then found the gale had passed. I forced myself out of the sleeping-bag, pulled on a soaking sweater, and went topsides to see a long swell fretted with small and angry waves that were the remnants of the wind's passage. I pumped the bilge till my back could take no more pain. I was hurting in every bone and muscle.

The cat protested that she had not been fed for hours. I slid back the hatch and climbed down into the soaked cabin. The cat rubbed itself against my legs. I no longer called her Angel, for every time I did Angela answered. I opened a tin of cat food and was so hungry I was tempted to wolf it down myself.

An hour later a Russian Aurora-Class missile-cruiser cleared the northern horizon. She was escorted by two destroyers which sniffed suspiciously towards *Sycorax*. I dutifully lowered and raised my Red Ensign. The courtesy over, and duly answered by the dipping of the destroyer's hammer and sickle, I switched on the VHF. "Yacht *Sycorax* to Russian naval vessel. Do you read me, over?"

"Good morning, little one. Over." The operator must have been expecting my call for he answered instantly. He sounded horribly cheerful, as though he had a bellyful of coffee and fried egg, or whatever else consituted a hearty Russian breakfast.

"Can you give me a position and time check?"

A minute later he gave me a position and a countdown to an exact second. He wished me luck, then the three grey warships slithered southwards through the fretting sea.

We'd done well. We'd cleared the tail of the Rockall Plateau, though I was further north than I'd wanted. If Bannister was doing half as well, in his faster boat, then he'd take the St. Pierre, so long as he lived to do it. My chronometer had stayed accurate to within a second, which was comforting.

"Who were you talking to?" Angela rolled over in her bunk.

"A Russian destroyer. He gave us our position."

"The Russians help you?" She sounded incredulous.

"Why on earth shouldn't they? Would you like some coffee?"

"Please."

Resurrection had definitely started. I made the coffee, then scrambled some eggs. Angela said she could not possibly eat any eggs, but five minutes later she tentatively tried a spoonful of mine, then stole the mug from me and wolfed the whole lot down.

"More?"

"Please." I made more.

She looked dreadful: pale as ash, stringy-haired and red-eyed.

"Good morning, beautiful," I said.

"I hope you haven't got a mirror on this damned boat." She had joined me in the cockpit and stared disconsolately round the horizon, seeing nothing but long grey swells. She frowned at me. "Do you really like this life, Nick?"

"I love it."

The cat did its business on the windward scuppers where it had somehow learned that the sea cleaned up after it, then stepped delicately down onto Angela's lap where it began its morning session of self-satisfied preening. "You can't call her Angel," Angela said.

"Why not?"

"Because I don't like it. Call her Vicky, after the Victoria Cross."

"That's immodest."

"She's called Vicky, and that's the end of it. Do I look really awful?"

"Absolutely hideous. What you do now is go below, undress, wash all over, put on clean clothes, comb your hair, then come out singing."

"Aye, aye, sir."

"Then open the forehatch to air the boat. Then sit here and steer two-eight-nine while I sleep."

"On my own?" She sounded alarmed.

"You can have Cat for company."

"Vicky."

She's been Vicky ever since.

THAT NIGHT THE SKY CLOUDED again. I was woken in the darkness to hear the water seething past the hull and I knew we were getting the spinning backlash of yet another gale.

Angela was sick again, but the next couple of days brought colour to her cheeks. We ran fast and saw no other sails, only a trawler steaming west and another warship heading north. We watched a whale blow its vents, and Angela stared like a child. "I never thought I'd see that," she said in wonder.

But most of the time she talked of her husband and I detected how desperately she needed to justify her presence on *Sycorax*. "He's more likely to believe the warning if he hears my voice on the radio," she would say. "He'll know it's serious if I go to these lengths to reach him, won't he?"

"Sure," I would say. My own belief was that Bannister would be mad as hell when he discovered his wife had sailed the Atlantic with another man.

"I can't believe he's really in danger," she said that evening.

"Danger's like that," I said. "It didn't seem real in the Falklands, either. We'd trained for war, but I don't think any of us really thought we'd end up fighting. I remember thinking how bloody daft it was. I was supposed to be counting the rounds I'd fired, but I clean forgot to do it.

140

Count so you knew when to change magazines, you see, but I was just laughing! It wasn't real. I kept pulling the trigger and suddenly there were no more bullets up my spout and this bloke with a submachine gun appeared in a bunker to my left and all I had . . ."

Angela was sitting next to me in the cockpit. "And all you had was what?"

I mimed a bayonet stroke. "Mucky."

She frowned. "You were shot then?"

"Not for another minute. I couldn't go back, because it would have looked as if I'd bottled out, so I kept on going. I remember shouting like a bloody maniac."

"Why wouldn't you talk like that on the film?"

"I don't know . . ." I paused. "Because I'd made a mess of everything, if you really want the truth. I was frightened as hell, and I panicked."

"That's not what the citation says."

"It was dark. No one could see what was happening."

THE WIND DROPPED NEXT DAY. There was still a modicum of warmth in the midday sun, but by early afternoon we were both swathed in sweaters, scarves and oilskins. That night, after I'd plotted our position, I called Angela on deck to see the aurora borealis, which was filling the northern sky with its curving and shifting colours. She was enchanted.

A great coral-coloured lightfall shimmered and faded in the twilight as *Sycorax*'s booms swung across in an involuntary but slow gybe. The sea was flattening to a sheen of gunmetal while Angela and I sat in the cockpit and watched the magic lights.

"Do you know what I forgot?" Angela broke our silence.

"Tell me."

"A passport."

I smiled. "I shall tell the Canadians that I kidnapped you."

She turned on the thwart so that she could lean against me. It was the first intimate gesture that either of us had made since she first stepped aboard. "Do you know why I came, Nick?"

"Tell me."

"I wanted to be with you. It wasn't because of your leg, and I'm not really *sure* that Tony's in danger. I know I should believe it, but I don't." She had brought a bottle of Irish whiskey from the cabin and she poured us each a glass. "Is this what's called running away to sea?"

"Yes," I said.

"I shouldn't be here, should I?"

"I wanted you to be here." I ducked her question.

She turned her face to mine. "I love you, Nick."

It was the first time she had said it, and I kissed her. "I love you."

"But . . ." she began.

"No buts," I said quickly, "not yet."

IT WAS IN THOSE MIDDLE DAYS of the voyage that Angela learned to sail *Sycorax*. She stood her own watches while I slept below. Life eased for me. And for her. The seasickness was gone and she seemed like a new woman. The strains of London and ambition were washed out by a healthier life. But I knew we must soon turn south to run down to the place where a girl had died. Day by day we could see the pencil line closing on the cross on the chart, yet it still did not seem real that we were sailing to a place of revenge.

What seemed real was the two of us. We were happy, and though neither of us forgot the cloud that waited beyond that western horizon, we stopped talking of it.

We were busy too. A small boat made of wood and powered by cotton generates work. I sewed sails and touched up worn varnish. Our lives depended on the boat, and there was a simple, lifesaving rule that no job should ever be deferred. It was a life that imposed its own discipline, and thus enjoyment. "But for ever?" Angela asked.

I was caulking the bridge deck where the mizzen had strained a timber. I leaned back on the thwart. "I remember waking up in the helicopter after I was wounded. I knew I was badly hurt. The morphine was wearing off and I was suddenly very frightened of dying. I promised myself that if I lived I'd give myself to the sea. Just like this." I nodded towards the grey-green waves. "That stuff," I said, "is the most dangerous thing in the world. If you're lazy with it, or dishonest with it, or try to cheat it, it will kill you. Is that an answer?"

Angela stared at the sea. We were under full sail, close-hauled and making good progress. "What about your children?" she asked suddenly.

"They've got Melissa and Hon-John, and the nanny, and their ponies."

"You're running away from them," Angela accused me.

"I'll fly back to see them." But she had touched a nerve. I did not have a proper answer.

We turned south the next day and our mood changed with the new course. We were thinking of Bannister again. Now, though, Angela spoke of his innocence, telling me again and again how she had insisted on hearing the truth before they married. Nadeznha, she said, had been killed when a wave swamped *Wildtrack*'s aft cockpit.

"If we don't find Tony," she said, "and he's all right, then can I fly home from Canada before he reaches Cherbourg?"

"Yes," I promised her. She was planning her departure from me and there was nothing I could do to stop it. My immediate worry was the glass. It had begun to fall fast, and I knew we were in for a bad blow and that, by sailing south, we were sailing towards the depression's vortex. But we got there before the gale reached us. We got to the featureless place where, a year before, a girl had died. The clouds were low and dark, the sea was ragged and flecked. I hove to at midday as a kind of tribute, but neither of us spoke. There was no ship in sight, nor any crackle on the radio.

"Are you in the right place?" Angela asked.

"As near as I can make it, yes."

"We don't even *know* that Kassouli planned to meet Tony here," Angela said. "We only guessed it."

"Here, or nowhere," I said. But the truth was that we did not know.

Angela pointed *Sycorax*'s bows to the west. I let her choose the course, and watched as she sheeted home the foresails and pegged the tiller. The cat sharpened its claws on a sailbag.

The seas were growing and the visibility was obscured by a spume that was being whipped off the wavetops. Angela, with new confidence, reefed the mainsail and stowed the staysail. The waves were running towards us; some of them smashed white on our stem and under their pounding Angela's confidence began to shred like the wavecrests. "Are we in for a storm, Nick?"

"Only a gale. That isn't so bad."

By twilight we were under the heavy canvas of storm jib and mizzen staysail alone. Both sails were tiny, yet they kept the heavy hull moving in the churning water. Angela and I were both oilskinned and harnessed, while the cat was imprisoned below as *Sycorax* staggered in troughs of green-black waves that were scribbled with white foam. That night was like an echo of creation's chaos.

The wind's noise is everything from a knife-sharp keening to a hollow roar like an explosion, which lasts for ever. The sea is the percussion to that mad music, hammering through the boat so that the timbers judder and it seems a miracle that anything made by man can live. But the sight of a gale-ripped sea is worse. It's a confusion of air and water, with foam stinging like whips in the sky, and through the chaos of white and black and grey the boat must be steered.

We staggered up the sides of ocean mountains and spilt at heart-stopping speed down to their foam-scummed pits. I felt the tug of the tons of cold water on her keel, and once I heard Angela scream as *Sycorax* lay over on her side and the mainmast threatened to bury itself in the grey-white water.

Water boiled over the decks, ran down the scuppers and swamped the cockpit drains. I made Angela pump, forcing her to do it when she wanted to stop, for the exercise made her warm. The cold would kill us before the sea did. I made her go down to the cabin to fetch the Thermos and sandwiches we'd made ready.

She brought me the food, then went below and stayed there, and I imagined her huddled in her bunk with the cat clutched in her arms. I sensed that this was not one of the great ship-breaking storms that could rack the Atlantic for days, but merely a snarling wildcat of a low that would skirt across the water and be gone. On a weather chart this gale would look no bigger than the one in which Nadeznha Bannister had died. Even before the night was out the wind was lessening. I opened the cabin hatch once and saw that Angela slept.

I hardened the boat into the wind, took down the aft staysail and hoisted reefed mizzen and main. The wavetops slashed across *Sycorax* and rattled on her sails. Angela still slept, but I stayed awake, searching.

My search was merely dutiful, for I believed we had missed *Wildtrack*. The odds against finding Bannister's boat had always been astronomical, and so I expected to see nothing. When, in the light of dawn, I did see something, I did not at first believe my salt-stung eyes.

I was tired and cold, and I thought I'd seen a lightning flash. Then I saw the reflected glow on the clouds above and I knew it was a red distress flare. It flickered out, then another soared upwards to burst against a dirty sky, and I knew that, by ill-luck or by God's loving mercy, we had come to the killing place.

Chapter 11

I pushed back the hatch and switched on the radio, but there was only the crackling hiss of the heavens. Angela was still curled in a corner of the bunk.

"I've just seen flares," I said.

It took her a sleepy moment to understand. "*Wildtrack*?"

"I don't know."

Angela struggled into her oilskins and came up to the cockpit. She hooked her lifeline to a jackstay and I saw her shudder at the height of the swell that was running down on us. *Sycorax* soared her way up the slopes and slalomed down again. At each crest I stared ahead, but saw no more flares. I began to think I had hallucinated, then Angela shouted.

I looked where she was pointing. For a second I saw nothing, then, a half-mile off, I spotted the yacht.

It had to be *Wildtrack*.

But not the *Wildtrack* we both remembered; not the proud and gleaming rich man's toy. Instead we saw a dismasted yacht, half swamped. For a second I dared to hope that this wreck was some other

144

boat, but then the sea momentarily bared the hull's flank and I saw the distinctive bold blue flash. We had sailed over seventeen hundred nautical miles and by a miracle we had found *Wildtrack*. But by a cruel fate we had found her too late.

I unpegged the tiller.

"Nick! Nick!" Angela's voice held a new urgency and I saw in *Wildtrack*'s aft cockpit a moving splash of orange, a man in oilskins. Alive. It had to be Bannister.

I scrambled down into the cabin, threatening the engine with death if it did not start. I staggered as the boat pitched, swung the handle, and to my amazement the cold engine banged straight into life. I bolted the companionway steps back over the motor compartment and climbed to the cockpit. *Wildtrack* had vanished in a wave valley, but as I kicked the motor into gear I saw her bows rise sluggishly on a wind-fretted ridge.

I turned head to wind, arrowing into the seas, and let the engine push us. Angela was staring, her mouth open. I did not want to know what she was thinking or what hopes, hers or mine, might be on the verge of being shattered.

The wind slewed viciously. We pitched on a crest and the motor raced like a banshee before the stern sank under water again. But while we were on the wavecrest I saw the orange figure in *Wildtrack*'s stern wave, then fall back. He was either hurt or so tired that he could hardly move.

"It's going to be bloody hard to fetch him off!" I shouted at Angela.

Being alongside a flooded boat in a high sea and a shifting wind would be a piece of seamanship that needed a Jimmy Nicholls or a lifeboat's coxswain. Worse, if Bannister was injured, one of us would have to board *Wildtrack* to give him aid.

It would have to be me. "You're going to have to steer the boat!" I called to Angela. "You'll have to lay us alongside, then sheer off once I'm aboard *Wildtrack*, understand? I don't want that hulk stoving us in!"

She nodded. She was staring at the figure in *Wildtrack*. His hood was up and his collar buttoned across his mouth.

"When I've got him," I went on, "you're going to have to come alongside again!" She'd become a good sailor, but this manoeuvre was like asking a passenger to land a jumbo jet.

I left her at the tiller while I tied all the fenders I'd taken from Bannister's boathouse onto *Sycorax*'s guardrail stanchions. *Wildtrack* and *Sycorax* would be pitching as they met and I feared I would crash my bows down on her deck or, worse, rip off my rudder and propeller with the force of the collision.

I let the mainsail fall and roughly lashed gaff and sail to the boom. I did not want Angela distracted by hammering sails as she tried to manoeuvre the boat. I left the storm jib sheeted taut, to stiffen *Sycorax* and to give

146

some leverage to the bows at the moment when Angela needed to sheer away. I took the tiller. "Are you hooked on?"

She showed me her lifeline. I accelerated. We were close enough to *Wildtrack* now to share the same valleys of sea. I wanted to circle the crippled boat and approach from the lee so that the wind would be pushing *Sycorax* away from the treacherous hull once I was aboard her. In choosing the course I risked *Wildtrack*'s trailing ropes tangling in *Sycorax*'s propeller, and I told a worried Angela that, once I was aboard, she was to put the motor in neutral and let the storm jib carry her clear. "Let the sheet run a bit, OK?"

It was clearly not OK. "Should I go across to him?" Angela shouted.

I'd thought of that, but I knew she did not have the physical strength to lift a helpless man. And Bannister was helpless. He was hardly moving except to follow our progress with his orange-hooded face. There was also another reason for me to go: if anything went wrong then Angela would be left on the safer of the two boats. I explained that I would clear the trailing ropes once I was aboard *Wildtrack* so that she need not worry about fouling the propeller on the second approach. "But if you can't get us off," I shouted, "then stay close if you can! If you can't, good luck! Go west! You'll find trawlers on the Grand Banks. And don't forget to feed Vicky!"

She gave me a frightened look. I grinned, trying to reassure her, then gunned the engine to spin *Sycorax* up into *Wildtrack*'s lee.

Angela took the tiller and I staggered forward to *Sycorax*'s starboard shrouds. I unclipped my lifeline from the jackstay and coiled it into a pocket. I put my good foot over the guardrail and held on for grim life as we rolled our gunwale under. We were six feet from the swamped boat, five feet, closing to three, two. Then the sea heaved the hulls together and I heard the crashing grind of wood on fibreglass. I jumped.

I pushed off with my left leg, which meant I landed on my right, and for the first time in weeks my knee buckled. I must have cried aloud, though I could hear nothing but the turmoil of water and wind. I sprawled heavily on *Wildtrack*'s slippery foredeck. Pain speared out from my back, then a wave broke and swept me towards the side. I grabbed a guardrail stanchion with my right hand and held on as the rush of cold sea slewed me round, but my left boot found a purchase on *Wildtrack*'s forehatch and somehow I held fast.

The sea began to stream off the deck and I lifted my head to see blood spewing into the flooded scuppers. I saw that I had slashed my left hand on a stub of metal shroud which had been sheared clean, and astonishingly sharp, with bolt-cutters. The cut was across the fleshy base of my thumb and there was nothing I could do about it now. I was cursing my leg as I pulled myself forward.

I slithered over the coaming into the flooded central cockpit. I was soaked through, but my fear and rage were warming me. The wind was lashing spray across the boat, and the great swells loomed steep above me, their sides like crinkling slopes of bottle glass. *Wildtrack* was sinking, and I was suddenly gripped with a terrible fear that she would go down before Angela could bring *Sycorax* back. I looked round for a life belt or raft, but when the crew abandoned *Wildtrack* they had taken all such equipment. And even if Angela did succeed in coming back, I did not know how I would transfer myself, let alone Bannister. My leg was useless. I tried to stand, fell again, and pulled myself to the cockpit's edge. The leg would have to look after itself while I dragged the trailing ropes from the water. As I pulled the last line aboard, a swell rolled the boat's stern up and the water in the cockpit surged forward. I saw the horror then.

The body floated forward with the ship's sluggish motion. It floated out of the rear cabin doorway until its shoulders stuck. Suddenly I knew it was not Bannister who waited for me in *Wildtrack*'s stern. I was looking at Bannister now, and he at me. Or rather his dead eyes were gaping at me. His throat had been cut almost to the spine.

Wildtrack's bows rose and the body mercifully washed back out of sight.

Using my arms, I dragged myself aft. It was then that the man in the stern cockpit turned his gaze on me.

It was Mulder.

Wildtrack shuddered under me as the sea poured off her topsides. I scrambled towards Mulder. "Can you stand?"

He shook his head, then pointed to his left leg which was bent unnaturally: it was broken. That made two one-legged men in a doomed boat.

"Where's the rest of the crew?"

"Taken off!" Mulder shouted back. "They're safe."

So another boat had stood by and rescued the crew? Mulder had clearly stayed on board to try to salvage the damaged ship and had then been marooned when the gale blew up. I wondered where the rescue boat was, and why it had not steered for the flares. "Is that who you were signalling?" I asked. "The rescue ship?"

"Get me off, Sandman! She's sinking!"

"I should bloody leave you. Why did you cut his throat?" I shouted the question as we reared up the side of a green cliff and tons of water smashed across us.

"Accident." He shouted the word vehemently.

He looked so damned smug that I hated him, and I tried to kick him, but my leg folded, so that I fell awkwardly in the cockpit. I fell over

Mulder's broken leg and I heard him scream. I rolled off him and pulled myself into a sitting position. "Why did you cut his throat?" I shouted again.

He just stared at me with hatred, so I lifted my left leg to kick his broken bone, and the threat made him babble in a desperate attempt to avoid the pain. "Because I couldn't push him overboard!"

"Did you kill his wife?"

He stared at me as if I was mad. "Get me off here! The boat's sinking!"

"Did you kill his wife?"

"No!"

I managed to kneel upright and unshackle his lifeline from a D-ring. He watched me, not sure whether I intended to push him overboard or save his life. I grabbed a braidline rope out of the tangle of wreckage in the cockpit and pulled forty or fifty feet free before the line jammed. "Knife!" I shouted over the sound of wind and sea. "Give me your knife!"

He handed me a sheath knife and I used the heavy blade to slash off the length of braidline. I tied a small bowline knot, then shackled the line of Mulder's safety harness to the bowline's loop. The other end of the rope went round my waist. Once Angela returned I would scramble on board *Sycorax*, then haul Mulder to safety. I explained that to him. "It's going to hurt you," I added, "but if you want to drown, then cut yourself loose." I tossed the knife back to him, then pulled myself to the lee rail.

I stood there, clinging for dear life to the guardrail stanchion, and willed my right leg to take my weight. I searched the broken seas for a glimpse of *Sycorax*. I waited, I prayed, and a moment later I saw her stern with the bright flash of the frayed Red Ensign. I knew Angela must be struggling to turn the old boat. She was already a quarter-mile off and I hoped to God she did not lose sight of us.

I crouched back into the small shelter of the aft cockpit.

"You're going to have to wait, Fanny."

"Who's sailing your boat?"

"A friend," I said.

Mulder looked worn out, grey-faced with red-rimmed eyes. "They lost us in the night," he said.

"Who lost you?"

"Kassouli. Who do you think?"

Who else? I should have known that Yassir Kassouli would be here at the kill. I clung to the handrail as a wave crashed over the coaming. I found a length of rope that I wrapped as a crude bandage round my cut hand.

"If Kassouli finds you here," Mulder said, "he'll bloody sink you, Sandman."

"He's deserted you, Fanny. He's left you here to die." I had to shout if

149

Mulder was to hear my words. "He's left you—but I'm going to save your miserable life. I'm taking you to where I can stand up in a courtroom and tell them about Bannister and his cut throat."

The South African stared at me with loathing, then shook his head. "Kassouli won't desert me."

"He already has." I pulled myself upright to search the southern horizon. *Sycorax* had turned, but she was still far off. There were no other boats in sight.

A gasp of pain made me turn. Mulder, the knife in his hand, had tried to lunge towards me, but the combination of his broken leg and the obstruction of his inflated life jacket had stopped his murderous thrust. It seemed he really did believe that Kassouli would return for him. I kicked at the knife in his hand to stop him trying again.

My kick missed, and once again the effort toppled me. My bandaged left hand slipped off the handrail so that I fell forward towards Mulder. I tried to regain my balance, but only managed to drop my right knee onto the thigh of Mulder's broken leg. He screamed, and the sound was whipped away by the wind. *Wildtrack* heaved up as I collapsed. Mulder was still moaning with the pain, but the strength of the man was extraordinary. He wrapped his left arm round my neck, and I knew that any second the knife blade would be in my ribs. Water sloshed up about us.

I rammed my head forward, smashing the bridge of his nose with my forehead, then screamed myself from the pain that clawed at my back. I glimpsed the knife and lunged for it with both hands. My right caught his wrist as my left was slashed by the blade.

He tried to jerk his hand away, but I clung to him. With my left foot rammed against the coaming, I used all my strength to force myself up. I let go of his hand and drove my bunched fists down onto the broken bone in his shin.

He screamed again, the knife forgotten. I plucked it from his fingers and scrambled desperately backwards. I jammed myself in the corner of the cockpit by the wheel and held my breath to let the pain ebb away.

Mulder lay exhausted and hopeless. I struggled upright, still holding the knife, and saw the spray from *Sycorax*'s bows. Angela was fighting towards us, still four hundred yards off.

I put my left foot against Mulder's broken leg. "Now," I said, "you're going to tell me what happened."

Because I had proved that I would use pain, he told me of Kassouli's revenge. The story came slowly, and I had to tease it out of him between the slashing assaults of the breaking waves.

Mulder had brought *Wildtrack* to this place in the ocean where, two nights before, while he was on night watch, he had sheared a port shroud. He had sabotaged a shroud before, trying to cast suspicion on me, and he had known that as soon as he put weight on the shroud the mast would bend and break. He had gone aft, tacked ship, and let chaos overtake the long hull. The crew had tumbled up from their bunks to find disaster—and salvation.

The salvation was *Kerak*, the supertanker. A Kassouli ship that had loomed with blazing lights out of the darkness. I imagined the terror Bannister must have felt when he heard, on the radio, the identity of the ship that had so fortuitously appeared.

The crew had been taken off, Mulder said, leaving only himself and Bannister on *Wildtrack*. "Bannister wouldn't leave."

That was a clever touch, I thought sourly. Bannister had chosen to stay with the one man he could trust: his own assassin.

Bannister and Mulder had cleared the mast's wreckage, then they ran westwards under engine power. That was when the gale had blown up. Mulder steered, following the tanker's lights, but at some time *Wildtrack* had been struck in the darkness by a cross-sea. Water, pouring through an open hatch, had swamped the boat, *Wildtrack*'s electrics had died, and the motor had coughed into silence. Mulder had clambered forward to start the engine by hand, but had slipped on the companionway and broken his leg.

They had drifted in the darkness until the tanker was lost from view. Sometime during that next long day Mulder had ripped his blade across Bannister's throat and thus fulfilled his contract. Then Mulder had waited for Kassouli, but because the swamped hull would not have shown on radar, he had waited in vain. He had slept for a time, waking at intervals to send up his last few flares.

Battered and shivering, I listened to Mulder's tale. I massaged my leg, feeling the slow return of life to the cold flesh. All I could do now was pray that *Wildtrack* did not sink before *Sycorax*, making painfully slow progress, reached us.

"What happened," I shouted at Mulder, "to Nadeznha?"

He had thought my interrogation was over, and I had to raise my left foot to encourage him. "I don't know!" he shouted. "I wasn't on deck. Bannister relieved me."

"You didn't say that at the inquest."

"Bannister paid me to say that I was on watch! He didn't want anyone to know he wasn't a watch captain. Me and Nadeznha, we sailed the boat, not him! But if anyone had known he was just crewing, he'd have lost face."

Good God, I thought, but it made such sense. Bannister's vanity would have made him insist that he was seen as the expert.

Mulder mistook my silence for disbelief. "As God is my witness"—he was shaking with fright and cold—"that's all I lied about. I don't know what happened. I wouldn't have killed her, I loved her!" I still said nothing, and Mulder construed my silence as a threat. "We were lovers, man, she and I!"

"Lovers?" I was incredulous. Yet it made sense, if I had bothered to think about it. "Did Bannister ever find out?"

"He never found out." There was pride in Mulder's voice.

But if Bannister *had* known about Mulder and Nadeznha, I thought, then his pride might have made him kill them both. "Did Bannister kill his wife?" I asked.

"I don't know." Mulder's voice was a whimper that barely carried over the noise of the sea. "In God's name, Mr. Sandman, I don't know."

"But you told Kassouli that he killed her."

"I told him I'd lied for Bannister at the inquest. It was Mr. Kassouli's idea that Bannister killed Nadeznha, not mine!"

"But you encouraged the idea?"

"I told him the truth. I told him Bannister hated Nadeznha. Behind her back he called her a spoilt bitch," Mulder babbled at me. "He was terrified of her!"

"But you don't know that he murdered her, do you?"

"Who else?"

"You bastard," I said. This whole star-crossed mess was because Kassouli had misinterpreted Mulder's lie at the inquest. Mulder had taken money for one lie, then seen that he could make more money by betraying Bannister and working for Kassouli. Now he lay shivering and broken in a sinking boat and, if I could save him, it would only be for a courtroom, and prison.

That fate suddenly seemed closer as *Sycorax* thrust her bows through the crest of the neighbouring swell. I hurled the knife overboard and struggled to the lee rail.

Sycorax surged down the wave slope, then a rolling crest came between us and all I could see was her topmast above the water. I held on to the guardrail for grim life as another crest slammed over *Wildtrack*, and when the water seethed away I saw that *Sycorax* was too close. She was rearing above us and I could see the copper sheathing at her stem. "Sheer off! Sheer off!" I shouted vainly as I felt *Wildtrack* rising, then *Sycorax* seemed to dip towards me as Angela saw the danger. She was too late. *Sycorax*'s bows crashed into *Wildtrack*'s hull.

"Nick!" I heard Angela scream and I knew she would never manage to make the run a second time. I took a breath, willed my legs to push me up, then lunged to seize *Sycorax*'s pulpit rails. If I fell between the hulls now my legs would be crushed to mincemeat. I hooked an arm over the rail, swung my left leg up, and suddenly I was clinging to the outside of *Sycorax*'s bows.

Angela thrust the tiller over to sheer off as I'd told her, and suddenly I knew she would accelerate the boat and she would not know that I was tied to Mulder. When the braidline jerked taut it would be me who was plucked into the sea, not Mulder. He was a great weight in a waterlogged cockpit, while I was clinging by weakened arms to *Sycorax*'s gunwales. I screamed for Angela to slow down, but my voice was lost in the wind. I had thrown the knife away, and all I could do was grab the trailing braidline with my right hand and reach under *Sycorax*'s guardrails to loop it round a cleat. I looped it once, twice, then it snatched taut and I heard the shout of pain as Mulder was plucked out of *Wildtrack*'s cockpit. The loops on the cleat had held, but were slipping now, and I let them slip so that the rope's tension helped to pull me inboard.

I dragged myself to safety. I was sobbing with pain and cold, and dripping blood, but there was no time to catch breath.

Sycorax dipped in a trough and water smashed me back towards the mainmast where I was stopped short by the braidline's tension. I kept that tension hard as I undid the bowline at my waist and knelt up to lash the braidline to a belaying pin. Angela was staring at me, her eyes wide in terror, but she had done all I had asked her to do, and done it well.

I crawled down the scuppers. "Hard to starboard! Engine out of gear!" Angela had turned to stare at the figure who was being towed in the water behind us. "Is that Tony?"

"Starboard the tiller now! Out of gear!"

Angela pushed the tiller over, kicked the throttle lever into neutral, and the strain vanished from Mulder's taut rope. I went forward to fetch a coil of rope from a locker in *Sycorax*'s cockpit. My right leg was shaking, but holding me. I harnessed myself with the rope, then leaned over the guardrails and tied my new rope to Mulder's with a rolling hitch. I released the braidline, then went back to the cockpit. The wind was screaming, or perhaps I screamed, for the pain was making me sob.

I pulled the braidline inboard, undid the rolling hitch, and fed Mulder's line through a block that hung from the boom gallows. Then I began to haul him alongside.

"Is that Tony?" Angela helped me pull.

"It's Mulder. Tony's dead." I could not soften the blow. I was at the end of my strength and I did not know how, in this welter of sea and wind, to break the news gently.

Mulder was too heavy for us. "Pull!" I said to Angela, and we pulled, but we could not hoist him over the guardrails. *Sycorax* rolled her gunwale under and Mulder tried to pull himself up, but he was as weak as we were. "Hold on!" I shouted at him. He nodded and gripped a guardrail stanchion. I cleated the braidline, then fetched my bolt-cutters from a locker. If I cut the guardrails away then a surge of sea would probably roll the South African onto our scuppers.

I cut the wires and was just loosening the braidline from the cleat when Angela screamed. I turned and saw, coming out of the grey-white murk, the bows of a giant ship.

It was a supertanker, a great black monster of the sea, and I saw she had the yellow kestrel-painted funnel of the Kassouli Line. It was the *Kerak*, and her great bulbous bow was heading straight for *Sycorax*. I suddenly remembered Mulder's threat—that Kassouli would sink us.

"Nick!" Angela screamed again.

"Hold fast!" I shouted at Mulder, then I banged the tiller across and throttled up. The great ship was closing at what seemed her full speed and I could do nothing but shout in impotent rage. *Kerak* must have seen us as I shouted, for she seemed to turn. We would not be rammed, but we still risked being swamped, and I instinctively wrenched my tiller to port so that our bows would meet the great tanker's wash head-on.

I turned *Sycorax* and, by doing so, I killed Mulder.

I had not meant to, but I killed him. Or perhaps, mercifully, he was already dead before I pulled the tiller across. I had released the two locking turns on the cleated braidline after I'd cut the guardrails away. I'd done it so that I could pull Mulder inboard, but my alarm at the *Kerak*'s threat had made me abandon the cleat. It still had three turns on it, but the braidline was made of slick synthetic fibre that slipped on the cleat's horns. The surge of our acceleration must have loosened Mulder's grip on the stanchion. He had let go, and his weight had dragged the braidline's loops inch by deadly inch, and with each lurch he had fallen further from safety. As I turned to port a wave had lifted our stern and he must have been thrust under the boat.

The first I knew of it was a chopping judder in *Sycorax*'s timbers, a quivering in the hull, and then I snatched the engine out of gear. Mulder's tethered body bobbed up on the surface and I jerked the rest of the braidline loose and throttled hard forward so that we would leave him astern and Angela would not see him. His skull had taken the propeller's blows.

Then the *Kerak*'s streaked and clifflike hull smashed past, to block out the eastern sky. Faces, made tiny by height and distance, stared from behind the bridge windows. A figure standing on the bridge hurled what I thought was a life buoy towards *Sycorax*. The thing twisted in the air, and red flowers shredded from it as it dropped to the sea.

A wreath for a dead girl.

The wake of the tanker was like a storm wave, breaking and running white. We pounded into the sea, rearing and plunging, and I hurled useless curses at the receding tanker.

154

"What happened?" Angela was staring at the cut guardrails where Mulder had been.

"He died," I said. "My fault." Our bows pitched into what seemed like a black hole in the sea.

"Who died?" Angela asked, and I realised that she was in shock.

"Mulder died."

Her eyes were vacant. "And Tony?"

"I'm sorry," I said. I didn't know what else to say. I was sorry for her, for her husband, even for the man who had died because I had undone the locking turns of his safety line. I would dream about those turns. A life had gone because I'd pulled a rope free. It was a foul dream to add to the one about the man who'd cried "*Mama!*" as my bayonet twisted in his gut.

Kerak had disappeared. I had turned *Sycorax* to face the swell when the squawk of the radio startled me. I forced Angela to take the tiller, pushed open the cabin hatch and leaned down to the set. The call sounded again from the speaker. "This is merchant vessel *Kerak* to yacht *Sycorax*, over."

"*Sycorax*," I responded.

"Is that Captain Sandman? Over." It was Yassir Kassouli's voice.

"Who else?" I snapped back.

There was a pause. "I could not see anyone on board *Wildtrack*. Did you get close enough to see anyone? Over."

"I got on board *Wildtrack*," I said. I was too tired, too hurt, and too cold to be bothered with radio courtesies. "There was no one there alive. No one. Bannister's dead. So is Mulder."

Kassouli's metallic voice sounded after another pause. "Who was the body being towed behind your yacht, Captain? Over."

"That was Mulder. I tried to save him. I couldn't."

"What happened? Over," Kassouli persisted.

"Mulder died," I said. "He just died." I raised my head to look for *Kerak*, but the tanker was now lost in the whirl of windborne spray. She'd be watching me on her radar, though, and I feared that she would turn and come back. "It was an accident," I said into the microphone.

"And Bannister's death? Over."

I hesitated. I wanted to vent my anger at Kassouli and accuse him of murder. I wanted to tell him that his perfect American princess had chosen Mulder for her lover. But somehow, in this stinging ocean, the truth seemed out of place. There had been too much killing, too much anger. Revenge breeds revenge, and I had the chance to end it now. So I hesitated.

"Are you receiving me, *Sycorax*? Over."

"Bannister's death was an accident," I lied, and only after I'd told the

155

lie did I wonder whether my motive was simply to stay alive for, if I'd accused Kassouli of murder, then the great leviathan might have returned and crushed me like matchwood. I pressed the button again. "All three deaths were accidents, Kassouli, all three."

Kassouli ignored my protestation that his daughter's death had been an accident. He was silent. There was nothing but the wind and the sea and the hollow emptiness of the gale's dying throes. Kassouli, I thought, had succeeded and his daughter's soul could fly free. It was over.

I killed the engine, took down the shredded storm jib and set the reefed mainsail while Angela hoisted the mizzen. She pegged the tiller, then helped me down to the cabin where, before I could put butterfly sutures on my cut hand, I first had to peel off my oilskins. I was shaking with cold and fatigue. Angela found the strength to heat some oxtail soup, to wrap me in a blanket, and then to hold me tight as though she could pour her own body warmth into me.

"Tony was dead?" she asked at last.

"He was dead."

"It was an accident?" she asked, and I realised she must have heard my words on the radio.

"It was." I shivered suddenly, remembering the slit throat. I closed my eyes for a second.

"Tell me the truth, Nick, please." But I did not know what cause the truth would serve now. It was over and Angela would live better in ignorance.

"What happened to Tony, Nick?" Angela asked. The seas were hammering our hull, shaking us.

"The boat was knocked over." I made the story up as I went along. "Mulder broke his leg. Tony was struck on the head. I don't think Mulder tried very hard to save his life, but it was an accident. I think Tony died of exposure in the end." I was shivering as I spoke.

"Mulder told you that?" Angela asked suspiciously.

"I saw the body."

I think Angela believed me. If I'd told her the truth about her husband then I do not think she could have resisted using it against Kassouli. Wherever her life went now, I thought, she did not need Yassir Kassouli's enmity to haunt her.

The metallic squawk of the VHF startled us both. "Yacht *Sycorax*. This is merchant vessel *Kerak*, over."

I did not recognise the man's voice.

Angela picked up the microphone. "*Kerak*. This is *Sycorax*, over."

The voice betrayed no surprise that a woman had answered his call. "Our determination is that *Wildtrack*'s hull is a danger to shipping. Can you confirm that there's no one aboard? Over."

156

Angela looked at me, I nodded, and she pressed the microphone button. "There's no one alive," she said curtly.

"Thank you, *Sycorax*. Over and out."

I slid back the coachroof and climbed to the bridge deck. Angela joined me. Neither of us spoke, but we both wondered whether the great tanker would come back to crush us for being inconvenient witnesses to a rich man's anger. We waited two minutes, then *Kerak* appeared from the grey north.

She had come back to finish her rotten task. I saw the swollen bow wave pushing ahead of her, evidence that the engines were driving the tanker at full speed. I could not see *Wildtrack* among the broken waters but the tanker could, and was aiming all her weight at the half-sunk yacht. Angela's face was expressionless.

"Is Tony's body still on board?"

I took her hand. "Yes."

Then the *Kerak* struck the floating hulk. I saw *Wildtrack* ride up the *Kerak*'s prow. She seemed to be caught there like a piece of driftwood. The *Kerak* ploughed on. The windscreens on the bridge looked like malevolent eyes. There were lights behind the windows, and figures moving there in the soft comfort of the huge boat.

Angela cried then. She had loved Bannister enough to marry him. She had put flowers in her hair for that handsome man, and now she watched the dream being sunk under two thousand fathoms of water.

Wildtrack freed itself from the tanker's bows. For a second the yacht's handsome, blue-streaked hull reared up, then, sliding and crumpled, the shattered yacht was sinking down to where Nadeznha Bannister's bones lay, down to where there are no storms, and no light, and only silence.

"Oh, God," Angela said, and it sounded like a prayer. I said nothing, but just watched the tanker recede into the grey nothingness of the ocean.

Only when it had at last disappeared did either of us speak again. "Is there an airport at St. John's?" Angela asked in a small voice.

I nodded.

"Nick?"

"It's all right," I said, "I understand." I'd always known that she was no girl for a small boat in a great sea, but I had dared to hope. Now I knew she would go home, so I set *Sycorax*'s bows towards the west. West towards Canada, west towards parting, and west away from the unmarked place where the dead would lie until the corroding salt made them a nebulous part of the very sea itself.

Sycorax dipped her bows to the sea and sluiced green water down her scuppers. She at least had come home.

We sailed on, in silence.

Epilogue

It was a hard winter. Frosts, fog and a cold to pierce the very soul. Yet it was a hard winter in a good place. I liked Newfoundland.

Sycorax's stem had been undamaged by the collision with *Wildtrack*. One copper sheet had ripped loose, but it took just a few minutes' work to nail it back into place. I re-rigged the guardrails and had a new storm jib made from heavy cotton. The sail took the last of my savings, but Vicky and I did not starve. I found work in a boatyard.

Vicky grew. A rat came aboard and lived just long enough to regret the transgression. Vicky stalked along the frost-rimmed scuppers with her tail aloft in victory. She was my company now; she and the photograph of Angela that I'd screwed to the bulkhead above my bunk.

I had read Angela's letter a dozen times, and now read it again. The verdict at the inquest was that the deaths of Bannister and Mulder were accidental. My notarised and sanitised affidavit had been given scarcely a glance. Angela thought the film about me could be cut into a fifty-minute programme, and would I consider taking *Sycorax* to England so she could shoot an end sequence? But she did not want me to go home just for that sequence. She had taken over Bannister's production company and she knew I could help her. Please, Nick, she wrote, come home.

I sat there getting cold, and staring into the shimmer above the brilliant ice. There was a temptation to go home to comfort and friendship and safety, but I had said I would sail to New Zealand. There was no reason for New Zealand; it might have been Utopia or La-la land for all that it mattered. It was just a goal. I'd gazed, one year ago, out of a hospital window and found a star to snare in a sextant's mirror, and now I was where the star had fetched me. I was alone with a sea cat, and happy. I competed with no one, felt no jealousy, and wished no man ill. Here at sea there were no bad dreams.

So here I would stay, for the time being. I released the foresail sheets and *Sycorax* dipped her bows as we turned, and Vicky pounced on the fluttering sheets of Angela's letter. I picked her up and scratched her under the chin as *Sycorax* caught the wind and drove forward.

"So, now that we've arrived," I said to Vicky, "where shall we go?"

BERNARD CORNWELL

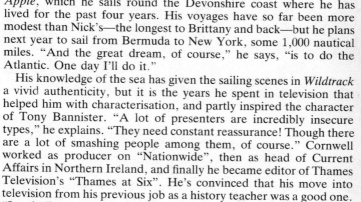

Wildtrack is a new departure for Bernard Cornwell, who is better known for his historical military novels, in particular for his series of stories about the Peninsular War, featuring Richard Sharpe of the South Essex Regiment. "I felt I wanted to do something completely different," he says. He came up with a gripping seafaring adventure which reflects his love of the sea and sailing.

Like his hero, Nick Sandman, Cornwell has his own old-fashioned boat: a gaff-rigged Cornish "crabber" named *Crab Apple*, which he sails round the Devonshire coast where he has lived for the past four years. His voyages have so far been more modest than Nick's—the longest to Brittany and back—but he plans next year to sail from Bermuda to New York, some 1,000 nautical miles. "And the great dream, of course," he says, "is to do the Atlantic. One day I'll do it."

His knowledge of the sea has given the sailing scenes in *Wildtrack* a vivid authenticity, but it is the years he spent in television that helped him with characterisation, and partly inspired the character of Tony Bannister. "A lot of presenters are incredibly insecure types," he explains. "They need constant reassurance! Though there are a lot of smashing people among them, of course." Cornwell worked as producer on "Nationwide", then as head of Current Affairs in Northern Ireland, and finally he became editor of Thames Television's "Thames at Six". He's convinced that his move into television from his previous job as a history teacher was a good one. "It suited me much better than dealing with Form 3C!"

Although Cornwell enjoys living down in Devon, looking to the future he says, "Now that I've got an American wife, and lots of family in America, I suppose it's inevitable that we'll go back there one day." He doesn't know exactly where, but emphasises that it must be "somewhere near the sea". Meanwhile, he intends to follow a busy schedule, writing a new *Sharpe* story every winter, and a contemporary novel every summer. The next won't be about Nick Sandman, though he admits that Nick might reappear one day. "He's still out there somewhere—getting wet!"

WINNER

A CONDENSATION OF THE BOOK BY

Maureen O'Donoghue

ILLUSTRATED BY JOHN THOMPSON

"Never let yourself be without the horses, daughter. They will run for you and bring you riches."

Macha Sheridan has never forgotten her father's advice. When, after his death, she is banished by her fellow gypsies for rebelling against their customs, she is determined to find those riches.

Undaunted, she travels through Ireland alone, begging for food and trading horses like her father before her. Until one day, to her delight, she finds she has a horse that possesses the rare gift of exceptional speed: a filly which, like Macha herself, has the makings of a winner.

Chapter One

The coffin was lowered, and as the first shovel of earth thudded onto its wooden lid Macha felt her eyes become bloodshot. The mourners gazed and shook their heads in sympathy, and she clenched her fists. It was a torment, trying not to laugh.

Hugh Mulligan pressed close and squeezed her. Smelling the porter on his breath, she stepped out of reach and turned to look straight at him. "Da's dead," she said in a low, emphatic voice. "So the wedding's off."

Only the priest's glare stopped the boy's protest. At the sound of his sulky grunt she lowered her head, and hoped the kinsmen thought her shoulders were shaking with sobs.

She was free! One week later she would have been married to Hugh Mulligan, with his pimples and pockmarks, his hair-grease and monkey eyes, and that would have been an end to it. But Da had died just in time.

Macha wanted to sing, and catch the fluttering red ribbons decorating the thornbush they were planting on the grave, and dance round it. She wanted to gulp down the flagon of liquor they were about to pour on the earth, and cause a scandal.

The ocean wind savaged them as the priest, hurrying through his lines, made the final sign of the cross and averted his eyes from the pagan bush. Tinkers! More heathen than Christian. He thought of the dumpling stew heating on the stove, and moved to leave.

The girl, Macha, was standing before him, her expression mischievous, reading his thoughts. He blessed her automatically and hurried away.

The company he left behind stood awkwardly round the grave, looking at one another. Then Hugh Mulligan's father pushed a coin into the soft earth; the poteen was poured, and they began to disperse.

Macha stared at the oblong mound and sighed. Now she wished she had not been tempted to laugh. She wished Da could have been brought here in a fine hearse drawn by plumed black horses. He would have liked being carried in style. "I'm sorry, Da," she muttered. "But everything else was done right."

That was true. His body had lain in its open coffin in a tent on the outskirts of the camp for several days. She herself had eaten only bread and water while he was unburied. He was dressed in his best clothes, and his drinking mug and fiddle and pocketknife were beside him. A round pebble had been set on his chest, and a handful of grain put in his pocket. Nothing had been forgotten.

They were calling her from the gate, their voices petulant.

"Macha, will you come!"

There was trouble brewing. Already she could see Hugh Mulligan talking urgently to his father and jerking his head in her direction.

"Come, child, or you'll be left to walk the road yourself."

She looked down at her father's grave for the last time, then turned and picked her way between the headstones and joined them.

The track was full of holes. A border of stone-walled swatches of grass separated it from the sea on the one side. On the other, the bog ran like a rust-stained tide all the way to the Twelve Bens in the distance, where clouds, heavy with rain, had already obscured the peaks.

"I've a throat on me as dry as a stone in an old shoe," Hugh's father, Michael Mulligan, complained. "Jack Sheridan, God's mercy on him, weighed worse than a knacker horse in that box."

"Hush yourself." His wife, Nan, cast a look at Macha, trailing behind. "It was a fine burial."

Macha heard their voices without registering what they were saying. With a mixture of melancholy and apprehension, she wished the day and night ahead were over and that everything was settled.

The village of Kilkieran came into view at the end of the road. Cousins had travelled over from Dublin; uncles, nephews and aunts had come up from the south to be at Jack Sheridan's funeral; and having done their duty, all now felt deserving of the succour obtainable at Flynn's bar. The pace of the Mulligan clan quickened. Nan took Macha's wrist to hurry her along too, and by the time they arrived, there were fifty or sixty travellers crammed into the back of the close, malodorous cave in the main street.

Mugs and tankards were filled, and there was that tender moment when everyone drew and swallowed his first drench, the contented sigh before the rest of the pint followed, and then the rattle of empty vessels slapping against oak.

The mirror over the fireplace reflected their slippery and demanding faces between the curlicues of its frosted lettering, which read "POWERS' WHISKEY. Estabd. AD 1791. 10 years old Extra Special". Other brands of whiskey lined the shelves on the opposite wall, and the Flynn of Flynn's bar, forewarned of the wake, had removed all other breakables and chairs, and was congratulating himself on having fixed the tables to the floor after the last local fair.

The drinking steadied to an even pace, and the sound of conversation increased from a growl to a smothering roar.

"The roads of Ireland will seem empty without Jack Sheridan travelling them," the panegyric began.

"And him so young! Why, the man was in his prime."

"Aye, and he could tell a tale fit to put a smile on the face of a ferret."

Annie Doran stroked Macha's hair in a motherly way. "And here's the angel child left an orphan."

"Our Hugh will mind her," Nan Mulligan said complacently. "No girl has time for sorrow when she has a man."

Macha sat down on a shadowy bench in the corner as they began to tease the boy about his forthcoming marriage and the number of children he would manage to sire. When he flushed and looked over, she glowered until his eyes slid away.

She stopped listening. It was all nonsense anyway. She was no orphan, her mother having run off to England with a Protestant after her birth, fourteen years ago; and far from being in his prime, her father had been well over sixty, the most unsuccessful horse dealer in all Ireland. He had drunk himself to death. And certainly she would not be marrying Hugh or any other Mulligan. But they were right about one thing. Jack Sheridan could tell wondrous fables.

He had been a large man, with thick grey hair which curved back in a luxuriant shag from his forehead to his shoulders, broad shoulders and a barrel chest. And he had a special voice, bass and expressive, which could purr of love, or crackle of perfidy, or breathe of unbearable sadness—a hypnotic voice, which she could still hear as though he stood behind her.

"You were born at midnight on May Eve, when the moon was so bright that scholars were reading books of Latin and Greek in their gardens and the Dublin shops forgot to close and were full of ladies not knowing they should have been sleeping."

When first he told her, he dandled her on his knee. Later, as she grew older, he had repeated the history over and over, each time further embellished and polished, until it reached the perfection of an ancient ballad, as they sat by the fire together.

"There was to be a great fair that day, and me with the only horse I had to sell lying sickly on the ground, and that creature all there was to save us from starvation. Midnight on the eve of May, the time of the gods, and as you were born, that dying horse scrambled to its feet and threw back its head like a warrior and neighed loud enough to be heard in Ulster, and the light came back into its eyes as though struck in a forge. It was a sign. Macha, the great mare goddess, was speaking and could not be ignored."

And then he would recount the legend from before the time of Christianity, of how Macha of the Horses had fallen in love with a mortal and turned herself into a woman to wed him. "And she was such a woman, tall and beautiful as no man had ever seen, with silver eyes full of mystery, like your own, and shining black hair and long, slim legs, like a true thoroughbred." It sounded like descriptions the child had heard of her mother, and her father's voice would deepen and soften at this point, as though talking to himself, and sometimes he would stop and stare into space before taking a deep pull at the whiskey bottle.

"But the man she espoused was an idiot fellow, and despite warning, he bragged of her grace and speed in front of the King of the Ulaid at the great fair, with the result that the king commanded this woman to run against his finest horse. She was brought before him heavy with child, and she begged that the race be postponed until after the birth. But the king would have none of it."

The funeral faded into the back of the girl's mind as she heard her father recite the tale again, telling of the gleaming, steaming flanks of the king's stallion and of the speed of the immortal; telling how the breath of the horse grew so hot that Macha's streaming black hair was scorched and turned red as she fled before it, and how the throng of fairground folk cheered with joy when the woman won.

"Then Macha fell to the ground in great agony," he would conclude. "And as the birth pangs gripped, she cursed the king and every man hearing her screams, that the men of the Ulaid would remain as weak as a woman in labour for nine generations. And before them all, the goddess gave birth to twin horses."

The day his only child was born, Jack Sheridan had sold his unsound horse for a miraculous sum of money, far beyond its value, and he had named his new daughter Macha in gratitude.

"Never let yourself be without the horses, daughter. They will run for you and bring you riches," he had often promised. "You will have great power over horses and great power over men."

Then, to her incredulity, he had disregarded all his predictions of her special future and, without word or warning, had traded her one night in a public bar to old Mick Mulligan for his pit-skinned son, in return for a couple of nags.

It was the custom at the turn of the century for traveller girls to be married early, sometimes as young as twelve years old. Usually matches were arranged between families related through blood or marriage, and as a first cousin, Hugh was considered a most suitable mate. It was irrelevant that Macha had despised him all her life. "He laughs like a donkey at nothing at all, Da," she had protested in vain. "And everybody knows he's backward. I don't want him."

The horse dealer had promised his daughter a thrashing if she complained again. The deal had been agreed. That was the way it was always done. Then, only days before the ceremony was due to take place, Jack Sheridan died.

Macha stared at the kinsfolk, by now more drunk than sober, and wondered what they would do that night, how they would react.

The women, their woollen shawls wrapped tight about them, looked like a pen of sheep as they spoke with lugubrious enjoyment of other deaths, but Macha had heard them scream with fury over slights and jealousies.

In the murk of the bar the men looked dangerous—black eyes like holes, red rising under their dark skins—and there was that atmosphere of anarchy that marked all meetings between them. Macha felt dread squeeze her breath, and she gulped down the porter.

An argument was developing in the opposite corner, between a Cauley and Manni Gorman. Their voices were already loud and their bodies tensed. The landlord began surreptitiously taking bottles from the shelves and placing them in a cupboard.

Manni's wife put her hand on his arm and was roughly pushed aside. A cousin intervened and was punched in the mouth. The first blood was drawn, and the bonds of the wake burst with female ululating and a violent smell of sweat.

The crowd collided. Old quarrels and rivalries were resurrected, with women clawing and screeching and male fists pounding flesh in an obscene travesty of brotherhood.

Macha had watched the scene before—men brawling over women, women fighting over men or money. Usually she relished the excitement, but this night, as people blundered and fell into her, she felt angry, as though they were belittling Jack Sheridan's memory. She edged along the bench to the door and pushed her way out into the village street.

Local people had already gathered in the dusk. She felt their indignation before she heard their insults.

"Will ye look at the scruff of her!"

"Dirty, filthy tinker."

There was the sound of breaking glass from the bar, and the group moved forward ominously.

"Listen to the drunken animals!"

"Aye, drunk on stolen money, you can be sure of that."

167

"They'd steal the button from your belly."

Macha stopped with her back to a shop wall, very still. The young men among them were restive, keen to join the fighting.

A woman at the back of the crowd shouted, "Let's be rid of the dogs! Run them out of Kilkieran!" And the young men looked at Macha, who was easy prey.

They began to close in. She could see their faces, the tight, right features of settled people. Their expressions were full of hatred. Made bold by their number, they wanted vengeance for their own superstitious fears and for the freedom of travellers. They moved as a pack.

Macha cursed them shrilly. "May God make you cough blood and have stillborn children, and may he drive the fish from the bay till you starve, if you cross a gypsy."

They stopped instinctively as, with profanity and commotion, two Doran brothers came battling out of the bar. The village gang swivelled to see the action, and Macha slipped away, keeping to the shadows, running with silent feet out along the coast road towards the heath where the travellers' tents and carts were drawn up.

By the time she slowed down to cross the stone bridge about two miles from Kilkieran, the ugly little incident had lost its importance. She was accustomed to the hostility of the settled people and the taunts their children shouted when they saw her. She had learned to pay little heed.

A half moon sprayed stars across the sky, and the rippled surface of Kilkieran Bay repeated its reflection infinitely. The fight in the bar would soon be over, and the bereaved would make their tipsy way back to the camp. She hurried to reach it before them.

A motley guard of dogs leaped out, snarling, as the girl arrived at the tents, only to fawn with recognition a moment later. Four horses were grazing at the edge of the bog, and grasping their head ropes, two in each hand, she ran them, stumbling in their hobbles, to where the only bow-top wagon on site was established in ostentatious prominence.

Bartered from an English gypsy, this bow-top had been Jack Sheridan's display of status. At a time when there were very few such vehicles in Ireland and most travellers slept in the hedgerows or under tents of bent hazel rods covered with felts, he would have starved himself and his child to keep it. It was proof that he was no tinker. It was the mark of his claim to be a half-blood Romany.

She hitched the horses to the rear of the bow-top, untied the two lurcher dogs from between its wheels and led them up the steps. The door opened to his familiar smell of tobacco and horses, so powerful it made him seem alive still. She sighed his name and let the first tears free. "Da. Oh, Da."

Macha had not been on her own since his death. For the past five days close kinsmen had fasted and kept vigil along with her, while others had come to view the body. Her Aunt Nan had fussed over the proprieties. There had been no time to resolve the conflicting feelings which stormed within her.

For weeks before his death Macha had been in a state of rage over the way he had matched her with Hugh Mulligan, and after the shock of his sudden sickness and dying had come a childish sense that she had outwitted him and that Macha the Immortal had delivered her namesake. The thrill of escape had persisted until now when, for the first time, she began to understand that she would never see her father again.

In the womb of the bow-top a sensation of isolation overcame her, and she cradled into the hay-filled bed and wept the noisy, gulping sobs of loss and guilt at last.

THEIR VOICES, STILL CANTANKEROUS with porter and whiskey, were carried ahead of them on the wind, and Macha dried her eyes and stood up, straightening her skirts and pushing her braided hair back. A last plea for forgiveness was whispered to the soul of the horse dealer. She knew what she had to do and wondered if it would send her to hell.

The lurchers growled and the men grumbled and there was a sharp crackling as someone threw wood on the fire. "Well, where is she, woman?" Mick Mulligan was heard to ask.

"I've not seen a whisker of her since Manni Gorman there set upon my man and near murdered him."

"Me murder him! Would I bother myself with the likes of him?"

"Shut your mouths, the both of you," commanded Michael Mulligan. "Now, where the divil is Jack Sheridan's daughter?"

"She said there was to be no wedding, Da," Hugh Mulligan said plaintively.

"That was the grief speaking, son," Nan Mulligan explained. "She's probably gone off to sorrow awhile."

"Well, we'd better get on without her, starting with the bow-top," the senior Mulligan decided. "Have you that torch aflame yet?"

Macha opened the door and saw a blazing brand raised from the fire.

"Will you look at that? Another instant and the child would have been kindled to death."

Macha glared at the company. "You will not burn the wagon, nor will the horses and dogs be murdered," she said shrilly.

"She's drunk, Nan. The girl's ranting drunk!" exclaimed her uncle, striding forward. The two dogs appeared, growling, beside Macha. As Michael Mulligan seized his niece round the waist, the lurchers catapulted into attack, one sinking its teeth into his thigh so that he tumbled backwards to the ground.

When the furore had died down, Macha spoke again. "This is my

169

wagon and those are my ponies and hounds now, and I say you will not touch them."

Nan crossed herself. "Macha, the belongings of the dead are destroyed by flame to keep their spirits from returning to haunt us all. You know all that."

"Jack Sheridan told me that the wagon must not be burned. It was his dying wish."

It might have been true, the mourners murmured angrily. The horse dealer had been excessively proud of the bow-top.

Mick Mulligan was outraged. "Now listen you here, you little heathen. Your father's dead, and you are charged to me as next of kin, and you will marry my son tomorrow, so come down out of there this minute, or I'll put fire to the lot, mongrels, nags, yourself and all."

Macha held her breath. The moment had come. She leaned forward and ground out the words. "You are no next of kin to me. And I'd sooner jump into the Shannon with a rock as big as a sheep round my neck than marry that half-witted idiot of yours. You've got no rights over me, Michael Mulligan, because I am not Jack Sheridan's daughter."

There was an indrawn breath from the crowd, and she glared down through the firelight at them. "I'm no orphan. I am *his* blood, the Protestant's blood, I am the child of the *gaujo* my mother lives with now in England. But she is still Jack Sheridan's rightful widow, and all his goods belong to her, and I am her nearest kin. Uncle Mulligan, you have no rights here, no rights at all."

"That's an infernal lie, you evil harlot!" Michael Mulligan rushed at her, roaring abuse. And then he was on her, his blows thumping against her head and her rib cage. She fell into the trampled mud of the enclosure and was hauled to her feet again. "Now take back that lie, ye filthy witch."

Macha shook her head. "It's God's truth," she swore, weeping. "Jack Sheridan himself told me . . . just . . . just before . . ."

"For a dying man, he seems to have done a deal of talking."

"He wanted me to know," she said quietly. "Just me."

The man released her and put an arresting hand on his wife's shoulders as she was about to go to the girl. "Leave the slut alone," he snarled, turning his back. "She is cursed. She is unclean—*mochardi*."

As he walked away the rest of the travellers began to disperse, until Macha was quite alone. Trembling, she climbed back into the wagon and onto the rustling hay again, to lie, ice-cold and staring at the direful knowledge that she had condemned her soul to eternal damnation. For it *had* been a lie, a vile, disgusting lie, and her father in purgatory must have heard her deny him. She had committed a foul sin and she knew she was beyond redemption.

It was many hours before sleep came and then only as a disturbance of dreams full of menace which made her flinch and moan. Jack Sheridan was there, marching nearer and nearer, making her cower, but he did not stop or even pause. He strode straight through her, as though she did not exist. And then faceless people came tramping after, and she screeched and covered her face, and the air shuddered with a hammering of hooves.

When she looked up, the people had gone. In their place stood an unholy woman with hair so long that it reached to the ground in labyrinths and mazes and whirlpools in which men were floundering and calling for help in faint cries. The hair hid half the woman, so that only one eye, one arm, one hand, one breast, one foot were visible. The woman neighed, brassy as a horn, and Macha awoke.

She was wet, her clothes clinging coldly to her back and chest. It was daylight. The camp would be alert, with men watering and feeding the beasts, and women cooking, and children running between the two. Her uncle had cursed her, called her *mochardi*. Had it not been so cold, she would have stayed out of the way, but her teeth were chattering, and pulling her shawl over her head, she opened the wagon door.

There was no one there. The site was deserted, the tents and carts and animals all gone, with no more than the black circle of the dead fire to show where the travellers had stopped. Followed by the lurchers, the girl ran to the back of the wagon. Jack Sheridan's horses were still tethered as she had left them. But everyone and everything else had vanished. And then Macha understood that this was the penalty. They had left her behind. She was completely alone—an outcast.

Chapter Two

Macha was frightened. Her life had been spent among the travellers. They had journeyed the roads of Galway and Mayo and Sligo together. She had never been alone.

The road was deserted. It was empty and muddy, and in both directions it appeared identical, seeming to lead nowhere. The village was too far off to be seen, and there were no houses in sight. Without the fire and the safe ring of tents, she felt bereft. The kinsmen had left no food, and the wagon contained no supplies. After the trouble at Flynn's bar, no traveller would be welcome that day in Kilkieran, and the nearest town was forty-eight hours away. Macha, with hunger cramping her stomach, imagined herself starving there by the desolate track.

None of the animals had been watered, and the morning was half over. A small inland lough lay a hundred yards off, and after untying the horses, she led them to it. They sank their muzzles into its water, and the filly plunged in while the older horses drank.

171

Their calm presence was comforting. In other travelling families women were not permitted to handle horses, but with only one child, Jack Sheridan had been forced to use his daughter's help with the ponies, especially at markets and fairs. Their curving bodies and flowing manes and tails, their elegant shoulders and knowing, bony heads delighted her, and her judgment and eye for good animals had become so acute as to be intuitive. Now, she was simply glad of their company.

The sun parted the clouds unexpectedly, and Macha sat on the grass to let the warmth flutter over her skin. She was a tall girl, still childishly spindly, with long, thin legs that folded awkwardly under her. Pale beside the dark-hued traveller children, she was so different she might have been a stolen child or a changeling, with her deep red hair and bright grey eyes.

The horses had begun to crop the sparse growth by the water, and the rhythmic sound reminded Macha of her own hunger. Already her feeling of panic had receded with the need to make decisions and the first independent moves in her life.

Travelling east would take her to the lodge at Screeb where Jack Sheridan used to stop to do outdoor tasks for the widow who lived there. The woman would certainly give her food, perhaps enough to last the journey to Galway, and there the horses could be sold.

She looked at them and grimaced. They were all too typical of her father's standard of trade—jades that no one would buy. The piebald was ancient, the grey gelding almost as old, his coat faded to white. He was lame as well, but there were tricks to make him seem sound, so he would probably find a buyer. The mare was required to draw the wagon, which left only the filly, who was too light to make a decent draught animal.

The filly wandered up and pushed against the pouch where she knew loose corn was kept. Macha offered her a handful, and the soft suede nose fidgeted over her outstretched palm as the grains were delicately removed. "Who's to say we can't find a blind man with a pot of gold to take you," said her mistress optimistically.

Macha looked all round. There was still no one in sight. Tucking her skirts into their waistband and catching hold of the mare she vaulted onto her back. The animal moved forward, and with her bare legs dangling against its warm sides, Macha was filled with a delicious sense of delinquency.

She was breaking one of the strictest interdictions—that females must never ride. Traveller men believed that women were all *mochardi* from the waist down and would contaminate their horses. Yet whenever her father had left her, she had ridden. Now she dug her heels into the ribs of the horse, which broke into a stately trot, to be followed by the other three back to the bow-top.

There was nothing left to do but harness up. Macha backed the mare between the shafts and tied the three-year-old filly and the other ponies to the back of the wagon. The lurchers were already in their running place between the wheels.

It was then that the girl realised it all truly belonged to her. She walked round the outfit with a swagger. There were few in Ireland travelled in such style, and no mere girls. She could never be forced to live in a tent with any man she did not want. The sense of ownership was exhilarating, and she began to understand just how Jack Sheridan had felt about the wagon. Now she could travel wherever she wished, deferring to no one.

Bobbing onto the driving ledge, she picked up the reins. The mare leaned her weight against the collar, and the bow-top lurched forward onto the track.

SHE HAD SPENT all her life roaming the province of Connacht, from Sligo to Athlone, and so she knew every twist and bend of the road and where each stream rippled into the sea.

This was one of the most desolate stretches of the coast. Here there was no soil, only bare stone and mighty outcrops and deserted, nameless loughs. But Macha knew them all, and the road was her home.

The mare set her own pace, and Macha rested against the frame of the bow-top with half-closed eyes, letting the emotional confusion of the past week fall away. The death of her father and the heinous lie she had told, the rejection by the family—all became part of the past on that day-long journey along the shore. It was almost dusk by the time she reached Screeb. The sea had turned the colour of weathered slate, and the old stone lodge in its surrounding trees was draped in mist, like a dream.

As was the way of all travellers, Macha attended to the horses first, leading them to drink at a stream before hobbling their forelegs with rope. By then it was nightfall, and an oblong of glass brightened at the back of the widow's house, showing that a lamp had just been lit in one of the ground-floor rooms. The hollowness in her gut made her daring, and she approached stealthily.

The back door was slightly open, and the appetising smell of meat wafted out as she peered in at the window. The room was a kitchen, and on a long table lay a whole leg of steaming mutton.

Macha drooled. Late or not, she would knock at the door. She turned and was hardly aware of the looming black shadow before she collided with it, to be clamped in the vice of its arms.

She squealed, and felt herself lifted off the ground and carried into the house, where she was dumped on the floor.

"Just as I thought, a snivelling little tink." The man's features were obscure in the shadows. "And what were you minded to lift, creeping right up to the place like a worm on a wet day?"

"May God cut out my tongue if I wasn't looking for the good lady, Your Honour." Macha's voice quavered from shock.

"And what lady would that be?"

"The widow lady who lives here, bless her for all her past kindnesses to a poor traveller," she gabbled. "Tell her it's Macha, sir. She'll know I've not come to rob."

"How should I tell her when she's been dead this year or more?" the man mocked. He seemed broad and powerful in the gloom, with a commanding moustache. He must be the new owner, she thought, and the fat odour of the joint encouraged her.

"I used to work for the lady, Lord rest her soul; fetch and carry and search out eggs. She was an angel of goodness and would think nothing of giving meself and me da a good feast of a meal."

"Hungry, are you? Always scrounging, you tinkers," the man said contemptuously.

From habit she ignored the insult and wheedled, "I could do the same work for a gentleman like yourself."

"I've no need of a slopeen to find a few eggs," he retorted, and gave her a shove towards the table so that she stepped into the light.

She turned and saw a balding head and an unshaven face with a mouth full of discoloured and broken teeth. He smelled of sweat. He was very drunk.

"Want some meat, do you?" he asked, putting his face so close to hers that she felt the heat of his skin. "Well, a tink like you knows how to earn it." His hand thrust under her cloak.

Macha, whose life had been governed by the strictest tribal taboos, designed to protect her virginity and value as a bride, was petrified.

Instinctively she struggled, making a frantic effort to get loose.

He lost his balance, and she whirled away. The door was open. Hesitating only long enough to snatch up the leg of mutton, she escaped into the night.

Down the slippery cobblestone path and between the clawing bushes she sped, bumping into branches in the moonless black. Already he was out in the darkness behind her, swearing and bellowing for vengeance. She reached the road, stumbled, and raced on towards the barking lurchers and the bow-top.

The man was close. The lurchers were baying uncontrollably. Macha crawled under the wagon, wrenching at the dogs' ropes. The man was there.

Then the first dog was free, and pounced. The second dog joined in. The uproar of growling and anguish was deafening, and under its cover, Macha scurried inside the wagon and bolted the door.

"You filthy strumpet! You'll suffer. I'll hunt you down and have you jailed." His threats ended in a yowl of pain which told her that the lurchers had renewed their attack.

Macha leaned against the door, gasping, and the noise of the fracas outside grew fainter and finally stopped. Within minutes the patter of feet announced that the dogs had returned.

She lit a candle, and cutting some pieces from the leg of mutton, she cautiously opened the top half of the door. The lurchers were standing at the foot of the steps, tongues lolling and tails wagging. She threw them some scraps.

The meat was cold now, but she was too famished to mind. She devoured more than half the joint, and by then she was exhausted. The past twenty-four hours had seemed longer than a month. She just had the strength to reach the hay-lined bed.

Macha slept so deeply that the sun had risen almost to midday before her eyes opened again. Angry with herself for having overslept, she darted outside to fetch the animals and be on her way. The horses could be watered later, when miles stretched safely between her and this miserable hamlet.

She caught the grey and the piebald and quickly tied them behind the van, knowing she should have moved on the night before, as soon as the man had gone. There was something wrong. The sense of danger was tangible, and yet she could not pinpoint what it was. The day was Sabbath silent. Then she realised that it was the very quietness that was wrong. Her attacker had promised reprisals. Yet there was no one in sight.

The filly was some distance down the track, and as Macha hurried towards her she snorted and backed away, stumbling in her hobbles. The mare was stretched out, basking, and the girl whistled to her. The mare was covered in mud and lying very still—too still.

The girl's heart thumped and her mouth went dry. She took a few swift steps forward, then stopped. The mud was red. The mare's head was flung back at an unnatural angle. Then she saw that a massive gash had almost hacked the head from the body, and the blood had gushed out to form a wide pool.

Macha closed her eyes to shut out the sight and wailed a harsh, keening note. The man had taken his revenge many hours before.

The filly was whimpering and shuddering, and Macha ran over, grasped the halter and examined her thoroughly. There were no wounds. With relief, she led the terrified creature back to the wagon and secured her close to the grey.

Although the vehicle was too heavy for the ancient piebald to draw, there was no alternative. She attached him to the traces, and they were on their way at last.

The coast rolled by, but she hardly saw it. Her face was wet with tears.

The mare had faithfully pulled the Sheridans round the West of Ireland in all weathers and had taught the girl to ride upon her patient back. Macha had lost a dear friend, and her head was heavy with thoughts of despair.

Freedom was not as she had imagined. Without the protection of the kinsmen, she was defenceless, and she began to believe she was being punished for the denial of her own father and the breaking of sacred customs.

The quietness as she travelled became intolerable. She longed now for the chatter and shouting of life on the encampment, for the acrobatic daring of the boys as they galloped past in races and for the companionship of the women and the girls.

She tried to imagine married life with Hugh Mulligan. He was not a horse dealer, only a maker of clothespegs and panniers, which it would be her job to peddle from door to door. She would tell fortunes and go begging in the streets and hand him the money she made. She would struggle against the wind and rain to set up the tent at each new camp, and when he was ready, he would come to her with his foul breath and runt's body.

She could not do it. She would not marry such a man. She would go her own way. The first day had been beset with problems because of her inexperience, but she would learn, and if she had to tell fortunes and beg, she might as well do it for herself as for a man she despised.

The road wound round Cashla Bay and through the little settlements of thatched two-room cabins. It was the spring equinox, and the mildness of the weather sweetened the coastal people after the relentless storm-blasted winter. At Keeraunnagark, a shopkeeper responded to her sad grey eyes with a pint of porter and a bag of old potatoes. A burdened girl about her own age promised milk, three eggs and a cabbage in return for a lift to the next village.

Macha camped on the river bank, where the horses could eat the first of the spring grass. Over the fire the potatoes in their skins boiled with the greens, and when she threw some of the leftover mash to the dogs, they bolted it down without chewing.

Refreshed and fed, she felt contented, and when an unbidden memory of the slaughtered mare flickered into her consciousness, she put it from her firmly. That had happened in the morning, and the morning was over.

PALM TREES AND LARGE HOUSES marked the approach to Galway. The roads leading to the town rumbled and rang with carts and carriages as the farmers and countryfolk crowded in for the two-day market and races. They drove small flocks of sheep or gaggles of geese or led a single cow. Everyone was in good spirits, and Macha enjoyed herself.

People admired her bow-top, with its intricate scrolls in scarlet and green and its brilliant yellow-and-red-painted wheels. Young bachelors sidled alongside with compliments, and men with small strings of Connemara ponies were good-humouredly rude about her horses.

Macha drove downhill to the fishing quarter of the Claddagh and found a patch of ground between two buildings behind the harbour. The horses were dirty from the journey, and she brushed the coats of the two she planned to sell, then washed them down with sea water and combed out their tangled manes and tails. Lifting a foreleg of the limping grey, she drove a nail between the wall and the shoe of the sound hoof with a stone. Being tender now in both feet, he appeared to walk sound. Jack Sheridan had always done that with a lame horse, and it rarely failed.

Forced to keep the piebald to draw the wagon, she left him tethered and led the other two over the bridge to the market.

There must have been five hundred horses and ponies round the market square. Young, unbroken ponies milled about, neighing in terror, and worn-out nags were provoked into action before prospective buyers by the heartily delivered sticks of their owners.

The grey was walking gingerly on his sore feet, picking them quickly off the ground after each step. It gave him a sprightly appearance, and Macha was well pleased with her ruse.

"If you've a nag to sell that looks like a mule, stand it next to a donkey so that it looks more like a horse," her father used to say. So she searched until she found a group of broken-down jades and stood her two animals next to them.

"Ten pounds for him," said a voice.

A very drunk farmer was standing in front of her.

"What?" She thought she had misheard.

"Fifteen pounds, then."

Fifteen pounds! It was a fortune. The grey was not worth half that. But Macha shook her head regretfully. "No. I couldn't do it."

The farmer ran his hand over the horse's shoulder, and she held her breath. "He would carry you home twenty miles and take your whole family to Mass next day," the girl said.

The farmer was impressed. "Eighteen pounds and ten."

Macha gambled. "No. No."

"Twenty pounds, then. 'Tis the best I could do."

She held up her hand for his slap before he had finished the sentence, then slapped his smartly in return to confirm the deal. He counted out the notes, and she grinned as the man disappeared into the throng with his horse.

It would not be long before he realised he had bought a jade and came looking for her. Leading the three-year-old, Macha moved to the most congested part of Market Street.

177

With money in her hand now, she bought big, bright pink candies and gobbled them down. Only then did she think about supplies, and purchased some whiskey, tea and sugar, paraffin for the lamp, loaves of bread, onions, carrots and a hare. Then she looked at the filly.

She had lost the will to sell. The afternoon was late, there was money in her pocket, and she had had enough of the crowds.

The fishing boats were putting out from the Claddagh under the moon when she returned. She put the money in a concealed cupboard of the bow-top and, after feeding herself and the dogs, lay down well pleased.

THE RACES STARTED at midday, but Macha was at the Ballybrit course well before that. She had time to visit the parade for the first race, place a bet on a powerful-looking bay and secure a prime vantage point. The horses had strolled around like gods, their eyes remote, their silk-skinned glamour unattainable.

Now, as they cantered down to the start with long, graceful strides, Macha checked her betting paper over and over. Frantic last-minute bets were made and the ring's runners waved wildly to each other until, to a great whoop, the thoroughbreds bounded away.

Everyone pressed forward, straining to see the distant bobbing colours as the horses cleared the fences. The gabble of cries crescendoed, and she heard her own voice join in. The horses rounded the bend, cleared the great bank and were beating towards the last fence, which came and went like a hiccup, and then they were in the straight, clods of turf at their heels like hornets. Everybody was jumping up and down, and to the accompaniment of an earsplitting cheer, the horses passed the post.

There had not been a nostril between number fourteen, the big bay, and number six, a chestnut. Macha hovered by the ring man. She had put a whole pound on fourteen to win at twenty-five to one. If the bay had won, she'd get her pound back plus twenty-five more. A labourer would have to work two years to earn that. She chewed her nails and felt the tension increase unbearably.

The second race started and finished before the word came via a man with a loudhailer. "The result of the first race first: number fourteen, second, number six ..."

She let out a yodel of delight and rushed forward, waving her receipt. A couple pushed ahead of her and as she waited impatiently she saw in the crowd the farmer who had bought the grey.

The bookmaker was counting out banknotes slowly enough to stop a clock and the couple insisted on recounting them before moving away. She handed up her slip. The farmer turned his head and recognised her. The ring man was examining the ticket and frowning. The farmer had begun pushing through the crush.

"Have we to wait until the Second Coming to collect?" grumbled an angry voice behind her.

The bookmaker muttered and thrust out a fistful of notes. The farmer was running towards her, his stick raised. Macha snatched the money and fled, zigzagging through the crowd, bumping into people and ignoring their curses. She could hear the farmer bellowing behind her, "Stop that thief. I've been robbed!"

Out through the gate, down the long road, with hair shaken loose and skirts impeding her progress, back into the streets of Galway she went. She looked over her shoulder and saw the man was no longer in pursuit, but she did not reduce her speed.

Breathless to the point of pain, she reached the bow-top and ran the startled piebald between the shafts. With the filly alongside, the wagon careered off over the bridge and onto the Lough Ahalia road. There the bow-top would be less noticeable than on a main road.

Once safely beyond the city limits she relaxed, letting the piebald set his own ambling rhythm as she counted out her winnings in her lap. She wriggled with pleasure. Altogether, there was enough to buy a string of cheap horses from isolated villages around the province to trade in the towns. The success of the past two days had completely obliterated the earlier feelings of failure.

The wagon followed the road until they came to a grassy semicircle bordering a narrow strip of white sand beach. Still elated by her good luck, Macha reined in, released the tired piebald and watched the dogs hurtle away down the strand.

The filly was jerking her head. The girl put a rope through her mouth, swung onto her bare back, and the animal sprang forward with a massive vault. Then, stretching out her neck and flattening her ears, she streaked along the beach.

The girl grasped the whipping mane as the wind hit her like a wall. She rolled her thighs and calves against the horse's ribs and crouched low in an effort to stay on. The filly increased speed, her stride lengthening until she seemed to flash parallel to the ground without touching it.

Then, miraculously, Macha felt that her flesh and her blood had become one with those of the horse, for they were racing the same joyous race, until at last there was no flesh and no blood and it seemed as though they had become elemental, part of the air and the water, the fire and the earth.

As suddenly as she had begun to gallop, the filly's pace shortened and slowed. The end of the beach rose in a dune before them, and when the rope was pulled the young horse obediently stopped. They stood together, slightly dazed and breathing hard, and Macha knew that she had found her purpose.

Chapter Three

"That horse could run before a train." A boy who had been sitting on a hump of the sand dune rose and walked towards Macha. "I bet she could beat Gallinule."

"She could." Macha looked down at the filly in surprise. Kept hobbled, and exercised only alongside the wagon, her astonishing speed had never before been displayed.

"What's your name?" the boy asked. He was sandy-haired and skinny, and his nose, which had been broken, had not mended straight, so that his face had a lopsided look. He appeared to be about ten years old.

"Macha Sheridan. What's yours?"

"Declan O'Brien." His attention was fixed on the filly, and he reached out to rub her muzzle. "I suppose you race her."

"I do," she claimed loftily, sliding off the hot, damp back.

He watched as she threw the rope over the three-year-old's neck, turning her about.

"Could I have a ride?" he asked abruptly.

"No." She was adamant. "You're too young."

"I'd be as old as you. I'm fifteen, and I'm a racing man," he responded with the defiance of one used to being teased about his lack of height.

But Macha was unmoved. "You still can't ride her, because she's as tired as an old bee now."

They returned along the beach towards the bow-top in silence, the girl wondering whether the speed of the gallop had been just an illusion. The notion of entering a race was unexpected.

"There's sweet water yonder." Declan reached out and took the rope from her. "I'll lead the way while you fetch the other."

He walked on, talking to the young horse so earnestly that Macha grinned. By the time she and the piebald caught up, he was rubbing the filly down with a twist of coarse grass.

He was uncommunicative, almost sullen, as he answered that he lived on a nearby farm, that it was tenanted to his father, that he had six brothers and six sisters.

"Where's her next race?" he asked.

"Killarney," Macha replied without hesitation. "And have you ridden many a race yourself?"

"A few."

"How many?"

"Not many."

"How few?"

"None, exactly."

She gave him a little push and laughed. "If you happen to pass this way in the morning with a pail of milk and a few eggs, you could ride the filly," she offered.

He was waiting at dawn when she opened the top half of the wagon door, and impatiently helped her light a fire and cook a mess of eggs.

With some cruelty, she ate slowly and deliberately before nodding permission to him to vault onto the filly's back.

Fine, dry sand flicked over Macha from the striking metal shoes, and by the time she had brushed it from her face, Declan O'Brien and the horse were meteorically diminishing in faint thunder to the distance. Macha ran to a better vantage point and watched them bend into the return gallop without a pause. From resembling a far-off rocking toy, the boy and the filly bowled back into focus as though wind-blown. They passed so close that Macha felt the filly's heat on her skin, and a twinge of fear that made her shut her eyes.

When she opened them a blink later, the boy was already dismounting. It had not been her imagination, after all. The filly was fast, very fast.

She was so distracted by the new conception of her young horse that she almost forgot to wave farewell to Declan O'Brien, left standing forlornly on the side of the road as she set off for the south in the bow-top. The filly looked fleet, seemed like a winner, but without others to run against there was no proof. She had to be raced, and as they travelled from sun into rain the girl pondered over where to begin, and who would ride her.

The land had changed from the barren rock and stone of Connemara into a rolling prettiness of wide, fertile fields where sleek cows grazed. Macha drove past a large camp of travellers, and arriving at the edge of Gort, she was glad to leave the bow-top in a clearing and walk among the people.

It was a fair-sized village, with rows of cottages, expanding unexpectedly into a garrison town with a spired church and a square of important buildings.

From a doorway a soldier shouted, "Clear orf, tinker! We don't want the likes of you round 'ere."

Townsfolk turned to stare and mutter. Macha felt her face burn, and she slid down a side road to escape attention.

The lane led to the deserted marketplace, its ground uneven and littered with empty wooden sheep pens. There was a board outside the only stone structure. Torn and out-of-date announcements of sales and auctions still clung to it, alongside a brash, fresh poster: KILLARNEY BUMPER AND PONY RACES AND HORSE FAIR, 1 MAY, 1895.

It had to be a portent. The day before, she had told Declan O'Brien that the filly would race at Killarney. Now she was being directed there. It was only five weeks off. If she went there immediately, the filly could be given a good gallop each morning and extra corn rations until the day of the race.

But after she returned to the wagon and was on the road again, she realised that the project was a practical impossibility. Apart from the fact that the other horses would be experienced—hunters and jumpers perhaps, against which the scruffy filly would not stand a chance—there was also the insuperable problem of having no rider. For not even the boldest horsewoman in the province would have been permitted to take part in a race.

She continued in the direction of Killarney anyway, worrying over this complication. Half the day was gone before the girl emerged from her reverie to notice that the old piebald no longer walked straight, but staggered unsteadily from one side of the road to the other. Then he stopped and sank to his knees. Jumping from her seat she hurriedly released him from the shafts. The pony slumped between them to lie groaning on his side.

Macha was stricken with remorse. "It's been the death of you. I should have bought a decent animal in Galway." She put her ear to his rib cage and felt the irregular heartbeat. "You're worn out as a granny's corset, you poor old soul."

She stroked the pony's head, and he looked back at her through eyes without lustre. She rubbed his ears with gentle regret as he buried his nose in a feed bag of corn. An animal that could not work was no good to her. He would have to go. The next day Macha managed to exchange the piebald for a tough, headstrong mule that was beyond the control of its elderly master. By the time she had reached Limerick, she had sold the mule to a young farmer as brawny and boneheaded as the animal and bought from him a good strong mare.

Macha drove along the north bank of the Shannon, looking at ships anchored beside a line of quays and, behind these, the houses of Limerick. The little party followed the river past castles and abbeys, heading for Kerry. At the kitchen entrance to a great house she was given bread, a bowl of soup and a bundle of clothes by a kindly cook, before being chased away by the butler.

Rumbling along soft earth paths, lighting dusk fires in woods dangling with catkins, galloping the filly down tracks and strands—all this formed the easy pattern of the journey. Evenings with golden skies deepened into rich sable nights, through which Macha slept untroubled, for she had lost her fear of being alone and no longer found the solitude lonely.

ABOUT A MILE short of Killarney they turned up a steep lane to where the view opened out over a magnificent lough to a range of awesome peaks, all overhung by one darkly purple mountain. The turf of the north bank stretched like baize for about two miles, and there was a ruined round tower and sheltering church walls—the perfect place to camp for the fortnight before the races.

The decision to run her horse had now become an obsession. The three-year-old, already fit from daily work and extra feed, would do her proud; yet there remained the impasse of having no rider. All travelling people would be aware of her disgrace by now, and they would not help her. There was no one else she could ask. Another day closed, and once again she sat impotently before the flames of the fire.

The lurchers, which had chased off after idly thrown chicken bones, returned, snarling over a large rag. Pulling it away from them, she saw it was a garment from the bundle given to her at the great house. As she held it out, a slow and beatific smile spread across her face. Here it was, the answer she had searched for. Now the filly would certainly race.

The morning of the fair, Macha stood looking at her horse. Then she looked at herself. They were both filthy. In such a state, it would be impossible to ride to the fair, let alone enter the filly for a race. With a noisy sigh she collected a can from the bow-top and led the filly to the edge of the lough. She slowly rinsed the mud off the saddle in the shallows. Then she took off her jacket and vaulted onto the filly's back. Clenching her teeth, she kicked hard and rode straight in.

Ignoring the whinnies of anger, she deluged the encrusted head and neck and swabbed them clean. All sensation had gone from her own legs. She filled the can with water and tipped it over her head. I'm a lunatic, she thought, sluicing the dirt away. If I'd married Hugh Mulligan, I'd never have needed to wash at all.

At last she steered the filly towards the shore. The rising sun cast a rosy path across the lake, and the horse and rider emerged like a legend, a silver armour cascading from them and shimmering ethereally in the clear light.

Macha returned to the bow-top to dress. From the bundle she had been given, she took out the clothes she would wear. The man's trousers were far too long, so she tied them up with string. Then she plaited her hair and stuffed it under the old cap. When she put the shirt and the tweed jacket on, she looked like a lanky lad in hand-me-downs and was ready to ride in any pony race.

THEY REACHED THE FAIR in good spirits, and although it was early, the racecourse was full of activity. She tied the filly to a hedge and worked her way round to the weighing room, where a number of officials scurried about.

"I want to put a horse in the races," she said, stopping in front of a man seated at a table, writing.

"Name of owner?" he asked, not looking up.

"Patrick Sheridan," she replied.

"Name of rider?"

She took a deep breath. "It's myself, Patrick Sheridan."

He entered the information without question.

"Name of horse?"

She hesitated. The filly had no name.

"Well?"

"Macha's Girl."

"Which race?"

"All of them, sir." She was enthusiastic.

"That's impossible. Are you selling her?" he asked crossly.

"No, she's not for sale."

"Then she can't run in race number two today or four tomorrow. Age?"

"I'm sixteen," she lied.

"Not you, you young dolt. The age of the horse."

"She's a three-year-old."

"Too old for the third race tomorrow, then."

Macha began to believe that the filly would not be permitted to enter at all. "She must run, Your Honour," she insisted desperately. "We've come all the way from Galway. She's got to race!"

"There's only the qualifying race for tomorrow's bumper left. That is the first race, twelve o'clock today. If she's placed in the first six, she can enter the fifth tomorrow." He was scribbling as he spoke. "That will be one guinea."

Macha counted the coins silently into his hand and concentrated on the coming ordeal. The filly had never been tested against others, and Macha had no idea what her tactics should be. Her lips were dry with apprehension.

There was no nonsense about weighing in or wearing silks for this race. Each rider was simply allotted a number, walked his mount once round in parade and then made for the distant end of the track.

All manner of nags and men were there, and they pushed, sidled and backed while the starter issued impossible orders in a vain attempt to arrange them in one straight line. The girl did not take her eyes off him, while the filly, amazed at the commotion, stood like a rock, with only her pricked ears betraying tension.

Eventually, hoarse and frustrated, the starter gave up the struggle and dropped the flag. The filly took off by mere instinct. Macha pushed her feet home in the stirrups and drove her mount on. The response was magical. The little horse stretched for the front runners, passing the third and second and drawing level with the leader with smooth, giant strides. The two horses ran nose to nose and Macha, hearing the other jockey shout, turned her head and felt a cutting pain across her neck. Her balance shifted, but Macha's Girl had winged ahead and was galloping straight and true for the post. The three-year-old showed no sign of stress and could have raced on to America. The winning post spurted by, and a huge bubble of excitement broke in sparkling effervescence over them.

They had won! Nothing in Macha's life had prepared her for that moment—for the glory and the crowds, the sunlight and the emerald grass, the rich steam rising from the filly's skin, her own thundering heart. The winning of that first race on the scrawny little beast was unique, and was to inspire all the rest of her days.

Someone took the reins and led them through the crowd. The onlookers stopped pushing and made way quite suddenly, their voices dropped, so that it became remarkably quiet.

Her neck ached where the jockey had slashed it with his whip. She put up her hand and withdrew it, covered in blood, and understood why the mob was backing off. What a sight she must be.

A very important person was approaching, beaming at everyone else without looking at her at all. "I have great pleasure in presenting the five-pound prize to the winner," he announced, then turned. His smile was replaced by a look of disbelief, followed by an expression of disgust. He stepped back.

"The sinfulness of it," Macha heard a woman say.

She could feel the blood trickling and looked down. Her jacket was open, and her shirt had been torn half off, baring her breast.

"Be jabus! That's no lad! That's a damn woman!" The exclamation came from the back of the gathering.

The very important person was shouting to a policeman, "Sergeant! Arrest that woman for gross indecency."

Macha dug her heels in hard, and the filly catapulted forward, scattering the functionaries. Ignoring the chaos, she headed for the fence and soared over as racegoers on the other side ducked to the ground beneath her.

Macha and the filly sped on to the wooded end of the course, and the police sergeant on a big, strong bay pounded after them.

The filly covered the soft earth without leaving a trace, not the mark of a shoe. The pursuer and the shrieking multitude shrank behind her. The trees rolled aside like parting waves and received her into their canopied and mysterious obscurity.

At last rider and horse felt safe enough to slow to a jog, putting the town behind them but going away from where the bow-top waited. By now the whole of Killarney would be agog at the outrage of the woman who had ridden half naked round the racecourse, and there was no possibility of her returning by the route she had come.

On the far side of the water Purple Mountain ascended aggressively within the dark and gloomy range of Macgillicuddy's Reeks, which seemed impassable. When they stopped to rest, Macha bathed her cut neck, buttoned her jacket securely over her torn shirt and wondered how she was going to reach her home.

Looking down the expanse of the lough, she saw a horse pulling a cart across a narrow isthmus that divided the lake. Sounds of singing came from the cart, and Macha cantered after it.

Three very drunk men were lolling and bawling in the back of the cart, while the horse walked with the purposeful resignation of one habitually left to find its own way home.

"The luck of the day to you all," said Macha politely.

They were dressed in bowler hats and homespun tweed suits—three farmers on an outing. "And you'll have been to the fair too?" the first said.

"Not I. My master wanted me for work," she invented. "Would you know if there's a way north through the mountains?"

"There's Moll's Gap to the chasm of Dunloe, but although fools have passed into it, there's not a one known to have passed out at the far side." The farmer waved vaguely towards a narrow fissure between two sheer precipices. "In there, rocks the size of churches tumble from the heavens, and tempests worse than at sea rampage for ever in the centre."

His companion, who had been watching her through narrowed eyes, reached out and caught the filly's reins. "If the crooks at the fair had paid out on the first race, I'd have cleared three guineas this day." His squint focused, and he pointed an accusing finger. "I know that one," he roared. "That's the winner! That's the devil's daughter that took the first race— and my five shillings."

The farmer tugged on the reins, and the filly reared and bolted, her rider clinging to her neck. The unfamiliar ground was strewn with shale that rolled beneath the horse's shoes and ricocheted, cracking like pursuing shot. The terrified animal tripped and swerved, then headed blindly up the winding path to Moll's Gap.

A waterfall gushed towards them through the opening. Boulders had been tossed from its course, leaving holes to become swirling pools through which they splashed and stumbled. The filly gave a huge lunge, and they were through the gap, into the ravine of Dunloe. Instantly, it was pitch-black. The young horse floundered and went down. In a burst of lights Macha hit granite as she crashed to the ground. She regained her senses briefly once, then settled back into oblivion.

Night became wan and smeared into grimy grey. It was morning at last. Macha felt the lump on her head and sat up, wincing, to find herself on a floor of algae-covered rocks, walled in by flat, wet slabs. There was no sign of the three-year-old.

186

Macha stood up, and reeled. The cut on her neck throbbed, and there was an ache behind her eyes. Not far ahead, a second waterfall plashed through the ceiling of mist. She made her way to it weakly, bent forward and cupped her hands, and drank until her stomach felt full. Then she began to look for her horse.

Overhead cornices and ledges were so delicately poised that it seemed the slightest sound or breeze would bring them hurtling down. Yet the draught echoed through the tunnel, and the water skirled and chorused from the interior ahead. The track plunged down and down and then opened into a wide and lovely glen, at the northern end of which was a lake. Standing up to her knees near the edge was the brown filly.

She nickered on seeing the girl, who ran to her, delighted. "What are you standing there for, you gossoon?" Macha scolded affectionately. "I thought I'd lost you." She took the reins and tried to draw her forward, but the filly did not move. "Come on, come on. I want a good feed, even if you don't."

The three-year-old staggered from the shallows on three legs, her offside foreleg dangling.

"Oh, what's happened to you?" Macha stared in dismay and put out an exploratory hand. The leg was burning to the touch and very swollen, and Macha wondered fearfully if the cannon bone was broken. There was no cure for a horse with a fractured leg, and the filly would have to be put down. Helplessly, Macha rubbed the velvet nose.

There was no alternative but to go on. "Come on, mavourneen. Macha will mind you." And with the reins over her arm, she set off, the filly faltering behind.

The rocks were dangerously slippery, and Macha lost her footing more than once. The young horse stopped at each stream and had to be cajoled to risk the crossing. After two hours they seemed to have covered very little distance, and they were both exhausted. Macha sat down and began to cry. Then there came a soft breath in her hair. The filly was nudging at her shoulder, gazing at her with wide, kind eyes.

"You're so much worse off than me and still as brave as a badger," Macha said, feeling ashamed of herself. "I'll get you out of here yet."

The way became so narrow there was barely space to pass. Then they rounded a bend, the gorge ended and wooded country stretched before them. The shores of the lough curved off to the remains of a monastery, and there, sheltered by its ruined church and tower, stood the bow-top.

MACHA GAVE THE FILLY a big bag of feed and pressed a water-soaked pad to the wounded leg and secured it with a bandage of rag strips. Only then did she go inside, change out of her wet clothes and get herself some hot tea laced with whiskey to stop her shivering

187

She climbed into the hay-lined bed and called the dogs. They jumped up, one on either side, and soon she felt their body heat wrap around her. The sensation of utter contentment and security was relaxing, and without further concern she fell asleep.

The dogs were gone when she woke. She could see stars through the doorway, and she waited, aware of fine hairs rising on the back of her neck. Not a whisper. Not a sigh. She reached above the bed for her father's shotgun, inching it from its rack and then swinging it to the floor. Two steps to the opening and a soundless drop to the grass.

He was there, furtive in silhouette against the moonlit lough.

"Stop where you are, mister, or I'll blow your belly open!"

He started visibly.

"Come over here," she ordered, and he came closer, close enough for her to see he was a young man, lightly built and not tall. His eyes glittered, unblinking, and his bold Romany face looked at her without a trace of alarm.

"What are you doing here?" she demanded harshly.

"It's nothing. I'm stopping for a day or two in the wood yonder and thought I'd just take a look at your pony."

The truth dawned. "You were stealing her, you scrub! You were stealing my horse." Macha was enraged, and the gun twitched dangerously in her hands.

"Will ye put that thing down!" he gasped, suitably nervous at last. "Wouldn't it look untidy to have the likes of meself spattered all over this lovely spot?"

His gaze flickered; she swayed out of reach a second before he struck out to seize the weapon. Her heart jerked with anger. She took a step forward and pressed the gun against his chest.

"I was not going to steal her," he said with apprehension. "I might have borrowed her for a while, that's all. She'd have won me a few races, Macha Sheridan."

That he knew her name was ominous. It meant that he knew all about her, where she came from, her behaviour after her father's death, the scandal of the Killarney race, everything.

He followed up on his advantage. "It seemed a shame that a brilliant beast like that could never run again because she hasn't a jockey."

"I'll find a rider," Macha said defensively.

"There's not a man in the land will ride for you, as well you know."

Certain that she would not shoot now, he lit his lantern and turned towards the filly. The light fell on her injured leg, still bulging under the rough bandage.

"What have you done to her?" he shouted at the girl. "The curse of hell on you! You've wrecked the best horse in Ireland."

"She fell. There was no helping it." Macha's voice was high-pitched in self-vindication.

"There was no helping it? Look at the mess of her." The man ran a hand tenderly down the filly's shoulder and began talking to her, his voice changing from rasping contempt to a crooning. He started to undo the rags, and the horse recoiled. "Steady now, steady, baby," he murmured over and over to the filly, easing the wet pad off and then cajoling her into the lough until the water reached to her knees.

"Keep her here till I come back," he ordered her owner, who found herself wading in barefoot to do his bidding. He strode off towards the woods without glancing back.

Macha's teeth began to chatter. The stranger was gone for a long time, and when he returned, it was so quietly that he was almost at her side before she was aware of it.

"Bring her up on the turf," he said, pouring some liquid from a bottle into his palm. He rubbed his hands together and then stroked down the filly's face to her nose. She half closed her eyes, and for the first time she lowered the crippled leg to the ground.

"Now hold her fast." The man opened a jar carved out of horn, and acrid fumes rose from it. He scooped out a dollop of the substance and spread it over the puffy flesh with quick fingers. There was no doubt he knew what he was doing.

The animal's eyes jerked open and she screeched and reared. Macha was sent sprawling. The stranger caught the rope halter and tied it to a wagon shaft, humming to the shocked filly until the snorting and shuddering finally stopped.

"Will she be all right? Is her leg broken?" Macha, covered in sludge, was on her feet again and staring at the horse.

"There's no saying till the swelling goes down, but I'd guess the tendon's torn."

The girl was abject. "Then she'll never race again."

"Oh, she might. Or she might do something better," he hinted cryptically. "Now, have you whiskey for a man, or do you not?"

Half an hour earlier he had been about to rob her. But now, concerned only with the fate of her horse, she realised she needed his knowledge and help. She led the way to the bow-top.

He hesitated at the top of the steps, afraid of Jack Sheridan's spirit. Deliberately she stood inside, a bottle of whiskey in her hand. He cleared his throat and entered.

She poured, then passed the mug to him.

He did not take it, but regarded her, unsmiling. "Drink it yourself, Macha Sheridan, to warm you," he said.

The whiskey, bitter as peat fire, blazed its way to her stomach.

"Now get rid of those soaked clothes," he instructed. "Wrap this about you." He pulled the thin blanket from the bed.

She had never undressed in the presence of a male before, not even her own father. She waited for him to leave the wagon, but he merely drew a pipe from his pocket, lit it and turned away.

She undressed, hiding herself with the blanket. Finally she pulled the wool tightly round her and sat on a bench.

The stranger took the bottle and drank directly from it. He poured some more whiskey into the mug and handed it to her. "Drink this, and sleep," he said. "I'll come back to see to the pony in the morning."

Then he left.

Whiskey and tobacco fumes seasoned the air in the bow-top, just as they always had during her father's time. She breathed in deeply and was somehow consoled.

Chapter Four

The man announced his arrival in the morning with tuneful whistling. The filly's injured leg appeared miraculously improved, but he was pasting on more ointment. This time his patient stood stock-still and unconcerned.

The girl was able to contemplate him without being observed. He was slim, but his shoulders and biceps curved powerfully under his heavy jersey. Thick, black, straight hair kept falling into his eyes and being tossed back impatiently as he worked. Macha blushed, remembering the night before. He looked up at that moment and smiled, reading her thoughts.

"What is that stuff?" she asked, pointing to the horn jar.

"Oh, just the feather of a toad and the juice of a dandelion and all my grandmother's beard." He grinned and talked down to her as though she were a child.

She decided she disliked him. "I will be moving today." She made the statement as a challenge.

"Yes. I was going to suggest you shift the wagon into the woods by my tent." He spoke as though he expected to be obeyed.

"And why would I move the bow-top under the trees when a ruby could not be better set in gold than it is in this place?"

"Because it must be visible for twenty miles." His eyes were full of amusement. "If the punters who lost their money on the racecourse find you here, you'll likely finish up in jail, or worse."

A cat on a silk cushion with a mouse under each paw could not be more smug, she thought, and flounced off to harness the mare.

EACH DAY THE MAN dressed the filly's wounds. By the end of the week the leg was reduced to its normal size, and against her will the girl was impressed. But she wondered why he was taking the trouble. The filly would surely not race again.

Meat was roasting over the fire one evening when he was suddenly there, standing in the dark, observing her through the smoke. "Do I get something to eat?" he asked.

She gestured for him to help himself.

"I knew Jack Sheridan well," he said.

"He never talked about you."

"How would you know that? You don't even know my name."

It was true; she had no idea who he was. It was obvious that he was a Rom, perhaps even a pureblood, but she had deliberately not asked questions. Now she waited, looking uninterested.

"Molloy, I'm called. Coper Molloy."

Molloy the Coper—the horse dealer—there was a name! Her father had said Molloy the Coper knew more about horses than any man living or dead. But she gave him a scathing stare. "What would Coper Molloy be doing in an old tent with not one horse of his own?"

"Is it horses you want? Well, I'll take you to them tomorrow, down beyond Kate Kearney's cottage." He tore off a piece of meat and nodded patronising approval of her cooking. "As for knowing your father, didn't he buy every broken-down pony I ever traded?" He laughed.

"That's a dirty lie!" Macha, roused by this slight on her father's reputation, threw a tin cup of water at him.

Molloy guffawed. "A lie, is it? What about that little brute that tossed so many buckeens off its back that Jack Sheridan offered a prize for whoever could stay on more than five minutes?"

A picture of Mick Mulligan being thrown repeatedly over a wall as he tried vainly to win the ten shillings invaded her mind. She gave in with a gurgle, and then laughter engulfed them. It shook the girl and rocked the man, and each time one managed to stop, the sound of the other still hooting was infectious.

Macha could see her father again, trying out ponies with his feet almost scraping the ground. And then she remembered his jokes and his stories, and her laughter turned to gasps, and she was sobbing out her grief piteously.

Molloy was there. She hung on to him for the smokiness of his jacket, for the hardness of his frame, for the marrow of his humanity. She did not want to stop weeping. She wanted to stay there against him.

His hand was on her head, smoothing her hair and her forehead, and then she was pressing her mouth against his palm and breathing very deeply. The sobs stopped, and a strange calm filled her. She opened her

191

eyes. Molloy smiled and went on talking as though it had not happened.

"How would it be if I took the little pony off your hands?" he offered unexpectedly, some time later. "After all, no one will buy her with that scarred leg, and she'll not race again."

It sounded a casual offer, but Macha, who had been waiting to discover his interest in her filly, was alerted. "No," she replied shortly. "And don't think to cod me, Molloy. You might as well tell me what you're after."

The coper looked at her with appreciation and asked, "Do you know where the filly came from?"

"Da bought the mare, her mother, in foal, but how would I remember where?"

"Well, I can tell you where, Macha Sheridan. He bought that mare from a tenant of a very important gentleman called Mr. Charles J. Blake, a steward of the Turf Club, no less—"

Macha interrupted. "What's so unusual about that?"

"Before she was sold, that mare had got loose and had a little adventure." He grinned. "The sire of your filly was the stallion Bel Demonio, the winner of two races in England worth one thousand pounds each. A local lad, who'd been party to the catching of her, gave me the tip, except that by the time I got there, she'd gone to your father and he wouldn't part with her."

Macha remembered being mildly puzzled that her father had not sold the foal after it was weaned.

"How would you like to go into partnership?" Molloy reached his purpose at last.

The girl was confused. "Share the filly with you?"

"No, not the filly. The filly's foal. When it's born next year."

Macha began to think he was deranged. "She's not in foal!"

"No. But she will be, and there's only one horse for her. With him she'll produce a real goer that'll make us our fortune."

"And which horse would that be?" There was no hiding the scepticism in her voice.

"Gallinule."

"Gallinule!" Macha gaped at him incredulously and then shrieked with laughter. Molloy was obviously quite mad.

She was still giggling at the thought of mating her scraggy three-year-old with the sire of the last Irish Derby winner, when he stood up.

"I've work to do," he said briefly, and walked off into the darkness.

"ARE YOU NOT UP YET?" The hoarse whisper woke her. It was not daylight, and she could barely see his outline as he stood in the doorway of the bow-top. "We should have been on the road half an hour back." He spoke urgently. "Now, let's be off."

192

Macha stumbled to the steps, rubbing her eyes.

Molloy ran past, leading a string of horses. "Come on, come on," he said.

Sleepily Macha began to collect the tins and utensils from around the ashes of the fire.

He came past again, this time with her horses, and thrust their halter ropes into her hands. "Hitch them up and follow me," he ordered. Then his cart rumbled by, outlined against the lough, and she found herself flapping the reins and rolling after him.

Molloy set a gruelling pace, so that the town was soon behind them. His cart was some distance ahead, and Macha wondered about him. With his sly black eyes and his jaunty walk, he looked like the kind of man who would have a lot of women. She felt unaccountably annoyed.

When he pulled off the road, she caught up. He pointed to the grassy river bank and said, "We'll rest there."

He quickly set up a fire, and to her amazement he put a griddle on the heat and added eggs and slices of smoked ham which he produced from the back of his cart. She had never seen a man prepare food before. Cooking was women's work, and she was embarrassed when he held out her share.

"Did you imagine I lived only on neat whiskey?" he teased. "Or do you think you're the only one who breaks the rules?"

This was the first time he had referred to her past, and she dropped her head and concentrated on eating.

"What about your own people?" She was curious why he travelled on his own.

"No family and no people," he answered. "Which is not to say I don't join up with others now and again. But it's best I'm on my own to deal with certain matters."

"Like trying to steal my horse," she could not resist saying.

He gave one of his quiet smiles and poked the fire. "The Connors and the Wards are good friends of mine, and remember the Maughams, if you're ever in need." He was looking at her seriously, but she was not sure what he meant.

When they had finished eating, he stood up. "Get a kettle boiled, Macha Sheridan. You've a lot to learn now that we're partners." And walking over to the grazing horses, he caught a black-maned bay with a white blaze and two white socks and tied him to the cart.

He fetched a large pair of scissors and hacked off the lovely mane. By the time he had shortened the tail by several inches, the water was hot. He added some reddish-brown powder in a glass jar to make a paste and mashed in oil and beeswax and some black drops from a small bottle. When satisfied with the colour of the paste, he began to paint it on one of the hind-leg socks with a short-bristled brush. Within minutes all traces of white were gone.

"Your turn." He handed the jar and brush to Macha. Now she knew why they had left with such stealth.

"Is this one of the horses that Kate woman was keeping for you?" she asked daringly, as she worked.

"Kate? Oh, you mean Kate Kearney's cottage." He beamed with inexplicable amusement. "Ah, well, it might be and it might not. You know how ponies come and go. Just like pretty cailins."

She would have liked to throw the dye all over him.

"Now," he said, "we'll just turn this blaze into a fine big star."

"Will the colour not wash off?" she wanted to know.

"Try and see." He pointed to the river.

Macha untied the rope and gave Molloy a sidelong glance that he could not translate. Without warning, she gathered her skirts into her waistband and sprang. She landed on the horse's broad back and whooped her mount on.

He felt a twist of terror and shouted out, but they had already cantered to the water's edge, entered without hesitation and started downstream with spray glittering over them. Her laughter vibrated above the wash as the hunter sped safely over the underwater rocks and carried her towards a bend in the river, round which they vanished.

Molloy leaned against the bow-top, shaken by his own reaction, and cursed himself for having brought her with him. For a moment he almost wondered if he were the victim of sorcery, caught in the trap of a spell cast by a witch.

With a splashing of hooves, the girl and the horse plunged back. They rose out of the water and lunged to stand over him—the horse gigantic, his red-hot nostrils blowing smoke, and Macha above, godlike, her clothes moulded to her in alabaster folds.

His heart was in his throat. He could neither move nor breathe. An uncontrollable desire coursed through him. He seized the girl's arm and dragged her from the horse, thrusting her against the wagon, forcing back her head until she was staring at him from a face as white as his own.

"Are you angry?" Her voice was tremulous. "I didn't think you'd be angry."

He took a step back and could hear himself saying, "No . . . no. I'm not angry." He felt violently sick. "I . . . I . . . was worried, that's all." He turned away. "It's time we went on."

A few miles further on, at a big house, the hunter fetched sixty pounds, an excellent price. But Molloy did not seem content. He pushed a few of the banknotes at her and slouched back to his cart, and they drove miserably past the shore and the colourful boats in Bantry Bay.

Since the scene by the river, Molloy had kept distance between them, hardly speaking, and refusing the food Macha had offered during the midday stop. She stared ahead at him, sitting loosely on the cart, and wished he would look back and wave or smile.

That evening, when they camped, Molloy fed and watered his beasts, then walked off without a word. Macha baked some potatoes in the embers of the fire, then ate them from habit, and waited. He did not return.

Restless, she remembered the smell of his clothes and the warmth of his breath as he had held her. Perhaps he was disgusted by her behaviour. Impossible images flooded her mind, nebulous and sinful—his naked back as he washed in the lough, his all-knowing eyes, meeting mouths.

Suddenly the dogs bundled from beneath the bow-top, yelping, and she heard his voice chastise them. He sounded drunk. Macha knew she should stay out of the way. Yet seconds later she was entering his tent. He had lit a lamp and was sitting on a straw pallet with a bottle in his hand, and he gave her a look she translated as hatred.

"Get away from here. Go back to your place," he shouted.

She knew if she obeyed he would be gone from her life for ever before morning. She swallowed and knelt on the grass beside him. "I'm sorry I rode the big hunter. It was *mochardi*, but I never thought you'd mind," she said humbly.

He looked at her in disbelief and shook his head. "Girl, you ride like a vision. What in the world is *mochardi* but old wives' tales? You were made to be with the horses. Don't let anyone on this earth ever try to stop you."

"But I thought you were in a rage."

He shook his head again and said in a hard voice, "You turned down Hugh Mulligan, your father's choice of a husband for you. Why?"

It was an unexpected question, and she did not know how to react. "I did not like him, and I did not want him," she said.

"Is it not a woman's duty to obey?" he demanded.

"But I could not. He was like a nasty white jellyfish, a pasty little slug," she protested.

There was a measureless silence, and then he looked at her deliberately. "And what am I like, Macha Sheridan?"

"You are ... You are like ..." she whispered, and sank against him, closing her eyes tightly and finding his mouth with hers.

Responding at last, he was almost ferocious, clamping her to him with a hard arm, then gradually becoming more restrained, more tender, until he was able to ease her away.

A deep flush covered her face. "Molloy?"

"I promised my mother I'd marry a virgin," he said with a grin.

"Amn't I a virgin any more?" she asked.

He felt shocked and enchanted at the same time and gently drew her back against him. "Of course you are. It takes more than a kiss to change that. But it's not good for you to travel about with me unwed. You need to be protected, and I would do that. Macha Sheridan, will you marry me?"

She was speechless. "And is that the reason you are proposing?" she finally asked.

"No, no, my silly filly!" The irrepressible smile spread again. "I'm going to marry you because we were made for each other, because I want you. Now, for the last time, will you marry me?"

She gave a squeal of excitement. "Oh, I will, I will!" She leaned against him, and in the light of the lamp his skin was glossy and his eyes glowed. "I know what you are like. You are like a fine, wild horse," she murmured. And then, as he pulled her closer she asked, "What would you do if I was not a virgin?"

"I'd marry you anyway, little goddess."

"Then, why do we wait? We could do what married people do, now," she said.

"You brazen baggage, and how would you know what married people do?" He glowered in mock disapproval.

"Oh, I know, all right. My cousin Kate Mulligan told me. They . . . they go to bed—" She took a noisy breath and added in a rush, "They go to bed together naked!"

Molloy howled with mirth and gave her a mighty bear hug. "And so will we, my darling girl, but for tonight, and for every night until the wedding, you will sleep in your bow-top. For no one is going to say Molloy took advantage of an orphan girl."

With that, he picked her up and carried her back to her wagon.

ON THE DAY BEFORE the Cork races Molloy had a furtive conversation in the bar with a man whose bow legs and leathery face proclaimed him a stablelad. "The mister," he introduced him cryptically to Macha, who was to learn that his tipsters were always called the mister.

On the third race Molloy won fifty pounds and gave it, all in notes and gold coins, to Macha. "Spend it on a fancy gown and trinkets for the wedding," he instructed.

"This much would buy the crown jewels of England," the girl said, intimidated by the idea of squandering it all on clothes.

Macha went off to a grand shop in South Mall, and as the shopgirls tried to block her way she slowly displayed the money and watched their faces change. A man in striped trousers and a tailcoat hurried to her side, bobbing his head deferentially.

She bought a length of bright pink satin and cards of coloured ribbon for a skirt, three white silk petticoats and a cream chiffon silk blouse with ecru embroidery. Then, at the jeweller's, the glint of sovereigns again worked magic, and in no time trays of necklaces, brooches, rings and bracelets were spread before her. Macha had never seen such treasures.

After an initial nervousness she relaxed and bought three gold bangles, a gold shamrock bracelet and matching brooch, and a gold bracelet with two moonstone hearts set in pearls.

A plain silver sovereign case lay at one end of the counter. The jeweller picked it up and handed it to her with a flourish. "With our compliments, madam," he said, and slid the remaining coins into it.

THE CROWDS LEAVING Cork Park cantered, red-faced and jolly, downhill to the bars in the town, impeding Macha's return with her parcels. By the time she reached the campsite, Molloy was pacing beside the harnessed horses.

"You can't pick and choose the time for these things, you know," he scolded. "If the filly's not at Brownstown Stud by next week, it won't be worth putting her to the horse this year at all."

"Why not?"

"You want to race the foal, don't you?"

She nodded.

"Well, racehorses take their age from the first of January, so the earlier in the year he's born, the better chance he has."

They left that same evening. Their route, past small, tidy fields, was lined with hawthorn and wild roses, and Macha was glad to have left the congestion of towns and racecourses.

Five more days and they reached the broad heath surrounding the Curragh, the racecourse on the road to Dublin where races had been held since kings ruled Leinster, and before. As they drove in with the dawn the girl jumped from the bow-top to stand on the sacred turf. It was as though she had returned to the birthplace of a previous self, in the age when war-horses trampled and unicorns tilted with golden horns.

"I have been here before," she said as Molloy came to see why she had stopped. "In another time, long ago."

He looked at her pale face and believed it, sensing in her a growing power that disturbed as well as attracted him. "We'll camp in a covert beyond Brownstown House," was all he said.

They passed training stables and stud farms and the beech-lined entrance to Brownstown, and were soon positioned in a small wood about a mile beyond.

"There are more eyes and ears around the Curragh than hairs on a bear," Molloy warned, "so when our man turns up this evening, keep out of it and don't look interested. He's not to be frightened off."

When the man arrived, she gave him whiskey, and he and Molloy walked behind the wagon.

"It'll take a deal more than that, man," the stranger said, scornfully refusing the proffered money. "If it came out, not only would Captain Greer sack me, but I'd never work again."

"Think about it, mister. Your usual groom's fee is only ten shillings, and I'm offering sixty—no, *seventy* pounds," the coper urged. "Why, you could buy out your Captain Greer with it."

"I'll tell you what, Coper Molloy," the mister said, after scanning the fan of notes with a mixture of greed and caution, "Gallinule might have an hour or two in the paddock at dawn the day after tomorrow—but no promises." So the money was handed over.

Molloy and Macha stayed on the site all the next day, behaving as tinkers were expected to do. She washed clothes, and he whittled at wood and whistled. But that night they padded the filly's hooves with rags to cushion the sound and led her by an elaborate detour to a field at the far side of Brownstown.

At five a.m. they heard the first activity in the stable yards.

"Will he come?"

"He'll come," Molloy confirmed. "Or we'll lay the gypsy's curse on him."

"We could have bought a cracking horse for all that money," Macha ventured.

"But it wouldn't be the same," he pointed out, chuckling and giving her a squeeze.

Then, as the sun blazed over the horizon, a boisterous bunch of yearlings were loosed into a lower paddock. Next, the broodmares stepped out with their foals. At last a man appeared, opened the gate and freed a big chestnut horse with a white blaze and three white socks into the field.

"That's Gallinule. That's the sire of the best," whispered Molloy.

For a second the great stallion stood with ears pricked and head raised, catching the morning. Then, with a ringing whinny, he began to canter round the perimeter of the field. In the brilliant light, he shone like living mahogany. He looked fit and hard, virile and strong.

Suddenly he stopped, facing them, his nostrils stretched and fluttering. The filly, which had been standing quietly, took a step towards the fence and nickered. Gallinule trotted forward excitedly.

Molloy lifted out the rails of the fence. "Now lead her in," he said.

The filly tossed her head, and the most magnificent stallion in all Ireland neighed, a primitive, brassy challenge. Then Macha's Girl stood calmly and received him.

Macha led her filly—a little mare now—out of the field as Molloy started repairing the fence. "Make her step out," he said, "we want to be well away while they're still over there in the yards."

Having watched the mating, Macha had become unexpectedly embarrassed and avoided Molloy. She had begun to realise that marriage could not be as simple as she had believed, and she found much to do inside her bow-top. Just before they started off again, he caught her arm and turned her quietly to face him. "We'll join up with others soon, for it's time you had women round you."

Macha felt a quiver of alarm. "They'll not want me. I'm *mochardi*. They'll cast me out."

"No one casts away Molloy the Coper's bride. So no more fretting yourself over what is to be a time of joy. All will be well." He spoke with infinite kindness, gazing into her worried eyes, and she was grateful for his understanding.

WITH MACHA'S GIRL preciously pregnant, they pushed along the lanes and byways leading north. They covered many miles and changed direction frequently. Once, Macha woke to see Molloy walking away through the trees. He looked furtive, and something stopped her from calling him.

The next evening at twilight two strangers visited Molloy. They were well dressed in suits and bowler hats and did not look like either travellers or racing people. There was an intensity about the meeting that made her keep her distance, and after they had left she decided not to ask Molloy about the visitors.

"We'll be there by morning," he said later.

"And where would that be?"

"Where kings ruled and fairies laughed and priests wore white and the goddess came to the fair," he answered.

Sometimes, with his puzzles and mysteries, there was no knowing him, she thought, and bit her lip in irritation.

THE HILL OF TARA was a low pillow on the night, and as they approached it the air became still and balmy. They left the bow-top and the cart and began to climb.

"King Laoghaire is here, buried upright in full armour, waiting for his army," Molloy's low voice told.

They climbed over two banks and found themselves enclosed by the circular earthworks that surrounded a bigger hummock on which stood a stone emitting an eerie green light. Petrified, Macha turned to escape.

"Wait," Molloy said. "We must touch the stone."

"No! I cannot."

"You must." He grasped her wrist and pulled her onto the mound. The light turned black and brilliant. Macha cried out as Molloy forced her against the stone.

There was a roar as she caught a glimpse of Death, with his hollow eyes turned on her. And then she saw beyond him, into a measureless radiance, an incandescence in the centre of which was the Power. Then silence, silence as reviving as a long, blessed draught, as cooling as a zephyr, and Molloy was sitting by her on the grass.

"You are of the ancient people, Macha," he said with awe. "*Lia Fail*, the royal stone, knows you and has revealed the secret to you. We'll be wed in Teach Miodchuarta, the banquet hall here at Tara, in three days' time."

Next day Molloy woke her by hammering on the door, and she was surprised to find the bow-top surrounded by tents, carts and even other bow-tops.

A woman stood beside Molloy, middle-aged and grave, with the straight eyebrows and full, curving mouth of a true Romany. "Biddy Connor," Molloy introduced her. "She'll look after you."

The woman nodded to Macha without smiling, and he left them, as though the situation needed no further explanation.

"Wild girls make poor wives. There was a tidy girl kept for a match with Molloy the Coper," Biddy Connor said. "But perhaps he needs more than that." There was a pause while they looked at each other. "And maybe you will do."

Macha felt as though she had passed a test.

Everyone present knew her background, but the fact that she was to be Molloy the Coper's wife seemed enough to overcome their reservations. Biddy Connor and her daughters helped to cut and sew the pink satin skirt and to stitch the yards of coloured ribbon round its hem. They all seemed excited by the prospect of the celebrations to come.

More families arrived daily. Everyone wanted to be at Molloy the Coper's wedding. But Macha did not see him at all, not even the night before the wedding, when she went nervously to bed in the Connor tent with all her jewellery and finery laid out in readiness. Biddy Connor snored comfortably beside her, there as official guardian of her virginity, and Macha was grateful that for once she had broken no taboo and done nothing to threaten her future life with Molloy.

IT WAS THE MORNING of the day, a dawn tingling with summer. The women crowded about Macha as she dressed. The girl, who had never before received such attention, preened and paraded. She felt proud and a little afraid. Then it was time.

The turf over which she walked was strewn with scarlet pimpernel and trefoil. Together with the women, Macha began to climb Tara. Molloy and the men were nowhere to be seen.

Teach Miodchuarta was a long, narrow hollow enclosed by parallel earthen banks, high enough to stop the wind and trap the sun. At the far end, Molloy was waiting. She walked slowly towards him, and when they met, they joined hands and turned to face the crowd.

"I, Cormac O'Neill Molloy, do take you, Macha Sheridan, for my wife, and I vow to honour and protect you all our days."

"I, Macha Sheridan, take you, Cormac O'Neill Molloy, to be my husband, and I promise to love and obey you all our days."

As she committed herself he did not smile, and she saw in his serious gaze another, stronger man, almost a stranger.

Someone handed them a small loaf of bread and two rose thorns. They broke the loaf in two, and Molloy pricked her thumb and she, with a little shudder, pricked his, and the drops of blood fell on the two halves of bread, and each ate the piece that held the blood of the other.

The fiddlers began to play, and with arms about each other, Molloy and Macha led the way back to the encampment, and the feast began. Mouth-watering smells filled the air, and they ate soup fragrant with herbs, and roast beef cut into succulent slabs. And it was all washed down with gallons of poteen. The fiddlers sawed out reels and jigs without pause, and when everyone else had dropped to the ground from exhaustion, Biddy's daughters and two boys spun into a fiery dance. Molloy, his face bright, clapped and stamped to the rhythms.

When the sky had darkened and the stars came out, the music stopped and the dancers drew aside, leaving the bride and groom alone in the centre of the arena. Then the married women ceremoniously unpinned Macha's red hair, letting it fall to her waist.

"Come," said Molloy at last, and she followed him gladly.

They did not go to his tent, but returned once more to the occult enclosure of Tara. "Kings married goddesses here," said the coper, before kissing her unhurriedly and gently, as though for the first time.

Together they sat on the grass by the stone. His skin was as dark and velvety as a rose under the moon, his hair like the wing of a raven, his eyes like garnets, and as he put out his hand Macha moved to him.

The fire they lit burned round them in a ring, illuminating the mystic hill, awakening the spirits of celestial lovers, reviving memories of epochs before St. Patrick. Then the night cloud extinguished the glowing moon, and in the bliss of love Macha and Molloy slept.

Chapter Five

Macha lost her look of bony immaturity, and the mare was no longer a gawky filly. Throughout the summer and autumn they travelled, and by the time they reached the outskirts of Dublin, both were round-bellied and quite matronly.

It had been a good year. Molloy had bought and sold horses very profitably, and the race meetings across the country had paid off well. He was a fine husband, caring, lusty and generous. There was no doubt that he worshipped Macha, fussing about her health and spoiling her with presents. Yet there was a part of him she did not know, a concern with matters he refused to discuss. Occasionally he would go away for a day or two and offer no explanation, and more than once she found his cart loaded with boxes that were too securely nailed for her to discover their contents.

Once, she asked him outright where he went and what he did. He replied that every man was entitled to keep his own counsel about private business. She continued to feel uneasy.

Instead of travelling throughout the cold months of the year, they stopped in an established winter camp to conserve Macha's strength and that of the little mare. Biddy Connor and some of the wedding guests were already on the site to the south of Dublin when they arrived, but they found a good position, slightly apart from the rest and out of the prevailing wind.

Rain fell week after week, and the mud on the encampment deepened. Then the snows came, at the beginning of the new year, and the temperature dropped so low that icicles hung on the inside of the bow-top windows each morning. Molloy bought thick woollens for Macha, and the stove in the wagon was lit.

As January dragged into February, tempers, always volatile among the travellers, became shorter. Wives picked on husbands, husbands replied with blows, and there were daily fights among the younger men.

Macha longed to escape from them all. She pleaded with Molloy to leave the encampment, but he insisted that this was impossible as he still had transactions to complete.

"I don't want my baby born here among the rats and the muck," she complained tearfully. "I want him born in Connemara."

He put his arms about her. "We'll be on our way at the first breath of spring," he promised.

Molloy kept his word. When April came at last, they were on their leisurely way once more, and in this final month of Macha's pregnancy he was by her side all the time.

They crossed over streams and brooks and rills and journeyed back to the luminous west. Macha, who had been away for more than twelve months, had not realised how much she had missed the region. To return was like a homecoming.

"We will stop here," she said when they came to Clew Bay, and the bow-top seemed to guide itself into the very haven on the bay where Jack Sheridan had drawn up every year since her birth.

THE GREY TOWN was busy that evening, and the bar was full. The couple did not see the young travellers in the far corner as they entered. But the Mulligan brothers and those with them saw Macha, and Hugh Mulligan swaggered up, stopped in front of her and deliberately spat on the floor.

Almost before he realised what was happening, he was pinned against the wall by the throat.

"That is my wife," snarled Molloy. "And you will grovel to her, boy."

They all watched as Hugh Mulligan struggled and received a winding jab below the ribs.

Molloy, wrenching the youth's arm hard behind his back, steered him to face her. "Now, what do you say to Molloy the Coper's wife?"

"I'm sorry," muttered her erstwhile fiancé.

"She has a name," prompted the older man.

"Macha Molloy."

"And don't you ever forget it, sonny." The coper released him, and the brothers trooped out sheepishly.

The incident took the enjoyment from the outing and left her depressed and tired. She was now so big with child that it was impossible for her to sit comfortably.

They returned to the site and there, in the fresh air, she was unexpectedly filled with energy and began turning out the bow-top. Despite his objections Molloy found himself directed to beat the mattress, while drawers and cupboards were emptied and cleaned.

Eventually he shooed her to bed, climbed in grumbling beside her, and was unconscious in minutes. But Macha, able to lie only on her back, stared up at the sky through the tiny window. Molloy had wanted to put up a special tent, as was the custom, but she had rejected the offer, determined to have her child in the bow-top. Now she wondered if she had been wrong, if breaking another taboo would bring bad luck. She felt restless, and her stomach was upset. She shifted her position to ease the cramps. Pain rumbled through her gut, and her muscles strained. Then another spasm gripped her, and she struggled to rise.

Molloy awoke to find her in tears. "It's all right, mavourneen," he comforted. "It's the baby coming. I'll fetch the doctor."

She held fast to him. "No! You mustn't go."

"You'll need help, Macha, and I'll be no time at all."

"Stay, Molloy," she shouted, but he had gone.

Rain crackled like fire over the wagon, and the hound of the wind clawed and howled at the door. Only yards away she could hear the Atlantic booming in the storm.

The contractions came quickly now, and shaking with fear she tried to pray. But she could only shout obscenities.

"Merciful heaven, are you alone?" The woman's voice sounded far off. "Where's the doctor?"

Macha opened her eyes to see her aunt, Nan Mulligan, and she grabbed her arm in frenzy. "Auntie Nan, something horrible is happening to me. I'm dying!"

"*Ach*, Macha, you've no time to go dying, with the baby arriving at any moment. Now, let me go. I've got to put a kettle on."

The woman shook her arm free and bustled noisily about the stove, stoking the embers and clattering the kettle.

Finally Macha let out a scream, and all at once Nan was there, holding up a damp, red, wailing boy baby, no bigger than a handspan.

Macha held out her arms feebly.

"Patience, girl." She heard water splashing, and then the baby, clean and wrapped in a shawl, was lying on her breast.

They dozed together for a time, and only the continuously rolling pain kept Macha from drifting into deeper sleep. When a sharper pang struck unexpectedly, she gave a yelp.

"Would you credit that!" Nan exclaimed. "It's to be twins." And the second child swam into the world like an otter. "You have a cailin this time," she said.

The door burst open, and Molloy pushed an unenthusiastic doctor through it. Nan rounded on them with a stream of abuse—for being too late and for daring to enter the bow-top at all at such a time.

The doctor gave Macha a cursory glance and left, with obvious relief. Molloy was banished to the weather.

Later, Macha, suspended between sleep and wakefulness, just caught her aunt's whisper. "I'll have to be away now, but don't ever let on to Michael Mulligan that I was here, or he'll kill me."

The girl nodded her gratitude, marvelling that her aunt would have crossed the cursed threshold.

When Nan had departed, Molloy crept in, dripping wet, and stood with awed eyes beside her. It was the first time she had seen him nonplussed, and as she smiled she caught a hint of her own capabilities and sensed that the balance between them had subtly changed.

THE TWINS WERE HEALTHY, and both their parents enjoyed them, Molloy even cradling them when he was certain no outsider would catch sight of him, for babies were women's concern. They named them Tom and Molly.

The days were lasting and lustrous on the road to Galway city. Leaf buds were fat on the twigs, and a green film of early growth flimsily dressed the uplands.

Then one white dawn the mare dropped her foal. When Molloy and Macha arose, the colt was unsteadily on his feet and suckling. He had the wide white blaze and three white socks of the champion. "Will you look at that. He's the image of Gallinule," the triumphant coper exclaimed.

They called him Gold, for his coat and his future, and as they drove on he trotted behind his mother across the world-famous grass of Ireland and grew almost as they watched.

In Galway, they pulled up on the waste ground in the Claddagh, and Macha, the twins held to her by her tied shawl, walked to the docks, where the air smelled of fish and salt and spices. Coasters and fishing boats were tied up at the quays. Two tramp steamers were unloading, and men were heaving bales, shouting and singing. Molloy was in among them somewhere.

That night he went off with the pony and cart. She ignored his instructions to stay in the bow-top, and followed him. On a deserted corner of the docks three men met Molloy, who was soon helping them lift boxes onto the cart.

"Cork, is it?"

"Cork it is."

Macha left and was waiting on the steps of the wagon when he returned. "You're to tell me now," she demanded.

"It's best that you know nothing," he parried.

"I must know."

"There are people I help out sometimes. People of the cause."

"What cause?"

"*The* cause. The cause of Ireland. *My* cause, Macha."

"Do you mean the Fenians? I won't believe you're any part of that demented rabble. What are they to you, a Rom?" Macha was incredulous. She knew travelling people were offered no clemency in any land, and in return they gave no allegiance.

"My father died in an English prison. Not for horse stealing. For being a Rom. And my mother died of hunger and cold in the winter of seventy-nine, when I was eight years old."

It was the first time he had talked of his family. Macha had heard stories of the famines, of the evictions and emigrations, of those who had taken to the road after the potato crops failed. But to her and to most travellers, the English were almost indistinguishable from the Irish. And who ruled the settled community was unimportant, for whoever rules harasses travelling people. However, she knew Molloy better now. She did not completely understand his commitment, but she admired him and would have helped had he permitted.

FROM GALWAY they followed a route south as far as Cork, where she woke one morning to discover that the boxes had gone from the coper's cart. Molloy was buoyant and happy and turned their vehicles to follow the coast to a small hidden bay. Soon they were running and splashing through the shallow waves. The babies were dandled with their tiny feet kicking the spray, and the dogs dived in after sticks and stones.

For a month they lazed by the sea. Wearing improperly few clothes, they would ride the horses bareback through the swell. The babies turned rosy and brown as two russet apples. The foal grew taller on legs like slender stilts. Macha wanted to stay there for ever and even caught herself imagining a thatch-roofed cottage on the edge of the strand, where they would all live. It came as a shock when Molloy began loading the cart one morning.

"Oh, could we not stay a few days more?" she pleaded.

"Then you might not get your present," he replied obliquely.

"What present?"

"The one I have to go back to Dublin to collect."

"You're teasing. Just a day longer."

"All right. You'll have your day. We'll leave tomorrow," he said, grinning. "And maybe you'll get the present as well."

So they swam and played with the babies; they kissed and made love and crammed a whole second month into that last day.

THEY DID NOT HURRY to Dublin, but zigzagged from town to town, trading horses. Finally they drew up on the banks of the River Dodder. The babies were left sleeping as Molloy drove Macha into Dublin in the cart. They arranged to meet at the foot of Sackville Street by the bridge, and he drove on, leaving her to wander up Ireland's most famous thoroughfare, to gape enviously at the well-dressed folk.

When he picked her up again, the cart was laden under the spread tarpaulin. They walked at the pony's head, and Molloy handed Macha a large envelope. "Your gift," he said.

She had pictured a dress, or maybe a brooch, and looked at the envelope doubtfully.

"Take a peek," he encouraged.

Inside, she could see documents.

Molloy was positively smirking. "They are the papers for Gold—pedigree, registration, everything he'll need to race."

"But how can you have a pedigree giving him as Gallinule's foal? Everyone will know it could not be."

"You're right," he agreed. "But here's the beauty of it." He paused, looking vastly pleased with himself. "I've arranged for him to be imported—from America. Our little colt is officially the offspring of a thoroughbred mare called Precious Stone and a stallion called Philosopher, retired to stud in Kentucky."

Macha gazed at him in open admiration.

"We won't always be living like this, goddess," he said. "One day we will be rich and you'll be covered in diamonds."

She giggled and took his hand, resting her head on his shoulder as they strolled. They did not see the black, horse-drawn van approaching rapidly from behind, until it passed and slewed across their path. The doors of the van swung open, and a dozen policemen leaped out.

"Go! Race for your life," Molloy yelled, giving her a brutal push. "Save yourself, Macha!"

A constable caught her wrist. She twisted and sank her teeth into his bare hand and tasted warm, salty blood before he swore with pain and released his grip.

Instinct and panic gave her speed. Fleeing across the wide street, she looked back over her shoulder only once. Molloy was surrounded. The cover had been pulled off the cart and the boxes exposed. No one was bothering to pursue her.

Macha slipped down a dark lane. A long way off, there was a small explosion.

She did not stop until she had reached the bow-top and locked the door behind her. She was shaking, too afraid to guess at the contents of the boxes but aware that Molloy was in serious trouble.

She tried to do what Molloy would have wanted, to calm down and concentrate. There was plenty of money, which could be used to help him, but the unthinkable kept pushing its way into her mind. Gulping back tears and feeling helpless and alone, she hunched for hours in a turmoil of impossible ideas, too distracted to light the lamps as evening spread across the city.

Then, suddenly, there was someone in the bow-top, and turning, she saw him standing by the door. "The Connors and the Wards are good friends of mine, and remember the Maughams, if you're ever in need." The ghost of Molloy repeated the words of long before, and then as she stared, he was gone.

The fretting of the babies invaded her reverie. She concentrated on them, spinning out the tasks to escape her thoughts. But once they were clean and fed and sleeping again, there was nothing more to do except wait, wide-eyed and motionless, until dawn.

THE ENCAMPMENT was still heavy with slumber when, jumping from the bow-top, she charged into Biddy Connor's tent, cast herself on the woman and hysterically blurted out the news.

Biddy's eyes pierced hers with glittering hatred. "Hold your noise this instant! Do you want the world to know?"

But the world had already heard, and women were stuffing infants into carts, and men were rounding up ponies and cursing and shouting in their haste to leave. As Liam Ward came running towards them Macha looked about the site in bewilderment.

"Why is everybody going?" she asked Biddy Connor.

"Because the police will be here in a trice, you stupid scrub." The older woman glared at her. "What did you mean by coming here and causing discomposure in us all!"

"Leave it, Mrs. Connor," advised Liam Ward. "Just get her and this thing away." He pointed at the bow-top. "I'll go into Dublin and see what I can discover. We'll meet tonight by Lough Tay."

He left, and without another word to Macha, the Connors packed up their cart and indicated that she should follow. They urged their pony to a canter, and the bow-top whiplashed dangerously as she tried to keep up. When they were well away from the city, they drew up in a secret valley in the heart of the mountains.

"You've got to tell me." Macha confronted Biddy Connor. "What has Molloy done?"

"Are you saying you don't know about Molloy the Coper?"

"I know he took messages sometimes for the Fenians."

"Messages, is it? That's the first time I've ever heard guns described as messages."

"Guns! Oh, Mother of God, no!" Macha felt her world shudder.

The woman, full of contempt, came so close that the girl flinched. "You brought this about, Macha Sheridan, tainting him with your *mochardi* ways, bringing that unclean wagon among us. It was Satan's day when he set eyes on you."

The Connor girls had gathered behind their mother, faces distorted with loathing, and Macha feared they were going to attack her. But Liam Ward arrived, his face white and drawn. "Leave me to talk with Mrs. Molloy," he said.

They moved back, and then she knew. She knew it all.

She must have spoken, although she did not hear a sound, but he was nodding and patting her arm pointlessly. "So you see, Macha, they never got him to jail. He put the pistol to his head and shot himself, God forgive him, right there in the street."

That distant little explosion as she had been running away through the alleys—it had been her man dying.

Liam was speaking urgently. "You'll have to get away, girl. They're hunting for you."

"Why?" she asked, confused. "What would they want with me?"

"You're his wife. You were with him, and they think you were in on it. You'll need to leave Ireland. They never give up the search when treason is involved."

She was floundering, quite uncomprehending, as Biddy and the man began to make plans over her head. She would have to go to Rosslare, cross the water to Wales and go on to England. They'd never think to find her there.

"Have you any money, girl?"

Macha nodded dumbly at the wagon.

"Well, fetch it and whatever else you want, for you will not be taking that monstrosity along."

"It's my father's bow-top. I cannot leave it," she protested.

"Leave it? We're going to burn it!" Biddy Connor shrieked at her, in grief and rage. "As it should have been destroyed long ago."

Biddy threw herself into the bow-top, and the contents came hurtling out. She finally emerged, panting, and thrust the tin box of money and jewellery at Macha.

"Get rid of it. Put the flame to it, Liam Ward."

The girls held Macha back as the man sprinkled the gaudy walls with paraffin and then lit it. With a boom the flames reared over the bow-top, and the fine scrolls and decorations split and blackened. As the blaze grew hotter, one by one the windows blew out, and with each she heard again the explosion of her husband's death.

They left her alone, and she crouched by the ashes, weeping bitter tears and listening to the terrible emptiness in herself where Molloy had been.

BIDDY BROUGHT OVER a bundle of Molloy's clothes. "Wear these," she said. "They'll not be searching for a boy. We'll put you on the road to Rosslare. Take only what you need."

"I know no one in England. How will I live?"

Biddy Connor indicated the tin box. "You won't starve."

"But I want to stay here." Macha began to cry.

The woman stood over her, her eyes cold. "There is nothing for you now in Ireland, girl. With Molloy gone, no traveller will welcome you. You have flouted our ways, and you are to blame for his death. You are not wanted here, Macha Sheridan."

It was an annihilating statement, implacable and icy. Without another word, Macha went behind a tent to change.

The clothes were warm, as though Molloy had only just discarded them. It was like climbing into his skin, and strangely, she gained strength from it. Returning to the fire, she began to push her hair under his old cap.

"That will not do at all. How will you keep your head covered day and night?" Biddy drew a pair of long scissors from a bag and, as the girl knelt obediently before her, hacked off the long red hair. Macha knew it was the woman's revenge.

Then they were on their way, the women and the babies piled in the cart, the man on a pony, leading her other horses in a clattering group behind. Macha sat with Molly and Tom in her arms, drawing comfort from their smiles and their trusting faces.

LATE THE FOLLOWING AFTERNOON they stopped outside Wexford. "There's a cattle boat leaving Rosslare at midnight," Liam told Macha. He and Biddy Connor exchanged a peculiar look.

"About the babies," the woman said grimly. "They cannot go with you. They must stay here."

"You're mad, Biddy Connor! I'd never leave my children." Macha was more astonished than outraged by the idea. Then her eyes narrowed. "And you needn't think you're getting them, you old witch, if that's your latest plot."

Liam moved between the two of them. "Macha, you can be certain the police know all about Molloy and you and your children. They'll be looking for a tinker with twin babies."

Macha swept the babies into her arms. "No! They're Molloy's and mine. He will not stand for you stealing them," she cried crazily. "I'll be dressed as a man. No one will guess."

"And what would a lad be doing with two infants? Of course they'll guess." He reached to take them, and she screamed. A pit was opening before her.

"What will happen to them when you're arrested?" Ward shouted. "When they lock you away, what will happen to them then? I'll tell you, woman. They will be put into an institution and brought up as orphans. Then they will have no mother and no family at all."

"Oh, Blessed Mary, Mother of God," Macha prayed.

"I will take the babies and look after them as if they were my own." Biddy, finally softened by the girl's anguish, put her arms around all three. "And in a while, when the fuss is over, we will send the children to you."

Biddy Connor took the babies from her at last. Macha, stunned, waited for a miracle. No miracle happened.

The Connor girls had packed two panniers with her possessions and strapped hazel rods and a canvas to Macha's Girl. The rest of the horses were roped together and ready to move. Liam Ward outlined the five-mile route to Rosslare and lowered his eyes superstitiously as she mounted astride. Macha, unable to see through her tears, reached blindly towards her children. Liam hit the mare on the hindquarters and sent her bucking away from them. By the time the girl gained control and looked back, the little group was already shapeless in the distance, and then they turned off the track and were gone.

Macha Molloy, at sixteen years old, had lost husband, children, home and country.

Chapter Six

Wales was funereal. The cattle boat docked under a pall of cloud after a crossing during which Macha was repeatedly sick. Numb from the dolour of the past days, she wandered through the hills, unaware of the dingy landscape or of anything beyond the annihilating shock that strangled her from throat to womb.

The ponies and the dogs scavenged for themselves. She did not know they were there. Rage would well up without warning—rage against Molloy for being dead, against herself for being alive. And just the thought of her babies would send her stumbling about distractedly with clenched teeth and covered ears, as though it were possible physically to escape her plight.

In a cart she'd purchased from a farmer, she moved across a land whose people spoke a tongue she did not understand, through villages and towns the names of which she could not read. She ate nothing and drank only a little and welcomed the rack of hunger.

It rained in Wales, rained without stopping, hiding the mountains behind a screen of vapour. She journeyed on to Abergavenny and finally turned towards England.

No wall or fence marked the border, and yet the difference was as emphatic as a change of world. England was luscious with autumn: her trees were hung with gilded fruit, her fields left butter yellow by the cut corn.

Macha did not hurry through the Cotswolds. She lingered in the woods and by the fresh streams, content to be seduced by their charms. England, with its gentle warmth and soft light, calmed and healed and renewed. Refusing to think of the past or the future, she lived from day to day, filling the hours with leisurely travel and the grooming and tending of her animals.

Once or twice she took casual work, picking apples and pears for orchard owners. The farms were prosperous, and trading was easy. In Stroud, she sold a couple of workhorses. Then she headed south.

Here was an unexplored country where no one had ever heard of Jack Sheridan or Coper Molloy or her past. Here she could do anything and be anybody she chose. It was not necessary even to be a traveller if she did not wish, and with that thought, she drew up behind a hedge on the edge of some common land and, still smiling at the idea, went to sleep inside the cart.

The next morning she decided to walk down the hill to nearby Bath. Grand houses lined the wide avenues, and there were shops full of exquisite fabrics and marvellous hats and shoes; shops selling only paintings or books; and then, most entrancing of all, a shop filled with toys.

Macha pressed her face against the glass in childish wonder. There were china dolls and wooden animals and puppets, and a doll's house with perfectly furnished rooms. Then she saw a merry-go-round in the corner of the window, seven gaily painted horses, with golden manes, beneath a red-and-white-striped roof. It was irresistible. Macha opened the door of the shop and entered.

"Out! Out!" A fat man leaped at her and waved pudgy hands. "No gypsies. What are you trying to do, drive my customers away?"

"But I want to buy something," Macha protested as he bundled her back to the door.

"I wouldn't sell you the crown jewels. Now, be off with you and don't come back!"

He gave her a hearty shove that sent her headlong into the street, to land in the gutter. A carriage threw mud all over her as it passed, and two arrogant ladies drew their furs more tightly about them, turning their faces away in disgust.

Shame gave way to rage as Macha stumbled back to the cart. She slapped down the welcoming dogs and fed the horses. Then she erected a tent and flounced inside. For a long time she lay staring up at the arch of hazel rods. Then she began to cry.

The two proud ladies, with their furs and scornful expressions, haunted her. She thought of all the other women she had seen that day, in balloon-sleeved jackets and bell-shaped skirts and feathered hats. No self-respecting girl would want to look so stupid. And yet, they were self-respecting—and respected. The toyshop owner would not have dared evict one of them.

Suddenly, Macha wished she had a looking glass.

Starting out in this foreign territory, she felt confused, and began to wonder about views she had always held, views about moving from place to place, about home being wherever she chose to stop on the open road. Without realising it, she was examining her beliefs about freedom.

Soon it would be winter, and the tent would be wet and bitter cold. Gold, her treasured foal, would need training, and that meant established roots and a daily programme that could not be postponed because there was nowhere to gallop or because of the usual harassment of travellers by the local authorities. By dawn, Macha had reached the most important decision of her life.

Stripping off all her clothes, she crouched in a nearby stream and washed herself, scrubbing her skin hard, until she emerged pink and tingling. Then, from her bundle of possessions, she drew out her carefully wrapped wedding garments and put them on: the petticoats, the cream chiffon blouse, the skirt with its trim of coloured ribbons. Pinning on the gold shamrock brooch, she descended once more to Bath.

At a secondhand shop she stopped to buy a plain navy-blue coat and a blue velvet hat with feathers. Dressed in these and feeling distinctly ill at ease, she straightened her shoulders and marched resolutely up the street and into the toyshop.

The fat man came scurrying forward, his puffy hands clasped together, and smiled obsequiously. "Can I help madam?"

He did not recognise her at all.

"I'll take the merry-go-round," she said haughtily.

"Certainly. Certainly." He bustled to the window to get it.

Macha coolly plucked the toy from him and held out the money. Then she was striding away in triumph. It was as though the wearing of a simple coat and hat had changed her into a different person.

She returned to the site. It had been a most extraordinary day. Now she started a fire, and as the potatoes charred in the hot coals she twirled the carousel and discovered a little key in the base. Turning it made the horses revolve, and then, to her delight, it began to tinkle a tune with silvery notes. A musical box!

To Macha, it was a sign of approval of her decision that morning. Her pluck returned, and she knew she would succeed.

IT SEEMED WISE to go where the winter climate would be most mild. The search began on the journey south. Her requirements were very specific— a wide, flat piece of open country, a large shed, no prying settled people nearby, yet not too far from good roads and possibly a railway. It did not cross her mind that such a location might not exist.

Meanwhile, to add to the money in the tin box, she traded horses as she travelled, fresh-legged youngsters and worn-out hobbies and jades. Along the way she dealt with rectors and doctors and numerous tradesmen, sometimes taking corn and hay as part of the price and once accepting a sidesaddle and a used lady's riding habit in return for a pony.

Then the end of the season came, and trading was over until spring. She counted up her profit and scrutinised the few animals carefully kept as future investment, and was pleased. She had done very well indeed. They would go on for a few more days, she decided, just to see what lay on the other side of the large port to the east. So, hitching the string of ponies behind the cart, she followed the waters of the Solent inland. Shortly she saw ahead the rolling contours of the Sussex downs—billowy, green and peaceful, unthreatened by crags or chasms, serene and timeless, undulating down to the sea, magical under the sinking sun. Macha drove into their folds as though magnetised.

A grove of yew trees grew in the vale where she spent the night. For the

214

first time since leaving Ireland she felt happy, sensing that the place she searched for was only a handspan away.

The next day she struggled into the riding habit, put the sidesaddle on a bay gelding and somewhat clumsily set out along the bridle path that led over the smooth slopes, so perfect for exercising a fine young horse.

Macha felt her pulse speed. The turf was springy, and the downs bowled before her for mile upon mile, like pale green clouds. Below, on the level coastal plain, lay villages of cottages clustered tightly as toadstools and a town, its harbour bustling with boats. Beyond it was the haze of the English Channel.

Then she saw, set on a ridge below, the white-railed elegance of a most beautiful racecourse. She had arrived.

Macha sat on her horse, absorbing everything. The air grew cold, but she did not care.

A very old man had ridden up unheard. He had a strong local burr, and Macha guessed he was a farmer.

"Ye've been here a time, missy. Be ye well enough?"

"I could not be better if I had grown twelve inches more," she replied with a smile. "It is a lovely scene indeed."

"What part do ye come from, then?" he asked, pulling at his beard.

"Ireland, sir. I lived there till my darling father was taken to heaven." She looked suitably tragic. "My dear mother brought me to Wales, and then she too went to the angels."

"And now you're all alone in the world, child?"

"There's just me and my brother. We are twins, sir."

Long before, she had worked out the answers to inevitable questions and, to prevent further enquiry, now changed the subject. "Could you do me the kindness of giving me the name of the racecourse down there?"

"Why, missy, where else would that be but glorious Goodwood?"

Macha gazed at the sweep of emerald with awe. Newmarket, Ascot, Epsom, Goodwood—Molloy had told her of them all. "My brother and I have a few horses," she said casually. "That's why we're here, searching for somewhere to live and keep them."

"Well, there are houses in this county of Sussex with stables and yards and paddocks aplenty," he said.

"Being orphans, we have not the means for such as you describe. No, sir. What we must find is a little cabin with a woodshed or two and the smallest piece of land, for rent."

"Well, missy, come ye with me and see summat," he said. "My name is Harold Locksash, and I was born no more'n a mile from here, eighty years ago. Some of that land yonder is mine."

He turned his mount and it began walking ponderously downhill. Macha followed, and they rode through a thick wood and then came quite suddenly upon a thatched cottage, beside which stood a low, L-shaped flintstone building comprising a cowshed, store and stable.

"How would this do ye and your brother?" asked Harold Locksash. "There's five acre goes wi' it."

Macha saw an almost secret place, sheltered from people by the density of Wildham Woods yet near wide, open gallops. She saw four stalls in the stable and grass for her horses' keep. She did not notice that the thatch was leaking. She asked his price.

"Well, 'tis a fine property, ye know." He gave her an enigmatic glance from milky eyes, and she realised he was almost blind. "Five pounds a year, missy. Now, what do you say to that?"

"I—we'll take it," she agreed, and they shook hands.

THIS WAS THE BEGINNING. She was a tenant and could no longer be harried by authorities or police from this, her chosen home.

The invention of a mythical brother had been a brainwave. She knew that a young, single woman would never be permitted to rent a property and live there alone. A brother provided protection, and in the guise of her brother she drove to Chichester the next day and bought a few cheap pieces of secondhand furniture.

The simple pattern of her life was soon established. Every day, regardless of the weather, the girl rode out over the downs, and she soon knew the countryside well.

Each fortnight, on market day, she went to Chichester to shop. The outing was intended as education as well as to buy food. Ladies choosing fabrics, ordering goods, meeting friends at luncheon were not aware of being watched, but Macha noted every detail of their clothes and conduct and copied what she could.

She purchased a loose cloak, two worn gowns and a pair of pliant brown leather shoes fastened by no fewer than twelve little buttons. But the overheard conversations between these well-bred women remained incomprehensible. Who was Hors d'Oeuvres? Apparently someone important, invited to dine everywhere. And what sort of house was a yacht? At times she returned to the cottage quite downhearted at her own ignorance.

Gold was her consolation. "He's a fine-looking horse," Harold Locksash said one day, when she was in the yard dressed in cap and corduroys.

"He's a thoroughbred, you know," she pointed out.

"I can see that." The old man studied him. "Reminds me a lot of one of your Irish stallions I saw run at Kempton Park—Gallinule were his name. Ye will have heard of him, maybe."

"Oh, yes." Macha could not quite keep the grin from her face. "I have heard of him."

THE ELMS IN GOODWOOD PARK had turned dusty pink with blossom. It was spring and Macha, who had enjoyed sitting by her warm stove during the February snows, suddenly found the cottage stifling and the five acres restrictive. Once, she built a fire outside and sat beside it, seeing ghosts in the shadows and hearing their laughter echoing down the years from her childhood. She remembered Connemara and the sea; she remembered the mountains and the tarns, and wept. Everything she had tried to forget returned to torment her.

Pictures of her children forced their way back into her mind. She could smell their milky breath again and feel their downy hair and peachy skins. Her angels. She wanted to crush them against her, to hold Molloy, to hold anyone. The human touch—all at once she was starved of it.

Like women before and after her, Macha sublimated her yearnings in work. She mucked out the stable, swept the yard, scrubbed the kitchen floor and painted the walls. Old Locksash noticed the work and was impressed. Arriving one morning as she was about to go into town, he issued an invitation.

"My daughter and her husband will be coming up from Wiltshire, Miss Sheridan, and it would please me mightily if you and your brother could take tea with us on Wednesday afternoon."

Macha looked at him in horror. There was absolutely no way she could refuse, yet if her brother did not appear, the family would be justifiably insulted and possibly suspicious as well. The only solution to this appalling problem was to leave the cottage and go back on the road.

Lying in her small iron-frame bed that night, she realised that was not what she wanted. She had grown to love Sussex and to enjoy the security of the old walls round her. She liked being clean and wearing gowns, and she liked the polite regard that came from being one of the settled people.

Early next morning she donned her disguise and brought Macha's Girl up from a paddock damp with dew.

This was to be their last hack over the downs, and as they neared The Trundle, above Goodwood, and saw other horses working there, Macha's Girl pulled and bucked. A pair of thoroughbreds had just started over the gallops. The mare jerked her head, and Macha shortened the reins and urged her on.

They thundered up the incline, quickly closing behind the two race-horses, whose lads looked back in surprise. The mare's stride lengthened, and her ears strained as she passed the second horse with a flourish. Skimming the turf like a swallow, body stretched, legs reaching, she drew alongside the lead horse.

A surge of exultation filled Macha. For one transcendent second they raced level with their thoroughbred rival, shoulder to shoulder, nose to nose.

It was enough. Macha's Girl slowed, and the two young sprinters sped ahead and disappeared over the ridge.

"You did that for me," said Macha, dismounting, and she moved unhurriedly downhill to cool and rest the mare. "Where's the fairness in having to leave here?" the girl muttered aloud to herself. "Macha of the Horses, how can I train the grandest colt in the land if I'm to be pushed about all the time? When are you going to put a bit of real luck my way?"

And Macha, the goddess, heard. A miracle happened.

A shouting figure ran out of the trees, arms waving, ragged and wild as a banshee. "Stop! Stop!"

Macha's eyes widened, and she stopped.

"I know that horse. I'd know that horse if you surrounded Tattersall's Sale ring with the cavalry and hid her in the middle. How did you get hold of her? You stole her, that's how. She that owns her would never have sold her, not if the Prince of Wales had made the order. You're a thief."

His clothes were torn and his eyes red-rimmed. Gawky and very young, he had obviously been living rough and starving. The girl backed behind the horse for protection. He came up very close and stared at her. Then his eyes filled with astonishment.

"But it's yourself! I'd know ye anywhere."

Then Macha recalled. So long ago—the boy on the strand who had once begged to ride the mare.

"Those clothes you have on are a scandal," he said with heavy disapproval.

"Just take a look at your own, Declan O'Brien," she retorted, and saw his face light up. "And I can't be standing here all day. The mare needs a feed, and so do I. What about yourself?"

"Yes . . . well, no. There's no need to go bothering about me."

"No bother. I've mutton enough for two," she offered airily.

He started to follow, and she turned. "No. Don't walk with me. It might look bad. Come by in an hour, and don't be seen. It's the cottage three miles on, beyond Wildham Wood."

In the stable, the girl worked quickly, and once the horse was fed and covered by a blanket she ran into the house. She pulled on one of her two gowns and her good shoes and jabbed her hair into place with pins before busying herself about the kitchen.

When she opened the door to Declan O'Brien, he entered hesitantly, confused by the change in her. But she put a plate of hot food before him, and he did not speak as he ate. Macha poured him English beer, and he drank it like a thirsty dog, drew nearer the fire and stretched out his legs with a noisy sigh of pleasure.

There was just time for her to learn, before he fell into a deep slumber, that he had come to England to work for a trainer who had then gone bankrupt. Ever since, he had been wandering from stable to stable looking for employment, and growing more and more desperate.

Macha did not forget to whisper thanks to her divine patroness as she watched the boy slumped in the chair. She laid out corduroy trousers, a shirt, waistcoat, jacket and hat and was standing before him when he finally woke.

"There's a pump in the yard. Take off those old things you're wearing and have a good wash."

He jumped up, flustered, and objected loudly as she shoved him out. "Scrub all over," she instructed. "You'll find decent clothes in the doorway when you've finished."

When he returned he looked clean, damp, thin and sheepish.

"You're a bit tall, but you'll do. Now, here's the plan."

"If it's a weddin' you're after, I'm not wanting a wife, tink," he said with a very frightened expression on his face.

Macha didn't know whether to be outraged or tickled. "If I could not do better than you, Declan O'Brien, I'd become a nun. And I'll thank you to remember that I might be a traveller, but I'm no tinker."

Crimson with embarrassment, he stared down at his feet and mumbled an apology, but Macha's amusement got the better of her and she burst into laughter. Taking a bottle of Scotch whisky and two cups from the cupboard, she waved him to a seat and told him of all her adventures in England. "So you see, it's not a husband I'm needing. It's a brother, and you're the very one."

"I'm not getting into this," he protested.

"What have ye against me?"

"We'd not get away with it. The whole world must know your so-called brother. No. You can have your clothes back, and I'll be on my way."

As he shuffled awkwardly to his feet she suggested casually, "Before you go, will you not take a peek at my few ponies?"

She led the way out of the cottage and across the yard to the lower paddock. "Now, what would you say to him?" Gold was grazing with the other horses, his coat burnished copper red by the brightness of noon. He moved gracefully on slim, straight legs, with white socks gleaming.

Declan stood shaking his head in silent admiration.

"He'll need a rider when he's ready to race," she said. "And who better than my own brother?"

There was a pause. Declan O'Brien gave a groan of defeat. "I'll do it," he said. "Though we'll be hounded to hell if it comes out."

AFTERNOON TEA AT THE FARMHOUSE was a success. The fact that the boy did not speak much was not unusual.

"I do declare ye've growed an inch or two since ye came to live here, young Mr. Sheridan," commented Harold Locksash as they were leaving. "Must be our good Sussex air."

They all laughed.

"Right," said Macha, when they returned home. "Now we can start some real work."

There were sales to attend, horses to buy and sell and, most important of all, the colt to train. There were also Macha's dealings between market and buyer, fascinating and shocking machinations from which Declan learned hitherto unimagined cunning. He was by nature reserved. He had an ineradicable sense of what was proper, and to him Macha was quite definitely improper. All they had in common was an obsession with horses, and he was torn between the terror of living with a fast woman and the desire to race her fast colt one day. Desire won, but he knew he would be damned for it.

EARLY IN MAY they spent a day at the races. Macha took much of her recent profits, and they drove the cart to Singleton station, from where the train took them to Salisbury, changing at Chichester and Portsmouth.

It was to be a plain meeting with no big prizes to attract the glamorous, but it was her first visit to an English racecourse and she was in a state of high impatience to arrive. The course was some distance from the city and had they not run the last quarter of a mile the first race would have been over, and with it they would have lost the chance which changed Macha's life.

As it was, the runners had left the paddock and already cantered down the mile-long straight to the start. Hurrying to the rails, she glanced at the runners-and-riders board, and saw only one name. It was a message just for her. She rushed to a bookmaker's stand.

"Hurry up, lady, or you'll be too late," the bookmaker urged. Without even having seen the horse, she handed him thirty pounds with shaking hands. "Irish Coper, to win," she whispered as the shouting crowd announced the off.

She could not look, could only hear the far-off rumble breaking up into staccato drumbeats, the sobbing breaths and oaths, the final cacophony of sound. She opened her eyes.

"Who won?" she asked Declan.

"Some outsider, at a hundred to one," he replied. "Irish Coper." She had won three thousand pounds!

"WHAT WILL YOU DO with it?" asked the flabbergasted Declan O'Brien as they sat in the train returning to Sussex.

"Everything. I'm going to do everything," she said happily. "I'm going to dress in lace and velvet. I'm going to be hung with jewels and wear hats with more feathers than a flock of birds. I'm going to mix with the quality, go racing and dancing and wining and dining."

He shook his head mournfully. "You'd be better off to buy yourself a little place and put the rest of the fortune away in safety. There's no good can come of all that squandering and frippery."

He could be very irritating, she thought.

Sitting by the cottage fire that evening seemed far too tame after the excitement of the day. She would have much preferred to go to some godless hall full of music and lights and handsome men and women and sin. But the port she and Declan were sipping was a splendid drink which touched her cheeks with heat and her mind with recklessness. She lolled in the chair and surveyed Declan through half-closed eyes.

"I am thinking that the fact that I am now a woman of wealth and able to bring a handsome dowry might make the divil of a difference to your ideas," she said capriciously.

"What difference? What ideas?" He was looking befuddled.

"Your ideas of a wedding, of course." She crossed the space between them like a cat. "Isn't every man wanting a rich wife?"

"What? What?" He tried to sit upright but failed.

Macha stroked his hair and knelt beside him and walked her fingers slowly up his arm. "Here we are, you and me, sitting in the same kitchen and then separated every night like sour milk. Do you not begin to think that is a pity, Declan O'Brien?"

"I do not. Will you get away!" His mien was one of sheer terror.

"Well, maybe you're right. Perhaps we should not be married yet awhile. But there'd be no harm in a little kiss or two."

At that, he hurled himself out of the chair. "You're a wanton jezebel, that's what you are, Macha Sheridan, but I will not commit sins of the flesh, not for all your gold." With which he reeled from the room.

Macha plumped down into her chair, whooping with laughter. What fun she would have had with Molloy on such an occasion. It was her last reflection, and as she slumped into unconsciousness two tears squeezed from her eyes.

When the light of day drove in through the window, Declan was standing over her, weighed down with solemnity and a small bundle containing his possessions. "I'll be off, then," he said mournfully.

She felt weak and rather sick. "Where are you off to?"

"On my way."

"Merciful heaven, Declan, what is this about you leaving?"

"After what happened last night, I cannot go on sharing the same roof with you and risking my immortal soul."

He looked piteous, and Macha began to feel twinges of guilt.

"Ah, it was only a game. Put down your things, and let's have tea."

"No. It was no game to me," he said stubbornly.

Something in his voice made her inspect him more closely. The boy had a face of character, not handsome, but a face many women would find attractive before long. Then, to her surprise, Macha saw in his eyes genuine pain, and all at once she understood something he did not know about himself—that he was desperately and impossibly in love with her. For although he was the same age, she was an adult, but he was still just a boy.

"Declan, please forgive me. I've been a fool, and I am sorry," she said simply.

Shy and deeply distressed, he flushed and shifted position.

"Don't leave," she continued. "I need you here. Take no heed of yesterday's blather and chatter. Though, make no mistake, I intend to enjoy myself. But what I want to do most of all is to buy the most promising thoroughbred filly we can find, and run her."

"We?"

"You and me. Who else can I depend on to help me choose the best?"

He gave her a hard and doubtful glare, and Macha cursed herself for being so cruel and insensitive. She had lost him.

Minutes passed. Then he took the singing kettle off the stove and made tea. "I will work with your horses and ride for you, Miss Sheridan," he said formally. "I will even act as your brother. But I will do no more. If you agree to that, I will stay on."

"I do," she confirmed at once. "And I am very grateful to you, Declan."

It was to be years before he used her Christian name again.

Chapter Seven

Mr. Toby Dodds was an exclusive court dressmaker in Chichester. Even ladies who spent the season in London often visited his establishment while in the country. He was a suitably august figure, tall and silver-haired, sartorially faultless, invariably courteous without ever being obsequious.

When Macha walked through the door in a perfectly dreadful puce garment and her relic of a coat, he knew he faced a challenge. He was an artist. Now he would create.

"I want the latest clothes," she stated frankly.

He nodded, and waited.

"And gloves and hats and shoes."

He smiled.

"And my hair dressed. I want . . ."

"You want to be beautiful, madam." His statement confirmed it as the most natural desire in the world.

222

"Yes," she replied, with a delighted grin.

"Leave it all to me, madam," he instructed, and she knew she had found a friend.

He had her measurements taken and recorded in a leather-bound book. He gave her fashion drawings and swatches of material to study. He arranged for a hairdresser's appointment that same afternoon and remained near at hand while her hair was cut, suggesting a style that would enhance her most fetching features.

Macha gazed into the looking glass in wonder. Her shining hair was piled sensationally on her head, with a fringe of the most delicious curls framing her face, which she had never noticed before was a charming oval shape set with wide silver eyes. "Oh," she said, and turned to Mr. Dodds.

"This is only the beginning, madam."

For weeks all her spare time was taken up with fittings and treatments, and even lessons. Mr. Dodds introduced her to a dancing master, a bootmaker, a milliner, and to the Honourable Mrs. Henry Wellington, a dowager whose glare could snap the mast of a ship halfway to France.

Only the almost imperceptible tightening of her eyelids hinted at Mrs. Wellington's feelings as she viewed her pupil for the first time, and, as widowhood in straitened circumstances made such an association necessary, she quashed those feelings with a self-discipline instilled in her from birth.

In a darkly shaded room, overfull of aspidistras, framed photographs and screens Mrs. Wellington taught Macha all the elements of society etiquette: when to call; when to leave her card; how to behave at tea, at supper, at a ball, at the opera. The rules were endless, and Macha knew she would never remember them all.

She also learned to curtsy.

"But what for? Isn't it only maids who curtsy?"

"You may be presented one day to Her Majesty the Queen, or to the Prince of Wales." Then Mrs. Wellington added, "It is a great pity you do not speak French."

"Oh, but I speak Irish," Macha offered.

The venerable lady paled, and produced a bottle of smelling salts. "Never tell anyone that. Irish is the language of peasants."

"You were right," Macha stormed to Declan when she returned home. "It is all frippery. Do you know they think Irish is the language of bogtrotters! I'm not taking any more. I will give all the dresses away tomorrow, and then I'll go back on the road."

"And what will happen to the colt?" he asked slowly.

Gold! Since becoming so preoccupied with manners and modes, she had not given him a thought. "*Ach*, it's all become a muddle. I seem to throw away time and money and get nowhere."

There was a pause as he looked at her. They were outside the cottage, and she was seated on a new wicker chair, dressed in a summer gown of white voile, her parasol carelessly discarded on the grass.

"It doesn't seem to me you've wasted either," he said. "All these frills and ways are becoming to a lady, a lady like yourself."

She was astonished and gratified, knowing he would never have made such a comment insincerely. "Me, Declan?"

"Well . . . usually," he added, with a rare touch of banter. "But maybe you should begin to put it all to use."

"This minute," she agreed, and hurried indoors, emerging shortly with a paper. "We'll send this off and have Gold registered. This is his birth certificate." She began to read from the paper. "'Born: 1896. Sire: Philosopher. Dam: Precious Stone.' And it's signed here. Look. 'G. H. Carter, Sheriff, Bowling Green, Kentucky.'"

Declan gave her a quizzical look. "Well, it doesn't matter whether he came from America or was born in Murphy's barn," stated the boy. "He's a champion, and he'll leave them all at the start." He looked Macha straight in the eye, and she knew that he knew the certificate was a fake.

IT WAS ALREADY the middle of June. They travelled all the way to Ascot in a smart hired carriage, taking the censorious Mrs. Wellington along as Macha's chaperone.

They started out the previous morning and stayed overnight at a coaching inn. Well before dawn on the third of the four days of the royal meeting, the little party drew near the famous course and managed to secure a perfect position drawn right up to the rails. A hamper of food had been prepared at the inn, and the coachman produced chairs and a table covered with a white linen cloth and laid out with china. They breakfasted on a pork pie, sliced ham and tea.

The course was like woven green cashmere. Bookmakers established their pitches with brash name signs, lists of runners and chalked prices. Touts in loud jackets and gaudy scarves appeared. Flocks of parasols and brigades of top hats began to wheel around the immaculate lawns opposite, as though taking part in a dance. Breathtaking horses were led by, visions incarnate.

Private drags and barouches, many with armorial bearings painted on their panels, swept into the enclosure alongside them, the male occupants sporting the enamelled badge of the exclusive Four-in-Hand Club and shouting greetings to one another. With a gunshot of a pop, Macha opened the first bottle of champagne to a chorus of encouragement. Turning, she saw that her new neighbours were lifting their glasses to her, with the exception of one young man who was busy scrutinising the horses through field glasses.

224

Mrs. Wellington hissed, and moved with remarkable alacrity to place her substantial bulk between her charge and the admirers, who gave an audible groan. "Ladies do not uncork wine. Allow Mr. Sheridan to do it if you should require more," she corrected crossly.

A mighty cheer rose from the crowd as the royal cavalcade, led by the royal huntsman and his whippers-in, entered the course at a fast trot. Behind came several landaus, each drawn by four horses with postillions. The first of these carried an imposing bearded man and his elegant wife, who waved and smiled genially to all.

"The Prince and Princess of Wales," quavered Mrs. Wellington, teetering dangerously into an attempted curtsy while perched in the carriage. Then she sat back, fanning her flushed face with a handkerchief and puffing quite alarmingly after the excitement of the experience.

The royal couple were soon in the royal box, and then horses loped past with their little burdens of silks, racecards were marked, money was passed from wallet to hand, field glasses were trained and the flag was dropped. There was a distant strumming and a whirl of colour, and the first race was over. Macha, with a most unladylike holla, rushed to collect her winnings.

The young man who had been studying the runners so earnestly from the next enclosure courteously stood back to let her reach the bookmaker's stand and watched as the coins and notes were counted into her gloved hand.

"Try Earwig in the next race," he advised.

"Oh, no," she responded. "Mr. Fairie's Eager will win that."

"You are so sure?" he asked with a mocking smile.

"Sure certain," she confirmed and, to prove it, put five guineas on the horse, at which moment Declan O'Brien and Mrs. Wellington found her and hustled her away, the latter lecturing her about never addressing anyone who had not been introduced.

"He spoke to me first," the girl explained.

"Then you should have ignored him," stated Mrs. Wellington.

Eager won by four lengths, and the gentleman perched on the next carriage inclined his head in acknowledgment of defeat. Macha pretended not to see him.

"Why don't you have a little flutter, Mrs. Wellington?"

"Ladies do not bet."

"But the next race is the Gold Cup, with the Prince of Wales's own horse Persimmon running," Macha enticed. "There can't be anything wrong in supporting the royal runner."

The widow was torn between allegiance to the crown and etiquette.

"I'll tell you what," suggested Macha, unabashed. "I'll put a sovereign on Persimmon for you with my own wager."

"Your brother, Mr. Sheridan, must deal with the bookmaker," protested Mrs. Wellington.

Macha relented and sent Declan with the money while she and the dowager crossed sedately to the paddock.

Persimmon won by eight lengths. All around, top hats and caps and bowlers were flung into the air. The prince appeared, beaming, to lead in his winner, and Mrs. Wellington fainted clean away.

Lying in her bed at the inn that night, Macha decided this had been the best day she had spent since coming to England. She had won more money, she had seen a prince and princess, and the horses, every one, had outshone her most fabulous ideal.

MRS. WELLINGTON ROSE the following morning to discover herself a devotee of racing. Her night too had been filled with echoes of that wonderful day—the mingling with royal personages; the return to society after the death of her dear husband, the brigadier, a decade earlier; and, not least, her small winnings from the Gold Cup. Now, she recalled that her late husband's nephew, Sir Frederick Wellington, had connections with the racing world, and she resolved to write to him forthwith.

Macha had no further difficulty in persuading the widow to accompany her to Sandown, Kempton, Brighton and Windsor, where they both benefited from the girl's winning streak. And each was surprised to discover a growing affection for the other.

Freddie Wellington, who was quite fond of his aunt, replied to her letter with an invitation to join him in the members' enclosure at Goodwood and to bring her ward, of course.

"Your ward?" Macha queried. "What does that mean?"

"It means," Mrs. Wellington explained, "you have someone who takes the place of your parents." It had been only the tiniest white lie, but Mrs. Wellington was unusually flustered. She certainly did not want it known that straitened circumstances had forced her to give lessons in deportment.

"Thank you," the girl said sincerely. "That is a great kindness."

"Then there is no time to lose." The widow dismissed the subject. "You must see Mr. Dodds and order your gown at once."

They chose a design in eau-de-nil silk, trimmed with cascades of cream lace. The minute waist and hip-skimming skirt emphasised Macha's willowy height, and the colour reflected in the silver of her eyes. The outfit was completed by long gloves.

Her arrival at Goodwood was sensational, causing monocles to be raised and questions to be asked by frosty matrons protective of their daughters' interests.

Freddie Wellington, on recognising the *grande dame* accompanying this ravishing young woman, became conspicuously proprietorial, and within half an hour Macha had met more people than would fill a winter campsite. But they all talked so much that, to her annoyance, she missed the first race, and as Freddie began steering her towards yet another group, she stopped.

"All your friends are very pleasant people, Sir Frederick, but could we not speak with them later?"

"What would you prefer to do, Miss Sheridan?" he asked.

"I should prefer to watch the runners," she stated decisively. "Is that not the reason for coming to Goodwood?"

"Many ladies come simply to be seen," he murmured.

"Well, not me," she retorted.

Freddie Wellington steered her towards the paddock and made another attempt to gain her favour.

"You might care to venture a sovereign on one of the races, Miss Sheridan," he said. "So, may I advise you on the horses?"

She listened carefully to his opinion of each, before asking, "And have you put money on any horse, Sir Frederick?"

"I have indeed," he answered. "Number six."

"Well, in that case, I'll risk a sovereign on him too. And would you put five guineas each way on number twelve as well?"

When Freddie's horse came in first and her choice third, she bounded about with hoydenish abandonment.

"We make a great team," she commented as he brought her her winnings. Poor Mrs. Wellington appeared close to apoplexy.

By the end of the afternoon Macha had happily agreed to return for the last two days of the meeting and had accepted an invitation from Lady Leconfield to a ball at Petworth House.

On her next day at Goodwood, Macha wore the gown she had worn at Ascot, and her delectable appearance, together with her astonishing good luck, increased her circle of admirers.

Professional and gentleman riders mixed in the second race, and one of the amateurs was up on a small brown gelding of such exquisite conformation that Macha found him irresistible. The bookmaker took her twenty-five pounds to win, and she focused her field glasses on the start. She saw the gentleman rider balance the horse within the first few strides, gradually draw up to the leaders and then dash for the winning post. The little gelding responded gamely and just managed to push his nose in front. Macha realised she had been shrieking him home like a fishwife.

"Of course, she is Irish, you know," someone said nearby, but walking among them, openly counting the wad of banknotes, Macha could not have given a tuppenny piece for their opinion.

The gentleman rider was introduced, and she recognised him. The Honourable James Melbaugh, who had just filled her hands with money, was the young man from the Four-in-Hand Club enclosure at Ascot.

"I see your eye for the best horse is still as keen," he said, bowing without relinquishing her gaze.

"Only a top horseman brings out the best." It was an honest compliment. "And you rode a cracking race."

"I trust you will be at the ball at Goodwood House tonight, Miss Sheridan?"

When she shook her head regretfully, he added at once, "Then neither shall I. That is, if you will dine with me instead?" He spoke very softly. No one but Macha had heard, and he did have fun in his blue eyes. Besides, she was thoroughly bored with the straitjacket of decorum.

"I will," she agreed.

Macha had the sense to refuse James Melbaugh's offer to send his carriage for her. Even she knew better than to leave herself completely vulnerable.

She wondered how on earth to persuade Declan O'Brien to drive her to and collect her from such an assignation. In the end, she guessed rightly that he would do it only for her own protection, but she had to tolerate his sulking all the way to Chichester.

Heavy crimson paper covered the walls of the supper rooms not far from the Assembly Rooms, and velvet curtains obscured the windows. Each table had a pair of candles with deep red shades and a bowl of dark, fragrant roses. Macha was relieved to see other girls of her own age dining. She had supposed the place would be full of harlots.

She sat down carefully and tried not to betray her uncertainty at the sight of three wineglasses and an array of silver. This was very different from light lunches in the teashops.

James Melbaugh signalled to a waiter, who came forward with a bottle of champagne.

"Is it Laurent Perrier?" she asked curiously.

He was surprised. "Do you like Laurent Perrier?"

"Oh, yes. I always drink it when I've done well at the races," she said, the truth being that it was the only name she knew.

"Take that away and bring some Laurent Perrier '83," he ordered the waiter. "Whatever you want, you shall have, Miss Sheridan, especially as you obviously know your champagne as well as you know your runners."

After the first glass her feeling of awkwardness vanished. They talked of horses, and he made her giggle with tales of racing and of the spills he had experienced as an amateur rider. Then, as he began to appreciate the depth of her knowledge and interest, he spoke of striving with back and arms and legs and heels, of the tension and heat in the middle of the rushing, crushing bunch. He described bolting into that unique moment of victory for which every thoroughbred had been raised. And Macha felt the breath at his heels and his hunger to win and win and win.

They stared at each other and then looked away, unwilling to travel so far yet. The evening passed so quickly that the waiter's announcement that her victoria was waiting came disappointingly soon.

"May I call on you?" James Melbaugh asked.

She looked at him with an eagerness that faded as she realised how unthinkable it would be for him to come to her cottage. "Mrs. Wellington—my guardian—would not permit it," she said slowly.

"Leave the gorgon to me, Miss Sheridan," he said, and his confidence left her too worried to notice Declan O'Brien's silent fury on the way home.

Macha went straight to her room and climbed into bed, sitting upright among the pillows and leaving the candle burning. It was where she always did her important thinking. After a while she went to the tallboy, took out and opened her tin box, and counted her money. In three months she had made nearly seven thousand pounds. It was time to put it to good use, she thought, picturing James Melbaugh once more, long-limbed and graceful, urging the little brown gelding past the winning post.

"DEAR MRS. WELLINGTON, you have been so good to me," Macha murmured while sitting in the widow's drawing room the following afternoon. "My greatest regret in being unable to return here will be the loss of your friendship."

"Unable to return, Miss Sheridan? Why ever not?"

"So many people at Goodwood have expressed a wish to call upon me. The quandary of it has kept me awake, and now I realise I have no alternative but to retire from society at once."

"Nonsense! Now, who is it wishes to call?" Mrs. Wellington was avidly curious.

"Oh, Mrs. Cookson and Miss Beresford and your nephew and the Honourable James Melbaugh. It is all quite dreadful."

"James Melbaugh! But that is wonderful, Miss Sheridan. He is most eligible, the younger son of the Earl of Watersmeet."

Macha gave an abject sigh. "But the problem is that they all believe I live here with you. In truth I live in very humble surroundings, such as I could not endure anyone to see."

The dowager looked puzzled. "I understood you had a house, and land, Miss Sheridan?"

"A rented hovel and two fields," Macha confessed. "It is the intention of my . . . cousin and myself to remove to Newmarket next spring, to buy a house and start a training stable—"

"Your *cousin?*"

"It seemed easier in the beginning to say that Declan was my brother, but the truth is he is the son of my mother's sister. His name is O'Brien, not Sheridan." She held her breath.

"But you must have servants? A maid? You mean you live entirely alone with your cousin?"

Macha nodded.

The widow sat with her mouth open for some moments. "Well, Miss Sheridan, such a situation cannot continue." Her voice sounded severe. "I am prepared to allow acceptable friends to call upon you here, but I should have to insist that you start searching for a suitable house as soon as possible."

Macha glowed.

On the following Sunday, Freddie Wellington, accompanied by his friend James Melbaugh, waited upon his aunt and her delightful ward.

Macha scrupulously divided her attention between them. They discussed the forthcoming ball at Petworth House, and each reserved dances with Macha in advance. They talked of her plans to buy a thoroughbred filly, a project on which both gentlemen were almost too eager to advise. It was finally agreed that all should attend the next auction at Tattersall's, in London.

"I didn't know all the world was going to have a say in this new horse," Declan O'Brien complained reproachfully on hearing of the proposed excursion to London. "I thought the filly was for us."

"For me," Macha corrected with asperity. "I shall be buying the filly, and you will ride her—that is, you will ride her if you stop all this huff. An old donkey would be better company than you have been since I had supper with Mr. Melbaugh, and I am putting up with no more."

"I don't want to see you destroy your good name, that's all," he muttered, kicking at the ground.

"It's not my good name you're minding, but me going out with a fine gentleman. Don't think I don't know, and it's to stop. You can't tell me how to run my life, even if I'm wrong." Her own harsh voice surprised her, and she felt a prick of remorse.

Declan was looking as though he'd never seen her properly before. He'd gone very pale. "Right," he said. "The mangers need filling."

"Declan," she said, as he reached the door, "we are friends."

"I know," he confirmed curtly.

He had recovered his normal dour demeanour by the time they took the train to London with Mrs. Wellington. James Melbaugh's coach met them at the station, and they drove in style to the vast premises of Tattersall's, where several dispersal sales of bloodstock were taking place.

"I've studied the catalogue and marked those I fancy," Macha said.

James Melbaugh gave her his own well-thumbed catalogue, and they began to compare notes, pleased and impressed with each other on discovering many identical choices.

Freddie Wellington looked over their shoulders and commented, "I see neither of you think much of Tulip Mary."

They had almost forgotten Freddie.

"At a trial last week she was very promising," he went on. "And she is a full sister to Captain Paul."

Tulip Mary was circled in their catalogues. Then Mrs. Wellington was made comfortable in one of the chairs provided in the gallery, and Macha, to her consternation, was left with her, while the men made their way to the vast glass-covered yard below.

The auctioneer's voice echoed through the building, punctuated by the shrill whinnying of the horses. "Eleven hundred. Eleven hundred. Twelve. Against you, sir. At twelve hundred guineas this filly is certainly a snip. One three. One four. Against you, sir. Last time. Any more anywhere? At fourteen hundred . . ."

This was not at all what Macha had expected. She had thought it would be a matter of haggling directly with the individual owners, and had been confident of striking a good bargain. Now here she was, completely excluded from the proceedings, glaring down on a mob of top hats and bowlers and caps, with not an owner in sight on whom to practise her wiles.

The filly was led out and another led in. The often incomprehensible tones of the auctioneer rattled off again.

"Three thousand guineas—three, three."

But Macha could see no one bidding. She glanced down to see Declan O'Brien looking panic-stricken by the whole business.

"The buyers make secret signs arranged beforehand." Sir Freddie had returned to her side and guessed the problem. "Watch how Bill Beresford there keeps stroking his beard. Many of them are regulars here, and the auctioneer knows what to look for."

"At three thousand five hundred guineas . . . Gentlemen, three thousand five hundred and cheap." There was a long pause, and then the sound of the gavel rapped through the silence.

It was an immense amount of money, and yet the auctioneer had called it cheap. Until that moment Macha had believed herself to be wealthy. As another gleaming, dancing animal was led in, it occurred to her that she was probably the poorest person there and that the purchase of a racehorse might not even be possible.

The names marked in her catalogue came and went. She shook her head at James Melbaugh's enquiring glances and remained very quiet. When the last crowd-drawing colt was sold—for six thousand eight hundred guineas—people began leaving, and Sir Freddie's recommendation was brought in, to very little attention.

Tulip Mary was an extremely pretty filly, with a shapely head and that slinky stride that indicates good action. Macha felt a familiar tremor sharpen her wits as the auctioneer began.

"Tulip Mary, a two-year-old filly by Gameberry. Full sister to Captain Paul. Am I bid four thousand? Three? Two? Start her off, gentlemen. One thousand five hundred guineas, one five, one six, one seven ..."

Macha waited. James Melbaugh was talking to an acquaintance and seemed oblivious to the auction.

"Two thousand. She's very small money at two thousand guineas. Two thousand ..."

Macha leaned over the railing with her arm out. The auctioneer stared and repeated, "Two thousand guineas, gentlemen."

Macha flapped her hand wildly, but again could not hold his eye.

"Two thousand guineas. Last time."

"Two thousand one hundred," she bellowed in a voice trained to carry across the loughs of Connemara.

The man looked up quizzically at Sir Frederick and then at her. "Are you bidding, madam?" he asked in astonishment.

"You know perfectly well I am. My bid is two thousand one hundred guineas," Macha retorted, without dropping a decibel.

The auctioneer looked behind to his superior. The man shrugged and nodded. "Two one," the auctioneer announced angrily, and then with relief, "Two two."

"Two thousand five hundred guineas," the girl called out, ignoring a restraining hand on her arm.

"Two five," the man echoed. "You're losing her, sir. She's worth more than this. Any more anywhere?"

He exhorted and bullied, spinning out her bid in a desperate but unsuccessful attempt to find a male buyer. Finally there was an agonisingly long pause before the gavel knocked. Macha's shriek of joy was audible outside the building, and the whole yard cheered.

"Oh, I can't thank you enough, Freddie—Sir Frederick." She remembered the proprieties too late to stop herself from grasping his hands.

"My dear Miss Sheridan, it was absolutely nothing," he disclaimed with unmistakable adoration.

"Let's hope the filly lives up to all this faith," Melbaugh put in sourly as they met and hurried towards the stables to organise transport.

Tulip Mary was waiting in a groom's charge. Declan O'Brien went straight to her as though mesmerised.

"What do you think, Declan?" Macha asked.

"You've done all right, Miss Sheridan," he said, beaming.

232

Chapter Eight

Society lost much of its appeal after the purchase of Tulip Mary, for Macha suddenly realised how much she had missed the daily routine and those carefree rides over the downs. The filly's arrival caused a transformation in Declan too. He fell in love with Tulip Mary instantly, and she with him. As he worked her, he took to whistling and did not even raise a protest when Macha appeared in trousers and an old jacket to ride out.

"You look like a sack of potatoes on a sidesaddle, anyway," was his only comment. He was certainly easier to live with.

They passed much time discussing Gold, who was ready for breaking, and the girl spent the next weeks working with him. This left less time to brood over the fact that there had been no word from James Melbaugh since the visit to Tattersall's. Although she was at home to callers one afternoon a week at Mrs. Wellington's house, he did not appear, seemingly having taken exception to her unladylike behaviour during the bidding.

Sir Freddie, meanwhile, was a regular visitor. He was not a dashing companion, but Macha became very fond of him, sensing a rather bashful man masked by superficial eccentricity.

As the day of the Petworth House ball drew near, the necessary fittings at Mr. Dodds's establishment resulted in an exquisite lemon-yellow chiffon gown adorned with clusters of ribbons. The bodice, sleeves and tiers of its skirt were edged with lace, and the satin train was decorated with hand-painted flowers. On Mrs. Wellington's advice she paid over twenty pounds for a necklace of pearl daisies with diamond centres and had her hair dressed with pearls intertwined in it.

On the evening of the ball their carriage drew up at the entrance to the long grey house with its windows all ablaze. As they made their way to the marble hall, Macha was speechless at the sight of opulence she could not have imagined. Quite forgetting her promised first dance with Freddie, she strayed away from the party, beguiled by the marble and the gold leaf, the paintings, murals and sumptuous furniture. Until this moment she had not appreciated the full meaning of the word rich.

"My nephew has been looking for you everywhere. It is not just thoughtlessness on your part, Miss Sheridan, but unforgivable discourtesy." Mrs. Wellington cut off Macha's ashamed reply by marching back to the ballroom, her ward bringing up the rear.

"Freddie, I want to apologise—" Macha began abjectly, as he revolved her expertly round the floor.

"Tell me more about this colt of yours," he put in quickly. "Your cousin

O'Brien tells me he's a real dandy." He was determined not to let her humiliate herself.

"They say he's just like Gallinule," she said, and gave his hand a grateful squeeze. "We want to take Tulip Mary and him to train at Newmarket, and I'm about to start hunting for a house there."

"My aunt should have told me your plan, for you may not have to search at all," he said eagerly. "I might know just the place."

"Where? Oh, tell me about it," Macha said.

As she spoke, James Melbaugh swept by them with a radiant girl, and Macha, watching as they swirled away, did not hear a word of Freddie's answer.

The next waltz on her programme had been reserved by Melbaugh. It was an arrangement he could not fail to honour, and it would give her the chance to put matters right between them, she thought. She found herself anticipating, with some fervour, how he would hold her.

Approaching her, Melbaugh bowed stiffly, and as they danced he maintained enough distance from her so that they could have raised their arms and simply allowed others to dance between them.

"Is this not a wonderful ball?" she said tentatively.

"Tolerable."

She tried again. "Have you been racing recently?"

"Of course."

"We have not, for several weeks."

"Really." He stared over her head with an expression of extreme boredom, which suddenly changed into a brilliant smile as his previous partner danced by.

Macha narrowed her eyes ominously. She apparently missed a step accidentally, stamped heavily on his foot and had the satisfaction of seeing him wince.

There was little satisfaction for her during the rest of the ball, although England's most aristocratic young men were so keen to partner her that she did not sit out a single dance. But then neither did James Melbaugh, who glided, twirled and spun past her, each time with a different beauty in his arms.

Macha laughed and tossed her head and trapped unwary gallants with a devastating mixture of flashing eyes, soft Irish voice and naively outrageous wit. Yet she was glad when the time came to leave, and she wandered into the fresh air with relief.

Just ahead of her, James Melbaugh, in scarlet-lined black cloak and silk top hat, sprang athletically into the driver's seat of his carriage, played the thong of his whip and skimmed off down the drive. She would not think of him again, she vowed.

But she thought of little else.

234

THE TRAIN CROSSED the autumn landscape, through the yellowing woods of Surrey with their flashing copper beeches; over the Thames and into the foggy, shrieking, packed, glass-vaulted chaos of a London station; then they were on their way to the heath where King Charles the First built a stand from which to watch the running of the Gold Cup—to Newmarket, the hub of English racing.

Rooms had been reserved for them at the Rutland Arms inn, and at first light next morning Macha dressed and went out into the hoof-clattering, wide-awake streets, through which the first strings of racehorses were wending their way towards the racecourse. Hundreds of thoroughbreds were converging on the gallops—bays, chestnuts, greys and blacks.

"I thought I'd find you here," said Declan O'Brien's voice by her side. "Was there ever anything like this?"

"Never." She drew in her breath with a sob.

The bells for matins rang out from All Saints, and still the horses came. "You'll be out there with them soon," Macha promised, reading his thoughts.

That afternoon Sir Freddie drove them out of the town and up Cambridge Hill, turning in to a short carriage sweep leading to a pretty, red-brick house.

"Is it for sale?" asked Macha.

"For rent," he replied, and when she looked doubtful, he continued. "I realise it may be too small, but such an arrangement would give you time to look for a larger property to buy."

Macha could not help smiling as she scanned the rows of windows and compared the building with her Sussex cottage. To her the house appeared palatial.

The door opened into a large oak-panelled hall with a staircase curving to a galleried first-floor landing. Macha was led from drawing room to breakfast room, dining room to smoking room, up and down stairs, until she was completely lost. She could not imagine how she would handle such a place. She was thinking up excuses to extricate herself as they followed the back drive to the yard, where her whole opinion changed.

Most of the stables were brand-new. There was a large tack room, a harness room, and a stallion box that was exactly right for Gold. The problems of coping with a large house vanished. The yard felt right, which was all that mattered. The rent for Ebberly House was agreed to, and all the way back to Newmarket Freddie kept exclaiming that everything was "top-hole".

Back at the inn, Mrs. Wellington retired to rest, leaving her nephew to show her ward round the town. The two strolled up the lane behind the inn to Palace House where the Prince of Wales usually stayed while visiting Newmarket. It was built of ordinary light-coloured brick.

"Why, it's not so different from my house!" Macha exclaimed in disappointment. "It's not a real marble-and-gold palace at all."

"Macha! My dear Macha!" Sir Freddie unexpectedly seized her hands and gazed down at her with a peculiar expression on his face. "Macha, I know I'm rather a chump, that is, in some ways not a particularly clever fellow, but I would treat you like a goddess."

Macha was taken aback to realise he was making a proposal, although it was unclear whether it was a marriage proposal or a less respectable one. She waited patiently as he floundered.

"The truth is, I've never met a girl like you, such a sport, y'know, and so pretty, d'you see."

"Freddie," she began, "what on earth are you trying to say?"

"Well, I'm asking you to marry me, of course, old girl," he blurted out. "I mean, we could have a topping time together. Plenty of horses—racing and so on."

"Oh, Freddie," she said, genuinely moved. "Freddie, I am truly honoured that you should want me for your wife. But I cannot accept your proposal."

"No . . . no. I did not think you would." He let her hands go, and his face fell into mournful folds. "Prefer Melbaugh, I expect. Good-looking chap and all that."

Macha did not answer.

By the time they returned to the hotel, Mrs. Wellington was waiting with an ill-concealed impatience. She sent her nephew off on some unnecessary errand and turned on the girl a face that would brook no prevarication. "Well? Did Freddie propose?"

"Why should you think such a thing?" Macha fenced.

"Because naturally he asked my permission first," retorted Mrs. Wellington. "Now, when is the wedding to be?"

Macha responded with singular lack of tact. "There's to be no wedding. I've turned him down."

"You've refused to marry Sir Frederick Wellington? Surely you cannot have been so foolish. Do you realise he has an income of twenty-five thousand pounds a year and is not only a baronet in his own right but also the sole heir to the Marquis of Angleton? He stands to inherit a fortune. Such an opportunity will never come your way again, you can be certain of that."

"Please don't be offended, Mrs. Wellington," Macha pleaded. "Sir Frederick is everything you say and much more. He's gentle and kind, and I know he's a great catch for a girl without background. But I also know we would not make each other happy. Besides, at only seventeen years old, I am too young for marriage."

They sat in uncomfortable silence. Eventually it was the older woman who spoke. "Well, you have made your decision, and I admit to being disappointed, but the matter will rest there." She stood up with dignified grandeur and marched from the room.

Freddie had returned in time to catch the end of the scene. "Do not concern yourself, Miss Sheridan. The dear old trout will soon be back on form again."

And his assessment was accurate. The next day Mrs. Wellington, followed by several servants, was driven to Ebberly House to embark on a ferocious programme of cleaning, measuring and ordering, in which appeared to lie the cure for her chagrin over the failure of her marital plans for ward and nephew.

IT WAS A WORKING WINTER. Society deserted Newmarket for the social imperative of London, leaving behind a community totally engrossed in the raising and training of racehorses.

At Ebberly House a locked room above the horse stalls was set aside for Macha to change in secretly, so as to ride out before the domestic servants were up. Gold would be waiting, his eyes like black marble and his white blaze luminescent.

He was already entered in the Brocklesby Stakes and the Darley Maiden Stakes at the beginning of the next flat season. He was now almost as big as his renowned sire. The nobility of the colt was always marvellous to her. Above all things she loved him, as though, like Macha the goddess, she had given birth to him herself. He was her last link with Molloy and her children, her tie to Ireland.

It must have been the wettest day of a wet, chilly spring. As Macha left the woods at the top of Long Hill, another horse and rider suddenly came up from behind and bolted past, causing Gold to rear in surprise and deluging them both with mud. Without a thought Macha dug her heels into the colt's side in anger, and the horse leaped to the challenge, swallowing the incline in massive strides and closing on the other like a vengeful missile. Gold had the bit between his teeth and his rival outclassed, and was not to be stopped until he was some lengths ahead. They flared past.

The unknown competitor was only halfway down the hill when Macha drew up at the foot and waited, a suitably coarse observation ready on her tongue. But as the rider drew nearer, she saw to her horror that it was James Melbaugh.

Wheeling Gold about, she started to canter away, but Melbaugh crossed the turf at an angle and cut off her retreat. He drew up directly in her path and stared. She ducked her head.

"Hiding your face will do you no good, Miss Sheridan."

She lifted her head and glared. "Right enough, James Melbaugh. And you can make of it what you will. Now get that nag out of the way and let me pass."

His laughter was wild, and then he asked unexpectedly, "Have you thought of me, Macha?"

"I have not," she lied stoutly.

"Well, I have thought of you constantly, and now here you are in cap and breeches, looking ... ravishing."

It was obvious that he was teasing. She threw him a look of contempt. "Poke fun all you like, Mr. Melbaugh, and tell all the world, but be sure and tell them at the same time how Gold and I thrashed you and your brute, for all your breeding."

"You did indeed, Miss Sheridan," he agreed. "You have a remarkable horse, and you are a very fine rider."

"I will be on my way," she said, and started to move off.

"Wait!"

She turned, suspicious.

"Marry me."

"What?"

"Marry me, Macha Sheridan. I must have you. Marry me tomorrow."

"Merciful heaven," she stormed. "You court me for a couple of weeks, then ignore me for long enough to grow an oak from seed and build a ship with it, and then you expect to marry me! Well, Mr. Melbaugh, I'd as soon hitch myself to a vagabond."

He drew alongside with a heartbreaking smile and looked into her eyes. "No, you wouldn't."

She looked into his compelling blue eyes. They glinted like cut sapphire and, behind the humour, other exciting qualities could be detected. She felt a surge of pure greed. "No, I would not," she echoed weakly.

"Marry me," he insisted.

Oh, she wanted him too. "I will," she consented unhesitatingly.

That was the moment Declan O'Brien chose to arrive on Tulip Mary, and a look of panic froze his face as he realised that Melbaugh was holding Macha's hand. "He knows. You're ruined," Declan burst out.

"Don't worry, dear boy, just congratulate me," Melbaugh drawled. "We're about to become cousins. Miss Sheridan looks so irresistibly delicious in her novel outfit that I had no option but to propose marriage at once, and she has accepted."

Macha was far too excited to notice the colour drain from Declan's face as he mumbled something about wishing her happiness and turned the filly to ride blindly away.

"I shall call on your guardian and we'll settle the matter at eleven," said James Melbaugh cheerily, as though arranging a picnic outing, instead of the most momentous occasion in their lives.

238

MACHA FLUNG OFF her cloak and the unbuttoned dress beneath and stepped into the bath of hot water which was always ready for her return from the gallops. Once dry, she sprayed herself with lavender water and rubbed grenadine into her lips, while a young maid tried to salvage the wreckage of her wet hair. Half a dozen frocks were brought out, tried on and discarded before she decided on the azure cashmere, a demure and pretty gown which she hoped would obliterate from James Melbaugh's mind the image of herself in breeches and boots.

At breakfast, she dropped her toast and spilled her tea and behaved so nervously that Mrs. Wellington was convinced she had a fever and began to talk of calling a doctor.

"I am perfectly well," Macha assured her breathlessly. "I am merely elated that Gold ran so superbly this morning, better than ever before."

She paused, before adding in what she hoped was a casual tone, "We met James Melbaugh, exercising a horse."

"Indeed!" Mrs. Wellington's fruity contralto exclamation made it clear that she was not fooled.

"Yes. In fact, he did mention his resolve to call today."

"What a pity we shall be out," said the dowager, rising from the table.

"Oh no! Oh please, Mrs. Wellington, we cannot be out!" Macha, too, jumped up in agitation. "It is most important that we are at home."

The widow waved an interested servant from the room before commenting with some severity, "My dear Macha, James Melbaugh has not made the slightest effort to see you for months. It would be most unwise if he were given the impression that you are eager for his company."

"But he wishes to see you . . . He has something to ask you." Macha was close to tears.

The old lady was imperturbable. "I am sure that whatever he wishes to ask can wait."

"It can't! It can't! He wants to marry me and I've said 'Yes'."

Mrs. Wellington carefully poured herself another cup of tea. Then she sat down again and sipped it slowly with slightly trembling lips.

"When did all this take place?" she asked, at last.

"This morning, as soon as we met again. He said he'd never stopped thinking of me." There was no point in lying.

"Well, his method of becoming engaged seems very bad form, if not actually peculiar, but a gel in your situation must find a husband and he is certainly an excellent match." Mrs. Wellington shook her head in some confusion.

"You will give us your blessing?" begged Macha.

"Are you quite sure this is what you want, child?" The old lady still looked very uncertain.

"Yes. Oh yes!"

"Then we shall wait for the young man to arrive and hear his intentions," was as far as Mrs. Wellington would commit herself.

However, two hours later, she was drinking a toast to their future, in sherry.

There could be no wedding until after Gold's first race in April, Macha told her new fiancé firmly, for she had to devote all her attention to training him.

"I never thought to find myself in competition with a horse for a lady's affections," he complained with a wry smile.

"But what a horse!" she responded, and he had to agree.

OCCUPIED WITH WEDDING PLANS, Macha and Mrs. Wellington went the following day to Regent Street in London, where they bought yards of ivory satin and flounces of Brussels-point lace to be forwarded direct to Mr. Toby Dodds in Chichester. Then they ordered lingerie and linen and, finally, visited the shoemaker, who was to make ivory satin shoes.

"Are you certain you would not prefer *white* satin, Macha dear?" the dowager asked. "The ivory shade is lovely, but a bride should be dressed in the white of purity."

Macha thought of Molloy. If he were able to see from beyond the grave, she knew he would not blame her for marrying again, but a virgin-white gown would seem like a denial of their marriage and their children. So she shook her head. "Cream is my favourite."

As they sat in the train on the way home again, she remembered the day in Cork so long ago when she had ventured into that smart shop and bought the bright pink satin, the coloured ribbon and the silk petticoats for her first wedding. She fingered the shamrock brooch that she always wore, for him.

THE ATMOSPHERE HEIGHTENED in Newmarket as the start of the flat-racing season drew close. At Ebberly, training intensified, and another stablelad and an old groom were hired.

James called daily and spent much time in the stables with Macha. Freddie Wellington became a regular visitor, and the experience of the two men was invaluable.

On the day of Gold's first race, the Brocklesby Stakes, Macha actually travelled in the train van with Declan and her colt, leaving the bemused party of Mrs. Wellington, Sir Frederick and the Honourable James Melbaugh to make the journey in a first-class passenger compartment.

At the racecourse, Declan was grim-faced and preoccupied. Macha gave him her last instructions as he mounted in the paddock. Then Gold, showing absolutely no sign of nerves, cantered down to the start with skittish enjoyment.

Macha's knuckles showed white as she raised her field glasses. She could not breathe as she saw Gold back away from the starting line. Then the flag was up. He gave a little bounce forward, and they were off. She picked up her colours—gold with emerald green—among the leaders, and then Gold was alongside Lord Rosefield's horse. They were neck and neck. She did not hear the full-throated roar or the thundering hooves. She watched Declan's hands and legs moving perfectly, like a part of the chestnut's own body. Gold thrust forward and stormed past Helm's Vintage, picking up a length, then two, and sprinting home to win the Brocklesby Stakes by three lengths.

Macha did not remember the tears streaming down her face, nor leading her horse through cheering onlookers, nor seeing Declan's ecstatic face. The explosion of the cork recalled her attention.

"Laurent Perrier," James murmured significantly in her ear.

His eyes were brighter than blue meteors, his lean face handsome as he smiled possessively over his bride-to-be and introduced her to dozens of strangers, who congratulated him on winning Macha and her on winning the race. Acquaintances bowed and smiled, not a few of the young women with very strained politeness, and Macha seemed to move several inches above the ground through the rest of the day.

"What do you think of the second week in June?" asked James as she leaned on his arm in a haze of euphoria.

"Derby week," she replied promptly.

"Oh, of course. That's out. What about the first of June?"

"The week before Derby week." She giggled.

"I'm talking about our wedding day, goose," he said, tapping her small nose. "Shall we marry on the first of June?"

"That would be lovely," she responded eagerly. "Then I can go to the Derby as the Honourable Mrs. James Melbaugh."

"And what about the honeymoon? I thought you might like to go to France for a month."

"During the flat season?" She came out of her reverie. "James do we have to? If we go to France, think what we'll miss here."

He shook his head, chuckling. "You're the only girl in Britain who would turn down a chance to visit Paris," he said. "All right, we'll postpone the honeymoon, but you'd better produce plenty of wins to compensate."

THERE WERE JOURNEYS to Gloucestershire and Hampshire to meet her fiancé's family: uncles who were captivated and aunts who were not.

Poldonith Castle, the family seat, was a thirteenth-century stone pile on the borders of Wales, clearly built for defence with battlements and towers, a drawbridge and a moat. James's mother was dead and his father,

242

the Earl of Watersmeet, was a kindly man, whose absent-mindedness put Macha at ease.

He seemed more concerned with the stock of partridge in his coverts than the future of his younger son. After all, his heir, Charles, had done the right thing by marrying an American with a multimillion-dollar fortune. There were also three small sisters in the schoolroom, and they were to be Macha's bridesmaids.

They made innumerable trips to London for more shoes and gloves, nightdresses and chemises. There were discussions with caterers, flowers to be chosen, invitations to be sent. At night Macha would flop onto her feather mattress and let her man drift through her mind, with his long, muscular legs and wide, straight shoulders. His wickedly inviting stare would be the last image in her head as she went to sleep.

On the day of the ceremony the wedding dress arrived at Poldonith Castle with the imperturbable Mr. Dodds. Seed pearls from five hundred oysters and mists of lace and satin were slipped over her head. The hairdresser gathered her thick hair round a wire frame, created a fabulous confection of curls and arranged the exquisite veil. Macha gaped at the ravishing transfiguration in the cheval glass.

"Did I not tell you to leave it all to me, Miss Sheridan?" The court dressmaker reminded her of his original promise to make her beautiful.

Mrs. Wellington, resplendent in mauve, dabbed at her eyes and sniffed loudly.

THE FAMILY COACH, with motto and heraldic bearings emblazoned on its panels, gave a jerk and then bumped off down the long drive, through the high iron gates and along the lane.

Macha was on her way to church, and passing the open common. There, drawn up on the turf, was the most ornate and elaborately decorated bow-top van she had ever seen.

"Stop! Stop!" she called to the liveried coachman, and the horses halted, snorting. The two vehicles stood side by side.

Macha stared at the magnificent bow-top. It had a scalloped frame and intricate scrolls of gold, carved and painted leaves and flowers, and tall wheels of crimson and yellow. On the door was a horse painted with gold leaf. She could not take her eyes off it.

A hand touched her arm, and she turned, full of an unbearable nostalgia. Declan O'Brien, who had generously offered to give her away, read her feelings and shook his head. "The past is gone. We must drive on," he said gently, and gave the instruction.

The church was crowded. The cream of the aristocracy and sporting society was waiting. Declan, very young and grave in morning coat and pinstriped trousers, gave Macha his arm. The organ sounded. Her bridegroom, so dashing and pedigreed, was standing before the altar. It was all totally alien. She had never felt so excluded. The country, the people, the setting, the ceremony, even the religion had nothing to do with her. Wildly, she started to turn, to run from the place, to return to the freedom of the road and never look back. Declan gripped her arm tightly against his side and took the first step forward.

Soon she heard herself repeating, "I, Macha, take thee, James George Sebastian, to my wedded husband . . ."

The expression on James's face was one of pure delight. Not even the solemnity of the vows could subdue his grin. He winked and squeezed her hand, the creases at the corners of his mouth deepened. All at once she was not thinking sad thoughts any more.

The wedding guests ate and drank heartily. And later, when James's hand closed over hers on the sword, to make the first cut in the four-tier wedding cake, Macha made her wish. It should have been to live happily with him for ever after, but instead she wished that one day Gold would win the Triple Crown.

There were toasts and speeches, and a girl in a daringly low-cut, clinging gown caught her bouquet and glared at her with transparent hostility. Macha had no idea who she was and would have asked James had the horses not jolted the carriage forward and thrown her into his arms.

The carriage rolled on, and she leaned drowsily against James in a way that only a new wife is permitted to do. Finally they were driven through a village twinkling with lamps and up a winding drive, past what seemed to be a tower, to an open oak door at which a butler was waiting.

"Where are we?" she asked.

"As Paris did not meet with my lady's approval, some friends have lent us their castle." He helped her to the ground with a playfully exaggerated gesture of courtesy.

Another castle! She was silent as the housekeeper led them through the great hall and up the heavily carved staircase and, to her puzzlement, showed her to one room and James to another.

As she stood alone, wondering what to do next, an adjoining door opened softly and James Melbaugh stood in its frame. Macha felt her colour rise.

"You are a coquette, a naughty coquette." He caught her round the waist.

"What's a coquette?" she asked, not struggling too hard to escape.

"A woman who drives men out of their senses with her wiles," he growled, still gripping her with one arm while taking the pins from her hair with his free hand.

He was light-hearted in his lovemaking, which freed her from the embarrassment of earnestness. His fairness, sunny skin and smooth,

244

broad chest were unexpected. She had always thought of men as being dark and knotted with muscles. James Melbaugh was fine-toned and strong, a golden thoroughbred.

There was no sleep that night.

Chapter Nine

In the following months they lived life at a frantic pace, training the horses, hurrying back and forth up and down England to race meetings, going to garden parties and to one country house party after another. It was an idyllic summer, danced through a succession of glittering ballrooms to the music of all the most popular orchestras.

She became quite an acceptable partner at bridge, a skill which was *de rigueur*, and she learned to play croquet ruthlessly. It was bizarre the way this game could rouse the phlegmatic English to such venomous choler. Old wounds were reopened, revenge for past slights was taken, and friends were turned into lifelong enemies when a shot knocked a ball out of play. Macha brought a steady hand, an unerring aim and a Celtic sense of mischief to the lawns, and entertained herself greatly watching the consequences.

Macha's horses ran well, with Declan O'Brien taking charge when she was away. Her husband's successes further enhanced his reputation as a gentleman rider, and the money poured in. Then it was August, and James announced that they were going to a friend's estate in Scotland.

"Gordon Mackintosh owns some of the best grouse moors there are. You will love it, my darling. All your friends will be there, and as we chaps will be out on the moors all day, you'll be able to gossip to your heart's content."

It sounded ominous. Wherever they went, she found herself in the same circle of single girls, to whom everything, especially every man, was "simply deevy", and married women who only talked of love affairs or about where they had been and who else had been there. They were a tightly bound group, held together by connections of background and marriage. In this, they were just like Romanies, Macha thought, and in their perpetual trundling from one house to another and their seasonal migrations to Ascot and Scotland and Monte Carlo, they were no different from travellers moving from site to site.

They arrived at a gaunt stone pile in Inverness. Even to Macha, hardy from years on the road, it was bitter cold. Fires, she was informed, were never lit in the bedrooms before mid-September. She changed in the room she had been assigned, next to James's room, and shivered.

As she descended to the sepulchral hall an outraged American voice sounded above her. "A fortnight? You mean we have to stay here for two whole weeks, Archie? With no fires and all that rain pouring down outside?"

Macha turned to see a couple crossing the gallery. The man's voice was too low to be heard, but the girl's reply was quite clear. "Yes, I know I said I'd love to visit a Scottish estate, but I did not say I wanted to die of cold on one."

Her husband was obviously English and obviously embarrassed, but his American wife was too appalled by her surroundings to care. She caught Macha's eye as they rounded the corner. "Do you have a fire in your bedroom?" she demanded.

The Irish girl grinned and shook her head.

"There you are, Archie. I told you it was no oversight," the other said triumphantly. She turned back to Macha. "And do you know that the men are going to be out all day, every day? If we don't perish of the polar temperature, we shall become moribund with boredom."

Seeing that his wife had attached herself to a female guest, Archie melted away thankfully.

"Daisy Fitzclarence." The American ignored etiquette by introducing herself and holding out her hand. "I was a Vanderbilt before I married Archie."

Macha took the hand and gave her own name.

"Oh, you're not English either." Daisy Fitzclarence was delighted. "Have you ever met such a lot of stuffed shirts?"

She was as tall as Macha and exceedingly pretty, with chestnut hair, a creamy complexion and large, clever hazel eyes.

Macha liked her at once, and they became allies for the rest of their enforced stay. By the second day they had decided that nothing would persuade them to sit about doing nothing for another minute, in such conditions.

"We could go into Inverness and shop," Macha suggested.

"Shop! Have you seen Inverness? My dear, skirts with bustles have only just arrived up here."

Then Macha had an idea. "I know! We'll do what they do."

"What's that?"

"Shoot, of course. Why didn't I think of it before?"

Her friend was doubtful. "They'll never allow it."

"They will so."

"You're right. We'll make 'em."

Lord Bentland, Daisy's husband, quailed at the idea, but James Melbaugh thought it had the makings of a capital caper.

"How good a shot are you?" he asked. "The truth now."

"Oh, I'm good enough," Macha replied airily.

246

It was a challenge he could not decline. "I'll ask Gordon Mackintosh if you can pot a rabbit or two in the glen."

After they had dined, they went to the glen. Quite a party accompanied them, the event being a diversion for the bored women and an amusing entertainment for the men. Gordon Mackintosh lent Macha an old shotgun he had used as a boy.

The heather smelled sweetly sharp after the rain that had been blown westward by a blustering wind. The glen was sheltered, peaceful and partly wooded. Macha missed the first rabbit, but then all the reflexes that had bagged her countless suppers in Ireland took over. In rapid succession she shot a hare, half a dozen rabbits, then a pigeon and a brace of woodcocks. There was a burst of spontaneous applause.

"You have an eagle eye, Mrs. Melbaugh," complimented Mackintosh.

"I'm out of practice, or I would have had that first rabbit," she confessed.

On the ride back, the gentlemen were full of cordial camaraderie. As they reached the great house they saw a brougham drawn up at the front entrance and a woman being helped to step from it. She turned, and Macha recognised the girl who had caught her bouquet at her wedding.

"Who is that?" she asked James.

"Victoria Paxton, of course. She was at our wedding. You cannot have forgotten, surely." He sounded testy, as though she had made a gaffe.

The ladies congratulated her on her day's sport with faultless politeness, but beneath it Macha clearly discerned disapproval. Afterwards, at bridge, she played forgetfully and therefore badly, to the annoyance of her partner.

"I have a little headache," she confessed to him apologetically.

James, who had overheard, came up to her side at once.

"Why don't you retire early?" he said.

"Will you not mind?"

"Of course not, sweet girl, and I shall not disturb you later."

He could be very kind and considerate, she reflected, as the maid unbuttoned her gown. How lucky she had been to find such a husband.

Her head ached and she lay in the dark unable to sleep. The hours went by. There were muffled sounds of others passing her door on the way to their rooms and then, later, the creaking of a floorboard as a gentleman crept towards the bed of his mistress, most probably Sir Henry Talbot going to Lady Anthony Arran, or Lord Anthony Arran tiptoeing to Baroness Radley's arms. She wondered if James was still awake and guessed not. It would be comforting to curl up against his warm, sleeping back. The inexplicable uneasiness she was experiencing would disappear. Reaching for her satin wrap, she crossed the room quietly, opened their connecting door, tiptoed towards his bed and slid under the eiderdown.

It was as cold as a glacier. She felt about with her hand and then sat up. The bed was empty. Lighting the candle on the table beside her, Macha stared round the room. James's shoes lay discarded on the floor. The bed had not been slept in.

Perhaps he had forgotten his pipe and returned downstairs, she thought, fear shredding such logic even as it presented itself.

Her throat constricted, and her hands tightened. Her mind was crackling with half-formed and horrible ideas. She gave a loud sob and lay back in the bed, sweating coldly. She knew, and could not bear to know.

Repeatedly the slim hand reached up and caught the wedding bouquet, followed by that look of deep dislike. The hair was sleek and blonde, the eyes cool and pale, the swanlike neck created, it seemed, to wear emeralds and priceless pearls. How amusing had been her conversation at dinner. Aristocratic, confident and beautiful. Victoria Paxton. Oh, Macha knew where her husband was.

She lay motionless, in a trance of misery, her eyes wide open and unblinking, her heart throbbing like a wound as the hours passed. She waited in limbo as the first bird fluted its sad, recurrent note. Then the door handle turned and James entered the room. She lay and stared at him.

"I awoke early and—" he began, and saw it was useless. "I—she—" He floundered again. "Don't look like that! It is unimportant, the way of the world. I've known her since we were children. . . . By gad, woman! It means nothing."

Macha rose from the bed and crossed the floor. At the door to her room she turned. "You are a whore," she spat, and he quailed before the scorn in her eyes.

A maid arrived in response to her summons and was instructed to pack her boxes and have them transported to Inverness station immediately. By the time her husband found the courage to come to her room, Macha was dressed in travelling clothes. He gazed at the packing operation, and there was an expression of appalled disbelief on his face. "What are you doing?"

"I am leaving." Macha tucked a strand of hair under her hat.

"That is quite impossible. It would be unthinkable to create such a scandal."

"Me create a scandal? I think not, James Melbaugh. It was yourself who created the scandal by fornicating all the night long with that Paxton slut."

"Macha, there is not one married man in our set who does not have a mistress. It is something every wife accepts."

"Not this wife."

"You cannot seriously mean to leave here over this business. I absolutely forbid you to go."

248

"Apparently you do not understand, James." Macha faced him calmly. "I am not simply leaving this place. I am leaving you."

James Melbaugh went pale. "Look, why don't you rest in your room today? It will give you time to recover yourself."

"I am leaving you, James," Macha repeated patiently.

"You'll be ruined, rejected by society. Don't you understand?" He gripped her arm and gave it a little shake. "No woman leaves her husband. You will become an outcast. You cannot survive."

"Oh, I survived well enough before I met you, and I shall doubtless survive again."

"Well, expect no help from me. I'll see you damned for this!" He slammed from the room.

A carriage was brought to the front of the house, and Macha's boxes loaded into it. When all was ready, she went downstairs. As she reached the breakfast room Victoria Paxton was just spooning a lightly coddled egg onto her plate.

Macha took the plate, laid it gently on the sideboard, and slapped the blonde hard across the face. "That is for stealing my husband," she announced. She clenched her fist and swung her arm. The punch landed on the well-bred nose. "And that is so that you don't forget!"

Blood flowed satisfactorily down the girl's chin. Macha turned on her heel before the speechless guests and walked out.

THE TRAIN STEAMED SOUTH, leaving Scotland behind. A jumble of memories and emotions suddenly crowded Macha's compartment—James's smile, which made her pulse race, the fun of him, that private look kept only for her, all lost, all betrayed. The bitter tears coursed, and with them came jealousy and rage, mordant as acid.

Eventually she reached Ebberly and the refuge of her boudoir, which she locked against the knocking of the servants and the anxious enquiries of Declan O'Brien and Mrs. Wellington. Trays of food were left outside and taken away untouched. Twenty-four hours later her husband came to shout and plead at the door and be ignored.

"If you do not open this door, I shall order it to be broken down," he bullied on the third day, and Macha lifted the shotgun she kept by the bed, just as her father had taught her, and blasted it in the direction of the voice. A blessed silence followed.

It was dark when Mrs. Wellington tapped on her door. "There is someone to see you, my dear. A friend who has come a very long way," she said nervously. "Do talk to her."

Then Macha heard a warm, young voice. "Honey, please let me in. It's worse than Siberia out here. The draughts in your English houses would freeze a penguin."

Macha opened the door to Daisy Fitzclarence. And then she talked and cried, and her friend held her hand and listened and poured out glasses of brandy until Macha's pain became blunted.

In the morning Daisy returned with a breakfast tray, insisting that Macha eat every mouthful.

"There," Daisy said, finally removing the remnants of the meal. "You are in a much better state to think sensibly and make proper decisions now, and I have a letter for you."

My dearest, darling girl,

Forgive me, I beg you. It was all a monstrous mistake brought about, I am sure, by too much port, and I am now demented with regret. Upon my most solemn oath such behaviour will never, ever occur again. Permit me to see you and talk with you, my angel, and I know I shall be able to make you forget the whole affair. I am waiting only for your word.

Your abject, but adoring husband,
James Melbaugh

Macha read it twice and then stared out of the window.

"What will you do?" wondered Daisy.

"Leave him."

"If you do, what sort of life do you think you'll have?" asked her friend. "It will not be the same as before. You will be ruined."

"But I have done nothing wrong. It is he who has been unfaithful."

"Men can do what they like." Daisy was resigned. "Look, Macha, you love him and he loves you. Why not forgive him, forget it and start again?"

Macha looked as though she were about to break down. "I know I will never be able to forget, and I don't think I can forgive either."

"Well, take time to decide. James has gone to his London house until he hears from you, so there is no hurry." Daisy gave her a hug. "You know, I really want to see you two together again, but may I give you a tip? If you feel, in the end, that you cannot take James back, then do not stay in England. Go to the United States. Life is not so restricted there. Anyone with guts and determination can be a success in America—and there are some very fine horses too!"

FLOWERS BEGAN ARRIVING in bunches and baskets and boxes, and eventually a whole carriage full of them. Chocolates and bonbons followed, then hats with plumes and veils and blooms and ribbons and seed pearls, then a diamond bracelet, and finally he telephoned.

"Are you at home tomorrow?"

She thought for a long moment.

"Darling?" he went on. "I want to see you, to talk to you."

250

"I will be home," she said reluctantly.

When he arrived, he hesitated at the door, then entered with some diffidence. Macha, sitting opposite him in the drawing room, listened as he made renewed apologies and promises and forecasts for their wonderful future together.

"We'll buy some more horses. I'll take you on that honeymoon to Paris. We'll forget what happened. Everything will be as it was before .. better, in fact."

But she knew it would not. Yet she hated seeing her golden, proud and laughing man humbled. She stood up and went to him, putting her arms round his neck and her head on his chest, and felt his own arms tighten about her.

"Thank God, Macha," he mumbled.

Chapter Ten

To her surprise James was right, for some time. The following months were as good as the first months of their marriage, and their life together was the same—their winning streak continuing, entertaining their friends and being entertained, dancing all night at the Duke of Devonshire's ball at Chatsworth. They removed to James's London house, and Macha spent all her time changing her clothes, from morning gowns to tea gowns to ball gowns. She never rode at all any more. James propelled them from one engagement to the next without pause. Declan O'Brien ran the yard at Ebberly now.

But after a while Macha found herself growing conscious of her own dissatisfaction at the thought of the years ahead containing nothing but dress fittings, chitchat and pointless pastimes. She wanted to work again, to feel the sweat run down between her shoulder blades and to ache with effort. She longed for serious discussions and planning, with men who smelled of horses and harness instead of scented soap. She was losing touch with her true aims and even losing touch with herself.

In January she returned to Ebberly House, leaving James to his London amusements. Newmarket Heath brought colour back into Macha's face, and within days she felt healthier.

"Don't think you're riding work until you've stopped all that huffing and groaning," Declan told her cruelly. "I'm not having a decent animal wrecked just because you've been sitting about eating like next year's bacon for six months."

From uncoordinated and bony boyhood, Declan O'Brien had become hard and capable, a man who had an affinity with the horses almost matching her own, and still light enough to race. Riding both for the yard and for other owners, he had had plenty of winners during the season.

Together they went over the prospects of her runners—the best races for each to enter, the distances and conditions, the possible rivals. She had complete confidence in Declan's judgment.

It was like old times. The routine of the yard dominated everything. James telephoned her quite often, but their worlds were so different now that there seemed to be little to say. She was too absorbed in her work, and his night with Victoria Paxton had effectively destroyed the prospect of abiding matrimonial love between them. Only lust was left, and that too burned less fiercely.

When he burst into her room before dawn one day, she thought at first he was an intruder and reached for her shotgun.

"Macha, darling! It's me . . . James." He fell across her body and began sobbing. He smelled of stale tobacco and alcohol.

"Mercy! Are you hurt? Are you ill? How did you get here at this time of night?"

"I drove the four-in-hand." He sobbed louder, like an angry child, and she grew vaguely frightened.

"James, tell me, for the love of God, what has happened?"

"I'm ruined," he said.

"Ruined? What do you mean, ruined?"

"I'm ruined. Don't you understand? I've lost everything—money, house, everything."

"No, I don't understand, James," she said slowly. "How have you lost everything? What do you mean?"

"I mean I've lost everything, at the gaming tables." He groaned.

"You've gambled away all your money . . . and your house?" Her mind ran over the news quickly, checking its seriousness. "Well, James, you've been a fool. It's as well I've some money and we've rented this house."

"Oh, God," he moaned. "How can you be so stupid? What's yours is mine in law, and I've lost everything, every penny. We'll have to move from here, sell the horses. There is nothing left."

"Sell the horses?" she screamed. "You're not selling my horses. I will shoot you dead, James Melbaugh, before I let you take one of my horses."

But despite her howling protests and her threats, most of the horses had to go. Only Macha's murderous fury saved Gold and the mare, his mother. It was fraudulently arranged that Declan O'Brien buy them for a token figure.

All the servants were sacked, and the grooms. Mrs. Wellington went tearfully back to Chichester, and most of the furniture was auctioned, along with Macha's furs and jewellery. She hid only the gold shamrock brooch she had worn at her wedding to Molloy.

James stayed drunk throughout the weeks during which the entire dismal process took place, and only showed signs of awareness when they finally climbed down from the hired carriage that had met them at Singleton station and carried them to the old Sussex cottage.

"Where the devil are we?" he asked blearily.

"Home," she said.

"Home? This hovel?" He stared at it aggressively. "You can't expect me to stay here. I'm a Melbaugh. My father is the Earl of Watersmeet."

"Then you can be an earl's son under the hedgerows, and you'll soon find out which is the more comfortable."

The cottage had stood empty since her departure to Newmarket, and Farmer Locksash had been happy to rent it to her again. It was still furnished with her two beds, table and chairs. James slumped into the chair nearest the stove in the kitchen, his only demand being a continual supply of bottles procured from the inn at West Dean.

Since word of James Melbaugh's ruin had spread, not one of his friends had called or sent any message offering help or even sympathy. A stiff accusatory note had arrived from his brother, Charles, and his father had paid his debts far too often before to be prepared to help him ever again.

"Not even the lowest tinker would have behaved like that to one of his own in trouble," Macha commented.

Declan agreed, and so they were both surprised when a coach complete with a pair of footmen lurched down the rough track and Sir Frederick Wellington stepped out, followed by his aunt.

"Oh, Freddie! You delightful man!" Macha flung her arms round him and then, with tears of joy, swept Mrs. Wellington into the embrace as well. She was overcome by their appearance. "I thought I'd never see either of you again."

"How could you have imagined such a thing of your friends?" Freddie sounded hurt. "Had I not been in the South of France, I should have called as soon as James got into this hole, but I only heard of it upon my return yesterday. Now, where is he?"

Macha grimaced and pointed to the cottage. As they went in, Mrs. Wellington gasped at the state in which they were living. James was unconscious again and snoring too loudly to permit conversation. Macha led the way to the next room.

"We've had to sell most of the horses, but we still have Gold," she said. "He'll win back our fortunes for us this year, for sure."

"Who's to ride for you?" Freddie asked after a moment.

"Declan and James, of course," she replied.

"Well, if something isn't done about Melbaugh, he'll be in no condition to ride. So I propose that I take him back with me and keep him off the wallop until he's fit to return to work."

I should have married Freddie, Macha thought, and, catching Mrs. Wellington's eye, knew she was thinking the same.

Freddie pushed a small roll of banknotes into Macha's hand. As she started to protest he whispered, "Take it please. Don't be proud with me. Give yourself a chance."

"Thank you, my friend," she said. "I shall repay it one day."

AFTER THE WELLINGTON COACH had driven off with James, Macha and Declan O'Brien counted the money. It came to one hundred pounds. "No windfall could have been better timed," commented Declan. "I'm down to my last few pounds, and we're almost out of corn."

"If it hadn't been for your savings, we'd all have starved," acknowledged Macha. "So I want you to know that when we're back on our feet, with our own yard again, you and me will be partners, fifty-fifty."

"Maybe," was all he said, but she knew he was pleased.

Some days later her husband returned, stepping like a dandy from a hired carriage and looking about him with obvious revulsion. He was his former elegant self, clean-shaven and immaculately dressed. Macha, dirty-faced and dishevelled from mucking out, caught his look.

"It would appear you've seen your tailor," she observed acidly.

"Freddie Wellington settled the outstanding account, so I ordered another couple of suits," he drawled.

"So you're in debt again." She was furious.

"Do you expect me to go about like some slum-dweller?" he snarled back. Then he stalked towards the stable, from which Declan appeared.

"I shall be riding Gold on Tuesday at Lingfield," Melbaugh told him.

"He needs a fortnight off," Macha protested.

"Good grief! You're not running a nag's rest home here. May I remind you that we are in bloody big financial trouble," he snapped. "That horse is in the three o'clock at Lingfield on Tuesday. It's no competition, so he'd better win."

Macha and Declan were dismayed, but James Melbaugh was already boarding the carriage again.

"I shall meet you at the course on Tuesday. If you have to contact me before that I shall be at my club."

With that the driver cracked his whip and the vehicle lurched noisily away over the potholes. Macha glared after it and cursed herself for having been stupid enough to marry such a man.

FAR FROM BEING no contest, as Melbaugh had claimed, the three o'clock at Lingfield included some very powerful opposition. The Duke of Westminster's Good Luck was the favourite in a strong field, but Macha decided to risk some money on Gold anyway.

The colt was sweating as Declan led him round the paddock, and Macha wondered if the journey had somehow upset him. He reared as James mounted, and she could see him fighting for his head all the way down to the start. When the flag dropped, he rampaged ahead of the field as though pursued by the hounds of hell, and not even the Duke of Westminster's classic colt came near his heels.

As Gold tore first past the winning post, Macha's field glasses were trained on his bulging eyes and froth-covered coat. When he went on careering round the course, she ran onto the turf in agitation. In the distance, leaning back with all his weight on the reins, her husband was trying to stop him. Suddenly, Gold veered without warning and, as his rider lost balance and fell off, crashed into the rails, sank to his knees, struggled up and began galloping flat out straight for Macha.

"Steady, Gold," she called, but he did not slow down. Then she saw, as he hurtled closer with ears flattened and teeth bared, that he did not recognise her. His eyes were blind and mad.

"Gold! No!" She felt his breath like a torch. People were screaming somewhere. He rose in the air before her. The whole length of his belly was streaked with foam and blood. He is going to kill me, she thought.

Then she was lying on the ground, and the horse was shuddering and groaning beside her, and Declan O'Brien was crossing himself and staring down at them both.

"It was a blessed miracle." He helped her up, and she saw that he was shaking. "The colt was in the air, his great hooves flailing down upon you. In that very split second—it's the sacred truth—he was lifted back. His head went up, and he was carried away from you by the hand of God. It was a miracle."

"Look at him! What's happened to him?" Macha was only concerned for her horse, stretched twitching on the grass, his shins bleeding profusely.

"He's been doped," Declan said.

A shadow fell over them as James Melbaugh walked up, covered with mud.

"You gave my horse dope?" She shrieked the question at him.

"He won, didn't he? And we've made a packet, haven't we?" was his contemptuous reply.

Macha stood up, straight and stony as carved vengeance. "I curse you, James Melbaugh, and I call on my father and my father's father to curse you from the grave. Your bones will crack, and your tongue will be swallowed into your throat. Your body will stiffen as though encased in ice, so that not even your little finger can move. You will hear and never be heard, see and go unnoticed. You will become the living dead." Then she spoke the words that must never be repeated.

James Melbaugh gaped and then gave a nervous laugh. "A gyppo—you're a gyppo. I should have guessed." He drew close to his wife, afraid some of the crowd might have overheard. "You may have fooled me into giving you my name, you filthy gyppo strumpet, but that's all you're going to get from now on," he hissed in her ear. "I never want to set eyes on you again." He stabbed a sharp finger against her ribs like a dagger.

"All your plans are dust, all your tomorrows are pain, James Melbaugh." Her eyes fixed upon him and seemed to pierce his angry gaze with slivers of glass and needles deadlier than venom.

He felt dizzy and put up a hand as though to ward her off.

"All your future is past, James Melbaugh."

THE JOURNEY BACK to Sussex was a nightmare. Gold, with his gashed legs bandaged, had to be tightly hobbled and blinkered to prevent him from kicking the horse compartment on the train to pieces. At the cottage, it took Declan and Macha over an hour to manoeuvre him into his converted box stall. There he was warmly rugged up and fed in total darkness, while Macha whispered to him until he was calm. She stayed with him all that night.

When the top door of the box was opened next morning, Gold stood with head down and dulled eyes and hollow flanks. They dressed his legs, Macha using the same ointment Molloy had once used to mend the filly's leg. For the next few weeks the colt was nursed and rested, and later allowed into the paddock to graze on the sweet summer grass.

His legs healed—leaving scars behind—and regained strength. Eventually he was able to canter again over the Sussex downs. But he was not the same as before. He shied at birds and rustling leaves, and any unexpected move near the stable made him squeal and roll his eyes in fear. Macha, gazing into his frightened eyes and remembering the mischievous, bold look of before, knew her virile and splendid horse was broken. She was sure he'd never race again.

A trainer at nearby Pulborough took on Declan in his yard, though the Irishman still came to the cottage to help out on days off. Macha returned to the buying and selling of ponies, just as she had in the beginning. Between them they made enough money to survive and even to put some aside for the coming winter.

Macha, mentally drained from the triumphs and devastation of the past two years, lived simply. After completing the daily chores she would go walking through the serene woods of Sussex with her lurchers, and she found the filtered green light soothing. But she did not permit herself to think too much.

In the autumn Declan was riding one of his new employer's horses at Goodwood, and she decided to go and watch. There was no question now of gliding graciously round the members' enclosure in a gorgeous gown. She bought cheap entry at the turnstiles and there mingled with the countryfolk, happy to be part of the company and noise after her seclusion.

Her pulse beat a little faster as the horses cantered past. It was like returning to a lover, glad and anticipatory. Then the multicoloured ball of the race bowled past and suddenly, on that balmy autumn day, Macha Sheridan became colder than snow.

Perfectly still, she saw her husband raise a flask to his lips, watched as he mounted his chestnut horse at the second attempt. The two passed before her, golden and exquisite in a spangled aura, almost floating down to the start. Macha Sheridan waited for the beating thunder and the rasping breaths, waited for the brawling, striving scrimmage of runners and raised her silver eyes. James was pushing his horse between two others, lashing out with his whip. Racing for the finish at thirty miles an hour, the three horses collided and lost balance. The chestnut stumbled and Melbaugh fell into the melee of hooves behind. For vital seconds his body was knocked about the turf, then left behind like a cast-off cloak. Macha went home.

They sent for her, of course, the Earl of Watersmeet and Charles, James's brother, and she journeyed to Poldonith Castle. The earl was vague and courteous, Charles Melbaugh stiffly polite. She was shown upstairs to a chamber overlooking the park and, as the door closed behind her, found herself gazing at the immobile figure of her husband, lying in a great canopied bed.

She stood over him. Splints encased his arms; his eyes did not blink or waver from their fixed stare. The icy cold that met her touch froze as deep as the marrow in his bones. He was the living dead. She felt no pity.

"Yes, it is the Romany woman," she said, knowing that he heard. "The filthy strumpet you married."

Taking a glass of water from a table by the bed, she put it to his lips. His mind gabbled against hers in terror.

The image of Gold, screaming and thrashing and bleeding, filled her head, and her look became stone. "You have a long way to go yet, my friend," she said, and turning, she left the room.

Chapter Eleven

Winter, crisp with frost and hard, bright days, feathered the downs white. Brittle twigs snapped off the trees, and the turf crunched under the horses' hooves. Animals and humans were invigorated by the tang of the mornings.

Macha invested in a cheap five-year-old retired racing mare that looked like a prospective steeplechaser. Declan O'Brien was not at all impressed with the purchase. He was right. There was no doubt that the mare could run and leap, but only when the mood took her, which was rarely indeed. Macha cajoled and whispered, bribed and bullied, but eventually gave up the struggle and turned her out into the paddock with the intention of getting rid of her in the spring.

It was her first failure with a horse, and it irked her as she sat by the stove in the evenings. Molloy would have known what to do, she thought, and it seemed she could feel his presence again, vibrant and wise, both father and lover, a true husband.

The twins were three years old now. She could see them as though they were in the room—Tom, black-haired and vital like his father; Molly, silver-eyed like her. She would put out her arms to them, but her arms were always empty.

Her nights were full of ghosts and guilt. James Melbaugh, too, came to her in her dreams, raging at first, and then, as the weeks passed, weeping with self-pity, later still, pleading for forgiveness, and at last begging to die. Thoughts of the future preoccupied her. She realised that her position was far worse than when she had first arrived in Sussex. Then, she had been beautiful, single and mysterious. Now she was society's reject. The paralysed figure of James Melbaugh lay across her way. She was manacled to him and he to her. If she released him, she would be free, and yet she could not do so. For as long as Gold stood whimpering in his box and trembling at the sight of the gallops, she could not forgive.

The snowdrops appeared, and Gold was taken to the lower pasture for the first time. She comforted him as he backed, shaking, from the open space. But the sweat broke out on his shoulders and flanks, his nostrils flared and his ears strained.

"Gently, gently, darlin'," she murmured, putting out a hand.

He plunged away from it and stood glaring over her. Then, to her amazement, the horse gave a deep, grunting whinny, the unmistakable sound of love. The nose of the sulky brown mare had appeared over the hedge. Gold galloped to the first break in the bushes and charged through.

The two horses stood, their nostrils almost touching, and as Macha watched, Gold slowly nuzzled his way up the side of the mare's face and along her scraggy neck. The ugly mare arched her neck and paid him the same compliment. For a long time they nuzzled and nibbled, and when the mare wheeled to canter off across the field, the stallion sped after her. For over an hour they galloped and shadowboxed, until at last they came to a halt and bent their heads and grazed, nose to nose.

From that day on they were inseparable, exercising side by side over the downs, where the stallion forgot all fear at last.

258

A fortnight later Macha journeyed to Poldonith Castle. James was lying exactly as when she had left him, his eyes fixed ahead, his arms, with the splints removed, transparent on top of the eiderdown. She drew up a chair and sat beside him.

"I cannot cure you, James," she said sadly. "That is not in my power."

Tears filled his eyes and ran down his face. She dried them with her handkerchief. "I know. I know." She could hear him pleading for release, although he was speechless. "There's been enough suffering. Don't fret no more, dear James."

She leaned over and put her arms about him. How cold he felt. She closed her eyes and joined her thoughts to his. "Yes, I forgive you, I forgive you with all my heart." Then she pressed her warmth to him and kissed his glacial lips. "It is over now. Be at peace."

His hand grew warm in hers. Colour, more delicate than a water tint, spread over his skin. His eyes looked into hers quietly. He was freed.

"Be at peace," she repeated, and left.

James Melbaugh died that night. The family sent word to the cottage and Macha attended his funeral, veiled in black. As the coffin was lowered, she remembered the laughing man of her hopes, her golden man, her spoilt child-man, and she wept.

THE UGLY MARE was in foal, and Gold, well aware of his achievement, was irrepressible. Though he would never race again, all his old conceit returned as he preened and strutted and herded the mare about. She grew matronly and actually pretty and on New Year's Day, when no one expected it, lay down in the paddock and gave birth to a colt as the stallion stood over her in a lather of excitement.

"Thank God, he takes after his father," commented Declan, viewing the new arrival. It flaunted the familiar wide blaze and three white socks passed down directly from the great Gallinule.

"Gaelic Gold," Macha named him with delight.

"Let's hope so," said Declan. "It's time we had some luck."

Queen Victoria's death in January 1901 was the end of an era, and the accession of Edward VII to the throne relaxed many of the stifling restrictions imposed upon society by the old order.

ON THE DAY Macha's first year of mourning finally ended, Sir Freddie's carriage rattled down the track to her cottage.

"Marry me," he demanded with resolution.

"Ah, Freddie. Was ever a man so desperate to reach the altar?" she teased.

"Marry me and you'll be adored and secure for the rest of your life. I'll give you all you could wish for," he vowed in one breath.

"Darling man, no one could have a more loyal friend, and I love you dearly."

His face brightened. "There you are, then."

"I'll always love you," she promised. "But not with the love a wife should feel for her husband, and without that, I cannot make you happy."

He took her face between his hands and looked down at her earnestly. "I'd be happy with anything you could give, so long as you were with me, and I shall ask you again and again, old girl."

She hugged him.

"In the meantime," he went on, "what say we go to the races? It's high time you came out into society again, and there's a meeting at Salisbury."

She laughed, and then remembered the rules of mourning. She was expected to wear black for two years more. "Oh, I've only rags of weeds to wear," she wailed.

"'Tis every lady's complaint," Freddie mocked. "But I think my aunt and Mr. Dodds may have a surprise in store."

The gown was velvet, trimmed with ribbon and with lace at the cuffs. Small panels emphasised Macha's tiny waist. It might be black in colour, but it was surprisingly daring in style, and her reflection showed a woman who would make heads turn.

"A little gift"—Mrs. Wellington smiled—"to mark the beginning of a new life."

Macha's throat was so tight that she could not reply. She pulled the old lady to her and burst into tears.

"How old are you, child?" asked Mrs. Wellington, flustered.

Macha gulped and considered. "I must be twenty-one now."

"Only twenty-one." Mrs. Wellington shook her head and sighed. "A widow so young."

Macha and Sir Freddie and Mrs. Wellington took the train from Chichester to Salisbury, the girl chattering nonstop, full of the memory of her first visit to this racecourse with Declan, and of the money she had won then. It was going to be her lucky day.

When they arrived at the station, some thoroughbreds were led from the van at the end of the train. As the trio watched, one horse reared and slipped off the ramp. His groom fell and let go of the reins, and the horse bolted through the screaming passengers. Without hesitation, Macha sped across the platform into his path, grabbed the flying reins and was dragged several yards before the terrified animal stopped.

"Easy, boy, easy." She had picked herself up and was already quieting the horse as Sir Freddie rushed up.

"Macha, my dear, my dearest! Are you all right?"

Another worried-looking man appeared close behind. "Is she hurt? My God! She might have been killed."

"I'm right as rain." She grinned at them. "Oh, if I haven't ruined my brand-new frock. Whatever will Mrs. Wellington say?"

But Mrs. Wellington had swooned and was lying on the ground, with several ladies waving smelling salts under her nose.

"Allow me to introduce the Earl of Ashreigney," Freddie said, remembering propriety at last. The stranger took her hand in his just as the red-faced groom ran up to lead the horse away.

"Stop! Don't move that creature another inch." Macha swung round and pushed the startled lad aside. She ran her hands down each of the thoroughbred's legs, carefully felt his quarters and shoulders and checked the head and belly.

She turned back to the Earl of Ashreigney. "There doesn't seem to be any damage done, but there's to be no racing for him today."

"I shouldn't dream of it," he agreed solemnly.

"And be sure the veterinary examines him."

"Of course." He smiled slightly.

Macha raised her eyebrows with dignity, unaware that her face was smudged with dirt and that she had lost her hat.

"Are you sure you are all right?" Sir Freddie enquired.

"A bruise or two. Nothing that a very large brandy could not put right," she replied.

"I should like to go home," said Mrs. Wellington faintly, still as pale as parchment.

"May I beg you to accept my sincerest apologies for the distress you have been caused?" Lord Ashreigney bent over her hand. "And allow me to suggest that you are in no condition for the privations of a train journey. Beckworth House is but a short distance," he continued. "Please permit me to have you conveyed there, where you and Mrs. Melbaugh may receive care and comfort."

"We could not possibly put you to such trouble," Mrs. Wellington protested.

"It would be the greatest honour, madam, and would enable me, in far too humble a way, to try to make amends to you both for everything you have suffered," said Richard Withington, the Earl of Ashreigney.

He was a tall, grave man with patrician features. He was quite old, Macha thought, at least twenty-eight, and with a face that was guarded to the point of austerity. She gazed into his haughty eyes and realised, with surprise, that it was not arrogance at all. In fact, he was a very shy man.

"Thank you, Lord Ashreigney." Macha gave him a radiant smile. "We should be delighted to join you."

And then she remembered. "You're the owner of the Beckworth Stud farm. Garnet Fox belongs to you."

He inclined his head with another smile, and by the time they reached his carriage and helped the still gasping Mrs. Wellington onto its leather seat, they were already far into that informed discussion that can keep two horse lovers talking for a lifetime.

"Oh, I would give anything to see the stud," Macha burst out. "You will show me round, Lord Ashreigney? I want to see everything."

Sir Freddie looked miserable, and Mrs. Wellington closed her eyes in despair at the girl's lack of modesty.

"First thing in the morning I shall show you every corner of my stables," promised the earl.

BECKWORTH HOUSE was not as forbidding as Poldonith Castle. It was built of old brick that glowed in the setting sun, and although it contained over one hundred rooms, it had the warm and friendly atmosphere of a much smaller dwelling.

As they drew up, Sir Freddie suddenly muttered something about having business to attend to and asked to be returned to the railway station. He was probably annoyed at having missed the day's racing, Macha guessed, and then she was so entranced by the sight of the house that she thought no more of it.

The original timber roof still arched over the great Tudor hall, and Macha and Mrs. Wellington were led up the wide staircase, across a large salon, and through a long gallery hung with portraits of Ashreigney ancestors. Finally, they were shown into adjoining bedchambers. A maid appeared, and Macha's torn garments were whisked away to be cleaned and repaired. They were replaced by a simple dark blue voile dress that somehow fitted perfectly.

They dined formally that evening. Lord Ashreigney answered all Macha's questions and was soon laughing without restraint at her stories of horses and racing. He added many of his own anecdotes. The footman, accustomed to his taciturnity, carried surprised reports back to the kitchen. It was the first time since the death of his young wife and baby in childbirth years before that they had seen their master so animated.

The following morning Macha struggled from bed, covered in bruises, experiencing the worst headache of her life. Mrs. Wellington was summoned and immediately bustled her back under the eiderdown. "I knew we should have called a doctor yesterday," she said.

"I don't like doctors and I will not see one," Macha responded with decision. "I'll be right as ninepence before you know it."

"Then give me your word that you will stay in bed and not move," Mrs. Wellington said reluctantly.

Macha waited until her footsteps had died away along the corridor, then tiptoed across the room to open the window.

Her room overlooked an immaculate topiary garden, the yews clipped into spheres and pyramids and cubes, all set on knife-edged lawns surrounded by a high hedge. A small crescent-shaped wood to the east sheltered the gardens, and to the west she could see the acres of Lord Ashreigney's paddocks.

The fresh air banished her headache, and she began to wonder where her clothes were. Hearing the sound of someone approaching, she scampered back across the bedroom and under the covers just in time. Mrs. Wellington entered, bearing an unpleasant-looking drink.

"I will be coming down to luncheon," Macha announced with determination. "And I should like my clothes, please."

As Mrs. Wellington demurred, Macha held up a hand. "I am perfectly well, and I cannot stand being cooped up here all day. I am bored to tears already."

The old lady sensibly saw there was no more point in arguing, and a little before noon a maid arrived and showed Macha into an exquisite oval dressing room with grey silk-covered walls. The maid opened a built-in cupboard cleverly concealed in the wall. It was full of gorgeous clothes. Mrs. Wellington had whispered of Lord Ashreigney's dead wife, and Macha knew that these had belonged to her.

"His lordship wondered if you would care to choose one of these for today," the servant told her.

Macha picked out a light green walking gown, and the maid produced a delightful matching green hat and a pair of gloves. "Madam may wish to take the air this afternoon," she explained.

"I certainly will." She could not wait to tour the stud.

The earl was talking to Mrs. Wellington in the hall as Macha descended the stairs. When he turned and saw her, he stopped in midsentence, and a muscle twitched slightly in his cheek. An awkward second passed before he stepped forward to greet her and enquire after her health.

During luncheon Lord Ashreigney was much quieter than he had been the day before, and she began to wonder whether he was finding their presence irksome. However, at the end of the meal he invited them to view the stud with marked willingness.

When Mrs. Wellington expressed a desire to rest, he escorted Macha to the main entrance, where a pony cart with a fringed canopy was waiting. "It would be inadvisable for you to overstrain yourself today," he explained, "so I thought it better to drive you round."

"That's very thoughtful of you, sir, but I'm as fit as a bug, you know." She grinned, and his face softened at last.

They drove to the paddocks. There the broodmares grazed gently over the rippling grass. Elegantly turned legs and long, sloping shoulders told of their impeccable breeding. The high-strung skittishness of youth was long behind them. Now they created an atmosphere of tranquillity, with their unhurried movements, their calm eyes and lazily swishing tails. Their foals lay stretched out in the warmth of the sun after the games of the morning.

Macha absorbed the scene in silence for a while, then turned to Richard Withington with a sigh of contentment. "Ah, there's nothing like it, is there?"

"No," he replied. And their minds were in harmony.

Leaving the pony cart, they walked towards a grass enclosure containing a number of upright square stones.

"It looks like a cemetery, only smaller," Macha observed.

"It is. A cemetery for horses."

He led her from stone to stone. Each was carved with a famous name, and he told her the histories, the races won, the legendary offspring sired.

"Hermitage. Now there was a holy terror, used to come out of his box kicking and bucking. No one wanted to go near him. Then a goat found its way into his paddock one day, and by Jove, if the horse didn't turn into a lamb from then on. It was most extraordinary. The old chap had been lonely, I suppose." His expression had become tender at the memory.

Lonely, just like you, Macha thought to herself and, taking his arm, she recounted the story of Gold and the ugly brown mare.

At last they reached the stallions' yard. It was much smaller than she had expected, with three horses in neighbouring box stalls. The stud groom brought out a stallion with a clatter of hooves. It was Garnet Fox, sixteen hands high, a superlative bay.

"Won the Arc, the St. Leger and the Gold Cup," Lord Ashreigney was murmuring. "He's a great horse."

Macha scarcely heard him. She caught her breath at the sight of the champion. Here was eminence, the culmination of centuries of breeding. She took off her glove and stretched out a hand.

The groom clicked his tongue in warning, and Lord Ashreigney made as though to restrain her, but Garnet Fox breathed delicately against her palm and, as she moved to him, inclined his head until their faces almost met and she was rubbing his ears. Then the stallion playfully pushed her hat off and nosed her hair.

"Well, my lord, I've never seen him do that." The groom was staggered. "He's a tricky customer, madam. I thought he was going to have your fingers there."

"Oh no," she said "They always tell you when they're going to misbehave, and he's far too good-mannered for that."

From a window, Mrs. Wellington watched the Earl of Ashreigney and Macha return across the lawn. She was waiting, seated on a sofa in the drawing room, when they entered. "It is time for tea," she said. "You have been away for almost three hours."

Richard Withington was immediately full of apologies, and Macha prayed he did not notice the sly and knowing look on the old lady's face.

ON THE WAY BACK to Sussex, there was no stopping Mrs. Wellington's twittering plans for Macha's future. "I could see how taken he was with you, my dear, and of course, he's one of the most eligible men in the country, and then you have so much in common, with your interest in horses. Oh, it would be the most perfect match."

"We may never see him again, yet here you are with us wedded already," Macha protested mildly. "And the truth is that I am not at all inclined to remarry."

"What a thing to say." Mrs. Wellington was horrified. "However will you survive otherwise?"

Macha did not argue further. In fact, she was not averse to seeing Richard Withington again. Admittedly, in some ways he was rather staid, and certainly her heart did not race as it had once over Molloy, but the hours spent in his company had been the most enjoyable she had passed for a long time.

When his invitation to attend an opera in London arrived the following week, she was delighted. Mrs. Wellington launched into a dissertation on how to behave at Covent Garden, and Mr. Dodds decided Macha must wear white, and produced a sketch.

"I thought widows weren't supposed to wear white," said Macha.

"Strictly speaking, madam is quite correct," he agreed. "But madam is so young that only a few old fuddy-duddies could object. And the Earl of Ashreigney should see madam looking her most—dare I say it?—virginal and luminous."

He was matchmaking too, she thought. It was a conspiracy. But the gown, when it was finished, was heavenly—white silk cut very low at the neck and with sleeves puffed at the elbow.

The opera turned out to be in an incomprehensible foreign tongue. "What is she saying?" Macha whispered to Mrs. Wellington as the soprano shrilled. Supper afterwards was much more fun. Romano's in the Strand was packed with theatregoers—fabulous women in sables and jewels; handsome, top-hatted men with silk-lined cloaks—and the sound of laughter filled the air. A stream of people greeted Lord Ashreigney and were presented to the ladies. Many names that meant nothing to the Irish girl produced a frenzy of quivering from Mrs. Wellington's fan, but Macha had certainly heard of Lord Salisbury, the prime minister, and her cheeks grew pink. Richard Withington thought she looked delicious.

He followed up the evening with an invitation to the colossal ball given

266

by the Duke of Richmond at Goodwood House at the end of the week's racing. Once again the mamas, who had seen him as a prize for their daughters, were scowling in Macha's direction.

There was no denying her pleasure at being out and about in company and lavish surroundings once more. But to return to this lifestyle on a more permanent basis was going to demand planning. She had no jewellery, and her wardrobe was a constant problem. She sold a few working horses at a profit and suspected that Mrs. Wellington was dipping into her own savings to help pay Mr. Dodds's charges.

When the earl insisted that she and Mrs. Wellington come to Beckworth House for Christmas, Macha incurred yet more expense. Her financial situation so preoccupied her that she was far quieter than usual throughout their stay.

On Christmas morning Richard Withington gave her a necklace of cabochon sapphires set in gold. She held it up and they sparkled with the cornflower-blue colour unique to the very finest stones. "Sapphires symbolise constancy, hope and heaven," he murmured as he fastened it round her neck.

Macha, to her shame, could only wonder how long it would be before she had to pawn it, or even sell it.

That afternoon he took her down to the stables. The box stalls were full of majestically pregnant mares. She fed them carrots and stroked their velvet noses and would have given her necklace for any one of them.

"The Christmases of the past are special. They are like roses, each with its own scent and colour," Richard Withington said unexpectedly. "One imagines they can never be repeated, and of course they cannot. But as each flower is different, it is also of equal beauty to the others, and so there will be other flowers, Macha."

She looked up, puzzled. He went on, "It is five years since my wife, Charlotte, died, and I do understand how hard it is to bear such loss. But please believe me when I say that time does heal."

Thoughts not of James Melbaugh but of Coper Molloy surged through Macha's mind. Her heart squeezed, and she closed her eyes.

"I know. Oh, I do know, my dear." He took her hand in both of his. "The past cannot be forgotten, but we have to learn to make life anew."

That night Macha lay awake and thought about Richard Withington. She was not in love with him. Yet that afternoon for the first time she had wanted him to take her in his arms and hold her.

He was a splendid catch. But he was also a good man who deserved an honestly caring woman. Macha could not bring herself to dupe him into marriage, and she was very unsure of her feelings.

"When is your birthday?" he wanted to know the next day, as they strolled back to the house from the stables.

"May Eve," she replied. "I shall be twenty-two."

He gave her a half-sad look, then went on. "May seems far too long to wait for your gift. Macha, would you accept a new filly as an early birthday present?"

"Oh, Richard, how wonderful." She skipped beside him and then put her hands up to his face and kissed him. "I can't thank you enough, but thank you."

He gave a little groan and pulled her head against him and held her tightly for several seconds. Then he released her as suddenly and walked ahead so fast that she had to run to catch him up.

It was the first time they had kissed, and she was taken aback at how shaken she felt. Catching sight of his remote expression, she wondered if she had upset him. He was lonely, and perhaps he thought of her only as a friend. Perhaps he would never want another wife. Macha, afraid of being hurt, decided to distance herself from him.

"But when is he going to propose?" Mrs. Wellington demanded impatiently. "Never mind gifts and jewellery and horses, welcome though they are. It is time you were betrothed."

"It is not the kind of friendship that leads to marriage," Macha replied.

They left for Sussex that afternoon, and although flowers and several affectionate but guarded notes arrived at the cottage, Macha politely refused Richard's suggestions to return to Beckworth.

This was not easy to do, for she missed him much more than she would have imagined. He seemed to be always on her mind, especially during the solitary evenings when she ate on her own and then sat by herself, reading or sewing, in the kitchen.

At Easter she treated herself to a day off. She packed a nosebag of corn for Gold and a saddlebag with bread and cheese and rode off through the woods for a picnic.

It was a blowy, noisy day, the clouds sweeping across the sky from the southwest. Gold whinnied and kicked up his heels as they cantered, and she gave him his head on the gallops. When Macha turned for home at last, she was tingling with the exhilaration of spring.

She went back through the woods behind the cottage, and so she was actually riding into the yard before she saw the strange horse tethered there. Thinking Freddie must have returned from France, she urged the stallion into a trot and then, to her horror, saw Richard Withington step out from the old farm buildings.

They stared at each other in appalled silence; Macha, dressed in old breeches, sitting astride the big chestnut, and the Earl of Ashreigney standing by the dung heap. Macha recovered first. Dismounting, she walked straight up to him, her face flushed and her eyes brilliant from the ride. "Sure, there couldn't be a better day to come visiting."

"Good heavens, Macha. What are you doing here?" He stared at her clothes.

"I live here," she said simply.

"But where is your house?" He looked about, uncomprehending.

"I've no house. Only this cabin. Come in and sit yourself down, and we'll drink some tea." She knew there was no point in trying to conceal anything. If the truth of her circumstances repelled him, then it was as well for her to find out now.

She quickly made the tea, pouring it into two cracked porcelain cups. Handing him one, she sat down in the chair opposite his, looked at him calmly and waited.

"I don't understand—" he began, and then stopped.

She said nothing.

"You live here?"

She nodded.

They sat for a long time while he regarded her and then the room and then looked back at her. Then his face crumpled. "I had no idea, no conception, that you were so destitute, that that swine, Melbaugh, left you penniless, that Watersmeet was permitting you to live in such conditions. I cannot believe it."

"It is my choice," she told him hurriedly. "And, in all truth, I did not care for my late husband . . . in the end."

"I'm not surprised. The man was a cad." Richard Withington stood up with an abruptness that startled her. "Macha, my dear, I beg you to forgive me," he said. "I know I had no right to make advances to you as I did at Beckworth. It was inexcusable, and I would not have distressed you for the world."

For a moment she wondered what he was talking about. Then she understood. He thought she had been affronted by his embrace. "But—" she began.

"I cannot allow you to live like this," he interrupted. "It is unbearable. Please allow me to help you. I could make you an annuity. You need never see me again, if you would only accept it, accept my help—"

"Oh, Richard, darling man, you're quite wrong." She managed to push her words into the flow of his wretchedness. "I wasn't in the least dissatisfied when we kissed. Quite the contrary. I thought it was you who thought me forward, a bold hussy."

"You believed that? Why, Macha, you are the most chaste and perfect of women." He was shaking his head in bewilderment. "Do you not know that I love you? I've loved you since I first saw you racing after that horse, with your bonnet flying off and your dear face all covered with mud. You were so beautiful, so impossibly brave. It is as though I've loved you since the day I was born. Don't you know that?"

Macha put out her arms, and he lifted her out of the chair into his. Their kiss was long and searching.

Then he stepped back and to her astonishment, actually went down on one knee. "Macha, will you marry me?" he asked.

"It's a fairy tale," she gasped. "And there's you, the prince."

"And you are the princess—and in every fairy story, the prince and princess marry. So will you be my wife, Macha?"

"And live happily ever after." She sighed with joy.

"Unquestionably." He was absolutely certain.

Chapter Twelve

Richard Withington's riches, status and love cocooned Macha. Magically, they swept her back to the pinnacle of society. Every door was open to her, and as though to make up for the privations she had suffered, he heaped jewels and luxury upon her.

Theirs was the wedding of the year, the ceremony performed in St. Margaret's, Westminster. Had the royal family not been in mourning for Queen Victoria, they would have attended. Others, not fortunate enough to receive an invitation, were so mortified that they felt obliged to leave London for the day.

The couple honeymooned in the South of France, and there, sitting under her parasol to protect her skin from the sun, Macha reached out every now and again to touch her new husband, as though to convince herself that he was real. He filled her with a sense of belonging, and made her feel more loved than ever before.

When they returned to England after six weeks, the walls of Beckworth House were rosy with welcome. Mrs. Wellington was waiting in a drawing room filled with flowers. Declan O'Brien was working for her again, and her horses were housed in the yards. Macha knew she had come home.

Her days took shape. The senior staff, old retainers, had worked for Lord Ashreigney all his adult life. Macha happily left the running of the household to them. She was able to spend nearly all her time with the horses or with Richard in the library, where they pored over the studbooks, tomes bound in morocco, with the ancestry of every one of his thoroughbreds.

At first Declan feared she might become bored with such an ordered existence. However, she stayed contentedly settled. Her movements became calmer and her expression more tranquil. Her body bloomed, and her face filled out and lost its hunger.

"I think the dear girl has a secret already." Mrs. Wellington so far forgot herself with excitement as to confide in Declan one day.

He thought so too, and before long everyone knew of Macha's condition, and she found herself pampered and cosseted by a husband both joyful about and terrified by her pregnancy.

UNLIKE THE BIRTH of the twins, this was an easy delivery—a boy. Macha and Richard were overjoyed. Macha clutched the baby to her with all the fierceness of a woman who has lost earlier children. Both she and her husband, each with the experience of past sorrow, were doting parents. This child was to have everything love could give and money could buy.

They planned a splendid christening, to be held in the chapel at Beckworth. Macha was so immersed in preparations for the ceremony that when an envelope bearing the royal seal arrived, she was taken by surprise.

Richard opened it in the library in a leisurely fashion, turning away as she tried to crane her neck over his shoulder. "Ah," he said without a glimmer of a smile. "Just as I thought."

"What does it say?"

"Hmm." He pretended to read it again and then shook his head.

"What? What? Is it bad news? What has happened?"

"His Majesty has agreed." He put the letter carefully back into its envelope. His eyes twinkled.

"Yes? Oh, Richard, you are being purposely perverse to torment me," she stormed. "Now, tell me what the King says."

"His Majesty, King Edward the Seventh, has agreed to be godfather to our son," he announced.

Macha whooped, and flung her arms round him, covering his face with kisses. "You arranged this, darling Richard. I know you did. You're more of a saint than Gabriel, so you are."

"It is a very great honour," he agreed with a smile.

HIS MAJESTY ARRIVED in a swirl of equerries. Thanks to Mrs. Wellington's rehearsals, Macha made a perfect curtsy and received gallant approval from the King's renowned roving eye. Knowing he was a man intolerant of boredom, she tried to keep him amused with jokes and tales throughout the visit, and his rumbustious laughter was proof that she had succeeded.

The child was named Edward Richard Percival. Standing by the font in the chapel, the rotund figure of the King watched as the godmother, the Duchess of Westminster, took Macha's son in her arms and passed him to the chaplain. Memories of two other babies crowded in. There had been no pomp and circumstance for them, no king's hand stretched out to them. Their baptism had been in the streams of Ireland, and now they were hidden by the mists of Macha's homeland, growing up without her. She would no longer be able to recognise them if she saw them. Her eyes filled, and at that moment her new baby grinned up at the monarch, who grinned back. The Irish girl blinked, and smiled with pride. To her, the royal vows made then were for all her children.

From an early age, young Edward accompanied his mother to the yards each morning. There was always plenty of activity, and the baby, sitting at first in his perambulator, and later toddling, watched it all. Before he could walk, they bought him a Shetland pony, and by the time he was three years old, he was fearlessly galloping around on its back. Edward was going to be a natural equestrian.

"WILL YOU LET GOLD stand for stud this season?" Macha asked Richard one day.

He gave her a penetrating look. "Do you think I should?"

She felt uncomfortable. "Well, you've seen his papers, his pedigree."

"Indeed." After a pause he asked her again, "What do you think?"

Since first coming to Beckworth she had spent countless hours in the library reading the studbooks. Richard insisted on only the highest standards of breeding. She had come to understand the value of the purity of the thoroughbred, and now she knew what she had to answer.

There was a long silence between them before she muttered, "Maybe better not."

"His sire was Gallinule, was it not?" Richard Withington was benignly certain.

"No. . . . I don't know. . . . Yes, Gallinule," she admitted.

He waited.

"My father dealt in horses in Ireland," she said by way of explanation.

"Ah." He did not ask for more details.

It was the end of a dream. That day she gave orders for Gold to be gelded. She knew that if he could never sire more progeny, his faulty genealogy would not be exposed. His colt, Gaelic Gold, would race as planned, and on him alone would depend the last chance for the renown schemed for by herself and Molloy in that secret pairing of the mare and the great Irish stallion.

Declan O'Brien now raced for other yards and did so well that he was much in demand. True to her word, Macha gave him a half share in any thoroughbreds she bought. She also made shameless use of his inside information to win herself some considerable sums of money. Richard occasionally counselled caution over the amounts she gambled, but her independence amused him, and he was intensely proud of her.

Macha, with her wicked and clever way of flouting convention, brought fun and even a little daring into his life, and during these early years together, they were very happy. They dined frequently at Windsor with the King, of whom she was a great pet, managing to deflect his flirtatious approaches without giving offence.

"You have a lovely little wife, Ashreigney," he would say, with an envious sigh. "See you look after her."

"I shall, sir," Richard would reply, gazing at her.

GAELIC GOLD won six races as a two-year-old and the next year showed something of his true running with a win at Salisbury. Yet, although he ran his heart out in the Derby, in the end he was beaten by three quarters of a length. This had been the last chance for Gallinule's secret bloodline to take the blue riband of racing, and Macha's disappointment was intense.

"He really is running extraordinarily well," Richard commented, seeing her look downcast. "I don't think you should give up yet. What say we enter him for the Grand Prix?" The Grand Prix de Paris was the championship, the most valuable race in Europe.

"We're far too late for that," Macha cried. "He'd have to have been entered last year, while he was still a two-year-old. Why didn't we think of it?"

"Well, as a matter of fact—" Richard sat back, looking smug.

"You did it. You entered him. You've known all along he was going to run in France and not said a word!"

MACHA AND HER FAMILY drove through the entrance gates to Long-champs racecourse, and were soon strolling towards the paddocks. The French bookmakers thought little enough of her horse to give outsider odds of twenty-five to one. Macha placed her bet, one thousand pounds to win, then returned to the paddock just as Declan O'Brien was mounting. Putting both hands on the horse's white blaze, she whispered close to his nostrils. Gaelic Gold tossed his head and took a couple of steps back before wheeling onto the course.

He made a good start, and Macha trained her field glasses on the bunch as it arrowed away. She thought she could see her green-and-gold colours quite well up, before distance blended horses and jockeys into a speeding cloud. Then she could not see Gaelic Gold at all and closed her eyes in despair.

"Look! Look!" yelled Richard, and she opened them again to see her colt going neck and neck with another for the post. There was a thunderous blur, and in the last three strides Gaelic Gold stretched his neck beyond his rival

"He won! He won!" they shouted in unison, running past disgruntled French punters to lead him in triumph to the winner's enclosure. The colt, descended from that illicit long-ago mating of Gallinule with Macha's Girl, had become the champion of Europe.

WHEN EDWARD WAS FOUR, they took him to the Boxing Day meet of the Wilton Hunt, although he was still far too young to take part. It was an earthy winter day, ginger sharp, and the horses stamped and mouthed their bits. Suddenly the hounds were away, and the followers streamed behind over the downs.

Macha was well up in front. In deference to Richard's wishes, she rode sidesaddle. Mounted on a gunmetal grey and wearing her new dark blue habit, she was like a song, her husband thought, rhythmically fused to the cadences of the hunter's motion.

Side by side they cleared the low hedges and chased through the woods. With the music of the hounds ringing up ahead, they spilled down a bank to the hedge below and took off simultaneously. Too late, Macha saw the fallen horse and huntsman on the other side. The grey twisted in midair to avoid landing on them. A branch hooked in the girth, wrenching the saddle round beneath his belly, and Macha, instead of being thrown clear, fell under him onto the stump which had caused the first accident.

It was a very bad fall, and the delay in her receiving medical treatment, caused by the distance from home, made matters worse. She had lost a lot of blood by the time the doctor came from her room to the library, wearing a serious expression.

Complete bed rest for at least two to three months, he directed. "She has severe internal injuries, and any movement at all could cause haemorrhaging. If you do not want to lose her, have a nurse with her day and night."

"Will she live?" Richard asked, white-faced with fear.

The doctor shrugged his shoulders. "God willing. But she is very ill indeed. And, Ashreigney," he added, as he prepared to leave, "there'll be no more children."

Macha dreamed she was back in Ireland. From inside the prison of her pain she called for her da and her Aunt Nan, for Molloy and her babies, Tom and Molly. But only strangers came and shook their heads at her and went away, leaving her searching and weeping for the faces of the past.

Richard sat by her bed day and night, until he began to grow ill himself for lack of food and sleep.

"Who are these people she begs to see?" he asked Mrs. Wellington. "Tell me, and I shall find them and bring them to her."

When the old lady could not answer, he brought in Declan. "You are her cousin. You must know. Who are Nan and Tom and Molly, and the one she calls Molloy?"

Declan wondered whether to confess that he was no blood relation to Macha. But at last he said, "Truth to tell, we lived at the other end of Ireland, and I've never heard of those you mention."

"Well, we must do something. If I have to contact every Sheridan in Ireland, I shall do so."

Fortunately, the Irish authorities replied that the task was beyond them, and just as the household began to fear for Richard Withington's sanity, Macha opened her eyes and looked at him with recognition.

"Oh, my dearest, dearest one," he sobbed openly. "If you only knew how happy I am to have you back."

"Well, you've a fine way of showing it," she whispered, and put up a feeble hand to dry his tears.

From then on, she began to recover and, to everyone's surprise, was most docile in her obedience to the doctor's orders.

Richard kept the news that they could have no more children to himself, and fussed round her daily and watched over her himself.

Winter passed, and Macha was allowed to bask in an invalid chair on the terrace in the first warm sun of spring.

"I tried to find them for you," Richard said one day. "I did everything possible, but could trace none of them."

"Who?" she asked.

"The people you cried out for, when you were ill," he replied. "You wanted your Aunt Nan, but I had no idea where she was. Tell me where she lives, and I shall bring her to you."

Macha closed her eyes for a moment, and her thoughts went back to Ireland. "It was long ago, too long ago," she said.

"But Tom and Molly?" he insisted. "And someone called Molloy. Who are they, my dear? They are important to you, and you shall see them."

The little flush created by the sun drained away. She wondered what she had babbled in her delirium, and stared at him to see if she had revealed all her secrets, but his eyes were full only of a loving anxiety to please.

"Dead," she said tonelessly. "All dead."

Her pallor so alarmed him that the nurse was called and Macha was hurriedly wheeled back to her boudoir and lifted into bed. Then, to her relief, Richard was banished from the room.

That night, as the nurse dozed in a chair by the fire, Macha lamented, bitterly and silently, her husband, her lost children, and Ireland.

IN TIME SHE COULD WALK again, and then she could run, playing with her son around the topiary and over the grass. She felt as free as an eagle.

In July they were included in the King's party in the royal stand at Ascot. It was Macha's first outing since her accident, and the monarch commanded cushions to be arranged that she might watch everything from the best and most restful vantage point.

"What you need now is to take the waters, my dear lady," the King said to her. "And we know just the place. Bad Ischl, in Austria. Bracing mountain air and mineral baths. You and your wife will join us there in August, Richard."

They travelled in the King's special train across Europe, and Macha was impressed by the deeply comfortable furniture, luxurious carpets, and the fully equipped bathroom assigned to her.

Within thirty-six hours of leaving home they were steaming along the shore of Lake Fuschlsee under mountains smoking in a heat mist. His Majesty loved travelling and approached each journey with childlike anticipation. He alighted at Bad Ischl railway station wearing an Austrian hat and stepped into a motor car that swept him to the Hotel Kaiserin Elisabeth. The royal party followed.

A tired Macha went straight to bed and awoke the next morning to find herself in an enchanting little town, surrounded by lakes and overhung by fir-coated steeps which rose to snowy peaks. The air reminded her of Ireland.

Opposite the hotel was the Café Zauner, a confection of mirrors, chandeliers, marble—and the lightest, most mouth-watering and intricately decorated cakes and pastries in Europe. She could hardly wait to finish breakfast each morning and hurry there for cups of hot chocolate and the first delicious titbit of the day. While sitting over a slice of sponge roulade that she was suddenly engulfed in shrill greetings, sable and scent.

"Honey! Whatever are you doing here? My, but don't you look just deevy in that gown. Worth, isn't it? And look at those emeralds! Do you like this?" A ring with a diamond the size of a meringue was flashed in front of Macha's nose as its owner went on, without pause, "Wilbur gave it me on our engagement. You have simply got to meet him. He is the sweetest man—a senator, you know."

"Daisy!" Macha gasped. "Daisy Fitzclarence! I thought you'd left Europe for good. I wanted to write to you, but no one seemed to know your address."

"Pretended not to know it, more like, after the scandal," Daisy said grimly. Her desertion of Lord Bentland had been the talk of the season a few years before. "Macha, I was never so glad to leave anything behind as those English stuffed shirts, and to get back to the States."

"Mm," Macha sympathised. "What are you doing here? Oh, it's good to see you again."

"Wilbur and I are on our honeymoon," the American girl explained. "I'm Daisy Schultz now."

Macha regarded her friend in disbelief. "But—but you're divorced," she blurted out, unable to stop herself. "No one marries a divorced woman!"

"They do in America."

Macha remembered her manners. "Well, I can't tell you how happy I am for you, Daisy," she said with genuine pleasure.

The two friends sat exchanging news and gossip about mutual

276

acquaintances until Wilbur appeared. He was a broadly smiling man with outstretched hand, and Macha was enveloped in the kind of immediate familiarity she had not experienced since living in Ireland.

The morning flew by unnoticed. It was as though the three had known one another since childhood, and when a shadow fell across the table, Macha looked up in the middle of laughter and saw her husband. "Oh, is it time for luncheon already?" she asked easily. "Well, I'm glad you've appeared, because look who I've met, and this is her brand-new husband, Wilbur Schultz."

Wilbur stood up and held out his hand. Richard Withington ignored him, and Daisy, who was waiting with an expectant smile. Instead, he glared angrily at Macha. "You will oblige me by returning to the hotel within the next five minutes," he said. Then he turned on his heel and left the café.

Macha was overcome with embarrassment. "I think my husband is ... indisposed," she muttered.

"I think he does not want you associating with a fallen woman." Daisy fixed a shrewd eye on her.

Wilbur was furious. "No one's going to insult my wife and get away with it. I'll have it out with that fellow and—"

"Forget it, Wilbur." Daisy pulled him down on the seat beside her. "You'll never understand the English, so don't try."

"I'm so dreadfully sorry." Macha was scarlet with shame.

Daisy took her hand in both of hers. "Dear Macha, don't be upset. I know all about it, remember? Now take this and don't lose it. One day you may need it, and you will always be welcome." She gave Macha her card.

"I'll write," Macha promised her friend.

As she crossed the street and stepped into the grandeur of the Hotel Kaiserin Elisabeth, Macha felt consumed with violence. She wanted to slap her husband's smug, arrogant face.

"How dare you insult the only reasonable and sincere woman I have ever met in your country." She was shouting before she had even slammed the door of their suite behind her.

"How dare you consort openly with a common American divorcée?" Richard was icy.

"Common!" she shrieked. "Daisy Vanderbilt comes from one of the richest families in the United States of America."

"Lower your voice." He looked down at her with contempt. "I have no wish for the whole world to discover that I am married to a fishwife. Now, listen to me very carefully. For several years I have tolerated the embarrassment caused by your uneducated behaviour. But this time you have gone too far." He bent over her with hard, cruel eyes. "I am prepared to accept the fact that you can provide me with no more children, Macha,

277

but your lack of any sense of propriety cannot continue. From now on you are to change your ways, and furthermore, I forbid you to see that person again."

Her anger was wiped out in confusion. What did he mean, she could provide no more children? But as she opened her mouth to ask, he turned and left the room.

She had been aware of a change in him, especially since her accident. Most English aristocrats, she knew, saw their wives principally as being there to bear heirs and to run their great houses with grace and efficiency. For companionship, they preferred the company of men. Richard seemed to have become more distant and absorbed in his own interests—the running of the estate, and his horses. Macha had attributed this to his upbringing and thought that perhaps it was to be expected.

Yet incidents she had previously ignored came into her mind: the time he had snapped at her for cutting instead of breaking the toast at breakfast, the way he seemed to have become more critical of her clothes, the anxious look she had caught sometimes when her irreverence was making the King chuckle. He had begun to turn down more invitations to court functions and she had imagined this was to protect her from strain. Suddenly it dawned on her that perhaps it had been to protect himself from what he appeared to feel was her unorthodox deportment.

Beneath these reflections a deep depression was growing at the idea that she could bear no more children. Tears fell coldly onto her cheeks.

That night he slipped into bed beside her in a way that indicated he wished for no contact. At first Macha pretended to be asleep. Then, as she felt his muscles relax, she asked, "Is it true?"

"Yes," he replied, without any hint of sympathy.

She thought of her children, of Tom and Molly and Edward.

"At least we have Edward," she offered diffidently.

"Yes."

"About this morning . . . I didn't think there was any harm in it," she said.

"That's your trouble," he retorted. "You seem to imagine you can flout convention with impunity, and it has to stop."

"But Daisy Schultz is my friend," she protested.

"I will not countenance hearing that woman's name again." His voice was bitter. "Nor do I wish to hear the names of any of your other nefarious friends from the past."

So that was it. With the click of a cog slipping into place, she knew precisely when he had begun to change towards her—after her recovery, when he had asked about Molloy and Tom and Molly and she had offered no explanation.

Throughout the journey back to England, Macha thought about her marriage. Her love for her husband had grown steadily since they were wed. He was the most gentle man she had ever met. In the beginning he had obviously enjoyed the fact that she was so different from the women in his circle. But the novelty had worn off with time, and her unpredictability had become merely a strain. Macha knew it was up to her to repair the damage, if possible, and so she resolved to change, to try to be more submissive and fit in with Richard's code.

It was not easy. After their return from Austria he remained remote, spending more time alone in the library. Their conversations were impersonal. Although she often longed to kiss him impulsively and shake him out of his mood, she did not do so. Her instincts told her the remedy for their problems lay in her self-control. He had to return when he was ready.

In her loneliness Macha could not even turn to her son, who now spent his days in the schoolroom with the governess, or otherwise with friends of his own age. His development was carrying him away from her.

Chapter Thirteen

The assassination of the Grand Duke Serge, uncle of the Tsar, in 1905 had caused no more than a ripple of gossip. The warnings of a possible German invasion were considered far-fetched. The demands from Ireland for Home Rule were treated with the impatience reserved by the English for Celtic aspirations. And Macha, although she certainly believed the English should get out of Ireland, had the sense to keep her opinion to herself.

In 1908 Richard Withington's father died, at the age of eighty-seven. Richard and Macha became the Marquis and Marchioness of Bridgemere. Their son, Edward, became Viscount Ashreigney. At that time Macha was twenty-eight.

They moved, not without regret, to Rapsleigh, where the Withingtons had lived for eight centuries. It was a vast, sprawling palace. Even Richard had no idea how many rooms it contained. Macha, exploring them over the first few days, was prey to a sense of unreality. She felt like an outsider, until Mrs. Wellington was persuaded to come to live with them as Macha's companion.

Macha and Richard had established a steady contentment. Perhaps their relationship had not returned to that innocent faith of before the scene in Austria. Part of him was always to remain concealed from her and she, having experienced the painful consequences of his disapproval, was more watchful of her deportment. But they were exceedingly fond of each other.

Then, in 1910, their dear friend King Edward VII died. He had been a merry monarch, loving pretty women and fine food, sport and good company. King George V was almost opposite in character from his father, and Macha felt that he was the herald of a different era, one that she could not imagine would be so enjoyable.

Then Richard insisted that Edward be sent away to Eton. Macha knew she could not win a struggle against tradition, and though the ache of her son's leaving remained with her, she kept her sorrow hidden. When the boy returned in the holidays, he was like a stranger, and she took her grief away on long rides over the Cotswolds.

By then the balance of power, both international and domestic, was shifting, and their world was beginning to shake. The Irish question had become a crisis with the formation of the Ulster Volunteer Force in the north and the Irish Volunteers in the south. The rebellion so preoccupied the politicians and the press that the German threat to Britain was of only vague concern.

When war was declared on August 4, 1914, Macha reacted with bewilderment. "War against who?" she asked Richard, thinking that England was about to attack Ireland.

"Germany, of course."

"Oh, them." She was instantly relieved.

She really had no inkling of the implications of the news until the young men in their circle joined the army as officers. Then the footmen and gardeners became soldiers and marched off, grinning with anticipation. Only the elderly and Declan O'Brien, who, like other jockeys, was too light to be of use to the armed services, remained behind.

Richard, at forty-two, was too old to be called up. As the villages and the land around emptied of able-bodied men, he became even more retiring than usual and, upon receiving news of the death of a nephew, shut himself away in the library.

The next morning the elderly butler reported that his lordship had left the house early. Macha thanked God for her husband's age for she guessed at once that he had gone to the recruiting office and she knew he would be rejected.

"I've joined the Grenadier Guards," he shouted on his return, bounding from the car.

"No!" Macha's stomach heaved as he ran across the terrace towards her like a boy. "They'd never take a man of your age."

"Ah, but they have," he answered in jubilation.

"What about the estate—and the horses?"

"Macha, you don't need me to run the estate. You're a highly capable woman. And you have Declan to help with the horses."

"What of me—and Edward?" She felt sick with dread.

"I shall be fighting to protect you both—to defend my country and everything I hold dear."

"But you are exempt from service. You don't have to go."

"I do have to go." He looked down at her, unwavering, and she saw he was already on his way. "I report to Wellington Barracks on Monday. They're making me a lieutenant."

The Brigade of Guards left for the front in February 1915. Macha and Edward travelled to Victoria Station to see them off. The three of them stood in a triangle, distanced from one another by Richard's uniform and the need to suppress all emotion. The platform vibrated under marching boots. Men shouted. A whistle blew. Lord Bridgemere shook his son's hand and turned to give his wife a brief embrace.

Macha gripped him to her with all her strength. "Oh, my Richard, take care," she whispered.

Then the station filled with steam, and he was gone.

HIS LETTERS HOME described billets, the food, the marches and patrols, but seldom mentioned the fighting. Occasionally he told her a friend had been killed; usually he asked simply about the land and his son and his horses.

Macha, too, kept much of real importance to herself. Rapsleigh was requisitioned for soldiers recuperating from injuries, and Macha was completely unprepared for their mutilations and, worse, their blank eyes. Trying to nurse and comfort them, she was filled with hopelessness. After dark they screamed of horrors beyond her imagining, and when they were mended, they were sent back to the living hell of their nightmares. None of this went into her letters.

But in their efforts to protect each other from the ugly truths of the Great War, they were doing more harm than good. As neither communicated well on paper, their letters were stilted and artificial and each was left feeling isolated from the other.

Although, of course, he was aware that Rapsleigh was now a hospital, when Richard came home on his first leave, the scale of the operation came as a shock. At a time when he most needed the private intimacy of his immediate family, there were strangers in every room. The daily evidence of suffering, which he desperately wanted to leave behind in France, filled his home.

Macha discovered that the husband she had always known as being of a rather shy and reserved temperament was now a man irrevocably changed, a man who had lived for months with barbarity and performed atrocities beyond his own conscience, who, to preserve his own sanity, was now locked inside himself by iron bands of self-control. He could not confide in her so she could not share the burden. Whatever she said he seemed to find trivial, and he himself rarely spoke at all. Behind a façade of old-fashioned formality, both were tormented by the situation which neither knew how to alleviate. When the time came for him to return to the war, they parted in speechless anguish, each feeling personal failure.

In April 1916 Macha read of the Easter Rising in Dublin. Irish Home Rule had become law a few weeks after the outbreak of war and was, she thought, what her countrymen had always wanted. That some had decided to take up arms against England at such a time seemed like treachery.

Then an unexpected telephone call from Richard announcing his arrival next morning put all else from her mind.

"What a lovely surprise. I'd no idea you were due leave," she said, tripping across the hall to meet him the following day.

His greeting was restrained, and he stared at her a little strangely, but as soldiers were often nervous and suspicious when they came home, she took little notice.

"It's not leave exactly," he said. "We're going away. Tell the servants to pack the trunk. I want to catch tomorrow's ferry."

"Where to?" she asked.

"I thought you might like to go to the Baldoyle Derby," he said.

"The Baldoyle Derby? But that's run in Ireland."

"Is there some reason why you do not wish to return to your homeland?" he demanded, almost aggressively.

"No ... no, of course not, Richard. It's a splendid idea," she said, but the truth was that she was overwhelmed by both pleasure and trepidation at the scheme. It was twenty years since she had fled from Rosslare, and the life she had left behind, the people and places of that past, filled her mind with disorder.

"I shall look at the bloodstock," he went on. "Perhaps we should visit Brownstown Stud and buy one of Gallinule's line."

Was that malice in his voice? She decided it could not be.

"And I imagine you will wish to see your childhood home."

"If there is time," she replied, a smile covering her wariness. Perhaps his passion for unravelling bloodlines and pedigrees had triggered some deep curiosity about her roots, she thought.

DUBLIN, WHEN THEY ARRIVED, was as Macha remembered it. Elegant streets of Georgian houses cut towards the centre, through which the River Liffey, thick as Guinness, curled darkly.

A light rain was blowing across the sea as they drove towards the Custom House and the bridge, the bridge where Molloy had met her on that final afternoon.

"One day you'll be covered in diamonds," he had said.

She touched the diamond spray at her throat, and her memories went back across the years, impressions from past and present collided. A ragged girl stopped to gaze at their motor car, and Macha saw herself. She became disorientated and displaced.

"Follow me along, m'lady, and I'll show you your room."

They had arrived at the hotel, and the porter was leading the way, loaded with their luggage.

"I reserved a suite," her husband told the man with hauteur.

"Sure, a suite's the best thing, Your Honour," agreed the porter.

Macha stifled a desire to laugh. The Marquis of Bridgemere's face was a study as he stuffed a coin into the man's hand.

"You're a topper, Your Honour." The man touched his cap with classic irreverence and left.

"I did not care for his manner. He was insolent."

"No, Richard. He was not insolent," she retorted firmly, "he was Irish. And the Irish are not given to kowtowing."

He directed another of those odd stares at her. "I have to go out," he said. "I shall be back in time for dinner."

At first she sent for some tea, and then left it untouched. She fidgeted with her hair, paced the rooms and went to gaze out of the window. Her own people. She recalled the bit of rough land to the south, the site where she and Molloy and Macha's Girl had camped in the rain and mud alongside the Connors, the Wards and the Maughams. It would be deserted, for at this time of the year travellers were always on the road.

She felt faint, and her head ached. She knew she should never have returned to Ireland. Years and years had passed since she'd had any connection with her homeland. She had survived and made a wonderful life for herself. She wanted no ghosts. She wished the past obliterated.

The rain had stopped by next morning, the day of the Baldoyle Derby, and the buildings and streets of Dublin were brightly polished with the sun. They went to fetch the car, and as Richard opened the passenger door a girl ran up to Macha with outstretched hand. "Your ladyship! Your ladyship!"

The girl was a tinker, with torn clothes and tangled, dirty hair, but Macha saw none of this, for as she turned to look, she found herself staring at her own reflection. The same oval face and ivory complexion, the same fine Celtic mouth and, most disturbing of all, the same silver eyes. The girl was her image as she had been twenty years before.

"Come along. Ignore the beggar." Richard seized her arm and hustled her into the car.

"But—" Macha was so shocked she could not continue.

Richard started the car. The girl began running after it. "Lady! Lady, wait," she was calling.

"Stop! Let me talk to that traveller," Macha said to Richard.

"Don't be absurd," he said, accelerating.

"Macha! Macha Molloy!" Her name carried like the peal of the wind, so loud all Dublin must have heard. "Macha Molloy!" Wrenching at the handle, she released the door, which swung outwards. The car screeched to a halt, with Richard swearing, and before she had time to get out, the girl caught up with them and stood panting beside her. "Help us, Macha Molloy. For the love of God, come to the aid of your own."

Macha jumped from the car and pushed the girl towards the pavement. "What is this? How do you know my name?"

"Save Tom Molloy!" The girl seized Macha's arm desperately.

"Tom . . . Molloy?"

"He's in Richmond Barracks, a prisoner, and no one can stop them hanging him but you, Macha Molloy." Tears were making clean streaks through the dirt on the girl's face.

Richard strode up. "Macha, come away at once!" He gripped her shoulders with angry hands and swung her round.

Macha pulled free from his hold and stared at him. "I cannot," she replied. "I must hear what this girl has to say." Turning her back on him, she spoke to the other. "Come with me." She led the way back to the hotel and then upstairs to their suite. Her husband did not follow.

"Now, sit down and tell me," Macha said.

The girl sat gingerly on the edge of the sofa, looking very frightened. "Tom Molloy took part in the Rising," she began slowly. "He was arrested. They say he killed a British soldier, and they—they are going to hang him. But I swear to you, lady, by the Holy Mother of God, that he never fired a shot."

"How would you know that?"

"I was there. There were not enough guns to go round," the girl explained. "He only had a big stick. That's the honest truth."

"And what has this to do with me?"

The girl looked at her with those long, unwavering eyes. Their power forced Macha to drop her eyelids.

"Who are you?" she heard herself ask at last, despite herself, knowing the answer.

"Molly—I am Molly Molloy."

The past had become the present, with her daughter as its living embodiment. There could never be any going back.

"Your husband has brought orders from London to Dublin Castle," Molly Molloy was saying. "Orders about the prisoners. He can talk for Tom. You are a great lady now and you can make him stop the hanging."

Macha went over to the girl and stroked her tangled hair. "Were they good to you?" she asked shyly.

"They were." The girl did not react to her touch.

"And did they tell you? About Molloy? About me?"

"Yes."

"Did you know where I was?"

"Yes. We always knew."

The guilt she had suppressed for so many years suffused her like sickness. "I should have looked for you, found you."

"No. You could not." Molly stood up and faced her abruptly. "Will you do it?" she demanded. "Will you speak for Tom? Save Tom? Only do that and we will never come bothering you again. We will leave you to your life."

Oh, it was too late for that.

"Will you do it?" Molly persisted.

"I will."

The girl started towards the door.

"Don't go yet," said Macha. "Stay a while."

"No."

"Where's your camp? Who are you with?"

"It's better for your own sake not to know. I'll be at the old south site, waiting, at noon the day after tomorrow." With that, her daughter slipped away noiselessly, as only a gypsy can.

Macha could not weep. Swept by emotion, she knew that her life of luxury no longer mattered. The son she had known only as an infant was now a man about to die. The daughter she had mourned for so long would be lost again. She had to act.

"Well?" Richard, who had returned unnoticed, was standing beside her. "I think you had better explain yourself."

"It's a long story. It goes back many years."

"I can imagine." He was glacial. "Sit down."

She began with the death of Jack Sheridan and her refusal to burn the bow-top. She told of travelling alone with her few horses, of begging and going hungry and cold, of the filly with the speed of a cheetah and the race at Killarney, of meeting Molloy—Molloy, with his black eyes and his knowledge of horses and his plan.

Richard Withington's expression did not change.

She described the mating of the filly with Gallinule and told of Tara, where she was first married. Even when she confessed to the birth of the twins, he remained like stone. But at the disclosure of Molloy's arrest for gunrunning and his subsequent death, her husband walked away from her to stare out of the window.

She was sobbing by the time she told of leaving her babies and escaping to Wales. As she talked, she relived the crossing of England again, meeting Declan O'Brien, the growth of her fortunes and James Melbaugh's courtship. "You know the rest, until today," she concluded quietly. She had held nothing back.

"And what of today?" He sounded like a complete stranger.

"The girl you saw is Molly, my daughter. My son, Tom—my son is in terrible trouble, in jail. Richard, he was in the rising, and she says they are going to hang him."

"Like father, like son," he commented viciously.

"Richard, he did nothing. He never fired a shot. He can't die. You can't let my son die. You can stop it, Richard. Richard?"

He had kept his back to her, and now he turned very slowly, his features so rigid that the words did not seem to be coming from him. "So. Our marriage has been one long lie."

"No," she protested. "I never lied to you, never."

"Never lied! You, a gypsy married to an Irish traitor, have never lied? Woman, your entire life has been a lie."

"No!"

"You inveigle your way into society, trick honourable men into giving you their name and position, and now you have the bare face to insist there has been no lie?"

He was the judge, and she was the condemned. Richard Withington was beyond compassion. "I knew there was something wrong about you from those ravings after your accident. I've known for years, and I've been too afraid of what I might discover if I enquired. What a fool I've been."

"Richard, forgive me. I never meant to do you harm. Help me. Speak for my son, for pity's sake."

"England is at war. The bodies of my dearest friends are smeared over France, their blood turning the earth to mud, and you dare even to mention the name of a traitor in my presence."

Macha went down on her knees, reaching up to him with her hands. "Richard, I love you. I've always loved you. I'll go out of your life for ever, if that is what you wish, only save my son."

"Don't blackmail me with the word love." He could no longer look at her. "Yes, you will leave my life. Of that you can be quite certain. From this day, you will never see me again."

"Richard," she cried.

He closed the door behind him and was gone.

Macha sat in a chair by the hearth, and somewhere in that anonymous time between three and five o'clock in the morning the fire went out, and still she sat, waiting for him to return. She knew how her story must have appalled him, but he was a humane man. He would think about everything she had told him, and he would gradually understand. He would be merciful.

Dawn came, and some time later a maid entered with a letter addressed to her in Richard's handwriting. She opened it with shaking hands:

By the time you receive this, I shall be on my way back to France. When you return to England, Edward will spend his school holidays with my brother-in-law's family in Northumberland and you may stay on at Rapsleigh until the war is over. At the end of the war I shall provide you with grounds for divorce and make suitable financial arrangements, on condition that you then live abroad and that you make no attempt to contact me. Should either condition be broken, you will receive no financial support and I shall pursue the divorce action myself. The gifts you have received from me during the period of our marriage shall, of course, remain your property.

Bridgemere

Cold. Cold. She reread the letter and felt numb with cold. The masonry of her life was falling about her again. Richard was lost, as Molloy had been lost, and the golden fantasy of James Melbaugh. But if she could do nothing else, she could fight for her son. Macha walked purposefully from the hotel, got into a hansom cab and was driven to Dublin Castle.

"LADY BRIDGEMERE, what you are asking is quite impossible." The official gave that fat, bland smile Englishmen reserve for women and idiots. "Military prisoners are not permitted visitors."

Macha took a deep breath. She had not intended to disclose her true connection with Tom Molloy, but now she was forced to change that decision. "Surely their families can visit," she pressed. "I am Tom Molloy's mother."

The official picked up a pen from his desk and began to fiddle with it. "Dear lady," he began, "your husband told me that your visit to Ireland has been rather stressful. Allow me to arrange for someone to escort you back to your hotel to rest."

"My husband talked to you?" she demanded.

"Richard Withington and I have known one another a long time," he explained. "Yesterday he told me of your anxiety over these prisoners, and being required to return to France immediately, he asked me to look after you during your stay here. In fact, my wife proposed to call on you later this afternoon."

Macha's heart sank, but she did not give up. "Listen! Tom Molloy is innocent. He needs a lawyer—"

"The legal requirements of the prisoners have all been taken care of, rest assured." He regarded her pityingly. "Now, dear Lady Bridgemere, I know my wife would be delighted if you would take tea with her."

"Damn your bloody wife! And damn you!" stormed Macha, and she rushed from the room.

Back in the street, she stumbled through the passers-by, choked with tears, hating herself for her inadequacy. Somehow she reached the privacy of the hotel suite and there released her misery in solitude.

"YOU'LL FORGIVE ME, my lady, but I let myself in." It was the porter, standing by her bed. Before she could speak, he went on, "My lady, take my advice and go back to England."

"There is something I have to do," she muttered, still hiccuping with sobs.

To her amazement, he replied, "It can't be done, my lady. There's nothing will save Tom Molloy."

"You know about Tom?" She stared at him.

"Sure, doesn't everybody know everything in Dublin?" He smiled at her naiveté. "Leave here, my lady. Ireland is no place for you. If you don't want to be locked up as a traitor alongside the others, take heed of me," he warned with deadly emphasis. "Now I'm going to send up a maid to pack your belongings, and the arrangements will be made. You'll be on tomorrow afternoon's ferryboat, with all this behind you before you know it."

Macha accepted defeat. "Thank you," she said humbly.

So the suitcases were piled ready by the door, and Macha, gaunt after a night of pacing the floor, went to the south Dublin campsite to face her daughter.

The girl came from a tent hidden in the scrub and looked into her face and learned everything.

"I tried," Macha said lamely.

"Yes," confirmed Molly Molloy flatly. "I hear your man went back over the water."

Macha nodded, trying to hide her own misery from one who had far more reason than her to lament. "Tom . . ." she began uncertainly. "Does he look like you?"

"No. They say he's the picture of Molloy the Coper."

"Ah." It was a sigh full of recollections.

They were awkward with each other, needing to make contact and not knowing how.

"I'm returning to England this afternoon," Macha told her. The girl made as though to go.

"Molly, come with me," she said on impulse. "I could give you the grand life."

The girl regarded her with eyes full of suspicion and shook her head. "I'll be off now."

"Don't go," Macha pleaded. "I'll never see Tom, but you're my child too. At least tell me something about yourself."

"I'm to marry Jim McDonagh this year."

"Oh." She was shocked. "Do you want him?"

Molly shrugged. "The Connors arranged it after Tom . . ."

"*Ach*, girl! What's a travelling man to offer?" Macha remembered the ways of the road—the leaking canvas, the drunken husband, the brood of children, the insecurity of the future.

"You married a travelling man," the girl said sullenly.

Realising that Molly was growing angry, Macha changed tack. "Take these," she said producing a handful of banknotes and one of her cards. "That is where I live. Don't let on to McDonagh about the money. It's yours. Enough to travel to me in England. If you're to stay on the road, I'll give you a dowry, whatever you need, but marry no man you don't want, daughter."

ENGLAND, THAT OTHER ISLAND, was a softer green than the harsh brilliance Macha had left behind. It was a relief to escape the insoluble tragedy of Dublin and be driven again through the familiar sprawling park that wrapped round the mighty defences of Rapsleigh like a fur.

After greeting Mrs. Wellington, she asked for Declan O'Brien. When he came into the library, she told him everything, almost as she had told Richard in Dublin, and the tears ran once more.

As she finished, he sat beside her and put his arms round her. "Why did you never tell me before?"

"There was nothing to be done about the babies," she said sadly. "I thought I could put it all away from me, and now I'm to lose everything—Richard and Edward and my home, even Molly and Tom all over again. God forgive me, but I can't face it."

"Now what sort of thinking's that?" He stroked her hair and cradled her in his arms. "You're not one to quit. Haven't I seen you pick yourself up and fight, over and over?"

"I'm tired of fighting," she said pathetically. "And anyway, what am I fighting for?"

"Macha, you can't do anything more for Tom Molloy, God save his soul. But you've not lost your husband or your second son yet, and there's still Molly."

"What's the use, Declan? Molly doesn't want me, and Richard is disgusted with me. He'll never forgive me."

"Listen here, Macha. It's not a fiend you're talking about. The man loves his home and he loves you. If he had been convinced of what he was saying in Dublin, you'd not be here now. He'd have put you out, bag and baggage. Am I not right?"

"I don't know," she muttered miserably. "I just don't know."

"Aye, well, I do know." He was adamant. "I'm not suggesting it's going to be simple, but you're a wily woman and you can win him round."

Macha hugged him tightly. "Where would I be without you, Declan?" she asked.

"I sometimes wonder." He grinned.

After he had gone, Macha reviewed their conversation. Declan's estimation of her husband had been astute. Richard was a deeply home-loving man, and if their relationship was not one of great rapture, she was sure he did love her. She walked to her desk, and picking up the gold fountain pen Richard had given her one Christmas, she began a letter. She wrote of her genuine distress at their estrangement. She was penitent for all the sins of her past. She told him how much she missed him and recalled shared incidents and times of happiness.

Macha knew that if he did not answer, all would be lost.

Tom Molloy's execution was drawing closer. There was no way of finding out the actual date of the fatal event, but one morning when she woke, she knew her son was dead. With that knowledge all her resolution crashed, and she gave way to hysterical grief, remembering the tiny babe she had left, blaming herself for having made no effort to find him, even when she had been blessed with riches.

It was in this mood of deep depression that she was staring out of her window one morning when Mrs. Wellington entered, white-faced. In her hand was a telegram.

RICHARD WITHINGTON, Marquis of Bridgemere, was dead. Killed in action in the Battle of the Somme. He had left her unforgiven.

Alone by the window, Macha was overcome by a compulsion to throw herself from it. Watching herself, as though an outsider, she could see her body lying smashed on the gravel below. It would be the end of the struggle. The hereafter could conceal no torments worse than this. Raising the window, she began to climb onto the sill. Then she was outside and clinging to the frame behind her. Slowly relaxing her fingers, she released her hold.

An arm seized her round the waist, and she was dragged screaming back into the room.

"*Ach*, Declan, let me die." She struggled against him.

He put her on the bed, pinning her down with his hands, glaring at her. At last he said through frozen lips, "Never do such a thing again. Never! Do you want to burn in hell?"

"Richard. And Tom—"she whispered.

"No," he interrupted furiously. "I don't want to hear. Macha, Macha, you're not alone." His eyes were gleaming with tears. "Whatever waits in the future, hurt or delight, you're not alone. Hold on to that. Hold on to Declan."

For a long time they clung to each other, and no word was spoken. At last Macha leaned back wanly against the pillows.

"How did you know?" She indicated the open window.

"I didn't," he admitted, his face crumpling slightly. "This was delivered, and I was bringing it to you."

He held out an envelope. It was in Richard's handwriting. Macha could hardly tear it open.

My dearest wife,

Your letter brought me such joy. I have thought of you constantly, and in this bloody battle, perhaps even because of it, I have grown to understand so much more. How very young you must have been when tragedy overtook you. No more than a child yourself when you lost husband and children.

Now you write and ask me for pardon, but it is I who beg on my knees for forgiveness. Thinking of the way I behaved towards you in Ireland, I have been overwhelmed with shame and have not known what to do to try to heal the wounds I must have caused.

My dearest darling one, can you find it in your heart to absolve me? When this terrible war is over, I vow to spend the rest of my life making you happy. Write, my Macha, and tell me all is right between us again.

Forever your loving husband,
Richard

"He forgave me, Declan," she whispered to him, caught between sorrow and ecstasy. "Before he was killed, he forgave me everything."

Chapter Fourteen

The new Marquis of Bridgemere came home from school for his father's memorial service and stood beside his mother in the village church hall, stiff with control. Afterwards Macha wanted to take him in her arms, but his withdrawn demeanour prevented it.

Later they sat opposite each other in the drawing room, ill at ease. School had long since broken the close bond between them.

"You'll stay a while? A week or so?" Macha asked.

"I think not, Mother," Edward replied. "There's a lot on at school at the moment."

"Well, it's not long before half term," she said.

"I shall be staying with Uncle Hal in Northumberland then," he told her. "Father came to see me at the end of his last leave and told me that was where I was to spend my holidays in future."

"Oh, but it's different now," she protested. "He would have wanted you to come home now."

"It was his last wish that I should spend the time with my uncle." Edward sounded distant and did not look at her.

Macha knew that despite his apparent unconcern, he was deeply upset, and she decided not to insist. "Well, we'll talk about it later," she said, covering her own feelings with equal control.

When he had gone, she told Declan.

"He's at an awkward age," he said. "He wants to be a man, but he's still a boy."

"Oh, Declan, what should I do?"

"Leave him alone for the moment," he advised. "He just needs a little time to himself. Let him go to Northumberland for half term and, nearer Christmas, write to them and explain that you'd like him here. They'll understand, never you fear."

As Declan had foretold, Edward did come to Rapsleigh for Christmas. But he had altered. Although his mother did her best to create a seasonal atmosphere, the visit was not a success. He was arrogant with the servants and behaved towards her with remote formality. Macha felt she no longer knew her own son. When he had returned to school, she withdrew into herself. Her conversations with Mrs. Wellington and Declan were polite but vague, as though her attention were elsewhere.

Some months later, when the Irishman told her he would be away for a few days, she smiled and wished him success at the opening race, not noticing his look of surprise. The flat season had started weeks ago.

"I'm going just in time," Declan told Mrs. Wellington.

"You're sure you're doing the right thing?" she asked.

"Quite sure," he replied.

A few days later he arrived back in a motor car with a companion, a young woman who walked a little clumsily and peered about her from under her brows. The old butler regarded her sniffily.

"I shouldn't have come," she muttered to Declan.

"Yes, you should."

They reached the door of the drawing room, and he pushed her ahead of him. Macha and Mrs. Wellington looked up from their tea and saw a pair of big silver eyes gazing back at them.

"Molly!" Macha leaped from the sofa and ran towards her. "Oh, Molly." Macha was brimming with delight.

The other two tactfully left the room, and Macha and Molly were left alone. The girl sat on the edge of her chair, snatching glances at the *objets d'art* and paintings. She was squirming with discomfort.

Macha watched her for a few moments and then said, "Come and sit here by me." Her daughter did so, full of distrust.

"So you didn't marry Jim McDonagh. Well, we'll do better than him for you, just you see," promised Macha, ringing for more tea.

Molly was quiet as a maid brought in a tray of tea and dainty crustless sandwiches. She was too diffident to help herself until urged on by her mother. Then she grabbed at the food and crammed it into her mouth with unselfconscious hunger.

Macha, who had decided that the sooner she put Molly in the hands of Mrs. Wellington and old Mr. Toby Dodds, the better, was careful not to criticise. "I'll show you round when you've finished eating," was all she said.

As they walked from room to room, between the beds of the sick soldiers and along the galleries and staterooms of the palace, it was difficult to discern what affected the girl more—the sight of the wounded or the grandeur of the architecture. Macha covered the silences with light chatter and then led the way round the garden. They reached the paddocks by the stables last.

The yearlings galloped up in a bunch and skidded to a halt at the gate, and her daughter laughed for the first time. When the stallions were led out, Molly could only sigh. Then she said, "The Connors would never let me go near the horses. I'd have liked to ride, but that's not for girls."

"What nonsense! You've horses in your blood. But it's not too late. I'll teach you myself."

A groom touched his cap as they passed, and a housemaid bobbed a curtsy as they crossed the hall. In the drawing room Molly stopped and turned to face her mother. "What are you going to tell them about me?" she demanded.

"Tell who?" asked Macha, puzzled.

"You know. All the flunkies and skivvies and such."

"Nothing." She smiled. "It's not their place to be told."

"What about your friends? What will you say?"

"That you're my daughter. What else?" Macha reassured.

"They'll not think it's right. They'll not like it." Molly's voice wavered. "Oh, I'll never fit here. I shouldn't have come."

Macha thought for a moment. She was sick of lies. The lies she had told in the past had caused only trouble in the end. Whatever happened she was determined to live openly and be herself at last. "It doesn't matter a tuppenny damn what people think, daughter," she said emphatically. "You're my blood, and I need you. I was the same as yourself, remember. Come here, and I'll show you there's nothing to fret about."

She took Molly up to her dressing room and handed her a gown of pale green silk. "Put this on," she instructed as she opened her jewellery box and took out a five-strand pearl choker. She fastened it round her daughter's neck. Then she positioned her in front of the looking glass. "See," she said, chuckling over the amazement on the other's face. "You're a lovely girl."

"Dear joy, I am so," Molly Molloy shouted, twirling about, trying to view herself from every angle.

"Bide a minute," said Macha at last, drawing her by the hand into the boudoir and making her sit in a chair. "Now Molly, I'm not going to transport you away from Ireland and the life familiar to you, without first speaking my mind. It wouldn't be honest if I didn't admit that there's many a time I've missed the freedom of the road. The English are a peculiar class of folk, especially the quality. Learning all their rules and etiquette is no simple matter. So, Molly, you're to make your choice. You can stay and try it out, or you can go back. I won't stop you. It's up to you."

The girl stared at the folds of the gown as they fell gracefully round her to the floor. "I don't know."

MOLLY REVEALED HER INTENTION by immersing herself in the nursing of the wounded who continued to pour into the household. She worked long hours with a skill and devotion that left her exhausted. Macha was touched to observe the care she lavished on the soldiers. Some of the men exchanged bawdy jokes with her; others, in their agony-ridden nights, cried in her arms. They asked for her when she was not there and visibly brightened when she returned. They loved her.

Nevertheless, society was not likely to value her qualities with the same simplicity as that of grateful soldiers. "You'll be introduced to people who judge by appearances," argued Macha when Molly protested at the idea of giving up time for such superficialities as elocution and dress fittings.

"Then I can do without them," the girl retorted.

"What about Edward and the rest of the Withington family? They'll turn up here sometime, and I want you to be accepted."

With reluctance, her daughter gave way.

For Mr. Toby Dodds, it was like being faced with the young Macha all over again, and a familiar gleam came into his eye at the challenge. Mrs. Wellington took on the pupil with unruffled professionalism, and between them, the designer and the old lady began to effect a transformation that was almost miraculous.

Macha introduced Molly into society and found herself once again listening to idle chitchat, playing endless rubbers of bridge and sitting watching her daughter dance by with one partner after another, and a look of undisguised boredom on her face which was all the more irritating because it precisely illustrated Macha's own reactions.

"How on earth will I ever marry you off if you won't bother with the most basic social graces?" She stormed at Molly, after spending an entire weekend engineering casual garden walks and accidental entrances into rooms so that her daughter could meet suitable young men.

"Who says I want to be married off at all? You told me in Dublin I shouldn't marry anyone I didn't want."

Molly flopped into a chair and then straightened her back, moved to the edge of the seat and folded her hands in her lap in the way she had been taught. Her reactions were the same as those of a high-spirited young horse which had been overschooled, Macha thought guiltily.

"Why do we have to stay here?" Molly demanded. "Why can't we go away?"

Macha misunderstood her. "Do you want to go home to Ireland then?"

"No." The reply was definite. "But I don't want to stay here, either. The English mean well, but they're not for me. You've put up with it, Mother, because you had to, but I don't think you like it any more than I do."

"So where were you thinking of going?" Macha humoured her with a smile.

"Anywhere! The world over can't all be the same. We could go to India."

"They drink a lot of tea there," Macha teased.

"Or China."

"They drink a lot of tea there, too."

"Will you be serious, Mother. Anywhere! Anywhere!"

"Is it so bad?" Macha stopped being flippant at the note of desperation in the young voice.

Molly dropped her eyes and blushed. "It would be all right ... if it was just for a while ... but not for ... settling."

The settled people. How well Macha remembered gazing at their cabins in Ireland with pity. To be confined between four walls and to one area had seemed a miserable fate. Yet, in a way, the limitations she had been imposing on her daughter were just as bad.

Suddenly an idea came to her. "America!" she said. "After the war we'll go to America." To the land Daisy Schultz had described in her letters. A land of hospitality and space and riches—and thoroughbred racehorses.

As another Christmas neared, Macha became increasingly restless and demanding of the household, in preparation for Edward's return. She had not written to him of the existence of his half-sister, believing it better to tell him in person. Yet now she was full of dread.

The servants lined up in the hall to greet Edward. Macha, in her boudoir, primped her hair and tugged at her own gown and then at Molly's. Nothing more could be done. She was thankful that the girl was a beauty.

The Marquis of Bridgemere stalked through the studded oak main door and stared at his tinker sister. Molly lifted her chin and stared back. They hated each other on sight.

"YOU'VE ALWAYS been an embarrassment, with your stupid Irish accent and never knowing how to behave." Crimson with rage, with loathing in his eyes, Edward loomed over Macha. "I've always been ashamed of you, ever since I can remember, and now this! How Father must have detested you! Not content with making a fool of him for fifteen years, you then had to produce some bastard girl from the bogs."

Macha's open hand slammed across his face. "Silence!" she commanded. "How dare you tarnish your sister's name!"

No sooner had she acted and spoken than Macha regretted it. Edward had gone white and still. She reached out her hand to him, and he flinched.

"Stay away from me! Don't touch me!"

She ran to her desk and took out Richard's letter. "You're so wrong about your father and me. Read this and you'll understand."

"I'll read nothing," he snarled.

"Then get out," Macha cried. "And don't come back until you've returned to your senses."

"Oh, I'll get out all right, Mother," Edward shouted. "And I will come back, just as soon as I am of age. I will come back to put you and that bastard of yours out in the streets where you belong."

"He'd have got a clout from me if I'd heard him," said Declan O'Brien when she reported the scene. "Edward's old enough to know how to conduct himself, and there's no excuse for it."

"Well, he's gone now, and he'll not relent."

"He's a cub trying out his strength. Tomorrow he'll be over it."

Macha shook her head. It had been many years since she'd been able to make any real contact with him, and today Edward had told her the reason. He was ashamed of her.

"Come down to the tack room; I've an idea," Declan said mysteriously. "What's needed round here is a bit of fun."

The smell of leather and saddle soap was evocative of her horses and autumn exercise on the gallops, and Macha drew in an appreciative breath. "I don't seem to get down to the yard much now," she observed nostalgically.

"It's time you gave less energy to thinking," he commented cryptically. "Try these on for size." He held out a pair of breeches, a black hunting jacket and boots.

"For heaven's sake, Declan, I can't do that," she protested. "What's all this about?"

"On New Year's Day they're putting on the first local point-to-point race round here since the start of the war, and I've entered old Red Rory. He's a good horse, and he'll show the rest his heels. How would you like the ride?"

"*Ach*, Declan, you've gone raving mad," she said. "I'm not a girl any longer. I'm a dowager. How can I be seen gadding about the country dressed as a man?"

"Oh, I see. You're too old, then?" he goaded.

"It's nothing to do with age. Apart from anything else, my hair's about three feet long. What am I supposed to do with that?"

"Bob it. Isn't that what all you women are doing nowadays?"

"Bob my hair?" she screeched. "My lovely hair. Never!"

"Ah, well, maybe you're right," he said with a philosophical shrug. "The soft living's done for you and no mistake."

This was too much. Macha drew herself up to her full height. "I'll show you who's soft, but that horse had better be in top condition, or you're sacked."

"Certainly, my lady." He touched his cap in mock deference.

Macha left the tack room and started towards the house, recalling the race at Killarney as though it had just taken place. She was urging on Macha's Girl again in her mind, and when she finally returned to her surroundings, her hands were damp with excitement. To feel as carefree and daring once more, she thought. To bolt over the jumps. To win! That would be one in the eye for Declan O'Brien, one in the eye for everyone, and what fun it would be.

She ran into the house, almost laughing aloud with glee. Picking up the telephone, she asked for a London number.

When the hairdresser arrived off the London train, Macha was sitting at her dressing table, her red hair loose down her back. "Cut it off," she instructed.

She avoided watching in the mirror as the long tresses fell to the floor. When it was done, her head felt light and cool, and she peeked at her reflection at last.

A very up-to-date young woman with an oval face and dazzling wide eyes looked back at her. She had lost years.

On the morning of the point-to-point, Macha, pleading a headache, let the party from Rapsleigh leave without her and then changed in the horse box driven by Declan. Knowing the whole county would be present at the event, she remained hidden there until the last minute, before being given a leg up on Red Rory and cantering to the start with head bent.

Leaning forward, she whispered in staccato breaths to her mount, who flattened his ears and jerked his head as the flag dropped. Up the slope they galloped, Macha keeping calmly in the centre of the bunch, waiting for the rest to spread out. One of Rapsleigh's tenant farmers took a fall at the first fence, and Macha began to move up stealthily. Red Rory needed no urging. The powerful muscles flexed under her, and he bounded over a stream, scrambling up the bank and over the fence at the top.

When the last fence was behind him, Macha gave him his head. Hunger gripped her, the hunger to win. Red Rory flattened himself past the remaining challenger, and as she lost her top hat they drew away and pelted for victory.

Molly reached her first, stretching up to pull on her arm, radiant with pride; then came Declan smiling his rare smile. Macha was so full of emotion that she was giggling like a child.

The news of her identity had passed through the crowd before the race was over. Not a few of the men were cheering loudly, and the other riders were running to officials to protest. Macha did not heed and did not care. She was as free as an eagle.

The silver chalice was being handed to a tall man. It would not be given to a woman, she thought without concern. The man turned and walked straight towards her, holding it out, and she saw with delight that it was Sir Freddie Wellington.

"Congratulations, my dear Macha, and well deserved," he said with a conspiratorial wink. "A race of perfection."

THE ESCAPADE DID MORE than release Macha from some of the weight of her bereavement. For the first time in many months she was filled with gaiety. She was still only thirty-seven years old; her appetite for experience was as ravenous as ever. She wanted to take risks, to try out the unknown. The obligation to live out the rest of her days in the staid role of dowager had become insupportable.

As she descended the stairs a few days after the race, her tangerine dress, its neckline plunging, was a blatant statement of her intentions. In throwing out her black weeds, she was also throwing out the past twenty years. "There's no cure for grief but to put it under your foot," she summed up her feelings to Declan. "I'm going to get on with it, my way."

Now, somehow, the differences between Edward and herself had to be healed. They would never be as close as she would wish, but with her whole heart she wanted his respect, and hoped for his love.

One afternoon Macha motored down to his school. Her son came into the headmaster's study pink-faced and refusing to meet her eye. She wanted to hug him to her, but the rigidity of his stance prevented it.

"Son ... Edward," she began tentatively.

He thrust his hands into his pockets and looked at the floor.

"Edward, it is because you are no longer a child that I am here, so that we can talk as two adults." Macha sat down and beckoned him to do likewise.

"Sometimes people born into privileged positions look down on those less fortunate than themselves. But they are not gentlemen, Edward. No gentleman ever despises others, whatever their status in life. A gentleman only despises dishonourable behaviour."

Edward looked confused.

"What I am trying to say is that your father and I were very different, having started out at opposite ends of society. Some of my ways were quite foreign to him and made him raise his eyebrows. But your father was a gentleman. He was quite incapable of looking down on me, or anyone else, because of their background."

"He didn't know about . . . that girl," Edward said.

"Molly? No, he did not know. And when he found out, he was very shaken and, yes, angry," she admitted. "But I swear to you, son, that we were not estranged in the end. He was a man with the breadth of vision and compassion to understand and to accept. We always loved each other."

There was a long silence, and she could see her son struggling with a flood of thought.

"Edward, you and I are different, and always will be," she went on. "But nothing would have made your father more unhappy than to know that we were alienated because of our disparity. I want you to consider that seriously. You are our only son."

He looked directly at her for the first time, his expression a mixture of doubt and vulnerability. He wanted to be persuaded, she thought with a little lift of hope.

"I'm glad Northumberland has become your second home. Uncle Hal is a good and wise man. His experience in running a great estate will be invaluable to you in years to come."

"So will yours, Mother," he said diffidently.

"Ah, son, you'll never know how pleased I am to hear you say that." She beamed at him in delight. "If ever you need anything, Edward, you only have to write."

"Write?" He looked puzzled.

"I have another reason for this visit," she said, and drew a breath. "When the war is over, I am going to live in America." She held up her hand as his face froze. "Now, it's not so far, and I'll come back to England and to Rapsleigh often, if you'll have me. And I hope you'll come over there. Every young man should see the New World."

He was dumbfounded. "What about me?"

"You'll be in the best of hands, and in any case, I'm not sailing tomorrow," she pointed out. "By the time I leave, you'll probably be up at university having a high old time."

"But—but, Mother, what about the horses?"

She grinned. They were not so different after all. "Do you know, there are stallions in America from some of the best bloodlines, and plenty of first-class racecourses. Mind you, it's a bit of a drawback that all the racecourses there are left-handed."

"Are they?"

Suddenly they were talking about racing in America and planning his first visit, and when the headmaster walked in, they were surprised to hear that over an hour had passed since her arrival.

Macha took Edward's arm as he escorted her to the car. To her joy, he ignored the line of windows behind him and gave her a brief, firm kiss.

THE CHURCH BELLS PEALED OUT on the eleventh hour of the eleventh day of the eleventh month of 1918. The war was over. There were services in every church, and parties all across the land.

Macha and Declan walked round evening stables and picked out the best broodmares and fillies, the ones she would take to America. Gold put his head out of his box stall and nudged her for carrots, just as he did every night.

"How old is he now?" wondered Declan.

"Twenty-two," she replied.

"Too old for the trip," he commented.

"Not at all." She rounded on him. "He's as fit as a yearling. Anyway, if he couldn't come with me, I wouldn't go."

There was a pause. It was the moment they had avoided for many months, each aware of what was in the other's mind and neither wanting to mention it first.

At last she rubbed her fingers against her mouth and asked hesitantly, "Have you made any plans yourself?"

"Oh, yes," he replied with an easy smile.

She waited, hoping he would enlighten her, but he just began whistling. "Would you be staying on here?" she probed.

"No, I won't be doing that."

There was a teasing look in his eye, which stung her into irritation. "Will you stop this shilly-shallying and tell me what you're going to do, Declan O'Brien?" she demanded.

"Well, you don't think I'm letting you go off by yourself on the high seas with my best horses, do you?" he retorted. "Someone's got to see them right. I'm coming to America, of course."

"Oh, Declan," she shrieked, grabbing him tightly to her. "Why didn't you say so? I've been worried sick."

"You didn't ask me." He grinned.

The voyage was booked. The boxes were packed. Rapsleigh was thrown open for a great ball, with Edward, the young Marquis of Bridgemere, as host. He even managed to dance one stiffly formal waltz with his half-sister, Molly, a gesture that moved Macha even more than the presence of royal princes.

Then it was the morning of the day, and the servants were lined up in the huge hall. Declan had gone ahead with the horses, and Sir Freddie and

Mrs. Wellington and Molly were already in the Daimler. Outside on the drive, gardeners and stablelads stood in a group and raised a cheer as the car purred slowly through the gates. Macha had never realised she was so loved.

Leaning out of the car and looking back, she saw the ramparts of Rapsleigh rising above the trees to the sky, mighty and permanent, like the great family they had housed for so many centuries. She gripped her daughter's hand.

THE *AQUITANIA* SOARED like a floating white castle above them; porters and passengers and seamen buffeted against them, so that they held tightly to one another to avoid being separated. Mrs. Wellington gave way to tears at last, and Macha clung to her.

"Don't worry, Macha, I'll take care of her." Sir Freddie's dear familiar face bent over them as he embraced them both. Then a siren sounded, like a dirge, and she was being pulled up the gangway by Molly. The air was full of streamers, and there was a band playing. The snowdrop of Mrs. Wellington's white lace handkerchief fluttered.

Declan's arm encircled her and held her tightly. He led her to the rail and raised her hand in his to wave to their friends.

The mighty liner slid out of port and into the Solent, past the very spot where she had once stood with her few rough ponies under the Sussex downs. The people merged into a tiny ball of colour, the city receded, England became a green jewel in the diamond sea.

"Oh, Declan," she said tremulously, "was there ever a time when you weren't by my side?"

"Where else would I be?" he smiled.

"How I love you."

"And I have loved you since I was a boy, Macha."

"Always?" she asked.

"Always," he confirmed.

Ahead lay America, the golden land of promise and refuge, offering hope and new life and freedom. They sailed to it together.

MAUREEN O'DONOGHUE

Authenticity is a passion with Maureen O'Donoghue. *Winner*, like her previous book, *Jedder's Land* (a Condensed Book selection in 1983), is the result of many months of careful research. Before starting her latest novel, the Scottish-born writer immersed herself in the history of thoroughbred racing. Even her journalist husband helped, she says, by sharing knowledge gathered from his own lifelong enthusiasm for the turf. But she also went to the experts in Newmarket, and to countless books and historical records, to discover how the sport was practised in Edwardian times. She tracked down stud and groom fees, studied bloodlines, learned about auctions at Tattersall's, London's famous horse market, and the races at Ascot, all of which, she says, re-created "the immediacy, exhilaration and beauty of the sport of kings, right there at my desk."

That desk is to be found in a lovely old farmhouse deep in the Devonshire countryside. Maureen O'Donoghue used to be a Londoner, and spent twelve years as a jet-set publicist in the film industry. "It was like a supercharged circus," she recalls, "frantic and fun." But now she has left all that behind her for a life of part-time farming. On a small, three-acre holding in Devon she and her husband grow their own vegetables, and breed pigs, chickens and sheep. "I've always been a countrywoman at heart," she says emphatically, and perhaps that explains the special vividness of her descriptions of the English landscape. As for Ireland, while the author is only half Irish, she maintains it is her more dominant half. Thus it is no wonder that she writes so knowledgably of Celtic folklore and of the Irish landscape as seen from a gypsy caravan. Add to those ingredients a spirited Irish heroine and a host of colourful characters, and the result is *Winner*, a superb portrayal of life, high and low, in the Edwardian era.

the English Eagles

A CONDENSATION OF THE BOOK BY
NIGEL SLATER

ILLUSTRATED BY GARY KEANE

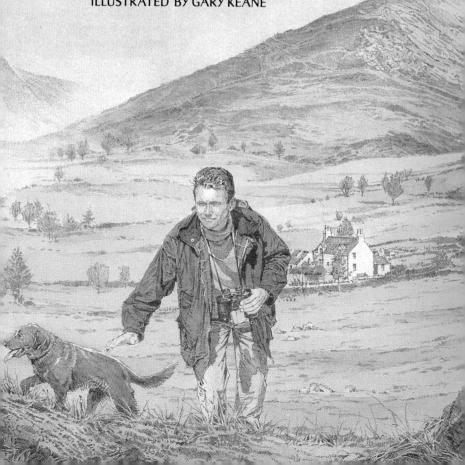

The two golden eagles were a magnificent sight as they soared over the pikes and crags of Skelmere: the first breeding pair in England for over two hundred years.

But it was not just their rarity that made them special. For Robin Woodford, who had come to the Lake District to escape his past, it was the freedom they represented. If only he too could be free, free from the painful memories that haunted him.

With overwhelming conviction Robin knew that the need to protect the eagles was as urgent as his own need to build a new life . . .

One

It was a blue and silver morning.

The two birds were no more than specks in the sky, circling and soaring over Westdale Pike. Buzzards? At a distance of over a mile they were too small to identify, dwarfed by the splendour of the snowscape. Jagged crags rose against a cloudless backdrop. Ice-cold streams tumbled like tinsel down the fell side and into the shimmering waters of Skelmere.

"Sir!"

The treble voice drew my attention back to the quiet classroom. Dawson had his hand up. It was always Dawson.

"Yes? What is it this time?"

"Question nine, sir. I don't quite see."

"You'd better come up."

You had to admire Dawson in a way. By the time I had explained the question, I had more or less given him the answer.

When I had joined the staff at Skelmere Grange Preparatory School the previous September, I had at first thought him slow. With his thick-lensed spectacles and hair sticking up at the back, he conveyed a permanent air of puzzlement. It took me a term to realise that he was an ace manipulator.

Dawson went back to his place, and silence returned to the classroom. I surveyed the twelve bowed heads in front of me. Form 4a—my own class—were finishing the General Knowledge test which I set them in the last period before lunch every Saturday morning.

With my limited academic qualifications (matriculation and one term at Oxford hardly counted), the headmaster had furrowed his brow before deciding on my specialist subjects of geography and scripture. His decision was based on the dubious strength of my experience as a rancher in South America and because I attended the village church at Skelham rather more often than other members of staff. The fact that I couldn't even hang a Dip.Ed. onto my name in the school prospectus had obviously worried him. "Geography and Scripture—Mr. Robin Woodford" looked a bit bald.

I'd grown fond of my eleven-year-olds. Inevitably, I suppose, a few favourites emerged. There was Barton, streets ahead of the others in class and captain of all three Colts teams; Hope-Atkins, who tried desperately hard and was still prone to tears when his parents dropped him back at school on Sunday nights; Dent, the cheerful hooligan. There were others, of course, who would never rank as teacher's pets. Smythe, the classroom lawyer; the hulking Green, already passing into puberty; and the unctuous Crawley, known by all as "Creepy".

Watching them work, I remembered my own time at Skelmere Grange, when—as a boy called Robert Wyndham—I had carved my own name on the very desk where Barton was now sitting. That would have been just after the war. There was rationing, and I wore long grey shorts that tickled the backs of my legs. I don't think, if I were honest, that the memories were particularly happy ones. I was overshadowed by two successful elder brothers, each head of school in his turn, and I suffered the stress of trying to compete with their reputations.

Now it was late January in 1969, over twenty years on. A decade was ending which I wanted to forget.

I glanced again out of the window and was confronted by my own image reflected in the glass. The face was too well travelled for a man in his midthirties. The lines were like wounds. Mostly self-inflicted.

The school's erratic central heating system was blasting out waves of warmth, and with the sun striking through the panes it felt oppressively hot. I opened the window and, ignoring the exaggerated chattering of teeth behind me, breathed in deeply.

The playing fields stretched down to the water's edge, the grass still white with frost under the trees. There was a strip of plantation on the far bank, giving way to hawthorn, birch and mountain ash as the ground rose sharply behind. Screes of shale sprawled down the slopes through stretches of dead bracken. Higher still stood rocky outcrops, black against the brilliance of the snow. The light was almost painfully bright to eyes accustomed to the grey Lake District winter.

Squinting, I watched the two birds wheeling above the Pike. There was something unfamiliar about their flight. It was too majestic, the slow wing beat too measured to be that of buzzards.

Oddly excited, I rummaged in my desk for a pair of Zeiss binoculars.

Dent had been given them for Christmas and I had confiscated them after he tried to insist that he needed them to read the blackboard.

"You can't borrow Dent's glasses, sir—they're confiscated!" Smythe protested. It was probably Rule 97, Subsection 2(c), I reflected. Smythe would know.

"It's freezing," Mather complained. He was a skinny child with bright red hair. "Can't we have the window shut, sir?"

"The next boy who talks," I said, lifting the binoculars to my eyes, "stays in after games this afternoon. And I don't care if that *does* mean his parents kicking their heels for half an hour."

The birds leapt into focus, magnified eight times by the glasses. They weren't buzzards. They were eagles. But eagles in the Lake District? Scotland was their natural habitat—at least in the British Isles. What on earth were they doing down here?

I tracked them as they drifted south along the jagged skyline. Eventually, they dropped from sight. Shutting the window, I returned to my desk, and when the bell rang at last I bustled the boys out. I was itching to ask Ken Wade about the eagles. Ken wore several hats, from that of deputy head to that of scoutmaster. He was also something of a naturalist.

I hurried down the corridors, absently registering the familiar school smells of floor polish, disinfectant and overcooked cabbage. Crossing the quad, I entered the Mastery.

"Hello, Rob," Ken said. "You look harassed."

He had known me as Robert Wyndham when I was a child and he a young member of staff fresh from the Arnhem battle, with an MC and a leg wound as mementos. He'd been quite a hero, and I still had a lot of time for him. Apart from the headmaster and the chairman of the governors, he was the only person at Skelmere Grange who knew my real background, and there were times when he puzzled people by referring to me forgetfully as Mr. Wyndham.

"Harassed? Not exactly. Just something I want to quiz you about."

"Take a pew." He settled himself into his favourite armchair, a glass of sherry beside him, and set about lighting his pipe. He had a squat, still powerful figure, the shoulders broad beneath the hairy tweed jacket. His study was as untidy as ever. "Well?" he asked, between puffs.

"You may think I'm mad, but I think I've just seen a pair of eagles over Westdale. Is that possible?"

"Probably buzzards," he said dismissively. "Tourists' eagles—that's what they call 'em in Scotland."

"I watched them through binoculars. I'm pretty sure."

"H'm. Well, to answer your question—yes, it *is* possible. I haven't seen any eagles round here myself, but there have been a few sightings reported since the war. From what I remember they were mostly immature birds, floating around before finding a mate. You can tell them by the pale markings under the tail and wings."

"The ones I saw seemed uniformly brown all over."

"And two of them, you say? It would certainly be quite something if they turned out to be a breeding pair. I don't suppose any eagles have nested in England for—well, God knows how long." But his interest was perfunctory. It was obvious Ken thought that all I'd seen was a pair of buzzards.

"But if they were eagles," I persisted, "where would they have come from?"

"Across the Solway, I imagine. I believe there are a few pairs nesting in Galloway."

The lunch bell rang.

"Ah, Summoned by Bells," Ken said. He was a Betjeman fan. "Just time for another quickie."

He heaved himself out of his armchair and limped over to his drinks cupboard. He knew better than to offer me one. Once again, I tried to shrug off the memory . . .

I HAD WOKEN UP at four in the morning, drenched with sweat. I had to have a drink.

I had slipped from the double bed, careful not to wake my Anglo-Argentine wife, Maria. Officially, no alcohol was kept at the ranch house—but I stashed it away, of course.

I padded into the bathroom and looked out of the window, trying to unscramble my brains and recall where there might be a bottle. I could just make out the shape of the corrals outside, with the Argentine pampas rolling silvery in the starlight beyond. The station wagon was parked beneath the window.

That was it. There was a bottle of whisky in the glove compartment.

I let myself out of the house, hardly noticing the sharpness of the gravel beneath my bare feet. Sitting on the passenger seat, I uncapped the bottle with shaking hands.

The raw spirit made me gag but I persisted doggedly, sipping until my stomach settled and the familiar warmth spread through me. My hands stopped shaking, the fear receded:

I needed half a bottle before I felt steady enough to return.

Entering the darkened room, my foot caught in the cable of the bedside lamp. It crashed to the floor. Maria sat up in bed.

"What the hell are you doing?" she demanded angrily.

"I couldn't sleep. It's just that—"

"You've been drinking, haven't you? I can smell it from here. I'm not surprised your big brothers are calling you back to England. No wonder you can't cope with the bloody job—you're smashed twenty-four hours a day."

"It's just a board meeting, that's all," I said weakly.

Wyndham's was a family business started by my grandfather, and had grown into a large chain of butchers' shops in northwest England with a ranch in the Argentine to supply the raw material. I ran the ranch, whilst my eldest brother, John, was chairman and chief executive at the head office in Manchester. Simon was the marketing director.

"Oh, yes?" she said, her voice rising. "I saw the letter from John about that cock-up you made with the shippers. *They* know you're hitting the bottle—don't kid yourself."

"Oh, get off my back!" We were both shouting now. The baby started to cry, next door.

"You've woken up Angela. God!" Disgusted, Maria went to comfort the little girl, and I was left alone. I already needed another drink ...

I STOOD AT THE HEAD of my table in Hall, waiting for grace. I had Dent and Green next door to me today—the boys moved places for each meal in rotation—and the rest of my saints and sinners were spread down either side. Jenny Stott, the new assistant matron, was at the other end with the plates and dishes ready for serving.

Jenny had joined at the beginning of term, and I hadn't really got to know her yet. She cut a trim figure in her starched white uniform with its broad black belt girdling a narrow waist. She had short springy hair, fair with a touch of gold, and the sort of skin that burnt easily in the sun. I thought that she looked terribly young, but perhaps that was just the freckles on her nose.

The headmaster mounted the rostrum and began to intone the grace— one of the longer Latin versions. He was an aloof and serious young man, destined to fly high in his profession.

He paused to draw breath halfway through, and Jenny started to sit down. Mather giggled and I tried to kill him with a look. After the "Amen", there was the usual hubbub of conversation and the scraping of benches and chairs. I looked up at Jenny. She was blushing.

Dent wanted a postmortem on the morning's test paper. Green joined in and shocked me by admitting that he hadn't known that Harold Wilson was Prime Minister.

"You're spastic, Green," Dent said witheringly.

I left them to it, and found my eyes roving over the Rolls of Honour on the wall. My brothers both featured during the war years as Heads of School and scholars to Sedbergh. The name of Robert Wyndham was conspicuous by its absence. As my eyes wandered, so too did my mind. I pictured again the two birds wheeling over the crags, utterly free, the sun gilding their plumage. I was *sure* they were eagles, and I was determined to find out more about them.

"... that question about the Holy Trinity—Mr. Woodford, sir?" I was miles away and Green was trying to attract my attention.

"Yes?" We'd reached the pudding stage, and I was pouring custard over a jam and sponge confection.

"Well, I knew the answer. It was Father, Son and Holy Ghost. But I don't get it, sir. How can God be all three at the same time?"

Green had surprised me again, the more so because his interest appeared to be genuine. I paused while I tried to find a simple answer to a very complex question. I didn't want to get it wrong. After all, I was the Scripture master.

I hurried to the library after lunch and pored over an old bird book. The eagle section was headed "*Aquila Chrysaetos*". The print was small and the prose turgid but my interest quickened with every line.

The clock tower over the main gates chimed the half hour and I was startled to see that it was already 2.30 p.m. I was in charge of Colts hockey, and there was a practice game that afternoon between the Probables and Possibles. The teams would be waiting for me.

Barton was the star, of course. As inside left for the Probables, he had netted three goals in ten minutes, and they were nearly into double figures by half time. As the teams rested, I saw Jeremy Ightam, the headmaster, making his way across the field. He had grown a moustache over the Christmas holidays and taken to smoking a pipe; both succeeded in making him look older.

"How are they shaping up, Robin?" he asked.

"Not bad, Headmaster. I think I've got it about right with the Probables. Barton's our key man, of course. We should give Keswick Hall a run for their money next Saturday."

"Excellent, excellent." He took his pipe out of his mouth. "I ... er, just thought I'd mention that the detailed plans for the new Assembly Hall have now been finalised. You might like to pop into my study to look them over some time. In view of your ... er, involvement in the project, I mean."

The headmaster had never quite known whether to treat me as a school benefactor or a subordinate.

"That's very kind of you, Headmaster, but I've seen the architect's impressions and I'm perfectly happy with the general design. I think it would be better if I kept my nose out of it, don't you?"

"As you wish, as you wish," he repeated. "Well, I'll leave you to your Colts. Keep 'em at it."

With his hands clasped behind his back, he returned towards the school.

The afternoon sun was only just above the western crags, but it lent warmth to the gaunt and forbidding structure. With its towers and neo-gothic windows, it was hideous even by Victorian standards. The new Assembly Hall tacked on to the south wing would give it a mongrel look, but I decided that it could only be an improvement. I blew the whistle for the second half.

My concentration was flagging when Green, playing full-back for the Possibles, intercepted a pass and cleared with a powerful volley. The ball rose and caught Hope-Atkins full in the mouth as he was following up.

He was rolling on the ground when I reached him, his hands to his face, and there was blood everywhere. The little ghouls gathered like vultures as I tried to examine the damage.

"Ooh! Do you think he'll die from loss of blood, sir?" one of them asked.

"Lucky it wasn't Barton," another one said heartlessly.

"That's enough," I said. "The game's abandoned. I'll take him to the surgery. The rest of you go and get changed."

I picked him up—he was light as a feather—and made for the school. He was fighting back tears. His mouth was a mess and it was just as well he couldn't see it. I called him by his Christian name and tried to make encouraging noises as I carried him across the field.

The surgery smelt strongly of antiseptic. I was laying him down on the couch when Jenny walked in.

"I'm afraid I've got a casualty for you," I said. "Hit by a hockey ball."

"I know. Crawley came and told me." He would, I thought.

Jenny gave Hope-Atkins a quick but professional examination.

"Poor old chap. Now let's see . . . split lip, wobbly tooth. Don't worry—nothing serious. We'll soon have you patched up."

Jenny was calm and efficient. The bleeding was staunched, and she cleaned him up and stuck a pad of gauze on the cut. What with the swelling, it gave him a lopsided and woebegone look.

"Thank you, Miss Stott," he mumbled.

"All in a day's work," she said and propelled him gently out of the door. "Run along and change. You don't want to keep your parents waiting, do you?"

"I suppose the damage usually looks worse than it is," I said, after he'd gone.

"Usually," she agreed, dropping the blood-soaked swabs into the bin. Then she dropped her eyes, and said, "I made a bit of a fool of myself at lunch today. Sitting down in the middle of grace, I mean."

"It must have happened to hundreds of people," I grinned, and changed the subject. "Going away this weekend?"

"No. My mother lives in Glasgow and it's a long haul for just one night." Yes, I thought I'd detected a slight Scottish accent. "And what about you?"

"Oh, I'll be at home."

"Home?"

"Southwater. It's down at the other end of Skelmere." I'd forgotten for a moment that she was new. "Just a couple of miles away. Far enough to be a bolt hole, but close enough to walk if I'm feeling energetic."

"That sounds ideal."

"You must come and see it some time." I meant it, too. I was proud of how I'd converted the house and she seemed a pleasant enough girl, though a bit shy. But we didn't make any firm plans, and I left her tidying up the surgery.

It was dark by the time the parents arrived to collect their children. Hope-Atkins's mother was helping her son into their car as though he were made of bone china. I told her that he hadn't been seriously hurt, but she shot me a look as though I'd belted him myself. I beat a retreat through the main gates and found Ken pinning up notices on the glass-fronted board in the quad.

"All the chaps gone home?" he said.

"Most of them. Peace at last. I'm just off myself. I thought I'd have a look for those eagles if the weather holds tomorrow."

"Needles in a haystack." His eyes twinkled. "Anyway, good luck."

I made my way to the staff car park and climbed into my Range Rover. It smelt conspicuously new. It was the first car I'd owned or driven for over three years.

I wound my way through Skelham—little more than a collection of cottages with a small church and a post office—and headed south down the narrow lakeside road. I only passed one building on the way, the two-star Skelmere Hotel, and then the road came to an end at the head of the lake. I bumped over the wooden bridge crossing Southwater Beck and lurched up the track before turning into my drive.

The house was built from local limestone and roofed with Coniston slate. I'd enjoyed doing it up inside, and the spree at Harrods had been fun. Ken had given it one look and observed drily that it was just as well I didn't have to live on my schoolmaster's salary. Fair comment: I paid more tax on my private income than I earned in a year's teaching.

Sally, my black labrador, gave me her usual effusive greeting, with her tail wagging fit to fall off as she followed me into the kitchen.

I put on the kettle, made myself a large flask of coffee and took mug and flask into the drawing room. There was a colour TV set in one corner. They'd only just come on the market and weren't easy to tune. Faces tended to be red or green.

I turned it on to watch the evening news. A pop programme followed, but I wasn't "with it", as the boys said. I switched off and decided to take Sally for a walk.

314

It was bitterly cold outside. Iced puddles crackled beneath my feet and the ground was like iron. It was too dark to go up by the Stones' farm and round the lower dale, so I settled for a brisk heel and toe to the hotel and back. Sally padded along beside me, and I think she was as glad as I was when we got home. I paused for a moment before going in. There was hardly any wind and the stars lent the snow on the crags a phosphorescent glow. The eagles were up there somewhere, in the silence and the stillness. I just knew it.

Feeling restless and impatient for the morning, I turned in early. Sally disgraced herself by worming under the duvet, and I drifted off, thinking that I really had to be firmer with her.

IT WAS LIGHT BY EIGHT. The crags stood cold and clear against the sky. Too clear—the weather would break before the day was out. I decided to play safe with a couple of thick sweaters under my Barbour.

Sally wasn't to be left behind. She tagged along, and I remembered that she was due to come into season. It was a bore. The farmer's dog was a randy devil, and I had to keep Sally virtually under house arrest when she was on heat.

These thoughts were crossing my mind when a collie bounded out from behind one of the farm outhouses. He dropped on his belly and wormed his way towards us, grinning from ear to ear and reminding me of "Creepy" Crawley. Sally stood over him, stiff-legged, tail wagging, and then pranced playfully round him. She was over seven now, and had matured into a middle-aged delinquent, but at least I'd taught her not to chase the sheep.

"Bruno! Here, Bruno!" It was a girl's voice, from the direction of the farm.

I'd never seen her before. She wore jeans, fashionably flared, and a shaggy goatskin coat. She was bareheaded and her hair fell long and raven-black round her shoulders. As she approached, I noticed her eyes; they were a Nordic blue, the sort of colour you don't associate with dark-haired people.

"They seem to be old friends," she said. The accent was mid-Atlantic.

"More than that. It's a tale of unrequited love." I hesitated, curious. "You're staying at the farm?"

It turned out that she was the farmer's daughter, and her name was Nera. Her father, Peter Stone, was a tough, taciturn type. We'd done little more than exchange the occasional greeting.

She asked, unexpectedly, if she could join me. Unaccustomed in recent years to the company of women, especially attractive ones, I hedged. I said something fatuous about it being a bit of a wild-eagle chase, but she seemed determined to come.

315

The walking was easy in the lower dale, but the ground rose as the valley narrowed. We laboured up the slope between the ridges, staying by the beck, and I managed to glean that she was a journalist on the *Manchester Herald*. She'd been working in America for a few years, which explained the accent.

I knew the *Herald* as a left-of-centre tabloid, with strong environmental sympathies, and I guessed that her interest in the eagles was as much professional as anything else. For my part, I told her that I taught at Skelmere Grange. I didn't go further back than that.

We encountered the snow line at around 2,000 feet, and there were another five hundred to go before we reached the plateau running parallel to the western side of Skelmere. There hadn't been much wind down in the dale, but I felt it now, slicing through my coat as we trudged north along the plateau. The going was easier and there was time to look round; our two houses looked diminutive beside the lake below; Scafell Pike was clearly visible to the west, and the Helvellyn crags to the east.

But no eagles.

"The last time I was up here," Nera was saying, "I was helping Peter dig out some of our sheep. It's amazing how Herdwicks survive." I couldn't help noticing she referred to her father by his Christian name.

"When was that?" I asked.

"Oh, five or six years ago and—oh, look, Robin!"

We'd found them. They were over the valley next to ours, and close enough to observe without binoculars. They were both wheeling in concentric circles when one of them dropped without warning. It fell with its wings half closed, gathering speed until it was far below us. Then, just when it seemed doomed to dash itself against the rocks, it spread its seven-foot span and soared up and up without a single wing beat. It hung poised above us before diving again. Soaring and swooping, it crossed the width of the valley. Rising on the thermals on the far side, it climbed to rejoin its mate. Then both of them fell. They tumbled like leaves, twisting and grappling in mock aerial combat. They dropped for over a thousand feet before breaking apart over the floor of the dale.

Wing tip to wing tip, they sailed majestically over the lake. I could just see the sun striking their golden crowns. Rising on the updraughts on the far side, they boosted their ascent with slow-beating wings until they were spiralling over the eastern crags. Higher and higher they rose, until they were lost from sight.

I was breathless.

"Fantastic!" Nera's eyes were alight. "The way that first one swooped and soared across the valley!"

"That was the male. It was a mating display."

"You sound quite an authority."

316

I had to confess that my expertise was based on twenty minutes' reading in the school library.

"Hey, we'd better watch out," Nera said suddenly. "We don't want to get caught by the weather."

She was right. Scafell was now completely obscured by cloud and it wouldn't be long before conditions deteriorated over the Skelmere ranges. It was quicker and easier going down. By the time the gradient flattened out in the dale, snow was beginning to fall, but we only had to follow the beck to the farm.

Nera asked me to join her and her father for lunch. There was a joint in the oven and plenty to spare. I was happy to say yes.

As we stood in the hall and shook the snow from our coats, Stone came downstairs. He was unshaven and wore a collarless shirt with trousers supported by braces. His acknowledgment of my presence was curt. "Oh, it's you," he said.

"I met your daughter when I was going for a walk," I explained. "She came with me."

"And I've asked Robin to lunch," Nera told him. "Oh, Peter, you'll never guess what we saw—a pair of golden eagles!"

"Aye, they've been here for about a week," he said. It was a bit deflating to realise that I hadn't been the first to sight them. "And the sooner they bugger off the better," he went on.

"Why's that?" I asked, following him into their sitting room.

"It's my lambs. The foxes and buzzards are bad enough, but I won't have eagles on my land. If they're still here in the lambing season, I'll shoot 'em."

"Don't you dare!" Nera called from the kitchen, and for a moment Stone looked chastened. I guessed that she ruled the roost when she was at home.

The threat to his lambs hadn't occurred to me. I had read that eagles' staple diet in Scotland included grouse, hares and rabbits. The nearest grouse moors were miles away, near Shap, and I hadn't seen a single hare since I'd arrived. As for the rabbits, the latest wave of myxomatosis had thinned out the warrens by the lake. I knew that eagles lived to some extent off carrion, but newborn lambs could easily tempt them in the absence of other prey. It was worrying.

"I think they're protected," I said cautiously.

"So's my stock," he replied. "You'll have a whisky?"

"No, thanks."

"Please yourself."

He hadn't offered me a chair, but I was tired and sat down anyway. Sally, too, had flopped down uninvited into Bruno's basket and was sound asleep. Stone was pouring himself a drink when Nera came back.

"That bottle was full this morning," she accused him.

"I've only had a couple, lass." His manner was defensive.

"I don't know how you do it after that skinful you had at the hotel last night." She shot her father an angry look, and returned to the kitchen.

It wasn't a comfortable meal. Stone ate for the most part in silence. I knew already that he was only a tenant farmer—I'd bought Southwater from his absentee landlord, Sir Graham Banner. Stone's three hundred Herdwick sheep were enough to make him a living and no more. He didn't have to spell it out; the shabby farmhouse told its own story.

"You mustn't mind Peter," Nera said as I was going. "He's not very good in company."

"The beef was delicious. Thanks, Nera." I wasn't going to comment on Stone's behaviour. Our dislike seemed to be mutual.

"When are you coming up again?" I asked.

"Next weekend with any luck. Peter's let himself slip a bit since my mother died last year. He needs me."

"Yes—well, I'll hope to see you again then. Maybe dinner at Southwater? It's my turn."

"That sounds lovely."

The snow was drifting through the open door, so I didn't hang about. Sally followed me down the half-obliterated track, gambolling through drifts and snapping at snowflakes. I wondered if she'd ever grow up.

Later that night, at evensong at St. Michael's in Skelham, there were just a dozen other people in the congregation.

It was a quiet service. My eyes were drawn to the eagle on the lectern. It stood as a symbol of strength, wildness and freedom, as old as the legends of Babylon and ancient India.

The candles on the altar flickered, mesmerising me. I drifted between dreams of the diving eagle and Nera's dark beauty.

"*DISCIPLINA EST LIBERTAS*. Who knows what it means?" I asked. "You, Crawley—you're in the headmaster's classics set."

"It's the school motto, sir."

"We all know it's the school motto, Crawley. That's not what I asked."

"Well, sir . . . it sort of means . . . well, discipline is freedom."

"Yes, but what does that really mean? Anyone?" Blank faces.

I was beginning to regret my choice of topic for the Monday morning debate. "OK, let's define the words first. Take discipline. Come on, Dent, we haven't heard a squeak out of you all morning. Anything wrong?"

"No, sir. Er, discipline. That's doing what the masters and prefects tell us? Obeying the school rules and all that jazz?"

"Partly. And that leaves you with a clear conscience, doesn't it? Right. Then let's move on to freedom. Let's have a definition from one of you."

318

"It's throwing a six to get out of jail." Dent went on. He grinned about him. He was just getting into his stride.

"Phillips? A sensible answer, please."

"D-Dent's right, sir." He tried to master his stutter. "It's being, well, f-free. Like w-wearing what you want in the h-h-holidays."

"Isn't it also freedom from fear and guilt? Having a clear conscience? Are you beginning to understand the motto now?"

There were a few cautious nods. "Right, let's go on with the debate. Usual teams. Barton's lot can propose the motion, and Smythe's can oppose it."

My throat was dry by break, and the coffee in the common room was more than usually welcome. Ken Wade came in, and I buttonholed him about the eagles.

"So you actually found them?" he said enthusiastically. "Gosh. I think you ought to tell the RSPB, you know."

"The who?"

"The Royal Society for the Protection of Birds. It's their sort of pigeon, as it were."

David Evans, the history and rugger master, was monopolising the pay-phone in the common room, and I counted my sixpences and shillings and waited for him to finish. Enquiries took ages to answer, and class was due to begin in five minutes—Form 3 Geography. I got the number eventually and rang the society.

The response was polite but muted. They'd had two sightings the previous week, from as far afield as Buttermere and Martindale. But the bloke perked up a bit when I mentioned the mating display. If I saw any evidence of nesting activity round Skelmere, they'd like to know straight away, but in the meantime there was nothing to be done. He thanked me, and rang off. I was left feeling disappointed, and the bell had gone, and I was late. I was hurrying down the corridor when I passed the headmaster. He didn't improve my mood by looking pointedly at his watch. I'd half promised the Third Form a chat about my ranching experiences in the Argentine—my cowboy stories always went down well. I decided instead to set them an essay on trade routes in Britain.

Two

The Alcoholics Anonymous meeting in Keswick that night ended in its usual fashion: "God grant me the serenity to accept the things I cannot change, courage to change the things I can, and wisdom to know the difference."

The church hall was spartan, with just a trestle table and chairs drawn round it in the middle. But the atmosphere was warm and friendly, and I never missed my Monday meetings if I could help it. Jim echoed these thoughts as we moved into the kitchen to join the others for coffee.

"If I didn't come regularly," he said, "I think I'd go spare. I need topping up with AA just as much as I did with booze."

"Yes." We had stopped drinking, but we were still alcoholics. There was no cure, no magic formula to turn us into normal, social drinkers. Jim was now a director of a major drugs company. As a young GP he'd lost a patient (and his licence to practise) through negligence. He'd been drunk, of course, at the time.

A gust of laughter came from across the kitchen. Marilyn was regaling the group with one of her theatre stories—she had once been a successful actress, but there had been too many gins in the dressing room, and her agent had finally washed his hands of her. It was good to hear them laugh, good to be reminded that there was life after alcohol.

I squelched back to my car through the slush, taking a short cut through St. John's graveyard. Keswick was drab on a winter's night. It was hard to imagine it as a tourist trap in high summer, the souvenir shops busy with trippers. But the surroundings didn't dampen my mood. As I drove out of town, I found myself looking forward to the weekend with the anticipation of a schoolboy before the Christmas holidays.

BUT IT BECAME a nervous anticipation.

By Saturday, I was behaving with all the emotional maturity of an adolescent on his first date. I ducked games that afternoon, and spent a couple of hours shopping in Keswick—smoked salmon, steak and imported asparagus from Sainsbury's, and a job lot of booze for my empty cocktail cabinet from an off-licence.

I was out to impress Nera, as I dressed for dinner. I was ready half an hour early, and was so keyed up that I jumped when I eventually heard her car door slam.

She'd parked her Mini Cooper beside my Range Rover, and picked her way between the puddles to the front door.

"Sorry. Meaning to put down new gravel on the drive for ages." I stumbled over the apology. That was a scintillating curtain raiser, I thought with annoyance.

"I'm used to it up at the farm," she said lightly. I helped her off with her coat, to find she was wearing a dark blue trouser suit. Very smart. Very sophisticated. I showed Nera into the sitting room and her eyes widened. "Wow! I didn't think the teaching profession paid this well."

"It doesn't. I've got a private income." Again, I felt myself apologising.

"Do you mean that I've been lured into a den of capitalism? I don't think my editor would approve at all."

"I suppose he subscribes to the view that property is theft?"

"Whole-heartedly."

"And you?"

"Only at the office." She smiled, and dropped her mocking manner. "It's a *lovely* room, Robin."

"What would you like?" I opened the drinks cupboard. "I've got most things, I think. Or there's some champagne in the fridge."

"I always think champagne should be kept for a special occasion." It was, for me, but I rode that one.

"Could I have a gin and tonic? I must say, you keep a well stocked bar for a nondrinker."

I didn't quite know what to say, and poured myself a Coke. Some ice and lemon made it look a bit more festive.

"Have you seen the eagles again?" she asked.

"No. It's dark by the time I get back from school. I rang up the RSPB on Monday and told them about the mating display. They were obviously interested, but there was nothing they could do until they knew if and where the birds are nesting."

"Wouldn't it be fantastic if they were!"

"Do you know—it'd be the first time that golden eagles have nested in the Lake District for over two hundred years? They're not exactly common in Scotland, even though it holds about twenty per cent of the world population. I mean there are only two hundred and fifty or so breeding pairs up there and—"

"You've been doing your homework," she laughed.

"Well, just imagine—English eagles breeding right here on our doorstep!"

"Quite a story," she murmured thoughtfully.

"Story?"

"For the *Herald*. It's right up our street. You know—conservation and all that."

That slowed me up. "Oh, I see. I—I think we'd have to tread carefully on any publicity. Splash a story, and we'll have an army of twitchers scaring the birds off."

"Twitchers?"

"Birdwatchers. Apparently they gather like flies round a jam pot when any unusual sighting is reported." My caution was selfish. I just didn't want to share my eagles with the world at large.

"Yes, but I'd have thought that a greater public awareness would help the eagles. You can't really pinch their eggs or take a pot shot at them if you're under the scrutiny of several pairs of binoculars."

We kicked around the pros and cons of the publicity angle until it was time for dinner. It was a good meal. Nera drank the better part of a decent bottle of Beaune I'd bought, and I noticed as only ex-drinkers can how her talk became freer and her eyes brighter. But her manner was infectious, and I found myself responding to her warmth and animation.

"Liqueur?" I suggested, as we moved back into the drawing room.

"Brandy, if you've got some."

I shoved another log on the fire, and we both lit cigarettes. "Anything you want to watch on the box?" I asked.

"Not specially. Not even in colour," she added with a smile. "Are you hooked on any of the Saturday programmes?"

"No, but Sunday evenings are sacrosanct. 'The Forsyte Saga'," I explained.

"Oh, didn't you see it a couple of years ago on BBC 2?"

"I missed it first time round. I was ... away, in nineteen sixty-seven."

"Away? I thought you came back from South America in sixty-six."

I hesitated, and then sat on the sofa beside her. An air of intimacy seemed to envelop us, and I found myself telling her about the missing years. About Robert Wyndham. About everything. She was a good listener.

"Do you ever hear from Maria?" she asked.

"Not since we were divorced. There's no point really. She's remarried, started a new life. I gave her a pretty rough ride, you know."

"But what about your daughter? She must be, what, four by now? No birthday cards, Christmas cards?"

"Angela wouldn't even know who I was. She was only a few months old when I left. We were never on speaking terms," I said, with a rotten attempt at humour.

"Poor Robin." She laid a hand on my arm.

I turned at her touch and kissed her. Or tried to. Our noses bumped and she averted her face.

It was awful.

"I'm sorry. I—I'm a bit out of practice."

"You really mustn't keep saying that you're sorry." Nera stood up, straightening her jacket.

"It was stupid of me. I—"

"Oh, for God's sake!" And then her face softened. "You're very sweet, Robin, but you hardly know me."

"You know everything about me." It seemed horribly one-sided.

"And I'm flattered that you told me—honestly. But that doesn't mean ..." For a moment she seemed at a loss, and then she went on, "Look, I know you've been out of touch—but just because women are more liberated now, it doesn't mean that every chick or bird you meet is an easy lay. *I'm* not, for starters."

"Obviously." I didn't look up. Silence.

"I think I'd better go," she said.

"Yes. It's getting late." It wasn't even eleven. I followed her into the hall and helped her on with her coat. "Will I see you again?" I asked.

"Oh, I expect so. Come on, Robin—do cheer up." She smiled, and rose on tiptoe to kiss me on the lips. Then she was gone. The exhaust of her Mini Cooper sounded a cheeky, almost derisive, note as the taillights vanished down the drive.

The weather was foul the following day, with low cloud and drizzle. I'd never have found the eagles, even if I'd had a mind to look for them. I skulked at home all day, half hoping that Nera would call, but too embarrassed to drop in myself.

Monday was no better, and even AA failed to work its usual magic that evening. I hardly listened, and didn't share, and when I got home the bottles behind the glass-fronted cabinet stood as symbols of my illness and its incurable nature.

The sensible solution would have been to pour them away, but then I wasn't in a sensible mood. By the light cast through the open kitchen door I smashed them one by one on the cobbles in the stable yard. Including the bottle of Krug. Then I swept up the broken glass, and let the rain do the rest.

"I SUPPOSE WE'RE BOUND to get it," Belinda Ightam said. She was a plain and nervous young woman, clearly dominated by her husband.

"Get what?" I asked, soup spoon halfway to my mouth.

"Asian flu. It's been sweeping the schools in the south."

"Oh that. Yes, I suppose we will."

It was Friday night, and I was dining at the headmaster's house. It was his practice to invite members of staff to dinner once a term on a rota basis. They were black-tie, duty affairs, and this time, it was the turn of the unmarried members of staff.

Ken and Jenny sat opposite, and Miss Winters beside me. She was a brisk spinster of fifty or so, and she took the First Form. Despite her no-nonsense attitude, the young ones adored her. She was a first-class teacher.

"Matron was saying that we might have to turn some of the dormitories into sickrooms," Jenny said. She looked fresh and pretty in a long Laura Ashley dress. It was the first time I'd seen her out of uniform.

"I might have to consider sending the boys home if it reaches epidemic proportions," the headmaster said. He dabbed at his lips with his napkin.

As the meal wore on, I became oppressed with the school-life chatter. Perhaps it was a feeling of mild suffocation that prompted me to change the subject and mention the eagles. Out of the blue.

"Eagles?" enquired Ightam politely.

"Yes. A pair of them. Right here, around Skelmere."

"Robin seems to have adopted them," Ken said. "He's rather hoping they'll nest in the local dales. I must say, it would be remarkable if they did. But with the number of hill walkers about, I'd say they're more likely to return north across the Border."

"Oh, I don't know," Jenny said. "This must be one of the remotest areas in the Lake District. When do they normally start building?"

"February, March. Any time from now, really," I said.

"And do you know what the breeding cycle is?" She sounded genuinely interested.

"They usually lay in late March. The chicks hatch at the beginning of May, and they generally fly around the middle of July."

"I'd forgotten what a long cycle it is. It brings us right into the tourist season. The eaglets would still be fledging," she said thoughtfully.

"You seem to know something about it?" I was curious.

"Only what I can remember from when I was a child. My father was a bit of a naturalist, and he once took me to see a nesting site in Galloway. Oh, it was marvellous!" She stopped suddenly, aware that we had been monopolising the conversation. "Well, I think it would be just grand if they managed to breed down here." It was a lame ending.

"That all sounds very interesting. Very interesting indeed," Ightam repeated smoothly. "We're indebted to you, Robin, for introducing such a fascinating new topic. I'm afraid we're all guilty of talking too much shop on these occasions. You're lucky to have had a father who shared his interests with you, Jenny. Now when I was a child . . ."

They took their cue from the headmaster, and reminiscences began to flow. That left me out. Effectively, I had no past. Ken and Ightam knew my background, but the others didn't. Ightam passed round a bottle of Graves with the lemon sorbet, and seemed to make a performance about refilling my glass with Perrier water. I was probably being oversensitive, but it only served to increase my sense of alienation.

The party broke up shortly after dinner, and Ken asked the three of us back to his rooms for a nightcap. Miss Winters declined, but Jenny and I took him up on the offer. It would be a relief to unwind.

Ken made a half-hearted pretence of sorting out the shambles in his study, but did little more than clear the sofa so that we could sit down. Jenny asked for something soft—I'd noticed that she hardly touched her wine at dinner—then Ken fixed himself a whisky and put the kettle on for me. He knew my poison: sweet, black coffee.

Jenny noticed some fly-tying equipment amongst the clutter on his desk, and Ken gave us a quick demonstration. Peering over his shoulder, I wondered at the deftness of his stubby fingers working on the minuscule hook and delicate hackles.

"There." He looked satisfied with the job and held it up for inspection.

"If that doesn't land me the Skelmere Monster, I shall take up tapestry."

"What are you going for?" I asked. I wasn't a fisherman.

"Char. It's a member of the salmon family that lives in these lakes. Not long before the season opens now. It'll be good to get out and about again."

"Yes. I'll be out on the crags on Sunday if the weather lifts."

"Eagle spotting? I must say, if it wasn't for my leg, I'd join you, but—"

"Can I?" Jenny's interjection was unexpected. It left me floundering.

"Well, I . . . I expect the cloud'll be too low, and—and Ken's probably right. They may have pushed off by now. Not much point really." It was a ham-fisted put-down. The truth was I was hoping to patch things up with Nera, and, jealously, I didn't want to share the eagles with anyone else.

"Perhaps some other time," Jenny said brightly. She finished her drink and left.

"Really, Rob," Ken said when she'd gone, "there was no need to pour cold water over her offer. I'd have jumped at it if I'd been in your shoes. Nice girl, Jenny. And you mustn't get to thinking that those eagles are your private property. Birds like that belong to no one but themselves."

"It's not that at all." But his accuracy was uncomfortable. I didn't stay long.

I steeled myself to ring the farm when I arrived home from school on Saturday evening. For some reason the number was unobtainable. But I had to find out if Nera was at home. I walked round. There was no sign of her Mini Cooper, and Stone confirmed what I had half expected—Nera wasn't going to be there that weekend.

I'd blown it, I decided. Put her off for good. There was a grim satisfaction in having my natural pessimism confirmed.

As though to mock my mood, Sunday dawned without a cloud in the sky. It was already warm for early February. The snows had retreated to the highest crags. The becks were in torrent down the fell side.

I set off up the dale with a packed lunch on my back and Sally racing on in front. We followed the same route as I'd taken with Nera, climbing up out of Southwater dale along the narrowing beck. After a last, punishing haul up the scree, I sat down to draw breath on the narrow plateau running parallel to Skelmere. There wasn't another human being in sight, not a single car on the road across the lake. The only buildings I could see below were the hotel, the farm and my own house. The school and the village at the far end of Skelmere were hidden in haze.

Time to push on. Giant ravines fell away on either side, broadening into dales. Walking north along the escarpment was like treading the spine of a massive skeleton, ribbed by ridges to left and right.

Stopping from time to time, I scanned them through my binoculars. There was little movement or life. A raven was circling over Breakneck

Crag, three red deer hinds were browsing in a distant gully. They saw me on the skyline and took flight, vanishing over the next ridge. Otherwise I found nothing.

Certainly no eagles.

I skirted Breakneck, keeping below the snow line, and stopped to eat my sandwiches under Westdale Pike. Then I started back. The descent into Southwater dale was familiar but still treacherous, and I had to watch every step.

So I don't know what made me look up and behind.

The sun was lipping the ridge and blinded me for a moment. The eagle seemed to fly from the very heart of its heat, and passed overhead as a big black silhouette. The wind whistled through its pinions. It seemed almost close enough to touch. The wing tips were swept forward and upward, the primary feathers splayed like fingers against the sky.

Its sudden appearance was shocking, its size awesome. And then I saw that it was carrying a branch. Fumbling with my binoculars, I tried to follow it down the dale. My hands were shaking.

The branch was unwieldy and weighing it down, but a single slow wing beat restored the height and momentum of its flight.

Halfway down the valley it swung in a broad arc towards a cliff face on the south ridge. There it settled behind a small rowan growing from a cleft in the rock.

The eagles were nesting. They had to be.

I waited, unable to move.

It flew off after a minute, unencumbered now, to glide down the dale with effortless ease, and over my house, until it was lost amidst the growing shadows on the slopes beyond. I waited, but it didn't reappear.

I was determined to investigate before darkness fell. Slipping and sliding down the scree, I scrambled across to the foot of the cliff face.

It seemed dauntingly sheer, but I was damned if I was going to give up. I'd had no experience of rock-climbing. If I had, I'd probably have gone home, put on the kettle and toasted some muffins.

The first fifteen feet or so were a doddle. The little ledges and handholds were tailor-made for a novice. I looked down the dale and couldn't believe my luck. The site was in full view of my house half a mile away. I'd have a grandstand view from my own bedroom window.

Looking up was less encouraging. I still had another twenty feet to go and there was a distinct overhang beneath the rowan tree. I inched my way up another three feet.

And there I stuck, my cheek pressed against the coarse, cold surface.

I scrabbled for a higher hold, but the rock was smooth. Worse, the angle had become vertical. With only my toes and the fingers of one hand supporting my weight, I knew I was going to fall. It was slow and

326

inexorable, a matter-of-fact observation. I even made a mental note to use it in class as an object lesson in Newton's Law of Gravity. And in what happens if you play silly buggers on the fells.

Then I lost my grip, and I was falling. Resignation turned to terror. I may have screamed. I can't remember.

IT WAS DARK when I came to, and a freezing fog was shrouding the dale. I didn't know what time it was. My watch had been broken in the fall.

Along with my left leg.

It was when I tried to stand that I realised what had happened. I nearly blacked out again as waves of pain swept over me and I collapsed in an untidy heap onto the rocks.

Whimpering, Sally pressed against me. I guessed she must have been cuddling up to me ever since I'd fallen. Without her body heat, I'd have been close to death from exposure.

Gingerly, I sat up to explore the damage. I could just see in the darkness that my foot was twisted at an unnatural angle. I probed my lower leg beneath my breeks with tentative fingers.

Nausea engulfed me. My fingers had touched a shard of bone sticking through the stocking. A compound fracture. I dropped my face into my hands. Dried blood encrusted my cheek and matted my hair. I didn't feel for the wound this time. The headache was bad enough.

I tried to take stock. It wasn't encouraging. I was stuck up the dale, half a mile from the house and the farm. It was well below freezing and the visibility was down to a few yards.

I started shouting, but the fog smothered the sound like a blanket. Then I looked at Sally.

"Go on," I urged. "Go and get help. Go on!"

She didn't move, just gazed at me with big wounded eyes. It was asking too much. She hadn't watched the Lassie films that I'd seen as a boy. I controlled my anger, remembering that I probably owed her my life.

I had to move. The temperature was dropping.

The waters of the swollen beck were just audible through the fog. I started slithering down the slope towards the sound. It hurt. Every time I pulled myself on I was sobbing with pain. It didn't matter. There was no one to hear.

A dry-stone wall loomed in front of me, bridging the beck. I'd forgotten it was there, and there was no way I could climb over it. Despair threatened to overcome me, yet I was grateful for the respite. I lay still, and the agony of my leg eased to a dull ache. I felt almost sleepy as a delicious numbness crept over my body.

It was Sally who saved me again. She whined and raked my cheek with her paw. I shook my head and forced myself to think. There were two alternatives: I could roll into the narrow stream and drag myself beneath the big lintel supporting the wall. Or I could dismantle the wall, here on the bank, stone by stone.

No, I decided, not the stream. The water was icy. My resistance was low enough already. The cold would kill me.

It had to be the wall.

Somehow I levered myself up and pushed the top stones down. They were light and insecurely wedged. Easy. But they grew heavier further down, bedded in lichen. I reached the base stones at last—rocks two feet high, weighing a hundredweight or more. They were sunk into the turf, and immovable. I'd have to go over them.

Walking normally, I would scarcely have broken my stride to cross them. Now they seemed an almost insurmountable obstacle. I hauled myself over them like a wounded worm, and lay gasping at last on the other side.

The wall served as a marker. I now knew where I was. And how far I still had to go. I'd only covered about a quarter of the distance.

I don't remember much about the rest of the journey. A few images remain. The tussocky grass, brittle and white beneath my face. Sally standing over me, her hot breath mingling with the fog. The sudden appearance of a Herdwick ewe, almost close enough to touch. Finally, the farm. I'd made it.

The buildings were in darkness, but Stone had left the front door open. Inside, I pushed myself up against a wall and reached for the light switch. The place was a mess, but I found the telephone on a corner table, half hidden under an old newspaper.

It was when I picked up the receiver that I saw the notice of disconnection beside the instrument, and remembered then that Stone's number had been unobtainable. Why the hell hadn't the feckless bastard paid his bill?

It was cruel. I hadn't made it at all. A ridiculous paranoia swept over me. Leaning on the table, I cursed my God.

There was an open bottle of whisky on the sideboard, but the sight had an oddly sobering effect. What an excuse, I thought wryly. The daddy of them all. I was confused and in shock, I had a broken leg and I was half dead with cold. But the very temptation served as a new source of strength. I wasn't going to give in to it. Or give up.

I eased myself to the floor again and dragged myself out. Only another two hundred yards to my own house, I told myself.

It might have been as many miles. The ruts on the track were frozen, sharp and cutting. It was so dark and foggy that I nearly missed the gateway. Then I was crawling up the drive.

Nearly there.

The blast of warmth from the central heating as I opened the door was like stepping off a plane in the tropics.

I was home.

Its comfort enveloped me. I had to thaw out before attempting to dial—my fingers were numb. I glanced at the carriage clock on the mantelpiece. Eight o'clock. I'd been out there for four hours, in that state.

"Which service, please?" The voice was impersonal.

"Ambulance. I had a fall on the fells." It was difficult to form the words.

"I'm sorry, caller?" Perhaps she thought I was drunk.

"Broken leg," I mumbled. "Bash on the head."

She asked for my name and address, and I managed to get it out. Then she said, sounding cautious and almost human, that there might be a delay; there'd been a pile-up on the A6 in the fog, and the ambulances were busy. I felt no resentment at having to wait, only a wild relief bordering on hysteria.

The euphoria of survival wore off. I tried to get comfortable on the sofa. My leg had been anaesthetised by the cold. Now it started to hurt like hell.

The ambulance took ages and I began to grow fretful. At last I heard its siren, whee-wheeing up the track. Quite unnecessary, I thought. The only thing they were likely to encounter was one of Stone's sheep.

PRE-MED DROWSINESS. Faces peering down at me in funny white masks and caps. The smell of surgical spirit. The smooth sound of rubber tyres on polished floors as they wheeled me into the operating theatre.

There was no pain. I clung to consciousness. Not to the dark memory of that terrible journey down the dale, but exultantly to the image of those outstretched wings. The power and glory, the freedom . . .

Three

"It isn't right, Mr. Woodford," my daily told me. "They should have kept you in hospital longer."

"I think they wanted to, mainly because I'd bumped my head, but I'm not a very good patient. I can't stand hospitals. Too regimented. A bit like prison," I added.

Every morning from Monday to Friday Mrs. Blenkinsop bicycled down from Skelham, and returned at lunchtime. Winter and summer, she wore a shapeless black coat and hogged the middle of the road. Her bike was an old-fashioned and sturdy machine. It had to be: Mrs. Blenkinsop couldn't have weighed less than fifteen stone.

It was Tuesday morning and she was making my bed while I sat in an armchair with my leg propped up on a stool. It was in plaster from below

my ankle to above my knee. There was a pair of crutches propped up against the chair.

I had watched the eagles flying to and from the cliff face all morning. Their activity hadn't been intense. Their flight was leisurely and long periods elapsed between their appearances. After landing at the site with a branch or a sheaf of grass, one or other of the eagles might perch for up to an hour on the rowan tree, motionless save for the swivelling of its head from time to time. I learned to differentiate between the male and female. The male was the darker and more compact. The female was tawny, her broad wings supporting with effortless ease the ten-pound weight of her body. I began to think of them as "he" and "she".

"..: oh, and before I forget," Mrs. Blenkinsop said, "I saw Mr. Stone this morning. He was complaining about the hole you made in his dyke. Some sheep escaped from his in-bye ground. That'll be his wall, I mean, and the lower pasture," she explained helpfully.

"Could you give him my apologies, Mrs. Blenkinsop? Perhaps he ought to have a bottle of whisky as well, if you wouldn't mind adding that to your shopping list."

"You shouldn't encourage him, Mr. Woodford! He's a terror with drink, is Mr. Stone. Well, if there's nothing more you need, I'll be away home." She plumped up the pillows.

"No, everything's fine, thanks. At least, with Sally away, we won't get her paw marks on the bed," I observed. Ken was looking after her.

"You spoil that dog, Mr. Woodford," she scolded, and waddled out, clucking disapproval like a mother hen.

I WOKE FROM an uncomfortable doze at eight that evening and clumped carefully downstairs in my dressing gown. Mrs. Blenkinsop had prepared a hotpot, and all I had to do was shove the Le Creuset dish onto the Aga and let it simmer for twenty minutes. As usual, she had made much too much. I was wondering how to dispose of the surplus without her finding out, when the doorbell rang. It was Jenny, with Sally.

The dog almost knocked me over. Her tail wagged like a metronome and she seized my wrist between her teeth in a soft, possessive grip. It was good to have her home.

"We thought you'd like to have Sally back," Jenny said. "Ken's on duty, so he couldn't come himself. Anyway, how are you?"

"All the better for seeing you both." I was, too. "Come in. Take your coat off and sit down." Jenny had walked from the school and her cheeks were flushed from the cold night air. She was still in her uniform. I tried to light the fire, but overbalanced as I bent down and had to make a grab at the mantelpiece.

"Here, I'll do it," she said, and knelt at the hearth with the matches. I watched in silence. The nape of her neck beneath the short fair hair was slender as a boy's. The flames soon took hold, and she stood up. "There. That's more cheerful."

"I'd offer you a drink, but I'm afraid I haven't got any," I said.

"That's all right. I don't really like the stuff. Oh, I mustn't forget to give you this." She delved into her pocket and produced a Get Well card from my form.

"Who put them up to this?"

"No one. It was their own idea. You're pretty popular, you know. They call you Woodie."

"Do they just? Cheeky devils." But I was secretly pleased. "Have they given you a nickname yet?"

"No. I think I'm too new—though I expect they'll come up with one. They've got names for most of the staff. The head's known as Sniffer, Ken's called Whistling Wade—"

"Sniffer? Whistling Wade?"

"Yes. Apparently Mr. Ightam always sniffs before he speaks, and Ken usually whistles in the corridors." They did, too, come to think of it. "Children always notice our idiosyncrasies," she added.

"And you mean they actually told you?" I was surprised.

"Oh, I think some of them regard me as their big sister," she laughed. "Anyway, you must tell me what happened. We're all dying to know."

I gave a somewhat shamefaced account of my attempt to scale the cliff, but didn't go into too much detail about crawling home. It was something I preferred to forget.

"It was a stupid accident, that's all," I said. "But what matters is that the eagles are nesting. At least I'm pretty sure they are."

"That's thrilling, Robin!" Then she went on seriously, "Would you like me to have a look? It's my day off tomorrow."

"You? Don't be daft, Jenny. I don't think anyone could get up that cliff."

"I wasn't suggesting climbing it, but it should be possible to abseil down. Don't worry." She laughed at my incredulity. "I know how to do it. I went on an Outward Bound course when I left school, and carried on rock-climbing when I was a student. I've got all my tackle at the Grange. I could give it a go. I'd like to."

So that was settled. I lowered myself onto the sofa and Jenny helped me to get comfortable. It was nice to be fussed over. Then she sat down, and looked round her.

"I can see why you prefer to live here than in the Mastery," she commented. I'd forgotten it was her first visit.

"It's much too big for me, but it was fun doing it up. When I bought it last year—" The pinger sounded from the kitchen. Supper was ready. I

332

said on an impulse, "Look, why don't you stay for dinner? There's masses—honestly."

"Well . . . sure?"

"Sure."

We spent a companionable evening. Jenny insisted on doing the fetching and carrying. I ate from a tray on my lap. I can't remember what we chatted about. The eagles, certainly, and what arrangements had been made for covering my classes at school. Afterwards, we played backgammon and she beat me. Time passed quickly, and I think both of us were surprised to hear the grandfather clock in the hall chiming eleven.

"Lord, I must go," she said, standing up.

"Look, why don't you borrow the Range Rover? I can't drive, so you can keep it for as long as you like."

"That would be marvellous." Her face was half hidden under the hood of her duffel coat.

"You're very welcome." I gave her the keys. "See you tomorrow?"

"Yes. I'll have a look at the nesting site and pop in afterwards. Good night, Robin. Thanks for a lovely evening."

We shook hands on the doorstep. It was very formal and proper.

"YOU WERE RIGHT—they *are* nesting!" She pulled off her bobble-hat and her hair sprang into shape. Her eyes shone and her cheeks were glowing.

"What does it look like?"

"A bit of a mess, really. Just a big jumble of sticks, wedged into the cleft and supported by the rowan tree." She took off her climbing boots and I followed her into the drawing room. She wore jeans tucked into thick woollen socks, and looked diminutive without any shoes on.

"What was it like, getting down?"

"No problem. There's a birch on top of the cliff to tie the ropes round."

"I wish I'd seen you. Well, this calls for a celebration. Tea?" I suggested inadequately. It was four o'clock.

"Love some. Oh, wait a sec—I've got something for you."

Jenny had arrived with a long box under her arm. She fetched it from the hall. It was a new Hawk telescope with a tripod, a zoom magnification of twenty to sixty, and a little finder scope on top.

"This is for me?" I could hardly believe it.

"I got it in Keswick this morning. I thought you could set it up by the window in your bedroom. You said last night that your binoculars weren't really strong enough. After all, you've lent me your car. I thought that one good turn deserved another."

"It's fantastic, Jenny." I was so touched I could have kissed her. "Come on, let's see if it works while there's still light."

Tea was forgotten as we set it up. I was experimenting with the zoom lens when the female eagle obliged by flying into the nest. She perched on the small rowan, the branch bending under her weight. I studied for the first time the ebony beak with its wicked hook, the fierce eyes set forward beneath a frowning, imperious brow; the powerful body; the legs trousered in feathers and extending to yellow claws each as big as a man's hand and armed with three-inch talons.

She started to preen, bending her head with its golden crown and running her feathers separately and delicately through her beak. Dipping it into her tail gland, she oiled and waterproofed her plumage. Grooming done, she "roused" and puffed out her feathers for the air to circulate, enhancing her bulk. Then, slowly and deliberately, she extended and stretched her wings and limbs, one by one, before settling down.

"Don't hog it," Jenny said. "Let's have a look."

"What? Oh, sorry." I moved aside.

Jenny watched her intently, neither of us speaking. The eagle flew after a minute or so, spreading her wings and dropping till she caught an up-current, then rising to soar in a spiral over the high plateau. Jenny tracked her as she drifted further away behind Breakneck Crag.

"It's beautiful," she breathed.

"She," I corrected. "That was the female."

"Know-all." And she made a face at me.

JENNY WAS ON NIGHT DUTY on Thursday and Friday; and then she used the Range Rover at the weekend to go and visit her mother in Glasgow, so I didn't see her at all.

Or Nera.

I nerved myself on Monday morning to ring the *Herald* in Manchester. Her office told me that she had been sent unexpectedly to cover the UN Assembly in New York. She would probably be away until the end of March.

I felt anger first—anger that she hadn't let me know. Then relief. My clumsy pass a fortnight ago wasn't the reason for her absence. She'd come back and we could start again.

I remembered when I put the telephone down that I had promised to contact the RSPB again if I saw the eagles nesting. I dialled the number. Their response had been lukewarm when I'd first called them. Their interest was now active. They'd like to send someone that very afternoon from their Newcastle office. They wondered, would I be available to show him the site?

THE RSPB MAN turned out to be a slow-talking Geordie, middle-aged and in ancient tweeds. But there was excitement in his eyes, despite his ponderous manner.

"You've hit the jackpot," he told me. His eye was glued to the telescope in my bedroom. "This is as big as the ospreys in Scotland."

The society, he said, would be sending a couple of wardens to mount a twenty-four-hour watch on the site. They'd probably arrive towards the end of March, a week or so before laying, and set up a hide in the dale.

"They could always stay here," I offered.

"That's very good of you, Mr. Woodford, but we find that a visible presence—a hide, a tent—helps to act as a deterrent against people approaching too close to the site."

"You'll have to clear that with Peter Stone—he's the farmer. He's not too keen on eagles, you know."

"He'll have to lump it," the Geordie said shortly. "We've got a statutory duty to look after them, under the Protection of Birds Act." When he'd gone, I sat and wrote Nera a long letter. It was mainly about the eagles. I mentioned my accident, but tried to keep things on a chatty and impersonal level. I addressed the letter care of the *Herald*, and posted it that evening on my way by taxi to the AA meeting. I felt more confident than I had for ages. I'd taken a positive step towards re-establishing contact with Nera, and the eagles' protection seemed assured.

It was a good meeting. There was a lot of laughter, and the warmth of fellowship. I slept well that night for the first time since the accident.

I'd been advised to take a couple of weeks off work, but I began to feel a bit of a fraud, so Ken and Jenny agreed to chauffeur me to and from the school. Sally came too, and the boys took turns in exercising her during break. She became a great favourite, and more spoiled than ever.

I was taken out of plaster at the beginning of March, which meant that I was independently mobile once more. It was a pity in a way. Jenny in particular had fallen into the habit of staying for supper after she'd taken me home, and I would miss her company. The boys also viewed my recovery with some ambivalence. Not only were they deprived of my dog now that I could take her for walks at home, but they had also become accustomed to my clumping dot-and-carry approach down the corridor. Keeping cave had been much easier.

Towards the end of the month a postcard came from Nera. She thanked me for my letter and said she hoped to be home at the beginning of April. That was all. It was better than nothing, but I felt disappointed. A letter came from the RSPB. The wardens whom they had appointed—a young husband-and-wife team—had both succumbed to Asian flu. Could I hold the fort until they arrived? Hold the fort? What was I supposed to do? Term had another ten days to run until the Easter holidays, and I couldn't keep a proper eye on the nest in the meantime.

It had become a habit first thing, if the weather was clear, to have a look through the telescope. If one of the birds was in the vicinity, I'd usually

335

find it perching not far from the eyrie—on the rowan, or a nearby rock. This time the female was actually in the nest. I could just see the golden crown of her head in the morning sunlight. And she was still there when I'd finished breakfast. Had she been injured? Or was she incubating? I had to find out, and rang Jenny at the school. I collected her before nine, and soon after we were tramping up the dale with her climbing tackle.

The female flew off when we were still three hundred yards from the site.

"Well, at least she's OK," Jenny said.

"I'd still like to know if she's laid."

"But she might desert any eggs if we take a closer look."

Jenny was right, but the compulsion to investigate overrode my better judgment.

It had begun to drizzle. We reached the top of the spur and made our way to the edge of the cliff. An overhang prevented us seeing down into the nest.

"That's the tree I used," Jenny said, and began fastening her ropes around the birch.

"I'll go down," I said suddenly. "You can tell me what to do."

"The rock's wet. Your leg's still not strong enough. You're crazy, Robin. Come on—I'll do it."

"No."

She knew I meant it, and harnessed me up with obvious disapproval. Her instructions were a jumble in my mind. Weight back. Legs apart. Don't look down. Take it slow. Keep at right angles to the rock.

You can't fall.

Oh no? I was frightened. Gradually leaning back into space, I regretted my impulse. The blue nylon ropes felt as tenuous as cotton in my hands. The surface beneath my boots was slick with rain. All the horrors of my fall rushed back into my memory. I'd only taken a tumble then from fifteen feet. Now I was hanging out over three times as high.

Slowly I gained confidence. With Jenny calling encouragement from above, I negotiated the overhang and lowered myself down the cliff. When I was level with the top of the mountain ash, I risked a downward glance.

The nest was an untidy construction of twigs and boughs, save for a shallow depression in the middle carefully lined with lichen, grass and feathers.

It contained two eggs, with pinkish spots and brown blotches.

"She's done it!" I shouted up to Jenny. I was as exultant as a father with his first-born. "Two of them. Big as goose's eggs and twice—"

I never saw the female approach.

I only heard the whoosh of her wings, and was buffeted by the wind of her passage. The onslaught was shockingly fast. I ducked instinctively, and my feet slipped. I slammed sideways against the rock face. Winded,

and dangling like a marionette, I watched her soar away. Then she was wheeling for a fresh attack.

Helpless, I saw it coming. She closed her wings into a delta configuration and began to plummet, rocking from side to side. Her head was sunk low between her shoulders, the beak aimed like an arrowhead. The feathers on her back were sucked upwards by the airstream, the wind whistled through them, rising to a roar as she spread her span within feet of me. Her legs and talons were thrust forward. Cringing against the cliff, I could almost feel them raking my scalp.

Then she was gone. Kicking and scrabbling with my feet, I regained purchase against the rock face and lowered myself to the bottom fast. The eagle soared in tight circles over the ridge. She didn't stoop again.

I unclipped the harness, my fingers shaking, and called up to Jenny that I was down in one piece. More or less. She released the ropes, and they snaked down to land in an untidy coil at my feet. Five minutes later, she joined me.

"Are you all right?" Her voice was edged with concern. "The eagle—"

"She missed me. She was only trying to scare me off. Succeeded, too." I found myself grinning inanely. Relief and joy flooded over me. Without thinking, I picked Jenny up and swung her round. She was as light as a feather.

"Wow!" she said breathlessly as I put her down. "It must have been quite an experience."

"Once in a lifetime. And not to be repeated," I added. "God, the size of her, Jenny! The speed!"

"I was worried silly. But tell me all about it back at the house. I think we ought to let her get back on the eggs, don't you?"

It was a gentle reminder, but enough to sober me up. My excitement died as we trudged home, and we spent an anxious half hour at the telescope in my bedroom before the eagle eventually returned to the nest. The male joined her, and perched on the rowan.

I was content and satisfied, as though I'd found my family.

"WHAT ARE THEY LIKE?" Jenny asked.

"The RSPB wardens? Oh, they're a pleasant couple," I said. "It took them no time to set up shop. The hide and the tent are about a quarter of a mile from the site. It's pretty primitive, but they use my house for baths."

It was the following Saturday, and school had just broken up. As was the custom, some of the staff were celebrating the boys' departure with a drink at the hotel.

"What are their names?" Jenny wanted to know. "The wardens, I mean?"

"Porgy and Bess." I laughed. "No, not really, but I can't help thinking of them like that. George is fat and cheerful, and Elizabeth is terribly serious. They're both very young, but they seem to know their stuff."

The bar was crowded. With Easter approaching, the season of hill walkers was beginning to burgeon. I couldn't help noticing one of them. He was about my age, and wore a fashionable Viva Zapata moustache, but it was the RSPB badge on his jacket which drew my attention. I was curious. "Not a bad day to be out on the fells," I said blandly.

"Aye. The visibility was good." The accent was flat and Lancashire.

"See anything?" I asked casually. I eyed his badge.

"Not really. A pair of peregrines nesting on Westdale Pike."

He was a cautious customer. We carried on fencing until we'd established our bona fides—and our mutual interest.

It turned out that he was secretary of the local branch of the RSPB. The society had told him about the eagles as a matter of courtesy, and in strict confidence.

I bought him a whisky and we introduced ourselves. His name was Hunter, and he owned a printing company in Preston. He'd built the business up from next to nothing, and it was obviously doing well. When the bar closed at eleven, he drove off in a flashy red E-type.

Ken drove Jenny back to the school. She was staying on for a week to tidy up, and she promised to drop in before she left for Glasgow. She gave me a cheerful wave as I set off to walk home. The night was balmy, with a suggestion of spring in the air. A full moon shone behind scudding clouds.

I was puzzled to see a light peeping through a chink in the drawing-room curtains. I was sure that I'd switched everything off before going out. The front door was open—the house was so tucked away that I never bothered to lock it—and I went in.

"I thought you'd never get back," she said. Her hair was as glossy as a raven's wing, her eyes improbably blue. She sat back in an armchair, in boots and a leather miniskirt. Her long legs were elegantly crossed.

"Nera!" I was astonished and delighted.

She stood up and put her arms round my neck. She kissed me as naturally as if we'd been lovers.

By midnight, we were.

I WAS STILL bewildered the next morning.

I could remember her pushing me away on our first meeting—and yet it was she who had led me upstairs last night, within minutes of my arrival. It was she who had initiated the swift ecstasy of our lovemaking.

Why? Instinct told me not to question her.

"What's your father going to say?" I asked instead, pouring her some coffee. I was wearing a paisley dressing gown she'd brought me from Bloomingdales' in New York, and she had on my old one.

"Peter?" She rested her elbows on the table in the kitchen. "He won't say anything. If he tried playing the heavy father, he'd be scared I'd pack my bags and leave."

"Couldn't he manage the lambing without you?" Nera had taken a fortnight's leave to help him.

"It's not that. He just doesn't want to lose me, period."

As the days passed, though, Stone's behaviour towards me grew increasingly hostile. It had nothing to do with moral outrage, it was jealousy. She spent the days with him, the nights with me, and he didn't like sharing her.

Mrs. Blenkinsop seemed to take a vicarious pleasure in our affair, and I suspected that it would soon become common knowledge in the village. When the bell rang on Good Friday morning, I had decided to ask her to be discreet, if only for Peter Stone's sake.

But it wasn't my daily on the doorstep. It was Jenny.

"I've come to say goodbye," she said. She wore a jaunty tam-o'-shanter. "You look surprised to see me—I said I'd call in. I'm on my way to Glasgow. How are the eagles?"

"The eagles?" I realised with a shock that I had hardly given them a thought all week. "Oh, they're fine. Porgy and Bess are keeping an eye on them now."

We were still standing by the front door. I should have asked her in, but Nera was in the bath upstairs, and for some reason I didn't want Jenny to know she was with me.

"Well, have a good trip," I said. "See you next—"

"Who is it, Robin?" Nera called. She came downstairs in my dressing gown, towelling her wet hair. "Oh, hello?" she said enquiringly.

I mumbled the introductions, and Nera offered her some coffee. I could see the colour rising in Jenny's cheeks. No, she couldn't possibly stay, thanks all the same. Ken was waiting for her in his car at the bottom of the drive.

"Oh, Lord," Nera said, flicking back her hair, "I'm afraid I embarrassed her. Is there something going on between you?"

"Don't be ridiculous." I was angry, and just as embarrassed as Jenny had been.

"Well, why not? There's nothing wrong. You're an attractive guy, and she's a wholesome little thing."

"That's a bitchy thing to say."

"I didn't mean to sound like that, Robin." She draped the towel on the banisters, and walked barefoot into the kitchen. I followed her, and she went on, "I had no business to ask. What you do here is your affair. In the same way, I have my own life in Manchester and abroad. Does that sound reasonable?"

"I'm not sure it does."

Nera lit a cigarette. She exhaled slowly, and looked at me through the smoke.

"Listen, Robin, if you want me, you'll have to accept me the way I am— as I accept you. Don't try and get possessive. It'll only hurt you. You know I wasn't a virgin, and I don't necessarily expect you to be celibate in my absence."

"So how many men did you jump into bed with in New York?" It was sarcastic and childish.

"Oh, for God's sake, Robin!" she flared back. "If I want to, I damn well will. I don't need your permission." Her voice softened, and she put her hand on my arm. "Just accept me. That's all I ask. You'll never change me, or the situation. You can only change yourself."

It was an echo of the AA doctrine, but that didn't make it any more palatable. I knew then that a feeling of uncertainty would rule our relationship for as long as it lasted. The honeymoon was over.

Four

Easter Sunday. It was chillingly damp and misty, and couldn't have felt less like spring. It was the sort of morning best spent in bed, but I was due to read the lesson.

Driving to church, I noticed Hunter's E-type parked in the turning bay at the end of the road. He wouldn't see much this morning, I thought.

I'd all but forgotten the eagles since Nera had come back. I felt unaccountably guilty, and after the service I went up to the hide for a progress report from Porgy and Bess.

"Damn this mist." Porgy sounded edgy. "It's swirling around, but it never lifts properly. I caught my first glimpse about an hour ago but she wasn't on it."

"Hunting, I expect," I said.

"Doubt it. Not in this weather."

The hide was no more than a prefabricated wooden box, less than ten feet square, and situated by the beck, midway between the farm and the eyrie. It offered a view of the site through a broad shutter, and a pair of powerful binoculars were clamped to its frame.

"Well, at least the weather should keep the hill walkers away," I said.

"Yes, that's something, I suppose."

The mist failed to lift all day, and I thought no more about Porgy's anxiety until the following morning. A stiff breeze had risen during the night and chased away the mist. There were rain clouds racing in from the west, but it was clear enough to see the eyrie through the telescope.

It was still empty. I hurried to the hide.

"I know." Bess's voice was grim. "She's deserted the nest. George has taken his climbing gear and gone to have a look."

"What on earth could have made her do that?" I felt sick with disappointment.

"God knows," she said bitterly. "Too much disturbance, I expect. Perhaps we'd been hoping for a miracle. I know it's pretty remote round here, but it's like Piccadilly Circus compared to most of the Scottish sites."

I looked through the binoculars. Porgy was abseiling down the cliff with enviable ease, despite his chubby build. Ten minutes later, he was back at the hide.

"No wonder she's gone," he said. He threw the climbing ropes angrily onto the floor.

"What do you mean?" Bess asked.

"Someone's stolen the eggs. From right under our bloody noses. There were fresh rope burns on the bark of the birch. It must have been done early yesterday, when the mist was down." There was silence between us.

"Stone," I said. "It must have been Peter Stone. He never wanted the eagles nesting here." I marched out.

"Hey—wait a minute!" Porgy called after me, but I didn't stop.

I banged open the door to the farmhouse, and found Stone taking a tea break in the sitting room. He rose to his feet, startled.

"The eggs have gone. It was you, wasn't it?"

"What do you mean? I haven't been anywhere near your nest!"

"What's all this about?" Nera came in from the kitchen.

"It's that fancy man of yours. He's accusing me of raiding his eagles' nest."

"The eggs have been taken," I told her. "We all know he's threatened to stop them rearing any young—he must have done it first thing yesterday morning, in the mist."

"Is that so, Robin?" Her voice was dangerously calm. "Then let me tell you that when I came up for the lambing yesterday, I could hardly wake Peter up. He was still in a stupor. He couldn't have moved since he'd fallen into bed dead drunk on Saturday night. Got it? Now, if you don't mind, I think you'd better leave."

"You heard what she said," Stone shouted. "And you stay clear of my lass in future."

I backed out, confused and still too angry to apologise. Porgy ran to meet me when I was on my way back to the hide. "Well?" he asked breathlessly.

"I've really messed things up. It couldn't have been Stone. He'd been on a bender on Saturday night, and was still comatose yesterday morning. Nera spent the rest of the day with him doing the lambing."

"I tried to stop you," he reminded me.

It began to rain heavily and I was soaked by the time we reached the hide. I was grateful for a steaming mug of coffee, and we started to play a futile guessing game. The trouble was that an alarming number of people knew about the eggs; colleagues at school, the people at the hotel, Stone's cronies from the village, the local RSPB members—"Hang on," I said suddenly. "Did that bloke Hunter come and see you yesterday morning?"

"Not yesterday," Bess said. "But he's been up to the hide two or three times before then. Why?"

"Because I saw his car parked at the end of the lane when I was driving to church. That must have been, oh—a quarter to ten."

"You're not seriously suggesting it could be Hunter, are you?" Porgy was appalled.

"Why not?" I argued. "Maybe he's an egg-collector as well."

"But it's illegal," Bess protested. "Look, you're jumping to conclusions, Robin. Anyway, it's more than our job's worth to hang an accusation like that round the neck of a leading society member."

"I'm not suggesting you do anything—apart from give me his address. It's a bank holiday, so he should be at home."

Bess looked up his address in the members' handbook. He lived in a little village on the edge of the Forest of Bowland, not too far from his printing business in Preston. I knew it vaguely.

"You won't do anything stupid, will you?" Porgy begged. "It was bad enough going off at half cock with Peter Stone, but—"

"All I'm going to do is nose around. But tell me something—if we *can* prove that he pinched them, what sort of penalty would the courts award on conviction?"

"Peanuts. Maybe a fine of a few hundred pounds."

"The punishment hardly fits the crime." I walked thoughtfully home. How on earth was I going to find out if Hunter had stolen the eggs? And what the hell was I going to do if he had?

I WAS NO CLOSER to any solution when I set off south that afternoon. I couldn't just charge in and ransack Hunter's house. The approach had to be diplomatic, if not downright devious. But if he had those eggs, I had to find them. They alone could provide proof of the theft.

Cruising down the A6, I fell to wondering why anyone should wish to steal the eggs. I knew that handsome prices were sometimes paid under the counter for young birds: the golden eagle had become a status symbol amongst falconers in the Middle East. But someone like Hunter didn't need the money, whether for eggs or fledglings. And the motive was more, surely, than one of collector's greed. He couldn't even display the eggs without risk of prosecution. Perhaps it was simple kleptomania, spiced by

343

risk and the rarity value of the English eagle. The sheer waste and futility of such an act made me grip the steering wheel in anger. I saw that I was travelling at over ninety, and slowed down.

Light was falling as I turned off the main road and struck east towards Longridge Fell and the Forest of Bowland. The country was less dramatic than the Lake District, but still wild in its way.

It reminded me of the moorland near Glossop where my eldest brother, John, lived; and the sense of *déjà vu* persisted as I drove slowly past Hunter's house, with his E-type parked in the drive. It was built in the same style as John's, a sprawling, hacienda-type bungalow, and similarly isolated on the edge of the moor.

I hadn't visited John since 1966. It was the night that the axe fell, the night that . . . again I tried to shrug off a memory. Then, as now, I'd been angry—and afraid.

I HAD LANDED AT HEATHROW that morning. A bottle of duty-free whisky had kept me company on the long drive north in my hired Corsair. Now it was finished. It was time to face the music. I knew in my heart that my job in the family firm was on the line.

I parked in the drive beside John's Rolls Royce. My other brother, Simon, had left his old Bentley roadster nearby. Fat cats, I thought sourly, but switched on a smile as I was let in.

"Hi—it's great to see you both again! God, it's good to be back!" I was full of bravado.

"Robert." John shook my hand gravely. With his three-piece suit and silver hair, he was every inch the managing director.

"Well, aren't you going to kill the fatted calf? How about a drink?"

"I think you've had enough already," John said.

"That's not very friendly, Big Bro." I had never liked John. I turned to my other brother. "What do you say, Si? Not much of a welcome, eh?"

"I think we ought to talk business first," Simon suggested tactfully. He was less aggressive than John. With his slight build and gentle manner, he was often taken to be the youngest.

"Sit down, Robert," John told me. He remained standing. "I won't beat about the bush. I think you know why we called you back. We want your resignation from the board, with immediate effect. I've got a paper prepared for your signature right here." He took it from his briefcase, along with a gold Parker from his inside pocket. "Sign it, Robert. It will be formally presented and accepted in your absence at the next meeting."

"No way."

"It's up to you. You can resign now, otherwise Simon and I will vote you off the board at the next meeting. I need hardly remind you of our two-thirds majority."

344

"My God, if Dad was still alive—"

"He'd have kicked you out years ago," John said. "You've been nothing but a liability at the ranch, Robert. It's been one cock-up after another—expensive ones, too. It's hardly surprising in view of your drinking habits. God knows how you expected to run a ranch when you were smashed twenty-four hours a day."

"I can stop drinking whenever I want." I was bitter.

"Good. Then this could be a heaven-sent opportunity," said Simon. "You'll have no business pressures—and certainly no money worries."

"What Simon means," John said, "is that we're prepared to buy you out at full market value. You'll be sitting on over half a million pounds. So sign it."

I looked at the piece of paper on the coffee table in front of me. Then I scrawled a shaky signature on the bottom.

"Satisfied?" I stood up. I felt hot and cold. Tears of bitterness and self-pity threatened to spill from my eyes. "God, to think that my own family—" I blundered from the room. Simon caught me up as I was climbing into the Corsair.

"Believe me, Robert, it's for your own good. Call it tough love, if you like, but—"

"Leave me alone, Simon."

I gunned the motor. The wheels spun, scattering gravel, as I swept down the drive.

BRINGING MY THOUGHTS back to the present, I parked in the road just short of Hunter's drive, leaving the sidelights on. It didn't take long to lift the bonnet and loosen one of the spark-plugs. I wasn't a mechanic, and I couldn't think of any more convincing excuse for a breakdown. It would have to do.

It was raining hard and I was soaked by the time I reached the porch.

The bell chimed a little tune, and Hunter opened the door. He was in jeans and a leather jerkin.

"I'm terribly sorry to bother you, but my car's broken down." Then I feigned surprise. "Good heavens! Isn't it—?"

"That's right. Wayne Hunter. We met at the hotel by Skelmere. Mr. Woodford? Robin Woodford?" He shook my hand but the smile of greeting seemed a shade defensive.

"What an extraordinary coincidence! I've been away for the bank holiday in Clitheroe, and I was driving home when the bloody car started misfiring. The engine died on me just outside your house."

"Probably the damp. Well, come on in, Robin." The welcome was noticeably warmer as he registered that I hadn't come hotfoot from Skelmere. He'd have guessed that there would be a hue and cry after the eggs were taken. He even had the nerve to ask me about the eagles, as he led the way into his living room.

"They were fine when I left on Friday. The female hardly ever leaves the eggs."

"That's great. Drink?"

"Something soft, if that's OK."

"Coming up."

There was a bar in one corner of the room, a wrought-iron and rattan construction in Spanish colonial style. As he set to work behind it, I couldn't help noticing the Hispanic flavour of the rest of the room, all a bit Costa Brava, but far from cheap.

"You like Spain?" I asked.

"Got a villa near San Antonio. We go out twice, three times a year." He gave me a tomato juice, and held up his tumbler of whisky. "Cheers, Robin."

"I'll bet the villa's not as grand as this."

"No. The villa was off the peg. This is architect-designed," he said proudly.

"I'd love to look round," I said.

"What about ringing the garage?"

"I'm in no hurry—unless you are, of course."

"No sweat. Come on, I'll give you a Cook's tour." As he spoke about his business and the Linguaphone lessons he was taking in Spanish, I hardly listened. My eyes were casing the joint. If he had the eggs, they'd be well hidden away. *If* he had the eggs ... perhaps I was barking up the wrong tree anyway.

"Well, that's it," he said finally. We'd ended up in his study. He indicated the telephone on his desk. "You can ring the garage from here, if you like."

"Thanks. Yes, I suppose I'd better—" I stopped. I recognised the walnut chest with its long narrow drawers. My father had owned one.

It was an egg cabinet.

Hunter followed the direction of my glance. "Butterflies," he said, too quickly.

"Oh, yes?" I tried to sound casual. "Mind if I have a look?"

Before he could move, I had crossed the room and opened the top drawer. Rows of eggs beneath glass in separate little compartments. Each egg was cocooned on a bed of cotton wool. Each compartment bore a label with the bird's Latin name.

I pulled out the next drawer, and the next.

There they were, side by side, with *Aquila Chrysaetos* written on the label in careful copperplate. I knew those markings well enough.

"Some butterflies!"

"I ... it's a collection I bought from a friend."

"Which just happened to include two specimens from the Skelmere site? I know those eggs, chum. I saw them in the nest."

Silence. Then Hunter made a rueful little gesture.

"Listen, Robin." His tone was friendly and reasonable. "I know that I may have come by some of those eggs ... well, illegally, but that collection's worth more to me than anything else I own. I've built it up since I was a kid. So what do you say to doing a deal? Forget what you've seen—and name your price."

I laughed. "I don't need money, Hunter. Certainly not yours."

"Then what do you want? You can't prove a damn thing if you go to the fuzz. Those eagle's eggs could have come from anywhere." His confidence was returning. "So what the hell are you going to do?"

The cabinet was surprisingly heavy. It took all my strength to topple it over. Glass shattered. The woodwork of the open drawers splintered. Broken eggshells littered the carpet. It was some sort of answer, at least.

"You—!"

Hunter's horror turned to fury. He charged.

My reflexes were slow, and I wasn't ready for him.

His shoulder caught me in the midriff. I was slammed back, winded, against the desk. Seizing the lapels of my jacket, he butted me full in the face. I was helpless, half blinded by blood and pain, and shocked by the ferocity of his onslaught. Sensing my weakness, he let go.

Instinct took over, sheer survival. I fought dirty. The knee to his groin made him gasp. He fell back into a crouch. With a strength born more of fear than rage, I swung at him wildly with my fist.

The impact jarred my arm. His head snapped back. His knees buckled. He sat down, abruptly and absurdly, amidst the broken glass and eggshells on the carpet. He was finished.

"I'll have you for assault," Hunter said thickly.

"No, you won't." I was surprised at the steadiness of my own voice. "You won't go to the police, and nor will I. You asked me to name my price. That was it."

I left him sitting there in the shambles of his study, and caught a glimpse of my face in the hall mirror as I left. My left eye was swollen and nearly closed, and blood from the cut above it was congealing on my cheek. I was no prettier than Hunter had been, but the face which stared back at me wore a satisfied grin.

"I THINK THAT CUT needs seeing to," Bess said seriously. She was bending over me as I sat by the fire at home. "It might need stitches."

"It's OK." I felt too drained to move, let alone drive to hospital. Porgy and Bess had struck camp and were staying the night. There was no point in their remaining in the hide, and they would be on their way in the morning.

I'd told them about finding the eggs, and a bit about what had happened.

"Do you mind if I ring my boss?" Porgy asked. "I don't know what he'll say, he doesn't even know that the nest was raided yet. I was waiting to see how you—well, got on with Mr. Hunter."

"Swimmingly." I could smile at the memory now. "If you want a bit of peace and quiet, use the upstairs phone." Bess made a fresh brew of coffee while he was on the telephone. My ribs ached and my face throbbed. But the pain was oddly pleasurable, like the bruising satisfaction of a good rugby tackle.

"Well, I've spoken to him," Porgy said, coming in again.

"Does he think we should have gone to the police?" Bess sounded anxious.

"No. He reckons that Robin deserves a medal. He doesn't think a prosecution would have succeeded, and it would have cost the society a bomb." Porgy was beaming. "Mind you, it's going to cost us money anyway. Our friend Hunter had apparently just taken out a new seven-year covenant for two hundred and fifty pounds a year. It's being sent back to him and his membership cancelled."

I made a simple calculation. Hunter's donation would have been worth £2,500 gross, with the tax back. Heaving myself up, I crossed to my desk and wrote out a cheque for that amount, payable to the RSPB, and gave it to Porgy.

"I say!" His eyes boggled. "But—"

"It was worth every penny," I grinned, and meant it. Then I asked him a question which had been at the back of my mind all day. "Do you think the eagles will stay, George?"

"I don't know," he said honestly. "A pair normally needs about twenty-five miles of territory, and there's no competition and plenty of room for them round here. But the hunting's not as good as in Scotland—hardly any grouse or hares. And there are too many people. But I suppose they might hang around and try to breed again next year."

"What about a second clutch this year?"

"They never lay twice in one year. The cycle's too long."

It was depressing. I wanted to go to bed, to sleep and forget all about it, but my day wasn't yet done. I still had to make my peace with Stone, and Nera.

HER HAND FLEW to her mouth as she let me in. "What happened?"

"I got into a fight."

"Robin!" She was half shocked and half amused.

"Yes, I suppose it was a bit out of character." I managed a rueful grin.

"But who with?" She was dying to know.

"The bloke who actually pinched the eggs. Look, that's why I've come."

"To eat humble pie? You'd better come in, then."

"What are you doing here?" Stone said, as I stepped into the living room. His tone was openly belligerent, and I could smell beer on his breath.

"I was just telling Nera that I found the culprit. The man who stole the eggs. I just wanted to say how very sorry I am to have accused you."

Stone ignored the apology. "He do that to you?" He was looking at my eye.

"Yes."

"I've half a mind to blacken the other one." He took a step forward. "You've got a nerve coming back to my house."

"Stop it, Peter!" Nera told him. "That's enough. You've said your bit, Robin. You'd better go home."

"Are you coming with me?"

"She stays here!" Stone shouted.

That was his mistake. No one told Nera what to do. Without a word she followed me outside.

We walked home a yard or two apart, and the silence was heavy between us.

Porgy and Bess sensed the atmosphere when we reached the cottage, and scuttled off to bed. I switched on the television. There was a late-night cops-and-robbers movie. It was noisy and mindless, but better than sitting in speechless confrontation with one another.

At last Nera could stand it no longer. She stood up. "It's those bloody birds!" she said.

"What do you mean?" I turned the television set off. "I thought you wanted to do a story on them."

"Oh, they're not worth more than a few column inches. Maybe if they'd succeeded in rearing any young, it might have been different ... Anyway, you asked me not to give them any publicity." She paused. "But that's not the point."

"What is?"

"What they've done to you. To us. They've driven a wedge between Peter and me." She shook her head in exasperation. "Why, Robin? Just what makes them so important to you? A respectable well-to-do schoolmaster taking the law into his own hands! It's ridiculous. What is it about those birds?"

"Their right to exist, if you like." Yet it was more, much more than that. I could have spoken about what they represented—nobility, beauty and, above all, freedom. But it would only have sounded sententious. I was

349

aching from fatigue, and I yawned. "Anyway, they've probably gone by now. There's nothing to keep them here. I'm off to bed. You?"

"Later." She threw another log on the fire. Nothing was resolved.

THE EAGLES DIDN'T LEAVE, although it was several days before I saw them again; the male quartering the northern ridge of the dale in search of prey, and the female circling high overhead. I felt curiously privileged by their continued presence, and grateful.

Nera's holiday came to an end. She had forgiven me for accusing Peter of stealing the eggs, but she'd warned me not to be possessive, and I knew better than to ask her when she would be coming back.

The house seemed quiet that night. I'd grown to value my solitude since moving into Southwater, but for the very first time I was conscious of a sense of loneliness.

Nera's departure didn't worry Sally: she was able to resume at last her rightful place under the duvet.

There was a freak spring snowfall the following weekend. It lasted all through Sunday, and most of the night.

I woke on Monday to find the dale white and still beneath a brilliant sky. But the Christmas-card effect was already changing. It was thawing fast by the time I'd finished breakfast. I was determined to climb the crags before the snow was gone. I hadn't seen either eagle for some days, and they might be easier to spot against a white background.

It was hard going. By the time I had climbed out of the dale, I was sweating freely in the warm sun. From my vantage point, the fells and crags spread about me like a crumpled white blanket, carelessly dropped.

The broad expanse of Skelmere stretched shimmering down the length of the plateau, and little tarns nestled like jewels on the other side. A steep and narrow valley dropped down to one of the tarns. On the bank, a red deer hind was pawing at the snow, searching for grass. Her calf, not more than a few days old, was trying vainly to suckle as her mother dug beneath the surface. They were about five hundred yards below me, and I focused my glasses on them.

The eagle's shadow raced into my field of view over the snow. The peaceful tableau disintegrated. The attack was so unexpected that I dropped my binoculars.

I watched the female eagle banking after her dive. The male flew in a tight circle overhead. The female swooped again. The hind reared up, striking out with her front hooves. The calf took fright. It skittered away on spindly legs, and floundered into a snowdrift. This was the male eagle's cue. He dropped pitilessly onto the little creature's back, enveloping it with his wings, the daggerlike rear talons driving deep into the calf's vertebrae. There was nothing I could do, even had I wanted to. Nor could the hind. Distracted by the female eagle, she saw too late what had happened.

The male stood crouched over his kill, his head thrust forward and wings half extended. The hind charged at him and he took off, seemingly unhurried. He joined the female in the branches of a hawthorn tree halfway up the slope. For perhaps a minute, no more, the hind nosed the dead body of her calf. Then she turned and trotted away, and didn't even look back at the little bundle beside the tarn.

The eagles waited until she had left the valley, then they descended. The calf was much too heavy to carry off, and they gorged themselves on the body where it lay.

The scene remained vivid in my mind as I drove back from the AA meeting that night. It had been savage and primitive, and yet uncomplicated. Since Nera's departure, I had sought to recapture some sense of serenity. In some ways, there was relief at her going. The tensions between us had been complex and unnatural, unlike the death of the calf which, violent as it was, had been in the natural order of things.

HENRY TETLOW had been the family solicitor for as long as I could remember. He dealt with all my affairs, including the stockbroking firm who handled my investments, and he also served as my only real contact with my brothers and my mother.

"Have you seen John and Simon lately?" I asked, as we sat down to lunch at Manchester's Piccadilly Hotel.

"They're flourishing, and so is Wyndham's. They're going into supermarkets now. You should have hung on to those shares, Robert." Like Ken, he found it hard to remember my new name.

"They gave me a fair price. Anyway, what about Mum? How's she?"

"I do wish you'd go and see her, Robert. She's getting on a bit, you know."

I had made a complete break with my family. It seemed cleaner at the time, and less embarrassing all round: black sheep are best forgotten. But there were moments when I missed them.

I changed the subject, and we got down to business over our Dover sole. There was a good deal to sort out: my first payment on the school building programme, little Angela's trust fund, and the question of changing my name formally by deed poll. Henry scribbled minute notes on the back of his menu, and passed me papers to sign across the tablecloth. It was altogether a far more pleasant way of doing business than in the dusty atmosphere of his chambers.

"Don't forget about your mother," Henry said, as I helped him into a taxi. "I know she'd like to see you looking so well. You really are a changed man, Robert."

"With a changed name," I reminded him. "At least, I will be when the papers are through."

He gave me a grin and settled back into his seat. I'd enjoyed our meal together.

There was nothing to keep me in Manchester, but I mooched aimlessly round the city centre for a couple of hours. Shortly before five I found myself in a grubby café opposite the *Herald* offices.

I think it had always been in the back of my mind to try to see Nera, though I had no idea what I'd say.

It wasn't until nearly six that she emerged. She wore a dark trouser suit, smart and businesslike. She skipped down the steps to the pavement, her hair flowing and shoulder bag swinging.

I rose quickly to my feet to try to catch her. And stopped. A man had stepped from a Volvo estate parked outside the office. I recognised him at once as Richard Fielding, one of the newscasters from the Granada television studios. I saw him on the box most nights, presenting the local magazine programme. He was assured, good-looking, and taller than I had imagined.

He held out his arms, and Nera smiled. They embraced. Then he opened the passenger door for her and they drove away.

I sat down again to finish my coffee. It was cold.

Nera had told me to mind my own business. Ignorance would have been bliss. What I'd seen served me right.

I returned slowly to my car by the hotel, but I still didn't drive home. I went east, not north. I took the Glossop road to the darkening Derbyshire moors. I found the pub without difficulty—the Tudor Rose. It wasn't far from John's house. I parked outside, but stayed in the Range Rover. I remembered it so well that there was no need to go in.

I HAD DRIVEN straight to the pub from my brother's house that night, and had drunk three double whiskies in quick succession. What was I going to do? Anger smouldered beneath the fear and resentment. Who did John and Simon think they were? Butchers. Tradesmen. That was all. The umbilical cord was cut, and I was better off without them.

"Got far to go, sir?" the barman asked me.

"What? Oh, Sheffield, London. I don't know." I had presumed that I would be staying with John. "Let's have another for the road."

"Do you think that's wise, sir?"

"I'm perfectly capable of driving."

The barman measured out the whisky in silence, and started polishing the glasses behind the bar.

I lit a cigarette and studied my surroundings. There was nothing Tudor about the Tudor Rose. The "timber" was moulded plastic, and the olde-

352

worlde decor was cheap and unconvincing. A jukebox belted out the latest Helen Shapiro hit. There was only a handful of other drinkers.

I decided to leave. It was a hazardous exit, and the fresh night air did nothing to sober me as I tried to remember where I had parked the Corsair. I stumbled about in the darkness until I found it.

The driving seat felt solid and supportive. I switched on and revved the engine. The chassis quivered with suppressed power like an excited racehorse. I felt as though I were flying. The Corsair swooped and soared over the rolling road. The needle on the speedometer quivered past the ninety mark. I had difficulty in focusing my eyes. The racing Cat's-eyes in the middle of the road sometimes split into two parallel lines like a narrow flight path. From half a mile back, I'd registered the thin beam of a cyclist's lamp turning into the main road from the right. Beyond it were the approaching headlights of a car. My foot remained flat on the accelerator. There was plenty of room.

The lights drew closer—the cyclist's red rear-lamp, and the twin beams of the car. A white roadsign flashed by—Bamford six miles to the right, and Sheffield straight on, ten miles.

The two cars and the cyclist all converged at the top of the next slope. The oncoming headlights were dipped, but they divided suddenly into four glaring eyes. They seemed to stretch across the full width of the road.

I swung instinctively to the left. Scarcely conscious of the sound or sensation of the impact, I saw for one brief appalling moment the cyclist flying over the bonnet. Spread-eagled against the sky. Silhouetted against the oncoming lights.

Then the Corsair slewed against the grass verge. It somersaulted and started rolling. Three or four times it flipped over, before settling with a crash on all four wheels.

I don't know how long it was before hands were reaching in to pull me out. There were already an ambulance and a police car on the road, their blue lights flashing. I was helped across the heather, and grew gradually aware of voices around me.

"He was all over the road, officer. Must have been doing nearly a ton."

"God, you can smell the whisky on him from here!"

It wasn't until I was sitting in the back of the police car that I said anything.

"What—what happened to the cyclist?"

"He's dead, sir," the policeman said shortly. "You killed him."

It didn't sink in for ages. I can remember little of what happened during the weeks that followed. I have dim memories of the magistrates granting me bail and of lengthy sessions with Henry Tetlow, the family solicitor. I stayed with Simon, though I might have been anywhere. The days passed in an alcoholic fog.

So the judge's sentence of three years imprisonment for manslaughter might almost have been passed on another man. It was unreal. And I remained anaesthetised in the prison hospital where the doctors doped me with heminevrin against the traumas of withdrawal.

But then they took me off the drugs and locked me up. I remembered what had happened, remorse and guilt engulfed me. I shaved under close supervision in the crude, communal washroom. Razor blades were sharp, and I was regarded as a potential suicide. My hand shook, and I couldn't bear the sight of my own face in the mirror.

BREAKING OUT OF my thoughts, I turned the Range Rover round, opening the windows wide. The cold night air rushed in, and I drove home nonstop, running from an old captivity. Yearning for the clean crags and the wheeling eagles. Hungry for a share in their perfect freedom.

Five

"How's your cricket, Rob?" Ken asked.

"Terrible. But you can put me down for tennis. I could take the boys sailing, too, if you want." I'd bought a fifteen-foot National during the Easter holidays, and built a jetty for the dinghy at the bottom of my garden.

"Splendid." Ken jotted it down. He was allocating games duties, and had cornered me in the common room on the first day of term. "What about swimming?" he went on.

Skelmere Grange didn't run to a pool, but there was a pontoon moored at the edge of the lake. For some reason—perhaps some Spartan ideal—the boys always swam in the nude. I could remember the black and icy grip of the water, how we shivered and shrivelled and pretended to enjoy it.

"Happy hols, Robin? Are you fit for the fray?" Jacques Thiery, the French master, asked.

"More or less. It was pretty peaceful on the whole." Well, some of it had been.

"And your beloved eagles?"

"As a matter of fact, there was a bit of a disaster. The nest was raided and the eggs were stolen," I said.

"What? Oh, no!" I hadn't noticed Jenny at my shoulder.

"Yes, I'm afraid so," I said, turning to her. "We caught the thief, but it means they won't be rearing any young this year. Still, they haven't pushed off. We'll just have to keep our fingers crossed for nineteen seventy."

Jenny seemed unusually shy. Our conversation was polite and stilted.

Her attitude puzzled me until I remembered the circumstances of our last meeting. I think we were both quite glad when the bell rang for the period after break. It was a pity, I reflected. We'd enjoyed such an easy and companionable relationship before.

"Right," I said briskly, as the form sat down. "Who can tell me the principal export of Australia? Or are your minds too woolly after four weeks' idleness?"

"Kangaroos, sir," Dent offered innocently, and Green sniggered.

"Ye gods! Do I have to spell it out?"

It was good to be back.

The term proceeded at a steady pace, and the routine was comfortable.

SO, FAR FROM WELCOMING Nera's return, I resented it. She threw me off balance.

"What on earth are you doing here?"

It was Speech Day morning, and I was marshalling the finalists for the Under-Elevens' hundred yards race.

"That's not much of a greeting." She kissed me in front of a milling crowd of boys and their parents. The mothers wore hats, and the summer setting made it look like a down-market Ascot. "As a matter of fact, the headmaster invited me. Or rather I wangled an invitation—told him the *Herald* was thinking of running an article on private education in the north. But I had no idea that I was going to witness your moment of glory."

"How do you mean?"

"As Lord of the Dance. Master of Ceremonies in natty blue blazer and white flannels. Very fetching."

It was my turn to inspect her.

The hat was a white Stetson and the enormous dark glasses were fashionably chic; the cheesecloth robe, flowing to her feet, was equally trendy. She looked like an expensive hippie.

"Do you know, I've never actually been here before? I must have passed the gates thousands of times." She looked round.

The school was at its best. The oaks and beeches were in full leaf, the grass mown and neatly marked with the running track. There was a cheerfully striped marquee beside the lake, and the Pikes rose grandly behind it. She went on, "So this is where you brainwash the poor little suckers into thinking they're God's gift to the nation."

"That's right," I said. "The cradle of elitism and privilege."

"Mr. Woodford's joking, of course." Ightam had materialised at her shoulder in his mortarboard and gown. "We mustn't give the press the wrong idea, must we? Now, let me tell you about our assisted places scheme."

"Don't worry, Mr. Ightam. Robin and I never take one another very seriously."

"You've met before?"

"My father farms Southwater dale."

"Really? What a delightful coincidence." He shot me an appraising look, then looked at his watch. "We seem to be rather behind schedule, Robin."

"I'll keep things moving, Headmaster."

"Anything I can do?" Nera offered.

"I'm sure Robin's got everything under control." He led her away, his hand on her elbow. They made an odd couple. He must have known that the *Herald* was dedicated to the destruction of the educational system which he championed. Perhaps the simple presence of the press, whatever its hue, helped to massage his ego.

It didn't do much for mine. The starting pistol misfired, and there was an undignified altercation between two sets of parents over which of their brats had won the obstacle race. With the wisdom of Solomon, I judged it a dead heat, which pleased no one.

I joined Nera for lunch in the marquee, and spotted Jenny with one of the parents across the big tent. She looked away.

The speeches and prize-giving took place in the dining hall. For the last time.

"As some of you may know, a generous and anonymous donation has enabled us to commission a magnificent new Assembly Hall."

The chairman of the governors was a retired field-marshal, diminished somehow in mufti. He looked clean through me, and carried on, "I am delighted to announce that it will be open in time for our Speech Day next year." Applause. "And now I will ask the headmaster to proceed with the prize-giving . . ."

NERA HAD SUPPER with her father that night, and turned up around nine. "Peter couldn't wait to go down to the hotel." She sounded depressed. "I don't know why I bother to come up here, sometimes."

"There's always me."

"Yes." She kissed me. "There's always you."

She had changed into jeans, and we went for a sail. It was a perfect evening, with just enough wind to give us steerageway.

"I'm away again next week," she told me, fingers trailing in the water.

"Now you see her, now you don't. New York again?"

"No. Rhodesia. To write rude things about Ian Smith."

"Don't you get fed up with being away so much?" I tacked, and the boom swung lazily over. "I do."

"Poor Robin." She smiled and touched my knee. "Yes, I do sometimes.

356

Actually, I'm thinking of leaving the *Herald*. Don't tell anyone, but I may be getting a job on television with Richard Fielding. You know, he does Granada's local magazine programme. I expect you've seen him.''

"Yes. Yes, I've seen him.'' Through the steamed-up window of a grubby café in Manchester.

"You don't seem very excited about it.''

"No, I think that's marvellous. You'd look terrific on the box. That's one way of seeing more of you, I suppose. Would you be free to come up to Skelmere more often?''

"Who knows?'' Tantalising.

I set a course for the jetty. It was growing dark and the midges were beginning to bite.

I didn't know where I stood. I wondered sometimes whether we really had anything in common.

I TOOK A VILLA ON HYDRA for the summer holidays, and wished I hadn't from the moment I boarded the hydrofoil at Piraeus. I was homesick. I missed Southwater and the eagles. I missed my friends in AA. And I missed Nera, for all the contradictions and uncertainties of our affair.

For two pins, I'd have packed my bags and gone straight home. But I'd paid the two months' rent in advance, and a sense of frugality which I hadn't known I possessed prevented me from making the grand gesture. Besides, the tourist season in the Lake District was at its height, and I didn't fancy having my privacy invaded by hordes of hill walkers carrying pocket editions of Wordsworth.

So I played the stoic and stayed on, reading the 'Waverley' novels. All of them. Cover to cover. I think it was some kind of penance.

"SIR!'' ENTWHISTLE WAS TALL for his age, an ungainly child who suffered the embarrassment of wearing shorts while everyone else in my new Form 4a had graduated into trousers. I'd heard that his parents were pushed to meet the fees. "Sir, I've run out of ink, sir.''

"You should have filled up before the beginning of prep. Thou foolish virgin,'' I added, and silenced the titters with a look. The class knew that it was a naughty word, but none of them had a clue what it meant, and they were just at that stage, at the beginning of the new school year, when they didn't quite have the nerve to ask me. We were still getting to know one another.

I took a bottle of Quink from my desk, and Entwhistle shambled up, grinning and blushing. Biros weren't allowed: the quaint notion persisted that they encouraged sloppy handwriting. He resumed his seat, and the silence was broken only by the scratching of nibs on paper.

They didn't seem a bad lot, I reflected, although some of them looked painfully young. I'd already spotted the saints and the sinners. Jefferson was the whiz kid of his year, like Barton before him. Wheeler monopolised the other end of the scale. He was lazy, feckless, and funny.

I wasn't sure what they thought of me, but I found that I cared. Jenny had told me that "Woodie" was regarded as "a pretty decent sort", which presumably meant that I was too soft on them. When the bell rang and they clattered off for supper, I hauled them all back. No running, I told them. There wasn't a fire. I didn't know whether I was proving to them or to myself that Sir could be strict.

I normally went home after prep unless I was on duty, but it was the first rehearsal that night for *Staff Laughs*, our annual Christmas review for the boys. It took place in the dining hall after lights out.

David Evans came into his own during the Michaelmas term. He was not only in charge of rugger, but he was also author, director and star of the revue. He'd slaved all summer holidays writing an appalling spoof of *Macbeth—Macdeath*, as he called it. He, naturally, took the title role, opposite an alarming Lady Mac in the form of Matron. Ken and Miss Winters were the two witches—we couldn't run to three. Jacques Thiery played Banjo, with a new member of staff as his page, Fleabite. I was cast as Macdufflecoat, and Jenny as Lady Macdufflecoat.

"And finally you, as King Doughnut, Headmaster. The last Ightam on the agenda." There were groans and the headmaster smiled bleakly.

David went on, "Don't worry, the script's much worse. And now, to coin a phrase, let's get the show on the road."

We read and walked our way through the play. It was like a bad pantomime, and I found myself giggling like a ten-year-old.

David didn't think much of my performance.

"For God's sake, man, look as though you mean it." Exasperated, he ran his fingers through his hair. "Try it again."

I was standing on the rostrum with my script in one hand and my other arm round Jenny's waist. She was stiff and unyielding beneath her uniform. I read,

> "Watch out for mad Macdeath—he seeks to slay
> Us all. Take care, dear heart, when I'm away.
> Thy love is sweeter to me than molasses.
> Farewell! For this my final kiss, alas, is."

I felt her relax as she started to laugh. It was impossible to go on.

"Right, that's enough for now. Same time next week," David said.

It was open house in Ken's study afterwards, and some of us gathered for a gossip. Jenny and I parked ourselves where we could amongst his usual debris, and agreed that David's *Macdeath* was unlikely to reach the West End. She was talkative and cheerful, an easy companion again.

358

WE WERE THROWN together, unexpectedly, at half term.

The school's central heating had been sounding a death rattle for weeks, and the break provided an opportunity to have it overhauled. There were always a few children who couldn't go home because their parents were abroad. November had already opened with the first frosts of winter, and they couldn't possibly stay in the school without any heating. The Ightams took three of them, and since there was plenty of room at Southwater, I agreed to have six. Jenny came too, and helped to look after them.

Hudson was the only boy from my own form. I'd thought him over-serious until I realised that he wore braces on his teeth and didn't like to smile. The rest were of mixed ages: the Thomas twins were in their first term, and liked to hold hands when they thought no one was looking; then there were the brothers Kingsley, one nine and the other twelve; and Lacy was a sixth-former, in charge of the group.

I had borrowed some extra beds from the school dormitories, and put the lads in two of the spare rooms. Jenny occupied the third. Like mine, it had its own bathroom, and she seemed to settle in very happily. So did the boys.

"This is better than home, sir. It's really fab," said Hudson, treating me to a full smile, tooth-braces and all. They'd watched a Western on TV, and it was the first time that some of them had seen a colour set.

"That's probably because your parents pack you off to bed at a sensible hour. Off with you, now."

Jenny came down after she had tucked them up and we had a mug of coffee together in the drawing room. We made plans, and Jenny sketched out her menus. We'd need to have a mammoth shop on Monday.

She yawned and stretched. It was time to turn in, and I went with her to the bottom of the stairs.

"It *is* nice here," she said. She stood on the lowest step, her face at a level with mine.

"I'm glad you're here. Good night, Jenny."

I went round switching off the lights and found myself smiling as I reflected wryly that I had nearly kissed her.

ON THE TUESDAY, we took them up onto the fells with packed lunches which Mrs. Blenkinsop prepared. She'd fussed at first and grumbled at the extra work, but it was a token complaint. She enjoyed it.

We climbed slowly—it was a struggle for the twins—but the boys were rewarded by the sight of a peregrine mobbing the male eagle. I felt sorry for him. He looked curiously cumbersome in comparison with the lighter, faster falcon. The peregrine stooped repeatedly, dropping hundreds of feet and sweeping like a scimitar over the eagle. The bigger bird weaved and flipped on his back in an ungainly aerobatic roll to present his talons to the diving peregrine. I could sense his frustration as he eventually found refuge, feathers and feelings ruffled, in the branches of a birch.

The boys were thrilled. The younger Kingsley drove us all spare in the drawing room that night by imitating the action of the peregrine. He wheeled round the sofa with his arms outstretched, making machine-gun noises.

"Grow up, Kingsley. That's a Stuka, not a falcon," Lacy told him. Then he wanted to know how birds could see where they were flying in a power dive. "I mean, doesn't it make their eyes water, sir?"

I explained about the nictating membranes, the transparent eyelids which protected their vision in flight. It was a little nugget of trivial knowledge which I'd never expected to display.

"Most impressive," Jenny told me later, when the children were in bed. "I wish I had been as quick on the draw when Kingsley asked me what the ram was doing in the tupping pen this afternoon."

"What did you tell him?"

"The truth, in the end. I couldn't think of a sufficiently convincing fairy story."

"You'll probably be regarded as a scarlet woman at school."

"Oh, Lord, I hadn't thought of that."

"They're terrible gossips. The twins have already married us off, you know."

"That's only because they're missing their parents," she said, and bent down to poke the fire. Perhaps it was just the flames that reddened her cheeks.

It was party time on Saturday—the boys' last night at Southwater. The shops in Keswick still had a few fireworks in stock, left over from Guy Fawkes' Night, and I managed to mount a decent display by the lake. The boys stuffed their faces afterwards with cakes and jelly, and we played games when supper was over: sardines, charades, pass-the-parcel and musical bumps.

By popular demand, there was a second round of musical bumps. The cushions were laid out in a circle on the floor, and Jenny, dressed simply in a denim dress and flat shoes, stood by the record player. The boys cavorted round in a circle. The music stopped in mid-bar. They dived for the cushions.

And Nera walked in.

The room was still, save for one of the twins who was looking disconsolately for a cushion to sit on.

"Oh, dear. I seem to have gatecrashed a party," she said.

Her ankle-length coat hung open showing the briefest minidress beneath it. She was smart and seductive.

"That doesn't matter. Come and join in."

"Thanks, but I'm not sure it's really my scene." She gave a brief smile, and left as suddenly as she had arrived. I shot a quick glance at Jenny, but her face was averted. I enjoyed a moment of grim amusement. The situation was a carbon copy of their last encounter, but the roles had been reversed.

"Come on, let's keep it going," I said, and removed a cushion. The room was filled once more with the crashing rhythms of the Rolling Stones.

It was after ten before we managed to pack them off to bed.

"They're much too excited to go to sleep," Jenny said. From the bottom of the stairs we could hear the whispering above.

"We'd better go up and read the riot act."

The boys had congregated in one room. The lights were out, and Lacy was telling them a ghost story. I waited for Lacy's bloodcurdling finale before breaking it up. I told him, without meaning it, that he ought to be ashamed of himself.

"Sorry, sir." He didn't mean it either. Then he looked unusually shy and hesitant. "Sir—"

"Yes?"

"I just wanted to say—that is, we wanted to say—well, we've had a jolly good time here. You've been awfully decent, sir. And Miss Stott."

"Hear, hear," said Hudson.

"Flattery will get you everywhere. Off to your own beds now, and no more talking. OK?"

"Yes, sir." In chorus.

Jenny and I returned downstairs and finished tidying up. The drawing room looked as though a small tornado had passed through it: there were cushions on the carpet and bits of paper from pass-the-parcel scattered everywhere.

"It's true, you know," Jenny said. She slipped a record back into its sleeve. "The boys have had a wonderful week."

"How about you?"

"It's been perfect, Robin."

Or it might have been, if Nera hadn't turned up.

IT WAS A QUIET CHRISTMAS but the sense of nostalgia was strong. I remembered my excitement as a child, the slow build-up throughout December, decorating the tree, and finally pulling the paper off my presents on Christmas morning. I missed it all.

Nera had given me a bronze cast of an eagle crouching over a dead hare. It was beautiful. We put it on the mantelpiece. It looked good there. She could hardly have found a better present.

I'd taken a gamble with Nera's. She'd said more than once that she

361

wanted a small dog, and I'd bought a Jack Russell from kennels in Grasmere on Christmas Eve. It was an enchanting puppy, with an excellent pedigree.

"Oh, Robin!" She was thrilled, and hugged the squirming bundle.

"You'll have to think of a name."

"Rat. We'll have to call him Rat," she decided, and examined the puppy more closely. "Sorry, her. Oh, she's adorable."

"I was a bit worried that you might not be able to look after her. With your foreign assignments, I mean."

"She'll be a splendid excuse not to go."

"That's rather what I was hoping." I smiled.

The puppy was trying frantically to lick her nose off. "Anyway, it looks as though the TV contract will be signed fairly soon for the local magazine programme. I'll take her with me to the studios."

I took the puppy and put her down on the carpet. Sally approached, sniffed the creature once, and retired in high dudgeon to her basket. It was clear that her nose was out of joint. I went to church, and Nera left for the farm to prepare the turkey. We were lunching with Stone.

"Come on, man, you'll have a whisky with me—it's Christmas Day!" he said. The bottle had already taken a beating by the time I arrived.

"Robin doesn't drink," Nera reminded him.

"I just thought we'd let bygones be bygones. Eh, Mr. Woodford?"

"Nothing I'd like more." I mustered a smile as the whisky fumes washed over me.

"Now, when are you going to make an honest woman of my lass, eh?"

"I think she's already married to her job."

"That's enough, you two." Nera pretended to be cross, but she was relieved that we weren't glowering at one another.

Nera and I crept out after lunch, leaving him snoring beside his living-room fire. We walked back to Southwater as the December light began to fade. Nera fell asleep later, curled up on the sofa like a contented cat. I stayed awake, drained and depressed. I wasn't growing any younger, and there seemed no future or real purpose in our relationship. It was as barren as the winter itself.

Then my eye was caught by the dull gleam of the eagle on the mantelpiece. I remembered the wild thrill of our eagles' courtship display. It wouldn't be long before they were mating again, before there was a new year and a new beginning. I could wait.

ON THE FIRST SUNDAY in February the eagles were nesting again.

They were both at it, shuttling to and fro across the dale with building materials. I watched them through binoculars, from a safe distance so as not to disturb them.

The new nesting site was further up the dale, but in an alarmingly open position, on a grassy bank at the foot of a large hawthorn bush. The branches would offer some protection from the elements, but that was all. The slope looked steep, but it would be an easy climb, even without equipment. I could see the black peaty ribbon of a sheep track running not fifty yards from the site. It was too accessible. Not only did the site offer an open invitation to the likes of Hunter, but there was a real risk of accidental disturbance. Its position near the head of the narrowing valley meant that the opposite ridge was only a few hundred yards away. It was a popular path to the plateau, and walkers on the skyline might well frighten the birds off.

Yet my anxiety took second place to a deep-rooted sense of satisfaction. They were nesting again. I was grateful and glad.

But my joy was short-lived.

The telephone rang as I was making my lunch. It was Simon. I hadn't spoken to him for very nearly two years, and at first I didn't recognise his voice.

He told me that my mother had died in the night. Yes, it was unexpected, but she'd gone peacefully in her sleep. The funeral was on Wednesday at the crematorium in Altrincham.

It was a family affair, though Henry Tetlow was there. I slipped into the chapel just as the service was beginning. I sat behind the others, and I don't think anyone realised that I had arrived.

It was a short ceremony, and Henry Tetlow was the first to speak to me as we drifted outside.

"I do wish you'd gone to see her before she died," he said.

"I know. So do I." I was filled with a sense of guilt, as well as grief.

"Robert!" It was Simon greeting me now. Despite his thick black overcoat he still looked slender and youthful, and the eyes behind his glasses were warm with welcome. "I wasn't sure you were going to make it."

"I'm afraid I was a bit late."

"You came, that's the main thing. You're looking marvellous. Fitter than I ever remember you. Look, you are coming to John's place, aren't you? He's laid on the lunch."

"I . . . I haven't spoken to John." Not since he fired me, I reflected.

"You're expected. That is, if you want to come," he added.

"Well, all right," I decided. There suddenly seemed no point in maintaining my self-imposed isolation for the rest of my life.

"Splendid. It's been ages! When did I last see you?"

"Just before they let me out," I reminded him bleakly.

"Oh, yes." He wasn't in the least put out by the memory. "It wasn't such a bad place, was it? Remember the first time I came to visit you?"

I DID. THEY HAD MOVED me from Strangeways to an open prison outside Macclesfield three months after I began my sentence. I had been dried out, and my mind was regaining its balance, although I still suffered bouts of deep depression.

Simon was waiting in the assistant governor's office.

"What's it like here?" he asked, after we'd exchanged greetings.

"Better than Strangeways, I suppose." I felt uncommunicative. There was only one thing I wanted to talk to him about. I had been put to work in the prison library, cataloguing the books. It was a peaceful job. In some ways, the library and institutionalised life reminded me of school, and it was perhaps this memory which had triggered the vague idea of becoming a schoolmaster when I was released.

"Teaching?" Simon looked surprised. "But you haven't got any qualifications."

"No—but I've got money. Look, it may sound crazy, but I've had a lot of time to think about it. What I've come up with is this: you know how Skelmere is always badgering us with appeals? I just thought that I could offer them something big—maybe an indoor pool, or a science lab. Whatever they need. In exchange for a job, Si. That's what I mean."

"It doesn't sound very ethical." Simon looked doubtful.

"Oh, I don't know. I think I could make a real contribution to Skelmere, as a teacher, not just a benefactor. And it's only a prep school. You hardly need a PhD at that level."

"But why do you want to teach at Skelmere? As far as I can remember, you weren't particularly happy there."

"Perhaps distance lends enchantment." It would have sounded corny to confess my longing for an organised existence, for a return to an age of innocence. "So what do you say?"

"I . . . don't know."

"Look, I know Ken Wade's still on the staff—he signed the last appeal. Will you have a word with him? Obviously, if they agree in principle, the donation would have to be made anonymously. So will you have a go? I mean, what else can I do? I'm a jailbird."

"You're also an alcoholic, Robert." Simon's reminder was gentle, but it deflated me.

"I haven't had a drink for three months. I'm not an alcoholic, for God's sake."

"You've only managed to stop because there *isn't* any booze round here. But could you stay stopped once you were out? It isn't a question of cutting it down—you know that doesn't work. Here, have a fag." Simon passed me a packet. Then he went on carefully, "Listen, you've asked me to act as your intermediary with Ken Wade. Fair enough, except— frankly, it just wouldn't be right to ask them to take on an alcoholic as a member of staff. Not even if you rebuilt the whole bloody school. So the answer is no."

"What?" All my old resentment erupted to the surface.

"Unless," Simon went on steadily, "you're prepared to accept help with your drinking. That's the first step. If you want, and only if you want, I'll have a word with the Governor or one of his sidekicks. I'm sure they'd be prepared to find someone to help you. But it's up to you."

"I don't mind." I felt listless and low.

It was the beginning of a depression which lingered on for weeks. One day followed another in a blur of dull detachment until there was a knock on my door one afternoon.

"Come in." It was an effort to get up and greet him. The stranger was dressed in a dark suit and a dog collar. He had a round red face, and his cheerful smile lent him the look of a superannuated cherub. Perhaps he's the new prison chaplain, I thought.

"Hello, Robert," he beamed. His accent was Irish, his handshake firm and warm. "My name's Noel, and I'm an alcoholic . . ."

It was Father Noel who was to help me break my chains, and begin to understand what real freedom was.

"DO YOU STILL GO to AA?" Simon asked me later, when we were at John's house for lunch. He eyed my glass of Perrier water.

"Heavens, yes. It's become a habit—a bit like booze, only better. They're a nice bunch."

"I'm so glad it worked," he said simply.

"You arranged it, didn't you? I've got a lot to thank you for, Si."

"Just call me Mr. Fixit." He looked a bit embarrassed, and helped himself to some caviare on toast. He munched, and went on between mouthfuls, "It's a pity that you and Mum couldn't have got together before she died."

"I wish I had seen her, if only to say sorry." I should have made amends to so many people, I reflected. Maria, my brothers. Above all, to the family of the cyclist I had killed.

His wife had won a £30,000 award which my insurers had settled, and I'd written to her from prison. She hadn't replied.

"I like your Range Rover," Simon said, changing the subject. We were standing by the big bow window overlooking the drive.

"Yes, it suits me fine. It's amazing how many boys you can bundle into it."

"You were damn lucky to get your licence back so soon. The courts are tougher now. I suppose they thought that a three-year stretch was punishment enough."

"Only eighteen months in the end," I reminded him. "But it felt like three years." John came across the room towards us. He'd put on weight, I noticed. Too many CBI lunches.

"Looking after yourself, Robert?" He was in a bluff, forgive-and-forget mood. "How's Skelmere?"

"I'm enjoying it."

"What do you do with all that spare time you lucky teachers get?"

"I walk. Climb the crags . . . as a matter of fact, I spend a fair bit of time keeping my eye on a pair of golden eagles which are nesting up the dale. They're terribly rare in England, you know. They haven't bred here for over two hundred years."

"Really?" He wasn't interested. "Well, give my best to Ken Wade when you see him." He clapped me on the back and drifted off to talk to Henry Tetlow.

I left as soon as I decently could, and Simon came outside with me.

"I'd love to come up and see you sometime," he ventured.

"I . . . well, the house is still a bit upside-down," I lied.

"I understand," he said, and I think he did. It was still too soon.

THE EAGLE CAUGHT us on the hop by laying early, a week before the RSPB team were due.

The days were lengthening by the middle of March, and it was light enough to see her through the telescope when I woke up that Saturday morning. She was still sitting on the nest after breakfast when I left for school.

"You look as though you've had twins," Jenny told me during break.

"Close enough! She's laid again."

"That's wonderful!"

"Are you free tomorrow?"

"Well . . . yes."

"Great. I'll pick you up after church. Say twelvish. We can have lunch at my place first. Oh—and bring an indelible pen with you. One of those ones you use for marking the boys' clothes."

"An indelible pen?" She looked bewildered. The bell rang for class, and I left her guessing.

She was ready and dressed for the dales when I collected her next day from the school. We'd asked Ken to join us. I knew how he hated his Sundays when the "chaps" were at home.

"Are you sure I wouldn't be in the way?" He looked half embarrassed.

"Of course not," Jenny said quickly.

We didn't linger over lunch. Afterwards Jenny and I left Ken and Sally snoozing in front of the fire, and made our way up to the site. Ken was too lame to come with us, and I hadn't taken Sally up the dale since the eagles started nesting. She was too inquisitive and uncontrollable.

Jenny produced the pen from the pocket of her anorak. "Now do you mind telling me what you need it for?"

"I thought I'd mark the eggs. It should discourage anyone from trying to pinch them."

"Do you think that's wise, Robin? I mean, you'll have to chase her off the nest, and you remember what happened last year."

"She was only warning me, and it didn't stop her sitting. I don't think one visit will do any harm." I had an idea that the eagles might recognise me now as a friend.

I thought that it would be better if I approached the nest alone. There was a crumbling wall running down the spine of the opposite ridge, and Jenny crouched behind it. She could see what I was doing through a gap in the stones.

It was more a walk than a climb, and I was scarcely out of breath when I reached the site. The female had let me come quite close before taking wing and settling on a rock higher up the fell. She was watchful at first, but didn't attack. Then she actually started to preen, as casually as though the dale was deserted.

It was a standard clutch of two eggs, with their now familiar mottled markings. They were warm to the touch and lay in a soft bed of lichen, dried grass and down. The whole nest was some five foot across, and it was awkward reaching across to the middle without disturbing it, but the job didn't take long. I soon joined Jenny further down the dale by the beck.

"She didn't seem to mind at all," Jenny said.

"I know." I was elated. The eagles appeared to have accepted me.

The sun had been playing hide-and-seek behind the clouds, and at that moment a shaft of light fell full on Southwater. It warmed the stones of the distant house, gilded the daffodils on the lawn and danced off the fringes of the lake. It was like an omen.

I should have known better than to believe it.

Ken had woken up and had been watching our progress through the telescope. He called to us from upstairs as soon as we came in: the female had flown off and hadn't returned to the nest.

The binoculars afforded a broader field of vision and I focused them on the top of the dale. I could see the bird circling over the high plateau. And I could also see why she hadn't come back.

Stone was standing on the opposite fell side, where Jenny had hidden. He was sticking up like a sore thumb, on an open ledge, in full view of the nest and a couple of hundred yards away from it across the valley.

"Look," I told Ken. "Up the other slope."

"Oh, yes. I wonder where he sprang from. Isn't he the local farmer?"

"That's right," I said grimly. "It's Peter Stone. He's keeping her off the eggs. Deliberately."

"You can't be sure of that," Jenny protested. "Let's wait and see if he moves on."

He didn't.

I checked on him occasionally for nearly two hours, until it grew dark. He made himself more comfortable on the ledge, sitting on a rock and reaching into his pocket from time to time for a hip-flask. The temperature up there must have fallen to near freezing, but it didn't seem to bother him.

"It looks like you were right, Rob," said Ken. "If it were a smaller bird, those eggs would be cold by now. Especially in this temperature."

"Do you think they'll be OK if the female comes back now it's dark?" I asked.

"They should be. But if he plays that stunt again for a longer period, they'll have had it."

"But what can we do?" Jenny wanted to know. "It's his land—well, he leases it. And he's not actually *doing* anything. Just sitting there."

"It's wilful disturbance. He's breaking the law," I said.

"So were you," Jenny pointed out. "But in his case, it would be damn hard to prove. When are the RSPB people coming? Couldn't they warn him off?"

"Knowing Stone, he couldn't care two hoots about any warning from them. Or from me, for that matter. There's only one person he'll listen to, and that's his daughter. I think I'll give her a call."

Nera was curt on the telephone. Judging by the background noises, she was giving some sort of party at her Manchester flat.

"I'll come up straight away," she said when I had finished explaining. "It's best that I see him. I'll be with you in a couple of hours." The line went dead.

I reported the gist of our conversation to Ken and Jenny, then I ran them both back to the school.

Jenny was subdued as I drove. Ken sensed the atmosphere and told a long and involved shaggy dog story. Jenny and I were so occupied with our thoughts that we both missed the point, but at least he bridged what might otherwise have been an uncomfortable silence.

It seemed longer than two hours, but it was only eight o'clock when Nera's Mini Cooper drew up in the drive.

"I hope I didn't break anything up," I said, as she walked past me into the drawing room. We didn't kiss.

"I just had a few friends round." She was very businesslike.

"Do you want some grub?"

"Maybe later. I want to see Peter first."

"I don't think he's up at the farm. There are no lights on."

"He'll be at the hotel. I'll go and see him there. If I wait until he comes home, he'll be too smashed to listen."

"I'm coming too."

"I thought you wanted me to fight this battle for you."

That was below the belt.

"It's not just my battle, Nera. Those eagles are struggling for their survival. They'll die out if they're not allowed to breed."

"All right," she said. "But let me do the talking. I haven't come up here to get involved in a bar-room brawl between you and Peter."

Nera wanted to walk. It had been a long drive and she needed to stretch her legs. There was a hint of rain in the air and it was cold. I pulled up the hood of my duffel coat and jammed my hands into the pockets as we turned out of the drive and onto the track. It was muddy, and we had to pick our way in the darkness. The trees beside the road were no more than vague shapes, and the lake was black. I couldn't even see the outline of the crags. The darkness was impenetrable.

After the cold night air, the hotel was suffocatingly warm and smoky. We found Stone playing cribbage at a corner table with Billy, the local postman. The farmer's face lit up with pleasure when he saw Nera.

"If it's not my lass!" He stood up. "I'd almost forgotten what you looked like. What can I get you?"

"It's all right. We can wait till you've finished your game," she said.

"No bother. We'll call it a day, eh, Billy?"

"If you like. 'Evening, miss. Mr. Woodford." The postman nodded to us both, and eased his way through the throng to the bar. Stone started to follow him.

"Well, lass, what's it to be?" he asked over his shoulder. "One of your fancy martinis?"

"Thanks, Peter."

"And a glass of milk for Mr. Woodford?" he said to me. He didn't disguise his dislike.

"Nothing for me," I told him.

He shouldered his way back with Nera's martini and another large whisky for himself.

"Sit down, lass," he said. "So what brings you up here to see your old man? We won't be lambing till next month."

"I can't help you with that this year, Peter, I told you. No, I'm here because you've been disturbing the eagles."

"I don't know what you mean."

"You spent most of the afternoon keeping the female off the nest," I told him. "You know damn well that she's just laid her eggs."

"There's no law against that."

"Oh, yes, there is. It's called Wilful Disturbance. You were deliberately preventing her from incubating the eggs. I don't know why you didn't just smash them."

"I don't have to take this from you," he said, rising.

"Shut up, both of you," Nera said quietly. Then she turned to her father. "Now listen, Peter. This has got to stop. You're to let those eagles breed in peace. Do you understand?"

"I told you, I wasn't doing them any harm. Just looking, that's all." But he had weakened, and couldn't meet her eyes.

"Come on, Robin. This place gets me down." Nera sounded weary. She knocked back her martini, and I rose to follow her.

"Will I see you at home, lass?" His eyes were still lowered.

She turned back and unexpectedly kissed his hair.

"If you're not too blind drunk," she promised, with a smile.

We walked back in silence. It had started to sleet.

"Did you mean that about seeing him back at the farm?" I asked. We had reached the house and were standing by her car.

"Yes. I'll wait for him there. He does need me, Robin."

"You're not coming in? Don't you think *I* need you?"

Nera looked up at me. "No, Robin, I don't think you do. You may want me, but you don't need me."

She kissed me quickly. Her lips were cold. Then she slipped behind the wheel of her Mini and swung the little car down the drive. She didn't wave or flash her light or honk her horn. She just went.

I felt relieved. It was over. It had never really begun.

Six

I was glad to see the RSPB had sent the same team. I liked Porgy and Bess. The only trouble was that Bess was seven months pregnant and would only be able to stay a few weeks. It was even money on whether she'd have her baby or the eggs would hatch first.

If they ever hatched, I reminded myself.

Porgy was as worried as I was about the exposed position of the nesting site. He spent much of his time on the high plateau, tactfully steering walkers away from the head of the valley, while Bess stayed in the hide and guarded the dale's lower approaches.

Porgy had built himself a crude shelter of stones and packed the gaps with peat. It was open to the skies but it afforded some protection from the wind.

"You must get bloody cold up here," I said. It was shortly after Easter, and a stiff northerly was trying to find its way through invisible crevices in his shelter. He'd put a kettle on his small camping stove.

"It doesn't worry me—I carry my own insulation," he said cheerfully. There was some truth in that: he had put on more weight since last year.

"Anyway, I can always take a stroll if I want to keep my circulation going. Care to come? The kettle takes ages to boil, and I want to check on what the birds have been eating. There's a roost not far from here which the male uses."

We reached it across a scree. It was a fingerlike rock embedded amongst the shale and it was covered in droppings. There was a bleached crow's skull lying at the foot of the rock and a few small bones. Porgy bent down to pick up a casting. It was about the size of a pullet's egg and he broke it open.

"Vole," he said. "See its claw?"

Feather as well as fur could be recognised in the dry, compacted material. The eagle had regurgitated the casting after using it as roughage to clean up his crop.

"There's no sign of lambs' wool, is there?"

"It's too early. There's hardly any been born yet. But they're bound to take one or two, especially when they're rearing the chicks."

"Let's hope Stone doesn't see them at it!"

We picked our way back to his shelter. It was cosy inside, after the open fell, and the tin mug was almost too hot to hold.

"When's Bess packing up?" I said.

"She wants to stay until the last minute." He leaned against the stonework and sipped his tea. "The society have promised a replacement, but—oh, listen!" A whistling *Kiiya! Kiiya!* cut clean through the sound of the wind, followed by a distinct and high-pitched yelping call. I peered over the shelter.

"It's the male," I said, watching him quartering the lower slopes. "I've only heard them call once before. Does it mean anything?"

"No one really knows."

I didn't often stump him. Porgy was a fund of eagle lore, from their average daily food requirement of two hundred and thirty grammes to the fact that one third of their body-weight consisted of wing muscle. One of his little nuggets was that a breeding pair only succeeded in rearing on average six tenths of an eagle each year. It was a somewhat gloomy statistic.

The call was repeated and Porgy's homely face was rapt with pleasure.

"It's a thrilling sound, isn't it? Wilder than geese—and rarer. But you wait till the eggs hatch and the chicks are hungry. You can hear them cheeping for miles."

I HAD ONLY TO WAIT a month.

It was a Wednesday afternoon in the middle of May, and I was taking three of the boys sailing: Entwhistle from my own form, with Stubbs and Acorn from the Lower Sixth.

"Look, sir!" Stubbs tugged at my sleeve. "Sir, there's someone on your pier. I think he's trying to attract your attention."

It was a bright afternoon, and I needed to shade my eyes against the glare to identify the tubby figure jumping up and down on the jetty. It was Porgy.

"We'd better head back and see what he wants," I decided. "You know what to do, Acorn."

"Yes, sir. Ready about, lee-oh!" His voice cracked nervously.

Our progress back was painfully slow. But I realised as we drew closer that I needn't have worried. Porgy was wearing the broadest of grins on his face.

"The eggs have hatched—both of them! Like to come and see?"

"Try and stop me."

I left the boys to deal with the boat. I told them to go to my house when they'd finished. There was a cake in the kitchen, and they knew how to use the television. I told them that I wouldn't be long.

Porgy and I took a detour up the north ridge, keeping low behind the stone wall running along its spine. We stopped opposite the eyrie, and the chicks' piping cries could be heard distinctly across the head of the valley. *Pee-UR! Pee-UR!* They sounded querulous and hungry.

Through binoculars, we looked down on the nest from our vantage point. The female stood over the two eaglets, feeding them tiny morsels of flesh with amazing delicacy. They seemed little bigger than sparrows, with outsize beaks and claws and covered in white down. The remains of the eggshells had been pushed to the edge of the shallow depression in the middle of the nest.

"They need to have more than their own weight in food every day," Porgy said quietly. "It's a full-time job being an eaglet's mum."

"Doesn't the male do any of the feeding?"

"He will when they're a bit older. He helped with the brooding, you know."

"They mate for life, don't they?"

"Yes. And they tend to be good parents—at least, they are to the chick which survives."

"How do you mean?"

"See that smaller chick on the left? It was the second one to hatch, and it'll be lucky if it lasts a fortnight. The bigger one will kill it—or grab all the grub."

I was appalled. "Couldn't we remove it from the nest, and rear it by hand?"

"No, it's best not to interfere."

The female remained unaware of our presence. It was a perfect observation area—the same spot from which Jenny had watched me marking the eggs. We kept our voices and our heads low, peering through gaps in the stone wall. Eagles have a fine sense of hearing, and their eyesight is seven times sharper than a man's.

I forgot the time. It was only when I grew aware of the shadows deepening in the dale that I remembered the boys. I looked quickly at my watch and was horrified to see that it was already six thirty. They should have been back at school half an hour ago.

"HONESTLY, KEN, he really is a pompous idiot," I told Ken, later.

Ightam had wanted his pound of flesh that evening. He'd kept me standing in front of his desk for a full fifteen minutes while he paced up and down, hands behind his back, and lectured me on my irresponsibility.

"Oh, I don't know. He was only doing his job," Ken said. He grinned. "Besides, it was a fair cop."

We were enjoying a late stroll round the grounds that evening. We paused by the swimming pontoon at the edge of the lake, and Ken lit his pipe to keep the midges at bay. "It looks pretty good from here, doesn't it?" he said between puffs. He was referring to the new Assembly Hall, seen dimly across the cricket field, a low and unobtrusive building attached to the south wing. The decorators had nearly finished inside, and it was due to be opened on Speech Day by the Lord Lieutenant.

"It'll pass muster in this light," I agreed.

"Was it worth it, Rob?" Ken looked at me from beneath his bushy eyebrows.

"Every penny. I like it here, Ken, despite the odd hiccup with Ightam. I'm really beginning to feel I belong." We started to wander back, dutifully skirting the hallowed turf of his cricket square.

"What about you and Jenny?" Ken asked suddenly.

"What about me and Jenny?" I was startled.

"Well, you seem to be putting down roots round here. Perhaps it's time you thought of starting a family."

"It's a friendship, that's all."

"I can think of worse reasons for getting married. Or are you still carrying a torch for that journalist girl?"

"Nera?" I laughed. "No, that died a peaceful death last term. On the night she came up to see her father about the eagles, as a matter of fact."

"I never thought she was your sort. Jenny is. She thinks the world of you, you know."

"Oh, come off it, Ken." I was nettled by his probing, and turned down his offer of coffee.

I was climbing into the car when something made me look up. There was a light burning in the dormitory wing. It was Jenny's room. I wondered what she was doing.

"IF YOU MUST KNOW," she said, "I seem to spend most of my spare time mending the boys' clothes—though Ken and I sometimes go mad and have a game of backgammon. What about you? If I may ask," she added pointedly, but with a smile.

"I'm sorry, I was being nosy. Me? Oh, nothing very exciting. Doing my own homework. Taking Sally for walks. Watching the box."

I'd been surprised to find Jenny sitting at the back of the church at matins and we were looking round the little graveyard after the service. It was a hot morning in late May.

"It's peaceful, isn't it?" she said. The crags were reflected in the waters of the lake.

"I wouldn't mind being buried here. Perhaps I should reserve a plot."

"Yuk!" Jenny pretended to shiver. "What a morbid thought on a day like this. Let's enjoy it."

"Fair enough." And I started to quote:

> "Look to this day,
> For it is life,
> The very life of life.
> In its brief course lie all
> The realities and verities of existence:
> The bliss of growth,
> The splendour of action,
> The glory of power—"

She took it up:

> "For yesterday is but a dream,
> And tomorrow is only a vision,
> But today, well lived,
> Makes every yesterday a dream of happiness
> And every tomorrow a vision of hope.
> Look well, therefore, to this day."

"How on earth do you know that?" I asked. It was an old Sanskrit proverb which appeared in my AA literature.

"I ... I read it in one of your books." Her cheeks were reddening. "I liked it so much that I memorised it."

There was a silence between us. "How long have you known that I was an alcoholic?"

"Ages. Does it matter?"

"I suppose not."

"I didn't want to say anything. You know, pry. I mean ..." She was confused. "I mean, not unless you wanted to talk about it. And you didn't, did you?"

"No." She might as well know the rest, I thought. I drew a deep breath. "Look, Jenny, there are one or two other things I ought to tell you ..."

She listened to it without interrupting.

"So there you have it," I said at last, and threw her own question back at her. "Well? *Does* it matter? You tell me."

"Of course not. You're what you are, not what you were." There was no hesitation in her reply. Then suddenly she smiled. "Anyway, I think that Robin Woodford is a much nicer name. I suppose you had to change it?"

"I think so. There was a great deal of publicity over the trial, and the Wyndham name is too well known at Skelmere. Someone would have put two and two together, and I couldn't see parents approving of an ex-con teaching their kids. Besides, I wanted a new name—it was for a new person. Does that make sense?"

"Yes," she said simply. "And I'm glad that you've told me."

I experienced a sense of lightness, as though I had shed a heavy load. "You'll come and have lunch, won't you? We can have a look at the chicks afterwards, if you like."

"Love to. But I'd better go back and change first if we're going up the dale." She was wearing a smart summer dress, the colour of ripe corn. Her arms were freckled beneath the short sleeves.

I drove Jenny to the school and waited while she changed. She emerged looking trim and boyish in towelling shorts and a T-shirt. I could see that she was wearing a bikini underneath.

"You're not thinking of having a swim, are you?" I asked. "The lake's icy."

"How do you know? You told me you never went in."

"Ah—but there was a boy called Robert Wyndham who did," I reminded her.

We concocted a picnic and took it down to the jetty. I'd slipped into swimming trunks strictly for sunbathing, and Jenny called me chicken before diving in. She rose to the surface, gasping.

"My God, you were right. It's freezing." She scrambled back onto the jetty, and stretched out to dry in the sun.

"You'll get burnt," I warned her.

"Just freckly. If I roast for long enough they'll all join together and I might even look brown."

She lay on her back with her eyes closed. With her small breasts and narrow hips, she looked about fifteen. Her short reddish hair was wet but still springy. The black bikini accentuated the fairness of her skin.

We ate our picnic sitting on the jetty with our legs dangling over the edge. We were about to clear up afterwards when I saw Porgy ambling across the lawn towards us. Bess was in labour, and his old Ford Anglia wouldn't start. Would I mind running her in to the hospital? I shot to my feet, knocking over our Thermos of iced coffee.

Porgy looked amused. "Don't worry, Robin. The pains are pretty infrequent. She probably won't have the baby for ages."

"Even so," I said nervously. "Where is she?"

"In the house. Look, Robin, I'd better hang around the dale. The weather has brought the Sunday walkers out onto the crags. I'll have to keep them away from the site."

"You mean you're not coming?" I had visions of trying to cope while Bess gave birth in the back of the Range Rover.

"I will," Jenny volunteered, sensing my panic.

"Thanks, Jenny," Porgy said cheerfully. "Perhaps you'll have a chance to earn a few Brownie points in practical midwifery."

I decided that he was mad, and dashed off to change. I saw Bess sitting calm and relaxed in the drawing room as I raced upstairs. She gave me a smile and a wave, and carried on with her knitting. I seemed the only one to think that we had a full-scale emergency on our hands.

Bess chatted comfortably to Jenny as I put my foot down along the occasional straight stretch, and only once did she draw a sharp intake of breath as a pain swept over her. We took her into the maternity wing of Keswick Hospital, and kicked our heels for a while until a nurse told us that there was no point in hanging around. Porgy had been right—the baby probably wouldn't be born before midnight.

We returned to Southwater and found Porgy in the hide with a couple of twitchers all the way from Sheffield. After they had gone, he complained good-naturedly that the Sunday trippers had turned the place into Piccadilly Circus, and he'd had to scramble up to the plateau twice to head off hill walkers.

"Still, it's one way of losing weight," he added.

378

"Elizabeth is fine," I told him. "I thought you might like to borrow my car to go and see her this evening."

"What? Oh, yes. Thanks." He accepted the keys absently, and continued scanning the skyline at the head of the valley. There was a solitary walker crossing the plateau. "Blast, there's another one."

"We'll see he doesn't get too close," I offered. "Jenny and I were going to have a look at the chicks from the north ridge anyway. You could push off now if you want. It's nearly five."

"No, I'd better hang on for a bit down here."

Jenny and I left him in the hide, and made our way up towards the plateau behind the cover of the north ridge. It was hard going and the day was still hot as we climbed higher. The walker seemed to have turned back. We pushed on to the top of the ridge, and crouched behind the stone wall. Looking down on the site across the valley, we could see through binoculars that the smaller chick was dead. It lay discarded at the edge of the nest, a pathetic little bundle of white down. I couldn't help feeling disappointment and sorrow.

The other eagle had grown remarkably since hatching. Still only ten days old, its hunger call had taken on an angry note, and it assumed an aggressive posture while waiting to be fed, with its rump high and head thrust forward. The female towered over it, shredding the carcass of a meadow pipit and feeding the morsels into the youngster's gaping beak.

"Who does the hunting?" Jenny asked quietly.

"The male, though she'll probably leave the nest and help him in a week or so, when the chick's a bit stronger."

We must have sat there for nearly an hour. At around six we saw Porgy making his way down along the beck towards the farm and Southwater.

"I ought to be going, too," Jenny said. "The boys will be getting back soon."

"OK."

I started to rise, when Jenny suddenly seized my arm. A vixen was stalking the nest.

With its belly to the ground and ears flat, it inched its way up the sheep track on the opposite slope. The eagle saw it. She launched herself off the eyrie and fell in a fast glide towards the intruder. She landed on the track no more than five yards in front of the vixen.

I had my glasses up again, and watched them confront one another. The eagle thrust one leg forward, and slashed the air threateningly with her talons. She held her head low, the ebony beak open. Her wings were half spread and her mantle rose like a ruff. The posture exaggerated her ferocity and size, though I knew that she was barely half the vixen's weight.

The fox bared its teeth. It gathered itself, hindquarters rippling with muscle, and leapt at the bird. The eagle sprang into the air and landed on its back. The vixen twisted and bit at her leg.

They tumbled down the slope, locked together in a welter of fur and feather. Wings thrashed, teeth snapped and talons grappled in a horrifying fight to the death. Now the fox was on top, now the eagle. There was a yelp—I couldn't tell which of them uttered it—then silence. And a sudden stillness.

I thought for one moment that they were both dead. Then the eagle was up, pulling a wing out from under the vixen's body.

She stood over her kill, weak and bedraggled, but still casting her glance savagely from side to side. Regaining her strength, she took to the air in a shallow glide down the dale. An up-current bore her aloft. One of her primary feathers was missing and she was trailing a leg. Three weary wingbeats took her back to the nest.

It was only then that I became aware that Jenny was pressed against me. Her face was buried in my chest, and my arm was round her shoulders.

"It's all right. It's over. The fox is dead," I told her, "and she's OK— well, more or less."

"I couldn't bear to look."

Her voice was muffled against my shirt. The skin beneath her short sleeves was hot, almost feverish to the touch. She gave a little shiver.

"I told you you'd catch the sun. I can feel it."

"Can you?" She lifted her face and I kissed her. It wasn't passionate. It was comforting and peaceful.

"I wish I'd done that a long time ago."

"Yes," she said.

So I kissed her again.

"I'M NOT KIDDING. I saw it happen with my own eyes," I told Stone. I'd caught him later that evening at the farm, just as he was leaving for his Sunday session at the hotel.

"A fully grown vixen? That's impossible. Those hill foxes are killers."

"Exactly. They're much more of a risk to your lambs than the eagles. They're real vermin, and you can thank the eagles for getting rid of one of them for you. Look," I went on, "I can show you if you want. You can see the fox for yourself. Dead as a doornail. Come on. It won't take long."

We hardly spoke as we climbed the north ridge, and neither of us mentioned Nera. We didn't even have her in common any more, I reflected.

But I didn't mind his silence, or his surly scepticism. The black peat was soft in places and bore the imprints of Jenny's sandals. It was as though she were still with me. I could sense her warmth, like the smell of summer. Nothing else mattered.

380

The light was fading by the time Stone and I reached the observation point behind the wall.

We both had binoculars and it was still possible to make out the shape of the dead fox on the opposite slope. I had half expected the eagles to have dismembered it and taken it up to the nest, but it looked untouched.

"See?" I said.

"Aye." There was a disturbing satisfaction in his voice. I glanced at him. He wasn't looking at the fox, but at the nest.

I lifted my glasses and focused on the female eagle. The magnified image seemed to dance and jump, and I was suddenly conscious of the evening chill. So that's why she hadn't bothered with the vixen's carcass, I realised. The male had brought her a more succulent kill. She was tearing at the body of a lamb. Its wool was white in the gathering gloom.

THE EAGLET WAS five weeks old at half term, and beginning to fledge. The cellophanelike tissue protecting the dark feathers had shredded away and the quills had started to push through the down. Blood still circulated through them and they were soft and tender. The young bird had a mottled and faintly comical appearance. Although it was now nearly half the size of the parent birds, its beak and claws were still too large for its body. It remained vociferous in its hunger, and aggressive when feeding. It was going through what Matron described as an "awkward age" when she referred to some of the ruder and less attractive senior boys. It lacked both the grace of a grown eagle, and the downy charm of a chick.

"I'm going to ring it this afternoon. Should be able to tell if it's a boy or a girl," Porgy said. "Care to watch?"

"Wish I could, but I've got Jenny and Ken Wade coming to lunch—you know, the deputy head. He's going to show me how to fish, afterwards."

I'd joined Porgy for a brew-up in the hide. It was Monday morning, and the boys had gone away for a week after Speech Day.

"You know that Peter Stone applied to the Nature Conservancy Council for a licence to kill the eagles?" Porgy said suddenly.

"No, I'd no idea." I was shocked.

"Don't worry. It's been turned down flat. He was notified at the end of last week."

"But I told him the lamb had probably died of natural causes anyway. Not that he believed me," I added.

"No, I don't suppose he did. He's also lost some sheep over a cliff—claims the eagles panicked them over the edge. We'll have to keep an eye on him."

"What do you think he might do this time? The parent birds are spending most of their time off the nest now, so there's no point in his playing his old game again."

"He could try anything. I'm thinking of doing a recce tomorrow to see if he's laid any poison or traps."

"I'll give you a hand. I'll try and rope Jenny in as well. She'll be off duty."

"That would be great. Thanks, Robin."

We talked shop for a while, remarking on how the female had made a complete recovery from her scrap with the fox, and was now strong enough to hunt. Then I asked him about Bess and the baby. He was a chip off the old block, Porgy told me proudly—growing fatter by the minute. Bess was staying with her parents in Birmingham for a week, but Porgy phoned her every night.

I returned to Southwater shortly after and found Ken's Morris Minor already parked in the drive. He and Jenny were down by the lake. There were two fly rods on the lawn, and a landing net.

"Not a bad day for it," Ken observed, casting an expert eye at the sky. It was overcast, but the cloud was high and threatened no rain.

"Aren't we going to have lunch first?" Jenny asked. "I could eat a horse."

"You need building up," said Ken. "Don't you think so, Robin?"

"Hadn't really noticed." I avoided looking at Jenny.

Ours was a vegetable love. We let it grow slowly and privately. We were like children sharing a newly discovered secret, and we were in no hurry to announce it. Ken could wait.

I told them over lunch about Porgy's plan to carry out a sweep of the immediate area on the following day, and explained that we didn't trust Stone not to lay poisoned bait or traps. Jenny was happy to join in, but Ken had to cry off because of his leg.

"It's a pity you're saddled with a neighbour like that," Ken said. He lit his pipe while Jenny and I stacked the dishes into the machine.

"Actually, I feel quite sorry for him in a way," I said. "But let's not spoil the day by talking about Stone. Come on, Ken, turn me into a Compleat Angler."

I stood on the jetty and practised casting, and realised why I'd found Ken such a good teacher when I was a boy at Skelmere. It was his patience, mainly. He didn't mind when I tangled the line into a bird's nest or cracked off one of his precious flies, or hooked the grass on the lawn behind me.

I went solo after half an hour or so, and tried my luck off the little bridge which crossed the beck where it fed the lake. With beginner's luck, I was into a fish on only my third cast. The surface swirled as it took the fly and I struck automatically. The line tightened, the rod bent, and I yelled for help. Ken limped over with the landing net.

The reel sang as the fish zigzagged away. The line cut through the water like a cheesewire. Ken talked me through it.

"Keep your rod up. Let her run. Mind those reeds. Reel her in when she's tired."

It was exciting while it lasted, but he soon had it netted for me. It was a small brown trout, little more than half a pound in weight. Ken knocked it deftly on the head and laid it down on the bridge. Just right for my supper, he observed. Its colours quickly faded and a thin film of dust settled on its eyes.

I wished that we hadn't killed it then, and Ken was disappointed not to have converted me into a fellow fanatic. He tried to persuade Jenny to have a go, but she said she'd rather watch.

"Poor Ken," she said, as we sat on the garden bench under the beech tree. "He probably thinks we're the most terrible wet blankets."

"He's got over it already. Look at him. Happy as Larry."

Ken was wearing waders, and stood thigh-deep in the water. He was casting with enviable ease, the long line snaking slowly behind him. He'd already landed a four-pound char, and he seemed to be in a world of his own.

"I'm glad that it isn't your scene, either," Jenny said.

"Oh, I can see the thrill," I admitted. "But we should have thrown it back. It was those dead eyes that got me." I ran my fingers down her bare arm. I could feel the small hairs rising.

"Don't," she whispered.

"You mean—stop it, I like it?" I grinned.

"That's exactly what I mean." Then she diverted my attention. "Where's your fish, by the way?"

"On the bridge."

"No, it's not."

Sally was making a meal of it not twenty yards away. We both burst out laughing. I couldn't have eaten it myself.

STORM CLOUDS DARKENED the dale. There was a roll of thunder overhead, followed by a flash of sheet lightning. The crags were thrown into startling relief. Rain drummed against the hide. The flimsy structure rocked in the wind.

We put our heads together to agree on a plan of campaign. Jenny was to cover Southwater dale, while Porgy and I would sweep the valleys on either side. We'd rendezvous at his shelter on the plateau at one. I'd lent Jenny a spare pair of yellow oilskin trousers which I kept for sailing. They were much too big for her. She wore a blue anorak with a peaked hood on top, and looked like Donald Duck.

We split up. I skirted the foot of the north ridge by the lake, and made my way up the next valley, climbing gradually towards the plateau. The rain was blinding, and the visibility poor. I passed the tree line at fifteen hundred feet, and was soon enveloped by swirling cloud. It was like climbing through a wet sponge.

I stopped for a smoke. The cigarette was sodden within seconds, and I tossed it away.

It landed beside the body of a rabbit.

I slowly registered the fact that I had never seen rabbits this high before—there were warrens down by the lake, but not on the crags. I picked up the sodden carcass. It had been shot through the head.

More significantly, the stomach had been slit open and the entrails left half protruding from its pale belly. It was a clean cut, the work of a sharp knife and not the talon or tooth of a predator. There was no sign of decomposition, and the rabbit's body couldn't have lain there long. I popped it into a plastic bag.

Reaching the plateau, I followed an old stone wall to Porgy's shelter. Jenny was there already, looking understandably cold and wretched. Porgy soon joined us. They had both drawn blanks, but my own find was ample evidence of Stone's work.

"Probably *alpha chloralose*," Porgy reckoned, examining the rabbit. "It's a common rodenticide. Or it may be strychnine, but that's not so easy to get hold of. I'll send it for analysis to the Newcastle office."

"We've got him this time," I said. "All we've got to do is confront him with the evidence and threaten prosecution unless he removes any other little delicacies he may have left lying around."

"He'll still try and wriggle out of it," said Jenny. "Probably claim he was trying to poison the foxes."

"That's illegal, too, except in Scotland," Porgy pointed out. "But you're right, Jenny—he's a slippery customer, and I'm not sure we'll frighten him off with a vague threat of prosecution. We'll have to bring some extra pressure to bear if we're going to stop him."

"Like what?"

We mulled over the problem as we made a sodden and dispirited return to Southwater. It was chilly in the house and I lit a fire. Jenny changed into one of my old sweaters and a pair of jeans which were also much too big for her, and sat on the sofa looking swamped. Her boots and socks were in front of the fire, steaming.

"Well?" Porgy asked. "Any ideas?"

"Perhaps." A possible solution had been forming in my mind. "Look, I bought Southwater off a bloke called Sir Graham Banner. Never met him—I dealt mainly with his local agent, but he is also Peter Stone's landlord. He might be the one to apply the pressure."

"Toe the line or get out?" Jenny said.

"That sort of thing. I'll bet you Stone would play ball if his tenancy was put on the line. It's his livelihood. His home."

"It sounds a bit extreme. Do you think Banner would agree?" Porgy asked. "What's he like?"

"I've no idea," I said honestly. "But I can give it a whirl."

THE TWIN-ENGINED PIPER trundled over the grass strip gathering speed, and rose slowly into the air. We banked over Penrith. The North Yorkshire moors stretched to the east, and there was a panoramic view of the Lake District to the west. It was a perfect morning, the sky a brilliant blue.

"You wouldn't have enjoyed this trip yesterday," Mike told me over the engine noise. "The turbulence was terrible."

Mike was an AA buddy who'd flown for BEA, until the booze got the better of him. Now he operated a one-man charter business from a private field near Penrith. He just about made ends meet, and was happier than he'd ever been.

We landed at Denham in under two hours. I agreed to meet Mike back there at five, took a taxi into town, and treated myself to a lobster lunch at Wheeler's before presenting myself at Banner's Piccadilly offices. He didn't keep me waiting, and I was shown straight in.

Banner couldn't have been more than thirty. His office was imposing, severely modern in design, but his easy confidence and casual clothes lent it an informal atmosphere.

"I'm delighted to meet you, Mr. Woodford. Do sit down. How are you enjoying Southwater?"

"Couldn't be happier there. I've done quite a bit to it."

"I expect you had to. My father kept it for the occasional holiday, you know. Lovely spot, but he never got round to installing central heating."

There was a percolator on his desk and he stopped to pour us both some coffee. "Now, what can I do for you? My secretary told me that it was urgent—something to do with the eagles."

"So you know about them?" I was surprised.

"Oh, yes. The RSPB needed my permission to put up their hide. I was obviously very happy to give it. So, what's the problem?"

I told him about Stone's vendetta, and that if he wasn't stopped, the chance of establishing the first breeding colony of golden eagles in England for two hundred years would be destroyed.

"So you want me to lean on him," Banner said thoughtfully.

"Yes." I was nervous.

"OK," he said suddenly. "According to my agent, the man's a lousy farmer anyway—sheep wandering, walls in disrepair. I could probably evict him just for that. But if he's actually flouting the law on my land by trying to kill the eagles, then I certainly don't mind threatening to terminate his tenancy. On one condition."

"What's that?"

"You draft the letter. You know the situation better than I do and I've got another appointment." He looked at his watch. "Five minutes ago. So you write it and I'll sign it later. You can take it up with you tonight. Fair enough?"

"Fair enough." I was delighted.

I was shown into a small office and spent half an hour composing the letter before giving it to his secretary to type. I pulled no punches, and half expected Banner to tone it down. But he signed it without altering a word, and even lent me his chauffeur-driven Rolls for the trip back to Denham.

We were in the air again at five, and I was delivering the letter by nine that evening. Stone was out, presumably at the hotel. I dropped it gingerly through his door and heard it fall on the mat inside.

I felt just as though I were lighting a firework which might explode at any moment.

IT BLEW UP on the Saturday evening, after I'd been out in the dinghy. But it wasn't Stone who confronted me on the jetty. It was Nera.

"This is your work, isn't it?" She had Banner's letter in her hand, and she was furious. "Here—read it."

I took my time tying up and dropping the sails.

"That won't be necessary," I said at last. "I wrote it, and Sir Graham Banner signed it."

"I guessed as much from the pedantic style."

"Look—do you want to talk sensibly about this, or have you just come down here to blow your top? I suggest we take a walk. The dogs can come."

We were silent as we crossed the lawn. I let Sally out of the house, and Rat sprang from Nera's car. We wound our way past the plantation and along the western shore of the lake, following a sheep track. Nera led the way.

"Why did you do it?" she said at last, over her shoulder.

"I'd have thought that was obvious. Your father was trying to kill the eagles."

We stopped and sat down. Nera perched on the trunk of a fallen birch, and I sat on the grass. There was a large clump of bracken nearby, and I could see the fronds waving as the dogs tried to sniff out rabbits.

"I know what Peter did was stupid and wrong, and so does he," Nera declared. "He admitted it all to Porgy, and removed the rest of his poisoned bait immediately. He's learnt his lesson. He *does* listen to me, Robin."

"If he's not too tanked-up to take it in," I said wearily. "Where is he, by the way?"

"Where do you think?" Her reply was bitter. The hotel was clearly visible across the water. "Oh, I know he was bad enough before you came to Southwater. But, believe me, he's worse now. Much worse. And that letter took him over the top."

"He brought it on himself, Nera."

"My God, you're smug! But you're not just smug, Robin. You're a damned bully as well. How would you feel if someone threatened your livelihood? If *you* were faced with eviction?" I didn't reply. There was no point. I shouldn't have let it hurt me, but it did. The viciousness of her attack was sour and unpleasant. I'd thought that our relationship had died a peaceful death, but now she seemed determined to end it all over again. It was nasty and unsettling, and I wished with all my heart that she had never returned.

I stood up, tired and dispirited.

"I don't think there's much future in—"

Then several things seemed to happen at once. A rabbit bolted out of the bracken. Rat scampered after it, yelping with excitement. And the eagle swooshed over our heads so low that I ducked instinctively.

I recognised at once the dark, compact configuration of the male. He was gliding fast, wings drawn in for extra speed. He rocked to and fro as he bore down on the two animals, talons outstretched. The rabbit dived into some brambles, but Rat was several yards behind. The eagle plucked the little dog from the ground, barely checking his flight, and soared upwards. The Jack Russell screamed pitifully.

I shouted. It was too late, but the sound must have startled the eagle. He dropped the terrier. For long seconds she fell end over end, before landing with a horrible thud on a flat rock not fifty yards away.

"Oh, my God," Nera whispered. Then she started to run.

I followed more slowly, shocked by the sudden savagery of what had happened. By the time I reached her, she was cradling Rat's lifeless body in her arms. The fall would have killed Rat anyway, but she had probably been dead even before the eagle released her.

"Nera, I can't tell you how sorry—"

"Then don't!" she flared. There were tears on her cheeks. "Look what you've done, you and your eagles. You and your—your magnificent obsession."

"Give her to me. I'll see to her, if you want."

The broken body seemed to fill her with a sudden revulsion. She almost threw it at me. "Take her back. Do what you want with her." She looked around wildly. "God, how I hate this place! I'll never come back to Skelmere again. Never."

"What about your father?"

"Peter? I've done what I can for him. He's on his own now—and I hope he does kill your bloody eagles. You won't be seeing me again, Robin, but I haven't done with you yet."

"How do you mean?"

"Don't worry—you'll see." Her voice was ugly with menace as, weeping, she turned and stumbled back down the track.

I buried Rat on the slope overlooking the lake, and left a small cairn of stones to mark the spot.

I sat down when I had finished and lit a cigarette. I couldn't rid myself of the image of Nera's face, distraught with passion and anger. Her words still revolved in my mind.

What had she meant?

Seven

"Bung the pill back, could you, sir?"

A cricket ball had rolled to a halt by my feet, and I threw it back to where Barton was giving Lacy some batting practice beside the pavilion.

It was the following Saturday, and Skelmere Grange had scored a dismal fifteen runs for six wickets against the Sedbergh Yearlings. Since we had already bowled the opposition out for only twenty-nine, it looked, as Ken observed gloomily, as if we were doing our level best to snatch defeat from the jaws of victory. Lacy was next man in, a slogger more than a stylist.

Ken and I sat on deck chairs on the boundary. He groaned as another wicket fell.

"Why can't they watch the ball? That's all I ask. Keep your eye on it, Lacy, we're counting on you," Ken called out to him, and Lacy looked back nervously as he approached the crease.

He didn't believe in playing himself in. The first ball was a full toss. His wild swing connected—four runs through mid wicket. There was a smattering of applause, and a high-pitched chatter of excitement from the boys in the pavilion

My attention wandered. It was a sleepy, bee-buzzing afternoon, and the longest day of the year. It was also Jenny's birthday. I was taking her out to dinner that evening, and I'd booked a table at the Keswick Hotel.

"A visitor for you, Robin," said Beryl Dean. Beryl was the school secretary, a helpful woman in her late twenties. There was a stranger beside her, tall and angular with thinning hair. He carried a briefcase.

I stood up and we shook hands.

"I must apologise if I've arrived at a very inconvenient moment, Mr. Woodford," he said with a Scottish burr. "My name's McLeod. I'm the editor of the *Herald*."

"Oh?" It was something to do with Nera. I felt cold and apprehensive.

"Could I tear you away for a wee while? Grand shot, lad!" he applauded. Lacy had swiped the ball high over square leg's head. Another boundary. "Three to win. Your boys have got it in the bag, Mr. Woodford."

"It looks like it. Shall we—shall we take a stroll?"

We started skirting the boundary.

"Look, is this about some article that Nera Stone has written? About the eagles?" I said.

"Aye, it is that." He stopped. "You look worried, Mr. Woodford."

"It's just that I'd rather you didn't print it."

"Oh? And why might that be?"

"Because the fewer people know about the eagles, the better their chances of breeding successfully."

"Is that all?" He gave me a quizzical look.

"No. There's more to it than that. You see, Nera thought I'd been victimising her father. I don't know how much she's told you, but Peter Stone farms the dale where the eagles are nesting. He's tried to kill them. Claims that they're taking his lambs. And we—that is, the RSPB warden and myself—well, we've tried to stop him. I got Stone's landlord to threaten him with eviction unless he left them alone. I'm not particularly proud of the fact, but it seemed like the only way."

"Go on."

"Nera and I had a blazing row about it last weekend, and to make matters worse, one of the eagles killed her pet dog. It wasn't pleasant."

"I can imagine."

"So it seems fair to assume that anything she's written might be less than complimentary—either about me or the eagles. It may be selfish, but that's another reason why I'd rather it wasn't published."

"H'mm." We resumed walking, and he went on, "You've been honest, Mr. Woodford. I knew the background of course, but I wanted to hear your side of the story as well."

There was uproar in the pavilion. Lacy had obviously hit the winning run.

"What *did* she write?" I wanted to know. "Do you have it with you, by any chance?"

"Aye."

"I don't suppose that I have a right of reply, but I'd like to see it, if I may?"

"I don't see why not," he said after a pause.

We sat on a bench, the gift of an old boy, and he produced three foolscap sheets from his briefcase. The copy was typed, double-spaced, with broad margins. It was headed *Where Eagles Dare*.

"He soars over the crags, with supreme confidence and effortless efficiency. With eyes seven times sharper than a human being's, he spots his prey. The magnificent marauder closes on his victim at nearly 100 mph. His merciless talons sink into warm fur like a cluster of stilettos. With lazy grace, he bears the body aloft and returns to his eyrie in the Lake District.

"Yes, the Lake District.

"For the first time in over two hundred years, golden eagles are breeding again in England. This secret has been as well protected as the birds.

"The *Herald* has always espoused the cause of conservation ... We stand by the law as embodied by the Protection of Birds Act, and we applaud the work of the Royal Society for the Protection of Birds ... But a clash of interests has arisen between the conservationists and the farmers. So bitter has the battle become that the *Herald* now feels bound to disclose the full story.

"It is being fought today amongst the picturesque dales surrounding Skelmere, one of the smaller and lesser-known lakes in Cumberland. It is here, under these cruel crags, that the local hill farmers eke out a meagre living from their small flocks of Herdwick sheep. They are good, hardy folk, and slow to anger. But now they are up in arms.

"For the eagles are taking their lambs and threatening their very livelihood. At least one dog has been killed as well—and a shepherd without his collie is like a conductor without his baton. One such farmer, who dared to express his opposition to the eagles, instantly found the big battalions of the Establishment mustered against him: prosecution may be pending, and his landlord has threatened him with eviction.

"We accept that the RSPB must do its duty, but it has entered into an unholy alliance with the eagle's chief champion. 35-year-old Robin Woodford is a wealthy newcomer to the Lake District and teaches in an exclusive preparatory school nearby.

"But there is more to Mr. Woodford than meets the eye. He is a self-confessed alcoholic. He has served a sentence in jail for manslaughter. He has neither educational nor ornithological qualifications. And his name is not Robin Woodford at all.

"He was born Robert Wyndham, grandson of the founder of the well-known butchers' chain. Convicted of manslaughter and drink-driving offences, he adopted his present alias to escape the ensuing scandal, and now hides in a remote area of the Lake District as an apparently respectable schoolmaster. He secured his position not by merit, but by the offer of a six-figure donation to a school already well endowed by the privileged and fee-paying few.

"We welcome the return of the English eagles, symbols of majesty and freedom. But must our long-suffering hill farmers stand idly by while their flocks are depleted?

390

"And is Robin Woodford—or Robert Wyndham, if you will—a worthy champion of the eagles' cause?"

I felt sick.

"You can't print this," I told McLeod.

"There's nothing libellous, is there? Are the facts not true?"

"Yes, but . . ." A sense of helplessness swept over me. It was wickedly one-sided and misleading, but there was no denying the accuracy of the facts as she had presented them. She may have sought to imply that a sheepdog had been killed, and that I was still a drunk, but these were just quibbles. I knew that I'd have to resign. I'd have to leave Southwater, and the eagles.

I wasn't sure that I had the strength to start a new life again. I handed him back the typescript, but he waved it away.

"Och, keep it if you like," McLeod said casually. "I'll not be running the story."

"What!"

"No, I wouldn't dream of it, Mr. Woodford. It's not up to Nera's normal standard. It lacks—what shall we say—balance? It was to have been Nera's swan song," he went on. "She'll be disappointed, of course, but there you are."

"I'm not with you."

"Do you not know that her ladyship has left the *Herald* for higher things?" He sounded caustic. "Aye, her pretty head has been hunted by the television tycoons. You'll be seeing her on your screen by the end of the year."

"Yes, I did know that that was in the air."

"Which is more than I did until last week," he said sharply. "I told her to clear her desk straight away and to hell with working out her notice. I taught that lass everything she knows, Mr. Woodford."

I sensed then that his refusal to publish the story was based less on its style and content than on Nera's unexpected resignation. He resented what he saw as her ingratitude.

"I'm most grateful to you," I said. "And thank you for coming. You've certainly set my mind at rest. Now I'm afraid you'll have to excuse me, but I'm supposed to be on duty."

"My pleasure. Aye, well, I'll leave you then, to your young elite." We shook hands perfunctorily. "I'll find my own way."

He turned and walked towards the school, straight across the empty cricket square. Ken would have had a fit.

I wandered down to the lake, dizzy with relief that Nera's story had been stopped. I took the sheets out of my pocket.

Kneeling down, I set fire to them on the shore. The ashes floated out over the water and settled on the surface like grey feathers.

"It's me again, Robin," said Beryl Dean from behind me. "I didn't want to disturb you when you had a visitor, but that RSPB warden phoned. Could you ring him back? He's at your house."

"Of course. Thanks, Beryl."

I hurried back to the school, to the common room. What had happened? Surely it couldn't be Stone again? I dropped my pennies into the coin box and dialled.

"Apparently Elizabeth left a message with Peter Stone. The baby's ill and she wants me down there straight away." I could hear the concern in his voice.

"I'm sorry, George. Anything I can do?"

"I was hoping you could cover for me this evening, when you get back?"

"Only till about eight, I'm afraid. Jenny and I are going out to dinner— it's her birthday."

"That'll do fine—it'll be pretty quiet by then anyway. Look, must go. And thanks, Robin."

I looked at my watch. It was six. By the time we got home, after Jenny had packed the boys off and changed, it would be nearer seven. We'd only be able to keep an eye on the dale through the telescope for about an hour, but perhaps that was better than nothing.

"VERY NASTY," was Jenny's comment about Nera's article. She preferred not to talk about her, and went on, "Poor Porgy and Bess. I do hope the baby's all right." She opened the French windows looking out on the lawn and stepped onto the terrace. I followed her.

"Probably some common-or-garden complaint."

We were both concerned, but I didn't want to let it spoil our evening. Jenny was wearing her Laura Ashley dress. I remembered the simple design, with its white cuffs and collar. She'd worn it—years ago, it seemed—at one of the headmaster's stuffy staff dinner parties. I told her that it was my favourite.

"Just as well," she said. "It's the only long one I've got. Aren't we going to look frightful lemons at the Keswick in evening dress?"

"They can put it down to midsummer madness. Anyway, it's your birthday. Talking of which," I added, "I've got something for you. I'll call you when you can come and have a look."

I slipped back through the house, out through the front door to the cobbled yard. There was a new MG Midget in the garage; Mrs. Blenkinsop had signed for its delivery that morning. The hood was back, and the green paintwork was shiny. I didn't start the engine, but pushed it out onto the drive in front of the porch and gave Jenny a call.

It took her some time to realise that it was hers. "This *is* midsummer madness," she whispered, and touched the leather-covered steering wheel tentatively. "How am I going to explain having a new car? Everyone knows that I haven't got two brass farthings to rub together."

"You could always say it was an engagement present." I hadn't planned it like this, but it seemed as good a time as any. "We can choose a ring next week."

Jenny didn't reply for a moment. "You do know what you're saying, don't you?"

"I'm asking you to marry me. Don't tell me you're surprised."

"No," she smiled, "but it's nice to be asked."

"Then how about saying yes?"

"Yes. Oh, yes!"

She kissed me, and we forgot about the car for a bit.

The grandfather clock in the hall struck seven thirty. We'd be late if I didn't go and get changed myself. I left her admiring the car.

Upstairs, I swept the dale quickly through the telescope. It was all quiet. I could see the male eaglet on the nest—Porgy had sexed him when he had ringed the youngster. There was no sign of the parent birds, but I knew that the female would return before dark.

I took a shower, and took my double-breasted dinner jacket out of the wardrobe. I took a last look at the dale before going down. The sun had sunk behind the plateau, but visibility remained good. I tracked the telescope slowly across the plateau's skyline and down the north ridge, and froze.

There was a man on a grassy ledge opposite the nest. I could only make out his body, in blue dungarees. He was pressed against the trunk of a small rowan tree, his head and shoulders partially concealed by foliage. I wouldn't have seen him at all had my eye not been caught by a slight movement: his hand reaching down to draw a hip-flask from his back pocket.

I knew it was Stone even before I increased the magnification to sixty. His face sprang into focus through the leaves. And it was then that I saw his rifle. A branch provided the perfect rest for a .22.

I guessed his strategy. He was waiting for the female to return, as she always did before dark. He'd take her first, and then the eaglet at his leisure. The male wouldn't stay around without his mate. The English eagles would simply disappear.

I knew, too, why he hadn't opted for an easier position, behind the wall above him. The ledge was at a level with the eyrie. He would have a clear shot, without any branches to deflect his bullet. The range was no more than two hundred yards. His telescopic sight would be zeroed in and it would be easier than potting plaster ducks at the fair.

I'd seen enough. I took the stairs two at a time and burst into the drawing room.

"I'm sorry, Jenny. You'd better ring the hotel and cancel."

"Why? What's up?" She looked startled.

"It's that bastard Stone. He's on the north ridge. Only this time he's got a gun."

"Perhaps ... well, perhaps he's just after a fox."

"Like hell. It's the eagles. And you can bet your boots that Bess never telephoned about the baby—Stone just wanted to get Porgy out of the way. I'm going after him."

"Don't be a fool, Robin! He's armed." She put out a hand, but I brushed past her. "Stop, for God's sake!"

But I was slamming out of the front door by then and only half heard her. It was a race. I had to reach Stone before the female returned. Sprinting past the farm, I found myself willing her to stay away.

I scrambled up the foot of the north ridge. The route was longer than the direct approach up the dale, but the going would be easier and faster. Though the gradient was for the most part gradual, my patent leather shoes were designed for dancing, not climbing. The soles were slippery, and several times my feet slid from under me. There was an element of farce: here I was playing cowboys and Indians on the fells in full evening rig.

I had to stop. There was silence save for the sound of my gasping. The crags were beginning to blacken into silhouettes. Soon it would be too dark to shoot, and I prayed again that the female would keep her distance until nightfall, but it was a vain hope.

I'd drawn to within a few hundred yards of Stone's position when I saw her. No more than a speck at first, she took shape as she flew closer. She wheeled over the dale and I noticed that she was carrying a crow.

She must have seen me running up along the wall, but even in my unfamiliar clothes, she seemed to have recognised me. For the first and only time, I bitterly regretted her trust and acceptance of my presence. I was going to be too late. She dropped towards the nest, spreading her wings at the last moment to brake the speed of her descent. And settled.

"Don't do it, Stone!"

I vaulted over the stone wall and kept running. I saw him emerge from under the rowan, and the eagle rose in alarm. I'd made it.

I stopped at last, panting, on top of the shale scree which rose behind him. My legs were like rubber.

From fifty feet below, Stone looked up at me. The rifle, held low, was pointing at my chest.

"You!" he spat out. "Why can't you leave me alone? You've already driven my daughter away—isn't that enough? You and your damned eagles! But you can't fly, can you?"

I knew then that Stone was going to shoot me.

I was an easy target against the skyline. He hardly had to aim. It was too late to regret jumping over the wall. Too late even to throw myself aside. I don't remember hearing the shot, but I saw the muzzle flash and felt a numbing blow above my right elbow. I spun round, and fell.

There was no pain, only shock.

Picking myself up, I saw him work the bolt. I had to reach him before he reloaded. I leapt down the scree in long bounds, and, hardly breaking my stride, launched myself at him.

I slammed him against the trunk of the slender tree and the rifle flew from his hand. He reached for my throat, his calloused thumbs squeezing my windpipe. With my right arm useless, I forced his head back with the heel of my left hand. I was conscious as we grappled of the stale smell of his working clothes, and the whisky on his breath.

He fought with a demonic strength. Exhausted by my race up the ridge, and with one arm crippled, I knew I was no match for him. I was choking, gurgling. Hooking an ankle round my legs, he threw me to one side. I landed on my right arm, paralysed by pain.

He kicked me. I saw the boot coming, but I couldn't move. It caught me in the lower ribs, and seemed to lift me bodily into the air. I rolled helplessly down the sloping ledge to within a foot or so of the edge.

The rifle lay nearby, but Stone pounced on it first. Winded, I rose to my knees as he seized it by the barrel and swung it like a club. I ducked instinctively. He missed. The momentum of his swing took him over the edge, and he fell, screaming.

The rifle clattered on the rocks a fraction of a second before I heard the thump of his body landing. Kneeling, I peered over the edge. He lay spread-eagled on his back at the foot of the cliff. The drop must have been nearly a hundred feet. It didn't need a closer inspection to tell that he was dead.

It hurt to breathe. My throat felt raw, my rib cage tender. But the pain and discomfort were nothing as I realised I was bleeding to death. The bullet had torn through my arm, severing the brachial artery. I could feel the blood pumping out against my sleeve and running from my cuff in a steady flow.

Desperately I dredged my memory for what little I knew of first aid. Pressure on the wound—that was it. I pulled off my jacket, oblivious to the agony as the sticky sleeve pulled away from the torn flesh. Folding the coat into a rough bundle, I pressed it between my arm and body.

I couldn't tell how much I had staunched the flow. I needed a tourniquet as well. Loosening my bow tie, I looped it round my upper arm and knotted it, using my teeth and my left hand. I pulled a stout twig from the rowan. Inserting it into the loop, I twisted it tight. Then I opened the front of my shirt and used it as a makeshift sling. It was the best that I could do.

With my left hand holding the tourniquet in place, and pressing my right arm against my body, I set off down the ridge.

I was nearly a mile from home, and I wasn't going to make it. My arm didn't really hurt, just throbbed. But I knew that each throb meant the loss of more blood.

My feet seemed to know the way. My mind wandered, and I imagined that Jenny was climbing up the foot of the ridge towards me. She vanished and reappeared. Then she seemed quite close, her face pale in the twilight.

"Oh, my God," she said.

My legs gave way and I sat down. She had spoken. It must be real.

"Stone's dead," I mumbled. "Shot me. Bleeding a bit."

"I saw it happen. I was watching through the telescope. But I didn't know . . ." She trailed off. She was looking at my shirt. The whole of the right side and the sleeve were red. Then she was helping me to my feet, pleading with me. "Come on, Robin! You can't stay here."

"Tired. Can't go any further."

"It's not far. You'll be all right. Come *on*, Robin!"

I remember little of our stumbling descent and our return to Southwater. I more or less collapsed in the stone-flagged hall, and that was as far as I got. I lay there with my head propped up on the bottom step of the stairs. I felt sleepy. Sally licked my face.

Jenny rushed into the kitchen for the first aid box. She removed the tourniquet, took the sodden jacket from under my arm and cut off my shirt. She didn't clean the wound up, but bound a pressure pad tightly against it with a bandage. Covering me with a blanket, she said I'd do.

Then she telephoned for an ambulance. And the police.

"What are we going to tell them?" I asked. "They'll think I pushed him. Why can't we just say we found him lying there?"

"And how do you plan to explain being shot?" she reminded me gently. "No, Robin. I saw what happened. We'll tell the truth."

I was too weak to argue. Anyway, she was right. I'd spent enough time lying already. Hidden too many bottles. Deceived even myself about myself. And my present life? My mind meandered, confused. Was that a lie as well?

No. I was Robin Woodford now. That was the truth, and that was what we would tell them.

THE YOUNG EAGLE left the nest in the middle of July, a week before the end of term. For days he had experimented with the rising currents, testing the breeze with his wings extended, hopping a foot or so into the air, and hanging on the wind before dropping clumsily back onto the nest.

Late that afternoon, the female swept tantalisingly to and fro in front of the eyrie with a freshly killed rabbit in her claws. The young eagle's hunger cries took on a deeper, more demanding note. She ignored them, and settling on a boulder far below she started tearing at the carcass with her beak.

This was too much. Launching himself from the untidy platform of twigs and branches, he sailed unsteadily down, wings wavering, and crash-landed on the grass beside her. Proud but pigeon-toed, he strutted forward to receive his share.

The young eagle was still there at nightfall, but he had flown by the following morning. I saw all three of them later that day, soaring on the rising thermals over the crags. The young one was scarcely smaller than his parents, but was easily identified by the pale markings under his wings and tail.

They wheeled ever higher and higher, with easy grace. In perfect freedom. Soon they were no more than dark dots against the summer sky, dwindling into the distance.

Epilogue

Our oldest—Simon, after his uncle—leaves Skelmere Grange at the end of next term, and Helen will join him at Sedbergh in two years' time. Both schools have now followed the trend of co-education, and I like to think of the two children staying more or less together. They're very fond of one another.

Skelmere is much the same, though there have been quite a few staff changes, of course. Sadly, Ken died shortly after he retired—he didn't have much to live for without his "chaps"—while Jeremy Ightam moved on to the headship of a large and expensive prep school in Sussex. I'm considered one of the old guard now

Jenny carried on working at Skelmere for nearly three years after we were married, and only stopped when Simon was on the way. She's thirty-eight now, though she doesn't look it. I may be nudging the half-century, but the difference in our ages has never seemed to matter.

Simon senior often comes to stay, a friendly ghost from the past, and last year, Jenny encouraged me to invite Angela for a holiday at Southwater. She has Maria's good looks, and has grown into an attractive seventeen-year-old. The visit wasn't a roaring success, but I was able to acknowledge our relationship and talk about her mother without opening any painful wounds.

We never heard from Nera, not even after her father's death. There was hardly any publicity. The coroner recorded a verdict of accidental death and that was that. Nera didn't attend the inquest. I think that with her new career, she simply wanted to put the whole episode behind her. She's on the national network now, with her own semiserious chat show, and she remains as beautiful as ever. But I can view her with detachment; it all happened so long ago.

A succession of new RSPB wardens has followed the departure of Porgy and Bess, and the new Wildlife and Countryside Act has tightened up the protective procedures. Porgy has been given a staff job with the society, and his ever-expanding bulk is squeezed behind a desk at their southern HQ. Bess has taken up motherhood in earnest—there were four children at the last count. Nothing, of course, was wrong with their first baby, and Porgy prefers to forget how he was duped by Stone. We still keep in touch.

I've almost forgotten how it was to crave alcohol, but I still go to AA. There are new faces, though we are the same people. We take the same comfort in sharing our experience, strength and hope. It helps me to remember the slavery of addiction, and to thank God for my freedom.

And the eagles? The talismans of my freedom? They still nest in Southwater dale, though it's a different pair now. There are three eyries on the south ridge, and they seem to use them in rotation. They have managed to rear a young one most years and their privacy is usually respected.

People say that there is now a second pair nesting in the western crags of the Lake District, but I don't suppose that there will ever be a real colony of English eagles: there's too much disturbance, too much people-pressure.

I've grown used to them now, but I don't think I'll ever take their presence for granted. We're lucky to have any at all.

NIGEL SLATER

Nigel Slater's lifelong interest in birds and animals was only part of the inspiration behind his writing of *The English Eagles*. The other half stemmed from his own personal experience of alcoholism, and it is perhaps this that gives the novel its particularly poignant character. The author knows only too well the difficulties of overcoming an addiction which one can never fully escape.

The story of *The English Eagles* is based on fact. It was indeed in 1970, after an interval of over two hundred years, that a breeding pair of eagles first succeeded in rearing chicks south of the Scottish border. Every year since then, at least one pair has nested and bred in Cumbria, under the watchful eye of the RSPB, and this year in May the most recent chick was born. The location of the nest is, Slater says, an "open secret" in that it is widely known among ornithologists, but kept under wraps from the general public so that these rare and beautiful birds will not suffer disturbance from too many visitors.

Born in 1944, Slater was educated at Wellington College and Cambridge. Later he was posted to the Foreign Office in Rome, and he then worked in the printing industry for several years before embarking on his present career as a fund-raising consultant for many different charities. He currently lives in Towcester with his wife and two young children.

The English Eagles is Nigel Slater's fifth novel. A previous one, *The Mad Death*, a story of a rabies epidemic in Britain, was adapted by the BBC into a successful television serial. Now Slater is researching a new novel about the "golden triangle" of drug dealers in the Far East. Like *The English Eagles* it will be concerned with addiction and the dreadful damage it can do to people's lives.

TRESPASS

A CONDENSATION OF THE BOOK BY

PHILLIP FINCH

ILLUSTRATED BY KEN LAAGER

"If you want to find out about someone, one day among the mountains is worth a year any place else."

Such is the conviction of Jonas Poague, head of his own successful computer firm, who has decided to put three of his employees to the test by taking them on an adventure holiday: Paul Travis, handsome and apparently self-assured, has a practised eye for the ladies; George Hollenbeck is a cheerful glutton, appalled at the prospect of a fortnight deprived of creature comforts; and Raymond Furlow is a self-confessed under-achiever who takes refuge behind a wry sense of humour.

The situation is clear to all of them: whoever performs best in the coming test of stamina and courage is likely to be Poague's successor . . .

PART I
DEPARTURES
CHAPTER ONE

For almost eight months the notebook lay in a kitchen drawer, in among some screwdrivers and pliers, rubber bands, a leaking tube of Super Glue and several Christmas tree bulbs of questionable integrity. Inglorious repose for so potent a talisman.

It is a spiral-bound pad, roughly three inches by five, about a hundred pages thick. Fifty-nine cents at any drugstore. In pencilled block letters on the front cover: GROUP JOURNAL. I don't know who wrote the words. Charles, maybe. Or Hollenbeck. It is exactly the dutiful, compulsive sort of gesture that Hollenbeck would have performed.

The first time I saw the notebook its covers were fresh and unmarked, the pages blank. There were nine of us then, most of us strangers to the others. We had met a couple of hours earlier, at the airport in Billings, Montana. Now we were near Red Lodge, in a meadow that was a front lawn to the fortress of the mountains. We were slightly bewildered, dazzled by the uncompromised colour and light and air. Gary Currey walked up and handed the notebook to me, and said, "On these trips we keep an informal log—everybody takes turns. After it's all over, we photocopy it in Billings—everybody gets one. Makes a nice keepsake."

I made the first entry and passed it on, and it came round to me again. At the end it was in the back pocket of my woollen trousers, and I found it several weeks later, when I was unpacking. No way could I open it then. Touching it was all I could manage, and then only long enough to take it into the kitchen. I shoved it quickly into the drawer and interred it with the junk.

Yesterday afternoon I went rummaging for a few loose nails, and it was there. I looked down at it, the wire spirals squashed, the cover turning up at the corners, edges water-stained. I thought of where it had been, what had happened around it.

I lifted it out of the drawer with the respect due to such a relic. Outside, there was plenty of commotion and warm sunlight. This was important. Fifty years from now I will still need warmth and light and life around me before I open the journal.

On my front porch is an old swing. I took the notebook there. Around me kids kicked a soccer ball in the street, and dogs yapped. The noise and the movement, the profusion of life, gave me courage to open the book. I went to the last entry, in what I knew was my own hand, though distorted by fear and fatigue.

Day Ten: Monday, September 15

We didn't come into these mountains expecting death. Blistered feet, yes, and aching backs. We expected to hurt, no more. But here we are. One dead. At least one more close to dying. Amend that. We are all close.

We don't seem shocked at what has happened. These are the mountains, and we have learned fast that here you are always close to something awful or magnificent. On the brink in every way. There is no place like a mountain for getting down to essentials, for handing you the consequences of your own mistakes.

It is so cold. Outside, the wind bucks and whines. Can't dwell on how high the snow must be, how deep we will stand in it tomorrow. If we can stand at all. Can't think of the endless miles, the tall rock walls. Makes us seem too inconsequential.

Instead I think of places where at this moment people are standing on sidewalks. Eating dinner. Sleeping beneath clean sheets. People who have no idea of cold, dark hell in the mountains and four dying humans pressing together, balled up like baby mice in a nest.

We are so cold.

We are so scared.

We are so alone.

Forgive the histrionics. Maybe a hero faces his demise with equanimity. We were just ordinary souls in deep trouble, unaccustomed to having death so near, quailing in its presence.

There were Hollenbeck and Travis and I, and Poague, and Charles and Donnie, and Eleanor, and Gary and Andrea. Somewhere among us was the truth of what happened in the mountains. I, Ray, am trying hard to get at it. I was there for much of it, so I can say what I saw, what I felt.

404

But that's just my truth, after all. I've talked to the others who are left, heard what they have to say. That's their truth, or what they choose to reveal of it. Some of it died with the dead, and I must deduce from their acts what they thought and felt. In the end, we're left with speculation.

This much I know. In the mountains there was only one truth. It allowed no doubt. Mountain truth sliced clean to the heart, and if I were a braver man I would go up there again for another chance to see the world and people the way they really are.

I SAY THAT WE WERE ORDINARY. But then I remember Paul Travis. He wasn't run-of-the-mill. He had been hand-crafted, a one-of-a-kind item.

Obviously, Travis had started with rare raw material: killer good looks so extravagant he had to be a freakish mutation. He had straight sandy hair, a slab of a stomach, wide, strong shoulders, with back and legs in proportion.

Travis must have grown up believing he was special. He must have remained convinced of it despite all life's attempts to kick him in the shins. Which life does to everybody—takes its cuts, tries to whittle you down. Any one of a thousand possible stumbles could have turned Travis ordinary, but he had avoided them all.

Travis transformed life into a collection of stylised set pieces: Travis the athlete, eyes intent with competition, a drop of sweat poised picturesquely in the cleft of his jaw; Travis the professional, sleeves of his fine-striped shirt neatly rolled up, gesturing to make a point to his colleagues; Travis the adventurer, looping the loop in his Pitts biplane, in a coppery evening sky; Travis the lover, slow-dancing in the darkness with a woman wearing pearls and a black sheath; Travis, charmed and charming. Confident and sure. Convincing.

FIRST, HOLLENBECK AND I were pals. We were in the same office, working for a company called Modern Data Concepts, in Bethesda, Maryland, a suburb of Washington DC. Which is to say that we were working for Jonas Poague. Then Travis joined the firm, and for some reason sought out Hollenbeck and me. He was impossible to resist. I became his friend, but we rarely tested the friendship with needs or demands. He seemed to want little from me beyond affable companionship. From him I expected nothing except the thrill of the exotic.

MDC designs computer systems. Travis, Hollenbeck and I were systems analysts, a job far less impressive than it sounds. We did not engineer computers or write programs. We knew as much about computer hardware as the average car salesman knows about cars—how to write a bill of sale, and how to stack the options. That is what we did, on a slightly elevated level. Computer systems analysts are like interior decorators. They make decisions for people with more money than sense. Most of the job is talk and persuasion.

There were twelve systems analysts at MDC. We occupied identical cubicles, a hundred and thirty square feet each, formed by partitions about five feet high. One morning in late June, Poague's secretary came out of the front-office suite, down the aisle outside our cubicles, and paused at Travis's, Hollenbeck's and mine. At each she left a typed memo: "My office. 11:50 today", signed JP. Clipped to the memo was a fold-out brochure. It was the first time I had ever heard of the Beartooth Mountains.

SPIRITREK WILDERNESS ENTERPRISES
Montana Mountaineering Adventure

GENERAL INFORMATION

SpiriTrek Adventures are a unique form of outdoor education, intended primarily for the novice. They are designed to promote leadership, confidence and self-reliance.

SpiriTrek Adventures aren't easy! Rather, they safely provide a distilled challenge that is frequently missing from modern daily life, a challenge that is as much mental and psychological as it is physical. A SpiriTrek Adventure may be among the most memorable events of your entire life.

COURSE SPECIFICS

SpiriTrek's Montana Mountaineering Adventure consists of a fourteen-day backpacking expedition through the Beartooth Primitive Area in the south central part of the state, near Yellowstone National Park. The terrain varies from pine forests at elevations around six thousand feet to a high plateau well above timberline, at an altitude of more than ten thousand feet.

This is a mobile course, with a different bivouac site each night. Knowledgeable counsellors will teach such necessary skills as wilderness navigation, campcraft and basic survival techniques. Activities will include a full day of rock-climbing on one of the sheer granite faces common in the area, as well as an attempted ascent of one of the numerous massive peaks that reach above twelve thousand feet. Total distance covered is ninety to one hundred miles.

WHAT YOU NEED

SpiriTrek will furnish all mountaineering equipment and food. Clients are expected to provide clothing. Severe weather is commonplace and clients must prepare to dress for all seasons. A full list of required clothing has been compiled by experts, and must be followed closely. A well-fitting pair of mountain boots is essential. They should be broken in before departure.

Perhaps the most important commodities on any SpiriTrek wilderness experience are perseverance and a sense of teamwork. The members of your group will be your constant companions for two weeks. A satisfying conclusion to the trip depends on your willingness to work with others and to extend yourself to your limits—which will expand every day.

Required clothing and equipment to be supplied by client:

1 pair mountain boots
2 pairs heavy wool socks
2 pairs inner socks or sock liners
1 heavy wool sweater
1 wool shirt jacket or synthetic-pile jacket
1 set of polypropylene thermal underwear
1 pair heavy wool gloves
1 wool hat
1 cotton turtleneck shirt
1 pair heavy wool pants
1 pocketknife
1 small torch
sunscreen, lip balm
toilet articles, personal items

Poague had a thing about the wilderness. During my five years with the company he had gone trekking in the Himalayas, rafting through Canyonlands National Park in Utah, backpacking along the Brooks Range in Alaska, cross-country skiing in Yosemite. A year earlier he had taken this SpiriTrek trip. Apparently he was going again, and he was asking the three of us to join him. Not once did I think it was a casual invitation. Nor did Travis or Hollenbeck, I'm sure. Everything Poague did was heavily freighted with significance for us.

You should know that most of us who worked for him feared Jonas Poague. He was a difficult boss, who fired people suddenly, and rarely for apparent reason. This alone would not have been so frightening. But Poague paid us generously, better than most of us deserved. Inevitably, we grew to need those inflated pay cheques, or thought we did, and we feared Poague the way a junkie fears his pusher. I was certain that he understood what a hold over us his largesse afforded him.

He was in his late sixties, lean and ascetic. His stern face—and grey hair, rimless glasses, taut skin—rebuked waste and excess. He daily wore a navy blazer, charcoal slacks, white shirt and bow tie. Tall and erect, he stalked the corridors at MDC, peering over shoulders, walking into conversations, intercepting memos. He was full of pointed questions that verged on rudeness.

The only clock in the office was a time code generated by the company's central computer. Each terminal in the place showed the time of day at a keystroke. I kept the display on the screen all that June morning, and at 11:49:30 I rose from my chair and put on my jacket.

Hollenbeck was already making his way up the aisle. Some fat men are said to move with an inborn dignity and grace. But not Hollenbeck. He walked as if slogging through ankle-deep mud.

A few seconds later Travis left his cubicle. We met in front of the walnut double doors that separated Poague from his hirelings, and his secretary showed us through to his office.

A topographic map was spread across his desk, and Poague stood over it. I had never seen a topo before. This one showed no towns or roads, only blue pools and green blotches on a field of white. There were elevation figures, names of mountains and lakes, and an indecipherable tangle of thin lines patterned like the combs and waves and whorls of a fingerprint.

"Gentlemen, the Beartooth Mountains," he said, without glancing up. "A truly magnificent place. As you may know, I was there last summer on an expedition. It was a most fulfilling fourteen days. I am returning in September, and I want you to join me."

We murmured yes, of course, be honoured, but Poague wasn't listening; he knew what our answer must be. He hadn't even asked a question.

"If you want to find out about someone," he said, looking up at us, "one day among the mountains is worth a year any place else."

His look passed over Travis, lingered for a moment on me, then settled on Hollenbeck.

"Prepare yourselves—mentally and physically," he said. "You will be challenged and exhausted in any event. But much benefit will be lost if the activities of each day drain you totally."

His eyes dropped, and he began speaking to the map again, about tests of character and the inner man. Finally I caught a drop in his voice, and I knew we were about to be dismissed.

"All expenses will be the company's," he said. "Buy what you need of clothing. It should be the best. Then submit the bills."

We filed out without a word. It was starting already, this business of deciphering what Poague had said, reading portents in it, each of us wondering what it might mean to himself individually. But the question of what the trip might mean never came up among the three of us. The implications were too large.

For a few days I tried not to think about it. Then I heard a rumour that in the fall Poague was going to create a director of systems analysis, promoting from within. It was a job that Poague had always held. Systems analysis was MDC's main service. The manager of that department—our department—would instantly become the second most powerful figure in the firm. And Poague was nearly seventy.

This was bombshell stuff. We were no cretins, Travis and Hollenbeck and I. We concluded immediately that Poague was taking us to Montana so he could choose his new director from among us. It made sense, if you knew the man. It was how he did things.

MY FATHER WOULD HAVE BEEN appalled to learn that it had come to this: that my prospects for even modest standing among men of substance finally had been reduced to piquing the whimsy of a Jonas Poague.

We are the Furlows of Prince George County, Virginia. The family home is a former plantation house that overlooks a rose garden and the James River. Old men in short sleeves still tip their hats from storefronts when my mother or my aunts pass by. For decades we have subscribed for the two front pews in a red brick Episcopal church with white pillars. At the age of six I was trundled off to a military boarding school in Greenville, South Carolina, where I lived for the greater part of the next twelve years.

The summer of the trip to Montana I turned thirty-eight. With bonuses my salary that year was sixty-three thousand. I have been married and divorced once. I own a house and a mortgage, and drive a leased Thunderbird. My tangible assets include an Individual Retirement Account worth about thirteen thousand dollars, and a hundred shares each of Coca-Cola, General Motors and Xerox. My father, a cardiac surgeon with practices in Richmond and Washington, would have scorned all this. Not because it was insufficient in itself, but because it was insufficient for his only son.

Whether I ever could have pleased him is a moot question, in that I seldom met even my own goals, far more modest.

At the military academy I was a lacklustre scholar, soldier and citizen. So paltry were my attainments that I ought to have been barred from the University of Virginia, a destination to which I had been ordained from birth. But the gravity of three generations of Furlow forebears, all graduates, pulled me through the thicket of the admissions board and into a premed curriculum.

I skated through the first three years. Fourth year, the ice broke under me. I left with a degree, and a set of marks too poor for even the most indulgent medical school.

To my father it was a disgrace beyond redemption. He stopped hoping, but he did not stop being disappointed. I could chant a litany of minor personal scandals, small humiliations, bad jobs badly done. My father heard the list for fifteen years; I always brought my defeats home with me. I was the bird dog of champion stock who bolts from pheasants to chase mice and chipmunks, returning finally to lay bits of vermin at the boots of its master.

Gentleman that he was, my father took his hurts quietly. I wish I knew why I bludgeoned him with the truth in this way. A perverse urge to lay waste his hopes, perhaps—my defence of last resort against his demands. Three years ago, at the age of sixty, he died. The morning we buried him I went to the church feeling some undefined expectancy. At the cemetery, my sense of anticipation was so strong that I can remember little but waiting, as if lightning had rent the sky and I were holding my breath until the thunderclap.

It was a drenched October day. Rain dripped off the canvas awning. The minister said his words, two of the undertaker's men lowered the casket down into the hole, and it was over. I kept an arm round my mother as we walked out to the limousine. We got in, and it carried us through the cemetery, through the gates, into the highway outside. I realised what I had been waiting for, and knew that it was never going to happen. Realised that nothing was changed, nothing would change. He was still in me, and he was going to be in me for ever.

THIS SPRING I bought a copy of the topo map that Poague had spread before him that day in his office. Took it home and studied its swirling contour lines. Tried to identify the eminences that had awed and punished us. And thought, Dear God, the suffering—that ought to be here somewhere.

MDC HAD A CORPORATE membership at a health and racquet club three blocks from the office. Piggybacking on the corporate account cost us half a normal membership, so Hollenbeck and Travis and I all joined. At least once a week we played cutthroat racquetball, a vicious game. There are three players competing against one another, and only one winner; thus, cooperation is fleeting and tenuous. About the only strategy is to hit the ball to the weaker opponent as often as possible. Good players can pick their spots, so vulnerabilities get exposed and exploited quickly.

Travis usually won our games. He was good enough to pick on the weaker player, but so much more skilled than both Hollenbeck and I that it didn't matter. Between the two of us I was better than Hollenbeck. I got to more shots because I was quicker and more willing to skin my knees. But in cutthroat racquetball, as in much else, there is very little point in second place.

LIFE IS TOUGH on fat boys. No, I take that back. Life doesn't care one way or the other. We, the people, are tough on fat boys. It starts when they're barely old enough to walk, never quite as steady as the rest of us at that age. By the time we're in kindergarten we have all learned that the fat kid can be pushed off his feet, that if we steal his candy or crayons, we can forever stay a few steps ahead of his waddling pursuit.

And it shouldn't be true, but usually is, that the fat boy is the one whose eyes are most likely to well up under provocation. That's all we need to see—tears on chubby, trembling cheeks. That's blood in the water for us circling sharks.

I've never seen the family album, but I would bet a bundle that George Hollenbeck was born a fat boy, grew up that way, and never changed. He was five feet eight, and that June he was at least forty pounds overweight. I had seen him heavier.

That summer I figured I would make some advance payments on the inevitable debt of physical misery that would come due in Montana. I tried to plod four miles a day on the indoor jogging track, twenty laps to the mile. In the infield of the track was an array of exercise machines, and often as I tramped round the banked turns Hollenbeck would be there, wrecking himself on the stationary bicycle or a rowing machine.

He was worried about the trip. Worried about making himself look like a fool, about feeling Poague's scorn, about being slower and weaker than anyone else. The worries made him work hard, but they didn't make him stop eating. I don't think he lost an ounce before September.

Two weeks before we left I went to dinner at his house. We did this about once a month. Hollenbeck and his wife, Anne Marie, fed me, and I hired a movie for their video machine.

Anne Marie brought out pizza and beer, and we ate in their furnished basement while we watched the movie. I passed on the third slice of pizza and the second bottle of beer. Hollenbeck had four of each. I watched him and realised that he was hardly aware of the movie. He nestled happily in an overstuffed chair. His eyes ceased darting, and his shoulders dropped to rest. The tension that he carried through the day sloughed off him as he bit through the stringy cheese and chewed, and licked the sauce off his upper lip. He was a genuinely joyful glutton.

After the movie we talked about the Redskins for a while. Anne Marie sat a few feet from Hollenbeck, bent over a square of bargello needlework. She was a small, pretty woman, with black hair that she wore cut close. Whenever Hollenbeck was present, she seemed maternally alert, warily monitoring what happened around her husband.

Hollenbeck said he had something to show me. He left the room and returned with a large canvas duffle bag. He opened it on the floor in front of us. It was full of new clothing, gear for the trip. He urged me to take it out and look at it. I dutifully fingered the fabric and examined the labels.

"What do you think, Ray?" he said.

"I think we've been spending Poague's money in the same overpriced outdoors store."

"Look at these." He held out a huge pair of hiking boots, slick and dark and tacky to the touch.

"It's snow wax," he said, after I had rubbed my fingers over them. "The guy at the store said it was good to waterproof them. You melt the wax and then smear it on. I've put on five or six coats."

The boots must have weighed nearly five pounds each, the leather as hard and unyielding as iron. I told him they were heavier than the ones I had bought. "You think they're too heavy?" He sounded anxious. "They cost a hundred and ninety. Poague said to buy the best."

"I'm sure they're fine."

"Have you been wearing yours to break them in?"

"When I remember. They're not bad."

"I've been wearing mine every day. I go out for a walk, eight or ten blocks at least." He looked at Anne Marie, as if he needed her to approve or affirm this statement. "They are kind of heavy. I got blisters at first, but I stayed with it."

I imagined Hollenbeck, his hands sticky with wax, clumping along on suburban asphalt in these fantastic gunboats.

"I'm a little concerned about the hiking," he said. He leaned towards me and spoke confidentially. "You know, the altitude, these mountains. It sounds rough. I'm not as fit as I should be."

"You'll be all right, George."

"Tell me the truth. Do you think I'm badly out of shape?"

I shrugged.

"I've been working out—you've seen me." It was a plea. "I try to get my heart rate into the target zone at least three times a week."

He was a gentle soul. But something about him grated on me now. His earnestness, the suggestion that he would be able to hustle up any mountain if only I would sanction his regimen.

"George, I know for a fact that you haven't had your heart in the target zone at any time during this decade. In two weeks you're going to be hauling yourself and seventy pounds of pack over some of the ruggedest country in North America. You're pretty sure you're not ready for it, and you want me to tell you it's going to be OK. I can't do that."

"You really think it'll be hard?"

"Sure, I think it'll be hard. I think our lungs will burn and our legs will feel like rubber. I think we'll regret every milk shake, every Big Mac we ever let slide past our tonsils. I think it'll be the worst two weeks of our lives. If we last that long."

412

Anne Marie had stopped her stitching and skewered me with a look. Hollenbeck sat heavily back in his chair. His face was drained. He looked stricken.

"A seventy-pound pack," he said.

The poor guy was such an easy mark. "Actually, I don't know for certain that they weigh seventy pounds. That's the whole point, George. I don't know any more about this than you do."

"Tell me the truth," he said. "Could you carry a seventy-pound pack? If you had to?"

"I have no idea. But I figure I'll be able to carry any pack they give me. This expedition thing is like basic training camp—it's supposed to look hard, but it's not designed to make people fail. What would be the point?"

"I was never in boot camp."

"Neither was I. What I'm trying to say is, they won't ask us to do anything we can't do. If they give us seventy-pound packs, it'll be because we can carry seventy-pound packs."

He was unconvinced. His movements were slow, reluctant, as he replaced the clothes and boots in the bag and took it away. I was alone with Anne Marie as she hunched over her work. The fingers of her right hand made severe jabbing and pulling motions with the needle.

"You could have been more kind," she said, with disgust.

As for me, I am five feet nine, with legs that are slightly stubby for the rest of me. My weight fluctuates within the limits that insurance companies deem healthy, so I am certifiably fit. But even though I met the standards of the insurers, I had by the age of thirty-five developed dimples on my buttocks and thighs, puckered goo that wouldn't go away for all the games of racquetball and turns round the track.

You may think I dwell unnecessarily, excessively, on the physical. It is not my usual focus. But as the trip got closer I found myself checking out the flab, skin tone and muscle mass of others. Envying Travis the striations of his calves and abdomen, feeling anger when I looked at Hollenbeck's corpulence.

Total distance covered is ninety to one hundred miles. Even Travis must have paused with some concern when he read that. So I was worried, too. Only I didn't let my worries bleed through, the way Hollenbeck did.

CHAPTER TWO

Charles and Donnie, Eleanor, Andrea and Gary. This is their story too, and by now you should have met them. You should know something of who they were and what they brought with them to Montana. When I saw them first, in Billings, they were ciphers to me, but soon I realised that Poague was right: a few days in the mountains will teach you a lot about somebody.

I keep returning to the last morning we were strangers, the hours before our lives became for ever altered. Some of what I learned they described to me. Some I got from clues as subtle as a gesture, but no less true for that. Some I heard under circumstances so solemn that any talk was testament. This is as true, as real, as I can make it. I see no percentage in falsehood.

EDDIE WILLIS WOKE suddenly and knew he had done wrong. The clock beside the bed said six thirty-five. He jumped up, pulled on his trousers, and went into the front room. His son, Charles, sat on the couch, dressed in his travelling clothes, his bony hands resting on his knees. On the floor beside his feet was a three-suiter valise.

"G'morning, Papa." Charles was sixteen years old, built painfully slight for his age. His clothes hung loose on him, gave him the appearance of a thin-limbed brown marionette.

"How much longer was you going to let me sleep, boy?"

"Till about a quarter of."

Charles's flight was at eight. The trip to the airport in Raleigh, North Carolina, would take about forty minutes.

"Cutting it kind of close, weren't you?"

"No, sir. You get ready right fast when you have to."

Eddie walked over to him and gripped his shoulders.

"Can you carry that suitcase?"

"Yes, sir, I better. I'm going to have to carry what's in it for the next two weeks."

"Then haul it out to the pick-up while I find my clothes. We have to get our butts on the road."

ELEANOR FARRIS SHUT the door on a big white house on piles, beside a canal on an island called Duck Key, about halfway along the crescent of the Florida Keys. She had spent nearly four months there alone. This was the last day of the longest summer she had ever known.

She turned her car up Route 1, with the ocean brightening on her right, the Gulf still dark to her left. The mainland was more than sixty miles away. She accelerated up the empty road. She had plenty of reason to be far from Duck Key before the sun got high.

HIS PARENTS WERE BOTH out of town the night before Donnie Lang left. Mother gave motivational talks to woman entrepreneurs, and that night she was in Arizona, motivating. Dad was a partner in an ad agency in

San Francisco. He pitched accounts better than anyone else in the agency, and that night he stayed on in Seattle after a full day of pitching. That meant Donnie and the Guatemalan maid were alone in the house above Tiburon. It was across the bay from San Francisco, high up on a high brown hill. The maid went to bed around ten that night. A few minutes later Donnie went down to the garage that was attached to the kitchen.

His sixteenth birthday present had been a Kawasaki motorcycle, a Ninja 900, a lithe, rippling panther of a bike that tried to shed him every time he twisted the throttle grip. The motor for the garage-door opener was loud, and might wake the maid, so Donnie lifted and pulled the bike up the steps into the kitchen. Then he pushed it across the floor, out onto the patio, and down the path to the street. He let it roll down the street in neutral, with the engine still dead. When he was a block from the house, ` he jumped onto the bike and ripped away down the hill.

He met his friend Trey at the north end of the Golden Gate. They rode to Sausalito, Donnie cruising beside Trey's Suzuki. Spotting a black Porsche in the municipal parking lot by the harbour, Trey insisted that it was a 930 and Donnie tried to tell him it was just a 911 with an accessory air dam and whale-tail spoiler. Donnie knew his Porsches; he had been driving a 944 Turbo in Santa Cruz when the police pulled him over. The 944 belonged to a Samuel Skinner in San Francisco. Donnie had never met the guy, but had definitely admired the automobile when he saw it parked with the keys still in it.

Donnie had been accepted into a diversion programme—no trial, no permanent record—on condition that he enroll in a wilderness leadership course. So he was going to Montana.

At around five a.m. Donnie rode home, put the bike away, got into the shower. He had to be at the airport by seven. Leaving because some judge thought two weeks of playing Eagle Scout would stop him from wanting to drive other people's Porsches.

A cab took him away while the maid still slept.

TWO CLIMBERS, AT OPPOSITE ENDS of a slim rope, on the face of a granite stub near Red Lodge. From across the valley the rock appeared sheer and seamless, the climbers clinging to it the way dust clings to a windowpane.

Andrea Simms was at the low end of the rope, and her face was about two inches from the granite. Her feet had found horizontal ripples in the rock, wide enough to catch with an edge of each boot. She had jammed one hand into a vertical crack. The other groped above her head. The rock was nearly eighty feet high.

"Left. Higher. There." A man's voice from the other end of the rope.

415

Gary Currey. Today, her climbing partner. He had suggested a morning climb before they drove to Billings. During the next two weeks they would lead the last SpiriTrek Montana Mountaineering Adventure of the season.

Her free left hand found a knob of stone. She tightened her fingers round it, pulled herself up, and joined him on a ledge. From here she could see the town, down-valley about six miles.

"We better shake it," he said. "Got to pick up the jerks."

"They're clients."

"They'll always be jerks to me."

The night before, in Red Lodge, after his fifth beer, Gary had told her how he felt about them. All summer he had herded them through the Beartooths, had seen their jiggling flab, heard their complaining. To him they had no more business in these mountains than a jellyfish had. Jerks, now and for ever.

Andrea knew that in Tuolumne Meadows, Yosemite, Gary's kind grew like fungus on the underside of a log. Lean and muscled, cocky, perpetually unemployed. The alpine equivalent of a surf bum. She guessed he was under twenty-five, which would make her at least six years older. She was afraid to ask.

The past winter she had guided canoe trips in the Everglades for SpiriTrek. This was her first trek in Montana. Gary had guided the trip three times this summer, and had been designated senior instructor. For two weeks he was her boss.

"You coming?" he asked now, as he began to climb again. Feet and hands moved, finding holds in combinations Andrea could never have imagined. In a few seconds he had both hands on the edge and was lifting himself over the grass at the top.

ON THE THURSDAY before we left, we had decided to drive together to the airport. Hollenbeck would pick up Travis, then me. He was supposed to be at my place by eight on Saturday. Eight fifteen came, and he still wasn't there, and I let myself wonder if he could really have been that hurt and angry.

We had had an argument the night before our departure. It involved the three of us, mainly me and Hollenbeck. Angry words, hasty judgments. Mainly my doing.

Two minutes later his Volvo wagon pulled up. He came out to open the back hatch so that I could put my bag in.

I said, "Good morning, George." Trying to sound casual.

He said good morning without looking at me.

I sat alone in the back seat. Travis was in front reading the *Post*. Hollenbeck got in and snapped his seat belt.

"Listen, you guys," I said. "I'm sorry. I was wrong."

"No big deal," Travis said over his shoulder.

Hollenbeck sat gripping the wheel with both hands, and looked out past the windscreen.

"George? I'm sorry."

"For what? Nothing happened."

"Come on, George. I'm trying to apologise."

"Don't say anything." Now he had turned to me; I couldn't remember ever seeing such intensity in him. His voice quavered and a deep flush rose from his cheeks to his temples. "Nothing happened. You have nothing to apologise for."

"Fine," I said. "I'm just trying to do the decent thing."

"I have more to worry about than that. So don't say any more."

And I didn't. None of us did. We drove in silence.

WE HAD A FLIGHT to Chicago, a stopover there, another flight direct to Billings. On both we occupied a full row of first class. Poague had a window seat and I was beside him, and then Travis and Hollenbeck across the aisle. This had been arranged before we got to the airport. I wondered—still do—whether Poague had asked to have me beside him. But he seemed indifferent to me during much of the trip, not unfriendly, but absorbed. When the 737 began a slow descent he came alive, peering through the window at the land that passed beneath the wing. He touched my forearm and pointed down. "The Little Bighorn River," he said. "Imagine." The plane banked over Billings, and a few minutes later we had stopped at the terminal. While we stood up and reached for jackets and bags, Poague sat still, seemingly unaware of all externals. Never had I seen him this way, without rigidity or raspy edge.

I recall a moment in Chicago, when we were waiting for the flight to Billings. In the office the old man was always called Mr. Poague to his face. That morning Hollenbeck spoke to him, addressing him as he always had. Poague corrected him at once.

On this trip, he told us, we would be expected to use first names among ourselves and with the rest of the group. It was a way of breaking down barriers. SpiriTrek insisted on it, and he thought it was a good idea.

"For the next two weeks I am not your boss," he said. "We are all equal. What is behind us is immaterial. Up there you create yourself, and nothing else counts."

CHARLES AND ELEANOR had arrived a few minutes earlier on a Denver connection, and they were standing with Gary to meet us. So when we came through the Jetway door, there were seven of us, shaking hands and making introductions.

These days I inveigh against the tyranny of first impressions. But I can try a few from that moment.

Gary intimidated. All athletic bone and sinew, carved calves, ridged forearms. As we spoke he rolled his shoulders and arched his back, while his biceps flexed and jumped. It seemed an unconscious display of arrogant beauty, and I told myself that if I had such a body, I would preen too.

Eleanor. Early thirties. Reticent eyes that flashed on me and then retreated, as if she feared lingering. A major-league tan and dancer's legs, long and trim and straight.

Charles was tucked behind her, easy to miss. As frail a child as I have seen, puberty alarmingly delayed. He could have been a scrawny twelve-year-old. And so grave. I am not a soft touch, but I wanted to embrace that kid and protect him.

Gary said there was one more client, a boy named Donald, who was on a flight from San Francisco and Salt Lake City that would arrive in half an hour. Andrea, the second instructor, was waiting for him.

We claimed our luggage and went to the men's room to change. I had never seen Poague wearing anything but business clothes. His must have been fitted to deceive; nothing had prepared me for the pipestem limbs and sunken stomach I saw as he put on his hiking clothes. He nearly caught me staring.

Travis finished dressing first, seeming to hurry. I didn't realise why until I walked out and found him beside Eleanor in the lobby. He was talking to her as if no other sight deserved his attention. She seemed flattered; I would have been.

Travis was telling her about his stunt plane, the weekend he flew at an airshow in Altoona. Her left hand was out of sight, tucked behind a flight bag at her side. I watched and waited, and finally the hand came up to sweep some hair behind her ear. Ring finger, below the last joint: a band of pink skin interrupting the wash of brown.

We waited. After a while Andrea appeared, introduced herself. She was about five feet tall, her physique almost as formidable as Gary's, though with an overlay of a woman's soft contours.

Behind her was Donald Lang, dragging a leather portmanteau. A dirty white dinner jacket draped from his shoulders. Baggy black trousers brushed the floor. Red canvas sneakers, a gold wire ring in his left ear, haircut a fusion of punkish spike and waxed flattop.

"I'm Donnie," he said.

We were nine.

Gary went to the parking lot while we lugged our bags out to the front sidewalk of the terminal. He came round in a van pulling a small covered trailer where we put the luggage. It all seemed random to me, the

418

standing around, hoisting of luggage, loading into the van. But when it came my turn to get in, and I looked round for Eleanor, she was already inside, Travis was beside her. Travis had contrived. He wasn't smarter than I was, only surer about what he wanted and how to get it.

Out of Billings we took an interstate highway southwest. Andrea turned round in the front seat and said there were some topics she wanted to cover. Before she could go further, Hollenbeck spoke.

"I was wondering about the name of these mountains where we're going," he said. "Are there bears in the Beartooths?"

"You bet there're bears. Black bears and grizzly bears. The mountains were named by men who thought they resembled the teeth of a bear. If you were trying to see a bear, this would be the best time. They forage heavily in September, fattening up before hibernation. You'd eat plenty too if you knew breakfast was six months away. They've got an excuse for being tubby." Andrea glanced at Hollenbeck and for the first time seemed to realise his size; she looked flustered, and I decided I liked her. She said, "They have great scenting ability, probably better than a dog. So we take precautions. That brings up ground rules.

"Below timberline we bear-bag all our food, put it in a sack, and hang it between two trees, high enough that a bear can't reach it. The best way to see a bear is to leave food around. For the same reason, we don't allow deodorant—it seems to attract them. Soap is out too. It pollutes the streams and lakes. SpiriTrek practises what's known as low-impact camping. The idea is that after we've left a campsite, somebody could come along and never know that we've been there. It doesn't always work, but we try. So, no soap. The water's too cold for bathing, anyway. After two or three days we all smell. You get used to it.

"The main thing you have to learn is that we're not nine individuals. We do things as a group. Every night after dinner we get together for a talk. If you've got a complaint, you don't like the way somebody combs his hair, that's the time to say it. Food always seems to be a problem. Whatever food we take up there belongs to everybody, no hoarding. We all eat out of the same pot.

"There are jobs that need to be done every day. Meals have to be cooked, and pots and dishes have to be cleaned. Every day, breakfast and dinner. For lunch we grab snacks on the trail. Gary and I are not porters; we're not cooks. We'll do our share, but no more. You come up with some kind of system—we don't care what, as long as the work gets done. Same goes with the shelters. No tents. We use plastic tarpaulins. Gary and I have one. There are two others. You set them up, you take them down. Sleeping arrangements are whatever you want—except for one thing. You four company guys spread yourselves out. We don't need to take any cliques up there.

"You will all be issued personal gear, besides what you've got with you now. And then there's group equipment. The tarps, the stove, climbing rope, a first-aid kit, pots for cooking. Most of all, food. It all goes with us. Between you, you have to get it parcelled out. We'll work on that tomorrow. Now, what else?"

Beside her, Gary said, "The water."

"Oh, yeah. You city people have probably been waiting all your life to drink some of that icy cold mountain water. But you can't. There's this bug, a parasite called *giardia*, which is deposited in streams by humans and other vile creatures who relieve themselves too close to the water supply. And I'll tell you, this thing will torture your intestinal tract. I had a friend who got run over by a truck when she was riding her bicycle. She got better. In six months she's on a hiking trip, she drinks the water, picks up some *giardia*, and she's in hospital again. She stayed nine days when she was hit by the truck. She was in for two whole weeks with the *giardia*. The bug hit her harder than the truck did.

"So you can't drink the water straight. We'll give you little bottles of iodine, and medicine droppers. You put three drops of iodine in every quart bottle of water, and then you wait half an hour before you drink it. We know it tastes awful, but use the iodine. You get sick up there, you'll be in real sorry shape."

"Evacuations," Gary said.

"I was about to get to that. Nobody will fly a helicopter into the Beartooths any more. The canyons are too narrow, the winds are crazy—it's just too dangerous. If anybody can't walk here, they have to be carried. I was carried on a rope litter once, for about a mile, and it was agony. And that was just practice; I was healthy at the time. I honestly think I'd rather die than get hauled ten miles with a compound fracture. So, don't get hurt. Simple. I'm not trying to scare you. Not much, anyway. Enough to get you to take this seriously. I want you to realise that up there we're on our own. You have to take care of yourself.

"That's all the rules. The rest is up to you. I've seen groups go out on a trip and be miserable for two weeks. Others have a great time. It's always hard work and problems. Question is, whether you let them beat you."

WHILE THE VAN ROLLED Andrea handed out what appeared to be nylon straps, flat ribbons of synthetic fabric about an inch wide and twenty feet long. She called it webbing, and we each got a length. We would use it climbing, she said. She wanted to show us a couple of knots.

"A bowline," she said. "Your basic, all-purpose knot for securing something to the end of a rope, among other uses. Anyone who has sailed will know this one. When we climb, you'll use it to tie yourself on the belaying rope."

420

We watched her do it a couple of times, and then tried it ourselves. I fumbled with it, thinking that in a few days I would be standing at the bottom of some very steep place, getting ready to climb, and there would be a rope dangling from above, and this is what I would do with it to keep myself from falling.

Travis, naturally, had done some sailing. I could see him with Eleanor, touching her hands—oh, so casually—to guide her.

Andrea looked at his bowline and said it was OK, could be neater, but that's usually the way it is the first time you try it with webbing. I wanted to thump her on the back.

At the edge of my vision I caught movement, quick and purposeful. Charles. His bony fingers swiftly tugged at the webbing, tying the knot and upsetting it and tying it again.

"Look at this one," I said to her. Charles looked up, startled.

Andrea reached for the knot. "You tied this off," she said.

"I thought you were supposed to." There was a thick drag in the boy's words, pine-woods Carolina. "I used a half hitch. Is that right?"

"Yes. The second one I wanted to show you is a water knot. Can you do that?"

"Yes, ma'am. A water knot is easy."

He took the webbing from her, worked his fingers over the fabric for a moment, and the bowline dissolved. Then he found the two free ends, bent and twisted them faster than I could follow, and when he pulled with both hands, he had another knot.

"You've been practising," she said.

"A little."

"You must have done some climbing."

"Oh no, ma'am."

"Then how did you learn?"

We were all looking at him. He slid back, fleeing to the corner of the van. Small fists clutched the webbing. His eyes panned slowly away from her face, across our eyes.

"Books," he said. "It's all in books."

THE MOUNTAINS FIRST APPEARED when we were about forty minutes out of Billings, grey-and-white wrinkles on the horizon. They grew, and we could see ragged tops. Seven miles south of Red Lodge, we turned up a dirt road. About a mile later the dirt road ended at a meadow, cut through the middle by a stream and fringed by pines. Two great half domes of granite embraced the meadow, and the mountains were visible in the split between them.

The van stopped at the meadow's edge, and Gary said, "We camp here tonight, move out first thing in the morning."

We got out and meandered in the dazed way you would imagine wandering through an oasis. The afternoon light had a clean sharpness that I had never before seen, and the air was purer than any I had ever breathed. It was how light and air should be.

Charles was beside me, oblivious of everything but the mountains. His face was fastened on them as if by some tropism, the seeking way a flower will turn towards the sun.

"Hey, blood, you figured out which way we're going?" Donnie had come up from behind us.

Charles pointed west to the citadel of peaks. "Right up there."

Donnie drew even with him and looked where he was pointing. "No. Come off it. Up there?"

"Look around. Cliffs over here, over here, behind us. We're not climbing those. We're not going back to town. This is the only way we can go."

Donnie turned round completely.

"You're right. Oh, man. I am in deep trouble now."

I heard Andrea tell Hollenbeck that here we were above six thousand feet, that the mountains ahead of us were over twelve thousand, and that they were about fifteen miles away. Montana miles, she said; you'll see the difference. I could almost hear Hollenbeck thinking that even a Bethesda mile was bad enough.

I looked at the mountains. From here I could see how broad and wide and massive they were, see how their bases spread over miles, a huge footprint of outthrusting buttresses, lambent in the afternoon sun, magical.

This is the last about beautiful mountains. I don't have it in me; once we began to climb, I became mired in detail and lost all sense of majesty. My memory of mountains now is the sandy texture of a boulder that scraped the skin off my palm when I stumbled and fell, or frigid water swirling round my ankles as I forded a stream. A tiger too is beautiful, but you wouldn't want to meet one on the wrong side of a zoo moat, where the reality of the animal is reduced to its fetid breath and the soulless objectivity of its eyes. The deeper we got into the Beartooths, the less we saw of their sweep, and the less beautiful they became.

LATER THAT AFTERNOON Gary left with the van and trailer. When he came back he had a passenger, and the van was full of food and equipment. The man with him was named Emmett Frye. He was a packer from outside Red Lodge, Gary said. We would see him again in a week, and we'd be glad of it—he was going to pack in our supplies for the second half of the trip.

We unloaded the van, and put the food and equipment into separate

422

piles under one tarp. Intimidating mounds—there was so much of it, and so few of us. In the trailer there was more—individual gear. We lined up to take our shares. First, backpacks. Then sleeping-bags; ponchos; climbing helmets; foam sleeping pads; rain pants; nylon gaiters, to keep pebbles out of our boots.

"Put it all in the packs," Gary said, and we did.

"Now pack everything from the suitcases that you're supposed to have," and we did. By this time my pack was nearly full, and we still hadn't touched the big piles under the tarp.

Finally Gary passed out large manila envelopes and pencils. "Write your name on the front," he said. "Now put in your valuables and wallets." At first no one moved.

He said, "Listen, jewellery just gets lost. There's no place up there to spend money, and bears don't ask for identification. Watches too. I keep one; that's all we need."

These things, the wallet especially and what the wallet carries, are as much a part of our existence as shoes. And I believe that was the point: we would shuck off what we were, or believed ourselves to be, and find out what lay beneath. I was queasy as I emptied my pockets into the envelope. The others seemed just as reluctant. I sealed the flap and passed the envelope to Gary, and felt shorn.

"OK then. Emmett's putting the suitcases and valuables into locked storage in Red Lodge. Get your luggage. Everything but what you're taking in the packs."

I put my suitcase into the trailer, and stood aside for the others to do the same. When it was full, the trailer contained all our links with what we knew, what defined us.

Frye got into the van, turned it round, and headed it down the dirt road. I watched it disappear, and knew that for the next two weeks we truly, unquestionably, belonged to the Beartooths.

FOR LIVID SUNSETS you can't beat our grimy eastern seaboard, where haze and smoke wring colour from fading light, and there are no annoying natural obstacles like twelve-thousand-foot peaks to hide the display. In the western high country the sun just slides behind a crest and takes its warmth with it, and you are in cold shadow. Most mountain evenings, even in summer, you can immediately see your breath's condensation.

That evening in the meadow it happened around seven, just before dinner. We scurried to our packs, pulled out sweaters and hats and mittens. I don't remember being totally warm again for the next two weeks.

Dinner was tuna and noodles. We sat on fallen logs, eating from flat,

423

wire-handled aluminium dishes that Andrea called Sierra cups. They are of a size to cradle in the hand, and we did that often during the trip, stripping off a glove so we could feel the food's heat radiating through the metal.

We had decided to rotate chores. Gary had given me the notebook, and on the inside back cover I listed the names in turn, and the dates we were due to cook or wash dishes. I drew cleaning duty after dinner. Poague said he would show me how to clean without soap or powder, and in the gathering darkness we knelt beside the stream, scrubbing with icy water and a steel-wool pad.

The old man saw them first. I caught him looking, followed the path of his gaze, and saw Travis and Eleanor. They were standing together about forty yards away, near the stream.

"He does like the ladies," Poague said, watching them.

"And the ladies like him," I said.

He nodded slowly. "I suppose you have to move fast if you want to beat him to a woman."

"Even in my dreams I don't move that fast."

He hacked a harsh, dry laugh.

"Is he your friend?" Poague said. When I didn't speak for a couple of seconds, he said, "It's a bad sign if you can't answer that one right away."

I still didn't speak. He dipped a pot into the stream, stood, and tossed the water in a sweeping arc across the meadow.

"I'm cold," he said. "Grab the cups and spoons."

I gathered them up; he stood looking at me.

"I'm glad you're here, Raymond," he said. "It will be difficult. Every time I do one of these, I tell myself it's the last. I get so tired. But I always come back. Staying away is harder than whatever we have to do here. Do you understand?"

"I think I do."

"You will. And you won't be sorry you came. That I guarantee."

A pregnant promise. He didn't let it hang there between us, but turned and began to walk. I followed him.

SLEEPING ARRANGEMENTS. Gary and Andrea found room beside the food and equipment under one tarp. Travis and Hollenbeck and Eleanor under a second shelter. That left the third for me and Poague and the two boys. We rolled out our sleeping-bags on a plastic ground sheet. Above us the tarp was stretched taut, the corners tied with line to tree trunks and stubs of rock that protruded from the ground. Poague slid his bag so that it was mostly out from under the tarp. He lay on top of the bag and stared up at the sky.

Charles was closest to Poague, and he caterpillared forward, holding his bag round him, until he was level with the old man. Then Donnie and I slid out to join them.

The sky was magnificent. In any metropolis and its suburbs you can almost count the stars that city lights do not obscure. Here we saw millions beyond reckoning, a profusion of white points wherever buttes and pines did not block the view.

I watched the sky for a few more minutes. Then I remembered the journal; I was supposed to make the first day's entry. I found the notebook, a torch, a pen, and I wrote sitting up, holding the torch between my teeth.

Day One: Saturday, September 6
We have bedded down outside Red Lodge in a meadow that epitomises the word "alpine". It looks like something from *Heidi*. The homes and lives that we left this morning seem very distant.

The mountains are inescapable. Even when they're out of sight we are aware of their presence. They look cold and very high, and we all feel some trepidation at the idea that we will be in them soon. This is not just another night, and these will not be just another two weeks.

All we have heard about the altitude is true. At six thousand feet a stroll across the meadow will get your pulse working. At twelve thousand feet . . . I hesitate to imagine. Andrea says we will acclimatise. Let's hope it happens soon.

I knew we were bound for misery. I could have guessed, tempest. If I had thought longer, I might even have seen death before us too.

PART II
CLIMBING
CHAPTER THREE

In the meadow the next morning there was a stillness before dawn when birds slept, and the night animals had bedded, and the wind was still. I was awake to hear it broken by dry pine needles snapping underfoot.

Gary Currey stuck his head under the tarp.

"Wake-up time. Everybody up."

During the night the tarp had sagged inwards, and it was rimed with frost from our breath.

Donnie croaked, "What time is it?"

"Don't worry about that—we don't need a clock. We go by the sun." He motioned to the east, where blue light edged the ridges. "And the sun says, time to roll."

When we had finished breakfast the sun was over the ridges and the meadow was brightly lit, shadows crisp. Andrea called us over to the piles of food and equipment. She had pulled away the tarp, and now we could see them fully. There were blocks of cheese, cartons of oatmeal and Granola, jars of jam, cans of tuna, boxes of crackers. And more. A week's food for nine. Beside the food were coiled ropes, the camp stove, three aluminium quart bottles of fuel for the stove. And more.

I'm not sure I can convey how daunting, how malevolent those stacks of goods looked to us. I had seen the Beartooths. I thought there was a chance that I could get myself up and down those mountains, given nothing to carry. Add a backpack and it became a less certain proposition. Throw in a share of food and equipment and it looked impossible.

"Time to do something about this," Andrea said.

"It all goes in the packs," Gary said. "Only way to do it."

We watched the piles like gawkers at the scene of a disaster.

"My pack's full already," Donnie bleated. "There's no room."

"Pack it tighter," Andrea said. "There's room."

I sensed we were being tested, that there were plenty of wrong ways to do this, and we would be allowed to make our mistakes.

"You tell us how," Hollenbeck said to Gary and Andrea.

"No. This is our trip," Poague said.

"There's no single right way," Andrea said.

For some reason I looked at Travis and saw that he had an idea to sell. He was looking at Poague, and I realised that he was trying to see how this would go over with the old man.

"Here's how we do it," Travis said. "We take turns grabbing something from the pile—something heavy the first few times. Take it to our packs, come back, grab something else. We keep doing that until it's all gone. It's the only fair way. We all agree?"

"It's not fair."

Charles Willis was almost hidden behind Hollenbeck. His voice was boyish, shrill, but it stopped Travis.

Charles moved so that the others could see him. "If we do that, it means we'll all be carrying the same weight."

"That's the idea," Travis said. "The same for everybody."

"The strong ones ought to carry more," Charles said. "I weigh about a hundred and ten. If my pack weighs forty pounds, that means I'm carrying almost forty per cent of my body weight. If somebody else weighs two hundred, then a forty-pound pack is just twenty per cent of their body weight. So it really isn't the same for everybody. See?"

There was logic to this. Why someone didn't speak up for the boy, I don't know. Unless we were all afraid that we'd be stuck with extra.

"We'll work it out," Travis said. Now he had a point to prove. He picked up a sack of instant cocoa and carried it away.

"What about freeze-dried food?" Donnie said. He hefted a block of Cheddar cheese and put it down. "This is crazy, man, carrying all this around. Freeze-dried weighs nothing."

"Not enough nourishment," Andrea said. "Also it has no taste. In a couple of days you'll be grateful for real food."

Charles walked past Donnie, pulled a large sack of brown sugar off one pile and carried it to his pack, hugging it to his chest with both arms.

YOU CAN STUFF sweaters and sleeping-bags tighter than you think. Half an hour later there was nothing left in the meadow except us and our jammed packs. We hefted them in the grass. I thought I would be able to walk with mine. For about a quarter of a mile.

Charles leaned over his bulging pack, bent at the knees, and slid his right arm through one of the shoulder straps. When he tried to get his left arm through the other strap, he reeled and nearly fell. He let the pack slide off his shoulder and drop.

Hollenbeck was trying his, walking in a small circle while he shrugged it to one side, then the other. I had already discovered that there is no magic spot where the straps don't bind and the weight becomes less burdensome. His face was red. He put the pack down and pulled out a big sack of raisins. I had seen it in the pile and figured it for at least five pounds. He carried it to where Travis was tightening the buckle of Eleanor's pack. His own was already loaded.

"Paul." Hollenbeck looked briefly at Eleanor, then back to Travis. "I need some help. I can't carry that pack."

"Come on, George. You haven't even tried. I don't like to see you give up so fast."

"Travis, please. Just this much. You said you'd help me."

Eleanor was looking at him. And he could see that others had stopped to watch. Me. Poague. Especially Poague.

I could see Travis wondering. What would Poague expect?

"Give it to me," Travis told Hollenbeck.

"Thank you," Hollenbeck said. "Thank you."

"No." It was Poague. We all turned to look.

"We had a plan," Poague said. "Now you want to change it. So let's change it the right way. Let's help the people who really need it." To Hollenbeck he said, "You can carry that."

I know that George didn't believe him. But he took the sack of raisins from Travis and took it to his pack.

"Now," Poague said. "What do we do? Do we stick with what we started with? Or do we help the weaker ones?"

Travis didn't answer at first. Then he mumbled, "It makes sense to help the people who can't carry as much."

And then he reached into Eleanor's pack and got a sack of flour, and put it into his own pack. I was standing closest to Poague, and I saw his face sour, then compose itself.

He motioned curtly to Charles. "Give me that rope."

Charles had taken one of the two braided nylon ropes, as thick as a man's thumb. Seven pounds at least. He handed it to Poague.

What I did next, I swear I didn't consider. I just did it. I took the rope out of Poague's hands.

"I can handle it," he said. The old man. His starveling's legs.

I said I could handle it too.

"OK, the jelly." A one-quart plastic container. Charles handed it over.

Then Donnie took a cooking pot out of Charles's pack.

Charles said, "Hey," and when Eleanor started to move towards the pack, he said, "That's all. That's enough."

While we all clinched and tightened our packs, Hollenbeck stood over his, testing the weight, miserably lifting it a few inches, letting it drop to

428

the ground. I walked over to him and said, "George, you'll be OK. You can do this."

"It's a little late for that, isn't it, Ray?"

Gary shouted, "Can we please get a move on?"

Two of us were ready, waiting. Poague and Charles were standing at the trailhead, among the trees at the western end of the meadow, and Poague was pointing beyond it, past the trees to where grey spires met the sky.

"Up there you create yourself," he had said, and it is true as far as it goes. But there are limits. Some baggage follows you wherever. I remember the moment, seeing Poague and Charles, Charles now standing straight under his pack. I remember because for the first time I realised that maybe not all of Jonas Poague's authority had been bought with cash.

NONE OF THIS BUSINESS with the packs happened in a vacuum. There had been the Friday before we left: the fight, for which I accept all due blame.

That afternoon we had a five-thirty court reservation at the racquet club. Poague had invited the three of us, and Anne Marie, to have dinner with him and his wife at seven. But the restaurant was close by and we had time for a full match. Travis normally didn't require more than about forty minutes to dispatch us.

At about a quarter to five Hollenbeck appeared at the entrance of my cubicle. "I'm headed over early," he said. "Got to get in at least eight miles on the Exercycle. If I'm still at it when you guys get there, start without me."

I told him I'd see him there, and he left.

The end of my working day came when I signed off the main computer. Everybody did it, an electronic version of punching a time clock. This allowed Poague to see what we were doing with our time. I called up the log program. The screen demanded, REASON FOR LOGGING OFF. I entered "1" from the menu of choices; it meant daily duties completed.

DATE AND HOUR YOU EXPECT TO LOG ON NEXT. I consulted a calendar and entered "09/22" and "08:30".

LOG OFF COMPLETE. NOW POWER DOWN TERMINAL UNIT.

I turned off the machine, got up, put on my sports coat, and walked to Travis's cubicle.

"School's out," I said. "George went over already."

"Another minute." I saw over his shoulder that he was logging off. "Just a quick call, OK?"

He was asking me to leave. So it wasn't business; otherwise he wouldn't have cared. I walked out into the aisle and strolled around for a few seconds, and then I saw that the cubicle beside his was vacant.

I would like to say that I at least grappled briefly with the idea. But I didn't have time for any monumental moral struggle. I just sat in the chair in the empty cubicle and wheeled it close to the partition to listen. Quietly, so that Travis wouldn't notice. I know, a rotten trick. But Travis led such an interesting personal life.

"It was great," he was saying. "I only wish we'd had more time. That's the only thing that kept it from being perfect. Absolutely matchless." There was silence on his end for a few seconds. I wished I could see whether he was keeping a straight face. Because he sounded sincere enough to convince a motorcycle cop. How do you get away with a phrase like "absolutely matchless"?

"I know you do the best you can," Travis said when he spoke again. It was at about this time that I sensed something awry. "I'm not trying to pressure you. I just want you to know how I feel. It's a compliment. I can't get enough of you."

Again a pause.

430

"No. I'm all packed," he said. "You're sure you can get away?" Now he seemed almost cautious. "I want to. Just be sure he won't miss you. A jealous husband is the last problem we need."

She was married. The idea shocked me. I had never known Travis to wade in that pond.

The conversation was ending. I got up, slipped out, and was standing beside my own cubicle when Travis came out.

"Let's get out of here," Travis said. "The old man got his money's worth out of me today."

I felt reasonably rotten as I fell into step beside him. You act like a thief, you feel like a thief. "Better rescue George before he does something rash on that Exercycle," I said.

"Yeah. He looked pretty serious when he left. If we don't get there soon, he might actually break into a sweat."

We walked outside into the summer heat. When we crossed the street, I could see bubbles where pure tar had been used to patch the asphalt. I tried to imagine wearing a sweater and thermal underwear. The idea seemed preposterous.

We reached the club and went in, and as we pulled on gym shorts and T-shirts I watched Travis. Adultery had a nasty sound, but it wasn't a hanging offence. They could have their reasons. Marriages went bad. It happened.

I decided that I was feeling the shock of discovery. Travis's philandering wasn't such a big deal, I kept telling myself, but it meant that once more I would have to revise my image of the way things are, how the world works. After you have lived for a while, you think you must finally have it right. But it's never so. Some gremlin always crawls out of the shadows to bite you.

We can skip the racquetball, which ended predictably. Skip drinks and dinner too. I keep returning to what happened as we finished dessert.

The restaurant was called "Les Cygnes". The head waiter had seated six of us along a red leather banquette intended for no more than five, rubbing knees and elbows, an arrangement much too intimate for the stiffness that had been introduced when Poague and his wife arrived. Stiffness, and more. Weird, eddying tensions that I didn't understand until later.

Poague perched on a curve of the banquette, with his wife almost invisible beside him. Her name was Noreen. She was his second, about twenty years younger than Jonas. I always believed that she would have been an ideal military spouse: dutiful, unobtrusive, conservative in dress and manner. Tonight she wore a blue seersucker shirtwaister. Her makeup was negligible. In five years of occasional meetings like this one, I had never once heard her speak spontaneously.

So, we were finishing dessert. Except to ask for the cream and murmur how rich the chocolate mousse was, no one had spoken for the past twenty minutes. The silence was becoming obvious.

Anne Marie, talking because nobody else would, said something empty about how lucky we were to be going into the mountains—such beautiful country.

Poague turned quickly towards her. "You like the mountains?" he asked. "You've spent time there?"

"Not recently," she said. "But I used to go to my grandparents' dairy farm in New Hampshire, and I loved those—"

Poague's look of distaste stopped her.

"Please," he said sharply. "You must not confuse our eastern foothills with such glorious creations as the Beartooths. A true western mountain is a most awesome and challenging place. We have nothing here to compare with it."

This became the launch pad for a lecture I had heard from him several times, about all the cushions we have built into our modern existence. Police to protect us, ambulances to rescue us, hospitals to heal us. Hotels and restaurants and all-night grocery stores. Saying these as if the nouns themselves offended him.

I watched Hollenbeck. His fingers worried the hem of a napkin while he pointedly, miserably, avoided Poague's glance.

"In the wilderness," Poague said, "if a person is to eat, he must provide himself with food. To be warm, he must have fire and shelter and clothing. These are the principal activities of a human in the wilderness: managing nourishment and making shelter. They also are the principal activities of any human in the modern world. Only we disguise them so well and construct so many fallback cushions against failure that even the unfit may thrive."

Poague's accusing eyes flicked over everyone at the table in turn. Hollenbeck sombrely picked crumbs from the tablecloth.

"That is the beauty of the wilderness: the total and utter clarity about what one must do to live another day. It exposes very neatly our shortcomings. The strong and intelligent being grows stronger, even in adversity. The weak one soon perishes. A more elegant and thorough test of a man's mettle I cannot conceive." He pursed his grim lips. "The trip we begin tomorrow is just such a test. This is not overnight camping in the Adirondacks or skiing in the Catskills. The Beartooths are a challenging place. People die there if they aren't prepared."

Poague showed as acid a smile as I had ever seen. "But we're not going to let that happen," he said. "It's not in the programme."

He leaned back in the seat. Around the table there was a silent expelling of breath. Poague drained his coffee cup, then stood.

"I must leave," he said. "I have five hours' work at my desk, and I must finish it before flight time tomorrow." He turned to his wife, who had stood up beside him. "Stay if you wish," he told her. But she said she was ready to drive herself home, and they walked out together.

We watched them until they were gone.

"You boys are going to have loads of fun camping out with that character," Anne Marie said.

I reached for a glass of wine. "To the Gold Card brigade," I said, "sallying forth into the wilderness."

"It'll be great," Travis said. "Like *The Call of the Wild*."

"More like *The Marx Brothers Go Hiking*," Anne Marie said.

Hollenbeck got up. His face was flushed. "I'll be back," he said. He pushed past me and left the table.

I followed him into the men's room about half a minute later. When I found him, he was vomiting his dinner.

"Leave me alone, Ray," he said.

I backed away. He flushed the toilet and went to a washbasin, and was splashing water on his face when Travis came in.

"Looking kind of rocky," Travis said.

"Feeling that way, Paul. Any time I get a little shaky about things, my stomach chimes right in. It's pretty stupid."

I could feel him opening up to Travis, just as quickly as he had shut me off. They were talking like confidants, the two of them seeming to pretend that I wasn't there.

Hollenbeck wiped his face with a paper towel.

"It's this hiking bit," he said. "Actually, I was thinking that instead of getting on the plane tomorrow, I could just tell Poague I was going to look for another job."

"You don't want to do that," Travis said.

"Oh, yes I do. But I won't. Poague would cut me to pieces, and Annie would kill me. I'd rather get eaten by a grizzly bear."

"The trip won't be that big a deal."

"You heard him just now. This is going to be some macho, man-in-the-wilderness thing. I wasn't made for it. And Ray—Ray was talking about seventy-pound packs . . ."

"Furlow doesn't know anything," Travis said. Neither of them looked at me.

"I keep thinking, at IBM they don't make you wrestle alligators. At AT & T they don't care whether you're into skydiving. Jonas Poague is the only boss I know who cares about that sort of thing. It's stupid. Tomorrow I could be driving up to watch the Orioles play the Red Sox. Instead I'm going to be hiking off to play explorers in some place that doesn't even have a zip code."

"It'll be a pain in the butt," Travis said. "You'll get tired out, lose a couple of pounds, come home and sleep for about three straight days. That's all. It'll work out OK."

"You think so?" Hollenbeck said. He was lapping this up. It was excruciating to watch, his eagerness.

"A month from now we'll be laughing about it. I promise."

Travis reached for Hollenbeck, held his neck in the crook of an arm, a brotherly act that made me feel even more unwelcome. "Quit worrying. I'll get you through it if I have to carry you and your seventy-pound pack the whole way."

Maybe I was angry, standing there watching this, being treated as if I were invisible. I guess I was envious also. Of Hollenbeck? Travis? I knew that I shouldn't speak, but I did.

"This is such bull," I said. "He can't tell you that, George."

They both stared at me. At last.

"Paul wants that promotion. Same as I do, same as you do." The first and only reference to the job, but they understood. In the mirror I caught a reflection of a jerk who looked like me, gesticulating, flapping his arms. He was a buffoon, but that didn't stop me.

"You think he won't be happy to see you fall on your behind? Cuts the odds to fifty per cent. How can you expect he'll help you look good? What's in it for him?"

I'd have figured that the anger would come from Travis. But he just said, "Better speak for yourself, Ray."

It was Hollenbeck who glared, and talked with sharp-spined bitterness. "That's your way, Furlow," he said. "Always ready with that knife. But not everybody's like that."

So for the second time in about five hours I felt like a class-A jerk. And the evening wasn't over yet.

I think Hollenbeck started to cry. I'm not sure; I turned and left, and Anne Marie was still there when I got back to the table.

"He'll be OK," I said to her. "He's being taken care of."

She stopped me before I could tell her goodbye. She wanted to know why I thought Poague was taking us on this trip.

"You know about the job," I said. "It's a good guess, to me. This isn't a method of promotion they recommend at Harvard Business School, but Poague has his own rules."

"I worry it's more than that. Less than that, I mean. I worry he wants George along for the entertainment value."

It took me a couple of seconds to realise what she meant.

"I was watching Poague," she said, "when he did his piece about the challenge of the mountains. He could see George going green, and he kept laying it on, watching him squirm. He knows George will do poorly

434

up there, and he can't wait to see it. It should keep him chuckling for the next six months."

I told her that would be pretty sick.

"He is not a nice old man," she said.

IN MY IMAGININGS I see Travis leaving the restaurant, walking three blocks to the new Hyatt hotel on Wisconsin Avenue. Into the lobby, to the bank of elevators, and up.

I don't know that it was the Hyatt. But it would have been his style. Maybe these details aren't important in and of themselves. But there were details not too different from this. And this is not all fanciful nonsense either. Some of this I know now.

He rides the elevator alone, gets off, and goes to the room she has already arranged. She has handled everything; she knows how to do these things.

Travis taps at the door. She opens it. She wears a pink satin robe tied loosely at the waist. Later I got a face to put on the body, but that night in my imaginings the face is in shadows, and it's just a figure in pink satin that Travis follows through the door. He shuts it without looking back. She pulls him to her. The bed is one step behind her, there to catch them as they fall.

Later she sits on the edge of the bed and watches him as he dresses, pulling on his slacks. Looking at him is the best part, she thinks. He really is a pretty one.

He turns up his collar, picks his tie off the floor, peers out of the window, down at the traffic below on Wisconsin Avenue.

"I really need that job," he says.

"You mean, you need the rise."

He's grinning crookedly when he turns back to her.

"That's part of it," he says. "Everything costs so much. The service charge on my apartment is more than I used to pay in rent when I first left college. Flying costs me almost sixty an hour. The loan on the Mercedes is over six hundred a month. It won't be so bad when I get the job and the money starts coming in."

She wants to say, "How can you be so sure?" But he seems incapable of self-doubt. Not a flattering posture, from her perspective. He's like a big kid, a high-school athlete who has never grown up. Grinning his way into middle age, affable but none too bright.

He sits beside her on the bed. She kisses him on the cheek and gets up to leave.

"I'll call when you get back," she says.

"Yes," he says. "Please, I need you."

More than you know, she thinks.

CHAPTER FOUR

This is hiking in the high mountains. If the weather has been wet, the trail is slippery, and if it has been dry, the trail is dusty hardpan. The pack sways from side to side, and the shoulder straps cut through skin and muscle to grip your collarbones. Your calves feel as if they've been slit vertically by a knife in need of sharpening. Feet smoulder inside boots, chafing against fabric and leather, rubbing raw. No breath is ever deep enough.

That second morning we followed the trail up from the meadow. Sometimes it climbed gently and sometimes it climbed steeply, but through the day it climbed. The stream ran beside it all the way, splashing over rocks and spilling into pools. The edges of the path were bordered by berry bushes and a scattering of tiny ivory wild flowers. The trail ran in and out of the trees, and when it was in the open the white tops of the great grey parapets were visible ahead. The trail was dry, and our boots puffed khaki-coloured powder when they fell.

I recall these details now, but at the time the overwhelming single impression was of moving one leg in front of the other, and drawing breath, and resisting the pull of the pack.

That pack. I battled with it the whole time. Every day I tried a different way of loading it, and all I ever found were different ways for the straps to pinch, for the weight to pull me backwards when I climbed or shove me forwards when I descended.

Andrea led us. Behind her Charles tottered under his pack, but he didn't complain. Poague was next. He looked puny, but the old man knew how to hike. Head up, shoulders back, his steps mechanical and unvarying. Eleanor followed him, listing to the right. Three times that morning we stopped so that she could straighten her pack. Minutes later it was tilted again, pulling her to one side. Travis was behind her, probably less taxed than the rest of us but still feeling the effort. Behind him Hollenbeck was gasping, noisily drawing in breath and expelling it with a rattle. The pack's hip-belt cut a furrow through his waist. Directly ahead of me was Donnie. His boots were loose, laces flapping in the dust—studied insolence, infuriating. Then me, walking my jerk's sloppy walk, dragging toes and the sides of my feet. Behind me I could not even hear Gary breathe. There was only the sound of his steps, heels striking the dusty ground.

You can see things in pain, through pain. I walked and hurt, and realised that I was walking because everyone else was. And they continued for the same reason. There didn't have to be any other reason; there was no other. We just kept walking.

436

IN THE AFTERNOON we began a long climb up through a forest. Beside us the stream cascaded, spraying a fine mist. Eventually the trail levelled into the bottom of a canyon, a deep, U-shaped notch that cupped the trail and the stream and a few trees. Here the stream spread wide, rippling past a sandbar.

Gary stopped us there to rest. Walk long enough, walking becomes easier than stopping; the legs keep moving involuntarily, almost a death twitch. So we halted by degrees, like a string of goods trucks rattling and bumping to a stop. Then we shrugged off our packs and scattered along the bank of the stream.

Charles perched on a flat rock and lowered his bare feet into the stream. I did the same, a few feet away; the water was cold, first numbing and then painful, vicelike. I pulled my feet out.

Donnie wandered up, walking stiffly, and sat near Charles at the edge of the water. He had been sullen with all the rest of us. But he seemed to assume that Charles was an ally.

"What'd you do to end up here, bro?"

"I got sent," Charles said.

"Just like me, I bet. Me and my buddy, see, we were in this Porsche. I was driving. My buddy said he wanted to go to the beach at Santa Cruz. Bad idea. Santa Cruz is full of cops. If you're going to break the law, you got to be cool."

"You were driving without a licence?"

"Hey, blood, it wasn't even my car. So what did you do?"

"I wrote a story about two people lost in the mountains," Charles said. "The teacher showed it to the principal, and the principal gave it to the school board, and they sent me here on an alternative-education grant."

Donnie's lips had the outline of a smile, but it was empty, and his eyes were mocking.

"Oh, man, that's great. A story." He stood up, laughing. "You're bad, all right. Charlie Too Bad, that's you." He went off baying, and his laughter echoed against the high cliffs of the canyon.

LATER THAT AFTERNOON, when we were all certain that we had gone as far as we could take ourselves, we reached the foot of a high, steep ridge. The trail climbed in a series of switchback turns that ended somewhere above, out of sight. I told myself that in the morning we would have a hard climb to start, certain that we would stop here for the night.

You have to understand that we hadn't been told where we were going or how we were supposed to get there or how far we were expected to travel. We were following Andrea, and she seemed to be doing what Gary told her to do. At the base of the ridge she slowed and looked back at him, and when I turned to look back at him too, he was pointing upwards, so we never broke stride. We followed Andrea up.

About fifteen minutes later we came out on a broad saddle between two knobbly prominences where the trail met the stream once more. "We came out on a broad saddle"—it sounds so easy. But I have a distinct memory of looking up at the last leg of the trail, before it flattened out, telling myself it couldn't be more than fifty strides long, and counting as I watched my boots crunch into grainy, decomposed granite. At fifty I looked up, and saw that there were still some steps to go, and those were the most difficult I have ever taken, because I had known that I had fifty in me, but no more.

Then we were over a lip, on a shelf where there were huge boulders, and some trees, and patches of grass beside the stream. Ahead of me the others were already out of their packs and collapsing, and I did the same.

We ate dinner in darkness. Soggy mung beans. I crawled fully clothed into the sleeping-bag, and my last sensation was the sad, hollow sound the water made as it plunged off the rim and down to the ridge below.

IT WAS NOT UNTIL much later that Charles told me, told anyone, what had happened to him that afternoon.

We had been at the saddle for nearly half an hour. Charles went to find the latrine, just a small slit trench scratched out with a folding shovel by whoever needed it first. "Up in that direction," somebody had said to him, vaguely waving towards a stand of pines. Charles picked his way through the trees and emerged in a small clearing dominated by a boulder the size of a house. He walked round the boulder and found Poague lying there, looking as if he had dropped on the spot.

Charles ran to him and knelt down by his head. The old man was breathing hard, spittle bubbling at one corner of his mouth. His gaze was unfocused, and for a few seconds he seemed unaware of Charles bending over him, saying, "Jonas, Jonas, what's the matter?"

Poague finally looked at Charles and said, "Nothing. I'm fine. Nothing's wrong. And don't say anything to anybody about this."

I can imagine how he said it, Poague when he really wanted something, even in this condition.

"Promise me," Poague said.

"I promise. But what's wrong?"

Poague didn't speak at first. He put out his hand, and Charles understood that he wanted to be helped up, so Charles stood and did what he could to pull the old man to his feet.

Poague rose, swayed, and leaned his shoulder against the big rock to steady himself. Then he straightened up, stood away from the rock, and looked directly at Charles. "Not today, boy," he said. "Maybe later. But not today."

438

ANDREA CAME ROUND to wake us. Or so I was told. I never heard her. It was Poague who brought me out of leaden, dreamless sleep, touching my shoulder and telling me, "Raymond, Raymond, wake up." Since it was Poague, I did. I opened my eyes.

Monday morning, I thought, and counted back two days. A weekend removed from Bethesda and racquetball and a restaurant banquette. It was as remote as childhood.

So was the future. The twelve hours before I could count another day gone seemed an impossible chasm: I was anchored by the inertia of the here and now. Muscles with the resilience of wet cardboard as I peeled away the nylon swaddling. An ache in one hundred joints as I stretched to put on my boots.

Breakfast was a gooey mess of oatmeal and raisins. As we ate, Gary lectured us about lactic acid. "Lactic acid is the reason you're all hurting," he said. "It builds up when you exercise hard, and if you don't work it out, you feel sore as hell the next morning."

Poague got up and left without eating much. I saw him go to his pack and take out his toilet kit and walk down to the stream. Travis wasn't even subtle; he watched Poague, immediately shoved the rest of the glop into his mouth, and then went to his own pack, got his kit, and followed the old man.

I put down my cup and spoon, hobbled over to my pack for a toothbrush, and went off towards where Poague and Travis had gone. When I saw them, I stopped. Poague was standing beside the stream unfolding a cutthroat razor. No mirror, no soap, no hot water; nobody else had shaved since we arrived. He bent and scooped some water from the stream, dashed it on his face, and began to shave. Travis was maybe ten feet away, brushing his teeth but watching this performance. Poague ignored him.

Travis took the toothbrush from his mouth. For a moment he seemed uncertain. Then I saw him gather himself up—an act that took place almost wholly within him, but I saw it anyway—and give a grin that I knew well, and cock his chin just so. He said something to Poague. I was too far away to hear, but I could guess—a witty trifle, slightly obsequious though not fawning.

Poague ignored him, continued to scrape at his cheek as if oblivious. Yet he had to be aware.

Travis waited, got no reaction, and then his posture changed again. A subtle hunch of his shoulders, a submissive dip of the head. He took a couple of steps closer to Poague, and again he said something. One second passed. Two. Poague deliberately dropped the hand that held the razor, and when the hand was at his side he turned his face to Travis and spoke. One sentence. A pause. Travis's face was set in an expression of bafflement. Poague said some more, turned away, and brought the razor up again.

Travis seemed about to reply. But he checked himself, took a step away, and stopped to look back. Finally he came striding up in my direction. I could not remember ever seeing him so flustered. He glanced at me and brushed past.

Down beside the water Poague moved the blade along his jaw in even, precise strokes.

THE TRAIL AND THE STREAM both ended about half a mile from where we had camped. We came out of some woods to find a droplet-shaped lake, nearly a mile long, with a pinched eastern end, from which the stream flowed. There the trail met a steep field of boulders that spilled from high bluffs down to the water's edge and covered the ground for as far as we could see. We climbed up and began to work across them. picking a path over them and sometimes through them, following the shoreline. It was the last we ever saw of a trodden path or trail.

The rocks were uniformly deep grey, ranging in size from steamer trunks to VW vans. Most had at least one flat face where we could plant a boot, sometimes squarely but more often at a tilt. To do it right you search out footholds two and three moves ahead. It tests the mind as much as the legs, a game of checkers played with soles on granite.

As long as we stayed level, climbing the boulders was tolerable. We were all capable of it in some fashion. For a few minutes probably we all believed that we could manage this for as long as we needed. Then we reached the end of the lake, and we looked up the long, long ramp of boulders that strained skywards from there, a great rocky funnel.

We had to go up—no other way. And we found that the vertical game is a much different game. No more hopping from perch to perch. No more smooth swinging of the foot from one boulder to another. This is no dance. When you climb a boulder field, you pay for every inch.

Gary and Andrea stood beside us and exhorted us and chanted instructions. "Use your hands for balance, but don't pull yourself up. Keep moving. Make your steps small. Don't stretch. Don't reach." They said the words, but the words didn't matter. It came down to this: some of us could do it, and others could not. I discovered that I could. It was almost an act of faith. Your right foot finds a small, scooped alcove in the stone, just where it needs to be, and when your left foot needs another platform, it is there, just where it has to be, and even when you are stymied for a moment, you find the rib of stone you must have to brace yourself. It is always there; you are never left grasping emptiness.

I could do it. Travis and Donnie and Hollenbeck could. Hollenbeck must have been euphoric.

So there were four of us, and Gary, and we began cheating our way up the boulders. It feels like cheating, the way it happens, the way the puzzle allows itself to be solved.

I paused and looked back once. The others had broken into two pairs. Andrea and Eleanor, Poague and Charles. Eleanor could not do it. I watched her try to pull herself up on a table of stone while her feet slipped and scuffed beneath her.

Nearby, Poague ascended two or three boulders, not quickly but with sureness, then stopped and turned to wait for the boy. Charles tried. But the pack rocked him from side to side, his child's fingers slipped, and his meagre legs folded under him.

Clearly, Poague could climb these rocks as well as any of us, and I thought that what he was doing was something very close to an act of love for the boy. I also know now that he had no choice. Poague was doing all he could, climbing a few feet and resting while Charles caught up. He had that, and no more, in his arms and legs. But we didn't know that then.

Eleanor made a noise—a grunt, a defeated whine—that was embarrassing to hear.

I wanted to flee from such struggle, and I did; I headed up and left them to their troubles.

You have to understand that when you climb boulders, there is a kind of sorcery in the way holds and niches present themselves to you, and you feel you must steal as much ground as you can before the magic abandons you.

I guess the jumble of boulders went on for half a mile before they topped out. In the Beartooths I lost all grasp of distance; the mountains are so big, and they can punish you so much in so little time. But I would say it took almost an hour to get to the top.

I stepped onto a grassy flat where the others were sprawled, exhausted; there was a touch of grimness even in Gary as he sat with his pack as a backrest. Before us was one last valley. It was mostly bare rock laced with trickling brooks, and when it ended, there were cliffs and more boulders, a second field higher and wider than the one behind us, and then the crest.

The peaks that had been distant in the meadow below now disclosed detail, and frightening scale. Huge, chiselled facets. Chutes that dropped thousands of feet, clogged with rock litter. Long rills where snowmelt plummeted in sparkling tendrils.

I looked up at the awesome peaks, and I knew we were interlopers. We weren't meant to be here, and if they couldn't stop us, the mountains would at least make certain that only the strongest and most determined walked among them and walked out again.

SOME THINGS I WILL NEVER be able to remember without anger. Knowing, the way I know now, that none of them had to happen. For we didn't die from snow or cold or stone, but from who we were. The woe we brought with us into that high country.

I recall Hollenbeck and Andrea sitting at the edge of the boulders. By then we had all struggled to the top, and Hollenbeck had asked Andrea how far we had climbed and how far we would still have to climb. She had brought out a map to show him.

There were only two sets of topographic maps, four to a set. Gary and Andrea kept the maps, and kept within themselves the knowledge of what lay ahead, what would be expected of us.

We had come a little less than a mile this morning, she told Hollenbeck. You couldn't go by that alone, though. The climb we had just made was worth five miles over open trail.

"Gary wants us to get to this small lake, right below the pass." She tapped the map, pointing to a notch between two sharp summits.

"Exile Lake," Hollenbeck said. "Wonderful."

"Just a name."

Hollenbeck looked at the mountains and then the map. "So how far is that?" he said.

"Here's the scale, at the bottom. It's an inch to the mile."

"That has to be about four miles." His voice was unsteady. "We can't do that. It took us all morning to do one mile."

"We have plenty of daylight. This morning the boulder field slowed us down."

"We've got another one ahead. I can see it."

"It'll be OK."

Hollenbeck stood, his shoulders slumped. "That's eleven thousand feet up there," he said to me. I could have been anyone; he just had to say it. "Two miles high. What are we doing here?"

When Hollenbeck left, Gary called Andrea's name. She went over to join him. They were alone, too far away for anyone to overhear. But she told me later what they'd said. I could have guessed.

"Things'll go easier if you put that map away," he said.

"He wanted to know where we were going."

"That's what they all want. If they needed to know, I'd have told them already."

"They have to get map and compass training."

"They'll get it in a week or so, when they've started to believe that they might make it to the end of this thing."

"On the other trips I've done we were very up-front about what was happening," Andrea said.

"That might work paddling canoes in the Glades. But these people are dragging. Right now the map just scares them. The miles scare them. Don't make it any harder on them."

"They have to know."

She remembered his answer. He said, "Not when I'm along they don't." She cried when she repeated the words to me.

HOW MANY MORE DESCRIPTIONS do you need of torturous, breath-sapping climbs? The lake was four miles distant, two thousand feet higher than the valley. The valley was three miles across; we covered that in about ninety minutes. The last mile, the ascent of two thousand feet, was mostly boulders, and it consumed all afternoon and all our strength. A cold wind blew down the slope, and by the last hour my lips were chapped and sore, I had a blister on my left foot, and I was moving on memory, on habit.

Sloping granite walls surrounded Exile Lake on three sides, like fantastic old tombstones, cracked and leaning. The walls were scrubbed brownish grey. The banks of the lake were brownish-grey clay. Not just a name. The place had the look and texture of a prison where a despot might send you to die.

The log showed that Donnie and I were to cook dinner that night. Poague had been carrying spaghetti and dehydrated tomato sauce. I sent Donnie for the food while I found a flat spot for the stove behind a rock, where the wind wasn't so strong. The stove was in the sack that carried the pans, cups and spoons, and the three aluminium fuel bottles.

When Donnie returned with the food, I gave him a pan and told him to mix the sauce. I took out the stove and put it on the ground to my left, where Donnie was. Then I took one of the fuel bottles, opened it, set its cap loosely on top, and put it beside the stove.

The stove was a loathsome little monster. Hard to start, difficult to fill. Not much to it—metal tank that sat on three stubby legs, regulator valve, jet burner. To fill it you needed a funnel. There was supposed to be a small plastic one. I bent forward to my right, to look in the bag.

To the left I heard a solid *clunk* of metal on hard ground. Heard a gurgle. Smelled fuel. When I looked back, the aluminium bottle was on its side and the fuel was burping out in splashes.

I could have moved faster. Donnie didn't move at all. He was stunned. I lunged and grabbed the bottle and righted it.

He said, "I hit it."

I must have shouted something, because Gary came over. For three days he had been watching us through a thick pane of mocking detachment. But he was not detached any more.

He took the bottle from me and shook it to hear the splash inside, took the stove and shook that, and said, "Damn."

444

I told him there were two more bottles.

"One's full," he said. "The other's almost empty. I checked."

"Don't we get more later?"

"At resupply."

"Is there enough until then?"

I thought he was about to give a real answer. But he swallowed it and said, "We'll be all right. Just don't fool around any more."

He got the funnel out of the bag and filled the stove. Then he handed the stove back to me, and looked at the bottle and the damp ground and at me and Donnie. He said, "I wish you hadn't done that."

IN THE MORNING, when I watched Poague and Travis beside the stream, I had tried to understand what it might mean, how much closer I might be to the job. But nothing happened. Jobs and prospects and ambition belonged to another reality.

That evening, at dinner and afterwards, Eleanor manufactured a sulk so formidable that even Travis couldn't breach it. When he tried to speak to her, she answered in a monotone and glanced at him dully. At another time I might have taken a petty pleasure in this failure of his charm. But I couldn't make myself care. Boy-girl games didn't matter.

I'm trying to convey the isolation that the mountains imposed. How thoroughly they removed us from all we had held important, and replaced those concerns with a complete set of others, far less ambiguous, much harsher and more real. You might imagine the nine of us in a lifeboat, becalmed in an empty sea, having jettisoned all our belongings. Stuck with the worst possible companions. Ourselves.

CHAPTER FIVE

Next day, all day, clouds covered the sky. Until now there had been sun when we walked. But that day, for the first time, there was no place to hide from the penetrating chill. Even when we walked we wore sweaters and wool trousers. The cold was constant, and it taunted us.

During breakfast Gary told us we had one more push to the top. Another half mile, another thousand feet higher, and we would be at the pass. Beyond that, Beartooth Plateau.

He jerked a thumb over his shoulder, towards a narrow chute between two of the granite walls. An impossible clutter of fallen rock choked the route, and it seemed to climb straight up. "Boys and girls," he said, "your stairway to the stars."

I hear him using the same line with every group. His smug delight in our pain and fear; I will never forgive him.

Breaking a bivouac camp and getting ready to leave takes longer than you might expect. Tape feet, cushion blisters, pack and repack so that the clothes and equipment you're likely to want will be ready when you need them. You might think there's comfort in having life reduced to simple chores, but the chores are endless, and they never go as fast as you think they should. Your fingers don't move right, your mind is contrary, you are cold and tired. Hike ten hours a day, and in the other fourteen you won't have a spare minute.

That morning we got ready more quickly than before, or ever again. I think we all wanted to be away from those walls. I began to fall in around the middle of the line, but Andrea came to me and said, "Ray, Gary is leading, and I want to be near the front today. Do you mind walking sweep?"

"I don't know." By now I had decided that I could survive this trip if it didn't get any tougher. But I wanted no uncertainties.

"It's easy. Just walk at the back. Don't let anybody get behind you. Only as far as the pass at the top. You can't get lost."

There was no good reason to refuse. So I stood aside to let the others gather in front of me.

Eleanor too hung back. While everyone else began to file out she spoke to me directly for the first time since we met. "So you got stuck with slug detail. What did you do to deserve this duty?"

I said, "Just lucky, I guess," and she turned away from me and trudged off after the others, and I followed.

We started up. The rock was looser here than on the boulder fields. It was rubble from the walls above, most of it with sharp edges, from pools of small chips to pointed chunks that jutted ten feet out of the rubble. It was hard going for everyone else; for her, impossible. She sank in past her ankles, and slid back eighteen inches for every step she took. Her floundering irked me; maybe I saw too much of myself in her.

"I could carry something from your pack," I said. Plain expediency. By now the others were out of sight, and I didn't want to fall too far behind. "Might make it easier."

She sat on the nearest flat rock and took off her pack. "Climbing is my problem. Not the pack."

"You might at least carry it straight."

"Why should it matter?"

"I don't know; it looks like you don't care."

"I don't. I want to get out of here, that's all."

Her eyes brimmed, and I got impatient.

"I don't need these problems," I said.

"I didn't ask you to be here." Her face was sulky. "I didn't ask for any of this."

446

"You think that makes you special? Nobody wants to be here. Except maybe one or two crazies. We just ended up here."

She looked at me as if I were a particularly backward child. "I do not want to be here," she said, the syllables precise to the point of insult.

I took a step closer, so that I was almost in her face. "I'll tell you what, Eleanor. That makes two of us. I don't want you here either."

"Thank you very much." No more pout. But hurt, real hurt. "You pig." She made a fist with her right hand and swung it at me. It didn't hurt— she held back at the last moment and opened her fingers, so it was just a loosely balled hand that slapped my sweater.

There was something pathetic but still funny about all that energy, that fury, expended with so little result. A corner of my mouth may have lifted, because she looked at me and hit me again, as hard as she could. That one I felt.

"You pig," she kept saying, crying as she did so, pummelling me, and I stood there unresisting, because I knew I had it coming, and I knew it helped and I could do this for her without cost to myself.

She stopped hitting me, but kept crying; she didn't lean towards me, but didn't resist either when I held her lightly to my chest.

Something came alive within me. How do I put this? This stranger to me—I *saw* her. A light shone abruptly from the deepest part of her, and through her translucence I could see layers of being, all revealed. I understood her stumbles, her crooked pack, her pouting and fists and tears, what was behind all that. I understood who she was and what she was and even some of what went into making her. Not the specifics—just the truth. I saw her. I loved her.

She moved her arms to tell me that I should let go, and I stepped back to re-create that narrow gulf between us.

"Well, now," she said. "That was loads of fun, wasn't it? You want to say something else nasty? We could try it again with rocks. We have plenty of rocks."

"We need to get up this hill," I said.

She looked up the incline. Directly ahead of us were about fifty yards of jagged, knee-high granite shards. An engineer could not have arrayed them more discouragingly.

She shook her head. "I can't go up there."

"Look, this is going to end. But before it does, we have to put up with a certain number of tough stretches like this one. It's like prison, but there's no parole and no pardons and no escapes. You walk in, you do your time, you walk out."

While the words came out I kept marvelling at this new warmth inside me. Of all times, of all places, I thought. That it had happened so quickly, or had happened at all, seemed perfectly natural at the moment.

Only since then have I questioned how and why. My best answer is that when you have relinquished all that does not directly pertain, you're on your way to being free.

"So what do you say?" I held my arms out, spread wide, palms up. "We take it slow and steady, it won't be so bad."

She sniffed, looked up the chute and at me.

"No," she said. She spoke very calmly. "I've decided. I am not going to leave this spot."

IF YOU DON'T get Ellie's story right here, I'll be way too far ahead of you. Because to me she was no stranger any more, and she shouldn't be to you.

For six years she had lived in a plush house in Key Biscayne. Her husband was a lawyer in Miami. Coleman Farris. If the name shimmers for you with Rolexes, and haircuts that cost more than most people pay for a pair of shoes, you're on the right track.

Then he announced that their marriage was finished. That was in May, four months before Montana. He suggested that she move to their weekend house on Duck Key. She had no job, after all, and she loved the Keys.

She had numbly acquiesced, and found herself living alone in that white stucco house built high on piles, overlooking the flats of the Gulf of Mexico.

She was thirty-two years old, and had always considered herself comely enough for most purposes. Every morning she studied her slim body, which was becoming burnished brown, and every morning she failed to discover the defects that her husband must have found in her. Then she would put on a yellow bikini and go outside to the chaise on the patio.

She had a radio and a TV and sometimes a magazine. When the sun was high enough, she filled a gallon jug with lime juice and orange juice and white wine, and put it in the shade under the chaise. The heat and the light and the wine were anaesthetic, and hours could pile up when she felt none of the hurt or confusion that always came upon her when she thought about her marriage.

At night she drank more wine and thought about Cole, and wondered what she had done wrong. She told herself that a man doesn't just kick away six years of marriage. She knew he must call soon, and she would leave Duck Key and return home.

He never called. A few times she telephoned him; he always sounded stiff—not hostile, but withdrawn, which was worse. Twice, a woman answered, and both times Eleanor hung up without speaking. Every night she cried.

448

In July her sister, Denise, had come to visit from Minneapolis. At the end of their first day together her sister promised to get her out of the house on Duck Key, if she had to use blasting powder. She had once been on a mountaineering trip in Montana, and she booked Eleanor on the same trek. She told her, "It will do wonders for your self-esteem."

Eleanor thought, The only thing wrong with me is that for some reason I'm not good enough for my husband.

She didn't fight, anyway. Her will seemed to have cooked away on the chaise, evaporated into tropical air. She called Coleman and told him she was going to Montana; not in weeks had she heard such pleasure in his voice as when he said, "Great! I'll send you all the money you need."

Then one morning, before the sun rose, she was in her car, heading up Route 1 to the airport, with a ticket to Billings. Before she got on the plane, she took off her wedding ring and put it into the coin pocket of her wallet. Three days later she was sitting on a flat rock on the flank of a mountain, bundled in wool, while the grey Montana sky festered above.

"I'VE DECIDED," she said. "I refuse to go any further."

I took off my pack and said, "In that case you'd better slide over and make room. If you don't walk, I don't walk."

She hadn't expected that. "You can leave—I don't care. Why don't you go ahead?"

"I was told not to leave anybody behind."

"It's your decision," she said, "not mine. So long as that's understood."

The rock was about the size of a coffee table. We sat side by side, at first without talking or moving. In her own way she had grasped the rules of the place, the logic of the immediate. When you can see no further than the moment, deciding to outwait a mountain isn't so absurd.

And I, I sat there and happily examined what was inside me, seeing it all the more clearly. It was like a gem, and I turned it over and over to catch the light, noticing all its facets. Thinking, Eleanor, I know something you don't know.

She was studying the wall on one side of the chute, its infinite network of cracks and faults, and she said, "It was cruel, what you said."

"I promise I'll make it up to you some time."

A question passed over her face. "That's an odd thing to say."

"Up here, anything goes. Haven't you figured that out yet?"

Mountain time moves like the moon across the sky. It is all stillness when you try to see it happen. We both watched a large bird—an eagle or some big hawk—turn about in the wind, skidding against it, fighting it with long and powerful strokes of its wings, and then land in a crevice high up on one wall.

"This starts to feel pretty dumb," she finally said.

"Your basic principle is fine. Digging in your heels if you think you're getting pushed around—that's OK. But this pile of rocks doesn't care about us or what we do."

We got down off the rock. I helped her on with her pack, then wriggled into mine. When we had finished, she said, "Ray, I'm going to be slow."

"Are you going to get there?"

"Yes," she said.

"Then if I stay right behind you, we'll get there together."

Strong and noble had a good feel, even if it was only pretence, even if I knew it was actually just me and therefore couldn't last long. I did enjoy the effect. She entered the thicket of toothed rocks and began to work her way through them. They swam loosely in the gravel. Tricky and unnerving—pressure from a foot or a probing hand might pry one loose. I moved to one side of the chute to stay out of the fall line. She did it right, never fully committing her weight to any one step. Twice, flaky rock broke under her feet, but she held on and tested for solid ground and kept going to the top.

I waited until she was there. From below I saw her straighten, lean into the wind, stare out ahead, then peer down at me.

"Ray," she said. "You'd better come quick."

SHE LEFT BEFORE I got there. When I reached the top, she was among the others, who were gathered in an uneven circle, almost as if in prayer, facing some object out of my sight.

I walked over, and stood beside her. In the middle of the circle were Gary and Poague, Poague sitting up against a boulder, Gary on one knee holding a gauze pad against a corner of the old man's forehead. There were dried dark smears on Poague's face. Gary took the pad away from an inch-long gash. At once blood welled up in it; he pressed the gauze to the wound again.

Poague saw that I was there. "I fell," he said. "Just down below. I was nearly at the top."

"Don't talk," Gary said.

A touch on my back. Andrea. She motioned me to follow, and we walked over to the edge, where I had just climbed up.

"How well do you know him?" she said.

"I've worked for him for five years."

"Have you noticed any changes in him lately?"

"No. He's always the same. There's nobody like him."

What she said next stunned me. "Has he always seemed this feeble?"

"Poague? Come on! He's not young, but the guy's in terrific shape for his age. For any age. He took this same trip last year."

450

"Not in this condition, he didn't." She must have seen my disbelief. "He's been nearly exhausted for at least two days. I'm surprised you haven't noticed."

"We're all exhausted." I felt the need to defend myself.

"No, you're not. You think you're wrung out, but there's plenty more in you if you need it. He has nothing left. He collapsed."

I looked down the chute, bumpy and studded with boulders.

"It happened there?"

"About ten feet from the top."

"That would be a bad fall. Will he be OK?"

"He'll bleed for a while. If there's a concussion, it's mild. But he can't go on, you know. I'll have to walk him down tomorrow."

"I'm sorry. I never noticed that he was having trouble."

"If it's any consolation, your friends didn't notice anything wrong either." Then, once more, she stunned me. "Have you had any reason to suspect that he might be seriously ill?"

I answered more quickly than the question deserved. "Absolutely not." That sunken stomach, his starveling's limbs.

"We'll rig shelters," she said. "We're not going anywhere today. Everybody can use the rest."

She walked away, and for the first time I noticed where I was, the immensity of it. I must try to describe it. The lie of the land was everything to us. Topography—daunting then—soon became a crushing physical reality.

I turned, and stood facing west. The climb up the last stretch of the chute had brought us to a shelf a few hundred yards wide. Immediately north and south of the shelf were twin pinnacles, perhaps three hundred feet higher than the pass itself. The shelf seemed to hang suspended between them. The pinnacles belonged to a line of peaks that I could follow to the horizon at both ends. The range had continuity; peak jostled peak, the furthest of them a craggy, crumbling version of a castle keep.

Spread before me, enclosed by the line of peaks, was Beartooth Plateau. Gary had mentioned the name, and I had let myself expect something flat. But beyond the crest the earth fell away to a stormy geological sea of troughs and upthrust ridges, valleys and violent buttes. In the morning we might descend from the shelf for a few hours, but after that, there would be more climbing.

For three days I had been thinking of this pass, this line of mountains, as a destination. I realised now that they were really a jumping-off point into the true high and wild. And that once we entered the plateau, the peaks would become a barrier containing us, standing between us and where we wanted to return.

The circle round Gary and Poague had begun to disperse. I went over and looked. This time when Gary took the gauze away there was no fresh blood.

Suddenly I became aware of a smell that had been there all along, waiting to be noticed. It was potent and acrid, something close to the odour in the cat house at a zoo, but even more direct.

I said, "Something sure stinks."

"Mountain goat," Poague said quickly. "They're ferocious territorial markers. Isn't it a wonderful stench?"

"An acquired taste, maybe."

"Oh, the scent is dreadful. But what it means, Ray! That old boy walks in only the highest of the high places. He breathes only the rarest air." Damp and bloody as it was, the old man's face was radiant. "And now we're on his turf. We've made it. We're here."

CHARLES AND I STRETCHED two tarps together on the lee side of a limestone slab. Seven sleeping-bags, side by side. Gary and Andrea had arranged their tarp over a wide notch in another chunk of limestone.

Among the lessons I learned on that trip: what bliss a warm sleeping-bag can be. I burrowed into mine, and through midday and the afternoon I floated between sleep and full consciousness, buoyant in the warmth that suffused me from outside and from within, the wonder that had come upon me down on the slope still opening petal by petal in the languor of the empty hours.

This ended when Andrea looked in and announced that we had to start dinner, that Charles and Poague were on the duty list, and that one of us would have to replace Poague.

Poague said something, and Andrea said, "No, Jonas. I want you to rest. They'll have to get along without us after tonight anyway. They might as well get used to it. Donnie, you're doing dishes tonight. We'll just move you up."

Charles was gone already. Donnie was slow to crawl out of his bag, but eventually he too left. The rest of us were stirring. Travis was already awake, and Poague was sitting up, pensive. Eleanor put on her boots and jacket and left. Hollenbeck put on his boots too, but Poague asked him to stay.

"We must talk," he said. "The four of us together." He kept his bag round his legs as he moved to face us, and the three of us shifted so we were sitting before him.

"You are all aware of a new job," he said. "I know you came up here with expectations. I should have told you they were unfounded, but that wouldn't have been exactly accurate, either." Then he said, "I'm not certain what I intended."

Nothing he might have told us could have astonished me more. Not even the awful fact that he had carried with him up the mountain, that even now he kept to himself.

"I have liked you all," he said. A choice of tense that should have alerted me; he always spoke with such precision. "It's my conceit that only individuals of value appeal to me. I have always hired and promoted those whom I like. We must have some standard, and mine hasn't failed me often. I asked you to be here because I thought you might all benefit from it and, selfishly, because I wanted you with me. If I were filling the position, I would consider each of you."

I knew he was trying to tell us something; I wanted to shake the old man and make him spill whatever it was.

Hollenbeck said, "There's no job?"

"Oh, yes there is."

Me: "Are we candidates?"

"I should think you are. But the choice isn't mine."

"Can you explain that?" Travis this time.

"No." Abruptly. I knew there was something more. "Tomorrow Andrea and I are returning to Red Lodge. Anyone who chooses may leave with us. If the thought of promotion, or of offending me, is all that keeps you up here, then you are free to leave."

None of us spoke.

"I don't know what else to say. Except that I have examined my motives, and I know they were good."

His features tightened. At first I thought the emperor in him was surfacing once more, but then I realised it was physical pain.

"I should rest," he said. "I'm in some discomfort. Forgive me if I have wronged you." He slid down into the bag, pulled it round him, and turned his back on us.

Travis and I got up together, put on boots and jackets and left. Hollenbeck sat on his bag and watched us leave.

The sky was low and ugly. Charles and Donnie had set up the stove behind a rock, and Gary and Andrea and Eleanor were standing round them. A natural reaction, to gather where there may be warmth. There was a place beside Eleanor and I filled it. Travis stood behind Donnie.

Charles was trying to start the stove. He struck a match, but the wind blew it out. He shielded the second one and the third with his body, but the jet only sputtered and spat fuel.

Donnie smirked beside him. "Charlie Too Bad, what's the matter? They didn't cover this in the books?"

His head was within reach of Travis's left hand. A striped blue ski cap, dirty blond hair. Travis knocked off the hat, grabbed the hair, and

453

roughly wrenched his head back. Donnie let out a long-drawn howl.

"You little punk," Travis said. "He's worth fifty of you."

He released Donnie with a shove and walked away.

OH, THE CONTORTIONS that pride put us through on that stony perch. Pride, stubbornness, maybe even greed, shaping us in their own twisted image.

After dinner we hid from the wind and sipped hot, liquid Jell-O. We were scattered behind every possible shelter. This time I had contrived that Eleanor and I sat together against an outcropping large enough for only two. We said very little. It felt unforced, both the silence and our being together.

Travis and Hollenbeck came up from behind us and squatted low to stay in the wind shield of the rock. Travis glanced once at her, and then spoke directly to me. He said, "George and I have been talking. We've never really discussed this job thing. But we've known it was there, right? And now that it's all blown up, this whole exercise starts to look pretty pointless, don't you agree?"

They wanted to go back with Poague and Andrea, I thought. No great deduction. I wanted to go back too.

Sometimes I had trouble seeing past Travis's relentless gloss. But I could always read Hollenbeck, and when I looked at him now, I saw that he was uncertain. George wasn't sure he wanted to end this right away. His face suddenly wasn't as chubby as usual. I remembered that he had pushed himself miraculously up the boulders, and I realised why he might want to continue.

Then it was Travis who wanted to go back. Travis and I.

"George feels we have nothing to prove. I have to agree."

Travis who wanted to go back. Travis, unwilling to admit that he was tired and that he wasn't fit to play mountain man.

I said, "Paul, what are you trying to tell me?"

"Why don't we go down with the others? Just bug out."

If only he had been willing to step out from behind Hollenbeck's frailties. If only I had been willing to let his vanity pass.

"You don't need me," I said. "Go ahead if you want to go."

"We ought to do it together." No surprise there; maybe Poague had conceived all this as some ultimate test. None of us wanted to fail without the others. "You actually want to stay?"

"All the same to me," I said. "I'm doing fine."

"I'm doing fine too. George is having a little trouble. I was thinking of him."

"George looks like he's holding up OK. Are you so anxious to get off this hill, George?"

454

"I guess not," Hollenbeck said.

"Then, maybe none of us really wants to leave," I said.

"Obviously not," Travis said.

He stood, and Hollenbeck stood, and they both started off. I watched them go, and I realised that even now, the right word shouted at their backs would have us off the mountain and home in time to see the football game on Sunday.

I watched them until they were gone, then turned to Eleanor. "How about you? Are you leaving?"

"Not now," she said.

"What does that mean?"

"What you told me earlier. I'm not going if you're not."

It should have made me feel good. Feel ecstatic. But I was under the weight of all three of them, staying because of my fool's jousting with words. Strong and noble seemed many miles distant.

THE EPISODE LATER that night had an unreal feel even then, an unfamiliar conjunction of the puzzling and the mystical.

I awoke without knowing why. Then realised a deeper cold than any so far. And saw two empty bags. Poague's, immediately to my right. Travis's, halfway down the row. Everyone else was asleep. I held my bag round my shoulders and slid out from under the tarp. Something outside.

For a few seconds I heard only the wind. Then it slackened, and I heard two angry voices, somewhere down the slope. Very clearly I heard Poague say, "She tells me everything." The last word vehement.

A surging gust of wind swallowed Travis's reply.

And then a sound that I had never before heard and surely never will again—an eerie cross between a cat's meow and a baby's distressed bawl. Somewhere close, to my left. I turned my head.

There was an elevated point of rock. A late three-quarter moon sat plump over the point and silhouetted a shaggy prominence that seemed at first to grow out of the rock. Until the prominence moved—a nervous shrug—and I made out furry shoulders, a dangling beard, a pair of horns with a scimitar's curve. Poague's mountain goat, made uneasy by the clamour below him. The animal twitched his head, shook his horns. He pivoted and made a small clatter of rocks, and was gone.

CHAPTER SIX

Eleanor's handwriting:

Day Five: Wednesday, September 10

This morning Jonas and Andrea left. Now there are seven of us instead of nine, and that will take some getting used to. After they left, we set off in the opposite direction.

This was our easiest day of hiking so far, but the worst in terms of group attitude. Everyone has a gripe or a grudge against someone else. The two teenagers aren't speaking to one another. Donnie isn't talking to anyone, but is especially angry at Paul, and the four supposedly adult males aren't getting along at all. I am upset at Gary, who answers all questions about destinations, resupply details, etc., with his infuriating grin. And somebody, I'm sure, is upset with me for some reason.

On the plus side, we actually walked *downhill* for most of the morning. The packs are lighter than ever—we keep eating food. Meanwhile, we seem to be getting stronger. Or we are just learning to ignore blisters, aching joints, etc., etc. At the end of the day Gary told us that we had covered at least nine miles—a record for the group so far! I don't want to get my hopes up, but maybe we have been through the worst of it.

Tomorrow we will be doing some rock-climbing. Tonight we are all practising the knots we learned last Sat. It seems like years ago. This afternoon we tried to get Gary to tell us how hard the climbing would be. He became impatient. Finally he told us, "Don't worry. We won't do anything interesting. The lawyers won't let us."

ELEANOR SAW PLENTY that day, missed plenty more. I've wondered how early she picked up the tension between Hollenbeck and Travis and me.

If hiking isn't too difficult, it leaves a lot of room for thought. At first I wasn't aware of the particular thought that bubbled in the background. Occasionally it boiled into my consciousness, taking form, distilling as I trudged. Until at one moment it became clear. What I knew and had witnessed, and intuition, and a knowledge of the way people are—all came together at once. This happened soon after we stopped for lunch. Already there was subtle discord among the three of us, a hangover from my word games the evening before, and my enlightenment didn't make me any more cordial. But I kept the revelation to myself for a few hours.

We descended to a creek and then went north along the creek's banks, following Gary up past a small waterfall until we stood on the gravelly sides of a bowl, with a dark crater lake at the bottom.

Along the lakeside the ground was too steep for a camp. But there were bluffs halfway up the bowl, with a few narrow flat spots where we could spread our bags and pitch the tarps.

To get water we had to go down a scree slope and then climb back up. Travis volunteered to fill some bottles. I said I'd help. I got my iodine and went with him to squat at the water's edge.

456

He filled the bottles one by one, and I added the iodine. I took one from him, replaced the cap, and shook the bottle. I said, "It's Poague's wife you've been seeing."

I had no proof. But I saw the look on his face, that first unguarded reaction of guilty surprise before he'd had a chance to compose himself behind the barrier of confidence and polish.

"You must be out of your skull," he said.

"Come on, Paul, you can confess. It's your old buddy Ray." I know I was smiling, but inside I felt vicious. "I knew you had something going with a married woman. I couldn't understand why. It's not as if you have to resort to that. In fact, I'd have said you were a man of principle in that area. But that'd be a pretty ridiculous statement under the circumstances, don't you think?"

"I think the altitude is starting to get to you." Playing it as if it were all in fun.

"But you weren't doing it to have her. It was for the job. I guess you thought she might be able to help."

"That's enough." He couldn't look at me to say it.

"What you didn't figure was that she'd tell Poague. But you should've known that. Poague gets people's loyalty, one way or the other. It was you she held out on. She didn't let you know something was screwy with the job. She used you."

"Why should she do that?"

"Why not? Look at you. Look at her. I would, in her place."

"No more," he said.

It might have ended there. It was all out, and in the open air it seemed far less monstrous than the beast that had growled inside me all afternoon. It might have ended there if Hollenbeck hadn't at that moment come grinding down the slope towards us.

He carried the cooking pots in his arms. Had come to fill them with water. He stopped where we were and looked down at us and said, "Jeez, what's eating you guys?"

His credulous presence kicked something over in me.

"Old Travis here has been playing backdoor games with Noreen Poague. Slap and tickle with the boss's wife."

"So what?"

"Think about it, George. He wanted the job. He was looking for an edge. Forget you and me. He was going for the big one."

"I'm not listening to this any more," Travis said. He stood up and started up the slope.

"Tell him I'm wrong," I yelled at his back. He kept walking away.

To Hollenbeck I said, "I know I'm right."

"I don't care," Hollenbeck said. His face showed me something like

457

pity. "I mean, I guess it's not right to sleep with somebody else's wife. If that's what he did. Maybe so. But he wasn't trying to hurt us."

"George, you have a blind spot where Travis is concerned."

"He is my friend."

"He's a jerk."

"Now listen." Hollenbeck's voice was fierce. "He has helped me. You know how I got this far up here? Because I believed. You don't get anywhere up here unless you believe, and he let me believe. He told me I could do it, and that if I had trouble, he'd help me. It's a hell of a lot more than I can say for you."

"George—"

"I don't want to hear it. He's my friend." He swiftly scooped up water into the pots. "He's your friend too, if you'd let him be."

He walked away, and the water sloshed, and his huge, dark gunboat boots crunched up, up, in the stones.

THE DEEPER YOU GET into the mountains, the less you see of their scope and range. The less you see of the world. Your view is of vertical rock that looms like a Dickensian taskmaster and conceals great portions of the sky. We saw nothing of other mountains. We saw nothing of the sunset that settled over those mountains.

Poague and Andrea did. He had found some strength that morning, and by the end of the day they had reached the head of the first long boulder field. Down that field, round the lake, and they would be back on the trail again.

She knew it might be no more than another long day's walk if Poague held up. She regretted having taken so much food—enough to feed them well for at least four days—and she wished she had checked her pack more carefully. If she had, she might not have forgotten to leave the set of maps that now sat in a side compartment of the pack. She didn't need them, and she thought that Gary might be more inclined to teach some trail navigation if he could use two sets of maps.

There in the broad valley Andrea and Poague could see the sunset and the clouds in front of it. Poague noticed the band of tufted furrows first. "Altocumulus," he said, and Andrea looked. She thought of us, somewhere up there, and hoped that when things got tough tomorrow, Gary wouldn't be too much of a jerk.

THE ELEVENTH OF SEPTEMBER, sixth day of our journey. This part I dread remembering, this and so much of what follows. It's one thing to retrace wrong paths taken, portentous mistakes, flawed judgments; they don't seem so dreadful if you manage to deal with them separately, out of their deadly succession. But eventually you get to results. At the end of every string of actions are consequences that stand alone—clear and unambiguous.

We're reaching that point now. The end of the string. What happened. Whenever I think of it, I become withered inside.

Gary woke us early, hustled us through breakfast. He said he wanted seven miles before lunch. Then we'd try rock-climbing.

We met sunrise when we hiked over the rim. All morning we hiked northwest towards the barrier of peaks in front of us. We clopped patiently up the one long stretch that we met, and strode across the rest; that morning was as close as we ever came to meeting the Beartooths on even terms.

Two moments are worth mentioning.

We had been walking for about two hours when Donnie yelled that he was going to bust a gut if we didn't stop. Gary said, "We took a break twenty minutes ago. You should have done it then."

And Donnie said, "I did it then, and I have to do it again."

We stopped, and Donnie got the trenching shovel and disappeared behind a rock.

Charles walked up to Gary, said something to him. There was a gravity about the boy that had to be confronted. Not even Gary could avoid it. Grudgingly Gary reached into an inside pocket of his poncho and brought out a map. He unfolded it and squatted. Charles hunkered down beside him and peered at the map. For maybe half a minute Charles's head snapped between the paper and the view around us, and for those few seconds he was not at all childlike, but intent, purposeful, his eyes searching the map even as Gary took it from him and put it back into the poncho.

One more, about half an hour later. We were walking hard, down a long, sloping grassy strip beside a stream. I was behind Gary, at the front of the line. The last time I had looked back, Travis and Hollenbeck were walking side by side at the rear. Neither of them had spoken to me since the evening before.

Now I heard heavy feet sweeping through the grass, a quickened pace. Hollenbeck drew alongside me. Not even breathing hard, I thought. And I noticed that the belt didn't cut nearly so deep a groove in his midriff. He said, "Ray, I want to talk."

"I'm not the one who's been avoiding it."

"I mean without anger. As friends."

"I always thought you were my friend, George."

"I am. We go back a long way." We tramped eight, ten steps further before he said, "You have to apologise to Paul."

"Forget it."

"Whatever he did isn't worth getting upset about."

"What he did was to stick a knife in my back and in yours."

"He didn't mean to hurt us," Hollenbeck said. "Even if he did do what you say he did, you have to understand why. He thought he had to have that job. He's a very proud guy."

All this time I had kept walking straight ahead. Now I stopped and turned to Hollenbeck, letting my voice carry back to Travis. "The man is all show and no go. You can be his friend if you want. But don't ask me. He's not the only one with pride."

"You're making a big mistake," Hollenbeck said.

But I ignored him, put my head down, and began to walk harder, faster. And did I ever feel righteous and full of myself.

WE DIDN'T EAT much lunch. We had stopped below a set of cliffs out of a John Ford western. Tall, straight columns mottled with dark mineral seeps and sienna streaks. When we spread out to eat, Gary said casually, "By the way, this is where you're going to pretend you're rock-climbers." So while we might have been eating we kept looking at the cliff face, studying its fastness.

We were going to climb straight up the wall, but you could also walk up to the top, and down from there. The cliffs and the butte they formed were half of a broad dome. Picture the dome sliced vertically in two, one half still standing and the other strewn in pieces of slag and rubble. From the base of the cliffs the direct way to the top was to climb straight up. But if you moved to either side, the wall dropped down, the dome sloping until finally its curve met the ground.

Gary went up that way. He took ropes and a bag of climbing gear. He worked up top for a while, dropped a rope over the edge. Charles watched it fall, and said, "Looks like about ninety feet." When Gary came down, it was straight down, clipped into the rope, rappelling in a single smooth descent that was so frightening, so beautiful, I had to remind myself to start breathing again when he was unhooked and walking among us.

We dragged out helmets and webbing. To each of us he gave three carabiners, big snap hooks with locking gates. He kept talking, and things began to happen—too fast for us to take it all in. Showing us how to use bowlines and loops to fashion a sling harness round our thighs, a water knot to secure round our waists. Instructions on where to snap the carabiners. How to tie into the rope. Belaying—securing the rope for the next climber. A call-and-response shout between the climber below and the belayer up top, something about giving rope and taking up slack. And climbing—don't lean into the rock, don't reach too high, let your legs do the work. So much. It flew in and bounced around my head and left me shuddering inside when it flew away.

A check of knots and harnesses, and he was going up again, walking up the curve of the dome. At the top, he clipped into some anchor we couldn't see, settled the rope round his waist and shouted, "OK, somebody has to go first."

We stood looking up at him, looking past helmets that tilted awkwardly on our heads, feeling the constriction of the harness.

After a second Donnie said, "Hey, I'll do it if nobody else wants to." He walked forward and tied the end of the rope to his harness. A quick hop, one foot up, then the other, hands grabbing, moving, and he was gripping the cliff with toes and fingers.

You're born knowing how to climb, Gary had said; then you spend your life forgetting how. Don't think about it; just do it. Donnie did, as if he had been born to do it. No pause longer than a heartbeat. Moving, moving, and up.

He stood there, untied the rope. Shouted, exultant, "That was fresh, Jack. That was sharp."

Charles next. On the rock, clinging. Long hesitations when a hand or a boot searched for holds.

"Charlie Too Bad, you got it—no problem." Donnie, kneeling at the edge and yelling down. "That crack right there. Uh-huh. Now you got it. Real easy—no problem."

They walked together down the curve of the dome where Gary had gone up.

The rest of us stood watching, our hearts shrivelling inside.

"Somebody," Gary said. "Anybody." When no one moved, he said, "Ray, you're up."

I remember standing at the angle where the cliff met the earth. Ducking the rope that Gary dropped down, finding the end, tying it to the harness. Breath coming short, shallow.

I remembered the litany and shouted, "On belay." Hollow voice that I didn't recognise.

From above, "Belay on."

"Climbing," I yelled.

"Climb," I heard, from far away.

The standing rock seemed to stretch and grow as I looked up. The rope was an endless strand, infinitely elastic. A few inches above my head was a horizontal crevice that could have been gouged expressly to give grip to a hand. I put both of mine in it, tightened fingers, found a protrusion with one boot, stepped up, found a nubbin with the other boot, and was on the rock.

One arm moved upwards, then a boot, and the others followed, obeying mental commands I couldn't hear over the roaring awareness of my sudden distance from the earth.

I moved, stopped, searched for holds and bulges, reached them and stopped again. The holds no wider than a pencil, the bulges subtle swellings. But I felt them. My fingertips alive, pulsing, understanding complexities of texture and friction and angle.

And all the time the insistent suction of the earth, not just the physical pull but the desperation of having left a place where I belonged, a place that wanted me back very badly. The rope was no comfort; to dangle free was as terrifying as a fall.

I clung to the stone and fled upwards.

"About ten more feet." Gary, sounding close. I worked my way up, head and shoulders rising into tweedy sky, flopped my torso forward, and reclaimed legs and feet from the cliff.

I turned over on my back and lay panting.

Gary said, "Hey, I need that rope, huh?"

I untied the bowline, started back down. The path was a crumbling ledge a foot and a half wide. A boulevard.

Hollenbeck went up, then Eleanor. I imagined her being where I had been a few minutes earlier, feeling the tug of the earth, her fingers tucked into the same creases.

Travis stood at the bottom, fumbled catching the rope, picked it up and began to tie in. Pulled at the knot, untied it, tried it again but stopped before he had finished.

From up top Gary yelled, "You people were supposed to have those knots taped. Ray—somebody—will you please do it for him?"

Charles got there before I could. Travis fixed on top of the cliff, never looked at Charles yanking the knot tight.

His eyes didn't move as Charles stepped away. Travis put his hands against the rock, leaned forward. I realised that he was waiting for something to happen.

"On belay," Charles said. "You're supposed to tell him."

Travis forced out the words, and Gary answered.

"Climbing," Charles said, and Travis repeated it louder, and Gary responded.

Nothing happened.

"Right above your head," I said. Some grudging wellspring of charity; I remembered how the wall had seemed to expand in front of me. "The crack right there—and you've got places for both feet."

Travis put his hands in the crack, got one foot up; the other dug and scratched before it held. A long pause before he moved. A hand. A foot. He was going up.

His climb was different from ours. In what way, I can't say exactly. I too had been slow going up. Charles also was uncertain when he felt for holds. Hollenbeck's feet, as well, slipped and pawed before they found a

462

rest. So we had had our problems. But we had made it to the top, and Travis wasn't going to. With about forty feet left, he stopped and leaned into the rock and rested his forehead against the wall.

From the top Gary said, "Hey, Paul, not too far now."

Travis's head moved from side to side in refusal.

"You've got a hold. I can see it. Good, solid ledge."

Again the quiet shake of the head.

We saw what was happening. Charles yelled up something brave, and Hollenbeck did the same. The kind of pep talk you might hear from kids in a playground ball game.

He didn't budge.

Donnie came out from behind a rock, carrying the trenching shovel. "Dinner last night," he was saying to nobody in particular. "Must have been something wicked in dinner last night."

He looked round, took in Travis on the rock and the rest of us watching and shouting. He said, "Yelling won't get him up there." He threw down the shovel and moved towards the cliff.

A short leap, one hand fastening, then the other, boots thumping into the wall and staying there. He was ten feet up before Gary could shout, "No, you crazy idiot! Get down, right now."

Donnie's hands and feet kept moving, sticking where he placed them, moving. A single snowflake drifted across my eye; I wished the speck away so I wouldn't miss anything. A dozen agitated snowflakes fell as Donnie climbed level with Travis.

They were talking. Travis's head didn't move. He spoke into the rock, and it swallowed his words, but I could hear Donnie telling him about the big ledge. Donnie said it was good and strong, he'd hung on to it himself—that's where you have to start.

I could hear Donnie's soft, confident tone. Travis moved his head away from the wall and looked at him.

I stepped back from the cliff so I could see better. A hundred snowflakes. Donnie, untethered, on the rock. Travis's left hand reaching for the ledge, grabbing it.

Snow patted wet against my face. I thought of my hands on the rock— dry rock—and thought of Donnie up there, his fingers and soles touching the slickness left by the snow.

Travis moving arms and legs. Gaining a body's length. In his motions I could read belief for the first time. He stood on the ledge, Donnie talking up to him now. Snow falling in my eyes. Falling in Donnie's eyes. He brushed it away.

Travis climbed, frantic to get off the cliff. At the top he put out a hand. Gary lunged for it, connected, pulled him up and over.

Donnie was alone. He raised his right arm, touched the wall, brought the arm down, wiped the hand on his pants, put it back. Wiped his left hand. The snowflakes a thick, swirling overlay. Behind it Donnie climbed, one move at a time now, tentative, tense. White pockets were collecting in the wall's recesses. Travis rolled over and sat up, and I could see Gary reaching back, unsnapping the carabiner that fastened him to his anchor.

Donnie got to the top, lifted himself over. He stood, and turned to go down the path. Gary was standing too, shouting something at Donnie. I could see Donnie turning and saying something surly over his shoulder. Snow so thick it muffled sound from the top of the wall. Gary making an angry gesture, stepping over Travis's legs at the edge, stepping towards Donnie.

There was loose rock up there—gravel. The rock must have been slippery with snow, and Gary must have skidded on it. Must have happened that way, but from where I watched, the cliff just seemed to spit him off.

One moment he was moving towards Donnie; an instant later his feet were out from under him and he was falling, twisting his body to keep the cliff's edge beneath him, hitting the edge and slipping off it and tumbling down.

I watched him fall, and waited for the tape to stop, reality to rewind itself and resume properly. But he kept falling through the snow, past the high, reaching rock, all the way to the ground.

Charles was closest to where he fell, and started towards the place. I wanted to get there first, wanted to spare the boy that. I tried to shout him away from it, but the denseness of the snow stifled my call and restrained my motions when I tried to run. When I finally got there, Charles was staring down. I could see his face, aghast. I forced my eyes down to see what he was seeing.

Gary lay chest down across a waist-high, sharp-peaked rock in a way I had never seen anyone lie before, a posture of violence personified. His head twisted impossibly to look back at me with dull eyes, his arms and legs at flagrant angles.

Eleanor was beside me, gasping, clutching my arm and crushing her face to my sleeve. Hollenbeck had Charles by the shoulders, trying to pull him away, but Charles resisted.

Donnie running up, stopping short. Travis behind him, open-mouthed, wide-eyed, panting. Donnie turning, head swivelling, shouting, "Help!"

He was shouting "Help!" into the great emptiness that the mountains filled. "Help!" at the horizon that the mountains rumpled and mocked. "Please, somebody help!" out into the mountains that contained us so utterly and completely.

PART III
DESCENT
CHAPTER SEVEN

For a while there we had crazy time.

Charles stared, unblinking, at the broken body. Donnie wailed for help, and nobody told him there was only us to hear. Eleanor took out a bandanna and pushed at the courses of the tears along her nose and down her cheeks. Hollenbeck turned his back and looked out towards the distance; he might have been waiting for a bus. Travis kept muttering something too low for me to make out. Sanity came apart, and you might argue that for as long as we were in those mountains we never again got it fully restored.

I had a sudden compulsion to see where it had happened. I climbed the path to the top of the dome. Rising above the shouts and tears and unblinking stares. I went to the spot where Gary had fallen. A morbid little pilgrimage, I knew. But it seemed important. I knelt and felt the edge that he had tried to catch after he slipped. I imagined his hands touching it and then being dragged away as he fell. The last instant when he might have believed he could save himself. My hands caressed in wonderment the last piece of earth he had touched while he was still whole and alive.

I looked over the edge, and I imagined his plunge down into that space, the earth hurtling up to meet him, what he must have seen. I jerked myself back, a violent spasm of the spine, and fell onto the solidness beside the edge.

When I stood up the footing tipped and pitched beneath me. The dome was coming alive, a quiescent beast stirred by our presence, or our arrogance. It had shrugged Gary dead, and now it was trying to do the same to me.

I wanted off. Had to get down that path, now snow-coated, now impossibly narrow. I went down on hands and bottom, sliding my seat and bracing myself with rigid arms. Finally, I could stand up and walk to the others.

Eleanor met me first. Her face was wet, but she wasn't crying any more. "He's dead," she said.

I nodded.

She summoned strength. "Ray, we have to do something," she said. "He's dead, and it's snowing like crazy." Her calmness held off the collapsing sky.

"I guess we have to bury him," I said.

"I guess so. We should put up shelter and get out of the weather too."

"I don't want to stay here tonight."

"No. Somewhere else. But we have to get started."

I clasped her to me and felt her substance. "It won't take all of us to get him in the ground," I said. "Me and one more. You take the rest and make a camp and get some food started."

That was something tangible; holding on to it kept me steady. We had started back towards the others when Travis stopped us.

He said, "Listen, this is not my fault. I don't know what happened. He was near the edge, and he went over. But he was past me, understand? I had nothing to do with it."

"Paul, nobody's accusing you."

"I want it known, that's all."

I realised this wasn't aimless raving. It was important to him.

"I could have made it, you know," he said. "The little punk didn't have to help me. I was just resting. I was going to make it on my own."

"I believe you. Nobody's blaming you. Here, you want to help us? We have to get things squared away here."

He followed us over to the others; out of the corner of my eye, I saw that he was avoiding the body, the sight of it.

The others were coming back on centre. Donnie silent, sitting near the peaked rock and holding his face in his hands. Hollenbeck pulling out his poncho and draping it over the body.

I said, "Don't bother. Donnie and I are going to start a grave. Everybody else can find a campsite and get it going."

Hollenbeck said, "There are some pines about a mile back. They'll give us a place to tie the tarps."

"Just the way we came," I said. "Not far back, right? Make sure that's the place. We'll have to find it when we're done, Donnie and I. We don't want to have to hunt for it."

"Let's go now," Eleanor said. They got their packs, the four of them. While Travis, Charles, and Hollenbeck waited Eleanor came over and said to me, "Hurry, OK?" Then they walked off into the snow.

Donnie and I and Gary's body. Us and the wall and the low afternoon light filtering dimly through the clouds. We had just the one shovel. We took turns digging, one working and sweating while the other stood and shivered as sweat evaporated. Donnie was into his second turn when he complained once more about what last night's dinner was doing to his stomach, so when he went off, I was working again, turning up moist loam that clung to the grass roots.

He returned, and I went over to the peaked rock to rest. I didn't want Gary to be alone. My reasoning was, I know he doesn't care for us, and maybe he'd rather be by himself, but he should have somebody with him at a time like this.

This is the sort of dangerous shunt your mind can make, up there, where matters are usually so clear. I can only conclude that clarity and craziness share the same deep wellspring.

We worked, and felt the sun dropping. We scooped and dug, taking out fresh snow with every spadeful of dirt.

We were about two feet down when Donnie hit the hard stuff. Slush for a couple of inches, mud laced with ice crystals, then ground that was frozen hard. He called me over. I took the shovel and scraped away some of the icy mud. What lay below was so hard I knew it must be permafrost. I had heard about it in the Arctic. Never in the real world—if the Beartooths qualify. Never in any place I had ever expected to walk.

I put my hand down and pressed against the firmness. Gary's resting place on frozen earth. It was almost marble. Even through my glove I could feel the utter unyielding cold that chills earth for ever. Cold was everywhere up here—in the air, the rock, the night, beneath the soil.

"Is it deep enough?" Donnie said.

"It has to be." I could make out a soft smear of brightness above the hills to the west. We had maybe an hour before sunset.

We walked reluctantly to the peaked rock and the body, which still lay where it had fallen. Without a word I went to the head and Donnie to the feet. Donnie said, "This isn't really him, right, Ray? He's gone."

"That's right. This is just something we have to carry over to that hole. A heavy package that we have to get over there."

Donnie held him round the legs, and I slid both hands under the neck of his poncho and held the fabric. My knuckles grazed the back of those magnificently muscled shoulders. I had never touched a dead man before. Donnie counted three, and we lifted. He was heavy.

We got him there. The hole had looked enormous, but he filled it up. I felt ashamed, seeing that, feeling that we ought to have done better.

Donnie took the shovel, I used my hands, and we scooped in the loose dirt. Finally, we had a rounded hummock of fresh earth. We tried to pat it firm. Then we covered it with stones. When we had finished, it looked like a real grave, not something done in haste, and that seemed important. The light was dimming when we stood and looked at our work.

"We did OK," I said.

Donnie said, "Ray, let's get out of here, all right?"

I saw Gary's pack leaning against a rock, topped with a dollop of snow five or six inches high. I swept off the snow and lifted it. At least thirty pounds. Fierce crampons strapped to the back. An ice axe, even more fierce, secured by a pair of loops. A headlamp and battery in one side pocket. Folded maps in the next. I thought, Thank God—maps. Of course, maps.

Donnie was looking at me. "Anything in there we can use?"

"At this point we can use everything." I swung the pack up onto my back. Donnie stuffed the contents of my own pack into his, and we started to leave. The light was definitely plunging now.

WE WALKED TOWARDS where the others had gone. Hollenbeck had figured the pines about a mile away. It seemed right to me. Maybe half an hour at a decent pace. There should have been that much residual daylight, and Donnie and I were hurrying.

But we walked into deep night. Donnie got out his torch, and I put on the headlamp. He said, "Do you know where we are?"

I said I thought so, but I wasn't sure.

Snow changes things. I'm talking about the way it obscures the clues by which we recognise our surroundings, softening abrupt edges, filling depressions, adding and subtracting until all is evenness. Under enough snow a tree is a truck is a house.

"I don't remember walking downhill like this," he said. "I mean uphill. I think it was more level than this."

"This is level."

"Uh-uh. I don't think so. I think we've been going down a little for the last ten minutes or so."

We couldn't see. Too much snow and darkness. The cold bit my nose; I could feel it in the extreme joints of my fingers. My toes didn't exist.

"I don't understand how we could have gone wrong," I said, arguing against the sense of something askew that had been rising in me for the last few minutes.

"I don't know either. But this doesn't feel right."

"We should have hit the pines by now," I said. "I don't think we missed anything, do you?"

"I don't think so."

"They they ought to be out here somewhere."

Donnie squinted in the headlamp's glare when I turned to him. He looked so young. A child, following my lead into deep night.

"We have to do something," he said.

"Let's walk the way we've been going for a few more minutes. I think we must be close."

We walked on, and night huddled round us. In the incandescence, wind-driven flakes gleamed and smeared our vision. I stopped. My futility was as obvious as the darkness.

"I'm sorry," I said. "I have no idea where we are."

I believed that I was apologising for our demise. No way could we survive fourteen hours of night and wind and snow. Already I could feel my warmth surrendering beachheads to the chill.

468

We began to wander, seeking direction. The falling snow seemed to pulse, raging and relenting and raging again. I could see Donnie's light to my right, faint when the snow burst down, more clear when it paused.

A shout. His voice. Saying, "Ray, c'mere."

I looked to my right. A solid cascade of flakes. No light.

"Ray. Hey, man."

I went towards the words. No light.

I called to him.

"Over here. This way." Gaps appeared in the fluttering white curtain. His light, poking randomly, disappeared, then found me, and held full in my face. I churned towards him.

"I lost you," he said.

"Let's not do that again for a while, huh?"

"But look. I saw a light."

We watched. The curtain convulsed and broke. Behind it a spot of brightness bounced with a plodding rhythm.

We ran towards it shouting. The bouncing spot rested on us, and Hollenbeck walked into our glare. I gasped, "George."

"Oh, there you are," Hollenbeck said. "Paul was getting worried. He sent me to look for you."

"We may have gotten a little off the track," I said.

"Well, you made it," Hollenbeck replied. "That's what matters."

"We're not anywhere yet," I said.

"Sure you are." He was walking away. We ran to catch him.

He covered maybe twenty steps, up a slight distension of the earth. At the top stood several dwarf pines, bending under the weight of the snow. Tucked within them, two blue tarps strung up to form a single tent, the ends pinched closed.

IT HAD BEEN Travis's idea to look for us. And I believed that Travis had been wrong.

Don't think me ungrateful. I knew that if Hollenbeck hadn't been out there, we might have walked past the trees without seeing them. Probably had. I knew how close we had been to a miserable death. When I crawled into the shelter, I felt only gratitude and relief. Not until later did I question the decision, the impulse, that had saved us.

The tent was chest level at its highest. It had about the area of a station wagon. One torch, for illumination, stood upright, wedged between Eleanor and Charles at their hips. They and Travis sat up, sleeping-bags pulled round their shoulders.

Charles said, "Hey, Ray, Donnie," his voice and his expression subdued. Eleanor was drained, but her face took on light when she saw us. And Travis . . .

"You're here!" Travis said. He skinned the sleeping-bag down to his waist, leaned forward, and thumped each of us on the shoulder, a peculiarly male gesture of bond and bravado.

"I've been feeling real guilty," he said. "Letting you two get stuck with such a rotten job. I had no idea it would take so long. I should've stayed behind. Then, when it got dark, I started to get real worried, so I sent George out to see what he could see."

The first time, out of Hollenbeck's mouth, it had escaped me. But this time I heard it. "I sent George out."

I thought, Who are you to be sending George into that?

"Anyway, you're here," he said. "Nice navigating. Better get into your bags. It's the only way to stay warm."

We did as he said. Travis had that way about him.

"I wish I could offer you supper," he said. "But we're getting low on provisions, and I thought we ought to save food and fuel in case we really need it, next couple of days."

"We were going to resupply on Saturday," I said.

"Uh-huh. But Gary was the only one who knew where. We're down to one full dinner of bulgur wheat. And snack stuff—about three cups of raisins, some cocoa, tea, Jell-O, a box of crackers, a few inches of hard salami and some Cheddar."

"This is bad," I said.

"It is bad. We're probably as deep into this country as we were going to get. Tomorrow makes one week. You've got to figure we'd have started making our way back tomorrow."

My mind worked through facts, realities. "We don't have that much food."

So softly his voice was almost inaudible, Charles said, "Maybe we ought to see what's in Gary's pack."

I opened it and dumped out its contents; Charles held the torch on what spilled out. Clothes, a sleeping-bag. A metal quart bottle that Hollenbeck opened, sniffed, found full of stove fuel. Two freeze-dried meals for three or four persons each. Half a dozen date-nut bars. A box of stubby candles. A third plastic tarp. First-aid kit; inside, the usual bandages, ointments, aspirin, and a small bottle of Percodan.

Maps. I remembered them in the side pocket. Before I could get them, Charles had them out, unfolding them in the light.

"He has an idea there's a quicker way out than the way we came," Travis said. Disapproving. "But I can't see it. I say we go back the way we know. We know what's there. And we're in better shape now. It won't take us as long as it did to get here."

The crinkle of the map pages. I heard it but watched Travis. I realised that he had taken over. He would. Of course.

"It isn't here," Charles said. "There's supposed to be another quad. The Alpine quadrangle. We're in the middle of it. I saw it today."

"Look again. It has to be in there," I said. I kept watching Travis. Remembering the guy whom fear had seized on the rock wall, his anxious muttering.

I told myself that he had done a terrific job of putting himself back together. Unless you knew him, and looked closely, you probably wouldn't have realised that it was a hasty, desperate task, that not all the important pieces were in place.

Eleanor started to search the pack's side pockets. "I don't think it's here," she said.

"Got to be," I said. "He had it out this morning. He showed Charles." The image returned, the boy and Gary bending over the map. Just a fragment. Then, unsummoned, the rest.

"Oh, no," I said. "He put it in his poncho. It was still there when I buried him. I didn't think to search his clothes."

"Doesn't matter," Travis said. "We know the way back." Nobody said anything. "I'm just telling everybody this. I have no intention of dying here. You follow me, I'll get you out."

I NEVER DID TALK to Travis about having sent George out into the storm. But I knew he had been wrong. Get enough of us wandering around in a blizzard and the dark, and somebody was sure to die.

Eleanor lit one of the candles. It gave light and a tinge of warmth. Heating water for cocoa was Eleanor's idea too. We had extra fuel now, she said. No point in starving completely. Travis listened and nodded, so we got cocoa.

But not until he consented; that was the point.

Afterwards Charles went outside. I followed him. The snow had nearly stopped. I motioned to Charles to follow me further away, where we wouldn't be heard.

I said, "I want to know about this route of yours."

"No route, Ray. I need the map for that. But there's a town or something on the other side of these mountains. I don't know how far— maybe a day and a half if we're walking fast. I remember seeing it on the map this morning."

"You know where?"

He gestured towards the northeast.

"That way," he said. "Somewhere. I'll bet the packer who's supposed to supply us starts out from there. We're probably supposed to meet him between here and there."

"You think we ought to try for the town?"

"If there's nothing in the way."

471

"Like what?"

"I don't know. A big gorge, maybe. Or if the pass is too hairy."

"Paul has kind of taken over."

"Every group needs a leader," Charles said. "It ought to be somebody who really knows what's going on. But if you can't have that, then somebody who everyone believes in. You don't have to know much if the others think you do."

"People believe in Paul. He's always had that going for him."

Charles didn't say anything. I felt reproached.

Foreboding squatted out there in that cold darkness, fat and ugly as a huge toad. I had to ask, "Are we in big trouble?"

"Maybe not." He sounded steady, almost detached. "If the snow stops and the sun melts what's on the ground, we'll be OK. We'll just walk out, and it won't matter which way we go."

"What if that doesn't happen?"

"If the snow gets much deeper, we won't be able to go back the way we came. It's too far. Nobody can walk thirty miles through two feet of snow in these mountains." Still detached.

"Are you worried?" I said.

"I'd feel a lot better if I could look at the map."

LATER WE LAY in our bags, waiting for the candle to burn itself out. None of us slept. Not a word among us for what might have been ten minutes, might have been an hour.

Charles reached into his pack, brought out the group journal and a pencil and held them out to Donnie. "Your turn," he said.

"Come on, we're not playing games any more. This is real life now."

"It's been real all along."

The notebook and the pencil were inches from Donnie's face.

"You're serious. You want me to write in that thing."

I heard myself saying, "Go ahead," and Eleanor did the same.

"OK," he said. "You got it," and he took them, and wrote:

Day Six: Thursday, September 11

Today we got dumped on but good. I don't see it getting better before it gets worse.

CHAPTER EIGHT

Down in Red Lodge, Poague was renting a car, getting ready to drive to Billings, fly home. He and Andrea had hiked out the afternoon before, and had hitched a ride into town. At dinner he had seemed quiet. She had thought that he must be fatigued.

472

Now he was almost brusque as he loaded his suitcase into the car and turned to tell her goodbye. He thanked her, shook her hand and was gone. All with such stiffness that she wondered whether she had somehow offended him.

His leaving felt wrong, she told me later. Of course, he was a busy man, and of course, the trip really was finished for him; but it still felt wrong, she said—the abrupt way he left.

I can imagine him disconnecting that way. That was the Poague I had always known. In the past I'd have called it boorishness. Now—after what I know, after all that happened—I'm inclined to say that he didn't accept defeat well, and that he would always turn away before he would show hurt.

I've thought about him leaving, about his being home while the rest of us floundered in the mountains. The image offended me when I first learned that he had left; though he could have changed nothing, it seemed to me that he ought to have been closer when the world came apart for us on the plateau.

I didn't know that his own world was already in pieces.

WE WALKED MOST of the next day, fuelled by a few raisins and that chunk of Cheddar, and we might have covered a respectable distance if Travis hadn't insisted on precisely following our old route. We wasted hours and miles. I could have told him about the way snow alters the land, but he wouldn't have listened.

The day before, we had hiked from the crater lake to the half dome in about four hours. The return took nearly eight. Twice, we wandered into territory that we couldn't recognise, and Travis demanded that we retrace our tracks until he was sure we were set right again. We reached the bowl around midafternoon. Miles yet to cover before we approached the pass. Even without delays tomorrow, we would have a hard pull all day up the summit.

What craziness this must seem to an outsider looking in. Charles knew there was a better way, and I knew there was, but we never protested.

Charles I can excuse. He was no leader. All the weight of his brains and knowledge couldn't balance his squeaky voice and his scrawny, puerile body. Somehow strength mattered; no coup ever succeeded on ideas alone. And as for me, I have since discovered any number of reasons why I didn't speak and act.

Here's a good one: clearly, Travis was wound tight and would not tolerate challenge. Any opposition was at the risk of his coming undone, so I tolerated his foolishness.

And another: Travis was so convincing. In the mountains and in every other world, he had a way of drawing others to him and keeping them

there. I was just Furlow, no match for his ability to make people want to believe him.

That one I can almost buy. But when I find the courage, I admit that I remained silent not because I believed that the others would never let me lead them, but because I feared that they might.

We were about an hour, two miles, past the crater lake when Donnie complained again about his stomach.

"It hurts," he said. "Cramps. Real bad."

Travis turned round and said he didn't want to hear any complaining. He was trying to save our lives. The least we could do was shut up and get serious.

What can you do when a hero invokes his own heroism? We shut up and got serious, and we kept following Travis.

An hour later we were walking through a ravine, downstream beside a small creek. The creek flowed away to the southwest, and we started a long climb up a ridge as hard and bare as any hunk of rock I have seen. It was at least a thousand feet high.

Donnie was directly in front of me as we climbed. Not far from the top he stopped. He stood holding his stomach, then folded in sections until he was sitting in the snow, bent at the waist, his head between his knees.

Eleanor and I squatted beside him. The other three were ahead of us, unaware. I called Travis's name, and they came over.

Travis said, "For crying out loud."

Donnie brought his face up. It was blanched and tightened, the face of someone in real pain. "I can't help it," he said.

"Can you walk?" Travis said.

Eleanor cut off Donnie's answer. "What a stupid question," she said. "Obviously, if he could walk, he'd be walking." I knew and Travis knew she wouldn't let him be pushed further.

After a moment Travis said, "It's getting dark anyway."

Charles found a nook in a granite outcropping, wedge-shaped, as if a big slice of pie had been lifted out of the ridge. It was just deep enough and wide enough to hold us all. We cleared the snow out of it. Charles and Hollenbeck stretched one of the tarps across the top and tied it down. The second tarp they fastened to the first, lacing the eyelets together down over the open end of the wedge. We put our packs inside the mouth of the wedge, holding down the loose end of the hanging tarp. Charles had piled snow against the other side of the tarp, leaving room for a crawlway entrance; the bank of snow blocked the wind and helped to trap our body heat inside.

George prepared the last of the Jell-O and then boiled the bulgur. Eleanor sat Donnie up, leaning him against her, and held a cup of the liquid gelatine to his lips. Soon he took it from her, drank it down, drank another cup. It seemed to help. His face loosened. Some colour returned. He looked at their shoulders resting together, lifted an eyebrow, and said if she was going to take care of him, he would have to get sick more often.

We were hungry enough that even the bulgur disappeared. We scraped out the pot and licked the cups clean.

Donnie got up, went outside, and returned a few minutes later.

"You feeling better?" Travis asked Donnie. The boy nodded. "That's good," Travis said. "Tomorrow we have to do some serious humping—I want everybody good and strong."

Nobody said anything. Eleanor lit a candle, and we settled into a quiet neutral consciousness that I have never experienced anywhere else. We consumed hours in this bivouac trance, clutching sleeping-bags round faces and necks to seal out the cold, thinking thoughts that leave no impression on the memory.

Later that evening Eleanor rustled, stretched her legs, and said she was thirsty, would somebody please pass her water bottle.

Hollenbeck was closest to the pile of packs. He unzipped a side pocket of one, took out a bottle, handed it to her.

She took a mouthful and said, "Whose water is this? It isn't mine."

A demand on our consciousness; we all shifted out of the trance. Hollenbeck said, "I thought this one was yours."

"From that pack over there?" Donnie said. "That's mine."

She said, "It's fresh. It doesn't have any iodine."

"Yeah. I tried it once. Couldn't take that taste."

Charles, naturally, found the handle first. "Donnie," he said. "You've got *giardia*."

Donnie said, "Hey, blood, I've known that for days."

BY MORNING we had had another foot of snow, and it continued to fall. Two foot deep or more, up to mid-thigh in places. There seemed no question of hiking through it.

Travis had been up at daybreak, and was now fully dressed, stalking aimlessly through the drifts outside. He stopped me when I went to get water.

He said, "I suppose everyone is very happy about this."

I groped for an answer suitable to such absurdity.

"It's a good excuse to stay put," he said. "We can all sit on our behinds and watch the snow come down."

"Even if we walked all day, we wouldn't cover five miles in this mess."

"I could feel it last night," he said. "I'm the only one willing to do what it takes to get out of here."

"Paul, I think you're mistaken."

476

He gave me a look of dry, pitying disdain that I felt drilling into my back when I walked away.

The only water we had found was a trickle down a crack in the rock, flowing under the snow. In one spot the water pooled in a depression about an inch deep, a foot across.

I shoved aside the snow from around the pool. With Gary's axe I shattered the ice that had formed on the top until I had a hole big enough to submerge a Sierra cup. Lift out the cup, pour its few ounces into a bottle. Sink the cup again, lift it out. Eight, ten immersions to top off each bottle. When the bottles were full, I held them against me and churned through the snow towards the shelter.

Travis still tramped about outside, stark and silly. I had to pass within a few feet of him. He stopped, stared as I approached.

"That's OK," he said. "I'll save you in spite of yourselves."

He came inside and got into his bag, and for the rest of the day he was tense and silent, an unsettling presence among us.

DONNIE TRIED TO JOKE about the *giardia*. He had been up and out of the shelter at least once every couple of hours, and every trip brought a fusillade of wisecracks. Eventually it stopped being funny. He was ill. By evening, after he had left one more time, he looked so unsteady that Eleanor said one of us ought to make sure he didn't collapse in the snow.

Donnie said, "Can't anybody have any privacy around here?" But he didn't complain later when he got up to leave again and Charles went out with him.

WE WERE BOILING WATER for a meal of freeze-dried turkey tetrazzini when the stove's jet popped twice and expired. Out of fuel. We still had Gary's bottle, so we filled the stove and finished heating the water. But those pops had the sound of emptiness and cold desolation.

One bag made half servings for the six of us. Donnie wouldn't eat his, but he drank as much water as the rest of us combined. That made sense when I thought about the fluids he was losing. Through dinner and afterwards, Travis kept watching him. Intensely, almost with hostility. Suddenly he said, "Can you walk, the way you are?"

"I'll go where anybody else goes."

Eleanor said, "It's ridiculous. We can't go anywhere."

"You want to sit here and let the snow bury us?" Travis said.

I said, "There are physical limits."

Sharply he snapped back, "You've never run into a real limit in your life. You never let yourself get that far." He slouched and withdrew, but inside he was coiled. I could feel it, the potential within him for a kickback that I couldn't name or predict.

Later, he all but told me, and I still didn't understand.

It happened that night, at some murky hour. The others were asleep. Travis and I lay beside the packs that held down the tarp's hanging end. I heard a rustling and raised my head. Travis was sitting, and when I moved, he looked at me—or had been watching me all along, I suppose. A candle's flame wavered beside him.

For an instant he was the Travis I had known once, across that eternity of the past eight or nine days: unshaken, controlled, sure of himself. All the pieces back in place, flawlessly finished.

He said, "Ray, you think you know. But you know only so much, and it's not enough." I was captivated by the softness of his voice. Like all the rest of him at this moment, it was almost unbearably beautiful. He said, "You'll see. That's all."

Obviously, he expected me to understand, but I had no idea what he meant. Before I could ask him to explain, I imagined him kissing Noreen Poague. Words would be wasted on that Travis. I set my face, turned over, and shut him out of my thoughts. Soon I was sleeping.

Since then I have wondered uncountable times what might have happened if I had asked what he meant. If I had bothered to think about him. If I had just bothered to care. This one question I find difficult to let go. If I had even listened.

At least I might not have been so astonished the next morning, when I looked over at the empty space where his bag had been, then pushed aside the tarp to see his tracks surging up the ridge, and realised that he had left.

He and Hollenbeck both. A page torn from the journal lay where Travis's pack had been. His handwriting:

Ray et al.
Gone to get help. Sorry. Can't sit around any more. Stay warm, don't leave. Won't be long. Somebody had to do something.
Paul

I dressed quickly and went out to follow the tracks.

A ripened dawn. For the first time in three days the sky was clear, air colder than ever before. The snow was above knee-high; it quadrupled resistance and effort. Long before I reached the top of the ridge, my breath was exhausted. My boots were soaked through, socks wet with melt. I thought of Hollenbeck doing this. No way could he go the distance. I saw him tagging after Travis like a kid after his big brother. I got angry at Hollenbeck for doing that, angrier yet at Travis for allowing it to happen. The anger carried me up to the top of the ridge. From there I could see the tracks stitching down across a valley. There was nobody else as far as I could see.

Eleanor was holding the note when I got back.

"Gone?" she said.

"Oh yeah. He's gone all right. George too."

"Can they make it?"

"Not George. Paul—who knows? He's in great shape."

She said, "Physically, maybe. For what that's worth."

I took off my boots and poncho, got into the bag. Charles shifted to face us. He had been awake to hear this.

He said, "They shouldn't have done that. In a survival situation the chance of success almost always goes down if a group divides."

I remember wishing that he hadn't used the term "a survival situation". Which it was, of course; but once correctly named, some realities become almost unbearably awesome.

Eleanor said, "They're out for themselves. They can't help us if pilots won't fly helicopters up here."

"They will for Travis," I said.

Charles said he hated to be cynical about motives, but we ought to check the packs, see how much food was gone.

I went through Gary's pack and found that they had taken the third tarp, a water bottle, two date-nut bars, a pack of matches.

Now Donnie was awake. He licked dry lips with a dry tongue and said, "Paul and George are gone?"

Charles told him yes. Gone to get help.

"Dumb jerks," he said. "Now what are we going to do?"

All three of them looked at me, waiting for me to speak.

The answer was simple, easily reached, but I hesitated; and when I spoke, the words felt ungainly.

"Just what we would have done anyway," I said. "We're going to sit and wait."

HOLLENBECK CAUGHT TRAVIS sometime in the afternoon.

He says he woke that dawn and found Travis gone, found the note. He dressed without waking us, and set out after him. Of course, Paul was stronger—but Paul had to break the trail, whereas Hollenbeck could follow in his tracks.

In the afternoon he came over a rise. Below him the terrain dipped and rose again, and he looked across the trough to the second swell. Where there should have been tracks the snow was unbroken. Travis hadn't been there yet. Hollenbeck ploughed forward, down into the dip, and at the bottom he found Travis kneeling at a frozen stream, pushing his bottle through a rupture in snow and shattered ice.

Travis stood up. When Hollenbeck approached him, he said, "No lectures, George. Please."

"Did I say anything?"

"I'm not trying to save my own butt."

"I believe that," Hollenbeck said. And he did.

"I know what they're thinking." Hollenbeck remembers him making a vague gesture towards the west, taking us all in. "I couldn't sit there feeling it. I couldn't stay."

"I understand," Hollenbeck said. "I really do."

Travis said, "What are you doing here, anyway?"

Hollenbeck thought, You're my friend and you're in trouble and you need looking after. But he knew he couldn't tell that to Travis, so he said, "I couldn't stay there either."

Travis said, "You can follow me if you want. But this is my play, George. It won't work if I have to think about you."

If he had said that to me, even on the best of days, I'd have told him, What's the matter, Paul—don't want to share the glory? But Hollenbeck said, "I can stay with you if you keep breaking trail all the way to the end. Can you do that?"

"I'm pretty sure. It's harder than I thought. But I feel good. Now that I'm away from the others, I feel real strong."

"I'm glad," Hollenbeck said.

"I hoped I could get to the pass by this afternoon. But it's too far. We'll find a place out of the weather tonight, head up there in the morning."

"You know where it is?"

Travis was bending to fill the bottle, capping it, putting it away. He said, "Somewhere east. We'll get within a mile or so, and find it when we're close."

Hollenbeck said, "You weren't that sure about it before."

Travis said, "It's different when people are watching." He turned, and started up the hill in front of him.

SOMETIME THAT DAY, that night, I realised that one of us might die. Life was ebbing in all of us. You can drain only so much energy before death starts to encroach upon the edges of life.

That evening we ate all the food that remained, all but a couple of inches of salami. Donnie picked at his share and put it aside. The rest of us gulped ours, then his leavings. We hadn't eaten fully in almost four days, and gulping that food was like flinging it into a canyon. In a couple of minutes the food was gone, but hunger was untouched.

Life was ebbing in all of us, but fastest in Donnie. Like turning down the wick of an oil lamp. Maybe we wouldn't have noticed if he hadn't burned so hot before.

Night clamped down on us. We huddled in candlelight, withdrawn into nylon and wadding. After a while Donnie got up to go outside moving slowly. He was in long johns, a poncho, unlaced boots. Charles got a torch, and they went together.

Eleanor had been opposite me, half hunched. Now she slid her bag over next to mine. "I think one of us ought to stay up with him at night." The wind thumped the tarp overhead. "To make sure he doesn't go out alone. It's nasty out there."

I told her we could take turns staying awake while he slept. Truth was, I didn't see the point. But I knew that sometime in the last few days, consciously or not, she had chosen him to care about. In a couple of minutes the boys came back and got into their bags. Before long they were dozing, then fully asleep. We were awake, she and I, watching this happen. This is going to seem crazy. But we were a family there—a man and a woman and their children. They were our charges, and we had to be strong and clever for them: they bound us.

The presence of death must have had something to do with it. Forcing us down to basics. In a low, calm voice Eleanor began to tell me about her husband and Duck Key. From me she got the basic short version of my life from adolescence on, abridged but not so disembowelled as to be falsely flattering. It even nibbled around my father. I know the thought of dying made that easier. What else will make trivia of failure and pain?

"One of us ought to rest," she said after a while.

"Go ahead. I'm fine. Sleep."

She shifted in the bag and lay with her head against my hip. "If you start nodding off, just wake me up," she said.

"Don't worry about me."

The three of them slept. Time became empty. I tried to fill it with thoughts and feelings, but it kept expanding.

The weight of her head against my hip. Their trusting sleep. Time at a halt. Creamy warmth inside the bag, skin melting into the fabric. Their trusting sleep. Their sleep.

You know what had to happen.

TRAVIS AND HOLLENBECK reached a small stand of woods around sunset, so they stopped for the night. Hollenbeck discovered a hollow under one large pine, a hole in the snow that the branches had sheltered. They strung the tarp over it and settled in.

George wanted to rest. Travis insisted on talking. He went on about racquetball and Poague and MDC. Hollenbeck didn't understand how Travis could think about anything beyond the crushing reality of the snow and the trees. But Travis didn't seem to require conversation, only an audience, so Hollenbeck shut his eyes and listened idly.

He was about to stop fighting weariness when Travis said, "This thing with Ray. About Poague's wife."

Hollenbeck nudged himself awake and opened his eyes.

"His facts are basically correct. I was up for the job. My two friends and myself. Or I thought we were. And I was seeing the boss's wife. It doesn't make me look real good."

When George didn't react, he went on.

"She was the one who came on to me. And this was before the thing with the job. But look, I won't lie to you. When it started to happen, I did ask myself what she might be able to do for me. I did hope it would kind of give me an edge."

Hollenbeck knew his face must be stunned, blank. Travis kept waiting for a reaction, but got nothing.

"Understand?" he said. "I did what Ray said I did."

Hollenbeck said, "I thought it might be true."

"Does it bother you?"

After a few seconds Hollenbeck said, "I feel like it happened to somebody else a long time ago."

"I don't want it to change anything between us."

"You get us out of here—all of us—and nothing else will matter to anybody."

"Hey, pal. That's the whole point entirely."

DONNIE WAS GONE and the candle was out and I was asleep.

When Eleanor stirred, I woke. She got her torch. In its light I saw Donnie's crumpled bag. I saw her reach into it. I saw from her face that the bag was cold.

She said, "Ray," in a way that was hurt, accusing, uncomprehending. My name has never sounded the same since.

Out into the night, the three of us, wincing against snow swirling off the ridge, blizzard-thick. We shouted for Donnie, waded through the snow, bent into the wind. Charles thought to look into a deep ravine that ran up the side of the ridge.

Donnie was at the bottom, inert.

He didn't move when I got there. I felt for a pulse, found a shuddering quiver; saw a gash over one eye; felt a swelling at the back of his head, another at mid tibia of his left leg. There were scrapes and contusions wherever the skin was bare and where the blue fabric of his long johns had torn away.

The only proper way to get him out of the ravine would have been with a neck brace, a litter, a winch and cable. I held him in my arms and began to carry him.

When I started climbing, he came to, and screamed a tortured scream that hurt my eyes and emptied me inside. The scream died to a horrible moan so low that only I could hear it. It kept passing over his lips while I

482

climbed through the snow, and rose each time I slipped or jostled him, and didn't end until I brought him into the shelter and laid him down and covered him with his bag.

"DON'T YOU LET him die," she said.

She expected me to do something. Me.

"I don't know what to do," I said.

"Just don't let him die." Her eyes made it a threat.

We knelt beside Donnie, the three of us. Charles at his head, Eleanor at one shoulder, I at the other. His eyes tried to follow us as we spoke, but they were slow to focus, slow to shift.

In a violent tremolo he said, "I'm real cold."

"Heat some water," I said. "We'll get him to drink some tea."

We covered him with all the clothes we could find. I zipped my bag open and draped it over his own.

There was so much wrong with him. And we knew so little. I got out the first-aid kit and opened it, looking for answers. Percodan. It would help the pain, but I didn't know what else it might do. Aspirin, yes. When the water was hot, I had Charles tilt Donnie's head up so he could take two with his tea.

Something returned from long ago. A summer job as a lifeguard: three days of training in first aid.

I asked him, "Can you move your arms and legs?"

His fingers flexed, his legs drew up tentatively. When he moved the left one, he said, "That hurts," in a shudder.

If the leg was broken, it had to be splinted. I took a knife, cut open one of the packs, tore loose the two steel shank supports in the back. Straightened the leg, wrapped it with foam rubber from a sleeping pad, and taped the shanks to either side of his calf.

We knelt round him and watched him shiver through a second cup of tea. His pulse was no stronger.

I told them it was shock and I didn't know what else we could do about it, but we had to get him warm.

Eleanor took off her poncho. I said that piling on more clothes wouldn't help, but she ignored me. She took off her boots, her gaiters, her pants, her shirt. Charles understood before I did. He too was removing his clothes, putting them aside.

By now I saw. Eleanor lifting the bags and the layers of clothing, moving into the space she had created beside him. Like a knowing lover she folded herself around his racked body.

Charles got in on the other side. He had been watching her, and now mimicked her movements, her posture, her care. After a few seconds I climbed into Eleanor's bag.

In the darkness I could hear breathing. Theirs was measured and soothing; Donnie's, chopped and pounding at first. But while I listened it became longer, lower, more even, until it matched theirs and I couldn't tell them apart any more.

Around dawn I fell into a brief and shallow sleep. Awoke to a pinstripe of muted daylight along the edge of the tarp flap. Eleanor, dressed again, sat vigilant at Donnie's head. Charles still stretched out beside him. She looked when I moved in the bag.

"We need water," she said. "There's plenty of light now."

There was no emotion in her voice. To say that she was cold would be flattering myself. She was neutral, impenetrable.

Donnie rested so solidly it couldn't have been sleep. I reached under his bag for his wrist.

"It's not good," she said.

His pulse boomed one beat, whispered the next.

I leaned closer, to thumb back his eyelids. As if I knew what I was doing. He didn't move when I touched his face.

The left pupil was open full, unnaturally large. Eleanor was looking; she wanted to know what that meant.

I said, "I don't know. It isn't right."

She might have answered, A lot of things aren't right. But she didn't say anything, only picked up a near-empty bottle and handed it to me.

"There's no more," she said. "He'll be thirsty when he wakes up. So get back as soon as you can."

I thought I'd be glad to get outside, away from her blankness. But beyond the tarp was the ravine. I couldn't avoid looking at it, imagining him in the dark, stumbling over the edge. Lying there unconscious while we slept. While *I* slept.

Early morning was warmer than night had been. I went down to the small pool where I filled the bottles, and I was back so quickly she let gratitude show through for a moment before she became opaque again.

CHAPTER NINE

Travis and Hollenbeck were up before daybreak. An hour later they were on a promontory, looking over several miles of the plateau to the crest line. They picked out the pass, and the shelf between the twin pinnacles. Hollenbeck got out his compass and took a bearing. One hundred and twenty degrees.

This was before the snow. Half an hour later big wet flakes descended thickly. Travis kept wading through the fall. He simply didn't stop; Hollenbeck thought his stamina was amazing. Then Hollenbeck remembered that he hadn't stopped either, that he was actually keeping up with Travis.

Around midmorning they hit the last long uphill gradient to the pass. The fresh fall was at least six inches thick by now, and Hollenbeck felt the urgency of a race—hurry, or be buried. Travis picked up his stride, and Hollenbeck let himself be drawn along. He felt giddy; the legs and the lungs that were making this happen had to belong to someone else. His own were incapable of such feats.

They pushed past the rock ledges where we had made shelter.

Travis was effervescent. "How about this?" he said. "On the nose, huh?"

"Let's not celebrate yet." Hollenbeck thought of the boulder fields. They would be full of snow. Couldn't make them any easier.

"Hey. From here we could roll down to the highway. Twelve hours from now we'll be in Red Lodge."

They reached the summit and crossed the shelf to the other side. Directly below and before them was the long chute where we had clambered up, now lush with trackless snow that filled in all the corrugations, cloaked the harshness.

Poague had fallen from near the top of the chute. Hollenbeck was telling himself that they would have to be careful on it when Travis grinned at him and whooped, and launched himself off the lip, as if from a springboard into a pool. He kicked in midair, spread his arms, and fell out of sight.

Hollenbeck ran over to the edge. Travis lay on his back, limbs splayed, awash in new powder, motionless. Hollenbeck thought, Stupid son of a . . . before Travis tossed up armloads of showering flakes and yowled, "Wow! That's one way to get down."

He bounced up and stood, hip-deep, and took several lunging steps down the slope, leaning forward, breasting the snow like a surfer paddling past breakers.

He yelled to Hollenbeck, "Take the plunge. Time's a-wastin'."

Hollenbeck hesitated at the top. He was looking at the snow in the chute, the deposits climbing up its sides. He thought that the chute looked pregnant—swollen, replete. Imminent.

He went down. The slow way. Travis was a couple of hundred yards ahead, pushing. On both sides of him piles of snow climbed the chute's high walls, thick even at the top, lying at improbable angles.

Hollenbeck noticed movement in the chute, a soft worrying, as if something bubbled beneath the fresh fall. It became a churning that spread wider as it chewed across the chute, up the other side, and then bore down on Travis. Building, gaining speed.

By the time it reached him, the rolling wave was twice Travis's height,

and growing. Hollenbeck was astonished that it made no noise. All that weight, that force—completely silent.

Travis glanced back at the instant the avalanche reached him. He existed, and then there was the wave storming, this soundless rampage that tossed and kicked snow dust in a billowing cloud, and the cloud and the wave kept boiling downhill, leaving empty the place where he had stood.

Hollenbeck started to go to the spot, wading through mudlike, slippery snow. He urged himself towards where he had last seen Travis. The snow began to move round him, began to flow with the deliberate firmness of wet concrete, sucking him along. He pumped his legs, but found no purchase underfoot.

Above him was movement. A bushel-sized package of fresh fall had separated from the side of the chute and was turning over, gaining mass and momentum as it snowballed. The pack was coming apart again, and it was taking him down with it.

Now the snow round him felt like a sluggish river. Hollenbeck forced himself to think. He told himself, If it's a river, I can swim. And that's what he began to do. A slow-motion mimicry of kicking and breast-stroking, pulling himself through the torpid white substance that wasn't snow any more, wasn't anything he could name.

To his right, along the side of the chute, was an island of solid pack that the movement hadn't dislodged. It was no more than a body's length away, but the flow was carrying him past it. Hollenbeck paddled and pulled. He reached for the island, dug the fingers of his right hand through the crust, and held; then, breathless, he hauled himself up onto its firmness.

IN THE SHELTER, Donnie lay before us like a festering wound. Most of the time he was unconscious, breathing without pattern.

That afternoon Eleanor tried to feed him salami that she had chopped and mashed in warm water. She cradled him and spooned it past his rubbery lips. His eyes were open, heavy-lidded, but he didn't seem to notice. The spoon shook in her hand, and I saw that she was crying, saying, "All you had to do was wake me up. I told you, if you get sleepy, just wake me up."

The food caught in Donnie's throat, and he gagged, and she had to stop. She wiped his chin, lowered his head. As she was turning away he said clearly, "Cut the poor guy some slack, huh? It isn't like he pushed me. Ray, my head hurts. How 'bout a couple of those Percs?"

So he was aware. His eyes followed me as I shook out a pill. He opened his mouth and put out his tongue to take it, and swallowed. Two minutes later he was unconscious again.

The wind was insistent, hectoring. Time ground slow and ponderous. Time and starvation and fatigue beat us down until we were less than we had been the day before, with the certain knowledge that a day later we would be further diminished.

You get surprised at what is worn away. Hunger. The first day of fasting is torture. After that the craving becomes just an imperfect memory. Bitterness and anger go too. They're emotional luxuries. When she reproached me, there was no bile in Eleanor. Only sadness.

I went out to brush snow from the overhead tarp, and was surprised to find day draining into night. Eleanor lit the stove, but it flamed out before the water was even tepid. Out of fuel. She asked how long it would be before Travis and Hollenbeck got through. Never suggesting that they might fail; like sadness, hope will root wherever it can, survive without sustenance.

I told her, "If they really hustle, they might get down in two days."

"So that would be tomorrow morning," she said.

"But nothing will happen until the weather is clear. Not even Travis will get a helicopter up in this mess." It had the feel of fantasy; any movement but our own labouring through the snow, any sound besides the wind and our voices seemed inconceivable.

WHEN I WOKE AGAIN, daylight was seeping into the shelter. Charles crawled to the entrance and threw back the hanging tarp to a blisteringly bright morning.

I went out, looked around, came back and dredged dark glasses from my pack. I cleared a place against an outside face of the granite that had hidden us, dug and pushed the snow until I was down to bare ground. I took off my poncho and sat. On the other side of the granite, within the cleft, were stink and dimness and dying. Some of the stench and a crust of despair clung to me too. But I could sense it crumbling under the bright pressure of the sun.

It seemed a good day for flying. I tried to imagine the arrival of a helicopter, its blades stirring up a false blizzard as it came to earth. Then Donnie and Charles and Eleanor and I on the chopper, the side of the ridge falling away from us as the machine rose. It was the last image on my mind before I melted into the only true sleep I had slept in uncountable hours.

A COLD SHADOW settled on my face. Charles stood at my feet, between me and the sun, now past its apex, descending.

"Ray, Eleanor asked me to make sure you were OK."

"I'm fine."

"We need water. I'll go if you want."

488

"It's my job. I know where it is."

I picked myself up and put on the poncho. The ice axe was in the shelter. I crouched and went inside.

Eleanor was at her vigil, stroking Donnie's head. She said, "Ray, he can't move his right side. He can hardly talk."

I scuttled the few inches to him. His left eye was alive, tracking me. The right one was motionless. They both showed fear.

"They didn't make it, did they?" she said.

"It's much too early to say." I picked up the bottles, searched for the ice axe.

"If they had, help would be here by now."

"We can't know that." I got the axe and left without looking at her again.

A V-shaped depression in the snow marked the pool. It was frozen over, but I could hear dribbling beneath it. I broke the ice, the water drained into the hole, and I bent to fill the first bottle.

I stood, and heard my name—a sound so tenuous, so indistinct, the tiny flow at my feet almost drowned it.

Once more, louder. From higher on the ridge. I saw a staggering bundle that flapped its arms and shouted, "Ray, Ray."

It was Hollenbeck. I fought uphill to meet him. A few feet away he stumbled, fell; the waist-high snow caught him, and I pulled him upright.

"Did it," he said. Breathless. "I can't believe I did it."

He seemed disappointed. As if he expected more from me than a casual hand up. But I was looking past him, up to the top of the empty ridge.

"Just me," he said. "Sorry. I'm all there is."

HOLLENBECK LOOKED at Donnie and asked, "What happened?"

Eleanor said, "The night after you left we fell asleep. He went outside alone and took a bad fall. It looks like he was out there quite a while before we got him in."

She left plenty of room to distribute blame. But Hollenbeck looked directly at me. He knew me, knew my ways. And knew enough to ask no more.

Instead, he said, "My muscles feel like jelly." He sat up against the rock, and while he kneaded his calves and his thighs he told us all that he had done and seen, all that he knew.

"I PULLED MYSELF UP on the solid part, where it wasn't moving," he said. "Then there was some bare rock, where all the snow had slid off. I climbed back to the top. I wanted to keep going down, but there was no way. I wouldn't have had a chance.

"I decided to come back here. I didn't know what else to do. For a while it was easy—just stayed with the tracks. But after a while I lost them on and off. They filled up with snow. So I used the compass. Three hundred degrees is the reciprocal of one twenty, right? And it worked. Once I got close, I knew where you were supposed to be. And you were."

He kept watching Donnie. Who lay so still he might have been dead. The spectacle of waste compelled Hollenbeck as it compelled the rest of us.

He said, "There's something we have to talk about." He looked round at each of us. "Here it is. We have to get out of the mountains. We can't count on help—we don't know that they'll start looking before it's too late. Without food we're not getting any stronger. This time tomorrow we'll be that much less able to do it. We have to get going. Anybody who can walk."

Eleanor said, "What about Donnie?" She was bending over him the way a mother suspends herself over her infant.

When nobody else answered, Hollenbeck said, "Donnie has to stay. The best thing we can do for him is to get help."

Now Charles and Hollenbeck began to discuss when we should leave and which route to take. Whether to wait until morning. I couldn't keep up. They were talking about the future, and I hadn't yet grasped a present where Travis did not exist.

Between them they decided that we ought to use the good weather; let Hollenbeck rest for an hour or two, then get moving. We could walk at night, use torches and the moon. And we could return to the pass that Hollenbeck had left. No other choice; we might wander for days trying to find another place to cross. Maybe the snow would be more stable when we got there. Maybe we'd have to take a chance.

"These boots," Hollenbeck said. He was taking them off to get into a sleeping-bag. "Thank God for 'em. And that snow wax. It was such a mess when I was putting it on."

"It worked?" I said. I remember my wet socks, frigid feet.

"Look." Toes wiggled in dry wool. "Kept me going."

"That's really good, George." I meant it.

"At the time you do it, you can't believe it'll ever make a difference. I felt sort of foolish, if you want to know the truth. It's one of those dumb tasks people say you should do. But nobody ever does except suckers. You know me. The suckers' sucker."

I took one of the boots, held it, felt its solidness. The weight and the hard-shelled leather were reassuring.

He said, "I can't believe it. For once there's a payoff—it actually made a difference. I guess it had to happen sooner or later."

490

I WENT OUT to finish filling the bottles. When I returned, Hollenbeck was outside the shelter, waiting for me.

"How bad is Donnie?" he said.

"About as bad as he could get and still be breathing."

"Is there any point in one of us staying with him?"

After a few seconds' thought I said, "He wouldn't be alone when he died. I don't know if that counts. The way he is now, I'm not sure he realises we're here, anyway."

"Better come in. She wants to stay with him."

I followed him inside. Eleanor seemed tiny at first, even in the midst of such confinement. Then I realised. She was not so much tiny as reduced in stature, the way a tremendous weight will bow its bearer's back. Her burden was the boy's suffering, and our misery, and the darkness and the squalor.

"I'm not leaving him," she said. "It's wrong."

"We have to leave," Hollenbeck said.

"I understand," she said. "Go. You don't need me. We'll stay here, Donnie and I, while you go for help."

"This is utterly stupid," Hollenbeck said. "The kid is dying. You want to sit up here alone and hold hands with a corpse."

"Enough," she said.

Charles said, "I know Donnie. If he could talk, he'd be telling you to get going with us."

"Unfortunately, he can't speak for himself."

Hollenbeck asked her, "If you knew he was up and talking, would that make a difference?"

"I don't know. Maybe."

"Then, why don't we give him a chance? I'm tired. Really. If we wait till morning, maybe we'll get this thing resolved."

Something out there had changed Hollenbeck. The miles, the snow, surviving where Travis had perished. But I could still read him. He was thinking, *Or it'll resolve itself.*

"Whatever you want," I said.

"As long as we don't wait too long," Charles said.

Eleanor said, "Do what you think is right. It's the only way."

DURING THE NIGHT I woke. I mean, just like that: woke so immediately and completely it could not have been happenstance. A part of me must have planned it.

All the others slept. I was alone with what had to be done. Why else should I have chosen the moment?

I knew exactly what I had to do and how to go about it. Under my head was my backpack. In a pocket was the headlamp, wrapped in a T-shirt that dimmed the light to a firefly smudge when I turned on the switch.

Already I lay beside Donnie; I could touch his face as easily as touch my own. Not even Travis had ever arranged so artfully.

I propped myself up on an elbow, and studied him longer and more closely than I ever could have done if he had been conscious, or even just asleep. Pain and paralysis had set his features. The filtered light softened them somewhat, and when I looked past the hurt, past the bruises and the scrapes and the puffy eye, I could see the beautiful child that he had managed to keep hidden from us. Youth that made me ache at the thought of it. Youth, and innocence too. He should have had years to dissipate them both.

He didn't move when I covered his nose and mouth with my hands and pushed down.

Some big-game hunters claim there's an instant before death when killer and quarry know each other completely, a moment of communion, total understanding. I'm not much of a hunter. But I believe this: I believe that Donnie heard me when I spoke to him in my mind. I love you. I'm sorry, but you have to go now.

Couldn't let her stay for him.

IN MY HEART I have snuffed him ten thousand times. It's always the same. While everyone else sleeps I wake beside him, I gaze at his face, I lovingly shut off his breath of life. When he is dead, I return to my slumbers knowing that in the ultimate judgment what I've done must prove right.

But it is a manufactured memory. Truth is, I lacked the will to keep my hands in place until it was done. Truth is that I am not nearly so confident of judgment's verdict.

You could say that at the moment of final decision I was unable to force myself to murder. You could also say that once more I failed to do what had to be done.

Eventually the others began to awake. It was morning, and Donnie remained unconscious, breathing, and Eleanor was still determined to stay with him.

Hollenbeck said, "This is stupid. Are you shooting for sainthood? Is that it? Martyrdom?"

"Just go, and leave us alone."

Even a week earlier she might have been bullied into coming with us. But now she resisted all duress.

Time was with her; while Hollenbeck argued, Charles gathered and sorted equipment, and there was only so much of that to do. Before long he was finished, and we were ready to leave, and she remained adamant. She had outlasted him.

Charles had divided the equipment—what little we were taking—into two backpacks. There were the sleeping-bags, the spare tarp, matches, compasses, a rope, the bag of climber's hardware. We took one water bottle and left the others.

The crampons and ice axe were strapped outside one pack. I told Charles that we should leave the axe, that Eleanor might need it to open the small pool.

"We could need it more," he said. At the time it struck me as selfish; a day and miles later I realised that he'd had a notion of what might be waiting. Instead he gave her a piton from the bag of climbing gear. It was an iron blade, dull and thick. He took her outside to the pool, showed her how the piton would gouge ice if she used it right. She said she'd make it work, don't worry.

The four of us stood in the snow. Hollenbeck put on one pack, and I had the other. To Hollenbeck she said, "Please don't be angry." She kissed him on the cheek.

"You take care of these guys," she said to Charles, and she put her arms round him.

I stood at a distance of maybe ten paces. Not by accident. I wasn't sure what she would say, what final disappointment I would sense in her, and I didn't want to find out.

I raised my right hand and waved once. She answered with the same motion, smaller.

Hollenbeck went up the hill first. When he passed me, he said we should take turns leading, let Charles follow; we would cover more ground that way.

I looked back once. She was at the entrance, watching us. Against the immensity of snow she seemed as vulnerable and lonely as anyone had ever looked to me. She crouched, and disappeared into the hole, and I wished, for the first of many thousands of times, that I had killed him when I'd had the chance.

WE WALKED, AND WE KEPT walking. My boots were soon soaked through; the cold marched in with the wet. The far mountains seemed to retreat before us. Yet we kept putting distance behind us, so that after a few hours we were far from where we had been, but hardly closer to where we were bound.

At first we rested every hour or so, but when we stopped moving, we stopped being able to gloss over discomfort and weariness. So during the afternoon we rested only twice.

Hollenbeck told us about the bivouac in the trees. He and Travis had reached it around sunset. But Travis had left before dawn that morning; our start had been at least two hours later.

493

Hollenbeck said we still had a way to go before we got to the trees, but it was worth pushing for. When darkness came, we let our lights lead us across the snow, and we kept walking.

I came apart at the oddest time. Hollenbeck was leading, so he was doing the really hard work. We were on a long descent, steep enough for gravity alone to pull our legs forward. The snow in this stretch was hardly calf-high.

None of that mattered. My legs gave way. I was astonished to find myself on my forearms in the snow, turning over, sitting, looking up at Hollenbeck and Charles.

"Are you hurt?" Hollenbeck asked.

I told him, "No. I'm just used up."

"Come on, then," he said. He put a hand down for me to grab.

I found the energy to shake my head. Understand, I wasn't being petulant. I thought my legs wouldn't carry me any more.

"There's nothing left," I said.

"Ah, don't give me that." His anger sounded genuine. "I'm still standing, and I've been up and down this track once already, and while I was out here doing it you were back there nodding off." He aimed that one for the quick, and it hit.

"I guess you're just a superman, George."

"We both know better than that."

Charles said, "We're getting cold. We need to keep moving."

Hollenbeck said, "Ray, this is how people get into trouble in the mountains. Fool around and get cold. Now, you come with us. We don't want to leave you out here."

"We won't do that," Charles said.

"The hell we won't." His answer startled Charles and me, and maybe even Hollenbeck himself. "I'm doing all I can to get out. If I have to leave either one of you behind to do it, I will." He knelt in front of me, and gripped my shoulders. "Here's the way it is, Ray. You're my best friend. If I lose you, it'll feel like my guts fell out on the sidewalk. But I'd rather be alive without you than dead here with you."

I wanted to cry, but I was empty of tears. All I could do was whimper, "It's all used up. I've got nothing to do it with."

"Sure you do. You've got *wanting* to do it. That's plenty. I've been running on that for the last couple of days. Now, let's go." He stood up, and extended his hand again.

There was a quality about the action, the way he did it. I could call it confidence, and that's part of it, but only part. He knew that this time I would take the hand and pull myself up.

I wondered how he could be so sure, when even I didn't know. While I was wondering I grasped the hand and came to my feet.

He began to walk down the slope. Before I realised what I had done, I was following him. This was new in him, this sureness. Travis too had had that way of informing you that he was on top of things you hadn't yet imagined.

Only one difference: when Hollenbeck told me, I believed him.

WE REACHED THE WOODS, and bedded down in the same hollow that had harboured Travis and Hollenbeck. I guess we slept five or six hours. Hollenbeck woke Charles and me; how long he had been up, I don't know, but he was ready.

At first his energy and alertness distracted me. Then I heard rain hitting the tarp. Rain, or something sharper. Sleet. I thought about hiking all day through freezing rain, through sodden snow. But the others didn't seem to notice the pattering overhead.

Hollenbeck said, "We put the tarp away, we'll be ready to go." We climbed out of the hollow and stood beside the tree.

We could have lost it right there. If one of us had moaned, "Now rain. When does this ever end?" everything might have crumbled. But we stood in the rain and the pellets of ice, and let them punch at us, and never acknowledged them. Not once all day.

We folded the tarp, Hollenbeck put it into his pack, and we started out of the woods.

CHAPTER TEN

Like supplicants approaching a throne, we made our way up the steep threshold of the pass, into tumbling clouds that hid the shelf and the twin pinnacles flanking it. We dug upwards, locking bent legs and pausing for breath after each step.

The grade became gentler, clouds less dense, footing solid. We were moving across the shelf, between the pinnacles. This was my second time here, and the site seemed even more disturbing than before. Partly, it was the weather's naked harshness. And there were fewer of us this time, so we were more easily swallowed. It was a place, and a moment, that you would want to put behind you.

Where the shelf ended we stopped, and looked over the edge. Below was the chute, paunchy and lush. The latest fall had covered all sign of the avalanche, and I knew that it must have covered Travis too.

"It looked like this before," Hollenbeck said. "Maybe it's not quite as bad today."

"Today is warmer," Charles said. "Wetter too."

"Does that make it less dangerous?" Hollenbeck asked.

"That depends. I'm not sure."

I said, "Can we go down there without getting killed?"

"I don't know, Ray," the boy replied.

Hollenbeck said, "I don't want to go down there. It looks too much like it did three days ago."

I felt pressure at my back, from Eleanor at the shelter and the miles we had walked to get here, from the necessity to do something. And another sort of pressure, the physical sensation that against our will we were being shoved into the chute.

See, the mountain had shaped our thinking, the cut and cast of the rock channelling our attention. If we let the flow of the land carry us along, we would be swept over the shelf and down the chute every time.

At the moment that I was thinking there had to be another way, Hollenbeck was saying it. And Charles was finding it.

The boy was looking at the pinnacles that straddled the shelf, taking them in together and then individually. I looked at them too, really seeing them for the first time.

The one to the south was an impossible obstacle, smooth-sided and precipitous. The other rose at the same angle, but its surface was broken and narrowly terraced in places.

Charles was looking at the one to the north. He said, "I wonder what it's like on the other side."

Hollenbeck said, "Can we get down that way?"

I said, "Getting down is easy; the trick is keeping solid ground under your feet while you're doing it."

He said, "Please, Ray, not now."

But it was no joke. It was not just the lie of the land, but the emptiness beyond, that kept funnelling us into the chute. Because the human reaction is to stay clear of the edges, away from those places where your next step may be a thousand feet deep.

The thought buckled my knees. Charles began slogging to the north. Hollenbeck was behind him, and I followed.

I joined the others where the shelf narrowed and blended into the pinnacle. Ahead, to the left, the ground fell away hard into the low, milling clouds. To our right was the pinnacle, scored and chunky. A jutting lip of granite formed a sill, now white-tufted, that joined the shelf a few feet from where we stood. It hugged the face of the pinnacle, curving round out of sight.

Where it met the shelf, the sill was almost as broad as a sidewalk. But gradually it contracted, until it was just a few inches wide as it disappeared behind the bend of the wall.

All this we comprehended during the space between heartbeats. Simple. Where we wanted to be was somewhere beyond that curve.

496

"Let me," Charles said. "I know what we're looking for."

He stepped up onto the sill. Before each step he swept a boot in front of him, clearing the snow.

Now he was well beyond the shelf, and the sill had narrowed so that he could no longer comfortably walk forward. He turned and faced the wall and began to edge along, pushing the snow out of his path with nervous, scuffing kicks. The sill tapered until it was no wider than the length of his boots. Hollenbeck and I moved as far as we could to keep him in view, and his next sideways step took him round the curve, out of sight.

We waited. Hollenbeck winced at a raw gust, and I thought of how it must be buffeting Charles on the far side of the pinnacle.

Where Charles had shuffled out of sight, first a boot, and then a hand, appeared. Then the rest of him, pressed against the wall. He was looking past his right shoulder, intent on the spot where he would slide his boot next.

As the sill broadened, Charles turned about, faced us, walked the last few feet. I realised what he had done, what I had seen. The image of him silhouetted against the sky that moment when he slid out of sight. I wanted to vomit.

He ran over to us.

Hollenbeck wanted to know how it looked. Could we do it?

"I think so," Charles said. "Here." He knelt, and swiftly scooped and packed a humpbacked loaf of snow.

"This is the mountain," he said. We got down with him so that the wind wouldn't carry away his words.

He pressed the heel of one hand into the top of the loaf—"The pass"—shaped a small peak beside the depression—"the summit right here"—with one finger slashed a deep lateral furrow—"the chute"—rubbed a thumb at the end of the furrow—"and Exile Lake at the bottom." His finger made a crescent round the summit, the route he had just taken.

"You get about halfway round, you climb down to a ridge," he said, words spilling out. "That's the top of the high wall on the north side of the chute. It looked pretty easy. But you can't see far, because of the clouds. Remember the third day, the flat part before we climbed up to Exile Lake? I bet the ridge drops into there. If we get lucky, we can walk down into that valley."

Hollenbeck said, "Great. Let's do it."

"Wait. The problem is, there are a couple of bad spots. First, the shelf gets narrow round the other side."

"How bad?"

"It gets down to a few inches. There's room to stand. But you can't belay. And it's a long way down." There was respect in his voice. "Then, when you get off the shelf, you climb down to the side of the ridge. And right there you run into a glacier you have to cross." He pointed to a place on the sculpted snow. "There's no way round it. It didn't look wide, maybe eighty or ninety feet. But it's real steep. We can't just walk it."

I wondered out loud how else we could cross it.

"One of us uses the ice axe and the crampons to get over to the other side. You can cut steps as you go, and carry over the end of a rope. So the other two have steps and a rope to hold on to."

Hollenbeck said, "How hard is that?"

"None of this is very hard if you believe you can do it."

"I know we can."

That was Hollenbeck. I looked over at the sill, imagined myself sidling into space as Charles had done. The idea made me sway.

"It's probably a better risk than the chute," Charles said.

"Ray, you have any better ideas?" Hollenbeck said.

I heard myself saying, "We have to do something. It's not getting any easier while we sit around talking."

We stood. Charles said he'd like to start, and he walked out onto the sill. This time when he faced the rock and began to sidle, I couldn't watch; I kept seeing myself out there.

"Some kid," Hollenbeck said.

"A great kid."

"My turn, I guess," Hollenbeck said. I looked up. Charles was edging out of sight. I decided that I didn't want to wait any longer, didn't want to watch Hollenbeck too disappear round that curve. If I didn't have him behind me, his expectation pushing me forward, I might never move off the bench.

I touched Hollenbeck on the sleeve and said, "Let me, OK?"

He said, "Sure, go ahead. See you on the other side." And in a tone as soft as the wind and the tension would allow he said, "Hey, Ray, remember: this is the way we get home."

I took three strides and hopped up onto the sill.

Charles's boots had left some pancake patches of snow. They were slush and ice now. Most of the sill was clear, but the freezing rain had given the bare rock an uncertain slickness.

I advanced one step, a second. To my left, when I passed the lip of the shelf, the rock seemed to withdraw, a curtain falling away. It revealed sky and clouds, and I was exposed.

The air left my chest, but I took a third step, a fourth, and more. Trying to stay fixed on the strip of rock in front of me. Trying to ignore the eternity beyond the brink, roaring like hurricane waves against a jetty.

The sill pinched in. I turned to the wall, raised my hands to shoulder

498

level, gripped what cracks and protrusions the wall offered, and shuffled to the left. A gust shoved me, tried to shake me off the rock; I grabbed what I could and held on until it passed.

The sill continued to narrow, and now it curved perceptibly with the wall. Past my left shoulder I could see it bend to the right, sweeping in front of open sky. My shuffle had become a sideways creep. Round the curve. Hollenbeck would have lost sight of me by now; maybe he was mounting the sill already.

Under my heels I could feel the edge of the sill. The open space chewed at my ankles. Still following the curve. Thirty, forty feet away, Charles was standing on a mantel that was maybe five feet across. Beyond was the glacier, nearly vertical, beyond that the raked flank of the ridge that slid into the clouds. The whole world was leaning and teetering. I wanted to go back to the shelf, where I could stand and sit and jump, and lie down to die.

Charles's mouth was moving, and when I stopped and watched his lips, I could make out the words.

"Careful," he was saying. "It gets tricky."

I dipped my left shoulder to see more. Ahead—six, seven feet—the sill receded to the width of a kerbstone. After about ten feet it protruded again. Somehow Charles had crossed those ten feet to stand where he was now.

"Oh, God, Charles." I yelled it into the rock. "You must be crazy."

"Easy," he said. "It's not so difficult."

His presence on the mantel seemed miraculous. I couldn't account for it. Nothing could exist beyond that narrow shelf.

I pressed my face against the stone.

"Ray, look at me."

I was shaking. The cold, I told myself. A series of muscular spasms ran through my arms to my fingertips. I tried to make myself part of the wall, use its solidness to stop the jerking.

"Ray, don't lock up. You can get over here. Really."

There was movement at my right. Hollenbeck, sidestepping towards me. He stopped within arm's length.

"Let's not get in the way of progress," he said. I could hear him trying to make it light, hear the effort it took.

"What are you going to do, George? Kick me off?"

"If I have to. But first we'll try less drastic methods."

The rain ran into my eyes as I tried to look at him.

"You haven't seen what we've got to cross. There's no place to put your feet. What're we supposed to do?"

"Listen to him. He got over. He says we can do it too."

From my left Charles was calling my name.

"At least look at him, Ray."

I turned my head so we could see each other, Charles and I.

"A nice hold for your left hand," Charles was saying. "A couple of steps further and you can grab that crack. Use it all the way across."

"Tell you how I plan to do it," Hollenbeck said. "I mean, after you're over. I'm going to stand where you are now and imagine myself being where Charles is. I'm going to see myself there. It's practically done already. I'm just about there."

It seemed like a good idea, one of those mental tricks that sound reasonable enough if you're sitting in a chair in a warm room. But I couldn't see myself on the mantel.

The wind slammed into us. I tried to blend into the wall.

"All right, this is crazy; this is enough," Hollenbeck said. He was shouting—not to overcome the gust. From sudden rage. "All you have to do is move. Charles made it over, and I'm going to. Move that damn leg. You can't even do that. You worthless puke."

It was hatred, pure and uncontrived and real. I had to get away from it. My left leg made an involuntary shuffle that my right leg matched, and I was maybe six inches closer to Charles.

"Go on," Hollenbeck said. "Don't stop now."

I began to shuffle towards Charles again, the sill tapering further, extracting itself from under my heels.

Charles was talking me over. He told me to wait. "There's the handhold. Grab it!" I reached. It was icy. My mitten slipped on it. I brought the hand down and pulled the mitten away with my teeth. Then the other, switching grips on the wall, until I had both mittens in my right hand.

I wanted to put them into the pocket of the poncho. But it didn't open right. I missed the slit, and the mittens fell.

"It doesn't matter," Hollenbeck said.

The hold was still icy, but with a bare palm I had a better grip. A couple of steps further along I found the crack, and I was across. I joined Charles on the mantel. So did Hollenbeck.

I SUPPOSE THE GLACIER should have frightened me at least as much. It was long and steep, and if any of us had misstepped, we'd have been gone, despite the rope.

It wouldn't have been possible without the crampons and the ice axe. The crampons in particular. Charles said they were nonadjustable, so whoever wore the boots that fitted the crampons best would have to lead across. I don't believe I was even surprised to find that they went on my boots as if they belonged there.

Charles told me to take a piton in my left hand, drive it into the glacier, and it would help to hold me. He told me how to use the front points, kick them in, use the crampons as a platform.

Hollenbeck gave me his gloves, and before I stepped out, he said, "Look at it this way. If we punch out now, at least we'll be choosing which way we die—not everybody can do that."

Crampons really do work. Almost miraculous the way they drive into ice and hold. I went across, stopping every couple of feet to punch out footwells for the others. I felt no panic. Maybe we all have an allotment of fear and I had exhausted mine.

By late morning we were at the head of the long boulder field. By midafternoon we had reached the end of the boulders.

The meadow, the trailhead, were pulling us down by then. I mean tearing at us. The snowpack thinned as we descended; feeling it ankle-deep was like throwing off shackles.

For more than an hour we lurched and stumbled down the trail, fell and picked ourselves up, and lurched again.

About a mile from the meadow Charles fell hard, bounced off a tree, and slid into the stream that ran by the trail. Hollenbeck and I got him out, but when he tried to stand, an ankle gave way.

"I don't believe this," he said. "You guys go. Go on, one of you, anyway. It's not far. I'll get there."

Hollenbeck didn't argue, but took off his backpack and emptied it into mine. All but a folding knife. He opened the blade. He asked Charles, "How much do you weigh?" as he hacked at the bottom of the pack.

"A hundred ten. Before I left home."

"You must be less now. I'll carry you on my back."

He made two holes in the bottom. He held the pack and told Charles to step in, one leg into each hole.

Charles refused, until Hollenbeck said, "If we're going to walk out together, I don't see any other way."

It slowed him some. Some. We got to the meadow just before dusk. I expected that we'd have that one last mile to walk, out to the highway. But during the afternoon the rain had turned to snow, and when we walked into the meadow, there were some teenagers with pick-ups and Jeeps. The kids were throwing snowballs, yelling and squealing.

One of them heaved a snowball our way, and they laughed; we were still some way off, and the evening was dense. We got closer, and they could see our faces, and after that there was no more laughing.

THEY TOOK US to a hospital. The truck engine's rumble was unnervingly loud, and in town the streetlights slapped my face.

At the emergency room an orderly put us into wheelchairs, and before things began to happen the three of us sat together for a couple of minutes. Under shadowless fluorescence I saw Charles and Hollenbeck as we must have appeared to everyone else. I saw the dirt, the lumps and bruises and dried blood. We could have been human debris. In a way, we were.

Hollenbeck glanced at me, and for that moment we were still up there, surviving, existing as we had existed for days: not so much in skin and muscle and sensation as in the mind. Then a doctor was standing over Hollenbeck, trying to talk to him. A nurse began tugging off my jacket so that she could take my blood pressure, and the orderly was wheeling Charles behind a curtain.

When I looked at Hollenbeck again, he was talking to the doctor. He was gone from me; and the mountains were gone, and the snow and the black wind and the desperation were gone.

The next couple of hours were a disjointed series of episodes separated by periods of oblivion. I kept passing out, and people kept pulling me back. The orderly bathed me, lifted me into bed. Finally Andrea was beside the bed, her face inches from mine, speaking words I either didn't hear or didn't retain. But I remember that she put her hand on my cheek, an inexpressible bleakness in her touch. I wanted to tell her about Gary, all the rest. I babbled something, but I could see that it didn't connect—I was exhausted, and there was really nothing to say, after all. Her sad face was the last I saw before I went under again. And then I slept.

CHARLES AND HOLLENBECK were in the room when I woke, Charles wearing a hospital gown, sitting up on the edge of the second bed, George in a chair between us.

I was glad to see them there—it was the first thing I felt, that we belonged together. Then I noticed grey light behind the venetian blinds. "How late is it?"

"Afternoon of the next day," Hollenbeck said. "You've been asleep about eighteen hours. The doctor let me go this morning. He wants to hold on to you two until tomorrow."

Only then, finally, did I remember unfinished business.

I said, "Eleanor—she OK?"

"She's still there," Charles said.

"Somebody has to get them down."

"It's been snowing since last night," Hollenbeck said. "Nobody's going up until it stops."

I counted back through sunrises and sunsets, through the sleet and the clinging to rock, through the hours and hours of walking. Three days and two nights since we had left the shelter. I thought of what can happen in three days.

Charles said, "Today's Friday. Friday the nineteenth. This was supposed to be the last day of the trip. We were going to be walking out right about now."

The idea of "supposed to be", of us intact, tramping to the end of the trail, made me think of Poague. I asked about him.

"Poague split a week ago," Hollenbeck said. "He's been back at work since Monday."

I said, "I guess that surprises me. I mean, I assumed he was hanging in there with us, you know? It's like he ran out on us."

"That's how it hit me," Hollenbeck said.

From over on his bed Charles said, "He didn't know what was happening."

I said I understood that. But it still didn't feel right.

"You don't know what's in somebody," Charles said. "People have their reasons, that's all I'm saying. You can't ever tell."

ALL THROUGH THE NEXT DAY the snow continued. The day after that, a Sunday, the snow turned to rain down in Red Lodge. But visibility was still too low for mountain flying. By then Charles and I were out of the hospital. The three of us had taken rooms in a motel. Andrea had been there all week. The lobby had a big picture window, a view of the mountains, and we spent hours there together, watching clouds mill round the peaks.

Nothing we had done in the past two weeks was more difficult, more excruciating than that wait. We had felt the lash of wind and sleet under those clouds, had felt the cold as it chased us into the burrow of our bags. We knew. Even worse, we could imagine.

On Sunday evening we went out to dinner. On the way back I stopped at the front desk to check for messages; the sheriff had said he would tell us when he planned to call for a chopper.

The desk clerk said to someone behind me, "This is Mr. Furlow."

I had glanced at him when I came in. A man about my age, my height—but not at all like me. Flawless teeth set off a uniform tan on a seamless face. A crew-neck sweater with a snowflake design across the chest, stretch ski pants, après-ski boots of furry cowhide. Perfectly arranged.

"I'm Coleman Farris," he said; but I think I guessed it before the words were out. "I'd have been here sooner, but I was out of town, and the sheriff had trouble getting in touch with me. I wanted to see someone who has seen Eleanor."

"Well, I saw her. That was Wednesday. She was OK then."

"This isn't an accusation," he said. "But how is it that you and the other two are here? And she's still there?"

At first I didn't answer. I knew I ought to be angry. But I didn't feel it.

I kept looking at his outfit. The clothes looked new, and it occurred to me that he might have bought them within the last couple of hours, after he arrived in Billings, so that he'd be acceptably dressed. His idea of mountain wear.

He said, "I guess you were afraid she might slow you down and none of you would get through."

"No. She'd have done as well as anyone else. We wanted her to leave with us. She wanted to stay."

"Why didn't you make her come?"

"She wanted to stay. Nobody could make her leave."

"Because of this boy?"

"Donnie."

"What's so special about him that she would do this?"

"He's just a boy. She thought he needed her."

He didn't understand. This wasn't about Donnie, or about her. All that counted was the place, what the place had done to us.

"This is a nightmare," he said. His arms were folded. I could see his ring finger—he wore a wedding band. I wondered if he had replaced it at the same time he bought the outfit. "I can't believe this is happening. My wife stranded in a place like that."

"They've got a good shelter," I said. "And she has a lot of strength. You probably don't believe that, but it's true."

"I hope you're right," he said. He left me standing there.

I was in my room ten minutes later when Andrea called. The sheriff had told her the front was clearing, the National Guard would have a helicopter ready at first light.

AT EARLY DAWN we stood on the airstrip. Andrea, Charles, Hollenbeck and me. Cole Farris. A sheriff's deputy. A paramedic. Two search dogs—Alsatians—with their handlers.

The chopper came out of the southeast, and landed in front of us at almost the exact moment of sunrise. There was room for the searchers and their dogs, for the deputy and the paramedic and for one of us, someone who knew where the shelter was. The deputy had already chosen Charles, to save weight.

Charles never went into much detail about the next few hours. All that really matters is the outcome, and that had been decided hours, maybe days, earlier, while the snow still fell up there.

Finding the ridge was no problem. Charles had the pilot hold three hundred degrees from the pass above Exile Lake. It was easy, Charles told me later, everything laid out below so plainly.

They found the ridge, but no sign of the cleft rock or the shelter. There had been much more snow. They swept back and forth until Charles saw a dimple in one white swell. They dropped to within eight, ten feet above it. He could see that the dimple was the shelter's crawlway, clotted with snow.

Charles kept waiting for Eleanor to come clawing towards the noise, but nothing happened. The pilot let the chopper down close to the surface, and they jumped out into chest-high snow. The deputy, the searchers with their dogs, the paramedic, and then Charles, last.

The deputy and the paramedic crawled into the shelter. A few minutes later they had pushed away the tarps and the snow. Charles tried to get closer. He saw the paramedic bending over someone. Over Donnie. There was nobody else.

They called the chopper close again, got a litter off one of the skids, strapped Donnie onto it. He looked dead, but Charles thought that the paramedic wouldn't have spent so much time with a cadaver. They lifted the litter, the paramedic jumped up with it, and the chopper was gone.

Charles fought through the snow until he was standing where the shelter had been. He saw two sleeping-bags among the debris. One of them had been cut open, to get at Donnie. The other one had to belong to Eleanor. He also saw the stove, two empty fuel bottles, a pack that lay almost flat.

The deputy asked him where she could have walked to. Charles told him there was no place to go. Then he remembered the small pool I had hiked down to when we needed water. He saw that there were no water bottles, and he knew where she had gone.

I CAN'T SEE belabouring this. I don't have the heart.

Travis's body stayed buried until the snow melted in the chute. Some hikers found it. That was in June.

Within an hour after the chopper had taken him off the ridge, Donnie was at a hospital in Billings; two hours later, on an operating table for neurosurgery. He survived, but would never walk or talk.

After three days of searching, one of the dogs found Eleanor, dead, about a mile south of the path between the shelter and the pool. She wore a backpack, and the water bottles inside it were full, frozen. She had gone to get water, had become lost in the storm, and died before she could find her way back.

Some images I refuse to assimilate. This is one: Eleanor lifeless. I won't let myself see it.

Not that I'm denying the fact of her death. I can tell you exactly the time when I realised it: the afternoon of the third day of the search, before the dog turned up her body but long past any real hope that she had survived.

That afternoon Andrea was driving Charles and Hollenbeck to the airport. Only Cole Farris and I were left, the two of us waiting in the lobby, standing a few feet apart, alone. A sheriff's deputy came in from outside. Cole saw him first, and went over to him.

I didn't have to hear the words. I could see Cole shrivelling where he stood, crumbling from the inside out until there was nothing to support the stupid snowflake sweater, nothing to fill those ridiculous furry boots. And I knew that she was gone.

CHAPTER ELEVEN

Hollenbeck got home on Wednesday evening, and was back at work Friday morning. I returned to DC six hours after he did, and I stayed away from the office for two and a half weeks. I slept late, read, browsed in the National Gallery, went to the movies. I didn't call in, didn't make excuses. I suppose I was daring Poague to fire me, but it didn't happen. Nothing happened. To my immense disappointment.

On the second Monday in October I drove into Bethesda, went to my cubicle and logged in, at eight forty-eight a.m. An hour later I looked up from my screen and caught Poague standing in the aisle, positioned in such a way that he had clear sight of me through the opening to my cubicle. His face showed nothing. Nothing. After a few seconds he walked away.

My return attracted little more notice than if I had been absent for a long weekend. After a week or so, all curiosity about the ordeal had been expended on Hollenbeck; to have survived a real-life wilderness adventure was no longer a novelty. Anyway, there was more substantial gristle to be chewed over. A few days after Poague came back to work he had ordered furnishings and equipment for a spare room in the office suite. The next day Noreen Poague walked in with him and occupied the office. She came to work every day after that.

She sat in on meetings in Poague's office and, like Poague, patrolled the aisles and policed the work spaces. Not as aggressively as her husband, perhaps—not so abrupt and grating a presence. But she was there. No more seersucker shirtwaisters, either. One morning, when she walked past my cubicle, I caught the scent of perfume, the hiss of silk, a flash of trim legs and emerald-green fabric, and I could almost believe that Travis had wanted her before he ever knew there was the new job.

The job. Hollenbeck got it, a couple of weeks before Christmas. But Poague's successor was clearly going to be Noreen. In late October some office memorandums had shown her initials beside his. By November most had borne hers alone, including the one announcing Hollenbeck's promotion.

So Hollenbeck had no grand illusions about ascending to the throne. He did get a good rise, and an impressive office behind the walnut double doors. I was happy for him. In Montana he had lost thirty-seven pounds. He promptly gained back nine, and stopped there. What's more important, he took the new job as if he deserved it. Which he did.

I left MDC within three months after returning to work. I went in one morning and knew I couldn't last to the end of the afternoon. I typed a letter of resignation on the computer, filed it with Poague's secretary and left. When I returned a couple of hours later, an envelope with my name on it sat on my desk.

It held a cheque for just under fifty thousand dollars, a year's salary less deductions.

I wanted to go to Poague and tell him that if this was severance pay it was too much, and if it was compensation for the Beartooths it could never be enough. But I didn't want to talk about the trip, least of all with Poague. So I just took the cheque and walked out and never went back.

After that I didn't see Hollenbeck so often. Even when we were still together in the office, some awkwardness had inserted itself between us. What had brought us close was gone, and nothing else felt right.

We didn't play racquetball any more.

I RESUMED THE ROUTINE of books, museums, movies. I didn't even think about another job. I tried not to think about Beartooth Plateau.

In January Poague died. Hollenbeck passed on the rumour of an inoperable malignancy in his brain.

I called Charles in North Carolina. After we had chatted for a few seconds, I said, "Charles, I have some bad news."

He said, "Jonas, right?"

"Somebody called you already."

"No. He told me when we were in the mountains."

"He *told* you?" I was shocked that Poague had confided in a boy, but not in Hollenbeck or me. "Why did he tell *you?*"

He snapped back, "I wasn't after any job." More softly he said, "I wasn't supposed to tell anybody else. I wanted to a couple of times, but I didn't. He really wanted to finish the trip. He said he was going to cancel it when he first found out, but he decided to try it again. He really loved the mountains."

"I know."

"He was a good guy, Ray. No kidding."

We talked for a couple more minutes, and the conversation wound down. I was ready to hang up. Before I could tell him goodbye, he said, "I think about you. You doing OK?"

507

"I'm fine."

"We all did our best. We couldn't make it come out the way we wanted. You just go on—that's the way I feel about it."

IN NOVEMBER I HAD MET a tall blonde named Karen. We dated several times before Christmas, and decided that before spring we would take a vacation together. We made reservations for seven days on Kauai, end of February.

We rented an apartment near the beach. For six days we sat in the sun and indulged ourselves. Our bedroom had a sliding glass door that faced the ocean. We kept it open after dark, to let in the warm breeze that blew off the water.

The last night the breeze seemed cooler than before. I closed the door. A window was open, and I closed that too. Karen looked curiously at me, but didn't say anything. I got into bed, pulled the sheet round me, but it didn't help; I kept getting colder.

I began to shiver. She got up and found a blanket. That didn't help, either. My feet ached. The last time they had hurt that way, I was standing in snow, wearing wet boots.

She was asking me, "Are you all right? Ray? Honey? Say something." Her voice was distant. I held the blanket round me; it had the feel of nylon, the bulk of a sleeping-bag. The cold was looking for a way into my skin; I could feel it nibbling at the fabric. I shook and shuddered.

It passed after a few minutes. But by then she was in a chair across the room, looking at me as if she were afraid I would come too close.

THE NEXT MORNING we left. The connection was through Los Angeles, with a stopover of about two hours.

A few minutes before we were supposed to board the flight to Dulles, I told her to go without me. She didn't argue.

I caught the first available flight to San Francisco. The cab ride to Tiburon was more than forty dollars. At the door, the maid told me the Langs were out of town, but if I wanted to see Donnie, that was OK. She showed me into the living room and left.

I heard feet on the carpet, and a soft mechanical squeak.

He was in a wheelchair. I had prepared myself for that. But I wasn't ready for Donnie. He had lost at least twenty pounds. Flaccid skin sagged over shrunken muscles in his face and his forearms. He sat in the chair as if he had been dropped there carelessly, randomly, arranged by someone other than himself.

Behind him was a tall man, pushing the chair into the room. He said his name was Ricky, and that he was Donnie's nurse.

"I'm a friend of his," I said. "I'd like to be with him for a few minutes."

"Sure. Whatever. He's all yours." He pushed the chair to face the sofa, and left. I was alone with Donnie.

He might have been dead, he was so still. All but his eyes. They followed me when I went over to the sofa. I sat in front of him. The eyes were as vivid as ever. He was alive inside them.

"I hope you don't mind," I said. "I had to see you. It seemed important. I don't know why."

He might have been angry, or joyous, or just bored. The eyes didn't change, only bubbled and flashed. They were surrounded by deadness.

"It seems like a stupid idea now. Maybe you don't even want me here. I never thought of that. I won't be long, I promise."

Nothing moved in him. His eyes were fixed on me, and I wondered what the world and I looked like from in there.

I began to tell him about the others, about Eleanor and Poague and the rest. For the first couple of minutes I felt as awkward as if I were talking aloud to myself. I tried to remember the boy I had known in the Beartooths, and told myself that he was still in there somewhere. That made it easier.

"George is doing great," I said. I told him about the job. "I talked to Charles a while back, and he sounded good. He's going to end up doing something terrific. I know it."

I stopped and let him watch me.

"Things have sort of fallen apart in my life. I don't mean to sound sorry for myself. I'm not blaming it on the trip. It's not like this is something that happened in the last few months."

For a while I didn't say anything. We just looked at each other. Then I said softly, "Do you do anything? At all?"

His arms lay on the side rails of the chair. At first nothing happened. Then I noticed a minute contraction of the fingers. They halted, in an open clench, then slowly relaxed.

I got off the sofa and knelt in front of the chair.

"I've been thinking about you a lot. I've been thinking about what happened. I can't talk to anybody else about it. With Charles and Andrea, on the telephone, it doesn't work. I see George every now and then, but I know it's over as far as he's concerned. He kept what he wanted out of it and got rid of the rest. I'm not knocking him. I wish I could do that. I have to do that."

I found my right hand holding the limp fingers of his left.

"The ones that are dead are gone. All the others are leaving. I feel like it's you and me, still up there."

Now the fingers were tightening. His eyes snapped and burned. I looked into them, spoke directly at them.

"Here's the thing about it. I've got to get down. That's all. I feel bad

509

about it. I feel like you're going to be alone up there again, and I'm sorry. I really am. But I can't stay there any more."

His fingers held me. I know his arm didn't move, but all the same I felt those fingers drawing me towards him. I held him with my free arm. I told him, "I'm sorry, I've got to get off the hill. It's just too real." His cheek was on my cheek. They were wet where they touched. Wet at first with my tears, then with ours.

A WARM AFTERNOON, spring on the verge of summer. I rock in the front-porch swing. Wind ruffles the trees, dogs bark, kids shout in the street.

I can remember being sure about life and people during those few days in the Beartooths. It was all so sharp-edged and defined. But down here the edges got dulled, the definite became ambiguous, imponderable. There's truth in the mountains, but it doesn't travel well. You can't spend that currency anywhere else.

But I can live with ambiguity; it's the one change I see in myself since I left the Beartooths. I might have wished that I had walked out stronger, or smarter, or more resolute. But I don't believe I did. The only difference in me is this: in human affairs, I no longer ask why.

Lately, without trying, I have thought a lot about my father. About his conviction that I had betrayed our station.

In truth, I have accomplished far less than I might have. For a long while I blamed his stifling expectations. I used to tell him that if he had asked less, I might have been free to deliver more.

It seemed a good argument, and I used it often. He would absorb it with a slow shake of the head and an infuriating smile. Now I know that he understood what I have only begun to grasp: that nothing is more ephemeral than intentions and motives, and that when those are gone, there remains the stark, enduring evidence of deeds done, or left undone.

PHILLIP FINCH

Phillip Finch's curriculum vitae reads like that of a man who has been around for a long time. Yet this prolific author of nine books, two documentary films and numerous magazine articles—this accomplished newspaper journalist whose interests include carpentry, rock-climbing, flying, and motorcycle racing—is only thirty-nine years old. For fourteen of those years he has been fascinated with mountain wilderness, and he once participated in a rigorous expedition in Montana's Beartooths, similar to the one he depicts in *Trespass*. "Being in true wilderness is unlike any experience in daily life," he explains. "You develop a tremendous sense of self-confidence from the knowledge that you can survive almost any situation."

The question of survival—who does survive and how—has interested Finch ever since his one-year stint as a member of a search-and-rescue team in California. Working alone, with only a Labrador retriever as a partner, Finch combed an area of up to ten square miles a day during rescue efforts. "Being on that team was one of the most meaningful experiences of my life," he says. "You must get into the skin of the person you're looking for, much as a writer does with the characters he creates." Reflecting on such *Trespass* characters as the cocky Gary, the panicky Travis and the bookish Charles, Finch adds, "There is a certain amount of me in every character of this novel. I know their emotions and thoughts because I had them all myself at one time or another."

Phillip Finch is currently at work on a new book, although he will not divulge its subject. "The best books are written out of intense personal knowledge and experience," he asserts. We can only wonder what his latest experience will yield.

R149